THE BOY IN THE PARK

THE BOY IN THE PARK

AJ Grayson

harper impulse

This novel is entirely a work of fiction.
The names, characters and incidents portrayed in it are the work of the author's imagination. Any resemblance to actual persons, living or dead, events or localities is entirely coincidental.

Harper*Impulse*
An imprint of HarperCollins*Publishers*
The News Building
1 London Bridge Street
London SE1 9GF

www.harpercollins.co.uk

A paperback original 2017
6

A catalogue record for this book is available from the British Library

ISBN: 978-0-00-823936-7

Set in Sabon 10.75/15 pt by
Palimpsest Book Production Limited, Falkirk, Stirlingshire

Printed and bound in the United States of America by LSC Communications

For Rachael

The Boy in the Park, Stanza 1

Little boy in the park,
Little boy standing, lost.
The waters quiet, the tree-wings
dance
For the little boy still, unmoving.
The little boy with stick in hand;
Little boy weeping . . .
Little boy weeping . . .

I am not certain I may ever know, ever understand, that which makes death what it is and sorrow so sadly, desperately haunting. I am not sure what it is that lingers, once everything else is gone. But I know the boy, alive through all his torments, and perhaps that is enough. Perhaps we are not meant to know anything more cosmic than one child, one face, one set of hands. In them, I have found enough grief to encompass the whole of creation.

—Dr Pauline Lavrentis
Interview notes

PART ONE

SAN FRANCISCO

1

Tuesday

My bench in the park is old, tainted from moisture, tinged a faint green by the growth of a moss that will one day consume it. A brass plaque that was once a colour other than tarnished black notes that it is dedicated 'To the Memory of Margaret Hoss, Beloved (1924–2008).' Margaret's bench, now mine. We sit together beneath the trees. We sit and we watch, and the world dances before us.

From Margaret's bench I am afforded the best view in the park. It is not off one of the great grassy quadrangles, nor the main paved walkways that criss-cross the gardens. To find it requires taking one of the thousand dirt pathways that branch away from these, spidering into densely planted greenery that's divided, for convenience, by continent of origin. My bench is in the hidden underbrush of Temperate Asia, and all around it are plants with names like Autumn Joy, *Nymphaea fabiola*, Emerald Cypress and Primrose Willow. The bench itself sits on a patch of wood chips – a place to rest one's feet in the absence of mud. A private retreat. And descending below, spreading out beyond my toes, is the pond.

The pond is tranquil, even beautiful. Not the blue-basined, sanitized sort of water feature too common in public spaces (there's one of those in the park, too, at the centre of its most obvious green lawn). The pond, though entirely manmade, is of a style *au naturel*. Just the right number of lily pads and watercress colour its surface. A few stones peek up from the brown water, often serving as perches for birds or even the occasional turtle. Surrounded by tall leafy trees, the pond is generally hidden from the breeze, and so almost always the texture of glass – and just as reflective.

I sit on my bench, the poet in the midst of poetry. It is an everyday thing, or almost everyday, this visit. I come with my little Moleskine notebook and stubby pencil, sometimes with a paper cup dredging coffee beneath a plastic lid marked with the brown imprints of my lips. And I, the poet, gaze into paradise. Outside the park, so close by, looms the paved wasteland of the city. I can hear it as I sit, there, out of sight. Cars (petrol, hybrid or electric, it makes no difference, really), skyscrapers, slums. But here, here a poet can come to sing his song to the greens and browns of nature, and witness it singing back.

A couple strolls by, arms linked at the elbows, smiling,

a Nikon camera dangling from the man's neck. There is a punctuated look in the woman's eyes. Romance, keyed in by the scents of begonias and rhododendrons. It's become a visible flush of redness on her face. I can tell she hopes it will become something more.

A chipmunk descends from a tree, marked by a small plastic sign as *Picea orientalis,* Oriental Spruce. He observes the layout before him, the inclines and dips of the soil. There is food here, a treasure trove of it; he seems fairly confident. A tail shivers in anticipation. Nearby a bird – a hermit thrush, I'm almost certain – swoops down and takes a perch on one of the rocks jutting up from the water. The breath from his wings ripples the surface, changing a still mirror into one of undulating motion.

There is a poem here. I can feel it. Woven into the greenery, the humanity, the natural ebb and flow of life. A poem, waiting to be found, waiting to be spoken. One that will sing of something brighter than the dark world that gives it birth.

And then, there in the distance, I catch it. The little brush of motion from the branches, customary and expected. I turn my head slightly, but I know what's there. I've known since before the motion came. It's familiar now, this sight, seen on eighteen months of afternoons just like this.

The little boy emerges from the boughs of the faux Asian foliage. He takes three steps to the edge of the manmade pond's crafted waterline, to where his toes almost touch. He wears the same worn overalls, the same once-white T-shirt beneath them that I've seen him wear more times than I can remember. His blond hair is dishevelled, as all little boys' should be. He holds a stick in his right hand and pokes it listlessly at the water's edge, sending new ripples across the pond. He gazes vacantly out at these results of his movements. The jade treetops bend in a breeze that doesn't descend to the tops of our scalps.

The boy is mesmerized. I am mesmerized. The bird on the rock clucks from somewhere beneath its beak then flaps its wings to take flight. The little boy doesn't notice. His gaze is still on the ripples of the water, meeting other ripples, colliding gently in the swell of a scene fabricated by man, yet hauntingly serene. Almost inhuman. Almost free.

And I cannot quite see his eyes.

2

Wednesday Morning

There is a rail workers' strike today. It's the third this year, and I feel as a result as if I'm becoming an old hand at dealing with them. Taking the train normally saves me thirty minutes of traffic and $28 in a day's parking charges, but a bus still beats out the car for second best. No reprieve from the traffic, but it's a $2.50 ride and there's a stop by the shop where I work, so I can hardly complain.

It's meant a morning on a hard, plastic bench seat rather than a padded one, and a bit more jostling of starts and stops than my generally impatient personality would prefer. But the wheels on the bus have gone round and round, and I'm fairly certain I'll get from point A to point B alive and unscathed.

I'd live closer to work if I could – the traditional commuter's lament. There's nothing in particular to recommend Diamond Heights, the neighbourhood south of the city that I call home, apart from the fact that it's outside central San Francisco proper and, therefore, the grossly overinflated San Francisco housing market. The Planning and Urban Research Association designed the district as part of the Community Redevelopment Law of 1951, transforming most of its shanties into liveable quarters, one of which I call my own. On a rental basis, of course. To be honest, I can't really afford living there, either, but it's a full three or four degrees less unaffordable than even the smallest flat in the city would be, and those are the kinds of maths that make the impossible seem feasible these days. So it's home. And it has the glamour of having diamonds in its name.

I can't say I entirely mind the commute. As the sun rises over the hills in the morning, its rays bouncing up off the sea, San Francisco's not a bad city to look at. I don't know if it's the beauty of the bay on its inland side, with its islands and hills and bridges, or the mystery of the endless, borderless ocean stretching out on the other, but something gives this city an aura – an otherness I've never felt replicated anywhere else. A sliver of land wholly encapsulated by the natural world, as if the earth herself had drawn a line around the silicon and steel and said, 'This far you may come, you may make your homes and monuments. This far, but no further.'

The bus rounds a corner, swerving its metal bulk to avoid a tiny, parked Nissan, and pulls onto Lincoln Way. I've taken this line before, I know the route, but even himself for an hour or less with the Princess," after which King Henry might carry her back again to England "unto such time as she should be thought [more] able."[9] Henry, however, refused to agree to either arrangement.

On April 30, "perpetual peace" was concluded between France and England: a pledge was made to declare war on Charles V if he refused to come to terms, and a French marriage between Mary and the French king, or his second son, the duke of Orléans, was agreed upon.[10] Mary was now betrothed to the House of Valois.

For two weeks, the Anglo-French festivities continued. These culminated on May 5 in a great court feast and a masque. A painted curtain was drawn back to reveal a stage, and Mary and seven ladies of the court emerged from a gold cave to the sound of trumpets. The princess was "dressed in cloth of gold, her hair gathered in a net, with a richly jewelled garland, surmounted by a velvet cap, the hanging sleeves of their surcoats being so long that they well nigh touched the ground." She looked radiant, wrote one observer; "her beauty in this array produced such an effect on everybody that all other marvellous sights previously witnessed were forgotten." She wore on her person "so many precious stones that their splendour and radiance dazzled the sight, in so wise as to make one believe that she was decked with all the gems of the eighth sphere."

Having descended from the cave, Mary and her ladies danced a ballet with eight lords. After the masque, festivities continued, with Mary dancing with her father at the heart of the revelry. Mary presented herself to Henry, who "took off her cap, and the net being displaced, a profusion of silver tresses as beautiful as ever seen on human head fell over her shoulders."[11] The evening entertainment culminated with the French ambassador dancing with Mary "and the King with Mistress Boleyn."[12]

CHAPTER 9

THIS SHEER CALAMITY

HENRY MAINTAINED THAT IT WAS A QUESTION POSED BY THE bishop of Tarbes, one of the French envoys, in the spring of 1527 that first made him doubt the validity of his marriage to Katherine of Aragon and therefore Mary's legitimacy.[1] During the course of negotiations for the betrothal of Mary and the duke of Orléans, the bishop had inquired whether in fact Mary was so great a prospect after all. Had not Henry married his brother's widow? Was that marriage valid? Was Mary legitimate? The envoy's questions struck a resounding chord with the king. Having toyed with the idea of advancing his illegitimate son, Henry now settled on a more radical solution to the succession. The lack of a male heir, the successive failed pregnancies that had left the forty-two-year-old queen seeming dowdy and dumpy, and the allure of the twentysomething Anne Boleyn all contributed to Henry's mounting disillusionment with his Spanish wife.

Attractive and vivacious, Anne Boleyn had grown up in the household of Queen Claude, the first wife of the French king Francis I. She was, as one observer described, "beautiful, had an elegant figure and with eyes that were even more attractive."[2] On her return to England in the winter of 1521 she joined the queen's household as one of Katherine's ladies-in-waiting. Three years later Henry began his courtship of her. He had previously ended an affair with her sister Mary. Now he looked to install Anne as his "sole" mistress. But Anne refused. Henry grew increasingly infatuated, sending her gifts of jewelry and letters in which he declared his love and made promises that he would "cast off all others than yourself out of mind and affection and to serve you only."[3] Still Anne resisted. Only if they were married would she give herself to him.

Henry now came to believe that his marriage to Katherine was contrary to divine law as stated in the Bible and that he was free to marry Anne. He looked to secure an annulment and cited Leviticus 20:21 to support his claim that in granting the dispensation for their marriage eighteen years before, Pope Julius II had breached the Word of God:

> If a man shall take his brother's wife, it is an impurity: he hath uncovered his brother's nakedness; they shall be childless.

On January 1, 1527, Henry and Anne secretly exchanged vows and pledged themselves to each other. It was at the Greenwich ball in May that they appeared in public for the first time. One moment the court was joyfully celebrating Mary's betrothal, the next she was all but forgotten, as all eyes and whispers turned to the subject of "mistress Boleyn." As Don Íñigo López de Mendoza, the new imperial ambassador, reported, the king was now "bent on divorce" and Wolsey was "scheming to bring it about."[4] Mary's life was about to change forever.

TWELVE DAYS AFTER the ball, Wolsey summoned Henry to appear before a secret tribunal at his town palace at York to answer the charge of unlawfully cohabiting with his dead brother's wife. In the days that followed, evidence was presented against the marriage, and Wolsey and William Warham, archbishop of Canterbury, were called upon to make a judgment.[5] It was a stage-managed trial, and the outcome seemed predictable. Yet on May 31, just when the verdict was to be delivered, Wolsey pronounced the case too difficult to call and referred it to a panel of learned theologians and lawyers.[6] News had reached England that an imperial army in Italy had mutinied for want of pay and had sacked and pillaged Rome. Pope Clement VII had taken refuge in the Castel Sant'Angelo and was now effectively a prisoner of the emperor.[7] Henry's divorce would be referred to Rome at just the time when the pope was at the mercy of Katherine's nephew.

Katherine had not been called to give evidence in the tribunal; she didn't even know it had taken place. It was not until June 22 that Henry went to her apartments to inform her of his intentions and to demand a formal separation. His conscience troubled him, he said; their marriage was invalid, and he was taking steps to have it annulled by the pope. He failed to mention his infatuation with Anne Boleyn, which was now an open secret. As Katherine began to cry, Henry lost his nerve: "all should be done for the best" he mumbled, and after begging her "to keep secrecy upon what he had told her," he beat a hasty retreat.[8]

But behind her tears the queen was "very stiff and obstinate." She confirmed that Arthur "did never know her carnally" and demanded counsel from both Henry's subjects and "strangers [foreigners]."[9] Wolsey immediately recognized the danger: Katherine was threatening to bring her nephew, the emperor, into the fight. "These were the worst points that could be imagined for the impeaching [preventing] of this matter . . . that she would resort to the counsel of strangers," and he "intended to make all the counsel of the world, France except, as a party against it."[10]

The queen hurriedly dispatched one of her Spanish servants, Francisco Felipez, to appeal to Charles to intervene. Henry ordered that Felipez be arrested, but the Spaniard eluded capture and reached the emperor at Valladolid at the end of July. Charles reacted quickly. He was shocked "to hear of a case so scandalous" and promised to "do everything in his power on her behalf." He told his ambassador in England, "We cannot desert the Queen, our good aunt, in her troubles and intend doing all we can in her favour." But, he added cautiously, "to this end, as the first step towards rendering help, it seems to us that this matter ought to be treated with all possible moderation, having recourse to kind remonstrances alone for the present."[11]

Charles wrote to Henry, asking that he halt the proceedings immediately, and to the pope, requesting that he revoke Wolsey's legateship and recall the case to Rome. He could not believe "that having, as they have, so sweet a princess for their daughter, [the King] would consent to have her or her mother dishonoured, a thing so monstrous of itself and wholly without precedent in ancient or modern history."[12] The fate of the king's marriage was not a merely personal affair but a public matter of European significance.

THE HUMANIST Juan Luis Vives, who had left England in May to spend the summer in the Netherlands, returned in late September to find Katherine "troubled and afflicted with this controversy that had arisen about her marriage." She "began to unfold . . . her calamity," weeping over her "destiny, that she should find him, whom she loved far more than herself, so alienated from her that he thought of marrying another; and this affected her with a grief the more intense as her love for him was the more ardent." She was unable to find out what Henry planned to do next, but the "report and common opinion was . . . that her cause was remitted to Rome."

Katherine instructed Vives to go to the emperor's ambassador, López, and ask the emperor on her behalf "that he would deal with the Pope that she might . . . be heard before his Holiness decided on her cause."[13] On October 26, López did as Katherine asked. "The divorce is more talked of than ever," he wrote to his master; "if therefore the Emperor really has the Queen's honour and peace of mind at heart, orders should be sent to Rome for a trusty messenger to bring us the Pope's decision."[14]

Cardinal Lorenzo Campeggio arrived in England on October 9 with orders from the pope to hear the case but to reach no decision.[15] He proposed that Katherine take vows of "perpetual chastity" and join a religious community, leaving Henry free to marry again without calling into question Mary's legitimacy or her claim to the throne. Katherine responded angrily: she would never take the veil as Campeggio had proposed and intended to "live and die in the estate of matrimony, into which God had called her, and that she would always be of that opinion and never change it." She held her husband's conscience and honor in "more esteem than anything in this world." She was, she said, the true and legitimate wife of the king and at the time of their wedding remained "intact and uncorrupted."[16] It was a protest she would make repeatedly for the next seven years.

Katherine would prove as defiantly committed to the legitimacy of her marriage as Henry was to its annulment. "She insists that everything shall be decided by [judicial] sentence," Campeggio reported.

"Neither the whole kingdom on the one hand, nor any great punishment on the other, although she might be torn limb by limb, should compel her to alter this opinion."[17]

AS THEIR MARRIAGE CRUMBLED and diplomats hurried between England and Rome, the king and queen continued to appear together in public at court. Mary lived as she had before her removal to the Marches, in houses adjacent to her parents, and regularly visiting them at court. With the outbreak of the plague in May 1528, the royal family, Henry, Katherine, and Mary, came together at Wolsey's house at Tyttenhanger, near St. Albans in Hertfordshire. For the twelve-year-old Mary, it was precious time spent with both her parents. In what is the earliest of her letters known to have survived, she thanked Wolsey for arranging for all of them to be together, telling him "I have been allowed for a month to enjoy, to my supreme delight, the society of the King and Queen my parents."[18]

It was but a temporary reprieve. Increasingly Henry would leave Katherine for days at a time to visit Anne. In advance of the Christmas festivities of 1528, Henry "lodged [his mistress] in a very fine lodging, which he has prepared for her close by his own." And, as Cardinal Jean du Bellay, the French diplomat, remarked, "Greater court . . . is paid to her everyday than has been to the Queen for a long time."[19] It was the way of things to come. But if Katherine knew all this, she chose to turn a blind eye. Perhaps she hoped that Henry's affection for Anne would wane. Certainly she took comfort in the fact that, as she confided to Mendoza, Henry continued "to visit her, and they dine and sleep together."[20]

ON MAY 31, 1529, the public trial of the king's marriage was held in the Parliament Chamber of the Dominican Friary of London, Blackfriars.[21] Both parties were required to answer their summons on Friday, June 18, but though Henry sent proxies, Katherine unexpectedly appeared in person. She entered the chamber accompanied by four bishops and "a great company" of ladies and gentlewomen. Then, "sadly and with great gravity," she read out a written statement protesting the cardinal's jurisdiction to hear the case.[22] The court was adjourned to consider her appeal and was reassembled on the Monday morning. Katherine arrived first, followed by Wolsey, Campeggio, and finally the king himself. Henry spoke briefly, asking for a quick decision "to determine the validity or nullity of his marriage, about which he has from the beginning felt a perpetual scruple." Wolsey spoke next, assuring the court, and in particular Katherine, that the case would be judged fairly. After Campeggio rose to formally reject Katherine's protestation and reassert the judges' jurisdiction, the court crier called, "Katherine, queen of England, come into court!"

Once again Katherine rejected the authority of the court and appealed directly to Rome: how could she, a foreigner, expect justice in England? She then turned to Henry. Though her address was public and in the austere setting of Campeggio's court, her words were intimate and imploring. Why did he now raise these scruples? she asked; "it was not the time to say this after so long silence."

In the face of Katherine's personal appeal, Henry was forced to respond. He had, he said, remained silent only because of "the great love he had and has for her"; he desired more than anything else that the marriage should be declared valid. Her appeal to Rome was unreasonable, "considering the Emperor's power there," but she had "the choice of prelates and lawyers." England was "perfectly secure for her," and that was where the case should be decided.[23] Suddenly the queen left her dais, walked across the courtroom, and knelt down at the king's feet. Twice Henry tried to raise her up, but she continued to kneel. Then, as Campeggio reported, "in the sight of all the court and assembly," she spoke "in broken English."

> [She begged] him to consider her honour, her daughter's and his; that he should not be displeased at her defending it, and should consider the reputation of her nation and relatives, who will be seriously offended; in accordance with what she had said about his goodwill, she had throughout appealed to Rome, where it was reasonable that the affair should be determined, as the present place was open to suspicion and because the cause is already [begun] at Rome.[24]

Katherine had turned Henry's protestations of love against him. How could he, if he was so keen for their marriage to be declared valid, object to her appeal to Rome? Katherine got to her feet, curtsyed to the king, and left the court ignoring calls for her to return.[25]

On July 31, Campeggio announced that the pope had adjourned the court.[26] While Henry immediately began petitioning for the court to be reconvened, Katherine and the Habsburgs urged Pope Clement to return a favorable verdict. And so events proceeded: high politics and diplomacy in London and Rome conducted alongside the personal reality of a marriage unraveling.

CHAPTER 10

THE KING'S GREAT MATTER

∴

The Queen writes that such are the King's disappointment and passion at not being able to carry out his purpose that the Cardinal will inevitably be the victim of his rage.[1]

—MENDOZA TO THE EMPEROR, JULY 25, 1529

WITH THE DIVORCE CASE REFERRED TO ROME, THERE SEEMED little prospect of Henry securing a favorable judgment. By the Treaty of Cambrai, Francis, Charles, and the pope had come to terms and ended French military efforts in Italy. France could no longer be used to put pressure on the emperor. While in Charles's custody, the pope had promised the emperor "not to grant unto any act that might be preparative, or otherwise, to divorce to be made to the King and Queen."[2]

It signaled Wolsey's fall from favor. He had failed in his efforts to free the pope from Charles's domination and to secure the annulment that Henry demanded. In his dispatch of September 1, the new imperial ambassador, Eustace Chapuys, reported that "the affairs of the Cardinal are getting worse and worse every day." Henry had banned him from receiving foreign ambassadors and prevented his coming to court. As the envoy continued in cipher, "the cause of this misunderstanding between the King and the Cardinal can be no other than the utter failure of the measures taken in order to bring about the divorce."[3] By October, Wolsey had been charged with *praemunire*, the illegal exercise of papal authority in England, in his role as legate. On the twenty-second, having resigned the lord chancellorship to the lawyer and accomplished humanist Sir Thomas More, Wolsey acknowledged his offenses and placed himself and his possessions into the king's hands.

Anticipating that the verdict from Rome would be hostile, Henry now embarked on an English solution to the annulment. Letters "of great importance," as the accounts of Sir Brian Tuke, the master of the posts, record, were sent to Henry's ambassadors in Rome, instructing them to inform the pope that neither he nor any other Englishman could be summoned to a Roman court because by ancient custom and privileges of the realm no one could be "compelled to go to law out of the Kingdom."[4] Over the next four years, under the stewardship of Thomas Cromwell, Parliament gradually eroded Rome's power in England: first to pressure the pope to make concessions, then to fashion a homemade settlement. By 1533, Henry would be the supreme head of the English Church and married to his new wife, Anne Boleyn.

AS THE CAMPAIGN against the Church reached a crescendo, relations between Henry and Katherine broke down irrevocably, with Mary remaining the only bond between them. In March 1531, Henry "dined and resorted to the Queen as he was accustomed, and diminished nothing of her estate, and much loved and cherished their daughter the Lady Mary, but in no ways would he come to her bed."[5] Mary lived in the midst of all this: sometimes at a distance in adjacent royal houses, at other times at court. At Christmas the previous year, Henry, Katherine, and Mary had been together; but Anne Boleyn remained a constant, tormenting presence. On Christmas Eve, Katherine directly challenged Henry about his relationship with Anne. His behavior was a personal affront to her: he was setting a scandalous example. Henry's response was curt: there was nothing wrong in his relationship with Anne, and he intended to marry her whatever Katherine or the pope might say.[6]

Anne was becoming equally bold. In conversation with one of Katherine's ladies-in-waiting, she declared that "she wished all the Spaniards were at the bottom of the sea" and added that "she cared not for the Queen or any of her family, and that she would rather see her hanged than have to confess that she was her Queen and mistress."[7]

Katherine now wrote to the emperor that she believed Anne alone stood in the way of a reconciliation with her husband and if she—that "woman [Henry] has under his roof"—were out of the way, their marriage might have a chance. Her husband's behavior displayed "not the least particle of shame."[8]

For Mary, separation from her father was proving hard to bear, and she continually petitioned to see him. In July 1530, she wrote asking to be allowed to visit him before he left for four months of hunting. On this occasion Henry agreed. He traveled to Richmond, where Mary was staying, and spent the whole day with her, "showing her all possible affection."[9] Suspicious of Mary's influence over her father, Anne Boleyn sent two servants to report on their conversation.[10] The following summer, Henry visited Mary again at Richmond "and made great cheer with her," speaking of her as he had when she was a young child, as a great "pearl."[11]

Such visits became more infrequent as Henry's views became increasingly colored by those of Anne. As Chapuys surmised, the king's apparent reluctance to see Mary was "to gratify the lady [Anne] who hates her as much as the Queen, or more so because she sees the King has some affection for her."[12] Chapuys believed that Anne was constantly scheming to have Mary moved as far away from court, and her father, as possible.[13] The child who had once bound the royal couple together was now used by Henry to pry them apart. The king demanded that Katherine choose between his company and that of Mary. He made it clear that if she visited the princess she might be forced to stay with her permanently and lose what little claim she had on Henry's companionship.[14] Desperate not to enrage Henry, Katherine "graciously replied that she would not leave him for her daughter, nor for anyone else in the world."[15] It was a painful and ultimately futile gesture of wifely loyalty.

AT THE END of May, a further attempt was made to force Katherine to submit to Henry's will on the divorce. A delegation of some thirty privy councillors was sent to see her in her Privy Chamber at Greenwich. Once again they made their case on behalf of the king, and once again Katherine's response was robust:

> I say I am his lawful wife, and to him lawfully married and by the order of the holy Church I was to him espoused as his true wife, although I was not so worthy, and in that point I will abide till the court of Rome which was privy to the beginning have made thereof a determination and final ending.[16]

The king would not approach Katherine again on the matter.

Henry and Anne left court for several weeks, leaving Katherine behind.[17] It marked the beginning of their public separation, though Katherine did not at first realize it. She sent a messenger to inquire about her husband's health, as was usual when they were apart, "and to signify the regret she had experienced at not having been able to see him before his departure for the country." Could he not at least have bid her farewell? Henry's reply was cruel and to the point. "He cared not for her adieux," he replied; "he had no wish to offer her the consolation of which she spoke or any other; and still less that she should send to him or to inquire as to his estate." He was "angry at her because she had wished to bring shame on him by having him publicly cited."[18] To both Katherine and the emperor's ambassador, it was obvious who was responsible: it "must have been decreed by her [Anne]."[19]

Mary and her mother stayed at Windsor, hunting and moving between royal residences. When Henry and Anne were ready to return, the king sent orders that his daughter should go to Richmond and the queen, banished from court, to Wolsey's former residence, The More in Hertfordshire.[20] It was the last time mother and daughter would see each other, though at the time neither realized it. Their separation would, it was hoped, force Katherine to accept a repatriation of the trial back to England. But, as Chapuys predicted, Katherine would never agree, "whatever stratagems may be used for the purpose."[21] Now, without her mother's comfort and support, the fifteen-year-old Mary would have to grow up alone.

Shortly after parting from her mother, Mary became unwell with sickness and stomach pains.[22] She wrote to the king that "no medicine could do her so much good as seeing him and the Queen, and desired his licence to visit them both at Greenwich." Chapuys reported that "this has been refused her, to gratify the lady, who hates her as much as the Queen, or more so, chiefly because she sees the King has some affection for her."[23] It is likely that Mary's illness was the onset of menstruation, with recurrent pains and melancholy exacerbated by distress and anxiety. It was a condition from which she would suffer repeatedly.

IN THE SUMMER of 1531, Mario Savorgnano, a wealthy Venetian, visited England from Flanders. His praise of Henry's warm welcome and impressive physique and intellect was tempered by criticism of his private mores. His wish to divorce his wife "detracts greatly from his merits, as there is now living with him a young woman of noble birth, though many say of bad character, whose will is law to him, and is expected to marry her." Having visited the queen, Savorgnano went to Richmond Palace to see Mary. The Venetian waited in the Presence Chamber

> until the Princess came forth, accompanied by a noble lady advanced in years, who is her governess, and by six maids of honour. We kissed her hand and she asked us how long we have been in England, and if we had seen their Majesties, her father and mother, and what we thought of the country; then she turned to her attendants, desiring them to treat us well, and withdrew into her chamber.
>
> This princess is not very tall, has a pretty face, and is well proportioned, with a beautiful complexion and is fifteen years old. She speaks Spanish, French and Latin besides her own mother English tongue, which is well grounded in Greek, and understands Italian, but does not venture to speak it. She sings excellently and plays on several instruments, so that she combines every accomplishment.[24]

Mary was acknowledged as a highly accomplished European princess. But in the years that followed such talents would be overshadowed by the need for courage and self-preservation. She would be forced to grow up quickly.

CHAPTER II

THE SCANDAL OF CHRISTENDOM

∴

Though the Queen has been forbidden to write or send messages to the King, she sent one the other day . . . a gold cup as a present, with honourable and humble words; but the King refused it, and was displeased with the person who presented it . . . it was sent back to the Queen. The King has sent her no present, and has forbidden the Council and others to do the same, as is usual. He used to send New Year's presents to the ladies of the Queen and Princess, but this has not been done this year. Thus they will lower the state of both, unless there is speedy remedy. He has not been so discourteous to the Lady, who has presented him with certain darts, of Biscayan fashion, richly ornamented. In return, he gave her a room hung with cloth of gold and silver, and crimson satin with rich embroideries. She is lodged where the Queen used to be and is accompanied by almost as many ladies as if she were Queen.[1]

—Chapuys to Charles V,
January 4, 1532

It was but a matter of time before Katherine's position as Henry's wife was entirely usurped, and steps were now taken to overcome clerical resistance. On May 15, 1532, the English clergy surrendered their last remaining independent legislative power: all new clerical legislation would now be submitted to the king. It was in direct breach of Magna Carta and of the coronation oath by which Henry had sworn that the Church in England would remain free. The following day, Thomas More resigned as lord chancellor in protest. Three months later, another staunch defender of the pope was lost with the death of the eighty-two-year-old William Warham, archbishop of Canterbury. Within weeks, Thomas Cranmer, an erstwhile supporter of the king's cause and ex-chaplain of the Boleyn family, was consecrated as his successor.

Henry now began to talk openly about the prospect of his remarriage. Anne Boleyn was made marchioness of Pembroke with a landed income of £1,000 a year. It was an unprecedented step: never before had a peeress been created in her own right. When Anne asked to have Katherine's jewels, the queen declared that she would never willingly give them up to "a person who is the scandal of Christendom."[2] When Henry sent a direct command, Katherine was forced to relinquish them.

As Henry took the last steps to repudiate Katherine and challenge the power of the pope and the emperor, he moved to shore up his alliance with France, concluded two years before. On June 23, a treaty of mutual aid was signed by which each party promised to send aid to the other if Charles invaded. An attack on England constituted an attack on France, and Henry knew that Charles would not be able to confront both.[3] Henry now prepared for a personal meeting with Francis designed to reenact the Field of the Cloth of Gold, to showcase Anglo-French amity and demonstrate to Charles and the pope the strength of their alliance.[4] On October 11, Henry and Anne Boleyn set sail for France with an entourage of more than two thousand.[5] For ten days the two kings feasted and jousted amid elaborate tents and pageantry. For now, at least, Henry had an ally and a means of applying pressure on the pope.[6]

Henry and Anne's six-week sojourn proved momentous. While they were away, Anne finally submitted to Henry's lustful advances and their relationship was consummated. By the end of December she was pregnant. They were married on January 25 in a secret ceremony presided over by Archbishop Cranmer. The formal dissolution of Henry's first marriage now became a priority. Katherine realized that time was running out. She wrote again to her nephew Charles:

> Though I know that Your Majesty is engaged in grave and important Turkish affairs . . . I cannot cease to importune you

> about my own, in which almost equal offence is being offered to God. . . . The prospective interview between the two kings, the companion the King now takes everywhere with him, and the authority and place he allows her to have cause the greatest scandal and the most widespread fear of impending calamity. Knowing the fears of my people, I am compelled by my conscience to resist, trusting in God and Your Majesty, and begging you to urge the Pope to pronounce sentence at once.[7]

Chapuys also made an urgent appeal on Katherine's behalf to the emperor:

> The Queen begs once more for the immediate decision of her case . . . she takes upon herself full responsibility for all the consequences, and assures Your Majesty that there need not be the slightest danger that war will follow. She believes that if His Holiness were to decide in her favour the King would even now obey him, but even should he fail to do so, she will die comparatively happy, knowing that the justice of her cause has been declared, and that the Princess, her daughter, will not lose her right to the succession.[8]

ON APRIL 5, 1533, the Convocation of English Bishops ruled that Pope Julius II's dispensation allowing Henry to marry Katherine had been invalid, "the same Matrimony to be against the law of God," and therefore "hath divorced the King's Highness from the noble Lady Katherine."[9] The Act in Restraint of Appeals decreed that England was now an empire, "governed by one Supreme Head and King" and subject to no outside authority.[10] There was now nothing to stop Henry from marrying Anne.

On May 23, Thomas Cranmer pronounced the marriage of Henry and Katherine to be null and void. It marked the failure of Katherine's long battle to save her twenty-four-year marriage. A week after Cranmer passed judgment, the visibly pregnant Anne Boleyn rode through the City of London to be anointed and crowned at Westminster Abbey. Chapuys recorded that along the procession route no one cried "God save the Queen!" and the "people, though forbidden on pain of death to call Katherine Queen, shouted it loud."[11]

Katherine was ordered to surrender the title of queen; her household was reduced in status, and workmen removed her arms from the walls of Westminster Hall and from the royal barge.[12] She was now the dowager princess of Wales, the widow of Prince Arthur. Lord Mountjoy, her lord chamberlain, at Ampthill Castle in Bedfordshire, was ordered to inform her of her demotion. Katherine rejected the title of princess dowager outright: she was and would always be the king's wife and the mother of his legitimate heir.[13] Henry's patience had run out. Katherine was to move to Buckden in Huntingdonshire, a remote palace of the bishops of Lincoln. The arrangement amounted to house arrest. She was forbidden to leave without the king's permission and prevented from seeing her daughter.

As Henry anticipated the birth of what he hoped would be his longed-for son, he began to harden his attitude toward his daughter as well. He forbade her to write or send messengers to Katherine, though Mary begged him to change his mind. He might, she suggested, "appoint someone next to her person to give evidence that her messages to her mother are only in reference to her health" and proposed that her own letters and those of her mother first pass through the king's hands, but Henry refused.[14]

When Mary was officially told of her father's remarriage in April, she displayed her developing self-preservation: she was "at first thoughtful" and then, "as the very wise person that she is, dissembled as much as she could and seemed even to rejoice at it. Without alluding in the least to the said marriage, and without communicating with any living soul, after her dinner the princess set about writing a letter to her father." On receiving the letter, Henry was "marvellously content and pleased, praising above all things the wisdom and prudence of his daughter."[15] As the imperial ambassador remarked, "As to the Princess, her name is not yet changed, and I think that they will wait until the Lady had a child."[16] For the time being Mary would be left alone.

Mary was a young woman caught between estranged parents and a new, hostile stepmother. Her mother, her role model, meanwhile, cast herself increasingly as martyr. In a letter to the emperor, the deeply troubled Katherine declared, "In this world I will confess myself to be the King's true wife and in the next they will know how unreasonably I am afflicted."[17] But as Chapuys said of Katherine, "wherever the King commanded her, were it even into the fire she would go."[18] Though mother and daughter were forbidden to communicate with each other, they sent letters secretly through trusted servants and the imperial ambassador. On April 10, Chapuys wrote of how Anne openly boasted that "she would have the princess for her lady's maid; but that is only to make her eat humble pie, or to marry her to some varlet, which would be an irreparable injury."[19] There was now an air of foreboding. Anne knew that both Mary and Katherine were held in great popular affection and that the majority of English people regarded Mary as "the true princess."

BY APRIL 1533, the imperial ambassador believed England was on the brink of civil war, and he implored Charles to invade:

> Considering the great injury done to Madame, your aunt, you can hardly avoid making war now upon this King and kingdom, for it is to be feared that the moment this accursed Anne sets her foot firmly in the stirrup she will try to do the Queen all the harm she possibly can, and the Princess also, which is the thing your aunt dreads most . . .
>
> I hear that the King is about to forbid everyone, under pain of death, to speak in public or private in favour of the Queen. After that he will most likely proceed to greater extremities unless God and Your Majesty prevent it.[20]

But Charles was preoccupied with the danger of the Turks in Hungary and the Mediterranean, the unrest in Germany, the intrigues in Italy, and the vengeful attitude of France.[21] Though committed in his support of Katherine, the emperor was not prepared to risk war with England; it was a private matter, and Henry had given him no pretext to intervene.[22]

CHAPTER 12

THE LADY MARY

∴

At three in the afternoon of September 7, 1533, the child that Henry had gone to such lengths to have legitimized was delivered. The king's physicians and astrologers had predicted that it would be a boy, and letters written in advance announced the birth of a "prince."

They had to be hastily altered. Anne had been delivered of a girl. As the imperial ambassador reported gleefully, "God has forgotten him entirely, hardening him in his obstinacy to punish and ruin him."[1] She was christened three days later at the Church of the Observant Friars at Greenwich and her name and titles proclaimed by the Garter King of Arms:

> God of his infinite goodness, send prosperous life and long to the High and mighty Princess of England, Elizabeth.[2]

For some, however, like Chapuys, she would always be "the Concubine's little bastard," the living symbol of England's breach with Rome.

Within a week of Elizabeth's birth, Mary's chamberlain, Sir John Hussey, received instructions "concerning the diminishing of her high estate of the name and dignity of the princess." Mary was to cease using the title immediately; her badges were to be cut from her servants' clothing and replaced with the arms of the king.[3] She was now to be known only as "the Lady Mary, the King's daughter": she was a bastard and no longer acknowledged as the king's heir.

Incredulous, Mary immediately wrote to her father:

This morning my chamberlain came and showed me that he had received a letter from Sir William Paulet, comptroller of your household . . . wherein was written that "the lady Mary, the King's daughter, should remove to the place aforesaid"—the leaving out of the name of princess. Which, when I heard, I could not a little marvel, trusting verily that your grace was not privy to the same letter, as concerning the leaving out of the name of princess, forasmuch as I doubt not in your goodness, but that your grace doth take me for his lawful daughter, born in true matrimony. Wherefore, if I were to say to the contrary, I should in my conscience run into the displeasure of God, which I hope assuredly your grace would not that I should.

And in all other things your grace shall have me as, always, as humble and obedient daughter and handmaid, as ever was child to the father . . .

By your most humble daughter
Mary, Princess.[4]

She had signed herself "Princess." Henry's response was immediate. A deputation led by the earl of Oxford was sent to visit her at the king's manor at Beaulieu (New Hall), in Essex, with a clear message:

The King is surprised to be informed, both by Lord Hussey's letters and his daughter's own . . . that she, forgetting her filial duty and allegiance, attempts, in spite of the commandment given . . . arrogantly to usurp the title of Princess, pretending to be heir-apparent, and encourages others to do the like declaring that she cannot in conscience think she is the King's lawful daughter, born in true matrimony, and believes the King in his own conscience thinks the same.

To prevent her "pernicious example" spreading, the earls were commanded to make clear "the folly and danger of her conduct, and how the King intends that she shall use herself henceforth, both as to her title and her household." She has "worthily deserved the King's high displeasure and punishment by law, but that on her conforming to his will he may incline of his fatherly pity to promote her welfare."[5]

In spite of the threats, Mary stood her ground.[6] When the delegation left, she wrote to her father, telling him that "as long as she lived she would obey his commands, but that she could not renounce the titles, rights and privileges which God, Nature and her own parents had given her." Compliance for Mary would mean acknowledging her own illegitimacy and the invalidity of her mother's marriage, and that she would not do.

ON DECEMBER 10, three months after her birth, Elizabeth was taken from court to Hatfield in Hertfordshire, a house some seventeen miles from London. Although there was "a shorter and better road . . . for great solemnity and to insinuate to the people that she is the true Princess," she was carried through the City accompanied not only by her new household but also by a distinguished escort of dukes, lords, and gentlemen.[7]

The following day, Thomas Howard, duke of Norfolk, was sent to Beaulieu to inform Mary that her father desired her "to go to the Court and service of [Elizabeth], whom he named Princess."[8] Mary responded that "the title belonged to herself and no other." Norfolk made no answer, declaring "he had not come to dispute but to accomplish the King's will." When Mary was told that she would be allowed to take very few servants with her, Margaret Pole—her longtime governess and godmother, who had been in Mary's entourage since the princess was three—asked if she might continue to serve Mary at her own expense and pay for the whole household. Her request was refused.[9] Henry wanted Mary, like Katherine, to be separated from those she trusted to encourage her submission. As Chapuys surmised, Pole would have prevented them from

> executing their bad designs, which are evidently either to cause her to die of grief or in some other way, or else to compel her to renounce her rights, marry some low fellow, or fall prey to lust, so that they may have a pretext and excuse for disinheriting her and submitting her to all manner of bad treatment.[10]

Mary was to be isolated in a household under the stewardship of Anne Boleyn's uncle and aunt, Sir John and Lady Anne Shelton.[11] Such was to be the princess's humiliation: she was to be little more than a servant—"lady's maid to the new bastard," as the imperial ambassador described it[12]—and prisoner.

As she prepared for her departure, Mary copied a protest, drafted for her by Chapuys, that declared that nothing she might do under compulsion should prejudice her status as princess:

> My lords, as touching my removal to Hatfield, I will obey his grace, as my duty is, or to any other place his grace may appoint me; but I protest before you, and all others present, that my conscience will in no wise suffer me to take any other than myself for princess, or for the King's daughter born in lawful matrimony; and that I will never wittingly or willingly say or do aught, whereby any person might take occasion to think that I agree to the contrary. Nor say I this out of any ambition or proud mind, as God is my judge. If I should do otherwise, I should slander the deed of my mother, and falsely confess myself a bastard, which God defend I should do, since the pope hath not so declared it by his sentence definitive, to whose final judgement I submit myself.[13]

On arriving at Hatfield, the duke of Norfolk asked her "whether she would not go and pay her respects to the Princess?" She responded that she "knew no other Princess in England except herself and the daughter of my Lady Pembroke [Anne Boleyn] had no such title." She might call her only "sister," as she called the duke of Richmond, Henry Fitzroy, "brother." As the duke departed, Mary requested that he should carry to the king the message that the princess, his daughter, begged his blessing. Norfolk refused, and Mary "retired to weep in her Chamber," which, Chapuys noted, "she does continually."[14]

Mary, like her mother, was now under house arrest. She was forbidden to walk in the garden or the public gallery of the house or attend Mass at the adjoining church lest the neighboring populace see her and cheer for her. Henry reproached Norfolk for going about his task "too softly" and "resolved to take steps to abate the stubbornness and pride" of the princess.[15]

Mary's resolve would prove hard to break; such were her love and commitment to Katherine. With the tenacity worthy of any Tudor, she determined to be as difficult as possible. For days she remained in her chamber, "the worst lodging of the house" and a place "not fit for a maid of honour."[16] She would eat a large breakfast to avoid having to eat dinner in the hall and often pleaded sickness as an excuse to have supper brought to her chamber. As soon as Anne Boleyn came to hear of this, she quickly stepped in, instructing her aunt that if Mary continued to behave in this way she was to be starved back into the hall, and if she tried to use the banned title of princess she was to have her ears boxed "as the cursed bastard."[17]

Over the next two years at Hatfield, Lady Anne Shelton would be repeatedly reprimanded for not being harsh enough and for showing Mary too much respect and kindness. Whenever Mary protested, she was punished: by the confiscation first of her jewels and then of almost everything else. By February 1534, she was "nearly destitute of clothes and other necessaries" and was compelled to ask her father for help. But even then she remained defiant: the messenger was instructed to accept money or clothing if they were offered, "but not to accept any writing in which she was not entitled princess."[18] Such was the hostility toward Mary that Sir William Fitzwilliam, treasurer of the king's household, was able to say with impunity of the king's daughter that if she would not be obedient, "I would that her head was from her shoulders, that I might toss it here with my foot," at which point, according to two witnesses, he "put his foot forward, spurning the rushes."[19]

CHAPTER 13

SPANISH BLOOD

∴

AROUND THE TIME MARY JOINED THE INFANT ELIZABETH'S HOUSEhold, she received a letter in secret from her mother. It was an extraordinary epistle, written in the most exceptional circumstances, born of Katherine's concern for her daughter's welfare.

Daughter,
I heard such tidings today that I do perceive (if it be true) the time is very near when Almighty God will prove you; and I am very glad of it for I trust he doth handle you with a good love. I beseech you, agree of His pleasure with a merry heart; and be sure that, without fail, He will not suffer you to perish if you beware to offend Him. I pray you, good daughter, to offer yourself to Him. . . . And if this lady [Shelton] do come to you as it is spoken, if she do bring you a letter from the King, I am sure in the self same letter you shall be commanded what you shall do. Answer with few words, obeying the King, your father, in everything, save only that you will not offend God and lose your own soul; and go no further with learning and disputation in the matter. And wheresoever, and in whatsoever, company you shall come, observe the King's commandments.

But one thing I especially desire you, for the love that you do owe unto God and unto me, to keep your heart with a chaste mind, and your body from all ill and wanton company, [not] thinking or desiring any husband for Christ's passion; neither determine yourself to any manner of living till this troublesome time be past. For I dare make sure that you shall see a very good end, and better than you can desire. . . . And now you shall begin, and by likelihood I shall follow.

I set not a rush by it; for when they have done the uttermost they can, then I am sure of the amendment . . . we never come to the kingdom of Heaven but by troubles. Daughter wheresoever you come, take no pain to send unto me, for if I may, I will send to you,

Your loving mother,
Katherine the Queen.[1]

It is the suggestion of a shared martyrdom that stands out. If matters did not improve on Earth, they would do so, Katherine reassured her daughter, in Heaven. The letter enshrined many of what would become Mary's guiding principles, not just for the next few torturous months but for the rest of her life: to dedicate her life to God, to remain chaste, and to accept struggles with good grace. Accompanying the letter, Katherine sent two books: *De Vita Christi* and Saint Jerome's letters to Paula and Eustochium, women who lived austere lives and dedicated themselves to God.

Katherine was then at Buckden. In mid-January, Chapuys reported that she had not "been out of her room since the Duke of Suffolk was with her [in mid-December], except to hear mass in a Gallery. She will not eat or drink what her new servants provide. The little she eats in her anguish is prepared by her chamberwomen, and her room is used as her kitchen."[2] Katherine was convinced that Henry and Anne were seeking to poison her. She trusted only the imperial ambassador, referring to him in correspondence as "My Special Friend."[3] Katherine continued to beseech the emperor that the pope do her justice. She and Mary were imprisoned "like the most miserable creatures in the world."[4] Charles accused Henry of mistreating them, but the king remained unmoved; "there was no other princess except his daughter Elizabeth, until he had a son which he thought would happen soon."[5] Still Henry hoped for a male heir.

ALTHOUGH MARY LOVED and respected Henry as her father, she refused to submit to his will as king, and at the vulnerable age of seventeen, this meant painful rejection. In January, when Henry visited the household at Hatfield, Mary was ordered to stay in her chamber.

Instead, Thomas Cromwell and the captain of the Guard were sent to Mary to urge her to renounce her title. Mary responded that she had already given her answer and it was useless trying to persuade her otherwise. She still craved her father's favor, however, and begged for permission to see him and kiss his hand. When she was refused yet again, she went out onto the terrace at the top of the house as her father prepared to leave. As he was mounting his horse he spotted her and, seeing her on her knees with her hands together, bowed and touched his cap.[6] Mary would not see him again for more than two and a half years.

Upon his return to court, Henry explained that he had refused to see Mary on account of her obstinacy, which "came from her Spanish blood." But when the French ambassador mentioned how "very well brought up" she was, "the tears came into his [Henry's] eyes and he could not refrain from praising her."[7]

Anne continued to resent Henry's clear affection for his elder daughter and persisted in conspiring against her. When she heard of Mary's defiance, she railed that "her answers could not have been made without the suggestion of others" and complained that Mary was not being kept under close enough surveillance.[8] When Anne went to visit her daughter at Hatfield in March, she wasted no time in humiliating her. She "urgently solicited" Mary to visit her and "honour her as Queen," saying that it "would be a means of reconciliation with the King, and she would intercede with him for her." Mary replied that "she knew no other Queen in England except her mother" but that if Anne would do her that favor with her father she would be much obliged. Enraged, Anne departed, swearing that "she would bring down the pride of this unbridled Spanish blood."[9]

According to a source close to Chapuys, Anne had been heard to say more than once that as soon as Henry was out of the country, leaving her as regent, she meant to use her authority to have Mary killed, "either by hunger or otherwise," even if she, Anne, was "burnt alive for it."[10]

CHAPTER 14

HIGH TRAITORS

∴

ON MARCH 24, 1534, POPE CLEMENT VII PASSED FINAL SENTENCE on the marriage of Henry and Katherine. It "was and is valid and canonical."[1] Katherine's cause had triumphed, but it was a hollow victory and had come too late to alter events. A week later, the Act of Succession received royal assent, endorsing exactly what the pope's sentence had rejected. Thomas Cranmer decreed in favor of Henry's marriage to Anne, and the succession was now transferred to Henry's male heirs by Anne or any subsequent wife. In default of a male heir, the throne would pass to Elizabeth. Mary was excluded from the succession. An oath to the act's contents was to be sworn by all the king's subjects, with refusal to swear treated as high treason:

> If any person or persons . . . do, or cause to be procured or done, any thing or things to the prejudice, slander, disturbance or derogation of the said lawful matrimony solemnised between your Majesty and the said Queen Anne, or to the peril, slander . . . the issues and heirs of your highness being limited to this Act . . . then every such person and persons . . . for every such offence shall be adjudged high traitors.[2]

On April 20, the Henrican regime made a very public display of its intent when Elizabeth Barton, known as "the Holy Maid of Kent," and five Carthusian priests met their deaths at Tyburn, a village just outside the boundaries of London. Tied to wooden planks, they were dragged behind horses through the streets of the city for the five-mile journey from the Tower of London. Barton, a nun famous for her prophecies, had made clear her sympathy to the cause of Katherine of Aragon and had foretold plagues and disaster if the divorce went ahead. She declared that by marrying Anne, Henry had forfeited his right to rule: in God's eyes he was no longer king, and the people should depose him. Among the charges made against her was that she had declared that "no man should fear" taking up arms on Mary's behalf and that "she should have succour and help enough, that no man should put her from her right that she was born unto."[3]

Barton had been used by opponents of the divorce, particularly by a number of monks of the Observant and Carthusian orders, who circulated accounts of the nun's prophecies. Now they were all to be made an example of. Elizabeth Barton died first, followed by her "accomplices," who, as priests, suffered all the penalties of the law of treason. The monks were hanged in their habits until they lost consciousness, then revived so that they could watch as they were castrated and disemboweled. Their entrails were burned in front of them and then each body was quartered and beheaded.[4]

On the same day the citizens of London were required to make the Oath of Succession.[5] The executions were intended as a warning to those who opposed the king's policies and reforms. Barton's head was impaled on a railing at London Bridge, and the heads of her followers were placed on the gates of the city.[6]

AS THE ACT OF Succession was passed, Thomas Cromwell, the king's principal secretary and chief minister, made a note to "send a copy of the act of the King's succession to the Princess Dowager and the Lady Mary, with special commandment that it may be read in their presence and their answer taken."[7] Commissioners were sent to Katherine at Buckden and directed to beseech her to have, above all, "regard for her honourable and most dear daughter the Lady Princess. From whom . . . the King's highness . . . might also withdraw his princely estimation, goodness, zeal and affection, [with] no little regret, sorrow and extreme calamity."[8]

In response to this clear threat made against her daughter, Katherine reiterated that Mary "was the King's true begotten Child, and as God had given her unto the King, as his daughter, to do with her as shall stand with his pleasure, trusting to God that she will prove an honest woman."[9] After refusing to sign the oath, Katherine told the commissioners, "If any one of you has a commission to execute this penalty upon me, I am ready. I ask only that I be allowed to die in the sight of the people." Weeks later, she was moved from Buckden to Kimbolton in Huntingdonshire, another gloomy fortified manor house, with thick walls and a wide moat.[10]

Meanwhile, Mary stood firm. As Chapuys described it, "Some days ago the King asked his mistress's [aunt], who has charge of the Princess, if the latter had abated her obstinacy, and on being answered 'No,' he said there must be someone about her who encouraged her and conveyed news from the Queen her mother." Lady Shelton suspected one of the maids of the household, who in turn was quickly dismissed. "The Princess has been much grieved at this," Chapuys reported, "for she was the only one in whom she had confidence, and by her means she had letters from me and others."

Faced with Mary's intransigence and realizing that he could get his way "neither by force nor menaces," Henry changed tack and began to beg her to "lay aside her obstinacy" on the promise that she would be rewarded with "a royal title and dignity." But Mary refused to yield: "God had not so blinded her as to confess for any kingdom on earth that the King her father and the Queen her mother had so long lived in adultery, nor would she contravene the ordinance of the Church and make herself a bastard." As the ambassador explained, "She believes firmly that this dissimulation the King uses is only the more easily to attain his end and cover poison, but she says she cares little, having full confidence in God that she will go straight to Paradise and be quit of the tribulations of this world, and her only grief is about the troubles of the Queen her mother."[11]

WHEN EMPEROR CHARLES V complained once more to Henry about his ill-treatment of Mary and Katherine, the king responded scathingly, "It is not a little to our marvel that, touching the fact, either the Emperor, or any of his wise council learned, or other discreet person would in anything think us, touching our proceeding therein, but that which is godly, honourable and reasonable."[12]

But the ill-treatment continued. By the middle of May, Katherine's household and Mary's remaining servants were made to swear to the act. Several men and women were committed to the Tower charged with holding private conversations with the Lady Mary and styling her "Princess." Of these, Lady Anne Hussey, formerly one of Mary's gentlewomen, was interrogated on August 3.[13] Questions were asked about her contact with Mary "since she lost the name of princess." Did she know that the Lady Mary was justly declared by law not to be a princess and yet she had called her so? Had she received any messages or tokens from the Lady Mary? She had, she explained, visited Mary only once since the king had discharged her from the lady's service the previous Whitsuntide. Hussey admitted that she had inadvertently addressed Mary as "Princess" twice, not from any wish to disobey the law but from having long been accustomed to doing so. She also confessed that she had received a present from Mary and that she had sent Mary secret notes and received tokens from her in return. After signing a confession and begging forgiveness, Hussey was released.[14]

The conditions of Mary's house arrest grew more restrictive. She received fewer and fewer visitors, and those who did visit her were heavily scrutinized and reported to the Privy Council. Often when people came to pay their respects to the infant Elizabeth, Mary was locked in her room and the windows were nailed shut. In February 1534, as she walked along a gallery, she was spotted by some local people, who called out to her as their princess and waved their caps, after which she was watched more closely.[15] Lady Shelton continued to torment Mary, saying that if she were Henry she would throw her out of the house for disobedience and that "the King is known to have said that she would make her lose her head for violating the laws of his realm."[16]

CHAPTER 15

WORSE THAN A LION

IN FEBRUARY 1535, TWO WEEKS BEFORE HER NINETEENTH BIRTHday, Mary fell "dangerously ill" with pain in her head and stomach. It was feared she had been poisoned. Few had forgotten Anne Boleyn's threats against her.

Henry was reported to be "as much grieved at her sickness as any father could be for his daughter"; he sent his own physician, Sir William Butts, and instructed Chapuys to choose one or two others to visit her. Their presence was to be strictly controlled: they were not to speak to Mary unless other people were present and then in no language other than English for fear that she would use them to convey messages to the emperor.[1]

Butts informed the king that Mary's illness was partly caused by "sorrow and trouble." He advised that she should be sent to her mother, arguing that it would be both less expensive and better for her health and that if anything did happen to her, the king would be free from suspicion. But Henry did nothing. It was a "great misfortune," he declared, that she was so stubborn, as she "took away from him all occasion to treat her as well as he would."[2]

When Katherine learned of her daughter's condition, she asked Chapuys to petition the king to reconsider. She had "grave suspicion" about the cause of Mary's ill health and insisted that "there is no need of any person but myself to nurse her . . . I will put her in my own bed where I sleep, and watch her when needful."[3] But Henry again did nothing. He blamed Katherine for Mary's "obstinacy and disobedience," asserting that "although sons and daughters were bound to some obedience towards their mothers, their chief duty was to their fathers." He believed that if Mary had the comfort of her mother, "there would be no hope of bringing her to do what he wanted, to renounce her lawful and true succession."[4] In this trial of wills, he hoped to break Mary's resolve by starving her of affection and blunt the threat that she and her mother represented. "The Lady Katherine," Henry declared, "is a proud, stubborn woman of high courage. If she took it into her head to take her daughter's part, she could quite easily take the field, muster a great army, and wage against me a war as fierce as any her mother Isabella ever wages in Spain."[5] It was a grudging acknowledgment of Katherine's resolve and her mighty political lineage.

Henry did agree that Mary could be moved to a house nearer Kimbolton, where her mother's doctor, Miguel de la Soa, could attend her, but on condition that Katherine did not attempt to see her. Writing to Cromwell, Katherine offered her thanks:

> Mine especial friend, you have greatly bound me with the pains, that you have taken in speaking to the King my Lord concerning the coming of my daughter with me. . . . As touching the answer, which has been made you, that his Highness is contented to send her to some place near me, for as long as I do not see her; I pray you, vouchsafe to give unto his Highness mine effectual thanks for the goodness which he showeth unto his daughter and mine, and for the comfort that I have thereby received . . . you shall certify that, if she were within one mile of me, I would not see her.

Katherine had wanted Mary to be brought to her, she said, as a "little comfort and mirth" would "undoubtedly be half a health unto her," explaining "I have proved the like by experience, being diseased of the same infirmity." Both mother and daughter suffered from "deep melancholy."

Katherine told Cromwell that she did not understand how Henry could distrust them or why he would not allow mother and daughter to be together:

> Here have I, among others, heard that he had some suspicion of the surety of her. I cannot believe that a thing so far from reason

> should pass from the royal heart of his highness; neither can I think that he hath so little confidence in me. If any such matter chance to be communed of, I pray you say unto his highness that I am determined to die (without doubt) in this realm; and that I, from henceforth, offer mine own person for surety, to the intent that, if any such thing should be attempted, that then he do justice of me, as of the most evil woman that ever was born.[6]

Mary received word through Lady Shelton that the king now regarded her as his "worst enemy." She had already succeeded in turning most of the Christian princes of Europe against him, and he believed "her conduct was calculated to encourage conspiracy."[7] Cromwell openly lamented the fact that, by their very existence, Katherine and Mary were preventing good relations between England and the Holy Roman Empire. If Mary were to die, it would do far less harm than good, as the immediate result would be a treaty of mutual goodwill between Henry and Charles.[8] If only God had "taken them to himself," Cromwell cursed, no one would have questioned Henry's marriage to Anne or the right of their daughter to succeed him; the possibility of internal revolt and war with the emperor would never have arisen.[9]

By early January 1535, Henry was losing patience. Mary was told that she must take the oath and "on pain of her life she must not call herself Princess or her mother Queen but that if ever she does she will be sent to the Tower."[10]

THE ACT OF SUPREMACY, passed in November 1534, authorized the king to assume the Supreme Headship of the Church and repudiated any "foreign laws or foreign authority to the contrary." Another act established an oath of obedience to the king, which involved a renunciation of the power of any "foreign authority or potentate"—that is, the pope—as well as an endorsement of the Boleyn marriage and the succession. Moreover, by the Treasons Act it was now treasonable, either by overt act or by malicious "wish, will or desire, by words or in writing," to do harm to Henry, Anne, or their heirs, to deprive the king of his titles (including supreme head) or to call him heretic, tyrant, or usurper.[11] To deny the royal supremacy, even to fail to acknowledge it, was high treason. The stakes had risen.

The first victims of the new treason laws were John Fisher, bishop of Rochester, and the humanist and former lord chancellor Thomas More; both were high-profile opponents of the royal divorce and supporters of Katherine and Mary. They were condemned for refusing to swear to the Act of Succession and for their denial of Henry as supreme head of the English Church. As he faced the block on Tower Hill in June 1535, Fisher addressed the gathered crowd: "Christian people, I am come hither to die for the faith of Christ's Catholic Church."[12]

Once he was dead, his naked corpse was displayed at the site of the execution, as Henry had demanded, and his head put on a spike. Nine days later, More's sentence of a traitor's death was commuted from disembowelment to beheading in deference to his former office. He was butchered on July 6 with one stroke of the ax. His corpse was taken to the Chapel Royal of St. Peter ad Vincula within the Tower, where it was interred; his head was parboiled and impaled on a pole on London Bridge.[13]

News of the executions shocked Europe. In Italy the bishop of Faenza described his horror on reading that the English king had caused "certain religious men" to be "ripped up in each other's presence, their arms torn off, their hearts cut out and rubbed upon their mouths and faces."[14] Meanwhile, Anne Boleyn urged Henry to mete out punishment to the real traitors, as Chapuys recounted: "She is incessantly crying after the King that he does not act with prudence in suffering the Queen and the Princess to live, who deserved death more than all those who have been executed and that they were the cause of all."[15]

Fearing for their lives, Mary wrote to the emperor, pleading for immediate intervention, while Katherine addressed the pope.

Most Holy and Blessed Father,

I have for some time ceased from writing to Your Holiness, though my conscience has reproached me for my silence. . . . [Now] once more . . . I do entreat you to bear this realm especially in mind, to remember the King, my lord and husband, and my daughter. Your Holiness knows, and all Christendom knows, what things are done here, what great offence is given to God, what scandal to the world, what reproach is thrown upon your Holiness. If a remedy be not applied shortly, there will be no end to ruined souls and martyred saints. . . . I write frankly to your Holiness, as one who can feel with me and my daughter for the martyrdom of these good men, whom, it comforts me to hope, we may follow in their sufferings though we cannot imitate their lives. . . . We await a remedy from God and from Your Holiness. It must come speedily or the time will be past![16]

Through a letter to Chapuys, Mary urged her cousin Charles to take action:

Now more than ever those services on your part are urgently required, considering the miserable plight and wretched conditions of affairs in this country, which is such that unless His Majesty, the Emperor, for the service of God, the welfare and repose of Christendom, as well as for the honour of the King, my father, takes pity on these poor afflicted creatures, all and everything will go to total ruin and be irretrievably lost. For the Emperor to apply a prompt remedy, as I hope and trust he will, it is necessary that he should be well and minutely informed of the state of affairs in this country. . . . I would dare to ask this favour of you, that you dispatch forthwith one of your men, an able one . . . to the Emperor, and inform him of the whole and beg him, in the name of the Queen, my mother and mine, for the honour of God, and the considerations above mentioned, to take this matter in hand, and provide a remedy for the affairs of this country.[17]

Mary was now desperate to escape England. A servant of the imperial ambassador who visited her at Eltham reported that "she thinks of nothing else than how it may be done, her desire for it increasing every day."[18] Chapuys had raised the prospect frequently over the previous two years, but then the immediate danger had receded and plans had not developed further. This time it was different: Mary felt the danger to be greater than ever. She sent word to Chapuys, "begging him most urgently to think over the matter, otherwise she considered herself lost, knowing they wanted only to kill her."[19]

Suspicious of Mary's intentions, Henry ordered that armed watches be kept around every house Mary stayed at and troops were placed at every seaport within a day's ride of these residences. On November 6, Chapuys wrote that according to Gertrude Blount, marchioness of Exeter, the king "has lately said to some of his most confidential councillors that he would no longer remain in the trouble, fear and suspense he had so long endured on account of the Queen and Princess" and that they "should see, at the coming Parliament, to get him released therefrom, swearing most obstinately that he would wait no longer."[20] All talk was of imminent martyrdom. Weeks later the imperial agent Dr. Pedro Ortiz wrote of the likelihood that Katherine and the princess would be "sentenced to martyrdom which she [Katherine] was ready to receive in testimony of the Holy Faith, as the Cardinal of Rochester and other holy martyrs have done."[21] Mary would, Chapuys feared, be made an example of, "to show that no one ought to disobey the laws" and that Henry meant to fulfill what "had been foretold of him; that is, that at the beginning of his reign he would be as gentle as a lamb, and at the end, worse than a lion."[22]

CHAPTER 16

SUSPICION OF POISON

My most dear lord, King and husband,

The hour of my death now drawing on, the tender love I owe you forceth me, my case being such, to commend myself to you, and to put you in remembrance with a few words of the health and safeguard of your soul, which you ought to prefer before all worldly matters, and before the care and pampering of your own body, for the which you have cast me into many calamities and yourself into many troubles. For my part, I pardon you everything, and I wish to devoutly pray God that He will also pardon you.

For the rest, I commend unto you our daughter Mary, beseeching you to be a good father unto her, as I have heretofore desired. . . . I forgive you myself, and I pray God to forgive you. . . . I make this vow, that mine eyes desire you above all things.[1]

AT TWO IN THE AFTERNOON OF FRIDAY, JANUARY 7, 1536, KATHERINE of Aragon died in her chamber at Kimbolton Castle. She was fifty years old. She had suffered with "pain in her stomach" for several months and had begged Henry to allow Mary to visit her.[2] Yet mother and daughter, separated for four years, were not to be granted the solace of a final meeting.

But Eustace Chapuys was given permission to visit. He arrived at Kimbolton on Sunday, the second, seeking to console Katherine as she prepared to die and to assure her, albeit falsely, that "the King was sorry for her illness."[3] For several hours each day he sat with Katherine, and they talked of the events of the previous years. Katherine thanked the ambassador for his good services and expressed regret as to "her misfortune and that of the princess," and for the "delay of remedy by which all good men had suffered." Chapuys reassured her that the mounting tide of heresy had not arisen because of her defiance, as she feared, but that God sent such trials "for the exaltation of the good and the confusion of the wicked." In response to the ambassador's words, "she showed herself very glad, for she had previously had some scruple of conscience because the heresies had arisen from her affair." Her nephew "could not have done better," given the "great affairs which had hindered him," and she declared it was "not without its advantages as the Pope now upon the death of the Cardinal of Rochester and other disorders, intended to seek a remedy in the name of the Holy See."[4]

The visit of the ambassador comforted Katherine, and for a while after she rallied a little. She managed to sleep; "her stomach retained her food" and, "without any help, [she] combed and tied her hair, and dressed her head"; but then her health deteriorated once more.[5] At dawn on Friday the seventh, she heard Mass, dictated her final letters to Charles and Henry, and prayed "that God would pardon the King her husband for the wrong that he had done her."[6] Having received Extreme Unction, she spent her last hours in calm reflection. By the early afternoon she was dead.

Later that day Sir Edmund Bedingfield, Katherine's steward, wrote to Cromwell, informing him of her death and detailing the arrangements that were to be made for the preparation of her body: "the groom of the chandlery here can cere [disembowel and embalm] her . . . and, further, I shall send for a plumber to close the body in lead."[7] Having embalmed the body, the chandler declared that her organs were sound, except for the heart, which was black all through and had "some black round thing which clung closely to the outside."[8] It was most likely a cancerous tumor, but her physician, Soa, concluded that she had been poisoned.

Katherine had been taken ill "about five weeks ago," according to the imperial ambassador. "The attack was renewed on the morrow of Christmas Day. It was a pain in the stomach, so violent that she could retain no food." He continued, "I asked the physician several times if there was any suspicion of poison. He was afraid it was so, for after she had drunk some Welsh beer she had been worse, and that it must have been a slow and subtle poison."[9] Katherine's supporters needed little persuading.

ACCORDING TO CHAPUYS, Henry greeted the news of Katherine's death with great jubilation. "You could not conceive," read his dispatch, "the joy that the King and those who favour the concubinage have shown at the death of the good Queen." That Sunday, Henry attended Mass in the Chapel Royal dressed entirely in yellow, signifying joy, except for a white feather in his cap. After dining, he went to Anne's apartments, "where the ladies danced and there did several things like one transported with joy." The ambassador continued, "From all I hear the grief of the people at this news is incredible, and the indignation they feel against the King, on whom they lay the blame of her death, part of them believing it was by poison and others by grief; and they are the more indignant at the joy the King has exhibited."[10]

Yet Henry was celebrating more than the demise of a former wife; Katherine's death had a far greater significance. On hearing the news he shouted, "God be praised that we are free from all suspicion of war!"[11] With the principal source of enmity between them removed, Henry believed the threat of war with the emperor had ended. He added a postscript to Cromwell's dispatch to the ambassadors in France to that effect: now that "the Emperor has no occasion to quarrel," they were to keep themselves "more aloof" and less ready to accede to the French king's requests.[12] Chapuys told the emperor:

> Cromwell was not ashamed in talking with one of my men, to tell him you had no reason to profess so great grief for the death of the Queen, which he considered very convenient and advantageous for the preservation of friendship between you and his Majesty, his master; that henceforth we should communicate more freely together, and that nothing remained but to get the Princess to obey the will of the King, her father.[13]

Katherine's death had altered Charles's position in relation to England. He was not bound to Mary as he had been to her mother, and now, as he resumed hostilities with France, he looked once again to court English favor. He wrote to Chapuys at the end of February that "a renewal of amity might be more easily effected now . . . with some suitable provision for the princess than during the Queen's life." It would be a means to "abate the insolence of Francis" and win time for Mary.[14]

Mary's status and welfare were, as they would always be, secondary to Habsburg strategic interests. Charles was not prepared to remain estranged from England over her disinheritance or ill-treatment, and he was soon in more pressing need of Henry's goodwill. In the spring of 1536, Francis invaded Savoy, triggering an imperial invasion of Provence. Both sides now sought an English alliance. Henry, who had risked war to be rid of Katherine, had apparently been absolved.

FOUR DAYS AFTER Katherine's death, Lady Shelton went to Mary and "most unceremoniously without the least preparation" told her that her mother was dead. That evening Mary requested that Katherine's physician and apothecary be allowed to visit her so she might hear of her mother's final hours and of the manner of her death.[15] As Charles told Isabella, his wife, Mary was "inconsolable at the loss she has sustained, especially when she thinks of her father's past behaviour towards herself, and the little favour she can expect for the future."[16] It was feared she would "die of grief" or with Katherine out of the way, Anne Boleyn might hasten "what she has long threatened to do, viz. to kill her."[17]

But Anne's intentions were far from clear. Although she had celebrated when informed of Katherine's death, rewarding the messenger with a "handsome present," thereafter she "frequently wept, fearing that they might do with her as with the good Queen."[18] Ironically, Katherine had been Anne's best protection. Henry was not likely to question his second marriage while his first wife was still alive. Fearing that Henry's affection was declining, Anne sought to be reconciled with Mary as a means of securing her own favor. She instructed Lady Shelton to tell Mary that "if she would lay aside her obstinacy and obey her father," Anne would be "the best friend in the world to her, like another mother, and would obtain for her anything she liked to ask and that if she wished to come to court Mary would be exempted from holding the tail of her gown." But Mary would not be swayed. As Lady Shelton informed Anne, she would "rather die a hundred times than change her opinion or do anything against her honour and conscience."[19]

By the new year, Anne knew that she was pregnant again, and, with her confidence renewed, she changed tack. Lady Shelton, Mary's governess, was instructed to ease the pressure, not to "further move the lady Mary to be toward the King's Grace otherwise than it pleases herself."[20] Anne felt sure she knew Mary's fate: "If I have a son, as I hope shortly," she wrote menacingly, "I know what will happen to her."[21]

Mary now raised once more with Chapuys the prospect of fleeing to the imperial court in Brussels. If she had something to drug the women with, she told him, she might easily escape and pass under Lady Shelton's window and then find some means to break or open the garden gate.[22] As the ambassador reported, "She is so eager to escape from all her troubles and dangers that if he were to advise her to cross the Channel in a sieve she would do it." Chapuys advised caution. Mary was then at Hunsdon, forty miles from Gravesend, from which she could be taken to Flanders. Any escape plan would necessitate her riding through many villages and towns, and she would be at high risk of discovery or capture. For now it was simply too hazardous an undertaking, and he recommended that she wait until Easter, when she would be moved again, hopefully to somewhere more convenient from which to escape.

In the meantime, Chapuys told Mary she should continue in the semiseclusion of mourning and, if approached by the king's officers, beg them to leave her in peace to grieve for her mother. If pressed, she might tell them she was thinking of entering a convent when she reached full age to stun them into indecision.[23] Mary was becoming increasingly hysterical, he added; "she is continually asking [me to] beg the Emperor to hasten the remedy, which she fears will be too late for her, for which reason she is daily preparing herself for death."[24]

CHAPTER 17

THE RUIN OF THE CONCUBINE

⁘

ON JANUARY 26, TWO WEEKS AFTER HER DEATH, KATHERINE OF Aragon's coffin was taken in procession, amid chaplains, gentlemen, ladies, and maids, on the nine-mile journey from the chapel at Kimbolton to Peterborough Cathedral. Three days later, Mass was said and a sermon preached by John Hilsey, the bishop of Rochester. He claimed that "in the hour of death" Katherine had acknowledged "that she had not been Queen of England."[1] In death, Henry claimed that Katherine had submitted to him as she had refused to in life. She was buried as a princess dowager and not as a queen:

> The right excellent and noble princess the Lady Katherine, daughter of the right high and mighty Prince Ferdinand, late King of Castile, and wife to the noble and excellent Prince Arthur, brother to our Sovereign Lord, Henry the 8th.[2]

On the day of Katherine's burial, Anne Boleyn was delivered of a stillborn son. Four days earlier, Henry had fallen badly from his horse during a joust, and Anne claimed the shock had brought on the miscarriage. As Chapuys reported, much to Henry's "great distress" the fetus "seemed to be a male child which she had not borne three and a half months."[3]

Gertrude Courtenay (née Blount), marchioness of Exeter, and her husband, the marquess, who was the honorific head of the Privy Chamber and Henry's first cousin, reported that Henry had shared with someone "in great confidence, and as if it were in confession" his doubts about Anne. "He had made this marriage," he said, "seduced by witchcraft and for this reason he considered it null; and that this was evident because God did not permit them to have any male issue."

He now believed that he might take another wife.[4] He had been "making much of a lady of the Court, named Mistress Semel [Seymour], to whom, many say, he [Henry] has lately made great presents."[5] Jane Seymour, the twenty-five-year-old daughter of a Wiltshire gentleman, had formerly been in the service of Katherine of Aragon and was now the focus of the king's affection. As for Anne, "her heart broke when she saw that he loved others."[6]

IN EARLY FEBRUARY, Mary changed residence. The imperial ambassador reported that the princess was well and "better accompanied on her removal and provided with what was necessary to her than she had been before." Her father had put "about 100,000 crowns" at her disposal to distribute in alms. It had been rumored that the king meant "to increase her train and exalt her position." But, as Chapuys wrote, this had been before Anne's miscarriage:

> I hope it may be so, and that no scorpion lurks under the honey. I think the King only waited to summon the said Princess to swear to the statutes in expectation that the concubine would have had a male child, of which they both felt assured. I know not what they will do now.[7]

Mary's supporters, including the marquess and marchioness of Exeter; Lord Montague (the son of Margaret Pole); Sir Nicholas Carew, the master of horse; and the imperial ambassador sought to capitalize on Anne Boleyn's loss of favor and looked toward restoring Mary as the rightful heir to the throne. Jane Seymour's sympathy for Mary was well known. Two years before, she had sent to Mary to "tell her to be of good cheer, and that her troubles would sooner come to an end than she supposed, and that when the opportunity occurred she would show herself her true and devoted servant."[8]

On April 29, it was reported that Sir Nicholas Carew was promoting

Jane Seymour and communicating with Mary, telling her "to be of good cheer, for shortly the opposite party would put water in their wine."[9] Carew and his allies at court coached Jane as to how she should behave to secure the king's affection, urging her "that she must by no means comply with the King's wishes except by way of marriage."[10] When, in March, Henry sent her a letter and "a purse full of sovereigns," Jane returned them unopened and, falling to her knees, begged that Henry "consider that she was a gentlewoman of good and honourable parents, without reproach" and that if he "wished to make her some present in money she begged it might be when God enabled her to make some honourable match."[11] As Gertrude Courtenay, the marchioness of Exeter, put it, "Henry's love and desire . . . was wonderfully increased."[12] It was claimed that "[Anne] and Cromwell were on bad terms, and . . . some new marriage for the King was spoken of."[13] Now, with the king looking to marry once more, Cromwell sought to bring about Anne Boleyn's downfall.

EASTER WEEK PROVED to be of fateful consequence. Two public rows—the first between Anne and Mark Smeaton, one of the queen's musicians, the other between Anne and Sir Henry Norris, the chief gentleman of the king's Privy Chamber—gave Cromwell the excuse he needed. The conversations had suggested that they were infatuated with the queen and desired the king's death. By the afternoon of Sunday, March 30, Henry had been told of the exchanges and had angrily confronted Anne. They both attended the May Day jousts as planned, but as soon as the tournament was over, Henry left for his town palace, Whitehall, formerly York Place, accompanied by Henry Norris. As Edward Hall's chronicle related, "of this sudden departing many men mused, but most chiefly the Queen." George Constantine, Norris's servant, reported, "[The king] had Mr Norris in examination and promised him his pardon in case he would utter the truth." Yet "whatsoever could be said or done, Mr Norris would confess no thing to the King."[14] The following day he was sent to the Tower, where Smeaton was already imprisoned. After four hours of torture and interrogation, Smeaton confessed to adultery with the queen.

On May 2, Anne and her brother, George, Viscount Rochford,

were taken by river to the Tower. To Henry, Anne was now an "accursed and poisoning whore" who had conspired to kill Katherine and Mary, Henry Fitzroy, and the king himself.[15] Two days later there were further arrests of members of the Privy Chamber: Sir William Brereton, Sir Francis Weston, and Sir Richard Page, together with the poet Sir Thomas Wyatt. A grand jury indicted all the accused, except Wyatt and Page, on charges of having committed adultery with the queen. At their trial days later, all except Smeaton pleaded innocent, yet all were found guilty and sentenced to death for high treason "upon presumption and certain indications," but, Chapuys noted, "without valid proof and confession."[16]

Two days later Anne and Rochford stood trial in the Tower before a crowd of two thousand spectators. Anne was "principally charged with . . . having cohabited with her brother and other accomplices," that there was "a promise between her and Norris to marry after the King's death, which it thus appeared they hoped for," and that she "had poisoned [Katherine] and intrigued to do the same to [Mary]." The ambassador continued, "These things, she totally denied, and had a plausible answer to each."[17] It made little difference; each member of the jury declared her guilty, and the duke of Norfolk, Anne's uncle, who was presiding as lord high steward, pronounced the sentence. The usual punishment for a traitoress was being burned alive, yet, "because she was Queen, Norfolk gave judgement that she should be burnt or beheaded at the King's pleasure."[18]

On Monday, May 17, the men condemned to death for high treason were executed. On the nineteenth, at eight in the morning, Anne was led out to the scaffold on Tower Green. Henry had decreed that she should be beheaded, not burned, and granted her one final "mercy": that she be beheaded by a French executioner's sword rather than an ax, as was the English fashion. Foreigners were prevented from attending the execution, and large crowds were discouraged by the delaying of the death from the usual hour. Anne begged the people to pray for the king, "for he was a good, gentle, gracious and amiable prince."[19] With one swing of the sword she was dead. She was buried in the Chapel Royal of St. Peter ad Vincula within the Tower.

The day before her execution, Anne asked Lady Kingston, the wife of the lieutenant of the Tower, to go to Hunsdon and on her behalf kneel before Mary and beg her pardon for all the wrongs she had done her.[20] On her way to the scaffold, as Antoine Perrenot, Cardinal Granvelle wrote to Chapuys, "the Concubine declared that she did not consider herself condemned by divine judgement, except for being the cause of the ill-treatment of the Princess, and for having conspired her death."[21] Two days after Anne's execution, Thomas Cranmer pronounced her marriage with Henry to have been invalid. Elizabeth, like Mary, now became a bastard. The love affair that had wreaked such havoc was over.

> The joy shown by this people every day, not only at the ruin of the Concubine, but at the hope of the Princess Mary's restoration, is inconceivable, but as yet, the King shows no great disposition towards the latter; indeed he has twice shown himself obstinate, when spoken to on the subject by his Council.[22]

On the day of Anne Boleyn's death, Henry VIII was betrothed to Jane Seymour. They were married ten days later in the queen's closet at Whitehall.[23] "She is," Chapuys told Antoine Perrenot, the emperor's minister, "the sister of a certain Edward Seymour, who has been in the service of his Majesty [Charles V]"; while "she [herself] was formerly in the household of the good Queen [Katherine]." The ambassador described Jane as being "of middle stature, and no great beauty; so fair that he would call her rather pale than otherwise." Her personal motto was "Bound to obey and serve."[24] On Whitsunday, June 4, she was formally proclaimed queen.[25]

For most of the three years that Anne Boleyn had been queen, Mary had lived in fear of death. Now, with a new stepmother whose patrons were Mary's leading supporters at court, there was hope of a return to favor and to the line of succession. Even before Anne's execution, Jane had, much to Henry's annoyance, begged for Mary's restoration, but Henry had resisted. "She was a fool," he declared, and "ought to solicit the advancement of the children they would have between them, and not any others." Jane was not deterred: "in asking for the restoration of [Mary as] Princess, she conceived she was seeking the rest and tranquillity of the King, herself, her future children, and the whole realm."[26]

Over the Easter holidays, April 14 to 17, Chapuys, supported by Cromwell, made overtures for a settlement between Henry and Charles V and a renewal of their earlier alliance. Three proposals were made: that Charles broker a reconciliation between Henry and the pope; that in default of male issue, "we would," as Henry recounted, "legitimate our daughter Mary, in such degree, as in default of issue by our most dear and entirely beloved wife the Queen, she might not be reputed unable to some place in our succession"; and that Henry help Charles against the Ottoman Turks and against the anticipated French assault on Milan.[27] But when, on the eighteenth, Chapuys was summoned for an audience, Henry dismissed each of the proposals and instead unleashed an attack on the emperor's fidelity. Charles would not "have acquired the Empire or enjoyed Spain without him" but had "treated him with neglect . . . tried to get him declared schismatic and deprived of his kingdom"; and he had not kept his promise "not to make peace with the King of France" until Charles had obtained for Henry the crown of France. As Chapuys reported, the "Chancellor and Cromwell appeared to regret these answers, and in spite of the King's gestures to them that they should applaud him, neither of them would say three words."

The next day, the whole of the King's Council was assembled for three or four hours, and, as Cromwell told Chapuys, "there was not one of them but remained long on his knees before the King to beg him, for the honour of God, not to lose so good an opportunity of establishing a friendship so necessary and advantageous." However, no one could change the king's mind: "he would sooner suffer all the ills in the world than confess tacitly or expressly that he had done you any injury, or that he desired this friendship."[28] He again made it clear that he would not tolerate interference from Charles:

> As to the legitimisation of our daughter Mary, if she will submit to our grace, without wrestling against the determination of our laws, we will acknowledge her and use her as our daughter; but we would not be directed or pressed herein, nor have any other order devised for her entertainment, than should proceed from the inclination of our own heart being moved by

her humility, and the gentle proceedings of such as pretend to be her friends.[29]

For Henry, to give Mary back her rights without terms was tantamount to submitting to the pope, to humbling himself before the emperor, and to climbing down in the eyes of his enemy, the king of France, and that he would never do.

CHAPTER 18

MOST HUMBLE AND OBEDIENT DAUGHTER

Master Secretary,

I would have been a suitor to you before this time, to have been a means for me to the King's Grace, my father, to have obtained his Grace's blessing and favour; but I perceived that no body durst speak for me, as long as that woman lived, which now is gone, whom I pray our Lord of his great mercy to forgive. Wherefore, now she is gone, I am the bolder to write to you, as she which taketh you for one of my chief friends. And therefore I desire you for the love of God to be a suitor for me to the King's Grace, to have his blessing and licence to write unto his Grace, which shall be a great comfort to me, as God knoweth; who have you evermore in his holy keeping. Moreover I must desire you to accept mine evil writing. For I have not done so much this two year and more, nor could not have found the means to do it at this time, but my Lady Kingston's being here.

At Hunsdon, the 26th of May.
By your loving friend,
Marye.[1]

AFTER THE FALL OF ANNE BOLEYN, MARY HOPED SHE MIGHT REGAIN her father's favor. She had waited at Hunsdon to be summoned to court, but when no word came she wrote to Cromwell asking him to intercede with Henry now that "that woman" was dead.

Four days later, Mary wrote again, thanking him for leave to write to the king and assuring him that "you shall find me as obedient to the King's Grace, as you can reasonably require of me." She trusted that this would be enough to withdraw her father's displeasure and permit her to "come into his presence."[2] Cromwell had been enlisted as mediator between Henry and Mary as Jane Seymour pressed for reconciliation. The king, however, remained determined that Mary submit. The price of his restored favor would be her complete subjugation to his will.

On June 1, Mary addressed a letter to Henry directly. In "as humble and lowly a manner, as is possible for a child to use to her father," she begged for forgiveness:

> I beseech your Grace of your daily blessing, which is my chief desire in the world. And in the same humble ways [ac] knowledging all the offences that I have done . . . I pray your Grace, in the honour of God, and for your fatherly pity, to forgive me them; for the which I am sorry, as any creature living; and next unto God, I do and will submit me in and all things to your goodness and pleasure to do with me whatsoever shall please your grace.

She prayed God to send him a prince, "whereof," she declared, "no creature living shall more rejoice or heartier pray for continually than I," and signed herself "Your grace's most humble and obedient daughter and handmaid, Mary."[3]

After she had been granted leave to write to him, Mary had assumed that her father had forgiven her and withdrawn his "dreadful displeasure." Yet her letter met with no response. She had submitted to her father "next unto God," but this was not enough. She wrote again, begging to receive some sign of his favor and to be called into his presence, but again there was no reply.[4] On the tenth she drafted another letter, this time sending a copy to Cromwell. In it she declared herself "most humbly prostrate before your noble feet, your most obedient subject and humble child, that hath not only repented her offences hitherto, but also decreed simply from henceforth and wholly next to Almighty God, to put my state, continuance and living in your gracious mercy."[5] As Mary added in her dispatch to Cromwell:

> I trust you shall perceive that I have followed your advice and counsel, and will do in all things concerning my duty to the King's Grace (God and my conscience not offended) for I take you for one of my chief friends, next unto his Grace and the Queen. Wherefore, I desire you, for the passion which Christ suffered for you and me, and as my very trust is in you, that you will find such means through your great wisdom, that I be not moved to agree to any further entry in this matter than I have done. But if I be put to any more (I am plain with you as with my great friends) my said conscience will in no ways suffer me to consent thereunto.[6]

Cromwell's letter does not survive, but his disapproval is clear from Mary's reply. He had taken exception to her qualified response and, enclosing a draft for her guidance, instructed her to write again to the king and to send him a copy:

> *Good Master Secretary,*
>
> *I do thank you with all my heart, for the great pain and suit you have had for me, for the which I think myself very much bound to you. And whereas I do perceive by your letters, that you do mislike mine exception in my letter to the King's Grace, I assure you, I did not mean as you do take it. For I do not mistrust that the King's goodness will move me to do anything which should offend God and my conscience. But that which I did write was only by the reason of continual custom. For I have always used, both in writing and speaking, to except God in all things.*
>
> *Nevertheless, because you have exhorted me to write to his Grace again, and I cannot devise what I should write more but your own last copy, without adding or [di]minishing; therefore I do send you by this bearer, my servant, the same, word for word; and it is unsealed, because I cannot endure to write another copy.*

For the pain in my head and teeth hath troubled me so sore these two or three days and doth yet so continue, that I have very small rest, day or night.

Your assured bounden loving friend during my life,

Marye.[7]

Mary copied Cromwell's draft "word for word" and then addressed the king once more. Having begged "in my most humble and lowly manner" for his "daily blessing" and permission to come into his presence, she continued:

I have written twice unto your highness, trusting to have, by some gracious letters, token or message, perceived sensibly the mercy, clemency and pity of your Grace, and upon the operation of the same, at the last also to have attained the fruition of your most noble presence, which above all worldly things I desire: yet I have not obtained my said fervent and hearty desire, nor any piece of the same to my great and intolerable discomfort I am enforced, by the compulsion of nature, eftsones to cry unto your merciful ears, and most humbly prostrate before your feet.

She signed off by petitioning for "some little spark of my humble suit and desire" and praying God

to preserve your Highness, with the Queen, and shortly to send you issue, which shall be gladder tidings to me than I can express in writing. . . . Your most humble and obedient daughter and handmaid, Marye.[8]

The king's response was direct and unequivocal. Within days he sent a delegation of councillors, headed by the duke of Norfolk, to visit Mary at Hunsdon to demand that she take the oath of allegiance and make a complete submission. The councillors condemned her for her earlier refusal to obey as a "monster in nature," a freakish departure from the natural obedience of a daughter toward her father. Any other man, they declared, would have sent her away, but, given Henry's "gracious and divine nature," he was willing to withhold his displeasure if Mary would now submit to him. Would she accept all the laws and statutes of the realm? Would she accept Henry as supreme head of the Church and repudiate the jurisdiction of the bishop of Rome? Would she acknowledge that her mother's marriage was invalid and accept all the laws and statutes of the realm?

Her answer to each was no. She was willing to obey her father in all matters except those that injured her mother, her present honor, or her faith, and in this she was steadfast. Norfolk angrily declared that "so unnatural" was she to oppose the king's will that "they could scarcely believe she was his bastard, and if she were their daughter, they would beat her and knock her head so hard against the wall that it made it as soft as a baked apple." She was a traitoress and "should be punished." They left, instructing Lady Shelton to keep her under constant surveillance, day and night, and to make sure she spoke to no one.[9]

Cromwell had pledged that he would secure Mary's submission, and he now feared for his own life. He confided to Chapuys that "he considered himself a dead man" for having represented Mary as "penitent and obedient."[10] Writing to Mary, he chastised her over her position:

> Knowing how diversely and contrarily you proceeded at the late being of his Majesty's counsel with you, I am both ashamed of that I have said, and likewise afraid of that I have done; in so much that what the sequel thereof shall be God knoweth.

He continued:

> Thus with your folly you undo yourself, and all that hath wished you good. . . . Wherefore, Madam, to be plain, as God is my witness . . . I think you the most obstinate and obdurate woman all things considered, that ever was, and one that so preserving, well deserveth the reward of malice in extremity of mischief, or at least that you be both repentant for your ingratitude and miserable unkindness, and ready to do all things that you be bound unto by your duty of allegiance.

He commanded her to sign the articles required and warned that if she refused he would "take leave" of her forever and desire her "never to write or make mean unto me hereafter. For I will never think you other than the most ungrateful, unnatural, and most obstinate person living, both to God and your most dear and benign father."[11] Mary still refused. It was the very apogee of her resistance. She had become a traitor to the king and his laws. Henry now insisted that she should be treated as such, as should her allies.

IN JUNE, THE MARQUESS of Exeter and Sir William Fitzwilliam were dismissed from the Privy Council as "suspected persons." Weeks later, Sir Anthony Browne and Sir Francis Bryan, two gentlemen of the Privy Chamber, were arrested and interrogated over their support of Mary.[12] Henry believed that such individuals were encouraging the princess in her defiance.[13] The examinations of Browne and Bryan implicated Sir Nicholas Carew, who had been in correspondence with the princess, and Thomas Cheney and John Russell, both gentlemen of the Privy Chamber. Bryan deposed that the rest of his "fellows of the Privy Chamber" were rejoicing at the fall of Anne and advancing Mary's claim should Jane Seymour fail to give Henry a son.[14] He claimed further that since the king's divorce they had been working against Anne Boleyn, supporting Katherine and Mary, liaising with Charles V, and working in defense of the traditional religion.[15] They were all now placed in the Tower along with Lady Anne Hussey, the wife of Mary's chamberlain.

The danger to Mary was now as great as it had been during the months before her mother's death. According to Ralph Morice, Thomas Cranmer's old secretary, Henry "fully purposed to send the lady Mary his daughter unto the Tower, and there to suffer as a subject, by cause she would not obey unto the laws of the realm in refusing the bishop of Rome's authority and religion."[16] Judges were commanded to proceed with a legal inquiry into Mary's treachery and sentence her as willfully defiant of the king's authority. Unwilling to use the legal system against her, they gave Mary one final chance. She was to be sent a document entitled "Lady Mary's Submission," detailing all points the king required her to agree to.[17] If she refused to sign those articles, legal proceedings would begin and she would be charged with treason.

Mary sent word to Chapuys, begging his counsel. He told her that "if the King persisted in his obstinacy, or she found evidence that her life was in danger, either by maltreatment or otherwise," she should "consent to her father's wish." He assured her that this was what the emperor wanted and that "to save her life, on which depended the peace of the realm, and the redress of the great evils which prevail here, she must do everything and dissemble for some time."

ON THURSDAY, JUNE 22, under threat of death, Mary signed the formal statement required of her. In "The confession of me the Lady Mary made upon certain points and articles under written," she acknowledged the illegitimacy of her mother's marriage, her own bastard status, and her father's Supreme Headship of the Church of England:

> First, I confess and [ac]knowledge the King's Majesty to be my Sovereign Lord and King, in the imperial Crown of this realm of England, and do submit myself to his Highness, and to all and singular laws and statutes of this realm, as becometh a true and faithful subject to do . . .
>
> (SIGNED) *"MARY"*
>
> I do recognise, accept, take, repute and [ac]knowledge the King's Highness to be supreme head in earth under Christ of the Church of England, and do utterly refuse the Bishop of Rome's pretended authority, power and jurisdiction within this realm heretofore usurped . . .
>
> (SIGNED) *"MARY"*
>
> I do freely, frankly . . . recognise and acknowledge that the marriage, heretofore had between his Majesty, and my mother, the late Princess dowager, was, by God's law and Man's law, incestuous and unlawful.[18]
>
> (SIGNED) *"MARY"*

In one stroke she had been compelled to betray the memory of her mother and the Catholic faith of her childhood. She had signed away all that her mother had resisted until her death; all that Mary herself had clung to and fought so hard to defend. It was in this moment of total and agonizing submission that the seeds of Mary's future defiance were sown.

CHAPTER 19

INCREDIBLE REJOICING

⁘

Most humbly, obediently and gladly lying at the feet of your most excellent majesty, my most dear benign father and sovereign lord, I have this day perceived your gracious clemency and merciful pity to have overcome my most unkind and unnatural proceedings towards you and your most just and virtuous laws; the great and inestimable joy whereof I cannot express. . . . I shall daily pray to God, whom eftsoons I beseech to send you issue, to his honour and the comfort of the whole realm, From Hunsdon, the 26th of June,

Your grace's most humble and obedient daughter and handmaid,
Marye.[1]

MARY'S CAPITULATION WAS GREETED WITH "INCREDIBLE REJOICING" at court. Restored to favor, she was acknowledged as the king's daughter once more and offered a sumptuous new wardrobe and a choice of servants.[2] Cromwell returned to Hunsdon with "a most gracious letter" from the king and, "kneeling on the ground," begged Mary's pardon for his former harsh conduct.[3]

Three weeks later, Mary journeyed to Hackney for a secret reunion with her father. It was their first meeting for five years. She had been a young teenager when Henry last saw her, and she was now a woman of twenty. Chapuys wrote that the kindness shown by the king to the princess was "inconceivable, regretting that he had been so long separated from her." He showed her "such love and affection, and such brilliant promises for the future that no father could have behaved better towards his daughter."[4] Jane Seymour gave Mary a diamond ring and Henry 1,000 crowns for her "many pleasures."[5] They spent one night together and parted on Friday, July 7, with Henry promising that she would be brought to court to take her place immediately after the queen.

Yet beneath the veneer of reconciliation there were, as Chapuys observed, "a few drachmas of gall and bitterness mixed with the sweet food of paternal kindness."[6] Before returning to court, Mary was forced to write to the emperor and his sister, Mary of Hungary, regent of the Netherlands, confirming her submission to her father as head of the Church; her acknowledgment of the statutes declaring her mother's marriage unlawful; and her decision to freely renounce her right to the throne.[7] For Henry it was a means of emphasizing his victory over the emperor. According to Chapuys, he had told the princess "that her obstinate resistance to his will had been encouraged and strengthened by the trust she had in you; but that she ought to know that your majesty could not help or favour her in the least as long as he [the king] lived."[8] Henry gave Mary a ring to celebrate her obedience. On one side was a relief of Henry and Jane, on the other a picture of Mary. The Latin inscription read:

> Obedience leads to unity, unity to constancy and a quiet mind, and these are treasures of inestimable worth. For God so valued humility that he gave his only son, a perfect exemplar of modesty, who in his obedience to his divine father, taught lessons of obedience and devotion.[9]

Mary's submission had cost her dearly. As Chapuys warned the emperor, "this affair of the princess has tormented her more than you think"; she had "escaped from the greatest danger that ever a princess was in, and such as no words can describe."[10] She now asked Chapuys to obtain a secret papal absolution, "otherwise her conscience could not be at perfect ease."[11]

> The princess is every day better treated, and was never at greater liberty or more honourably served than now . . . she has plenty of company, even of the followers of the little Bastard, who will henceforth play her court. Nothing is wanting in her except the

name and title of Princess, for all else she will have more fully than before.[12]

On June 30, 1536, just days after Mary's submission, a new Act of Succession was introduced into the House of Lords. Yet neither Mary's legitimacy nor her position as heir was restored. The succession was conferred instead on the heirs of Jane Seymour or, as the act declared, "any subsequent wife." Both of Henry's first marriages were declared invalid, and Elizabeth was stripped of the title of princess and removed from the line of succession. Henry was granted unprecedented powers to nominate whomever he pleased as his successor, irrespective of illegitimacy, should he have no children with the queen.[13] He might have intended to promote his bastard son Henry Fitzroy, duke of Richmond, but three weeks later, just after Parliament was dissolved, Richmond died, probably of tuberculosis. "Few are sorry," wrote Chapuys to Perrenot de Granvelle, "because of the Princess."[14]

Those who wished for a return to the old order in England now looked to Mary's influence to bring it about. "It is to be hoped," the ambassador wrote to the empress Isabella, "that through the Princess's means, and through her great wisdom and discretion she may hereafter little by little bring back the King, her father, and the whole of the English nation to the right path."[15]

In October there was unrest in Lincolnshire, and over the following weeks rebellion spread across the northern counties. Under the leadership of the lawyer Robert Aske, the rebels, some forty thousand in number, demanded the return of the "old faith"; the restoration of the monasteries ransacked in the dissolution of the past year; the return of the old religion; and "that the Lady Mary may be made legitimate and the former statute therein annulled."[16] Among the rebels were Lord Hussey, Mary's old steward, and Lord Darcy, who had for many months been petitioning Charles V to intervene in England. As Aske related in his subsequent examination, "both he and all the wise men of those parts much grudged, seeing that on the mother's side she came from the greatest blood in Christendom." The statute declaring her illegitimacy would "make strangers think." It was "framed more for some displeasure towards her and her friends than for any just cause, while in reason she ought to be favoured in this realm rather than otherwise."[17]

When news reached Rome of the rebellion, Pope Paul III appointed Reginald Pole cardinal and commissioned him as *legate a latere* to go to England and raise support for the rebels.[18] Pole was a cousin of the king and a son of Margaret Pole, countess of Salisbury, Mary's godmother and former governess. He had left England in 1532 following Henry's break with Rome and in 1536, in answer to Henry's request for his views, had sent him the treatise *De Unitate Ecclesiae* (In Defense of the Unity of the Church). The tract had turned Pole from Henry's protégé into his bitterest enemy. In it he appealed to the nobility of England and the emperor to take action, and he called on Henry to repent for having broken with Rome. He warned that the king would not get away with repudiating Mary and that among "such a number of most noble families" any disruption of the succession would lead to sedition.[19] By the time Pole left for England, the rebellion had been put down. Henry demanded Pole's extradition from France as a traitor and to have the cardinal "by some means trussed up and conveyed to Calais" and then to England.[20]

MARY WAS TO SPEND Christmas at court for the first time in years. On December 22, Henry, Jane, and Mary rode from Westminster through the City of London to Greenwich, preceded by the mayor and aldermen of the city. In Fleet Street, four orders of friars stood in copes of gold, "with crosses and candlesticks and censers to cense the King and Queen as they rode by." The choir of St. Paul's, the bishop of London, and two priests from every parish church in London stood outside St. Paul's to watch the royal procession.[21] "The like sight," Richard Lee wrote to Lady Lisle, formerly a maid of honor to Jane Seymour and wife of Arthur Plantagenet, "hath not been seen here since the Emperor's being here [in 1522]." He noted the presence of Chapuys, "the ambassador to the Emperor," with the royal party, which "rejoiced every man wondrously."[22]

In April, the Privy Council recommended that Mary and Elizabeth be "made of some estimation" and since Mary was the elder, "and more apt to make a present alliance than the other," it "might please the King to declare her according to his laws" so that she might be more attractive as a bride, as a means of ensuring that the king "may provide himself of a present friend."[23] Although Charles pressed for a match with Dom Luis of Portugal, the young brother of the king of Portugal, the advice was not taken. Jane was pregnant, and Henry was optimistic that it would be a son. Any negotiation for a betrothal would now depend on public recognition of Mary's illegitimacy.

CHAPTER 20

DELIVERANCE OF A GOODLY PRINCE

∴

Right trust and well beloved, we greet you well. And forasmuch as by the inestimable Goodness and grace of Almighty God we be delivered and brought in child bed of a Prince conceived in most Lawful Matrimony between my lord the King's Majesty and us, doubting not but that for the love and affection which ye bear unto us and to the common wealth of this Realm the Knowledge thereof should be joyous and glad tidings unto you, we have thought good to certify you of the same.[1]

—Jane Seymour to Cromwell,
October 12, 1537

At two in the morning of Friday, October 12, 1537, Jane Seymour gave birth to a son at Hampton Court. Born on the Feast of Saint Edward the Confessor, he was named after the royal saint.

By eight o'clock Te Deums had been sung in every parish church in London; bonfires were lit, and the firing of the Tower guns continued well into the evening.[2] Messengers were dispatched around the country and to courts across Europe proclaiming the birth. "Here be no news, but very good news," wrote Thomas Cromwell to Sir Thomas Wyatt, the ambassador to Spain, who had been imprisoned after the fall of Anne Boleyn. "It hath pleased Almighty God of his goodness, to send unto the Queen's Grace deliverance of a goodly Prince, to the great comfort, rejoice and consolation of the King's Majesty, and of all us his most humble, loving and obedient subjects."[3] Finally Henry had a legitimate male heir.

Anticipation of the birth had been growing since the spring. On May 23, Jane's pregnancy was made known at court, and four days later a Te Deum was celebrated at St. Paul's upon the "quickening" of her child.[4] The king added a nursery to the building works at Hampton Court in preparation for the queen's confinement, and Mary was summoned to attend on the queen.[5] On Sunday, September 16, Jane took to her chamber, where she remained for three weeks before going into a prolonged and arduous thirty-hour labor. A solemn procession was made at St. Paul's "to pray for the Queen that was then in labour of child."[6] On the following morning, Jane was safely delivered. As news of the birth rang out from the bells of St. Paul's, Henry hurried back from Esher in Surrey, to which he had been forced to move on account of the plague, to begin a round of celebratory banquets.[7]

Three days after the birth, Mary stood as godmother at the font in the newly decorated Chapel Royal at Hampton Court as Thomas Cranmer, archbishop of Canterbury, performed the rites of baptism over the infant prince.[8] Although the plague limited the size of the retinues coming to court, it was a lavish ceremony. Some three or four hundred courtiers, clerics, and foreign envoys formed the midnight procession from the queen's chamber to the chapel. After the prince had been baptized and confirmed, the heralds proclaimed him "Edward, son and heir to the King of England, Duke of Cornwall, and Earl of Chester." Amid a torchlit procession, Mary led her four-year-old sister, Elizabeth, back to the queen's apartments for the giving of the baptismal gifts.[9] Mary presented a golden cup, which she gave, along with £30, to Edward's nurse, midwife, and cradle rockers. Great fires were lit on the streets of London, and bells rung across the country.

WITH THE REJOICING barely over, Jane fell seriously ill with "a natural lax"—heavy bleeding.[10] The week of celebrations ended with a general procession at St. Paul's for "the health of the Queen," and the Chapel Royal was filled with courtiers praying for her safety. By the evening of the twenty-fourth, her condition had worsened and she received Extreme Unction. She died in the early hours of the morning of puerperal fever, having suffered a massive hemorrhage and contracted septicemia. Henry withdrew to Windsor, where, as the chronicler Edward Hall recorded, "he mourned and kept himself close and secret a great while."[11] Writing to Francis I in acknowledgment of the French king's congratulations on Edward's birth, Henry described how "Divine Providence . . . hath mingled my joy with the bitterness of her who brought me this happiness."[12]

In the days immediately following the queen's death, Mary was too grief-stricken—"accrased"—to take part in the initial obsequies, and the marchioness of Exeter had to take her place.[13] But as she gathered her composure, she appeared as chief mourner at dirges and Masses in the Chapel Royal, accompanied by her ladies. On November 8, she rode behind the coffin at the head of the funeral cortege, her steed covered in black trappings, as the procession made its way from Hampton Court to Windsor. Upon the coffin was an effigy of Jane in robes of state, a crown upon her head and a scepter in her right hand. Four days later, she was buried between the stalls and altar of St. George's Chapel. Above the vault the Latin inscription heralded her as a phoenix, her personal emblem, which in death had brought life:

> HERE A PHOENIX LIETH, WHOSE DEATH
> TO ANOTHER PHOENIX GAVE BREATH:
> IT IS TO BE LAMENTED MUCH,
> THE WORLD AT ONCE N'ER KNEW TWO SUCH.[14]

In a letter of condolence, Cuthbert Tunstall, bishop of Durham, reminded Henry that though God had taken his queen, Henry should not forget "our most noble Prince, to whom God hath ordained your Majesty not only to be father, but also as the time now requireth, to supply the room of a mother also."[15]

Edward spent his first Christmas with Henry at Greenwich and was with him again in May 1538 at the royal hunting lodge at Royston, where the king "solaced all his day with much mirth and joy, dallying with him in his arms . . . and so holding him in a window to the sight and great comfort of all the people."[16]

But it was Mary, then twenty-two, who would be most involved in Edward's early upbringing. She would be his most frequent family visitor. Residing for much of the time at Hampton Court, she was just a barge ride across the river from her brother's nursery at Richmond. She visited him in November 1537 and in March, April, and May the following year.[17] As Jane Dormer, one of Mary's gentlewomen, later noted, when Mary came to see him "he took special content in her company . . . he would ask her many questions, promise her secrecy, carrying her that respect and reverence, as if she had been his mother." She would offer him advice "in some things that concerned himself, and in other things that touched herself; in all showing great affection and sisterly care of him."[18]

Lady Lisle visited all the royal children at Hampton Court in November. "His grace [Edward]," she wrote to her husband, "is the goodliest babe that ever I set mine eye upon. I pray God to make him an old man, for I think I should never weary of looking on him. . . . I saw also my Lady Mary and my Lady Elizabeth."[19] Edward was acknowledged as the king's heir, and the rivalry between Mary and Elizabeth abated. All three siblings were now brought together under one roof.

CHAPTER 21

THE MOST UNHAPPY LADY IN CHRISTENDOM

The King . . . is little disposed to marry again, but some of his Council have thought it mete for us to urge him to it for the sake of his realm.[1]

As Henry mourned the death of Jane Seymour, the French king and the emperor agreed upon a truce and began peace talks mediated by the pope. Now, with the growing threat of a Catholic offensive against him, the search for a new wife for Henry and a husband for Mary was used in an effort to forge an alliance that would keep France and the empire apart. "Since the King [Francis I] my brother, has already so great an amity with the Emperor, what amity should I have with him?" asked Henry. "I ask because I am not resolved to marry again unless the Emperor or King prefer my friendship to that which they have together."[2]

Offers of marriage alliances were made to the empire and France for a match between Mary and either Dom Luis of Portugal or the duke of Orléans. Henry considered the prospect of marriage with the dowager duchess of Milan and for a time with Mary of Guise, though Henry delayed too long and in May she was betrothed to King James V of Scotland, thereby renewing the "Auld Alliance" between France and Scotland. At Nice in June, Charles and Francis came to terms, signing a ten-year truce, and some months later they pledged themselves to cooperate against the enemies of Christendom. Henry now moved to secure his position at home and look for new friends abroad.

Though publicly reconciled, Henry still regarded Mary and her supporters with suspicion. In the summer of 1538, Cromwell sent her a letter of warning. She had taken some "strangers" into her house. The incident had been relayed to the king in such a way to put her trustworthiness in doubt.[3] Mary responded, "I fear it hath been reported to the worst, nevertheless I will promise you, with God's help, from henceforth to refrain [from] it so utterly that of right none shall have cause to speak of." She assured Cromwell that she would not lodge anyone in her house again and added that she would rather endure physical harm than lose even the smallest part of the king's favor.[4]

Amid renewed fears of war, Henry sought to alienate Mary from the emperor and draw her more securely to him. At the end of August 1538, she was instructed to complain to the imperial ambassadors, Chapuys and Mendoza, about the emperor's failure to conclude the Portuguese alliance and the miserable terms he had offered. Cromwell wrote to Mary outlining the supposed grievances that she was to present to the ambassadors when they visited her at Havering. Upon their arrival on the twenty-sixth, Mary dutifully protested about the "dissimulation" employed by the ambassadors, the offer of a miserly "dower," and the emperor's failure to show her the cousinly kindness and friendship she expected of him. "She was a woman only and could not help saying these things." But "after so many overtures and fine words, nothing had been concluded."[5]

Later Mary made clear her real feelings. She told Chapuys that she held the emperor in high esteem, as a "father and mother," and "was so affectionately attached" to him "that it seemed almost impossible to her to have such an affection and love for a kinsman." She did not believe what her father said about him, and she stood ready to do whatever he asked of her in the issue of marriage.[6] Fearing for her safety, the ambassador raised again the prospect of escape. Mary was hesitant: "It might happen," she said, that her father "might hereafter show greater consideration for her, or cause her to be more respected and better treated than she had been until now." If that were the case, "she would much prefer remaining in England and conforming herself entirely to her father's commands and wishes."

When quizzed by Cromwell on her meeting with the ambassadors, Mary displayed some political astuteness, saying only that they had reiterated the emperor's support for her and had urged her to remain "in the obedience and goodwill of my father."

HENRY NOW TOOK action against the old Catholic families of royal Plantagenet blood, the Poles, Nevilles, and Courtenays, who had long been objects of suspicion for their loyalty to Katherine of Aragon and Mary. Reginald Pole had denounced Henry's tyranny and heresy in the bitterest terms and, according to reports by the emperor's agents, had hoped that the unrest in England might lead to "his marrying the princess himself."[7] As John Wroth wrote in a letter to Lord Lisle, who was in Calais on May 18, "Pole intended to have married my old lady Mary and betwixt them both should again arise the old doctrine of Christ."[8] It was such a union, or a rising in support of Mary against Edward's succession, that the regime particularly feared.

In late August 1538, Sir Geoffrey Pole, the younger brother of Reginald, was arrested for treason and imprisoned in the Tower. Under interrogation he implicated his elder brother Henry Pole, Lord Montague; Sir Edward Neville, Montague's brother-in-law; and Henry Courtenay, marquess of Exeter—the king's cousin—in an alleged conspiracy that sought to deprive the king of his supremacy and marry Mary to Reginald Pole. By November 4, Exeter, his wife, Gertrude, and their twelve-year-old son, Edward, were committed to the Tower. Soon after, the elderly countess of Salisbury was interrogated and her house searched. She was convicted without trial of aiding and abetting her sons Henry and Reginald and of having "committed and p[er]petrated div[er]se and sundry other detestable and abominable treasons" and was imprisoned also.[9] On Monday, December 9, Montague, Sir Edward Neville, and Exeter were tried and, having received unanimous guilty verdicts—on the basis of remarks such as "I like well the proceedings of Cardinal Pole"—were executed at Tower Hill.[10]

Two days after Christmas, Reginald Pole set out again secretly from Rome to rally the Catholic powers against "the most cruel and abominable tyrant" the king of England.[11] In the Pact of Toledo in January 1539, Charles and Francis agreed to make no further agreements with England. It seemed that a crusade, termed the "Enterprise of England," was about to begin.[12] The pope was determined to "chastise the irreverence and extravagance of the King of England."[13] Counties were mustered, defenses were strengthened, and the country prepared for war. Meanwhile, diplomatic overtures were made to the Schmalkaldic League of German princes and any other rulers opposed to Charles or the pope.

On New Year's Eve, Sir Nicholas Carew, a onetime royal favorite, was apprehended and questioned. A letter had allegedly been found at the home of the marchioness of Exeter that implicated him in the treason for which the marquess had been executed earlier in the month. Carew was tried and convicted on February 14, 1539, and beheaded on Tower Hill three weeks later. For Mary, the execution of so many of those who had supported her and her mother served as a sharp reminder of her father's capacity for vengeance and cruelty. As Chapuys reflected, "It would seem that they want to leave her as few friends as possible."[14]

WITH RENEWED FEARS of war against him, Henry was keen to secure alliances among the Lutheran princes in Germany. In mid-January 1539, the English ambassador Christopher Mont was sent to the duke of Saxony to discuss the prospect of a double match between Henry and the duke of Cleves's eldest daughter, Anne, and between Mary and the young duke of Cleves himself.[15] Cromwell instructed Mont to make clear that although Mary was "only the King's natural daughter"—meaning she was not of "princely status"—she was "endowed, as all the world knows, with such beauty, learning and virtues, that when the rest was agreed, no man would stick for any part concerning her beauty and goodness."[16]

Though the negotiations for a marriage with Mary and the young duke of Cleves came to nothing, by the autumn an alliance had been secured between Henry and Anne, the sister of Duke William of Cleves. The duke was a natural ally for Henry: a committed Habsburg opponent yet not a Lutheran. Agreement was reached in October, and, as negotiations continued for a match with Mary and another of the German princes, Anne of Cleves began her journey to England.

Meanwhile, Thomas Wriothesley, the earl of Southampton, was

sent to Mary to instruct her that she should entertain the prospect of marriage with the Lutheran Duke Philip of Bavaria, who was in England in advance of Anne of Cleves's arrival.[17] Mary responded that although she knew the matter was of "great importance," she "would wish and desire never to enter that kind of religion, but to continue still a maid during her life," although she "committed herself to his majesty, her benign and merciful father." On December 22, she agreed to meet the duke in the gardens of Westminster Abbey. Speaking partly in German with an interpreter and partly in Latin, the duke declared his intention to take Mary as his wife, if it were agreeable to her, and was bold enough to kiss her.[18] When he left England in the new year, Duke Philip believed he would soon be returning to marry the princess. The French ambassador, Charles de Marillac, expected the wedding to take place within "ten or fifteen days," and in December a draft treaty was drawn up.[19]

By January, word reached Rome that Mary had already married "without the advice or knowledge of the Emperor." Chapuys sought desperately to learn if rumors of her marriage to a Lutheran duke were true. They were not. For Henry the negotiations had never been intended as anything more than a ploy to strengthen his hand against the emperor at a time when he feared a Catholic crusade against him.

Steps were also taken to suppress popular heresy and to appease conservatives at home. In the Parliament of 1539, the Act of Six Articles was passed, intended to head off the rising tide of heresy. It reaffirmed the Catholic doctrine of transubstantiation, with denial punishable by death by burning; rejected Communion in both kinds for the laity; required priests to remain celibate; and advocated the continued use of private Masses and auricular confession. Since the break with Rome, only John Lambert, an Anabaptist and one of Europe's most radical heretics, had been burned for heresy. The passing of the Six Articles was intended to reassure Europe's Catholic rulers that Henry, despite the schism, was fundamentally orthodox and they need not respond to the pope's calls for a crusade against him.

In any event, no invasion came. The pope withheld the promised bull and recalled Cardinal Pole to Rome.[20] France was unwilling to take action without a commitment from Charles, and the emperor, faced with the threat of the Ottoman Turks and the Lutherans in Germany and deteriorating relations with France, was not prepared to act against England.[21] Instead, negotiations for an English alliance and a marriage with Mary were reopened with both sides.[22] Yet as Marillac, the French ambassador, observed, "The King will not marry [his daughter] out of England, lest the crown of England should be claimed for her as legitimate by the Church and not of those born since the withdrawal of obedience to the Holy See, like the prince."[23] Moreover, as Henry made clear to Marillac, "I love my daughter well, but myself and honour more." He would not declare Mary legitimate and refused to allow the invalidity of his first marriage to be doubted.[24]

Mary, then twenty-six, expressed her situation to one of her chamberwomen, an informant of Marillac. "It was folly to think that they would marry her out of England, or even in England," she said, "for she would be, while her father lived, only Lady Mary, the most unhappy Lady in Christendom."[25]

CHAPTER 22

FOR FEAR OF MAKING A RUFFLE IN THE WORLD

∵

On DECEMBER 27, 1539, ANNE OF CLEVES ARRIVED IN ENGLAND. "The day," the duke of Suffolk reported to Cromwell, "was foul and windy, with much hail [that blew] continually in her face."[1] She journeyed to Canterbury and then to Sittingbourne and Rochester, where she remained for New Year's Eve. The following day, a party of six gentlemen went unannounced into Anne's chamber at Rochester. All were disguised, yet one was the king. He had been scheduled to meet Anne formally at Blackheath on January 3, but curiosity had gotten the better of him.[2] "How ye liked the Lady Anne?" Cromwell asked the king on his return to Greenwich. "Nothing so well as she was spoken of," Henry replied, adding, "if [he] had known as much before as [he] then knew, she should not have come within this realm." He now asked his minister, "What remedy?" To which Cromwell responded, "I know none, he was very sorry therefore."[3]

The twenty-four-year-old was not the beauty that Hans Holbein's portrait, sent to England before her arrival, had portrayed. Henry immediately questioned her virginity, observing that she had the fuller figure expected of an older woman rather than the slender figure of a maid. He believed she was already married to François, heir to the Duchy of Lorraine, to whom she had been betrothed at the age of twelve.

The marriage was postponed while Cromwell investigated whether the Lorraine match had been properly broken off. Two days later, with assurances from the Cleves ambassadors, Henry reluctantly resumed preparations for the wedding. Francis I and Charles were celebrating the New Year together in Paris, and Henry needed to maintain the alliance with the German princes. As he later declared, "If it were not . . . for fear of making a ruffle in the world—that is, to be a means to drive her brother into the hands of the Emperor, and the French King's hands, being now together, I would never have married her."[4]

When Anne made a solemn declaration before the Privy Council "that she was free from all contracts," Henry urgently petitioned his chief minister. "Is there none other remedy," he questioned, "but that I must needs, against my will, put my neck in the yoke?" Cromwell hurried away without offering a reply.[5] Within a few months the cost of Cromwell's blunder would become clear.

AT EIGHT IN the morning on Tuesday, January 6, 1540, the Feast of the Epiphany, Thomas Cranmer, archbishop of Canterbury, celebrated the marriage of Henry and Anne of Cleves in the Chapel Royal at Greenwich. Both Mary and Elizabeth attended the service.[6] The next morning, Cromwell visited the king in the Privy Chamber. "How liked the Queen?" he asked, to which Henry replied, "Surely, as ye know, I liked her before not well, but now I like her much worse. For I have felt her belly and her breasts, and thereby, as I can judge, she be no maid." The king continued, "[The] which struck me so to the heart when I felt them that I had neither will nor courage to proceed any further in matters. . . . I have left her as good a maid as I found her."[7]

For the next six months, despite repeated efforts, the marriage remained unconsummated. As Henry explained to his physician, "He found her body in such sort disordered and indisposed to excite and provoke any lust in him. Yea, [it] rather minister[ed] matter of loathsomeness unto [him], that [he] could not in any wise overcome that loathsomeness, nor in her company be provoked or stirred to that act."[8] Now he lamented the fact that he would never have any more children for "the comfort of the realm, if he should continue in marriage with this lady." Cromwell responded that "he would do his utmost to comfort and deliver his Grace of his affliction."[9]

By the summer, Henry had decided to sever his ties with the

German princes and to seek an annulment. He could afford to break the alliance. The Franco-imperial entente had become strained, and another phase in the Habsburg-Valois conflict had begun. Some weeks before, he had started an affair with one of Anne's maids, Katherine Howard, a niece of the duke of Norfolk. "The King is," the French ambassador reported, "so amorous of her that he knows not how to make sufficient demonstrations of his affection." He "caresses her more than he did the others" and lavished her with jewels.[10]

As Henry's infatuation with Katherine grew, his calls for a divorce from Anne became more strident. The leading religious conservatives, Norfolk and Bishop Stephen Gardiner, saw an opportunity to install a queen supportive of their cause and effecting the downfall of their great enemy, Thomas Cromwell. As Marillac wrote, "The King, wishing by all possible means to lead back religion to the way of truth, Cromwell, as attached to the German Lutherans, had always favoured the doctors who preached such erroneous opinions and hindered those who preached the contrary." Having been recently warned that he was working "against the intention of the King and of the acts of Parliament," Cromwell had "betrayed himself."[11]

When letters from the Lutheran lords of Germany were found in his house, the chief minister's fate was sealed. "The King was thereby so exasperated against him that he would no longer hear him spoken of, but rather desired to abolish all memory of him as the greatest wretch ever born in England."[12]

AT 3 P.M. ON SATURDAY, June 10, 1540, Cromwell was arrested in the Council Chamber by the duke of Norfolk. His goods were seized and confiscated, and he was sent to the Tower, charged with heresy and treason and of plotting to marry Mary.[13] He had lost Henry's confidence, and the king had disavowed him.

From the Tower Cromwell wrote to Henry protesting his innocence and begging for mercy, signing himself "with the heavy heart and trembling of your Highness's most heavy and most miserable prisoner and poor slave."[14] He was condemned on June 29 as "the most false and corrupt traitor, deceiver and circumventor against your royal person and the imperial crown of this realm that had ever been known in your whole reign." Cromwell was paying the price for the failed match, for his reformist inclinations, and for the rise in ascendancy of the conservative Howard family. He was kept alive only to recount all that he knew about the king's marriage to Anne of Cleves and of Henry's conversations with him as to the nonconsummation of the marriage.

On June 24, Anne of Cleves was ordered to go to Richmond Palace, ostensibly to avoid an outbreak of the plague.[15] The convocation of the clergy was instructed to examine the king's marriage after doubts had been raised about its validity. The investigation concluded that Anne had been precontracted to the prince of Lorraine, that the king had wed her against his will, and that the whole nation desired the king to have more heirs. On the twenty-fifth, the king's commissioners visited Anne and informed her that her marriage was invalid.[16] She consented without protest, agreeing to the divorce proceedings and confirming that the marriage had not been consummated.[17] Her acquiescence was rewarded: she was endowed with lands to the value of £4,000 annually and Richmond and Bletchingley manors, and was thereafter known as "the old Queen, the King's sister." On July 9, the convocation found their marriage to have been unlawful given its nonconsummation, her precontract with the duke of Lorraine, and the fact that Henry had acted under compulsion. Four days later, Parliament confirmed the verdict and Henry was declared free to remarry.

On July 28, Cromwell was finally taken to the scaffold on Tower Green. Maintaining his innocence to the end, he denied that he had supported heretics but accepted the judgment of the law. He knelt, prayed, and, laying his head on the block, "patiently suffered the stroke of the ax," it taking a number of attempts to remove his head. Two days later, three well-known reformers, Robert Barnes, William Jerome, and Thomas Garret, were burned as heretics at Smithfield. At the stake, Barnes utterly denied his guilt: he was condemned to die, "but wherefore I cannot tell."[18] The others made similar declarations. On the same day, three defendants of the old faith were put to death: Edward Powell; Richard Fetherstone, Mary's former schoolmaster; and Thomas Abel, Katherine of Aragon's chaplain, were hanged, drawn, and quartered for treason. All had refused to acknowledge the Act of Supremacy. The heretics and traitors were dragged facedown on sheep hurdles through the streets of London, a heretic and a papist strapped to each.[19] The king would not tolerate opposition of any kind. A major inquisition for heresy now began.

CHAPTER 23

MORE A FRIEND THAN A STEPMOTHER

∴

ON JULY 28, 1540, THREE WEEKS AFTER THE ANNULMENT OF HIS marriage to Anne of Cleves, Henry married his fifth wife, Katherine Howard, at Oatlands Palace in Surrey.[1] She was the nineteen-year-old niece of Thomas Howard, duke of Norfolk. By November, Marillac was writing to the French king, "The new Queen, has completely acquired the King's Grace and the other [Anne of Cleves] is no more spoken of than if she were dead."[2]

Yet Anne was "loved and esteemed" by the people and, having readily accepted her new status as the "King's sister," was welcomed at court. She arrived at Hampton Court on January 3 and was admitted to the queen's presence. "Lady Anne approached the Queen with as much reverence and punctilious ceremony as if she herself was the most insignificant damsel about Court . . . all the time addressing the Queen on her knees." Katherine "received her most kindly, showing her great favour and courtesy." The king then entered the room and, "after making a very low bow to Lady Anne, embraced and kissed her." They all sat down to supper at the same table with "as good a mien and countenance and look[ed] as unconcerned as if there had been nothing between them," as the two queens danced and drank together.[3]

Relations between Mary and Katherine Howard were initially fraught. The new queen was a cousin of Anne Boleyn and five years younger than Mary. On December 5, Chapuys told the emperor's sister that the queen had tried to remove two of Mary's attendants because she believed that the princess was showing less respect to her than to her predecessors. Mary's behavior evidently improved, as it was soon reported that she had "found means to conciliate" Katherine and "thinks her maids will remain."[4] Though they were too different in temperament and too similar in age to ever be close, relations began to settle down. "A week ago," on May 17, the imperial ambassador reported, "the King and Queen went . . . to visit the Prince [at Waltham Holy Cross in Essex] at the request of the [Lady Mary], but chiefly at the intercession of the Queen herself." It proved a successful visit, and "upon that occasion" the king granted Mary "full permission to reside at Court, and the Queen has countenanced it with a good grace."[5]

But ever present were reminders of her father's vengeance and the price Mary might pay for her perceived disloyalty. The following year, sixty-eight-year-old Margaret Pole, the woman whom Mary had referred to as her "second mother," was taken to the scaffold on the slope of Tower Hill. She had been attainted in 1539 without ever having been tried. At seven in the morning of May 27, 1541, she was brought out to die. She commended her soul to God, prayed for the king, and requested to be remembered to the "Princess Mary." She then placed her head on the block. In the absence of the usual Tower executioner, "a wretched and blundering youth . . . literally hacked her head and shoulders to pieces."[6]

> Thinking now in his old days, the King felt after sundry troubles of mind which have happened unto him by marriages, to have obtained such a jewel [Katherine] for womanhood and very perfect love towards him . . . and showed outwardly all virtue and good behaviour.[7]

Yet unbeknown to the king, Katherine had had relationships before she was married, when she had been part of the household of her step-grandmother the dowager duchess of Norfolk: first in 1536, when she was fourteen, with her music teacher, Henry Manox, and then two years later with Francis Dereham, a kinsman of her uncle the duke of Norfolk. Upon becoming queen, Katherine resumed her illicit liaisons. Dereham returned to court as her private secretary, and Thomas Culpepper, a gentleman of the king's Privy Chamber, began regularly meeting with her in her chamber. By October 1541, Cranmer, the archbishop of Canterbury, learned of Katherine's continuing behavior, and, on November 2, he presented Henry with a written statement of allegations. The king was initially disbelieving, but after Manox and Dereham were questioned, he was forced to accept the fact of Katherine's adultery.

Five days later, at Hampton Court, Katherine was interrogated by her uncle, Norfolk, and Cranmer. At first she denied the allegations, but then she admitted the truth. In a letter of confession to the king, she begged for his mercy, describing her relationships with Manox and Dereham and explaining why she had not told him before they were married: "I was so desirous to be taken unto your grace's favour and so blinded with the desire of worldly glory that I could not, nor had grace, to consider how great a fault it was to conceal my former faults from your Majesty."[8]

In January, Katherine and Lady Rochford, her lady of the bedchamber, who had arranged illicit meetings, were declared guilty of treason. On February 10, Katherine was moved from Syon to the Tower, passing first beneath London Bridge, where the heads of Dereham and Culpepper, executed the previous year, were still displayed. Two days later, Sunday the twelfth, she was told to prepare herself for death. According to Chapuys, "she asked to have the block brought in to her so that she might see how to place herself, which was done, and she made trial of it."[9] Early the following morning, her preparations complete, Katherine knelt at the scaffold and her head was struck off.[10]

"This King has wonderfully felt the case of the Queen his wife," Chapuys wrote. "He has certainly shown greater sorrow and regret at her loss than at the faults, loss or divorce of his preceding wives."[11] By April, it was reported that, since learning of his late wife's conduct, he had "not been the same man" and was often to be found "sad, pensive and sighing."[12]

Following Katherine Howard's execution, Mary enjoyed far greater favor and presided over court feasts as if she were queen. As a New Year's gift Henry presented her "with rings, silver plate, and other jewels" among which were "two rubies of inestimable value."[13] However, during those months, the princess suffered repeatedly from chronic ill health, linked to anxiety, depression, and irregular menstruation, although the symptoms varied widely from one episode to the next. In March and April, she had a "strange fever" that brought on heart palpitations and so afflicted her that at times "she remained as though dead."[14] On April 22, Chapuys told the queen of Hungary, "the princess has been seriously ill, and in danger of her life."[15] Yet Mary recovered and on December 17 was summoned to court for the Christmas festivities "with a great number of ladies . . . they work day and night at Hampton Court to finish her lodging."[16] Chapuys reported that the king "spoke to her in the most gracious and amiable words that a father could address to his daughter."[17]

ON JULY 12, 1543, Mary and Elizabeth attended their father's sixth wedding, in the queen's Privy Closet at Hampton Court. As Thomas Wriothesley, secretary of the Privy Council, reported to the duke of Suffolk:

> The King's Majesty was married on Thursday last to my Lady Latimer, a woman in my judgement, for virtue, wisdom and gentleness, most mete for his Highness, and sure I am his Majesty had never a wife more agreeable to his heart than she is. Our Lord send them long life and much joy together.[18]

It was a small ceremony with some twenty people in attendance, presided over by Stephen Gardiner, bishop of Winchester.[19] Henry's bride, the twice-married Katherine Parr, a former member of Mary's household, had come to the king's attention during Mary's frequent visits to court. Katherine had long-standing connections with the princess. Her mother, Maud, had been one of Katherine of Aragon's ladies-in-waiting, and she had been named after the queen, who had stood as godmother at her baptism. It was soon apparent that Katherine Parr, only four years older than Mary, was to be "more a friend than a stepmother." She sought to improve relations between Mary and her father, and soon Chapuys was reporting, "The King continues to treat her [Mary] kindly, and has made her stay with the new Queen, who behaves affectionately towards her."[20] Mary and Katherine were both learned women, and, despite Katherine's evangelical sympathies, they enjoyed a close relationship and studied together.

In 1544, under Katherine Parr's influence, Mary took up the translation of *Erasmus's Paraphrases on the Four Gospels.* The scholar Nicholas Udall was the editor of the book; Katherine funded its publication, and Mary was one of the translators. Ill health prevented Mary from finishing work on the book, and her chaplain, Francis Mallet, eventually completed it. In a letter of September 20, Katherine inquired as to whether Mary wished it "to go forth to the world (most auspiciously) under your name, or as the production of an unknown writer?" adding, "You will, in my opinion, do a real injury if you refuse to let it go down to posterity under the auspices of your own name, since you have undertaken so much labour in accurately translating it for the great good of the public and would have undertaken still greater (as is well known) if the health of your body had permitted." She continued, "I do not see why you should repudiate that praise which all men justly confer on you."[21] In his preface to the *Paraphrases,* Udall paid tribute to "the most noble, the virtuous, the most witty, and the most studious Lady Mary's grace," calling her "a peerless flower of virginity."[22]

Based at court, Mary thrived in the favor of an intelligent and benevolent queen. When in February 1544 a ball was held during the visit of the Spanish grandee the duke of Nájera, Mary danced elegantly, dressed extravagantly in a gown of gold cloth under a robe of violet velvet with a coronal of large precious stones on her head. As Nájera described her:

> The princess Mary has a pleasing countenance and person. It is said of her that she is endowed with very great goodness and discretion, and among other praises, I heard of her is this, that she knows how to conceal her acquirements; and certainly this is no small proof of prudence, since the real sage, who is aware of the extent of knowledge, thinks his own learning of too low an estimate to be boasted of, whilst those who have only a superficial acquaintance with learning exhibit the contrary, as they pride themselves in proportion to their acquirements and with-

> out imparting their knowledge, allow no one to be learned but themselves. The princess is much beloved throughout the kingdom, that she is almost adored.[23]

Despite being twenty years younger than Mary, Edward was fiercely protective of his elder sister. Writing to his stepmother, the six-year-old urged her to keep a careful eye on the princess: "preserve her, therefore, I pray you, my dear sister Mary," from all the "wiles and enchantments of the evil one" and "beseech her to attend no longer to foreign dances and merriments which do not become a most Christian princess."[24] At the same time he praised Mary, telling her, "I like you even as a brother ought to like a very dear sister, who hath within herself all the embellishments of virtue and honourable station." In the same way that he "loved his best clothes most of all, though he seldom wore them," he explained, "so he wrote seldom to her, but loved her most."[25]

CHAPTER 24

THE FAMILY OF HENRY VIII

His Majesty therefore thinketh convenient before his departure beyond the seas that it be enacted by his Highness with the assent of the lords spiritual and temporal and the commons in this present Parliament . . . that in case it shall happen the King's Majesty and the said excellent Prince his yet only son Prince Edward and heir apparent to decease without heir of either of their bodies lawfully begotten . . . then the said Imperial Crown . . . shall be to the Lady Marie the King's Highness' daughter and to the heirs of the body of the Lady Marie lawfully begotten . . . and for default of such issue the said Imperial Crown . . . shall be to the Lady Elizabeth the King's second daughter and to the heirs of the body of the Lady Elizabeth lawfully begotten.[1]

IN FEBRUARY 1544, PARLIAMENT PASSED A NEW AND RADICAL ACT of Succession. The previous law, passed in 1536 following Henry's marriage to Jane Seymour, had bastardized both Mary and Elizabeth and settled the succession on any son born of Seymour or "by any other lawful wife."[2] Yet now, as Henry visibly aged and the six-year-old Edward remained his sole heir, a real uncertainty hung over the Tudor succession. As the new act declared, "It standeth in the only pleasure and will of Almighty God whether the King's Majesty shall have any heirs begotten and procreated between his Highness and his . . . most entirely beloved wife Queen Katherine" or whether "the said Prince Edward shall have issue of his body lawfully begotten."[3] Although still regarded as illegitimate, Mary, and then Elizabeth, were placed in the line of succession after Edward and his heirs.

On June 26, the royal children came together with their father at Whitehall for a lavish reception—a *voyde*—at which wine and sweetmeats were served. It was the first public outing of the reconciled royal family.[4] The reunion was commemorated in the portrait known as *The Family of Henry VIII,* painted by an unknown artist. The picture is dominated by Henry, sitting on his throne between his son and heir, the six-year-old Prince Edward, and, to emphasize the line of dynastic succession, Edward's mother, the long-since-dead Jane Seymour. On the left stands Mary, on the right Elizabeth. Both are dressed similarly, with Mary distinguishable only by being the taller sister. Despite having played a part in brokering the reconciliation between Henry and his children, Katherine Parr is omitted from the scene. This was more than just a family portrait, however; it was to commemorate the political settlement enshrined in the Act of Succession. This was the Tudor family as Henry had decreed it: the king's heirs in degree of precedence. It would shape the English monarchy for the rest of the century.

WITH THE SUCCESSION settled, Henry looked to recapture the glories of his youth by going to war with France. The emperor and the French king had resumed hostilities, and both sovereigns once again began to compete for Henry's favor. Chapuys reported that the French "now almost offer the English carte blanche for an alliance," and he advised that England must, at whatever cost, be secured for the imperial interest.[5] Henry would indeed make a secret treaty with the emperor, in February 1543, that provided for a joint invasion of France within two years.

But Henry first needed to secure the northern border by mounting a campaign against Scotland. At Solway Moss in November 1542, the English inflicted a humiliating defeat on the Scots. Three weeks later King James V died, leaving the kingdom to his week-old daughter, Mary. Henry then sought to subdue Scotland in advance of his invasion in France, and in July 1543 a treaty of peace and dynastic union was signed at Greenwich with Prince Edward betrothed to Mary, queen of Scots.[6] But within five months, the entente had broken down as the Scots reaffirmed their alliance with the French.

Preparations were now made for war on two fronts: with Scotland

and with France. While the emperor sought to make Francis relinquish his claim to Milan and support the German princes, Henry looked to force him to abandon the cause of Scottish independence. In May 1544, 14,000 troops were sent to Scotland, and a month later, an English force of some 40,000 men invaded France. On July 11, Henry, despite his greatly expanded girth and swollen, ulcerated legs, left Whitehall for France.[7] In his absence, Katherine Parr was appointed regent of England, to rule the country in the name of the king as Katherine of Aragon had done some thirty years before. She managed the five-man council that Henry had appointed to assist her and oversaw the supply of men and money for the war. Writing to Henry's council, Katherine adopted the full royal style: "Right trusty and right well-beloved cousins, we greet you well." She signed herself "Katherine the Queen." In letters to Henry she used the submissive tone of a royal wife "by your majesty's humble obedient servant."[8] She was a model of wifely queenship.

As Katherine governed from Hampton Court, Mary was with her, and later Edward and Elizabeth too. Both stepdaughters witnessed a woman governing and imposing her authority on her male councillors. It would prove formative for both.

ON JULY 14, HENRY arrived in Calais, ready for the planned siege of Boulogne, which began five days later. After weeks of laying siege, the Council wrote to Katherine on August 4, informing her that "Yesterday, the battery began, and goes lustily forward, and the walls begin to tumble apace." They anticipated that Boulogne must fall shortly.[9] Six weeks later, the town surrendered and Henry entered in triumph. Yet on the same day the emperor, who sought to concentrate his efforts on Germany, had concluded a treaty with the French at Crépy and abandoned England. Henry was left to fight Francis alone. The French king now pledged "to win as much as the Englishmen had on this side of the sea," to capture a town on England's southeast coast that could be exchanged for Boulogne, and to send troops into Scotland for an invasion of the north.

On May 31, 1545, a French expeditionary force landed at Dumbarton in Scotland, and on July 19, a French invasion fleet of more than two hundred ships entered the Solent. Fires were lit across England, raising the alarm.[10] In the skirmishes that followed, Henry's warship the *Mary Rose* was sunk with the loss of 500 men. Two days later, 2,000 French troops landed at Bembridge on the Isle of Wight and burned several villages before being forced to retreat. English shipping in Portsmouth harbor was attacked and the towns of Newhaven and Seaford were sacked until the French forces were driven back across the English Channel. The following day Henry ordered processions throughout the realm and prayers to be said to intercede for victory.[11]

"We are in war with France and Scotland," warned Bishop Gardiner;

> we have enmity with the bishop of Rome, have no assured friendship here, and have received from the Lansgrave, chief captain of the Protestants, such displeasure that he has cause to think us angry with him. Our war is noisome to our realm and to all our merchants that traffic throughout the Narrow Seas. . . . We are in a world where reason and learning prevail not and covenants are little regarded.[12]

By September, as both sides sued for peace, negotiations were revived with the emperor. On October 23, Bishops Gardiner and Thomas Thirlby were commissioned to present a three-pronged plan: Charles V would marry Mary, Edward the emperor's daughter, and Elizabeth his son, Philip. Charles did not respond favorably.[13] It was clear that Henry was seeking better relations with the emperor merely to secure a stronger negotiating position with France, and the proposals came to nothing.

IN MAY 1546, the ailing Eustace Chapuys prepared to leave England after sixteen years as ambassador. On May 4 he went to the palace of Westminster to bid farewell to the queen and Mary. Katherine expressed her desire that the friendship between England and Spain be maintained. "She . . . begged me affectionately, after I presented to your majesty her humble service, to express explicitly all I had learned here of the good wishes of the King towards you." Mary, meanwhile, thanked him for the emperor's "good wishes towards her," and, "in default of her power to repay your Majesty in any other way, she said she was bound to pray constantly to God for your Majesty's health and prosperity."

At a final audience, Chapuys and Henry spoke about future relations between England and France. Henry "observed that he would very much prefer a settled peace to a truce . . . but, after all, if your Majesty would aid him, in accordance with the treaty, he did not care very much either." The king stressed "the importance of the treaty of friendship . . . that I would report very fully and use my best endeavours, in every way, to induce your Majesty to declare against the French."[14]

Finally, on June 7, 1546, French and English commissioners signed a peace treaty in which it was agreed that Boulogne would be returned to France in eight years' time on payment of 2 million crowns. In the hope of exploiting the new accord, the pope sent an envoy to England, Gurone Bertano, to propose terms for Henry's reconciliation to Rome. Pope Paul had hoped that the prodigal son might now submit to papal primacy, but Bertano's overtures were firmly rebuffed.[15]

CHAPTER 25

DEPARTED THIS LIFE

∴

Sir, I am confused and apprehensive to have to inform your Majesty that there are rumours here of a new Queen, although I do not know why, or how true it may [be].[1]

—AMBASSADOR FRANÇOIS VAN DER DELFT TO THE EMPEROR, FEBRUARY 27, 1546

IN FEBRUARY 1546, A PLOT WAS HATCHED TO DESTROY THE QUEEN. Her evangelical beliefs and her growing influence over the king had made her enemies among the religious conservatives at court. With Henry's deteriorating health, and his temper growing ever shorter, he became increasingly irritated by Katherine's debates with him over religion. "A good hearing it is," he retorted to Bishop Gardiner, "when women become such clerks; and a thing much to my comfort, to come in mine old days to be taught by my wife."[2] Seeing an opportunity to gain the ascendancy at court and halt the progress of religious reform, Gardiner and his fellow conservatives moved to convince Henry that Katherine was to be feared.[3] Gardiner murmured to the king that the queen's views were heretical under the law and that he,

> with others of his faithful councillors, could, within a short time, disclose such treasons cloaked with this heresy that His Majesty would easily perceive how perilous a matter it is to cherish a serpent within his own bosom.[4]

Gardiner secured Henry's agreement for Katherine to be investigated for heresy and for treason. Her chief intimates, the ladies Herbert, Lane, and Tyrwhitt, were to be questioned and their closets searched for anything that might incriminate the queen.[5]

In the spring, Anne Askew, a young Lincolnshire gentlewoman who held evangelical opinions and who associated with Lady Hertford and Lady Denny, both high-ranking women at court, was taken to the Tower. There she was interrogated in an attempt to extract information that could be used against Katherine. Did not the ladies of the court share her opinion? Could she not name "a great number of my sect"? She conceded nothing. She was put on the rack and tortured and, refusing to implicate anyone, was revived and racked again. The lieutenant of the Tower would not perform the second torture, so her interrogators, the chancellor of the Court of Augmentations and the lord chancellor of England, "threw off their gowns" and became "tormentors themselves." As a gentlewoman, Askew should have been protected against torture, and the Council was "not a little displeased" when news of the racking spread. So desperate were the conservatives to implicate the queen that the lord chancellor of England himself had broken the law.

On July 16, 1546, Askew's broken body was carried on a wooden chair and she was bound to the stake, together with Nicholas Belenian, a priest from Shropshire, and John Adams, a tailor. All were accused of heresy for refusing to accept the Real Presence in the Eucharist, as the Act of Six Articles had decreed.

Although Askew failed to incriminate Katherine, Gardiner managed to procure evidence regarding the discovery of forbidden religious books and a warrant of arrest was issued. Katherine was warned by her physician, Thomas Wendy, of the action to be taken against her and advised to submit before Henry; she should "somewhat . . . frame and conform herself to the King's mind." If she would do so and "show her humble submission unto him . . . she should find him gracious and favourable unto her."

Fearing that she faced the same fate as her predecessor, Katherine took Wendy's advice and acquiesced to the king, protesting her weakness as a woman and the God-given superiority of men: "Must I, and will I, refer my judgement in this, and all other cases, to your Majesty's wisdom, as my only anchor, Supreme Head and Governor here in earth, next under God." Henry relented. "Is it even so, Sweetheart? And tend your arguments to no worse end? Then perfect friends we are now again, as ever at any time heretofore."[6]

When Chancellor Wriothesley arrived the following day with a detachment of the guard to arrest the queen, Henry berated him as a "Knave! Arrant knave, beast! And fool!" and ordered him to "*avaunt* [leave]" his "sight."

THE COLLAPSE OF the plot against Katherine Parr signaled the end of the conservatives' brief period of ascendancy. With Henry's health deteriorating rapidly, the Seymour faction, led by Edward's uncle Edward Seymour, earl of Hertford, acted to destroy its enemies, the Howards and Bishop Gardiner, and take control of the government. "Nothing is done at court," reported the newly arrived van der Delft, "without their intervention and the Council mostly meets at Hertford's house. It is even asserted that the custody of the Prince and government of the realm will be entrusted to them; and this misfortune to the house of Norfolk may have come from that quarter."[7]

Mary, meanwhile, was untouched by these shifts of power and remained in relative peace at court as Henry continued to show her every sign of favor. One of the last entries in the king's accounts is the purchase of a horse for Mary, "a white grey gelding."[8]

On December 12, Thomas Howard, the foremost peer of the realm, and his eldest son, Henry Howard, earl of Surrey, were arrested on grounds of treason and sent to the Tower. Surrey, a descendant of Edward III, had boasted of his Plantagenet blood and declared that when Henry died, his father would be "metest to rule the prince." He had planned, it was alleged, to disband the Council, depose the king, seize the young Prince Edward, and display his own heraldry as the royal arms and insignia, an indication of his ambition for the throne. It was upon this last charge that he was tried and found guilty of high treason.[9]

Meanwhile his father, Norfolk, was questioned and imprisoned in the Tower. On January 12, he confessed that he had "offended the King in opening his secret counsels at divers times to sundry persons to the peril of his Highness . . . [and] concealed high treason, in keeping secret the false acts of my son, Henry, Earl of Surrey, in using the arms of St Edward the Confessor, which pertain only to kings."[10] Surrey was executed on January 19 on the scaffold at Tower Hill. A week later Thomas Howard was attainted without trial and awaited execution.

ON THE EVENING of December 26, Henry ordered his will to be brought to him. He wanted to make some changes to the list of executors. "Some he meant to have in and some he meant to have out." The crown would go directly to Edward and any lawful heirs of his body and in default to Mary "upon condition that she shall not marry without the written and sealed consent of a majority" of Edward's surviving Privy Council. In the event of Mary's childless death, Elizabeth would succeed. The succession would then be conferred on the Grey and Clifford families, descendants of Henry's younger sister, Mary.[11] Sixteen executors were to act as Edward's councillors until he reached the age of eighteen. They included Edward Seymour, the earl of Hertford; John Dudley, the earl of Warwick; Sir William Paget, the royal secretary; and Sir Anthony Denny, chief gentleman of the Privy Chamber. Stephen Gardiner, bishop of Winchester, was excluded, and Katherine's position as regent was revoked. Instead, the voices of all the executors were to be equal and decisions were to be taken by majority vote.

Though he had suffered for some time from ulcerated legs, obesity, and gout, Henry's health had declined rapidly since the New Year and he remained confined to the Privy Chamber with a high fever. On January 10, the French ambassador, Odet de Selve, wrote to Francis I that "neither the Queen nor the Lady Mary could see him."[12] His doctors had known that death was approaching but for fear of punishment had held back from telling him. Sir Anthony Denny finally volunteered to inform the king of his imminent demise. He was "to a man's judgement not like[ly] to live." He should, Denny advised, now "prepare himself to death."

"Yet is the mercy of Christ able," Henry asked, "to pardon me all my sins, though they were greater than they be?" He ordered that Archbishop Cranmer be sent for to hear his confession, first declaring that he would "sleep a little." He woke an hour later, "feeling feebleness to increase upon him." By the time the archbishop arrived, Henry was unable to speak. So when Cranmer asked him his faith and assured him of salvation, he urged him to "give some token with his eyes or with his hand, that he trusted in the Lord." Henry squeezed his hand and wrung it "as hard as he could."[13]

By two in the morning of January 28, 1547, Henry was dead. He was fifty-six. Apothecaries, surgeons, and wax chandlers were immediately summoned to "do their duties in spurging, cleansing, bowelling, searing, embalming, furnishing and dressing with spices the said corpse." The body was wrapped in fine linen and velvet and tied with silk cords before the plumber and carpenter cased the corpse in lead. The coffin was then laid out in the middle of the Privy Chamber at Whitehall, watched over by Henry's chaplains and gentlemen.[14]

For three days the king's death was not made public and was kept secret from all except Henry's councillors. Life at court continued without interruption. Henry's meals were brought into the great hall as usual to the sound of trumpets; Parliament remained in session, and those who requested audiences with the king were told that he was indisposed. As van der Delft wrote to the emperor, "I learn from a very confidential source that the King, whom may God receive His Grace, had departed this life, although not the slightest signs of such a thing were to be seen at court."[15] The imperial ambassador subsequently wrote that Mary had been very displeased with Edward Seymour because "he did not visit her or send to her for several days after her father's death."[16] Only when Edward's succession was secure would Mary be told of Henry's passing.

Finally, on the morning of January 31, the tearful Lord Chancellor Wriothesley announced Henry's death to the dumbstruck Parliament, and a section of his will, dealing with the succession of the crown, was read out.[17] Meanwhile, on the twenty-eighth, the day of the king's death, Edward Seymour, the new king's uncle, and Sir Anthony Browne, master of the king's horse, had ridden with a force of 300 mounted troops from London to Hertford Castle to inform Edward of his father's death and pay homage to him as the new king.[18]

PART TWO

A King's Sister

CHATPTER 26

THE KING IS DEAD, LONG LIVE THE KING

∴

Edward VI, by the grace of God King of England, France, and Ireland, defender of the faith and of the Church of England and also of Ireland in earth the supreme head, to all our most loving, faithful, and obedient subjects, and to every of them, greeting.

Where it hath pleased Almighty God, on Friday last past in the morning to call unto his infinite mercy the most excellent high and mighty prince, King Henry VIII of most noble and famous memory, our most dear and entirely beloved father, whose soul God pardon; forasmuch as we, being his only son and undoubted heir, be now invested and established in the crown imperial of this realm.[1]

—Proclamation of King Edward VI,
Westminster, January 31, 1547

At three in the afternoon of Monday, January 31, 1547, nine-year-old King Edward VI entered the City of London to take possession of his kingdom. Guns fired from ships on the Thames as the nobility of the realm accompanied the boy king to his lodgings.[2]

The following day the Privy Council gathered in the Presence Chamber, where Edward sat in a chair of estate, and Henry's will was read out. The executors announced that it had been "agreed with one assent and consent" that Edward Seymour, the king's uncle, should be "preferred in name and place before others" and become lord protector. This was not as Henry had decreed. The sixteen executors were to have formed a regency council with all men having equal status; now Seymour emerged as the foremost councillor. Two weeks later, amid a general granting of lands and titles, Seymour would become duke of Somerset. "There was none so mete . . . in all the realm as he," the House of Lords declared.[3]

Having sworn oaths to the king, his councillors cried together, "God save the noble King Edward!" Edward thanked them heartily and doffed his cap.[4] He would remain in the Tower for the next three weeks until after his father's funeral had taken place and preparations had been made for his own coronation. From there he wrote letters of condolence to his stepmother Katherine Parr and this to his sister Mary, then thirty-one, who remained in the dowager queen's household:

> Natural affection, not wisdom, instigates us to lament our dearest father's death. For affection thinks she has utterly lost one who is dead; but wisdom believes one who lives with God is in happiness everlasting. Wheretofore, God having given us such we ought not to mourn our father's death, since it is his will, who works all things for good . . . so far as lies in me, I will be to you a dearest brother, and overflow with all kindness.[5]

On Wednesday, February 2, between eight and nine at night, Henry's body was moved from the Privy Chamber to the Chapel Royal at Whitehall. Ten days later it was taken to Windsor in a gilded chariot pulled by seven horses, all bedecked in black velvet. The roads had been cleared and widened to allow the easier passage of the procession, which stretched over four miles. In front were 250 poor men, dressed in mourning gowns and carrying torches, followed by gentlemen bearing the king's standards and heralds with the king's helmet, targe (sword) shield, and coat of arms. Upon the coffin, draped in cloth of gold and blue velvet, was a life-size, lifelike effigy of King Henry, a scepter of gold in his right hand, in his left the ball of the world with a cross. On his head rested the imperial crown, and around his neck was the collar of the Garter.[6] According to one observer, it "looked exactly like that of the King himself . . . just as if he were alive."[7] Behind the coffin rode the king's chief mourner, the marquess of Dorset, constable of England, and the king's guard, all in black, their halberds pointing to the ground.

The procession reached Syon, the former Bridgettine house on the banks of the Thames in Middlesex, at two in the afternoon. There, after Masses were said, the corpse remained overnight. One account describes how, at Syon, "the leaden coffin being cleft by the shaking of the carriage, the pavement of the church was wetted with his [Henry's] blood." When plumbers later came to solder the coffin, they saw a "dog creeping, and licking up the King's blood."[8]

At seven the following morning, the procession resumed its slow progress to Windsor. Funeral knells were rung, and townspeople lined the route through each town it passed. Finally the gilded chariot arrived at the chapel of the Order of the Garter, where the coffin was placed in a hearse thirty-five feet tall and covered with tapers and candles. The next morning, February 15, Henry's burial took place. Stephen Gardiner preached the funeral sermon, and sixteen yeomen of the Guard lowered the coffin into the vault next to that of Jane Seymour, just as Henry's will had instructed.[9]

As Edward Hall wrote in his chronicle, "The late King was buried at Windsor with much solemnity, and the officers broke their staves, hurling them into the grave. But they were restored to them again when they came to the Tower."[10] With Henry laid to rest, Edward's reign could be formally inaugurated.

AT ONE IN THE afternoon of Saturday, February 19, Edward left the Tower, dressed in white velvet and cloth of silver embroidered with precious stones, to ride on horseback through the city to Westminster.[11] Before him went an ordered procession: his messengers walking side by side; his gentlemen, chaplains, esquires of the body, and nobles; and his councillors, each paired with a foreign ambassador. The marquess of Dorset walked ahead of the young king, bearing the sword of state. Bringing up the rear were the gentlemen and grooms of the Privy Chamber, the pensioners, and the Guard.[12]

Along the route were pageants celebrating Edward's arrival, many echoing those that had greeted the last boy king, Henry VI, on his entry into London in 1432.[13] Edward was heralded as "a young King Solomon," charged with "rebuilding the Temple"—that is, continuing his father's reformation.[14] In one pageant, a phoenix, representing Edward's mother, Jane Seymour, emerged from an artificial Heaven of suns, stars, and clouds to be met by a crowned golden lion (Henry). Two angels then crowned their offspring; the phoenix and the old lion vanished, leaving the cub to rule on his own. The highlight of the pageantry, in nine-year-old Edward's eyes, was an acrobat who "came sliding down" a rope strung from the uppermost part of the steeple of St. Paul's to an anchor in the garden of the dean's house. The tumbler stood up, kissed Edward's foot, then walked back up the rope, "tumbling and casting himself from one leg to another."[15] By the time the procession reached Westminster, it was nearly six in the evening, five hours after it had set off from the Tower.[16]

Early the following day, noblemen were summoned to accompany the king to Westminster Abbey and attend the coronation.[17] Edward was taken by barge to Whitehall and dressed in a robe of crimson velvet, "furred with powdered ermines throughout." At the abbey a scaffold seven stairs tall had been erected, on top of which was set the throne, a white chair covered with damask and gold. Two cushions had been placed on the seat, one of cloth of tissue, the other black velvet embroidered with gold, upon which the diminutive boy king would sit.

Edward was not the youngest king to be crowned; Henry VI had been just eight at his coronation in 1429. However, his would prove to be the most radical English coronation in its thousand-year history. He would be the first monarch to be anointed "Supreme Head of the English Church," and though the coronation would broadly follow the *Liber Regalis*—the Book of Kingship—which had dictated the ceremony for kings since 1375, there would be some significant departures.[18]

The week before, the Council had announced its decision, "upon mature and deep deliberation," that the "old observances and ceremonies [should] be corrected" on account of the king's "tender age" and so that they might conform to the "new laws of the realm," particularly concerning the supremacy and abolition of papal authority. A new king would traditionally swear to confirm laws and liberties that had been granted to people by kings before him and to observe "such laws as . . . shall be chosen by your people."[19] This was drastically altered. It was now left to the king to decide which laws and liberties he would obey. The clause ensuring the protection of the liberties of the clergy was entirely omitted, and the final part of the oath was rewritten: the people, not the king, now had to consent to the new laws.

As Thomas Cranmer, the archbishop of Canterbury, explained in his sermon, the oaths Edward had sworn were not to "be taken in the bishop of Rome's sense," and the clergy had no right to hold kings to account ("to hit your Majesty in the teeth").[20] Although Edward was to be anointed, Cranmer made clear that this was "but ceremony." He was king "not in respect of the oil which the bishop useth, but in consideration of their power which is preordained . . . the King is yet a perfect monarch notwithstanding, and God's anointed, as well as if he was inoiled." Edward had come to the throne "fully invested and established in the crown imperial of this realm."[21]

Now the young king was called upon to do his princely duty:

> Your Majesty is God's vice-regent and Christ's vicar within your own dominions, and to see, with your predecessor Josiah, God truly worshipped, and idolatry destroyed; the tyranny of the bishops of Rome banished from your subjects, and images removed. These acts be signs of a second Josiah, who reformed the church of God in his days.[22]

Edward was to model himself on the young biblical King Josiah and purge the land of idols. The coronation was an opportunity to showcase the Protestant aspirations of the new regime.

With the oaths made and litanies sung, Edward was anointed and crowned with the crown of Edward the Confessor, the imperial crown—styled as such since the reign of Henry V—and a third crown made especially for his small head.[23] Normally the imperial crown was not part of the crowning ritual; its inclusion here emphasized the imperial status of the king and echoed the triple crowning of the pope.

The spurs, orb, and scepter were then presented to the young king and Te Deums were sung as the lords spiritual and temporal paid him homage.

Recalling the coronation in his journal, Edward noted only that he had sat next to his uncle Edward Seymour and Archbishop Thomas Cranmer and that he had worn "the crown on his head."[24]

CHAPTER 27

FANTASY AND NEW FANGLENESS

∴

THE EMPEROR AND PAPAL CURIA DID NOT IMMEDIATELY RECOGnize the new king. In the eyes of Catholic Europe, Edward was illegitimate and Mary the lawful heir. Charles returned Edward's greetings without explicitly acknowledging his title. "We went no further than this with regard to the young King," he explained to Ambassador van der Delft, "in order to avoid saying anything which might prejudice the right that our cousin the Princess might advance to the throne."[1]

Similarly, Charles's sister, Mary of Hungary, regent of the Netherlands, wrote to van der Delft, "We make no mention at present of the young prince, as we are ignorant as yet whether or not he will be recognised as King. . . . We likewise refrain from sending you any letters for our cousin, the Princess Mary, as we do not yet know how she will be treated."[2] Meanwhile, the French, always keen to drive a wedge between English and imperial interests, claimed that the emperor planned to make war on the English in support of Mary's claim.[3] As it was, Mary accepted her brother as Henry's rightful heir and made no challenge.

In his will, Henry had confirmed Mary in her right to the succession and granted her and Elizabeth a yearly income of £3,000 "in money, plate, jewels and household stuff" and, upon their marriage, a dowry of £10,000 each. But amid the general sharing of lands, titles, and estates among the regency councillors, aimed at securing their support for the new regime, Mary received a much more generous provision. She was granted lands and estates in East Anglia and the Home Counties valued at £3,819 18s. 6d.[4] Most of her endowment consisted of properties in Norfolk, Suffolk, and Essex, including Hunsdon and

Beaulieu (New Hall), where she had spent much of her time, and Kenninghall in Norfolk, the home of the Catholic Thomas Howard, duke of Norfolk, before his attainder on the eve of Henry's death. In all, Mary received thirty-two principal manors and a number of minor ones, which were later exchanged for Framlingham Castle in Suffolk.

Now thirty-one, Mary was one of the wealthiest peers in England and a significant regional magnate. She could choose her own household personnel and surrounded herself with Catholic men local to her estates, such as Sir Francis Englefield, Sir Robert Rochester, and Rochester's nephew Edward Waldegrave, who shared her commitment to the faith. Many of the women she chose, such as Jane Dormer, Eleanor Kempe, and Susan Clarencius, had been in her service and would remain with her for many years. Mary's household would become a bastion of Catholic loyalty. Ordinances were drawn up at Kenninghall providing for religious services. Particular importance was attached to the observance—by all her servants—of Matins, Mass, and Evensong. "Every gentleman, yeoman and groom not having reasonable impediment" was to be at the services every day.[5] To be in Mary's service was to live as a Catholic. Service and sanctity were inextricably bound together.

IN APRIL 1547, Mary left Katherine Parr, with whom she had remained since her father's death, and journeyed north to her new estates. Within weeks, Katherine had rekindled her relationship with her old love Thomas, Lord Seymour of Sudeley, and in May they were secretly married. Seymour sought to win Mary's approval, but she responded with thinly veiled disapproval, declaring that "being a maid," she was "nothing cunning" about "wooing matters." Henry was "as yet very ripe in her own remembrance," and she found it "strange news": "it standeth lest with my poor honour to be a meddler in this matter, considering whose wife her grace was of late."[6]

Initially relations between Mary and the Edwardian regime were distinctly amicable. The lord protector, Somerset, had previously been in the service of the emperor at the imperial court, and Anne, duchess of Somerset, formerly in the household of Katherine of Aragon.[7] Mary addressed her as "my good gossip" and "my good nann" and signed off a letter to her "your assured friend to my power, Mary."[8] As Christmas approached, Edward wrote to Mary, inviting her to spend the festive period with him and Elizabeth at court:

> *Right dear and right entirely beloved sister,*
>
> *We greet you well. And whereas our right dear and right entirely beloved sister, the Lady Elizabeth, having made suit to visit us, hath sithence [since] her coming desired to remain with us during all this Christmas Holydays, like as we cannot but take this her request in thankful part, so would we be glad, and should think us very well accompanied, if we might have you also with us at the same time.*

However, Edward concluded with the suggestion that if Mary's health was not good, she might postpone her visit to another occasion "when both the Time and your Health shall better suffer."[9]

ALTHOUGH THE NEW evangelical establishment was determined to overturn Henry's Act of Six Articles, at first it proceeded cautiously. Negotiations for peace with France had ended with the French king's death at the end of March, and in April Charles had defeated the German Protestants at Mühlberg. England was diplomatically isolated; it was not a good time to champion religious reform. But such prudence was short-lived, and the government was keen to press ahead with the process of reformation.

On July 31, 1547, new Church "Injunctions" were issued in the king's name and a general visitation ordered for the whole Church. Though the wording on the Mass was cautious and conservative—"of the very body and blood of Christ"—it was ordered that "abused" images be destroyed, processions abolished, the ringing of bells and use of rosary beds condemned, and the lighting of candles on the altar forbidden.[10] The same year *The Book of Homilies,* which set out the Lutheran doctrine of justification by faith alone, was written by Cranmer and issued to be read in all churches. A translation of Erasmus's *Paraphrases* on the Gospels—which Mary had had a role in translating under the sponsorship of Katherine Parr—was also to be placed in every church. Within three months, each parish was to possess the Bible in English. Sermons were to be preached regularly and priests instructed to recite the Lord's Prayer, creed, and Ten Commandments in English. When Bishops Edmund Bonner and Gardiner protested against the Injunctions, they were imprisoned. It was the prelude to further change. In Edward's first Parliament, which opened on November 4, 1547, the Act of Six Articles and Treasons Act were repealed. Marriage was made legal for the clergy, and the laity were to receive Communion in both kinds.

As the practices of the "old religion" came under attack, Mary made her Catholic devotion stridently clear, hearing up to four Masses every day in her chapel at Kenninghall.[11] In a dispatch of October 4, 1548, Jehan Dubois, the imperial secretary, described how Mary had just returned from Norfolk, where she had inspected her estates "and was much welcomed in the north country and wherever she had the power to do it she had Mass celebrated."[12] Mary wrote to Somerset, protesting at the "fantasy and new fangleness" and declaring that the Henrican religion had been established by parliamentary statute and it was illegal to defy it. Her father, she claimed, had left the realm in "Godly order and Quietness," which the Council was now disrupting with innovations.[13] No change should be made to the religious settlement imposed by the Act of Six Articles until the king came of age and was old enough to make his own decisions about religion. Somerset professed astonishment at Mary's attitude, believing that her words could not have "proceeded from the sincere mind of so virtuous and wise a lady, but rather by the setting on and procurement of some uncharitable and malicious persons." Henry had, Somerset continued, died before he had achieved all that "he purposed to have done" in religion.[14]

AS THE ACT OF Uniformity made its way through Parliament in January 1549, making the Book of Common Prayer the only legal form of worship, confrontation between Mary and the Edwardian government seemed inevitable. While maintaining doctrinal conservatism, the book represented a significant break with the past. The number of saints' days was reduced; only plain vestments were to be worn by the priest; and the Latin Mass was to be said in English and was now described ambiguously as "the supper of the Lord and the holy communion commonly called the mass."[15] The Elevation of the Host was abolished and the Catholic doctrine of the sacrifice of the Mass omitted.

When van der Delft visited Mary in late March, she complained bitterly of the changes brought about in the kingdom and of her private distress, saying she would rather give up her life than her religion. Once again she looked to the emperor for protection against the law that was shortly to come into effect. She explained how "in these miserable times," Charles was her "only refuge."[16]

Days later Mary addressed a letter directly to the emperor:

> We have never been in so great necessity and I therefore entreat your Majesty, considering the changes that are taking place in the kingdom, to provide, as your affairs may best permit, that I may continue to live in the ancient faith and in peace with my conscience.

She feared that, except by way of his Majesty, the emperor, she would "not be permitted to do so, judging by what has been settled in Parliament," and she reaffirmed her commitment "that in life and death I will not forsake the Catholic religion of the Church our mother."[17]

Charles was determined that he would "suffer no pressure to be put upon her [Mary], our close relative, or allow religious innovations to cause them to assume a different and less suitable manner towards her."[18] He ordered his ambassador to obtain a written assurance,

> in definite, suitable and permanent form, that notwithstanding all new laws and ordinances made upon religion, she may live in the observance of our ancient religion as she has done up to the present, so that neither the King nor Parliament may ever molest her, directly or indirectly by any means whatever.[19]

His dispatch to his ambassador on June 8 underlined his position:

> With regard to the Princess our cousin, the Protector and all other worthy people must understand that, her near kinship to us and close affinity, the perfect friendship we have always felt

> and feel for her, make it impossible that we should ever desist from our endeavours to save her from molestation in the free practice and observance of her faith . . . the Protector's answer that the Princess must obey the laws of the realm, is too bare and harsh to our cousin, the King's own sister . . . neither we nor our brother, the King of the Romans, nor any of the relatives of the Princess could tolerate such attempts, as the Protector might well suppose.[20]

Under instruction from the emperor, van der Delft went to Somerset to try to get a guarantee of Mary's freedom of worship. Somerset made it clear that "it was not in his power to act against the laws passed by Parliament" and that the ambassador had "asked for something dangerous to the kingdom":

> If the King and his sister, to whom the whole kingdom was attached as heiress to the crown in the event of the King's death, were to differ in matters of religion, dissension would certainly spring up. Such was the character of the nation . . . he [Somerset] hoped the Lady Mary would use her wisdom and conform with the King to avoid such an emergency and keep peace within the realm.[21]

Keen to preserve his good relationship with the emperor, Somerset was conciliatory. Though he could not act against statute and would not grant a formal dispensation for Mary to be immune from the laws, he made it clear that he had no intention of inquiring into the worship of her household until the king came of age.[22] Many on the Privy Council, however, disagreed, and they demanded that Mary submit to the law.

CHAPTER 28

ADVICE TO BE CONFORMABLE

⁛

ON JUNE 9, 1549, THE DAY THE FIRST ENGLISH PRAYER BOOK became law, Mary celebrated Latin Mass in her chapel at Kenninghall amid incense, candles, and the chiming of bells. In doing so she publicly signaled her opposition to the religious changes and defied Edward's authority as king. The Privy Council responded swiftly. In a letter dated June 16, Mary was given "advice to be conformable and obedient" to the law: Mass was no longer to be celebrated in her house. Her comptroller, Robert Rochester, and her chaplain, Dr. John Hopton, were summoned to court to receive further instructions.[1]

A week later, addressing Somerset and the rest of Edward's Council, Mary responded directly to their charges:

> My Lorde, I perceive by the letters which I late received from you, and all of the king's Majesty's council that you be all sorry to find so little conformity in me touching the observation of his Majesty's laws; who am well assured that I have offended no law, unless it be a late law of your own making, for the altering of matters in religion which in my conscience, is not worthy to have the name of a law, both for the King's honour's sake, the wealth of the realm . . . and (as my conscience is very well persuaded) the offending of God, which passes all the rest.

She would not change her practices and would obey only her father's laws, and she trusted that the Council would "no more to trouble and unquiet" her with "matters touching her conscience." She excused from obedience the two men whose presence the Council had demanded: Hopton because of his ill health, Rochester because "the chief charge of my house resteth upon his travails."[2] In a subsequent letter to Somerset and the Privy Council, she expressed her anger and disappointment: "For my part I assure you all, that since the King my father, your late master and very good Lord died I never took you for other than my friends; but in this it appeareth co[n]trary."[3]

Days later, Lord Rich, the lord chancellor, and Sir William Petre, the first secretary, were sent to visit Mary at Kenninghall. Their brief was to challenge the points she had made in her previous letter, to induce her to comply with the new regulations, and to make her servants aware of the danger of disobeying the law.[4] In their "Remembrance for certain matters appointed by the Council to be declared to Dr Hopton to the Lady Mary's Grace for Answer to her former letter," the Privy Council rebuffed her objections point by point, yet Mary remained immovable and resistant to any such pressure.[5] She was determined to defend her servants' rights to the free practice of their religion. She described her staff as "worthy people, ready to serve their King after their God to the whole extent of their power"; they were "as her own kin" whom she would stand by. When Rochester and Hopton were instructed that they must persuade their mistress to conform, they explained that they would not and could not. Rochester protested that "it was nowise suitable that a servant should act otherwise than in obedience to his mistress's orders, and discharge of his domestic duties," while Hopton declared that "he was the Lady Mary's servant and obeyed her orders in her own house."[6]

As in years before, Mary gave the emperor a powerful hold over English politics, with the threat of war hanging over the country.[7] Sir William Paget was to be sent to the imperial court to "renew and make fast the amity with the Emperor" and make a formal proposition of marriage for Mary and the Infante Dom Luis of Portugal, the emperor's brother-in-law and a longtime suitor for Mary's hand. Rich and Petre were to ask Mary to draft, in her own hand, a letter of recommendation introducing William Paget to ensure that he gained the emperor's favor. Mary took the opportunity to defend her household. She would write the letter, but if the councillors spoke to her servants as they had threatened, she would add an account to the emperor of how she was being treated in religious matters.[8] The commissioners departed with "soft words having made no declaration or inhibition to her servants."[9]

When Paget arrived at the imperial court in late July, Charles expressed "great astonishment" at the pressure that had been put on Mary to accept the changes in religion. He stressed that, even if she were inclined to accept the reforms, he would do his "utmost to dissuade her, our close relative; for we and those to our blood would grieve exceedingly if she were to change." He repeated his request for an assurance "in writing or otherwise, that she should not be included in the regulations made by Parliament about religion or be kept in suspense on the matter."[10]

THE DAY AFTER the Prayer Book was introduced at Sampford Courtenay in Devon, local villagers petitioned the priest to defy the government. As John Hooker described it in his contemporary account of the rebellion, the priest "yielded to their wills and forthwith ravessheth [clothed] himself in his old popish attire and sayeth mass and all such services as in times past accustomed."[11] The news spread; a considerable force of Cornishmen angry at the religious changes gathered at Clyst St. Mary near Exeter. "We will," the manifesto of the western rebels demanded, "have the mass in Latin, as was before"; "we will have holy bread and holy water made every Sunday, psalms and ashes at the times accustomed, images set up again in every church, and all other ancient, old ceremonies used heretofore by our mother the Holy Church." The rebels insisted that the Act of Six Articles of 1539 be reintroduced until Edward came of age and described the new Prayer Book as a "Christmas game."[12]

There was violence too in Hertfordshire, Essex, Suffolk, and Norfolk, as the rural poor protested against the economic hardships brought about by Somerset's policy of land enclosure. Fences were pulled down and deer killed, and chaos engulfed the countryside. In Norfolk, rebels led by Robert Kett called for all bondmen to be free and emphasized that Thomas Howard, the third Duke of Norfolk, who had been imprisoned in 1547, "had used much more extremity than his Ancestors did towards them." Since many of the rebellions occurred in East Anglia, near Mary's estates, suspicion naturally fell on Mary.

On July 18, the Council warned her that certain of her servants were reported to be "chief in these commotions." One of her staff had been active among the rebels at Sampford Courtenay in Devon, and another, Thomas Poley, was declared to be "a captain of the worst sort assembled in Suffolk."[13] Men spoke of her complicity and of her plan to overthrow the present rulers of England. In a letter to the secretary of state, William Cecil, Sir Thomas Smith disguised his accusations not only by writing in Latin but also by referring to Mary in the masculine form: "Marius and the Marians; the fear which torments me to the point of destruction."[14]

Mary replied immediately, denying all charges made against her. The uprisings, she countered, "no less offend me, than they do you and the rest of the Council." As for her chaplain being at Sampford Courtenay, "I do not a little marvel; for, to my knowledge, I have not one chaplain in those parts." Poley had remained in her household, she claimed, and "was never doer amongst the commons, nor came in their company."[15]

IN THE MIDST of rebellion and as the French king declared war, Mary was able to continue to flout the law. As Somerset noted, "whereas she used to have two masses said before, she has three said now since the prohibitions and with greater show."[16] The government needed to maintain the imperial alliance, and it was considered prudent that for now, Mary be left alone to practice her religion. "If she does not wish to conform," Somerset reasoned, "let her do as she pleases quietly and without scandal."[17]

Yet as Edward wrote to Mary in August:

> We have somewhat marvelled, and cannot but still marvel very much, what grounds or reasons have or do move you to mislike or refuse to follow and embrace that which, by all the learned men of our realm, hath been so set forth, and of all our loving subjects obediently received; and knowing your good nature and affection towards us, we cannot think any other matter in this your refusal than only a certain grudge of conscience, for

want of good information and conference with some goodly and well learned men for remedy.[18]

Mary would receive corrective instruction. Such men would be chosen and sent to her, after which it was expected that her attitude would improve. Both the king and the lord protector clung to the hope that in time Mary would come to embrace the religious reforms.

Mary's conscience had driven her into a position of direct opposition to the government. The girl who had been broken down and forced to yield her soul and the honor of her mother in fear of her father was now a mature woman of thirty-three. She was a landed magnate with a following of her own and the support of Emperor Charles V. Her brother, the king, was a child. She would not succumb again.

CHAPTER 29

THE MOST UNSTABLE MAN IN ENGLAND

∴

"MATTERS IN THIS REALM ARE RESTLESS FOR CHANGE," VAN der Delft wrote on September 15, 1549. Somerset's handling of the rebellions and the continuing war with France and Scotland had lost him the confidence of the nobility and gentry. "The people are all in confusion, and with one common voice lament the present state of things."[1]

It was the beginning of the end of Somerset's protectorate. Dudley and the conservative nobles, Thomas Wriothesley, earl of Southampton, and Henry FitzAlan, earl of Arundel, were plotting against him and the country was drawing close to civil war. Matters came to a head on Saturday, October 5, when Somerset issued a proclamation commanding men to come to Hampton Court "in most defensible array" with harness and weapons, to defend the king against "a most dangerous conspiracy."[2] Dudley and his supporters immediately took up arms riding through the city, their retinues following behind "attending upon them in new liveries to the great wondering of many."[3] Letters were sent to other members of the nobility across the country, ordering them to ignore Somerset's proclamation and repair to London armed. Somerset moved Edward to Windsor as chaos engulfed the capital. Four days later, faced with overwhelming opposition among the ruling elite, Somerset surrendered. On October 14, he was arrested and sent to the Tower, charged with treason.

Dudley and his allies had asked Mary to support the coup against Somerset, but on the advice of the emperor she had declined to get involved. "As for certain councillors' machinations against the Protector, it does not for the present seem opportune that such an important change take place in England," wrote Charles; "it would be exceedingly hazardous for the Lady Mary to take any share in such proceedings."[4] There now developed a struggle for power on the Council, raising hopes among Mary's Catholic supporters. Van der Delft cautiously rejoiced, for "religion could not be in a worse state, and that therefore a change must be for the better, and that it was not made by the enemies of the old religion."[5] Wriothesley reassured the ambassador that Mary would be allowed to hear Mass, saying "those who have molested her will do so no more, and even though they were to begin afresh she has many good servants of whom I hold myself to be one."[6]

How they were deceived. Dudley emerged as leader of the government and lord president of the Council and, despite earlier indications of conservative sympathies, soon became a supporter of more evangelical reform. Mary was to come under renewed pressure to conform to the new religious practices. By the end of October, a proclamation announced that the government would "further do in all things, as time and opportunity may serve, whatsoever may lend to the glory of God and the advancement of his holy word."[7] When van der Delft visited Mary early the following year, she told him she considered Dudley to be "the most unstable man in England" and that the conspiracy against the protector had "envy and ambition as its motives." She was anxious and fearful of what lay ahead: "You will see that no good will come of this move, but that it is punishment from Heaven, and may be only the beginning of our misfortunes." It was for this reason, she declared, that she wished herself "out of the kingdom."[8]

IN DECEMBER, EDWARD once more invited Mary and Elizabeth to spend Christmas at court. He wanted all three siblings to be together for the festivities, but Mary suspected a trap.

> They wished me to be at court so that I could not get the mass celebrated for me and that the King might take me with him to hear their sermons. I would not find myself in such a place for anything in the world. I will choose a more convenient time to go and pay my duty to the King, when I need not lodge at court,

> for I have my own establishment in London. I shall stay for four or five days only, and avoid entering into argument with the King my brother who, as I hear, is beginning to debate the question of religion . . . as he is being taught to do.[9]

Mary made her excuses on the ground of ill health. It was a wise decision. On Christmas Day, the king and Council, heavily influenced by Dudley, publicly pledged to further the reformation. In a letter written in the king's name to the bishops, Dudley challenged those "evil disposed persons" who, since the "apprehension" of the duke of Somerset, "have bruited abroad that they should have again their old Latin services, their conjured bread and water, with such like vain and superstitious ceremonies, as if the setting forth of the said book had been the act of the Duke only." The bishops were commanded to order the clergy to gather up all service books besides the Book of Common Prayer and to "deface or destroy them," and send to prison anyone who refused to obey. Further, "excommunication or other censures of the Church" were to be imposed on any layman who refused the new Communion service.[10] By late January, pressure was mounting on Mary once more. England had signed a peace treaty with France, at the cost of Boulogne, and the necessity to appease Charles V receded.

Yet Mary continued to say Mass and keep a strict Catholic household, its daily routine based around the Mass. As van der Delft described the situation following a visit to Kenninghall:

> It is a pleasure to see how well kept and well ordered is her household in the observance of our ancient religion. Her servants are well to do people and some of them men of means and noblemen too whose boast is to be reputed her servants, and by these means they continue to practise the said religion and hear God's service . . . six chaplains . . . say mass in her presence every day.

Mary was now "more than ever afraid that the Council would attempt to disturb her."[11] She wrote to Charles, declaring that she trusted in his goodness and regarded him as her father in "spiritual and temporal matters." She then asked him what she must do: "Our kingdom is daily approaching nearer to spiritual and material ruin, and matters grow worse day by day."[12] She had heard that her household servants would in future be excluded from all Catholic services held under her roof, and soon she would be ordered to conform to the Act of Uniformity. The emperor again demanded an assurance from England that his cousin "should be permitted to continue in her observance of the ancient religion, and in the enjoyment of the same liberty that had been hers at the time of the death of the late king her father."[13]

Mary now waited for the ax to fall, "being neither summoned nor visited by the Council." Meanwhile, Elizabeth, who had conformed to the statutes, remained in high favor. As van der Delft observed, "It seems that they have a higher opinion of her for conforming with the others and observing the new decrees, than of the Lady Mary who remains constant in the Catholic faith."[14]

CHAPTER 30

WHAT SAY YOU, MR AMBASSADOR?

∴

They are wicked and wily in their actions, and particularly malevolent towards me, I must not wait till the blow falls.[1]

—MARY TO VAN DER DELFT,
MAY 2, 1550

AT THE END OF APRIL 1550, MARY SUMMONED VAN DER DELFT TO her residence at Woodham Walter Manor, near Maldon in Essex. She was in despair and had resolved to leave the country. "If my brother were to die," she told the ambassador, "I would be far better out of the kingdom, because as soon as he were dead, before the people knew it, they would despatch me too." She feared what was to come:

> When they send me orders forbidding me the mass, I shall expect to suffer as I suffered once during my father's lifetime; they will order me to withdraw thirty miles from any navigable river or sea-port, and will deprive me of my confidential servants, and having reduced me to the utmost destitution, they will deal with me as they please. But I will rather suffer death than stain my conscience. . . . I am like a little ignorant girl, and I care neither for my goods nor for the world, but only for God's service and my conscience. I know not what to say; but if there is peril in going and peril in staying, I must choose the lesser of two evils. . . . I would willingly stay were I able to live

and serve God as I have done in the past; which is what I have always said. But these men are so changeable that I know not what to say. What say you, Mr Ambassador?[2]

Mary, then thirty-four, had been contemplating escape for some time. In September the previous year, before Somerset's fall, she had sent the emperor a ring and a message that she wished to flee England and seek refuge with him.[3] Charles had responded cautiously, declaring it a matter in which Mary "should not be encouraged" because of the difficulties of getting her out of the realm and the cost of supporting her at the imperial court.[4] Now, faced with her continued persecution and her ever-shriller protests, Charles cautiously agreed to support her in her wish, "for we have the best of reasons and have done all we could do to protect our cousin's person and conscience." He had held back as long as possible from "this extreme measure" but agreed it had "now become imperative to resort to because of the attitude adopted in England."[5]

It was arranged that Mary's escape should coincide with a change of imperial ambassador in mid-May. Van der Delft had been in England for six years, and his recall would not cause suspicion. Once he had formally taken leave, his ship would be diverted to waters off the Essex coast for long enough to meet a boat bringing Mary from Maldon. But with the plan set, fear of renewed popular unrest led to extra watches being placed on the roads near Woodham Walter. There was no chance of her passing unrecognized; another scheme had to be devised.[6]

On the evening of Monday, June 30, 1550, three imperial warships arrived off the coast near Maldon under the command of a Dutchman, Cornelius Scepperus, admiral of the imperial fleet. The next day, Jehan Dubois, secretary to the imperial embassy in London, rowed ashore disguised as a grain merchant. The plan, devised over the previous months, would see Mary escape under cover of darkness from Woodham Walter to the sea two miles away. She would then be rowed out to the waiting ships and taken to the Low Countries and the court of Charles's sister, the regent Mary of Hungary.

In the early hours of July 2, Dubois arrived in Maldon, but there was no one to meet him. He sent an urgent, detailed dispatch to Robert Rochester, one of Mary's senior household officers:

> Sir . . . I arrived here this morning in a six-oared boat. Yesterday I sent my brother, Peter Marchant, to announce in this town that we had brought the corn, and were coming with the next tide; and this I did in order that you might the sooner be advised of my arrival. However, as far as I know, there was nobody there to take the corn or receive the said Peter. Therefore I am obliged to write now to point out to you that there is danger in delay, especially as M. Scepperus is now coming to Stansgate with a warship, and near Harwich there are three other ships waiting and moreover four larger ships are out to sea. Consider therefore whether we must not hurry. There is yet another reason as well: the water will not be as high tomorrow night as tonight, and will be lower every night until next moon, and we now have the advantage that the tide serves our purpose late at night and towards morning, that is, about two o'clock. By that hour or immediately afterwards all ought to be here, so that we may be on our way while the tide is still rising . . . I will sell my corn at once, and be ready tonight. Please let me know your intentions. . . . I must add that I see no better opportunity than the present one; and this undertaking is passing through so many hands that it is daily becoming more difficult, and I fear it may not remain secret. However I will yield to a better opinion, and I pray God to inspire you now; for the Emperor has done all he could.

Hours later, Dubois and Rochester met on the pretext of trading grain. Though Dubois expected them to confirm the final details of the plan, Rochester called the whole scheme into question. He said he thought Mary's imminent flight was unnecessary, as she would be "in no way molested before the end of the Parliament that was to meet the following Michaelmas at the earliest," at which point she would have the advantage of being at her house at St. Osyth, also in Essex, which had a garden from which it was easy to reach the open sea. It was, he argued, simply too dangerous for Mary to attempt her escape with a watch posted on every road near Maldon. "If you understand me," Rochester explained, "what I say is not that my Lady does not wish to go, but that she wishes to go if she can." Dubois demanded clarification. "The thing was now a question of Yes or No." A decision had to be made. The men of Harwich had seen their ships, and it would not be long before the Council was informed of their presence.

That evening Dubois rode in secret to visit Mary. Rochester voiced his concerns again, and the imperial secretary grew frustrated. "The whole business was so near being discovered that it was most improbable that it could be kept secret." Rochester replied, "For the love of God, do not say that to my Lady! She is a good woman and really wants to go; but neither she nor you see what I see and know. Great danger threatens us!" As Mary stowed her possessions into hop sacks, she expressed fear as to "how the Emperor would take it if it turned out to be impossible to go now." She would not be ready until the day after next. On Friday morning, just after the watch retired, she would leave her house on the pretext of going "to amuse herself and purge her stomach by the sea."

As the plan was agreed, word came that the bailiffs of Maldon wished to impound Dubois's boat on suspicion that it was associated with the warship at Stansgate. According to Dubois, Mary started to panic, asking "What shall we do? What shall become of me?" She feared "how the Emperor would take it if it turned out impossible to go now, after I have so often importuned his Majesty on the subject." Dubois urged that they should take Mary immediately, but Rochester declared that it would be impossible: the watch was going to be doubled that night and men would be posted on the church tower. At this point Mary became hysterical, repeatedly shrieking "But what is to become of me?" It was decided that Rochester would contact her again within ten or twelve days with an exact date when they would be ready to put the plan into action. But no further attempt was made. Dubois suspected "that the Comptroller had made out the situation at Maldon to be more dangerous than it was in reality."[7]

To have fled would have been to gamble. If Edward died when Mary was abroad, she would have no hope of succeeding. If she stayed, she might be deprived of her household and be left to face dangers alone. There was both "peril in going and peril in staying." Having set the plan into motion, Mary procrastinated, then changed her mind. She accepted that to win her rightful throne and restore Catholicism, she needed to be in England. She resolved to stay and fight.

CHAPTER 31

AN UNNATURAL EXAMPLE

∴

The Lady Mary sent one of her servants to me today to tell me that a publication was recently made in that part of the country where she lives, forbidding, as she hears, chaplains or others to say mass or officiate at all in her house according to the rites of the ancient religion, under certain heavy penalties both civil and criminal. She requested therefore that I should remonstrate with the Council on the first opportunity and declare that she demanded and would persist in her demand to live according to the ancient religion, in virtue of what had passed in this matter. She requested me also to inform your Majesty and the Queen [Dowager of Hungary].[1]

—AMBASSADOR JEHAN SCHEYFVE TO THE EMPEROR, JULY 26, 1550

WITH THE ESCAPE PLAN ABORTED, MARY PREPARED TO LEAVE Woodham Walter and sent her chaplain, Francis Mallet, ahead to Beaulieu to arrange Mass for her arrival. When Mary was delayed, Mallet performed the service anyway with many of her household servants in attendance. The incident gave the Council the pretext it had been looking for. Orders were dispatched for Mallet's arrest, and Mary was summoned to court. Again she refused to attend, claiming ill health—"being the fall of the leaf"—and petitioned the Council to rethink the enforcement of the statutes.[2] The Council responded that the dispensation regarding Mary's freedom of worship had been made to the imperial ambassador

> for his sake and for your own also, that it should be suffered and winked at, if you had the private mass used in your own closet for a season, until you might be better informed, whereof there was some hope, having only with you a few of your Chamber, so that for all the rest of your household the service of the realm should be used, and none other. Further than this the promise exceeded not.[3]

Mary made a fresh appeal to the emperor, who instructed Scheyfve to secure unconditional assurances. As he added in his dispatch, "You will persist in your request at all costs. Give them plainly to understand that if they decide otherwise, we will not take it in good part, or suffer it to be done."[4]

BY CHRISTMAS, MARY had run out of excuses to avoid attending court and all three Tudor siblings gathered for the reunion, postponed from the previous year. Edward, now twelve, rebuked Mary for hearing Mass in the chapel. She continued to argue that he was not yet old enough to make up his own mind about religion. He demanded her obedience, she resisted, and both were reduced to tears. Writing later to the Privy Council, she blamed its members for turning her brother against her:

> When I perceived how the King, whom I love and honour above all things, as by nature and duty bound, had counselled against me, I could not contain myself and exhibited my interior grief. . . . I would rather refuse the friendship of all the world (whereunto I trust I shall never be driven), than forsake any point of my faith.[5]

But though Edward protested that he thought "no harm of her," he remained determined that she submit. He would "inquire and know all things." On January 17, 1551, Mary received letters from the Privy Council ordering that Mass must no longer be heard in her household. While claiming her "general health and the attack of catarrh in the head" did not permit her to answer their points "in detail, sentence by sentence," she vehemently disputed the assertion that no promise had been made to Charles V as to the practice of the Mass:

> God knows the contrary to be true: and you in your own consciences (I say to those who were then present) know it also . . . you accuse me of breaking the laws and disobeying them by keeping to my own religion; but I reply that my faith and my religion are those held by the whole of Christendom, formerly confessed by this kingdom under the late King, my father, until you altered them with your laws. To the King's majesty, my brother, I wish prosperity and honour such as no King ever enjoyed . . . but to you, my lords, I owe nothing beyond amity and goodwill. . . . Take this as my final answer to any letters you might write to me on matters of religion.

Once again she emphasized her poor health in an attempt to bring the confrontation with the king to an end: "were you to know what pain I suffer in bending down my head to write," she said, he would "not wish to give me occasion to do it. My health is more unstable than that of any creature and I have all the greater need to rejoice in the testimony of pure conscience."[6]

A week later Edward wrote, advising Mary that he would see that his laws were obeyed:

> *Dear and well-beloved sister,*
>
> *We have seen the letters recently sent to you by our Council, together with your answer thereto, concerning the matter of certain chaplains of your household, who have committed a breach of our laws by singing mass. We have heard their good and suitable admonitions, and your fruitless and wayward misunderstanding of the same. We are moved to write to you these presents, that where the good counsel of our Councillors have failed to persuade, the same advice given by us may haply produce some effect. After giving all due consideration to the matter, it appears to us to stand as follows: that you, our nearest sister, in whom by nature we should place reliance and our highest esteem, wish to break our laws and set them aside deliberately and of your*

own free will; and moreover sustain and encourage others to commit a like offence. . . .

. . . it appears by your letters that you have persuaded yourself that you may continue in your erring ways in virtue of a promise which you claim to have received, though we truly know that the said promise was not given with the intention you Lend to it. My sister, you must learn that your courses were tolerated when our laws were first promulgated, not indeed as a permission to break the same, but so that you might be inclined to obey them, seeing the love and indulgence we displayed towards you. We made a difference between you and our subjects, not that all should follow our ordinances, and you alone disregard them, but in order that you should do out of love for us what the rest do out of duty. The error in which you persist is twofold, and each part of it so great that for the love we bear to God we cannot suffer it, but you must strive to remedy it; nor can we do otherwise than desire you to amend your ways, for the affection we bear you . . . knowledge was offered to you, and you refused it.

Mary would be permitted to "speak frankly" and would be listened to, provided she agreed to abide by Edward's response. As for the second part of her offense—"the transgression of our laws"—Edward made it clear that he would not tolerate the abuse of his office as king:

We have suffered it until now, with the hope that some improvement might be forthcoming, but none has been shown, how can we suffer it longer to continue? . . . Your near relationship to us, your exalted rank, the condition of the times, all magnify your offence. It is a scandalous thing that so high a personage should deny our sovereignty; that our sister should be less to us than any of our other subjects is an unnatural example; and finally, in a troubled republic, it lends colour to faction among the people.

He summed up his position in a postscript written in his own hand: "Sister, consider that an exception has been made in your favour this long time past, to incline you to obey and not to harden you in your resistance." He could not "say more and worse things because my duty would compel me to use harsher and angrier words. But this I will say with certain intention, that I will see my laws strictly obeyed, and those who break them shall be watched and denounced."[7]

Mary was stunned. Replying two days later, she declared that his words, accusing her of being "a breaker of your laws" and "inciting others to do the same," had caused her "more suffering than any illness even unto death." She had been promised free expression of her faith and implored him to command his ambassador in Brussels to learn from the emperor "the truth concerning the said promise" so that he could see that she was guilty of no offense. She beseeched him "for the love of God to suffer me to live as in the past" and reiterated that rather than offend him and her conscience she would "lose all that I have left in the world, and my life too."[8]

The same day Mary sent another hastily written letter to Francesco Moronelli, a former servant of van der Delft, who had traveled in secret to meet her at Beaulieu months before. At the time she had made him promise that if she were ever in trouble he would travel to Flanders to tell the emperor's ministers that help was urgently needed. That moment had now arrived.

> *Francisco, you must make great haste concerning the message, for since your departure I have received worse and more dangerous letters than ever before from the King himself, written in haste the 3rd of February.*
> *[Postscript]: I request and command you to burn this note directly after you have read it.*[9]

Charles again made representations to the Privy Council through Scheyfve, but Edward remained firm. In March, to affirm his determination, he summoned Mary to court. No further disobedience would be tolerated.[10]

CHAPTER 32

NAUGHTY OPINION

∴

ON MARCH 15, 1551, MARY ARRIVED IN LONDON, RIDING TO HER house at St. John's, Clerkenwell. Fifty knights and gentlemen in velvet coats and chains of gold rode before her; some four hundred gentlemen and ladies followed behind. As Henry Machyn the London diarist recorded, each carried a "pair of beads of black"—a rosary. It was a dramatic display of Catholic defiance and the scale of Mary's power and support.[1] By the time she reached the gates of the city, there were more than four hundred people in her train. It was, in Machyn's assessment, the greatest demonstration of loyalty in living memory: "The people ran five or six miles out of town and were marvellously overjoyed to see her, showing clearly how much they love her."[2]

The following day, Mary was met unceremoniously at the court gate at Whitehall and led into the Presence Chamber, where the young king and his Council waited to receive her. She was charged with disobedience and ordered to obey. In his journal, Edward described the meeting:

> The Lady Mary my sister came to me at Westminster, where after salutations she was called with my Council into a chamber, where was declared how long I had suffered her Mass [against my will; *crossed out*], in hope of her reconciliation and how now, being no hope, which I perceived by her letters, except I saw some short amendment, I could not bear it. She answered that her soul was God['s], and her faith she would not change, nor dissemble her opinion with contrary doings. It was said I constrained not her faith, but willed her [not as a King to rule;

inserted] but as a subject to obey. And that her example might breed too much inconvenience.[3]

When Edward warned her of the dangers of continuing to practice the old religion, Mary put it to him again that he was not yet old enough to be making decisions, assuring him "Riper age and experience will teach Your Majesty much more yet." This time Edward snapped back, "You also may have somewhat to learn. None are too old for that." Mary reasoned that even if there had been no assurance to hear Mass, she hoped that, as her brother, he "would have shown her enough respect to allow her to continue in the observance of the old religion, and to prevent her from being troubled in any way." Did he want "to take away her life rather than the old religion, in which she desired to live and die?" Edward responded that "he wished for no such sacrifice."

The meeting broke up unresolved. Mary left beseeching Edward not to listen to those who spoke ill of her, "whether about religion or anything else," and assuring him that he would always find her his obedient sister, something, Edward replied, "he had never doubted."[4]

Soon after Mary's visit to court, two prominent Catholics, Sir Richard Morgan and Sir Clement Smith, were summoned before the Council, accused of having heard Mass two or three days earlier in the princess's house at St. John's, Clerkenwell.[5] Days later, Sir Anthony Browne was questioned about the same offense and admitted that he had heard Mass "twice or thrice at the New Hall, and Romford, as my Lady Mary was coming hither about ten days past, he had heard mass."[6] All three men were imprisoned in Fleet Prison on Farringdon Street.[7] Some weeks later Francis Mallet, Mary's principal chaplain and almoner, was arrested. He was condemned for reoffending and for persuading others to embrace his "naughty opinion" and imprisoned in the Tower.[8]

Mary immediately wrote to the Council, claiming that "he [Mallet] did it by my commandment . . . none of my chaplains should be in danger of the law for saying mass in my house" and asking them to "set him at liberty."[9] The Council rejected her appeal: "To relieve him would take the fault upon yourself; we are sorry to perceive your grace so ready to be a defence to one that the King's law doth condemn."[10]

ON MARCH 19, Charles V threatened war if Mary were not given freedom of worship. Edward noted the event in his journal: "The Emperor's ambassador came with a short message from his master, of war if I would not suffer his cousin, the princess, to use her mass. To this no answer was given at this time."[11]

Meanwhile, a diplomatic row broke out at the imperial court in Brussels between Charles and the resident English ambassador, Sir Richard Morison, an outspoken evangelical, who argued on behalf of the English government that envoys to Brussels should have the right to exercise their evangelical beliefs. With Jehan Scheyfve continuing to assert that a promise had been made that Mary "might freely retain the ancient religion in such sort as her father left it in this realm . . . until the King should be of more years,"[12] diplomatic relations reached a crisis point. Edward insisted that he would not give way on a matter "that touched his honour as head of the family." He would "spend his life, and all he had, rather than agree and grant to what he knew certainly to be against the truth."[13] The bishops Thomas Cranmer, Nicholas Ridley, and John Ponet instead advised the king that "to give licence to sin was to sin; to suffer and wink at it for a time might be borne." The Council now feared that the emperor might take action as he had threatened and that the whole realm might be in peril. They persuaded Edward to send Nicholas Wotton, dean of Canterbury, to the imperial court to try to reason with the emperor. He was instructed to make it clear that no assurance or promise had ever been made by the king regarding Mary's right to hear Mass but that he was only "to spare the execution of the laws for a time, until he saw some proof of her amendment."

As pressure came to bear on Mary once more, the emperor challenged Wotton:

> Ought it not to suffice you that ye spill your own souls, but that ye have a mind to force others to lose theirs too? My cousin, the Princess, is evil handled among you; her servants plucked from her, and she still cried to leave Mass, to forsake her religion in which her mother, her grandmother, and all her family, have lived and died. I will not suffer it.

Wotton replied that Mary had been well treated when he left England and he had heard of no change, but the emperor insisted:

> Yes by St. Mary . . . of late they handle her evil and therefore say you hardly to them, I will not suffer her to be evil handled by them. I will not suffer it. Is it not enough that mine aunt, her mother, was evil entreated by the King that dead is, but my cousin must be worse ordered by councillors now.

Though Mary had "a King to her father, and hath a King to her brother, she is only a subject and must obey the law," Wotton countered. "A gentle law I tell you!" snorted the emperor. Wotton then asked if Sir Thomas Chamberlain, English ambassador to Mary of Hungary, might be permitted to have the service of the Book of Common Prayer in his house, at which Charles exploded, "English service in Flanders! Speak not of it. I will suffer none to use any doctrine or service in Flanders that is not allowed of the Church." He ended the audience by saying that if Mary were not allowed her Mass, he would provide her with a remedy. And as Charles made clear: "We would rather she had died ten years ago than see her waver now; but we believe her to be so constant that she would prefer a thousand deaths rather than renounce her faith. If death were to undertake her for this cause, she would be the first martyr of royal blood to die for our holy faith, and for this earn glory in the better life."[14] The emperor had raised the prospect that Mary might be sacrificed as a Catholic martyr.

CHAPTER 33

MATTERS TOUCHING MY SOUL

∴

ON SUNDAY, AUGUST 9, 1551, TWENTY-FOUR LORDS OF THE PRIVY Council met at Richmond, as Edward noted in his journal, to "commune of my sister Mary's matter." It was agreed that "it was not mete to be suffered any longer." In July a new Anglo-French alliance had been concluded, with Edward betrothed to Henry II's daughter Elizabeth. Dudley now felt confident to confront the issue of Mary's disobedience.[1] Mary's senior household officers, Robert Rochester, Francis Englefield, and Edward Waldegrave, were all summoned before the Council at Hampton Court to receive instructions ordering the princess to conform.[2] Upon their return to Mary's residence, Copped Hall, near Epping in Essex, on Saturday the fifteenth, Mary forbade them to speak with her chaplains or her household and required them to return to London with a personal letter to the king:

> I have by my servants received your most honourable letter, the contents whereof do not a little trouble me, and so much the more for that any of my said servants should move or attempt me in matters touching my soul. . . . Having for my part utterly refused heretofore to talk with them in such matters, trusted that your Majesty would have suffered me, your poor humble sister . . . to have used the accustomed Mass, which the King your father and mine, with all his predecessors did evermore use; wherein also I have been brought up from my youth, and thereunto my conscience doth not only bind me, which by no means will suffer me to think one thing and do another, but also the promise made to the Emperor, by your Majesty's Council, was

> an assurance to me that in so doing I should not offend the laws, although they seem now to qualify and deny the thing.

Mary maintained that although the letter was signed by Edward's hand, it was "nevertheless in my opinion not your Majesty's in effect," and she restated her belief that "it is not possible that your Highness can at these years be a judge in matters of religion." She petitioned him "to bear with me as you have done, and not to think that by my doings or example any inconvenience might grow to your Majesty or your realm . . . rather than to offend God and my conscience, I offer my body at your will, and death shall be more welcome than life with a troubled conscience."[3] When the household officers arrived back in London, they were each commanded separately to return to Mary and do what had been asked of them. They all refused, Rochester and Waldegrave saying that they would rather endure any punishment and Sir Francis Englefield declaring that he could find it "neither in his heart nor his conscience to do it."[4]

ON AUGUST 28, the lord chancellor, Lord Rich; Sir Anthony Wingfield, comptroller of the king's household; and Sir William Petre were sent to Mary at Copped Hall with instructions from the king:

> His Majesty did resolutely determine it just, necessary and expedient that her Grace should not any ways use or maintain the private mass or any other manner of service than such as by the law of the realm is authorised or allowed.[5]

Mary treated their authority with contempt. She would hear no service than that left by her father, though when the king came of age and maturity of judgment he would find her conforming to his laws. Her chaplains might do as they wish, but if they read the new service she would leave her own house. Again Mary stated that she was prepared to die for her faith:

> First she protested that to the King's Majesty she was, is and ever will be his Majesty's most humble and most obedient

> subject and poor sister, and would most willingly obey all his commandments in any thing (her conscience saved); yea, and would willingly and gladly suffer death to do his Majesty good, but rather than she will agree to use any other service than was used at the death of the late King her father, she would lay her head on a block and suffer death.[6]

Mary lamented, "You give me fair words, but your deeds will always be ill towards me."

The commissioners then called the chaplains and the rest of the household and gave them "straight commandment upon pain of their allegiance, that neither the priests should from henceforth say any Mass or other Divine Service than that which is set forth by the laws of the realm." As their subsequent report to the Council stated, "Her chaplains, after some talk, promised to obey all the King's Majesty's commandment signified by us." As the men were leaving, Mary called out that she needed her comptroller, Robert Rochester, to be returned to her, adding that since his departure "I take the account myself of my expenses, and how many loaves of bread be made a bushel of wheat . . . my father and mother never brought me [up] with baking and brewing, and to be plain with you I am weary of mine office, and therefore, if my Lords will send my officer home they shall do me pleasure."[7] But the Council ignored Mary's plea and sent Englefield, Waldegrave, and Rochester first to the Fleet and then to the Tower.

With the situation at a deadlock, security around the princess was tightened. Edward recorded in his journal that "pinnaces were prepared to see that there should be no conveyance overseas of the Lady Mary, secretly done." Meanwhile, the lord chancellor, the lord chamberlain, the vice chamberlain, and Secretary Petre "should see by all means they could whether she used the mass, and if she did that the laws should be executed on her chaplains."[8]

IN OCTOBER 1551, Henry II of France declared war on Charles V with the intention of recapturing Italy and securing European supremacy. The renewal of Habsburg-Valois hostilities brought an increased fear of imperial intervention in England. Mary of Hungary,

Charles's sister, was certain that England would join France in the war and so proposed an invasion of England to gain a strong port from which to defend the Netherlands and to place Mary on the throne.[9]

With her fortune ever tied to events in Europe, pressure eased on Mary. When Mary of Guise, the dowager queen of Scotland, visited Edward for several days in October, Mary was invited to court "to accompany and entertain" her, while Edward sent his own message, that he would enjoy the pleasure of Mary's company. Once again Mary pleaded ill health to avoid being put under religious pressure by her brother.[10] Over the next few months the conciliatory overtures continued. In March 1552, Rochester, Englefield, and Waldegrave were released from the Tower and returned to Mary's household. Two months later, Mary rode through London to St. John's "with a goodly company of gentlemen and gentlewomen" and went by barge to Greenwich to visit her brother.[11]

In April, Edward had written in his chronicle, "I feel sick of the measles and the smallpox." He made a quick recovery, but by the winter of 1552 he was seriously ill once more, his body racked by a hacking cough. It was clear that the king was suffering from "consumption"—tuberculosis. The Council made no further overt attempts to suppress Mary's Masses. With Edward's health deteriorating, it was prudent to conciliate one who stood so near to the throne.

CHAPTER 34

MY DEVICE FOR THE SUCCESSION

THE YEAR 1552 SAW THE CLIMAX OF THE EDWARDIAN REFORMATION. In the Second Book of Common Prayer and Forty-two Articles, the Real Presence in the Eucharist was rejected outright; altars were stripped from churches throughout the country and replaced by Communion tables; and images were whitewashed.[1] The long-term survival of the new Protestantism was, however, under threat. By the terms of Henry VIII's will, Mary was Edward's heir, but it was clear that she would halt the process of reformation and restore Catholicism. It was a prospect that Edward would not countenance. He needed to overturn his father's will and the parliamentary statute of 1544 that had decreed Mary his successor.

On February 10, 1553, Mary rode to court along Fleet Street, accompanied by more than two hundred lords and ladies. She was met on the outskirts of the city by John Dudley and knights and gentlemen, who escorted her to the gates of Whitehall. There she was "more honourably received and entertained with greater magnificence" than ever before, "as if she had been Queen of England."[2] But for several days, Edward could not see her, having contracted a "feverish cold." Following Mary's visit, the fifteen-year-old's health deteriorated further, though his decline was concealed from both his sisters. Mary heard falsely that he was better and sent a letter giving thanks for his recovery and praying "with long continuance in prosperity to reign."[3] It would be her final contact with her brother.

Among the Council there was a growing sense of fear that the king would soon die. His doctors believed he had a "suppurating tumour" of the lung, exacerbated by a hacking cough and a fever. "The sputum which he brings up is livid, black, fetid and full of carbon; it smells beyond measure; if it is put in a basin of water it sinks to the bottom. His feet are swollen all over. To the doctors all these things portend death, and that within three months, except God of His great mercy spare him."[4]

Writing at the end of May, Scheyfve described how Dudley, who had become duke of Northumberland in October, "and his party's designs to deprive the Lady Mary of the succession to the crown are only too plain. They are evidently resolved to resort to arms against her, with the excuse of religion among others."[5] By mid-June, it was obvious that Edward did not have long to live. Another successor needed to be found.

In early spring, Edward had drawn up in his own hand "My Device for the Succession" by which he sought to direct the succession and, specifically, disinherit his sisters. Mary and Elizabeth were excluded on the grounds that they were both bastards. The line of succession was transferred to the family of Edward's cousins the Greys—the male heirs of Frances Grey, duchess of Suffolk, the daughter of Henry VIII's sister Mary, and the male heirs of her eldest daughter, Lady Jane Grey.[6] Women were, Edward determined, unfit to rule in their own right and through marriage might subject the realm to foreign domination. Edward was relying on a yet-unborn male heir. It was a last-ditch attempt to avert a female succession.

On May 21, Lady Jane Grey was married to Guildford Dudley, Northumberland's son. But within days, Edward's health deteriorated rapidly. There would be no time for Jane to become pregnant. Edward was forced to overcome his misogyny and, in his own hand, to alter his device. Whereas originally he had left the crown to the "Lady Jane's heirs male" he edited the text and changed it to "Lady Jane and her heirs male."[7] The Protestant Lady Jane was preferred as Edward's successor to the throne.

Three weeks later, Sir Edward Montagu, the lord chief justice, and other senior lawyers of the King's Bench were summoned to the king's bedside at Greenwich. To make the succession legal, they were required to draw up letters patent to give legal effect to the terms of the revised "device." Montagu refused, declaring he would not be involved with any changes to the succession and asserting that letters patent could not overturn statute; Parliament needed to meet. There was, he warned, "the danger of treason." He suggested a compromise: Mary should be allowed to succeed if she pledged to "make no religious change." Northumberland and Edward were furious. The plan was sharply rejected.[8] As Edward explained, neither Mary nor Elizabeth was acceptable as his heir:

> I am convinced that my sister Mary would provoke great disturbances after I have left this life, and would leave no stone unturned, as the proverb goes, to gain control of this isle, the fairest in all Europe, my resolve is to disown and disinherit her together with her sister Elizabeth, as though she were a bastard and sprung from an illegitimate bed. . . . Therefore, to avoid the kingdom being weakened by such shame, it is our resolve, with the agreement of our noblemen, to appoint as our heir our most dear cousin Jane . . . for if our sister were to possess the kingdom (which Almighty God prevent) it would be all over for the religion whose fair foundation we have laid.
>
> For indeed my sister Mary was the daughter of the King by Katherine the Spaniard, who before she was married to my worthy father had been espoused to Arthur, my father's elder brother, and was therefore for this reason alone divorced by my father. But it was the fate of Elizabeth, my other sister, to have Anne Boleyn for a mother; this woman was indeed not only cast off by my father because she was more inclined to couple with a number of courtiers rather than reverencing her husband, so mighty a King, but also paid the penalty with her head—a greater proof of guilt. Thus in our judgment they will be undeservedly considered as being numbered among the heirs of the King our beloved father.

Lady Jane, by contrast, would support "the religion whose fair foundation we have laid."[9]

Finally, confronted by Edward's frail figure, the judges relented and agreed to help the king draw up his will.[10] The letters patent were countersigned by Edward in six places and then by more than a hundred signatories, including judges, peers, nobles, and other dignitaries.

Edward made his final appearance at the window at Greenwich Palace on Saturday, July 1. It was clear to all that death was little more than hours away. "He was doomed, and that he was only shown because the people were murmuring and saying he was already dead, and in order that his death, when it should occur, might the more easily be concealed."[11]

THE FRENCH NOW urged Northumberland to commit to war against Charles in return for their support for Jane's accession; the situation in England had turned to their advantage.[12] With Edward in poor health in the spring of 1553, both rulers had sent ambassadors to England. Antoine de Noailles represented the French king, and Simon Renard, who would become the resident ambassador, came as part of a three-man embassy from Brussels. The emperor's mission, as Charles outlined in instructions drawn up on June 23, was to "preserve our cousin's [Mary's] person from danger, assist her to obtain possession of the Crown, calm the fears the English may entertain of us, defeat French machinations and further a good understanding between our dominions and the realm of England."[13]

Noailles feared that Northumberland had made a deal with Charles V to hand over Mary to be married, possibly to his eldest son, "a thing which is more to be feared than a thousand others which might happen in this affair."[14] In desperation he presented the Council with further "honest and fine offers" from Henry II, pledging his military support. Northumberland thanked him, saying that he hoped for the support of French troops "when the occasion presents itself," and a letter was sent to the French court, stating, "We shall never forget this great friendship in so difficult times, although we doubt not but that the estate and power of this realm shall, by God's goodness, prevail against all manner of practices or attempts either by the Emperor or any other, either foreign or outward enemies whatsoever the same be."[15]

A year earlier, Henry II had extended the frontiers of France almost to the Rhine by seizing the bishoprics of Metz, Toul, and Verdun. His great ambition was to win back the last English territory in France, Calais. An alliance with England would tilt the balance of power decisively in favor of either Henry or the emperor. For the French, it would provide a base from which to launch an invasion of the Netherlands, while for the emperor it would mean the encirclement of France and security of the sea route between Spain and the Low Countries. England now stood as a potential battleground between the Habsburg and Valois kings.

AS EDWARD LAY on his deathbed, struggling to breathe, Northumberland took the first steps to execute the plan. He needed to ensure that Mary did not become suspicious of his intentions for the succession and sought to lull her into a false state of security, regularly sending her news of the king's health and promising that if he should die she would be queen with his assistance. At first Mary believed him, but then she learned the truth. On or about July 1, her closest advisers told her of Northumberland's deceit.

Mary acted swiftly. She feigned ignorance and tricked the duke into thinking he could get possession of her whenever he pleased. She was then staying at Hunsdon in Hertfordshire, no more than twenty miles from his grasp. Yet her household servants had already formulated a plan for her escape. She had been summoned to Edward's bedside, but on July 3 she received a tip-off from a spy at court that the king's end was near. On the night of the fourth, she fled with six attendants, four men and two women. The pretext was the illness of her physician, Rowland Scurloch, which forced her to move household for risk of infection. Through the night Mary and her party traveled, riding north through Hertfordshire to Sawston Hall in Cambridgeshire, the home of Sir John Huddleston, a local Catholic gentleman. At first light, Mary rose, heard Mass, and then set out once again. There would be perilous consequences for Huddleston's loyalty to the princess: when Northumberland's men arrived the following day and realized that Mary had fled, they burned his house to the ground.

Instructions were hurriedly dispatched to lieutenants and justices across the country, notifying them of Mary's escape and ordering them to prepare to muster troops at an hour's notice and to maintain continual watch:

> These shall be to signify unto you that the Lady Mary being at Hunsdon is suddenly departed with her train and family toward the sea coast at Norfolk, upon what occasion we know not, but as it is thought either to flee the realm or to abide there some foreign power . . .
>
> Wherefore to avoid the danger that may ensue to the state and to preserve the realm from the tyranny of foreign nations which by the said Lady Mary's ungodly pretenses may be brought into this realm to the utter ruin and destruction of the same, we have thought good to require and charge you, not only to put yourselves in readiness after your best power and manner for the defence of our natural country against all such attempts, but likewise exhort you to be ready upon an hour's warning with your said power to repair unto us. . . . From Greenwich, the 8th of July.[16]

From Sawston, Mary rode the next twenty-eight miles virtually nonstop. Finally she reached Hengrave Hall, the seat of the earl of Bath, just outside Bury St. Edmunds. There she rested briefly before continuing on to Euston Hall, where she was met by the dowager Lady Burgh. When she had been informed of the king's death on the previous day, the sixth, she had reacted with cautious suspicion: the messenger, Robert Reyns, had been sent by Sir Nicholas Throckmorton, a gentleman of Edward's Privy Chamber who was known for his Protestant sympathies. Whatever the truth, the message had made flight more urgent. Mary hurried on to her seat at Kenninghall, Norfolk, where the news of the king's death was confirmed.

CHAPTER 35

FRIENDS IN THE BRIARS

∴

The 10. of July, in the afternoon, about 3. of the clock, Lady Jane was conveyed by water to the Tower of London, and there received as Queen. After five of the clock, the same afternoon, was proclamation made of the death of King Edward the sixth, and how he had ordained by his letters patents bearing the date the 21. of June last past that the Lady Jane should be heir to the Crown of England, and the heir males of her body, &c.[1]

As LADY JANE GREY WAS PROCLAIMED QUEEN, "NO ONE SHOWED any sign of rejoicing, and no one cried 'Long live the Queen' except the herald who made the proclamation and a few archers who followed him."[2] As the Genoese merchant Baptista Spinola continued, "for the hearts of the people are with Mary, the Spanish Queen's daughter."[3] One young man, Gilbert Potter, who had shouted out that Lady Mary was the rightful queen, was arrested and sent to Cheapside, where his ears were nailed to the pillory and then cut off.[4]

All hope of Mary's accession looked to have been lost. The Armory, Treasury, and Great Seal were all under the control of the duke of Northumberland, and with Lady Jane in possession of the Tower, the capital seemed to be secure. Warships had been dispatched to the Thames, and "troops were stationed everywhere to prevent the people from rising in arms or causing any disorder."[5] Mary had neither soldiers nor sufficient funds; she was an isolated figure in East Anglia, surrounded only by her household servants. The ambassadors sent by the emperor were pessimistic about her safety. Believing Northumberland had secured French support, they feared nothing could be done to prevent Jane's accession and considered Mary's chances "well-nigh impossible."[6]

But Mary was determined to proclaim herself queen, a resolution the ambassadors believed was fraught with danger. "All the forces of the country are in the Duke's hands, and my Lady has no hope of raising enough men to face him, nor means of assisting those who may espouse her cause."[7] They sent agents to advise her not to issue a proclamation but to wait to see if any support was forthcoming.[8] Now only the English people could put Mary on the throne.

ON JULY 9, MARY wrote to Jane's Council from Kenninghall, demanding that it renounce Jane and recognize her as queen, as her father's will had decreed:

> You know, the realm and the whole world knoweth; the rolls and records appear by the authority of the King our said father, and the King our said brother, and the subjects of this realm; so that we verily trust that there is no good true subject, that is, can, or would, pretend to be ignorant thereof.

Mary made it clear that she knew of the plot against her:

> We are not ignorant of your consultations, to undo the provisions made for our preferment, nor of the great bands, and provisions forcible, wherewith ye be assembled and prepared—by whom, and to what end, God and you know, and nature cannot but fear some evil.

She called upon them to display their loyalty to her "just and right cause" and declared that she was ready to pardon them in the hope of avoiding bloodshed and civil war.[9]

After presenting the dispatch to the Privy Council, Mary's messenger, Thomas Hungate, was sent to the Tower. The Council replied in a letter of the same day, addressed to "my Lady Mary" and criticizing "your supposed title which you judge yourself to have." They asserted that Jane was queen of England by the authority of letters patent executed by the late king and endorsed by the nobility of the realm. They reminded her that by an act of Parliament she was illegitimate and unable to inherit and urged her to submit with assurances that "if you will for respect be quiet and obedient as you ought, you shall find us all and several [ready] to do any service that we, with duty, may be glad with you to preserve the common state of this Realm."[10] Meanwhile, circulars hurriedly drafted by Northumberland were sent to justices of the peace, ordering them to "assist us in our rightful possession of this kingdom and to extirp, to disturb, repel and resist the fained and untrue claim of the Lady Mary bastard."[11]

The duke of Suffolk, Jane's father, was nominated to lead an army of reinforcements to East Anglia to capture Mary, though Jane "with weeping tears made request to the whole Council that her father might tarry at home in her company," and Northumberland declared that he would lead the charge himself.[12] On the evening of July 13, three carts rumbled out of the Tower, laden with "great guns and small; bows, bills and spears." Before he left, Northumberland bade the Council farewell: "Well, since ye think it good, I and mine will go, not doubting of your fidelity to the Queen's Majesty, which I leave in your custody," not to leave them your "friends in the briars, and betray us." They were fighting for "God's cause" and for "fear of papistry's re-entrance" into the realm.[13]

The following morning, Northumberland set out from Durham Palace with munitions, artillery, field guns, and more than 6,000 men. The imperial ambassadors wrote to Charles V, "We believe that my Lady will be in his hands in four days' time unless she has sufficient force to resist."[14] Yet as he rode eastward Northumberland noted, "The people press to see us, but not one sayeth God speed us."[15]

Within days Richard Troughton, bailiff of South Witham, Lincolnshire, who was attempting to win support for Mary in Lincolnshire, had submitted a petition to the Privy Council stating that Northumberland had poisoned King Edward and would now "go about to destroy the noble blood of England." He was confident that "over a hundred thousand men would rise" in support of Mary, believing "her grace should have her right, or else there would be the bloodiest day . . . that ever was in England."[16]

CHAPTER 36

TRUE OWNER OF THE CROWN

This attempt should have been judged and considered one of Herculean rather than womanly daring, since to claim and secure her hereditary right, the princess was being so bold as to tackle a powerful and well-prepared enemy, thoroughly provisioned with everything necessary to end or to prolong a war, while she was entirely unprepared for warfare and had insignificant forces.[1]

—ROBERT WINGFIELD, *VITA MARIAE*

FOR FIVE DAYS MARY STAYED AT KENNINGHALL, RALLYING FRIENDS and supporters among the East Anglian gentry and commons. The core of her support was her household. Many, like Robert Rochester and Edward Waldegrave, had served her throughout Edward's reign and had consistently defended her and her right to hear the Catholic Mass. Now they moved to defend her right to the throne. As Robert Wingfield, an East Anglian gentleman, wrote, they "did not hesitate to face an untimely death for their Queen." Each played an important role in mobilizing members of the local gentry and their tenants. The first gentlemen to arrive at Kenninghall, Sir Henry Bedingfield, Sir John Shelton, and Sir Richard Southwell, were from the same group of conservative East Anglian magnates as the men in Mary's household. The arrival of Southwell and Henry Radcliffe, earl of Sussex, with money, provisions, and armed men would greatly expand Mary's meager forces. Southwell was a knight, the wealthiest of his rank in Norfolk, and his commitment did much to raise the morale of Mary and her supporters.

On July 12, with her forces growing, Mary moved southeast to another of her principal houses, Framlingham Castle in Suffolk, the ancient seat of the Howard family. It was far larger than Kenninghall and, as the strongest castle in the area, an ideal place from which to defend against, or indeed engage, a determined enemy. Built by the old duke of Norfolk, it had come into her possession only a few months before. Now it would witness Mary's stand against the might of central government. As she journeyed to Framlingham, many of the local gentry and justices, together with a crowd of country folk, gathered in the deer park adjacent to the castle to await her arrival. "A great concourse of people were moved by their love for her to come and promise to support her to the end and maintain her right to the Crown, bringing money and cattle as their means enabled them."[2]

Finally, at eight in the evening, she arrived. Her standard was unfurled and displayed over the gate tower. It was a defiant gesture on the eve of what looked to be imminent conflict. Northumberland was said to have had 3,000 men and the whole of the royal armory to draw on. Mary's forces and supplies were thin in comparison. Again she sent a desperate appeal to the imperial ambassadors: "She saw destruction hanging over her" unless she received help. But the emperor believed Mary's chances of coming to the throne to be "very slight," and he sent nothing.[3]

For a number of days Mary's fate hung in the balance. In many towns it was a confused picture of shifting and changing allegiances. In Ipswich, Sir Thomas Cornwallis, the sheriff of Norfolk and Suffolk, together with Thomas, Lord Wentworth, and other prominent Suffolk men, initially declared for Jane, on July 11. But then one of Mary's servants, Thomas Poley, arrived in the town's marketplace and proclaimed Mary "hereditary Queen of England." It was only then that Cornwallis saw where the sympathies of the people lay and declared for Mary. As Wingfield described it, the public outcry against Jane was so great that Cornwallis actually stood "in grave peril of his life." Although a lifelong religious conservative, Cornwallis, like many other East Anglian gentry, had bet against Mary, given Jane's access to superior military resources. Yet they too had underestimated the popular support for Mary. At Framlingham, Cornwallis humbly prostrated himself before her and begged her pardon. For Cornwallis, as for many others, factors other than faith or principle led him to declare for Mary.

In Norwich, where the town authorities had on July 11 refused to open the gates to Mary's messengers, saying that they did not yet know for certain that the king was dead, they not only proclaimed her the following day but also sent men and arms. Gradually events began to swing in Mary's favor. A squadron of five ships of the late king, laden with soldiers and weaponry, had been forced into the safety of Orwell harbor by bad weather. The crews mutinied against their officers for disowning Mary and put themselves under the command of Mary's ardent supporter Sir Henry Jerningham. Many others flocked to Mary's side. Henry Radcliffe arrived at Framlingham with a cohort of horsemen and foot soldiers. He was followed by John Bourchier, earl of Bath, another noble figure, who also arrived with a large band of soldiers including Sir John Sulyard, knight of Wetherden, and Sir William Drury, knight of the shire for Suffolk. All leading figures in East Anglia, they, together with Sir Thomas Cornwallis, were important gains that would prove crucial to Mary's success. Yet one figure eluded her. To secure her position in eastern Suffolk, Mary needed to win the support of Thomas, Lord Wentworth, a prominent and respected nobleman. She sent two of her servants, John Tyrell and Edward Glenham, to Nettlestead to negotiate with him. She warned that forsaking her cause would lead to the perpetual dishonor of his house. He paused and reflected. Finally he declared for Mary. It was a great coup. Wentworth arrived at Framlingham on the fifteenth, clad in splendid armor and with a large military force of gentlemen and tenants.

It was just in time. Northumberland was en route to Bury St. Edmunds, just twenty-four miles from Framlingham. Five hundred men were appointed to guard Mary within the walls of Framlingham Castle. Mary was focused and resolute. She summoned her household council, ordered her field commanders to prepare her forces for battle, and issued a proclamation asserting her authority, making clear her defiance:

> We do signify unto you that according to our said right and title we do take upon us and be in the just and lawful possession of

> the same; not doubting that all our true and faithful subjects will so accept us, take us and obey us as their natural and liege sovereign lady and Queen.[4]

Now, as her army mustered, Mary declared that she was "nobly and strongly furnished of an army royal under Lord Henry, Earl of Sussex, her Lieutenant General, accompanied by the Earl of Bath, the Lord Wentworth, and a multitude of other gentlemen." She condemned Northumberland, that he "most traitorously by long-continued treason sought, and seeketh, the destruction of her royal person, the nobility and common weal of this realm," and finished with a rallying cry:

> Wherefore, good people, as ye mindeth the surety of her said person, the honour and surety of your country, being good Englishmen, prepare yourselves in all haste with all power to repair unto her said armies yet being in Suffolk, making your prayers to God for her success . . . upon the said causes she utterly defyeth the said duke for her most errant traitor to God and to the realm.[5]

Within days an unskilled and disorganized mob had been turned into a disciplined army, obedient to order and eager to meet the enemy. On the twentieth, Mary rode down from the castle to review her troops. Standards were unfurled and her forces drawn up in battle order; helmets were thrown high in the air as shouts of "Long live our good Queen Mary!" and "Death to the traitors!" rang out across the Suffolk countryside. Mary dismounted and for the next three hours inspected her troops on foot.

SINCE NORTHUMBERLAND'S departure from London, the privy councillors had begun to waver in their support for Jane as queen, "being deeply rooted in their minds, in spite of these seditions, a kind of remorse, knowing her [Mary] to be, after all the daughter of their King Henry VIII."[6] By the eighteenth, their resolve had crumbled. Ships' crews off Yarmouth had deserted, and rumors had spread that Sir Edmund Peckham, treasurer of the Mint and keeper of the king's privy purse, had fled with the monies to Framlingham. Now a proclamation was drawn up offering a reward for the arrest of Northumberland: £1,000 in land to any noble, £500 to any knight, and £100 to any yeoman bold enough to lay his hand on the duke's shoulder and demand his surrender.[7]

The following day, a dozen or so privy councillors, including the earls of Bedford, Pembroke, Arundel, Shrewsbury, and Worcester, and Lords Paget, Darcy, and Cobham, broke out of the Tower, which had been locked, and rendezvoused at Pembroke's house, Baynard's Castle. There they took the final step. In a speech before the Council, Arundel declared:

> This Crown belongs rightfully, by direct succession, to My Lady Mary lawful and natural daughter of our King Henry VIII. Therefore why should you let yourselves be corrupted and tolerate that anybody might unjustly possess what does not belong to him? . . . [8]
>
> If by chance you should feel somehow guilty proclaiming now our Queen My Lady Mary, having acclaimed Jane only a few days ago, showing such quick change of mind, I tell you this is no reason to hesitate, because having sinned it befits always to amend, especially when, as in the present circumstances, it means honour for your goodselves, welfare and freedom for our country, love and loyalty to his King, peace and contentment for all people.[9]

At five or six in the evening of the twentieth, as Arundel and Paget set out to pledge their fidelity to Mary at Framlingham and petition for pardon on behalf of the whole Council, two heralds and three trumpeters rode from Baynard's Castle to the Cross at Cheapside. With the streets full of Londoners, the heralds announced that Mary was queen.[10] "There was such shout of the people with casting up of caps and crying, 'God save Queen Mary,' that the style of the proclamation could not be heard, the people were so joyful, both man, woman and child."[11] For two days all the bells in London, "which it had been decided to convert into artillery," rang; money was "cast a-way," and there were banquets and bonfires in the streets.[12] "It would be impossible to imagine greater rejoicing than this," the imperial ambassadors reported.[13]

> From a distance the earth must have looked like Mount Etna. The people are mad with joy, feasting and singing, and the streets crowded all night long. I am unable to describe to you, nor would you believe, the exultation of all men. I will only tell you that not a soul imagined the possibility of such a thing.[14]

Upon hearing the news, Northumberland, then at Cambridge, was forced to admit defeat. He threw his cap into the air and acknowledged Mary as queen. The coup attempt was over. That evening the earl of Arundel arrived to arrest Northumberland in the queen's name.[15]

PART THREE

A Queen

CHAPTER 37

MARYE THE QUENE

∴

Days before she was to be crowned at Westminster Abbey, Mary called together her Council for an impromptu and improvised ceremony. Ensconced in the Tower of London, she had been preparing for the coronation to come, rehearsing the oaths and changes of clothes and regalia and pondering the responsibilities of office. Kneeling before her councillors, Mary spoke of how she had come to the throne and what she considered to be her duties as queen. It was her solemn intention to carry out the task God had given her "to His greater glory and service, to the public good and all her subjects' benefit." She had entrusted "her affairs and person" to her councillors and urged them to be faithful to the oaths they had sworn and to be loyal to her as their queen. Mary remained on her knees throughout. So "deeply moved" were her councillors that "not a single one refrained from tears. No one knew how to answer, amazed as they all were by this humble and lowly discourse unlike anything ever heard before in England, and by the Queen's great goodness and integrity."[1] It was an astonishing sight, yet these were extraordinary times: a woman was now to wear England's crown.

The first queen to rule England was a small, slightly built woman of thirty-seven. With her large, bright eyes, round face, reddish hair, and love of fine clothes, she cut a striking figure, though one marked by age and ill health.[2] She suffered bouts of illness, heart palpitations, and headaches, was exceedingly shortsighted, and was prone to melancholy. Although for most of her adult life she had known neither security nor happiness, she was regarded as "great-hearted, proud and magnanimous." Highly educated and intelligent, well versed in languages, and quick of wit and understanding, her frequent acclamation was "In thee, O lord, is my trust, let me never be confounded. If God be for us, who can be against us?"[3]

Mary had secured the throne against the odds. It was a victory, Wingfield wrote, "one of Herculean rather than womanly daring."[4] A female accession had been a prospect her father had gone to great lengths to avoid, but on Edward's death all the plausible candidates for the English throne were female. In default of male heirs, Edward had had to accept Lady Jane Grey as his Protestant successor. Yet Mary had managed to win support across the religious spectrum as the rightful Tudor heir. Notably it was a victory won without direct foreign aid; the English people had put Mary on the throne. The anonymous author of "The Legend of Sir Nicholas Throgmorton" put into the mouth of his hero the sentiments of many:

And though I lik'd not the Religion
Which all her life Queen Mary had professed,
Yet in my mind that wicked Motion
Right heirs for to displace I did detest.[5]

Her victory was widely celebrated. She was as popular as any English sovereign who had ascended the throne before her, and her triumph was one of the most surprising events of the sixteenth century.[6] She had preserved the Tudor dynasty, and now both the French king and the emperor sought to ingratiate themselves with her.

"This news," wrote Charles V to his ambassadors, "is the best we could have had from England and we render thanks to God for having guided all things so well . . . [you will] offer our congratulations on her happy accession to the throne, telling her how great was our joy on hearing it." The emperor now sought to justify his lack of intervention: "You may explain to her that you were instructed to proceed very gradually in your negotiation, with the object of rendering her some assistance, and that we were hastily making preparations, under cover of protection of the fisheries, to come to her relief."[7]

Meanwhile the French, who had conspired with Northumberland, were now forced to declare their belief in Mary's legitimacy and deny their part in the coup.[8] Many Englishmen believed that France had been set to invade in support of Northumberland. As Noailles reported, "You could not believe the foul and filthy words which this nation cries out every day against our own."[9] Henry II now feared that England might join the war on the emperor's side and sought to emphasize Charles's lack of support for Mary in the July crisis. "In all her own miseries, troubles and afflictions," wrote the French ambassador, "as well as in those of the Queen her mother, the Emperor never came to their assistance, nor has he helped her now in her great need with a single man, ship or penny."[10]

AS BELLS ACROSS the country rang out the news of her victory, Mary left Framlingham to begin her slow and triumphant progress toward London.[11] Along the route and at her various stopping places, she received the homage of her subjects. At Ipswich she was met by the bailiffs of the town, who presented her with "eleven pounds sterling in gold," and by some young boys, who gave her a golden heart inscribed with the words "The Heart of the People."[12] Having spent two days in Ipswich, Mary moved to Colchester, where she stayed at the home of Muriel Christmas, a former servant of her mother, Katherine, and then journeyed to her residence Beaulieu in Essex. There she was presented with a purse of crimson velvet from the City of London, filled with half sovereigns of gold, "which gift she highly and thankfully accepted, and caused the presenters to have great cheer in her house."[13] From Beaulieu she rode on to Wanstead, east of London, where she was joined by her sister, Elizabeth, who had ridden from the Strand to meet her, accompanied by countless gentlemen, knights, and ladies.[14]

Leaving Wanstead on the third, Mary began her journey into the city, stopping en route at Whitechapel at the house of one "Mr Bramston," where she "changed her apparel."[15] As Wingfield described the occasion:

> Now indeed her retinue reached its greatest size . . . nothing was left or neglected which might possibly be contrived to decorate the gates, roads and all places on the Queen's route to wish

her joy for her victory. Every crowd met her accompanied by children, and caused celebrations everywhere, so that the joy of that most wished for and happy triumphal procession might easily be observed, such were the magnificent preparations made by the wealthier sort and such was the anxiety among the ordinary folk to show their goodwill to their sovereign.[16]

CHAPTER 38

THE JOY OF THE PEOPLE

∴

AT SEVEN IN THE EVENING OF AUGUST 3, 1553, MARY ENTERED the City of London, accompanied by gentlemen, squires, knights, and lords, the king's trumpeters, heralds, and sergeants at arms with bows and javelins.

She was dressed in a gown of purple velvet, its sleeves embroidered in gold; beneath it she wore a kirtle of purple satin thickly set with large pearls, with a gold and jeweled chain around her neck and a dazzling headdress on her head. Her mount, a palfrey, was richly trapped with cloth of gold.[1] As the imperial ambassadors reported, "her look, her manner, her gestures, her countenance were such that in no event could they be improved."[2] Behind her rode Sir Anthony Browne, "leaning on her horse, having the train of her highness' gown hanging over his shoulder," followed by her sister, Elizabeth, the Duchess of Norfolk, the Marchioness of Exeter, and a "flock of peeresses, gentlewomen and ladies-in-waiting, never before seen in such numbers."[3] It was a spectacular display of dynastic unity, of power and authority: the first formal appearance of England's queen regnant. According to one estimate, some ten thousand people accompanied the new queen into the capital.

Mary was met at Aldgate by the lord mayor and aldermen of London. Kneeling before her, the lord mayor presented the scepter of her office as a "token of loyalty and homage" and welcomed her into the city. She returned the scepter to the lord mayor with words "so gently spoken and with so smiling a countenance that the hearers wept for joy."[4] Mace in hand, the lord mayor joined the cavalcade next to the earl of Arundel, who bore the sword of state. At St. Botolph's Church, a choir of a hundred children from Christ's Hospital, all dressed in blue with red caps on their heads and sitting on a great stage covered with canvas, sang choruses of welcome.[5]

All along the procession route the streets had been swept clean and spread with gravel so that the horses would not slip; the buildings had been decorated with rich tapestries, and spectators crowded onto roofs, walls, and steeples. As the procession moved through Aldgate, trumpets sounded from the gate's battlements. Lining the streets through Leadenhall to the Tower were the guilds of London, all wearing their livery hoods and furs, all paying homage to their new queen. Wherever the queen passed, placards declared, *"Vox populi, vox Dei"*—"The voice of the people is the voice of God."[6] The streets thronged "so full of people shouting and crying 'Jesus save her grace,' with weeping tears for joy, that the like was never seen before," reported the chronicler Charles Wriothesley.[7] The imperial ambassadors agreed: The "joy of the people" was "hardly credible," "the public demonstrations" having "never had their equal in the kingdom."[8]

With cannons sounding from every battlement "like great thunder, so that it had been like to an earthquake," Mary arrived at the Tower. There the lord mayor took his leave and Mary was met by Sir John Gage and Sir John Brydges, constable and lieutenant of the Tower, respectively, standing in front of rows of archers and arquebusiers. Kneeling on the green before the Chapel Royal of St. Peter ad Vincula within the Tower precinct were Edward Courtenay, who had been prisoner since the age of nine and whose father, the marquess of Exeter, had been beheaded in 1538; the aged Thomas Howard, duke of Norfolk, still under sentence of death since the last months of Henry VIII's reign; and the deprived bishops of Winchester and Durham, Stephen Gardiner and Cuthbert Tunstall. In the name of all the prisoners, Bishop Gardiner congratulated Mary on her accession. "Ye are my prisoners!" exclaimed the queen. Raising them up one by one, she kissed them and granted them their liberty. Courtenay and Norfolk were restored to their rank and estates, the deprived bishops to their sees. Then, as her standard was raised above the keep, Mary entered the Tower.[9] "The people . . . are full of hope," wrote the imperial ambassadors, "that her reign will be a godly, righteous and just one, and help to establish her firmly on the throne."[10]

NOW IN POSSESSION of her kingdom, Mary could begin the task of governing. She had won the throne at Framlingham with a small council of her household officers, including Robert Rochester, Edward Waldegrave, and Henry Jerningham, together with figures such as the earls of Sussex and Bath, who had arrived in the early days of the coup. All were of proven loyalty, but few had political experience. Then, as Mary journeyed to London, she had been besieged with apologies and pledges of fidelity from the Edwardian councillors who had been so closely involved with Edward's Protestant reforms and who had, just days before, conferred the crown on Lady Jane Grey. Some had displayed reluctance in agreeing to Northumberland's plan, but all had eventually signed Edward's "Device for the Succession." Though Mary doubted their loyalty and their motives, most upon their submission were restored to royal favor.

To her existing council of household servants, Mary appointed experienced men such as Sir William Petre, Lord William Paget, the earls of Arundel and Pembroke, Sir John Mason, and Sir Richard Southwell. The earl of Arundel became lord steward; William Paulet, the marquess of Winchester, retained his office of high treasurer. By the time Mary reached the Tower, she had a Privy Council, a hybrid of trust and experience, of some twenty-five members.

Mary also appointed to her Privy Council men who had suffered for their views and faith under the previous regime, including those she had freed from the Tower. Stephen Gardiner was appointed to the Privy Council the day after his release and three weeks later became lord chancellor. Though he had been principal adviser to Henry VIII in the king's divorce from Katherine of Aragon, he had become increasingly conservative in his religious views during Edward's reign and had developed a hatred for Northumberland after being imprisoned in 1551. As far as Mary was concerned this sufficiently redeemed him, though he would never come to enjoy the queen's full confidence. Yet Mary's political pragmatism was resented by many of the councillors. "Discontent is rife," the imperial ambassadors reported on August 16, "especially among those who stood by the queen in the days of her adversity and trouble, who feel they have not been rewarded as they deserve, for the conspirators have been raised in authority."[11] Although their commitment to Mary varied, they all shared a fundamental loyalty to the Tudor regime.

In all, Mary's Privy Council numbered some forty councillors. While it was among these men that a core group formed to govern and administer the realm, it was as much in the halls and corridors of the royal household, in whispered conversations and secret meetings with the queen, that decisions were made and policies formed. Unlike the Privy Council, the upper echelons of the royal household were an exclusive preserve of trusted Catholic loyalists whom Mary relied upon. Members of Mary's "princely affinity of proven loyalty" replaced all those who had acted against her in the succession crisis. Sir Henry Jerningham, who had been in Mary's service since 1533, became vice chamberlain and captain of the Guard; the long-serving Robert Rochester became comptroller of the household; Edward Waldegrave, master of the great wardrobe; and Sir Edward Hastings, master of the horse. John de Vere, the earl of Oxford, whose defection to Mary in the succession crisis had proved decisive, recovered the "hereditary" position of lord great chamberlain from the marquess of Northampton.

THE ACCESSION OF a queen regnant necessitated changes in the monarch's private apartments. The male servants of Edward's entourage were replaced by female attendants, many of them long-serving servants from her princely household, such as Jane Dormer, Mary Finch, Frances Waldegrave, Frances Jerningham, and Susan Clarencius, who became chief lady of the Privy Chamber. Their positions close to the queen gave these women a measure of influence, especially in the early months of the reign, a fact that was of concern to the emperor. "If you have an opportunity of speaking to her without her taking it in bad part," he instructed Renard, "you might give her to understand that people are said to murmur because some of her ladies take advantage of their position to obtain certain concessions for their own private interest and profit."[12]

But it was Simon Renard, building on Mary's familial ties and attachment to the emperor, who would enjoy an unprecedented role as secret counselor and confidant. From the start, Mary had expressed her uncertainty as to how to "make herself safe and arrange her affairs," and, as the ambassadors reported, "still less did she dare to speak of them to anyone except ourselves. She could not trust her Council too much, well knowing the particular character of its members."[13] Just a few hours after the imperial ambassadors' first public audience, on July 29, and within days of her accession, the queen sent all three ambassadors word that one or two of their number might go to her privately in her oratory, "entering [by] the back door to avoid suspicion."[14] The task was delegated to Renard, who from then on acted as a secret counselor, advising and admonishing Mary as to decisions to be made and actions taken. He quickly won the queen's trust and confidence and was frequently consulted by her in secret, when none of her English advisers was present. On religion Renard told her:

> not to hurry . . . not to make innovations nor adopt unpopular policies, but rather to recommend herself by winning her subjects' hearts, showing herself to be a good Englishwoman wholly bent on the kingdom's welfare, answering the hopes conceived of her, temporising wherever it was possible to do so.[15]

Huddled under a cloak, Renard would slip quietly in through the back door of the queen's privy apartments. She would encourage him to come in disguise and under cover of darkness.

> Sir, If it were not too much trouble for you, and if you were to find it convenient to do so without the knowledge of your colleagues, I would willingly speak to you in private this evening. . . . Nevertheless, I remit my request to your prudence and discretion. Written in haste, as it well appears, this morning, 13 October. Your good friend, Mary.[16]

To consult an ambassador as though he were a secret counselor upon the domestic affairs of the kingdom was a highly unusual step for a monarch to take. But from her earliest days Mary had pledged herself to the emperor. On July 28, when the imperial ambassadors had journeyed to meet Mary at Beaulieu, she had declared that "after God, she desired to obey none but" her cousin Charles, "whom she regarded as a father."[17] After her accession, she wrote thanking him for his congratulations, adding, "May it please your Majesty to continue in your goodwill towards me, and I will correspond in every way which it may please your Majesty to command, thus fulfilling my duty as your good and obedient cousin."[18] It was a sign of things to come.

CHAPTER 39

CLEMENCY AND MODERATION

∴

A WEEK BEFORE MARY'S CEREMONIAL ENTRY INTO LONDON, JOHN Dudley, the duke of Northumberland, and his accomplices, Sir John Gates and Sir Thomas Palmer, were brought back to London under heavy guard.[1] Despite a proclamation ordering citizens to allow the prisoners to pass by peacefully, the mounted men at arms struggled to hold back the large crowds.[2] As they made their way to the Tower from Shoreditch, Londoners filled the streets to watch, throwing stones and calling out "Death to the traitors!" and "Long live the true queen!" Pausing at Bishopsgate, the earl of Arundel made Northumberland take off his hat and scarlet cloak to make him less conspicuous among the group of prisoners. For the rest of the journey to the Tower, he rode bareheaded through the streets, his cap in his hand.[3]

Two weeks later the duke was tried and condemned to death. During his time in the Tower he was assailed by remorse for his sins, begging to be pardoned and professing his adherence to Catholicism: "I do faithfully believe this is the very right and true way, out of which true religion you and I have been seduced this xvj years past, by the false and erroneous preaching of the new preachers."[4] His apostasy did not save him. He went to the block with Gates and Palmer in front of a huge crowd on August 22.[5]

None of the other July rebels was executed, and both Lady Jane Grey and her husband, Guildford Dudley, remained in the Tower in honorable imprisonment. The emperor urged Mary to act against them, but she "could not be induced to consent that she should die."[6] Jane had written a long confession explaining that she had known nothing of the plan to declare her queen until three days before she was taken to the Tower and had never given any consent to the duke's intrigues and plots. Upon the proclamation of Mary's accession, she had, she claimed, gladly given up the royal dignity as she knew the right belonged to Mary.[7] Mary acknowledged her submission and showed a spirit of temperance toward her. Her mother, the duchess of Suffolk, was a long-standing acquaintance and had spent Christmas with Mary the previous year. "My conscience," Mary declared to the ambassador, "will not permit me to have her put to death."[8]

On July 31, upon the petition of his wife, Frances, Mary released the duke of Suffolk from the Tower, even though he had been strongly implicated in Northumberland's coup to place Jane on the throne. As Renard reported, "many who judge her actions impartially, praise her clemency and moderation in tempering the rigour of justice against those who plotted her death and disinheritance, in staying their punishment, and, moreover, in forgiving their misdeeds and extending her grace and mercy to them."[9]

FIVE DAYS AFTER Mary had taken possession of the Tower and a month after the king's death, the coffin of the late Edward VI was carried from Whitehall to Westminster Abbey. Mary had initially expressed her intention to have him buried "for her own peace of conscience" according to the "ancient ceremonies and prayers" of the Catholic Church, fearing that if she "appeared to be afraid" it would make her subjects, particularly the Lutherans, "become more audacious" and "proclaim that she had not dared to do her own will."[10] But in a confidential memorandum, Renard advised caution: if Mary inaugurated her reign in this fashion, she would "render herself odious and suspect." Burying Edward, who had lived and died a Protestant, with Catholic rites might "cause her Majesty's subjects to waver in their loyal affection."[11] Mary agreed to compromise. On August 9, while Mary and her ladies heard a Requiem Mass for the repose of his soul in a private chapel in the Tower, Edward was buried in the abbey in a Protestant service conducted by Thomas Cranmer, the archbishop of Canterbury.[12]

Outside the Tower, there was evidence that religious change had

Henry VIII by unknown artist c. 1520: THE YOUNG HENRY IN THE EARLY YEARS OF HIS REIGN.

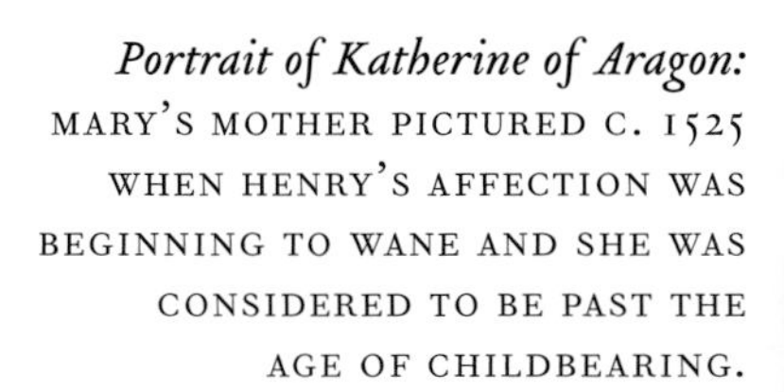

Portrait of Katherine of Aragon: MARY'S MOTHER PICTURED C. 1525 WHEN HENRY'S AFFECTION WAS BEGINNING TO WANE AND SHE WAS CONSIDERED TO BE PAST THE AGE OF CHILDBEARING.

The Family of Henry VIII by Horenbolt: THE PAINTING COMMEMORATES THE RESTORATION OF MARY AND ELIZABETH TO THE LINE OF SUCCESSION. MARY IS ON THE RIGHT, ELIZABETH ON THE LEFT, WHILE EDWARD AND JANE SEYMOUR STAND NEXT TO HENRY. KATHERINE PARR, HENRY'S WIFE AT THE TIME WHO WAS CHILDLESS, IS NOT PICTURED.

Lord Cromwell, Wearing the Order of St. George, by Hans Holbein: THE KING'S CHIEF MINISTER, WHO BROKERED MARY'S RECONCILIATION WITH HER FATHER IN 1536.

Princess Mary: THIS PORTRAIT MINIATURE WAS PAINTED AT THE TIME WHEN MARY WAS BETROTHED TO THE EMPEROR CHARLES V. THE LETTERS OF HER BROOCH SPELL OUT "THE EMPEROUR." THE PORTRAIT WAS ALMOST CERTAINLY INTENDED AS A GIFT FOR CHARLES.

The Emperor Charles V on Horseback in Muhlberg by Titian: MARY'S COUSIN, UPON WHOM SHE RELIED THROUGHOUT HER LIFE AS HER "SECOND FATHER."

Michaelmas Plea Roll (1553): MARY AS A TRIUMPHANT QUEEN HAVING WON THE THRONE IN JULY 1553. SHE IS PICTURED IN THE FULL PANOPLY OF A QUEEN REGNANT.

Mary Tudor curing the King's Evil: MARY IS PICTURED HERE PERFORMING THE ROYAL TOUCH TO HEAL THOSE SUFFERING FROM THE "KING'S EVIL" (SCROFULA) AND DEMONSTRATING THAT SHE WAS INVESTED WITH THE TRADITIONAL QUASI-PRIESTLY POWER OF MALE MONARCHS.

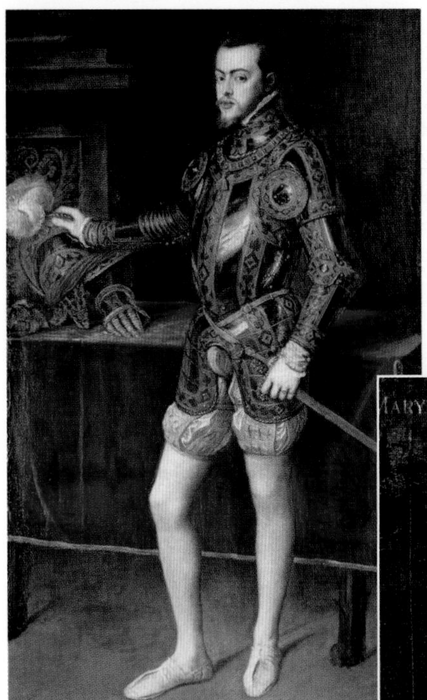

King Philip II by Titian c. 1550.

Queen Mary I of England by Antonio Moro: MARY PAINTED AS A HABSBURG CONSORT. THE FLOWER IS ASSOCIATED WITH BETROTHAL AND MARRIAGE. SHE IS WEARING A JEWELED PENDANT THAT SHE HAD RECEIVED FROM PHILIP ON THE EVE OF THEIR MARRIAGE.

Michaelmas Plea Roll (1556): THE KING AND QUEEN PICTURED TWO YEARS AFTER THEIR WEDDING. PHILIP ASSUMES THE DOMINANT POSITION ON MARY'S RIGHT WHILST A CROWN FLOATS BETWEEN THE TWO, SUGGESTING SHARED ROYAL POWER.

Simon Renard by Giacomo Antonio Moro c. 1553: THE IMPERIAL AMBASSADOR UPON WHOM MARY DEPENDED AS HER CHIEF CONFIDANT DURING THE FIRST YEAR OF HER REIGN.

Philip II and Mary I by Hans Eworth c. 1558.

Cardinal Reginald Pole, Archbishop of Canterbury: MARY'S COUSIN AND THE SON OF HER FORMER GOVERNESS, REGINALD POLE ABSOLVED ENGLAND FROM ITS SCHISM WITH ROME. MARY RELIED HEAVILY ON HIM IN PHILIP'S ABSENCE DURING THE LATTER PART OF HER REIGN.

"A Lamentable Spectacle of three women, with a sely infant brasting out of the Mothers Wombe, being first taken out of the fire, and cast in agayne, and so burned together in the Isle of Garnesey," from Foxe's Book of Martyrs (1563).

The Burning of Thomas Cranmer, Archbishop of Canterbury, from Foxe's Book of Martyrs (1563): IT HAD BEEN MORE THAN TWENTY YEARS SINCE CRANMER HAD PRONOUNCED THE MARRIAGE OF MARY'S PARENTS TO BE INVALID AND HAD MARRIED HENRY TO ANNE BOLEYN. MARY NEVER FORGAVE HIM.

Queen Mary I by Hans Eworth: A PORTRAIT OF A MAGNIFICENT QUEEN. SHE LOVED TO DRESS EXTRAVAGANTLY AND KNEW THE IMPORTANCE OF DISPLAYING A STRIKING IMAGE OF ROYAL MAJESTY. MARY IS AGAIN PICTURED WITH THE PENDANT JEWEL THAT SHE HAD RECEIVED FROM PHILIP.

The signature of Mary I.

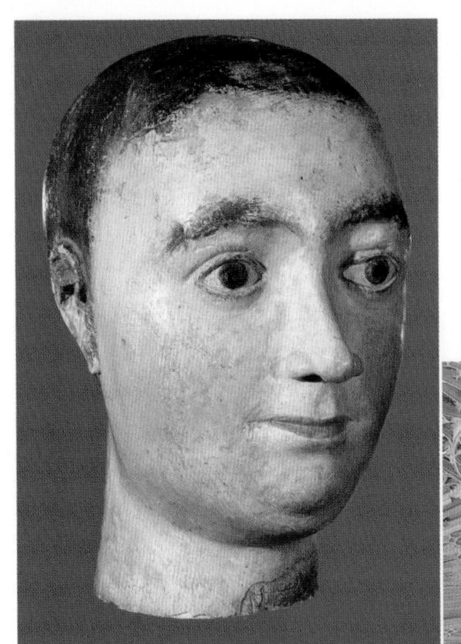

The head of Mary's funeral effigy, displayed at Westminster Abbey.

The tomb of Mary and Elizabeth at Westminster Abbey: ELIZABETH'S BODY WAS MOVED HERE BY JAMES I, THREE YEARS AFTER HER DEATH, BUT MARY'S PRESENCE IS BARELY ACKNOWLEDGED.

already begun. Even before Mary had reached London, altars and crucifixes had started to reappear in the city's churches, and Matins and Evensong were being recited "not by commandment but by the devotion of the people." As the chronicler Wriothesley described, at St. Paul's "the work that was broken down of stone, where the high altar stood, was begun to be made up again with brick." And on Saint Bartholomew's Day, August 24, a Latin Mass was said there.[13]

But amid such demonstrations of enthusiasm for the old religion, violent disturbances erupted across London. On Sunday, August 13, during a sermon at St. Paul's Cross, Gilbert Bourne, chaplain to the bishop of London, was "pulled out of the pulpit by vagabonds" and "one threw his dagger at him."[14] The following Sunday, crowds there were met by the captain of the Guard and more than two hundred guardsmen to protect the preacher. Defamatory pamphlets exhorting Protestants to take up arms against Mary's government littered the streets. "Nobles and gentlemen favoring the word of God" were asked to overthrow the "detestable papists," especially "the great devil" Stephen Gardiner, bishop of Winchester.[15] A number of leading Protestant figures, including John Bradford, the prebendary of St. Paul's, and John Rogers, the canon of St. Paul's, were arrested, and leading reformist bishops such as John Hooper, bishop of Worcester and Gloucester, and Hugh Latimer, bishop of Worcester, were imprisoned some weeks later. In September, Thomas Cranmer, the archbishop of Canterbury, was imprisoned for treason for his role in Lady Jane's attempted coup.

In mid-August, as violence and alarm spread, Mary issued her first proclamation, intended to avoid "the great inconvenience and dangers" that had arisen in times past through the "diversity of opinions in questions of religion":

> Her Majesty being presently by the only goodness of God settled in the just possession of the imperial crown of this realm and other dominions thereunto belonging, cannot now hide that religion which God and the world knoweth she hath ever professed from her infancy hitherto, which her majesty is minded to observe and maintain for herself by God's grace during her time, so doth her highness much desire and would be glad the same

> were all of her subjects quietly and charitably embraces. And yet she doth signify unto all her Majesty's said loving subjects that of her most gracious disposition and clemency her highness mindeth not to compel any her said subjects thereunto unto such time as further order by common assent may be taken therein.

Mary called on her subjects "to live in quiet sort and Christian charity" and told them that further religious change would be settled by "common consent," by act of Parliament.[16] In the midst of popular unrest and fear of change, Mary had responded with moderation and pragmatism.

YET WHILE MARY publicly temporized, she made secret steps toward restoring Catholicism. In August, she addressed a private letter to Pope Julius III, petitioning him to remit all the ecclesiastical censures against England that had been imposed when Henry broke with Rome. As she wrote to Henry Penning, the pope's chamberlain, she had "always been most obedient and most affectionate towards the Apostolic See and his Holiness had no more loving daughter than herself." She declared that within a few days she "hoped to be able to show it openly to the whole world" and would first need to "repeal and annul by Act of Parliament many perverse laws made by those who ruled before her."[17]

On learning of Mary's accession, the pope had appointed as cardinal and papal legate Reginald Pole, the son of Mary's former governess Margaret Pole, in order to arrange the reconciliation of England to the Catholic Church. Pole began petitioning for an immediate and unconditional return to Roman obedience, for "The Queen, or at least England, was assuredly [ship]wrecked when she threw herself overboard . . . into the sea of this century." As he had "drawn a picture of the danger; her Majesty will judge whether it is time to deliberate, or rather to act as ordained and prescribed by divine and human counsel."[18] With Parliament summoned for the beginning of October, Pole demanded that the issue of papal supremacy and monastic property be quickly resolved and on August 10 launched a series of exhortations to the queen, begging her to end the schism without delay.

Yet Mary had come to realize the scale of her task. On September 11, she wrote to the cardinal of Imola, informing him that no legatine mission should be sent until the time was more propitious. She was aware of the dangers of introducing religious changes before they could be sanctioned by Parliament. For now she dissembled, maintaining that she did not want to coerce people into going to Mass. As Mary declared to Renard, "she had so far found no better expedient than to leave each free as to the religion he would follow. . . . If some held to the old, and others to the new, they should not be interfered with or constrained to follow any other course until the coming Parliament should decide by law."[19] There was, however, one notable exception.

WITHIN TWO WEEKS of Mary's entry into London, Renard reported that he had raised with the queen the presence at court of the Lady Elizabeth, who might, out of "ambition or being persuaded thereunto, conceive some dangerous design and put it to execution, by means which it would be difficult to prevent, as she was clever and sly."[20] Writing to Mary in late August, the imperial ambassadors, M. de Courrières, M. de Thoulouse, and Renard, advised her "not to be too ready to trust the Lady Elizabeth" and urged her

> to reflect that she now sees no hope of coming to the throne, and has been unwilling to yield about religion. . . . Moreover, it will appear that she is only clinging to the new religion out of policy, in order to win over and make use of its adepts in case she decided to plot. A mistake may perhaps be made in attributing this intention to her, but at this stage it [is] safer to forestall than to be forestalled and to consider all possible results; for there are clear enough indications.[21]

Aware of such suspicions against her and "perceiving that the Queen did not show her as kindly a countenance as she could wish," Elizabeth asked Mary for a private audience. They met at the beginning of September at Richmond, in one of the galleries of the palace; Mary was accompanied by one of her ladies, Elizabeth by one of her maids. Falling on her knees before the queen, Elizabeth wept, saying she knew the queen was "not well disposed towards her, and she knew no other cause except religion." She begged for understanding. She acted out of ignorance, not obstinacy: she had never been taught the doctrine of the ancient religion. She asked for books so that "having read them she might know if her conscience would allow her to be persuaded; or that a learned man might be sent to her, to instruct her in the truth."

Glad to see such "good resolves," Mary granted her request.[22] Meanwhile, as she had promised, Elizabeth attended Mass in the Chapel Royal on September 8, the Feast of the Nativity of the Blessed Virgin. It was clearly under duress. She had tried to excuse herself on grounds of ill health and had complained loudly of a stomachache all the way to church.[23] It was a rerun of the earlier clashes between Mary and Edward, when he had implored her to submit to his authority and accept the Protestant changes. But unlike Mary, Elizabeth had no desire to be a martyr.

No one, least of all Mary, was fooled by Elizabeth's display of compliance. Within days the imperial ambassadors were reporting that "last Sunday the Lady Elizabeth did not go to mass," adding "the Queen has sent us word that she has half-turned already from the good road upon which she had begun to travel."[24] Mary continued to press Elizabeth as to the purity of her motives, questioning whether she really believed, as Catholics did, "concerning the holy sacrament," or whether she "went to mass in order to dissimulate, out of fear or hypocrisy." Elizabeth replied that she was contemplating making a public declaration "that she went to mass and did as she did because her conscience prompted and moved her to it, that she went of her own free will and without fear, hypocrisy or dissimulation."[25]

Although she continued to doubt Elizabeth's sincerity, Mary allowed her sister to remain at court and to attend her coronation. But underlying tensions remained. Within weeks Renard reported that Mary was considering barring her from the succession on account of her "heretical opinions and illegitimacy, and characteristics in which she resembled her mother." As Anne Boleyn "had caused great trouble in the kingdom," she feared her daughter might do the same "and particularly that she might imitate her mother in being a French partisan." She told Renard that it "would burden her conscience too heavily to allow a bastard to succeed."[26] Mary increasingly suspected that Elizabeth went to Mass only "out of hypocrisy; she had not a single servant or maid of honour who was not a heretic, she talked every day with heretics and lent an ear to all their evil designs."[27]

Finally, in early December, Elizabeth asked for permission to leave court. The sisters parted on affectionate terms. Mary gave her a coif of rich sables, and en route to Hatfield, Elizabeth stopped to write to Mary asking her for copes, chasubles, chalices, and other ornaments for her chapel. The queen ordered all these things to be sent to her, "as it was for God's service and Elizabeth wished to bear witness to the religion she had declared she meant to follow."[28]

CHAPTER 40

OLD CUSTOMS

As to the establishment of the Queen upon her throne, the preparations for the coronation are going forward apace for the first of October.[1]

—IMPERIAL AMBASSADORS TO THE EMPEROR, SEPTEMBER 9, 1553

FROM THE EARLIEST WEEKS OF HER REIGN, PLANS WERE PUT into place for Mary's coronation.[2] Fabrics and cloth were purchased and delivered, clothing was made ready, the nobility was summoned, and triumphal pageants were composed. By mid-September, the citizens of London had begun decorating the city; arches, scaffolds, and scenery for the pageants were erected and painted, and wooden rails were installed along the coronation procession route to hold back the crowds.[3] At Westminster Abbey a great stage had been constructed for the crowning, and banners hung all around. It was as it had been for countless coronations before.

Yet amid the following of "old customs" there existed unease.[4] Though everyone had resolved to make the ceremonies "very splendid and glorious," the manner and form of the ceremony were uncertain. There were no precedents for the crowning of a queen regnant, let alone a Catholic bastard.[5] The fourteenth-century guide *Liber Regalis* and the "Little Device," first used for the coronation of Richard III, outlined only the procession and ceremony of a queen consort. And after weeks of religious unrest and plotting in the capital, there were fears of further violence.

As Renard reported, "arquebusers, arrows and other weapons were being collected in various houses," giving rise to fears that during the coronation procession "some attempt might be made against [the Queen's] person."[6] A number of former Edwardian councillors called for unprecedented change, arguing that the coronation should be postponed until after Parliament had met and confirmed Mary's legitimacy.[7] The imperial ambassadors believed that such "novelty" was intended to "cast doubts upon and put in question the Queen's right to the throne, to render her more dependant on [her] council and Parliament than she should be [and] bridle her so that she cannot marry a foreigner." It was a proposal born of the fears raised by accession of the country's first female sovereign, and one that Mary rejected outright.[8]

The coronation had been set for October 1, a Sunday, according to tradition. Although the 1552 Act of Uniformity remained in force and Mary was to be crowned supreme head of the Church, the coronation ceremony was to proceed as a full Catholic Mass. Recognizing the potential illegitimacy of the ceremony, Mary requested that Pole, the papal legate, absolve her and her bishops on the day of the coronation so that they might be able to say Mass and administer the sacraments without sin.[9] Moreover, concerned that the oils to be used in the anointing, which had been consecrated by an Edwardian minister, "may not be such as they ought," she asked the imperial ambassadors to write to the bishop of Arras, Charles's chief minister in Brussels, to secretly prepare specially consecrated oil for her anointing.[10] The conservative Bishop Gardiner, recently freed from the Tower, was chosen to perform the rite in place of Thomas Cranmer, archbishop of Canterbury, who remained imprisoned. With the amendments made, all was ready for the pageantry to begin.

ON THURSDAY, September 28, Mary departed St. James's Palace for Whitehall, accompanied by her sister, Elizabeth, now heir apparent, and their former stepmother Anne of Cleves. At Westminster, Mary boarded her barge and was escorted down the Thames to the Tower by the lord mayor, the aldermen of London, and the companies, their boats festooned with banners and flying streamers.[11] As the flotilla approached the Tower, a salute was fired. At the Watergate, Mary thanked the city officials, and then, amid a cacophony of trumpets, musicians, singers, and the pounding of cannon, she entered the Tower.[12]

On Saturday, the eve of the coronation, a symbolic chivalric ritual dating back to the fourteenth century was performed. Fifteen young nobles were created knights of the bath. A ceremony of naked bathing, shaving, and prayer marked their coming of age as warriors.[13] It was a male rite of passage, an exercise in chivalric kingship, and a means of rewarding loyalty and service to the Crown. Many of those given the honor were those of Mary's servants who had acted in her defense in the succession crisis, men such as Sir Henry Jerningham and Robert Rochester. Not for the last time, Mary's gender necessitated the redefining of ritual as the lord steward, the earl of Arundel, deputized in Mary's place. On Saturday morning the chosen gentlemen plunged naked into a wooden bath in the chapel of the Tower before reemerging to kiss Arundel's shoulder.

At three that afternoon, as guns fired from the ramparts and bells rang from the churches all around, Mary departed the Tower for the coronation procession. The event, another tradition dating from the reign of Richard II, was an opportunity for Londoners to see their sovereign before the coronation the following day. First, the queen's messengers rode out from the courtyard of the Tower, followed by trumpeters, esquires of the body, the knights of the bath, heralds, bannerets, and members of the council and clergy, some in gold, some in silver, their horses covered in plate. Then, in rank order, came the Garter knights, the rest of the nobility, the foreign ambassadors, each paired with an Englishman, merchants, soldiers, and knights; behind them the queen's personal entourage, the earl of Sussex, her Chief Server, carrying the queen's hat and cloak; and "two ancient knights with old-fashioned hats, powdered on their heads, disguised," representing, as was traditional, the dukes of the former English territories of Normandy and Guienne. Gardiner and Paulet followed with the seal and mace; the lord mayor in crimson velvet carrying the golden scepter; the sergeants at arms; and the earl of Arundel bearing Mary's sword.[14]

Then came Mary herself, riding in an open litter pulled by six horses in white trappings almost to the ground. Official accounts describe her as "richly apparelled with mantle and kirtle of cloth of gold . . . all things thereunto appertaining, according to the precedents."[15] Mary was dressed as a queen consort. On her head she wore a gold tinsel cloth and a jeweled crown, which was described as being "so massy and ponderous that she was fain to bear up her head with her hands."[16] Around Mary's litter rode four ladies on horseback: Edward Courtenay's mother, the marchioness of Exeter; and the wives of the duke of Norfolk, the earl of Arundel, and Sir William Paulet. Next came the carriage carrying Elizabeth and Anne of Cleves; then lines of peereses, ladies, and gentlewomen, some in chariots, some on horseback, and the royal henchmen dressed in the Tudor colors of green and white.[17]

For a mile and a half, the grand procession wound its way through the graveled streets of London. The aldermen of the city stood within the rails; behind them the multitudes, "people resorted out of all parts of the realm, to see the same, that the like have not been seen before."[18] The procession was, Renard reported, "a memorable and solemn one, undisturbed by any noise or tumult."[19]

From the Tower to Temple Bar, Mary was greeted by an array of civic pageantry. At Fenchurch Street, Genoese merchants had created a triumphal arch decorated with verses praising Mary's accession: as she passed, a boy dressed as a girl and carried on a throne by men and "giants" delivered a salutation.[20] At Cornhill, the Florentines paid tribute to Mary's triumph over Northumberland's forces by invoking an image of Judith, the Israelite heroine, saving her people from Holofernes, the Assyrian leader, and of Tomyris, who had led her people to victory against the all-conquering Cyrus. In the pageant, an angel clothed in green, trumpet in hand, was strung up at the highest point between four gigantic "pictures." As the angel put the trumpet to his mouth, a trumpeter hidden within the pageant "did sound as if the noise had come from the angel, to the great marvelling of many ignorant persons."[21] In Cornhill and Cheap, the conduits ran with wine and pageants were performed in which people stood singing verses in praise of their queen.

At St. Paul's, Mary was addressed by the recorder of London and the chamberlain before being presented with a purse containing a thousand marks of gold, a gesture of goodwill "which she most thankfully received."[22] At the school in St. Paul's churchyard, the playwright John Heywood, sitting under a vine, delivered an oration in Latin and English; and at the dean of St. Paul's Gate, choristers held burning tapers that gave off "most sweet perfumes."[23] At Ludgate, minstrels played and children sang songs of joy. Then, passing through Temple Bar by early evening, Mary finally reached Whitehall and took leave of the lord mayor. The following day she would be crowned queen of England.

CHAPTER 41

GOD SAVE QUEEN MARY

∴

AT ELEVEN IN THE MORNING ON SUNDAY, OCTOBER 1, 1553, MARY proceeded to the south transept of Westminster Abbey for her coronation. It was a sight not seen before and combined elements of both precedent and novelty. The queen, dressed as a male monarch in traditional state robes of crimson velvet, walked beneath a canopy borne by the barons of the Cinque Ports; the duke of Norfolk carried the crown, the marquess of Winchester the orb, and the earl of Arundel the ball and scepter. Before her, in pairs, walked an ordered procession of gentlemen, knights, and councillors, headed by the bishop of Winchester and ten others, all with miters on their heads and crosses in their hands.[1]

In the center of the abbey a raised walkway led to the royal stage and then steps to a higher plinth bearing the coronation chair. It had seated every monarch at coronations since Edward the Confessor more than five hundred years before. Now, for the first time, it would seat a queen regnant. Two noblemen led Mary to each corner of the dais so the congregation might see her. To this assembly Gardiner made his address:

> Sirs, Here present is Mary, rightful and undoubted inheritrix by the Laws of God and man to the Crown and Royal Dignity of this realm of England, France and Ireland, whereupon you shall understand that this day is appointed by all the peers of this land for the consecration, injunction and coronation of the said most excellent Princess Mary; will you serve at this time and give your wills and assent to the same consecration, unction and coronation?

The gathered throng answered as one: "Yea, yea, yea! God save Queen Mary!"

Mary went before the altar and, as she lay facedown on a velvet cushion, prayers were said over her. From the side of the stage she listened to the sermon of George Day, bishop of Chichester, on the subject of the obedience owed to a monarch. Then, kneeling in front of the altar, Mary prepared to make her oaths, pledging to defend her subjects, maintain peace, and administer justice throughout the realm. She had feared that the oath would be tampered with so that in some way she would be called upon to condone the new religion, and she therefore added the words "just and licit laws" to the traditional form. "Will ye grant to keep to the people of England and others your realms and dominions, the *just and licit* laws and liberties of this realm and other your realms and dominions?" Mary was asked.[2] Then, lying prostrate before the high altar, the choirs sang "Veni Creator Spiritus."

After the choir quietened, Mary moved to a curtained traverse at the left-hand side of the altar, accompanied by some of her ladies. Here she made her first change of clothing in preparation for her anointing. This, the most solemn part of the ceremony, was intended to mark the monarch with the indelible stigma of divine majesty. Her mantle of crimson velvet was removed, and she returned to the altar in a simple petticoat of purple velvet. She lay again before the altar, a pall held over her by four knights of the Garter, and she was anointed by Bishop Gardiner on her shoulders, breast, forehead, and temples with the holy oil and chrism secretly obtained from Flanders.[3] Returning to the traverse dressed in her robes of state, Mary was led to the altar, where she received the ornaments, her symbols of power: the sword, the scepter, and the orbs. She was crowned with the crown of Edward the Confessor, the imperial crown of the realm, and with another specially made for her, a vast yet simply designed crown with two arches, a large fleur-de-lis, and prominent crosses. The choir then burst into a Te Deum.[4]

Mary was crowned in a fashion similar to her male predecessors: "girt with a sword as when one is armed a knight, and a King's sceptre was placed in one hand, and in the other a sceptre wont to be given to queens, which is surmounted by doves."[5] Finally, the crimson mantle furred with ermine was fastened on her shoulders. Arrayed in her regalia, Mary was seated in Saint Edward's Chair, where she received the nobles, led by Gardiner, who paid homage to her as queen.[6]

At four that afternoon Mary emerged from the abbey as queen of England. Carrying the orb and scepter, which "she twirled and turned in her hand," she proceeded back along the carpeted path to Westminster Hall for a ceremonial dinner. Gardiner sat to her right, Elizabeth and Anne of Cleves to her left, though at a distance.[7] Four swords were held before her as she ate, and according to custom she "rested her feet on two of her ladies."[8] The earl of Derby, high steward of England, and the duke of Norfolk, high marshal, rode around the hall on chargers trapped with cloth of gold, overseeing the banquet and maintaining order. After the second course, the banquet was interrupted by a horseman, the queen's champion, Sir Edward Dymocke, who entered dressed in bright armor, ostrich plumes in his helmet, with a surcoat of armorial bearings. He read out a challenge: "Whosoever shall dare to affirm that this Lady is not the rightful Queen of this Kingdom I will show him the contrary, or will do him to death" and threw down his glove.

Returning to the queen, he proclaimed that seeing that "none was found who dared to gainsay him or take up his glove, he hailed her as the true and rightful Queen."[9]

CHAPTER 42

INIQUITOUS LAWS

∴

FOUR DAYS AFTER HER CORONATION, MARY OPENED HER FIRST Parliament. As she looked on from her throne, Bishop Gardiner, the lord chancellor, made his opening address in which he "treated amply of the union with religion," demonstrating how many disadvantages had befallen the realm owing to its separation. "Parliament," he declared, "was assembled by her Majesty and the Council to repeal many iniquitous laws against the said union, and to enact others in favour of it."[1]

In one of its first acts, Parliament declared that the marriage of Mary's parents, Katherine of Aragon and Henry VIII, had been valid and that Mary was therefore legitimate. The queen's title was vindicated from "the corrupt and unlawful sentence" that had divorced her father and mother and from subsequent laws that had declared her illegitimate. It was what Mary had fought for since the years of her adolescence. Finally she had restored her mother's memory and confirmed her own legitimacy.

Next came the repeals of the Edwardian religious legislation that had pronounced on the Prayer Book, the sacraments, and married priests, thereby restoring the Church settlement to that of the final years of her father's reign. All offenses defined as treasonable during Henry and Edward's reigns were repealed, and the law was taken back to its basic definition of 1352, with evidence of guilt now lying once more in action against the monarch rather than in a denial of the royal supremacy.

To make the bills acceptable to the House of Commons, all allusion to the pope had to be avoided. Holders of monastic and chantry lands, whatever their doctrinal beliefs, feared that a return to Rome would threaten the property that they had received following the dissolution of the monasteries during the 1530s. Writing to Pole, Mary explained that the Commons would not hear of "the abolishing, specially of the law that gave the title of the supremacy of the Church in the realm of the crown, suspecting that to be an introduction of the Pope's authority into the realm, which they cannot gladly hear of."[2]

Although the bill was eventually passed, it demonstrated that though Parliament was willing to restore church services and religious ceremonies to the pattern of the 1540s, it was not prepared to sanction the abolition of the Supreme Headship and the return of papal authority in the realm. The Commons would not sacrifice their property and revenue from ex-monastic lands; these would need to be safeguarded before a return to Rome could be achieved.[3] "There is difficulty about religion, the Pope's authority and the restitution of Church property," Renard explained, "so much so that a conspiracy has been discovered among those who hold that property either by the liberality of the late Kings Henry and Edward, or by purchase, who would rather get themselves massacred than let go." Renard's message to the emperor was clear: "The majority of Parliament refuses to admit the Pope's authority or to come back into the fold."[4]

Mary was forced to curb her zeal; for now she would remain supreme head of the Church. As she wrote to Pole on November 15:

> This Parliament was to make a full restoration [of obedience], but we now need another in three or four months. You will hear that all Edward's statutes about religion have been annulled, and the state of religion put back where it was at the time of the death of King Henry, our father of the most pious memory.

Yet Pole still pushed for an immediate and full restitution: "He [God] destroyed the government that displeased Him without any human action, and gave power to a virgin, who trusted in Him," he railed, yet Mary "thinks that temporal matters should be taken care of first. She must not be so ungrateful . . . nothing more neglectful than putting off religion to the end. Her impudent councillors must not intimidate her." And he implored Mary, "[God] did not give you such great courage so that you might become fearful as Queen."[5] In a subsequent letter he told her, "You have given your enemies good argument that you [are] schismatic, since [you] have taken Parliament's authority for most important confirmation of your claim." It was "no excuse" that some of Parliament had proved resistant. Her adversaries could say that she was "no better than Northumberland" with regard to obedience. "You look weak now," he ended; "these acts establish schism."[6]

Despite Pole's insistence, Mary knew she could not move too fast. Yet she dared not show "the intent of her heart in this matter," given the opposition expressed.[7] On the day that Parliament rose, a dead dog with a shaved crown, representing a tonsured priest, a rope about its neck, was slung through the windows of the Queen's Presence Chamber.[8] Mary was indignant and warned Parliament that "such acts might move her to a kind of justice further removed from justice than she would wish."[9]

AS OF DECEMBER 20, religious services were to be conducted and sacraments administered as they had been in the last years of Henry VIII's reign. It marked the beginning of restoration and reform. Although Mary did not use the title, she did use her authority as supreme head to press for reform. In royal articles of March 1554, she ordered the strict observance of the traditional ceremonies and the repression of "corrupt and naughty opinions, unlawful books, ballads, and other pernicious and hurtful devices." Married priests were to be deprived, all processions were to be conducted in Latin, all "laudable" ceremonies were to be observed, and "uniform" doctrine was to be set forth in homilies.[10]

The restoration of the Mass and of Catholic ceremonies demanded the return of all that the Edwardian government had had stripped out of the churches. In articles designed for the visitation of his diocese in the autumn, Edmund Bonner, bishop of London, outlined a program of reconstruction to be adopted by bishops. The articles specified what his church now required, and parishioners were ordered to return property still in their possession:

> Whether the things underwritten (which are to be found at the cost of the parishioners) be in the church: it is to wit, a legend, an antiphoner, a grail, a psalter, an ordinal to say or solemnize divine office, a missal, a manual, a processional, a chalice, two cruetts, a principal vestment with chasuble, a vestment for the deacon and sub-deacon, a cope with the appurtenances, it is to wit an amice, alb, girdle, stole and fannon, the high altar with apparel in the front and parts thereof, three towels, three surplices, a rochet, a cross for procession with candlesticks, a cross for the dead, an incenser, a ship or bessel for frankincense, a little sanctas bell, a pix with an honest and decent cover, and a veil for the Lent, banners for the Rogation week, bells and ropes, a bier for the dead, a vessel to carry holy water about, a candlestick for the paschal taper, a font to christen children with covering and lock and key, and generally all other things, which after the custom of the country or place, the parishioners are bound to find, maintain and keep?[11]

Bonner's investigation was minute in its detail, from issues of dress to clerical residence and morality. But it also focused specifically on seeking out heresy. He wanted to know about the doctrine taught by the clergy, about seditious or heretical books in circulation, and about priests who administered any sacraments in English. In addition, Bonner wanted the names of any laity who, at the moment of consecration, "do hang down their heads, hide themselves behind pillars, turn away their faces, or depart out of the church," any who "murmured, grudged or spoke against" the Mass, the sacraments, or ceremonies, and any who "made noise, jangled, talked or played the fool in church."[12] He demanded the names of any circulating "slanderous books, ballads or plays, contrary to the Christian religion." He wanted to know about any who refused to take part in rituals such as procession on Sunday, and issuing of the pax, and any who had eaten flesh on the traditional fasts or vigils. Pictures on the walls of churches were to be removed that "chiefly and principally do tend to the maintenance of carnal liberty" by attacking fasting, good works, celibacy, or the veneration of the Blessed Sacrament.[13]

Gradually, signs indicating the return to Catholicism were visible across the country. In November 1553, Saint Katherine's image was carried around the steeple at St. Paul's on her patronal feast day, and on Saint Andrew's Day there was "a general procession . . . in Latin with *ora pro nobis*."[14] As Machyn recorded in his diary, "The viii day of December was [the] procession at [St.] Paul's. When all was done my lord of London [Bonner] commanded that every parish church should provide for a cross and a staff and cope to go to the procession every Sunday, Wednesday and Friday, and pray unto God for fair weather through London."[15]

Outside London, Robert Parkyn, a Yorkshire priest, described how

> it was joy to hear and see how these carnal priests (which had led their lives in fornication with their whores and harlots) did lower and look down when they were commanded to leave and forsake their concubines and harlots and to do open penance according to the Canon Law . . . all old ceremonies, laudably used beforetime in the holy Church was then revived, daily frequented and used.[16]

The process of Catholic revival, resisted by some but welcomed by many, had begun.

CHAPTER 43

A MARRYING HUMOR

⁙

So as to restore the succession and continue the line, they [the Council] considered it necessary for the good of the kingdom that the Queen should enter into an alliance, and marry; and the sooner the better, because of the state of her affairs and her years.[1]

—Renard to the Emperor,
October 5, 1553

Upon Mary's accession there was general expectation that she would marry. No one expected a woman to rule alone. It was important that she have an heir to ensure a Catholic succession and someone to assist her in government.[2] Mary now accepted the need to marry: "I have lived a virgin, and I doubt not, with God's grace, to live still. But if, as my ancestors have done it might please God that I should leave you a successor to be your governor."[3] At thirty-seven Mary would have to wed quickly if she were to stand any chance of conceiving.

Despite the contemporary belief that a queen needed a consort, there was also apprehension. It was assumed that a husband would exercise power. Under English law not only would a woman's property, titles, and income pass to her husband upon marriage, but she would also cede governance of her person. For Mary, any prospective bridegroom had to be of royal blood and a good Catholic.

English hopes came to focus on the twenty-five-year-old Edward Courtenay, a great-grandson of Edward IV. His father, the marquess of Exeter, had been executed by Henry VIII in 1538; his mother, Gertrude Courtenay (née Blount), the marchioness of Exeter, remained one of

Mary's most trusted intimates. Chief among his supporters was the lord chancellor, Stephen Gardiner, who had spent a number of years imprisoned with Courtenay in the Tower. Although Gardiner was supported by almost all the other privy councillors, Mary quickly made it clear that she had no intention of marrying Courtenay or any other of her own subjects. Dom Luis of Portugal, the brother of King Juan, who had been suggested as a husband many times over the previous years, now renewed his overtures. Maximilian, the son of the emperor's brother, Ferdinand, also emerged as a possible candidate; while Charles V intrigued for a match between Mary and his own son, Philip, prince of Spain.

The prospect of Mary's marriage was of great importance in the struggle between the Houses of Habsburg and Valois. If Charles could succeed in establishing his son, Philip, upon the throne of England as Mary's husband, the sea route between Spain and the Netherlands would be secured, the Netherlands themselves would be saved from falling into the clutches of the king of France, as they seemed likely to do, and France would be encircled.[4] Moreover, it would provide a counterweight against the intended marriage of the French dauphin to Mary, queen of Scots.

To the French an Anglo-Habsburg marriage was deeply alarming and had to be prevented. As Noailles wrote to the French king, the queen's marriage would be "to the great displeasure of all, with perpetual war against your Majesty, the Scotch and her own subjects, who will unwillingly suffer the rule of a foreigner." He continued, "It was a perpetual war against the King [of France] that the Emperor wished her to espouse rather than his son."[5] The final outcome of the long struggle between Habsburg and Valois seemed to depend on developments in England: at stake was the hegemony of Europe.

IT WAS ON JULY 29, at his first private audience with the queen at Beaulieu in Essex, that Simon Renard raised the question of the queen's marriage. The emperor, he declared, was mindful of the fact that a "great part of the labour of government could with difficulty be undertaken by a woman" and urged her to "entertain the idea of marriage and fix on some suitable match as soon as possible."[6]

Mary had told Renard that she had never thought of marrying before she was queen and "as a private individual she would never have desired it, but preferred to end her days in chastity." Katherine of Aragon, in one of her last letters, had urged her daughter "not thinking or desiring any husband for Christ's passion."[7] However, as she now occupied "a public position," Mary was determined to follow the emperor's advice and said she would "choose whomsoever you might recommend." At his second audience two weeks later, Renard reopened the subject by mentioning Mary's duty to the nation and implying that a foreigner would best help her fulfill the obligation. At this Mary laughed "not once but several times, whilst she regarded me in a way that proved the idea to be very agreeable to her."[8]

Meanwhile, Charles wrote to his son, Philip, that he was "glad to see our cousin in the place that is hers by right, to strengthen her position and to aid the restoration of Catholicism." He told him he was contemplating marrying the English queen himself, as he had some thirty years before: "I am sure that if the English made up their minds to accept a foreigner they would more readily accept me than any other, for they have always shown a liking for me." But ill and aged, Charles had no real intention of marrying Mary. As his letter continued, he wondered whether Philip might be a better choice. He asked his son "to consider it privately and keep the matter a close secret."[9]

A month later, Philip, who had been in negotiations for a possible match with the Infanta Maria of Portugal, finally responded to his father's letter: "All I have to say about the English affair is that I am rejoiced to hear that my aunt has come to the throne . . . as well as out of natural feeling as because of the advantages mentioned by your Majesty where France and the Low Countries are concerned." He continued, "As your Majesty feels as you say about the match for me, you know that I am so obedient a son that I have no will other than yours, especially in a matter of such high import."[10]

Awaiting further instructions from Brussels as to the advancing of Philip's suit, Renard questioned Mary about Edward Courtenay and the "common rumour" that she was to marry him. Mary was adamant that she "knew no one in England with whom she would wish to ally herself" and asked whether the emperor had yet selected "a suitable person." Renard responded that it would be much easier for the emperor to advise if "she could inform him of her inclinations." Mary had expressed her desire for someone "middle aged"; Renard had mentioned several Catholic princes, but she had responded that she "was old enough to be their mother."[11]

On October 10, Renard knelt before Mary and formally offered the hand of Prince Philip. He assured her that "if age and health had permitted," the emperor would "have desired no other match, but as years and infirmity" rendered him "a poor thing to be offered to her," he could think of no one dearer or better suited than Philip, "who was of middle age, of distinguished qualities, and of honourable and Catholic upbringing."

Philip was twenty-six, eleven years Mary's junior. She was the granddaughter of Ferdinand and Isabella; he was their great-grandchild. He had already been married to his cousin Infanta Maria of Portugal, who had died in childbirth in July 1545. Their son, Don Carlos, was now nine years old. For Mary the prospect of marriage to Philip represented her imperial destiny, a chance to join the family that she had long since relied on for support and protection. Moreover, it would put England at the center of European politics.

Mary was thrilled, calling it a "greater match than she deserved." But, she said, "she did not know how the people of England would take it." She also expressed fears about what the marriage would entail; "if he were disposed to be amorous, such was not her desire, for she was of the age your Majesty knew of, and had never harboured thoughts of love." She would, however, "wholly love and obey him to whom she had given herself, following the divine commandment and would do nothing against his will." But, if he wished to "encroach in the government of the kingdom, she would be unable to permit it, nor if he attempted to fill posts and offices with strangers, for the country itself would never stand such interference."[12] Mary would attempt to separate her duties as Philip's wife and her responsibilities as queen, as her grandmother Isabella had before her.[13]

For a month the court was an agitated ferment of secret meetings, hushed conversations, and exaggerated rumor. William Paget and Renard lobbied councillors in favor of Philip, and Gardiner pressed the claims of Courtenay. On October 20, Gardiner and a number of Mary's trusted household servants approached her to speak of the

English candidate. As Mary told Renard, because their actions were "dictated by whole-hearted affection and devotion to her service," she could not "take the advice of such trusty counsellors in bad part."[14] Gardiner had stressed that "the country would never abide a foreigner; Courtenay was the only possible match for her"; Francis Englefield added "that his highness had a kingdom of his own he would not wish to leave to come to England and that his own subjects spoke ill of him." Edward Waldegrave argued that if the queen "wedded his Highness the country would have to go to war with the French."

But Mary begged them all to "lay aside their private considerations" and to "think of the present condition of affairs, the French plottings, the marriage of the French Dauphin with the Queen of Scotland, what benefit the country could look for were she to marry Courtenay, and what profit might accrue to it if she chose a foreigner."

Robert Rochester and other of the household servants were given letters from the emperor in which he feigned to care for their opinions "as to what alliance would be best for her [Mary] and the country," suggesting that he would be guided by their advice. Meanwhile, by intrigues, bribes, and promises, and drawing on a web of agents and informants, Noailles sought to make the idea of a Spanish alliance hateful to the people of England. When Henry II heard rumors of the impending betrothal, his "countenance was sad, his words few, and his dislike of the match marvellously great." Speaking to the English ambassador, Nicholas Wotton, the French king remarked that "a husband may do much with his wife" and that it would be hard for Mary, as for any woman, "to refuse her husband anything that he shall earnestly require of her."[15]

FINALLY, ON THE EVENING of Sunday, October 29, Mary sent again for Renard. He found her in her chamber alone, save for Susan Clarencius, her trusted lady-in-waiting. The room was barely lit. A lamp shone in one corner, its glow illuminating the Holy Sacrament, which stood on the altar before them. It was a momentous decision for Mary, both as a woman and as a queen. Her Council and even most of her trusted household servants opposed the match; it could be expected that the country would too. Ever since the emperor's letter had arrived, she had not slept. Instead she woke, weeping and praying for guidance. Now all three knelt before the sacrament, singing "Veni Creator Spiritus"—"Come, Holy Spirit, eternal God." Rising to her feet, Mary announced her decision. She had, she declared, been inspired by God to be Prince Philip's wife. "She believed what I have told her of his Highness's qualities," Renard explained, "and that your Majesty would ever show her kindness, observe the conditions that would safeguard the welfare of the country, be a good father to her as you had been in the past and more, now that you would be doubly her father and cause his highness to be a good husband to her." Now that her mind had been made up, "she would never change but love him perfectly and never give him cause to be jealous."[16]

Two days later Mary hastily wrote to Renard, revealing her anxious excitement:

> *Sir: I forgot to ask you one question the other night: that is to say, are you quite sure that there has never been any contract concerning marriage between the Prince and the daughter of Portugal, for there was much talk to that effect? I request you to write me the truth, on your faith and conscience, for there is nothing else in the world that could make me break the promise I made to you, so may God of His grace assist me! I also pray you to send me your advice as to how I shall broach this matter to the Council, for I have not yet begun to do so with any of them, but wish to speak to them before they speak to me.*
>
> *Written in haste, this All Saints Eve,*
> *Your good friend, Mary,*
> *Queen of England.*[17]

CHAPTER 44

A SUITABLE PARTNER IN LOVE

∴

In the beginning of November was the first notice among the people touching the marriage of the Queen to the King of Spain.[1]

—RESIDENT OF THE TOWER OF LONDON, 1553

ON NOVEMBER 16, 1553, MARY FACED A DEPUTATION OF SOME twenty members of the Commons seeking to dissuade her from marrying Philip. She had postponed the meeting for three weeks, claiming ill health; now she could delay no more. As Sir John Pollard, the speaker of the Commons, put it, it would displease the people to have a foreigner as the queen's consort. If Mary died childless, her husband would deplete the country of money and arms. He might decide to remove Mary from the kingdom "out of husbandly tyranny," and if he were left a widower with young children, he might try to usurp the crown for himself.[2] Instead, the speaker argued, it would be better for the queen to marry an Englishman. Mary listened to Pollard's long speech with exasperation. As she later told Renard, his discourse had been "so confused, so long-winded and prolific of irrelevant arguments," that she had found it irritating and offensive.

Finally, when Pollard had finished and without waiting for the chancellor to answer on her behalf, Mary rose to address the assembly. She thanked it for encouraging her to marry but, as she went on, she said that she did not appreciate the idea that it should attempt to choose "a companion" for her "conjugal bed." As she declared, "I now rule over you by the best right possible, and being a free woman, if any man or woman of the people of our realm is free, I have full right and sufficient years to discern a suitable partner in love"—both someone she could love and someone who would be to the benefit and advantage of the realm. It was, she told them,

> entirely vain for you to nominate a prospective husband for me from your own fancy, but rather let it be my free choice to select a worthy husband for my bridal bed—one who will not only join with me in mutual love, but will be able with his own resources to prevent an enemy attack, from his native land.[3]

She warned that "if she were married against her will she would not live three months and she would have no children." Her affairs had been conducted by divine disposition, and she would pray to God to counsel and inspire her in her choice of husband, "who would be beneficial to the kingdom and agreeable to herself . . . for she always thought of the welfare of her kingdom, as a good princess and mistress should."[4] Her riposte was so extraordinary that Pollard was rendered speechless and the deputation retired.

Mary suspected that Gardiner had inspired the speaker's words and afterward challenged him directly. "She would never marry Courtenay," she told him; "she never practiced hypocrisy or deceit, and had preferred to speak her mind, and she had come near to being angry on hearing such disrespectful words."[5] Mary asked him crossly, "Is it suitable, that I should be forced to marry a man because a bishop made friends with him in prison?" Courtenay was, she said, of "small power and authority," and, given the intrigues of the French and the poverty of the kingdom, would not be the most desirable match.

Gardiner tearfully admitted that he had spoken with Pollard but now accepted that "it would not be right to try to force her in one direction or another." He now swore to "obey the man she had chosen."[6] The Commons' petition proved futile; Mary had already made her decision. On the day after Parliament was dissolved, her betrothal was made public.

❧

MARY'S REBUTTAL OF the Commons' challenge enhanced her authority. Never before had a Tudor ruler flaunted popular opinion, as expressed by Parliament, so openly. In the face of the Commons' delegation, Mary had claimed the right to marry whomever she wished. By maintaining that she would marry as God directed her, "to his honour and to our country's good," she argued that her private inclination and the public welfare were compatible. But many within and outside the court remained discontented. As one contemporary observed, "This marriage was not well thought of by the Commons, nor much better liked by many of the nobility."[7]

At end of the year, Mary wrote to Henry II, assuring him that her marriage to Philip would not alter her desire for amicable relations with France. Henry was not convinced. He told Sir Nicholas Wotton "that he clearly saw that she was allying herself with the greatest enemy he had in the world, and he knew marital authority to be very strong with ladies. He had not thought she would choose a match so odious to him."[8] As Renard reported, the French ambassador "is plotting openly against the alliance, and has spoken to several councillors and nobles to whom he has rehearsed all imaginable disadvantages," spreading fears that England would be forced into war against France and that the country would become ever more subject to Spanish rule.[9]

When the imperial delegation arrived in the City of London to sign the marriage treaty on January 2, 1554, it was received coldly. The people, "nothing rejoicing, held down their heads sorrowfully." As the retinue rode through the capital, "boys pelted them with snowballs; so hateful was the sight of their coming in to them."[10]

Henry, meanwhile, instructed his ambassador:

> If you see that the Queen is resolved to marry the Prince of Spain and also that there is likelihood that Courtenay has the will and means to upset the apple-cart, you may say still more confidently that you are sure that for such a great benefit to the realm [of England] I would not deny my favour either to him or to the other gentlemen who know the evil which the marriage

> could bring to the realm and would like to oppose it. However, since things are as they are, you must act prudently and with great caution.[11]

On December 1, Mary wrote to the emperor:

> I would begin this letter by offering my excuses for not having written before . . . and would repeat in detail all my conferences with your Majesty's ambassador, were it not that your letters show that he has omitted nothing, so I feel sure that he has explained all and freed me of the necessity.
>
> He assures me that he has sent you accounts of the progress of the marriage negotiations he has conducted with me, telling you of my reply and professions of goodwill and affection for the Prince, my good cousin; the reasons founded on my zeal for my kingdom's welfare, towards which I have the duty your Majesty is aware of, that moved me to give my consent; my belief in the Prince's excellent qualities, and confidence that your Majesty will ever remain my good lord and father, and will offer terms in accordance. He also avers that he has not forgotten to transmit to your Majesty my most humble and affectionate thanks for the honour you have done me by proposing so great an alliance, for the mindfulness of my kingdom and myself and constant care for all my interests and concerns.[12]

As a token of the new accord, Charles had sent Mary "a large and valuable diamond"—"in witness of the fact," he told his ambassadors, "that beyond our old friendship and in respect for her position, we now consider her as our own daughter in virtue of this alliance." Their union saw the climax of Mary's long-standing relationship with the emperor and the revival of the Anglo-Spanish entente established by Mary's mother on her marriage to Prince Arthur, fifty-three years earlier.

On January 14, the terms of the treaty were officially proclaimed at Westminster "to the lords, nobility, and gentlemen" by the lord chancellor. As Gardiner explained, Mary had made her decision to wed Philip "partly for the wealth and enriching of the realm, and partly for friendship and other weighty considerations."[13] They should, he continued, "thank God that so noble, worthy, and famous a prince" would "humble himself as in this marriage to take upon him rather as a subject than otherwise; and that the Queen should rule all things as she doth now; and that there should be of the counsel no Spaniard."[14]

It did little to allay fears. After Gardiner's declaration of the terms of the marriage treaty, one chronicler described how the news was "very much misliked . . . almost each man was abashed, looking daily for worse matters to grow shortly after."[15]

CHAPTER 45

A TRAITOROUS CONSPIRACY

⁘

The King of France . . . is fitting out his best ships, so that before Easter arrives there shall be such a tumult in England as never was seen.[1]

—RENARD TO THE EMPEROR,
DECEMBER 11, 1553

IN LATE NOVEMBER 1553, A GROUP OF CONSPIRATORS, LED BY SIR Thomas Wyatt, a Kentish gentleman and the son of the poet of the same name; Sir James Croft, the head of a Marches family; and Sir Peter Carew, a soldier and Devonshire landowner, met to discuss the overthrow of the Marian government. Their plan would see a four-pronged rising in Kent, the Midlands, the Southwest, and the Welsh Marches, followed by a march on London. Mary would be deposed and the Spanish marriage thwarted; Elizabeth and Edward Courtenay would be married and both placed on the throne.

The rising was timed for Palm Sunday, March 18, to coincide with the start of Philip's journey to England. It was a scheme backed by the French in what was a final attempt to thwart the Spanish marriage. As Henry II wrote dismissively, the conspirators "have to do only with a woman who is badly provided with good counsel and men of ability, so it should be easy for them to guard against discovery if they are prudent enough and have blood in their nails."[2]

By the new year reports had spread of a "traitorous conspiracy" fostered by "certain lewd and ill-disposed persons."[3] Sir Peter Carew's return to Devon during the Christmas festivities raised suspicions, which seemed to be confirmed when he failed to obey a summons to attend the Privy Council.[4] On January 18, Renard informed Mary that a French fleet was assembling off the Normandy coast and pressed her to take immediate steps to protect herself.[5] Mary ordered that troops be raised and an oath of loyalty be administered to each member of the royal household "in order to ascertain the real feelings of each one." As the oath requesting "obedience and fidelity to his Highness" was read out, "all raised their hand." The same was done with the mayor, magistrates, aldermen, and men of law of the city, who "did not openly show any opposition."[6] Circulars were sent out across the country with copies of the treaty's provisions and orders to proclaim them, "lest rebels be inspired under the pretence of misliking this marriage, to rebel against the Catholic religion and divine service within this our realm, and to take from us that liberty which is not denied to the meanest woman in the choice of husband."[7]

On the twenty-first, Courtenay confessed his role in the affair to Gardiner. As Renard reported in a letter to the emperor, Courtenay had been approached by certain individuals who had sought to influence him "where religion and the marriage were concerned." However, "he had never paid any attention to them." Three days later, the details were revealed and the plot began to unravel.[8] The rebels were forced into action two months earlier than expected. Three of the anticipated risings failed. Carew fled to France, and the duke of Suffolk, who was to have led the rising in Leicestershire just weeks after he was pardoned for his support of Northumberland's coup, was arrested and taken to the Tower. Sir Thomas Wyatt, meanwhile, succeeded in raising a substantial force in Kent.

ON THURSDAY, JANUARY 25, Wyatt raised his standard at Maidstone with 3,000 men and issued a proclamation declaring the realm to be in imminent danger. He appealed to the townsmen to "join with us," maintaining that he meant the queen no harm "but better counsel and councillors" to preserve liberty against the Spaniards.[9] He declared he had taken up arms solely for the love of his country, fearing that the Spanish match would reduce the realm to slavery, and called upon "every good Englishman" to help him. The Spaniards had "already arrived at Dover," he said, and were "passing upward in

London, in companies of ten, four and six, with harness and arqubusers, and marions, with matchlight."[10] By Thursday the twenty-fifth, Wyatt had taken Rochester for the rebels.

The queen was at Whitehall when she heard of Wyatt's proclamation, and a band of citizens was quickly drawn together under the command of the eighty-year-old Thomas, duke of Norfolk.[11] On Sunday, the twenty-eighth, Norfolk set out for Rochester with a detachment of the Guard and five hundred city whitecoats, accompanied by one of the queen's heralds.

Upon reaching Wyatt's forces, the herald pronounced that all rebels who would desist from their purpose would be pardoned. With great shouts the rebels declared "they had done nothing whereof they should need any pardon." A commander with the city whitecoats, Captain Alexander Brett, addressed his men, telling them, "Masters, we go about to fight against our native countrymen of England and our friends in a quarrel unrightful and partly wicked"; the rebels were assembled to prevent Englishmen from becoming "slaves and villeins," to protect against Spanish designs "to spoil us of our goods and lands, ravish our wives before our faces, and deflower our daughters in our presence." Many of the whitecoats deserted, proclaiming "We are all Englishmen!" and expressing fear at the prospect of rule by the Spaniards.[12]

Norfolk and the remnant of his forces retreated to London. One chronicler wrote, "You should have seen some of the guard come home, their coats torn, all ruined, without arrows or string in their bow, or sword, in very strange ways."[13]

The desertion of the city whitecoats threw into question the loyalty of the whole of the capital. Wyatt's forces were rumored to be near, moving along the banks of the Thames toward Blackheath and Greenwich. Guns were set at each of the city gates, and a watch was kept day and night. The queen sent privy councillors Sir Edward Hastings and Sir Thomas Cornwallis to establish the cause of the commotion. If it was a question of the Spanish marriage, they were to point out that it was the duty of true subjects to sue by petition and not by force. If the rebels would lay down their arms, Hastings and Cornwallis were to offer to negotiate.[14]

They encountered Wyatt at Dartford, but he dismissed their conciliatory overtures, declaring that he would not lay down arms before he had secured control of queen and capital, and proceeded to march on London. "I am no traitor," he declared, "and the cause whereof I have gathered the people is to defend the realm from our overrunning by Strangers; which follows, this Marriage taking place."[15]

The Privy Council was divided as to how to protect the queen's person. Mary had been urged to withdraw to Windsor or the Tower but chose to remain at Westminster with a guard of 500 men, well armed and with all the necessary provision for defense. "She even asked to go and fight herself; that however was not permitted to her."[16] Instead she put her faith in Londoners to defend her. On the thirty-first a further proclamation was issued, condemning Wyatt and his company as "rank traitors."[17] The livery companies were informed that 2,000 men were needed for the defense of the city, and every householder was instructed to "raise for his family . . . on pain of death" and arm immediately for the defense of London "and not elsewhere at their peril."[18]

MEANWHILE, MARY took the initiative. At three in the afternoon of February 1, she ordered her horse to be brought to her and rode with her armored guard, heralds, trumpeters, and Council and a company of ladies along the Strand, through Ludgate to the Guildhall, "addressing the people as she went with wonderful good nature and uncommon courtesy."[19] There, beneath the cloth of estate and with scepter in hand, she gave a stirring speech to rally London to her cause, her voice, as one ambassador later described, "rough and loud almost like a man's so that when she speaks she is always heard a long way off."[20]

> I am come in mine own person to tell you what you already see and know, I mean the traitorous and seditious assembling of the Kentish rebels against us and you. Their pretence (as they say) is to resist a marriage between us and the prince of Spain . . . by their answers, the marriage is found to be the least of their quarrel; for, swerving from their former demands, they now arrogantly require the governance of our person, the keeping of our town, and the placing of our councillors. What I am loving subjects,

ye know your Queen, to whom, at my coronation, ye promised allegiance and obedience, I was then wedded to the realm, and to the laws of the same, the spousal ring whereof I wear here on my finger, and it never has and never shall be left off.

She was the rightful and true inheritor of the English Crown, she said. She was her father's daughter and the kingdom's wife. She told them:

I cannot tell how naturally a mother loveth her children, for I never had any, but if the subjects may be loved as a mother doth her child, then assure yourselves that I, your sovereign lady and your Queen, do earnestly love and favour you. I cannot but think you love me in return; and thus, bound in concord, we shall be able, I doubt not, to give these rebels a speedy overthrow.

She now addressed the subject of her marriage:

I am neither so desirous of wedding, nor so precisely wedded to my will, that I needs must have a husband. Hitherto I have lived a virgin, and I doubt not, with God's grace, to live still. But if, as my ancestors have done, it might please God that I should leave you a successor to be your governor, I trust you would rejoice thereat; also, I know it would be to your comfort. Yet, if I thought this marriage would endanger any of you, my loving subjects, or the royal estate of this English realm, I would never consent thereto, nor marry while I lived. On the word of a Queen I assure you, that if the marriage appear not before the court of Parliament, nobility and commons, for the singular benefit of the whole realm, then I will abstain—not only from this, but from any other.

She finished:

Good and faithful subjects, pluck up your hearts, and like true men stand fast with your lawful prince against these rebels both

> our enemies and yours, and fear them not, for I assure you that I fear them nothing at all.[21]

She was loudly cheered. Londoners rallied to her defense, throwing their caps into the air. So eloquent was her speech that people cried out that they would live and die in her service and that Wyatt was a traitor.[22] It was inspired rhetoric. Her queenship, which had lacked precedent, was defined in these moments with clarity, conviction, and originality. She had pledged herself to her country in entirely feminine terms but with an invocation of motherhood that was strong and resolute. It was an extraordinary moment. Hearts and minds were won over. "God save Queen Mary and the prince of Spain!" cried the crowd.

William Herbert, earl of Pembroke, was appointed as chief captain and general against Wyatt, and preparations were made for the defense of the capital. The following day, Candlemas, the inhabitants of London were "in harness."[23] Five hundred peasants were said to have deserted Wyatt on the night of the queen's speech alone.

ON SATURDAY, February 3, Wyatt reached Southwark and set up two cannon against London Bridge. Finding the bridge's drawbridge up and defended strongly against him, he laid siege for three days, waiting in vain for the bridge to be opened. There were a number of anxious days as the loyalty of the queen's subjects hung in the balance. When Wyatt heard that the lord warden, Thomas Cheney, was pursuing him and that George Neville, Lord Abergavenny, along with Pembroke and Edward, Lord Clinton, intended to cut off his retreat and attack him from three sides, he broke camp. On Tuesday the sixth, he headed for Kingston, where he crossed the river during the night.

The climax came the following day, Ash Wednesday, as Londoners received news that Wyatt was upon them. By the early hours of the morning volunteers had been armed and called to rendezvous at Charing Cross. The musters were summoned immediately. "Much noise and tumult was everywhere; so terrible and fearful at the first was Wyatt and his armies coming to the most part of the citizens, who were seldom or never wont before to have or hear any such invasions to their city."[24] But the queen would not let the guns of the Tower be turned against the rebels, lest innocent citizens in Southwark be caught in the fire.

Earlier that morning Mary's councillors had awakened her and urged her to flee by boat. She immediately requested Renard. He advised her to stay, arguing that if she fled she risked losing her kingdom. If London rose, the Tower would be lost, the heretics would throw religious affairs into confusion and kill the priests; Elizabeth would be proclaimed queen, and irremediable harm would result. The Council was divided; some pleaded with her to depart, others to stay. But Mary ignored their words of despair. She remained at Whitehall Palace in Westminster, praying, as some of her ladies wailed, "Alack, alack! We shall all be destroyed this night."

Troops were mustered, trenches dug, artillery was positioned, and three squadrons of cavalry and 1,000 infantry were drawn up.[25] Mary ordered Pembroke to lead out his infantry at first light and Lord Clinton, commander of the cavalry, to send a detachment of horse against Wyatt's troops while they were disorganized and fatigued by their march. The queen's main forces waited at Charing Cross. It was known that the rebels planned to pass through the area in the hope of gathering more sympathizers or splitting the queen's forces before attacking Whitehall.

By nine in the morning, Wyatt was mustering his forces in Hyde Park, within six miles of Westminster and St. James's. Again Mary was urged to flee, but again she refused and sent word that "she would tarry there [Westminster] to see the uttermost." So great was her determination that "many thought she would have been in the field in person."[26]

At around midday, Wyatt led his forces down St. James's, past Temple Bar, and along Fleet Street, passing citizens armed at their doors. The mayor and aldermen stood paralyzed "as men half out of their lives."[27] Wyatt found Ludgate barred against him with cannon. He retreated toward Charing Cross and was attacked by the queen's soldiers at Temple Bar. By five in the afternoon, Wyatt was captured and taken by boat to the Tower. Altogether, forty people were killed in the fighting in London, only two of them the queen's men.

Celebrations were held across the capital

> for the good victory that the Queen's grace had against Wyatt and the rebellious of Kent, the which were overcome, thanks be unto God, with little bloodshed, and the residue taken and had to prison, and after where divers of them put to death in divers places in London and Kent, and procession everywhere that day for joy.[28]

As in July 1553, the citizens of London had shown that they were not prepared to support a usurper against their rightful queen. Mary had triumphed over the rebels. A fortnight of fear, panic, and danger had passed.

Though Mary had displayed clemency with the Northumberland conspirators on her accession, this time she could show no mercy. Stephen Gardiner used his Lenten sermon at court on February 11 to petition Mary to exact extreme justice. In the past she had "extended her mercy, particularly and privately," but "familiarity had bred contempt" and rebellion had resulted; "through her leniency and gentleness much conspiracy and open rebellion was grown." It was now necessary for the mercy of the commonwealth that the "rotten and hurtful members" be "cut off and consumed." His meaning was clear. As the chronicler noted, "All the audience did gather there should shortly follow sharp and cruel execution."[29]

CHAPTER 46

GIBBETS AND HANGED MEN

At present there is no other occupation than the cutting off of heads and inflicting exemplary punishment. Jane of Suffolk, who made herself Queen, and her husband have been executed; Courtenay is in the Tower; and this very day we expect the Lady Elizabeth to arrive here, who they say has lived loosely like her mother and is now with child. So when all these heads are off no one will be left in the realm able to resist the Queen.[1]

—RENARD TO PHILIP,
FEBRUARY 19, 1554

IN THE DAYS AND WEEKS FOLLOWING THE DEFEAT OF THE REBELLION a stream of rebels were arrested. Prisons overflowed and churches became jails as hundreds of suspected traitors were questioned and tried.[2] Gallows were erected at each of the city gates and at principal landmarks in Cheapside, Fleet Street, and Smithfield, on London Bridge, and at Tower Hill. The whitecoats who had gone over to the rebels were hanged at the doors of their houses in the city. As the executions continued, the smell of rotting corpses polluted the air. Renard wrote that "one sees nothing but gibbets and hanged men"—a warning to citizens of the cost of rebellion.[3]

Yet in the midst of this wave of retribution there was clemency too. As the London diarist Henry Machyn recorded, some of "the Kent men went to the court with halters about their necks and bound with cords," walking two by two through London to Westminster; the "poorer prisoners knelt down in the mire, and there the Queen's grace looked out over the gate and gave them all pardon and they cried out 'God save Queen Mary!' as they went."[4] Mary's victory was secure, the defeat and humiliation of the rebels total. The public spectacle of reconciliation underscored the scale of her triumph.

FIVE DAYS AFTER Wyatt's surrender, Lady Jane Grey and her husband were put to death. Although neither Jane nor Guildford Dudley had taken part in Wyatt's rebellion, they were now too great a threat to live. Both had been found guilty of high treason and condemned in November the previous year, but then Mary had protested Jane's innocence and maintained that her conscience would not permit her to have Jane put to death.[5] Now the involvement of Jane's father, the duke of Suffolk, who was also to be executed, sealed his daughter's fate.

At ten o'clock on Monday, February 12, Guildford Dudley was beheaded on Tower Hill. The seventeen-year-old Lady Jane watched as her husband departed from his prison in the Beauchamp Tower for the scaffold and then afterward as "his carcass, thrown into a cart and his head in a cloth," was brought back for burial in the chapel in the Tower precinct. It was, as the London chronicler described, "a sight to her no less than death."[6] An hour later, Jane was collected by Sir John Brydges, lieutenant of the Tower, and, dressed in black, led out to the scaffold on Tower Green. She prayed as she went. Two gentlewomen accompanied her, both weeping as they approached the gallows.

At the block Jane addressed the crowd before her: "Good people, I am hither to die, and by a law I am condemned to the same." She confessed her guilt for her part in Northumberland's attempted coup but denied her involvement in Wyatt's rebellion, claiming to be "innocent before God, and the face of you, good Christian people, this day." After removing her headdress, gloves, and gown, she bent down, begging the executioner to "despatch me quickly," and asking him "Will you take [my head] before I lay me down?" The hangman answered, "No, madame." After tying a handkerchief around her eyes, she groped for the block. Panicking, she called out, "What shall I do? Where is it?" Taking pity on the young woman, one of the bystanders led her to it. She laid her head on the block and said, "Lord, into thy hands I commend my spirit." The ax fell; with one sweep her head was removed.[7]

AS THE EXECUTIONS continued, attention turned to Elizabeth, in whose name the rebels had acted. On January 26, the day after Wyatt had raised his standard at Rochester, Mary had written to her sister, requesting that she come to court:

> *Right dear and entirely beloved sister,*
>
> *We greet you well. And where certain evil-disposed persons, minding more the satisfaction of their own malicious and seditious minds, than their duty of allegiance towards us, have of late foully spread divers lewd and untrue rumours . . . do travail to induce our good and loving subjects to an unnatural rebellion against God, Us and the Tranquillity of the realm, we, tending the surety of your person, which might chance to be in some peril, if any sudden tumult should arise where you now be, or about Donnington, whither as we understand, you are minded shortly to remove, do therefore think expedient you should put yourself in good readiness, with all convenient speed, to make your repair hither to us . . .*
>
> *Your loving sister, Mary the Queen.*[8]

Elizabeth had excused herself from the queen's summons, citing ill health. Now, with the rebellion quashed, the government acted. On February 9, three councillors were sent to Elizabeth's residence at Ashridge in Hertfordshire, charged with bringing her to court. The two royal doctors who had been sent ahead to report on her condition concluded that she was fit to be moved, despite her protestations. Three days later she left Ashridge, bound for London.[9] On the same day, February 12, Edward Courtenay, the man the rebels had hoped to place on the throne with Elizabeth, was taken to the Tower as a prisoner.

After a slow journey to London, which took eleven rather than the five days planned due to Elizabeth's apparent illness, she arrived in the city in an open litter, dressed in white to proclaim her innocence. From Smithfield and Fleet Street she proceeded to Whitehall, passing the gallows and city gates decorated with severed heads and dismembered corpses, and followed by great crowds of people. A hundred horsemen in velvet coats rode in front of her; another hundred behind in scarlet cloth trimmed with velvet.[10] Renard wrote, "She had her litter opened to show herself to the people, and her pale face kept a proud, haughty expression in order to mask her vexation."[11]

Upon her arrival at Whitehall, Mary refused to see her. She was lodged in a remote and secure part of the palace, adjacent to the Privy Gardens, from which neither she nor her servants could go out without passing through the Guard. Renard made clear what he thought should happen to Elizabeth: "The Queen is advised to send her to the Tower, since she is accused by Wyatt, named in the letters of the French ambassador, suspected by her own councillors, and it is certain that the enterprise was undertaken in her favour . . . if now that the occasion offers, they do not punish her and Courtenay, the Queen will never be secure."[12]

Meanwhile, as more leaders of the rebellion were arrested and questioned, the evidence against Elizabeth mounted. It emerged that Sir James Croft had stopped at Ashridge on his way to raise the Marches and that he and Wyatt had advised Elizabeth to move to Donnington, her castle two miles north of Newbury. Her servant Sir William St. Loe, who had been sent with a letter to Wyatt, was subsequently found with two of the rebel leaders at Tonbridge. Equally incriminating was the fact that a copy of Elizabeth's letter excusing herself from the queen's summons to court had been found in the seized dispatches of the French ambassador, Noailles. Elizabeth had, at the very least, been in contact with the conspirators, though as yet there was no evidence that she had approved of their designs or known of their plan. In the Tower, Gardiner pressed Wyatt to confess concerning Elizabeth, but the rebel leader would disclose nothing. At his trial, Wyatt admitted only that he had sent her a letter advising her to get as far away from London as she could, to which she had replied, though not in writing.

It was the flimsiest of evidence, but for the Council it was enough. On Friday, March 16, Elizabeth was formally charged with involvement in Wyatt and Carew's conspiracies. The following day, she would be imprisoned as a suspected traitor.

WHEN THE MARQUESS of Winchester and the earl of Sussex arrived to take Elizabeth by barge to the Tower, she begged to be given more time and the opportunity to write to Mary, a request the commissioners granted.[13] Addressed "To the Queen," her letter sought to secure her freedom and save her life:

> If any ever did try this old saying—that a King's word was more than another man's oath—I most humbly beseech your Majesty to verify it in me, and to remember your last promise and my last demand: that I be not condemned without answer and due proof: which it seems that now I am, for that without cause provided I am by your Council from you commanded to go unto the Tower; a place more wonted for a false traitor, than a true subject. . . . I never practiced, counselled or consented to any thing that might be prejudicial to your person any way, or dangerous to the state by any mean. And therefore I humbly beseech your Majesty to let me answer afore your self, and not suffer me to trust to your councillors . . .
>
> Yet I pray God, as evil persuasion persuade not one sister against the other; and all for that have heard false report, and not hearken to the truth known. Therefore once again, with humbleness of my heart because I am not suffered to bow the knees of my body, I humbly crave to speak with your highness.

More than half of her second sheet of paper was left blank; she scored it with diagonal lines so that no words could be added and attributed to her, and then she added a final appeal:

> I humbly crave but only one word of answer from yourself, Your Highness's most faithful subject that hath been from the beginning and will be to my end, Elizabeth.[14]

By the time she had finished her plea, the tide had risen and it was too late to depart. Her imprisonment would have to wait for the following day. Mary raged at Sussex and Winchester for granting her permission to write: "They would never have dared to do such a thing in her father's lifetime," and she "only wished he might come to life again for a month."[15]

At nine the following morning, Palm Sunday, Elizabeth was conducted downstream to the Tower, the place where her mother had met her death. At first Elizabeth refused to land at Traitor's Gate, saying she was not a traitor but came "as true a woman to the Queen's majesty as any is now living, and thereon will I take my death."[16] She was given no choice and entered the Tower across the drawbridge, passing the scaffold on which Lady Jane Grey had been executed. She was taken to the royal palace within the Tower precinct, where the councillors left her, turning the keys in the door as they went.[17]

Days later, Elizabeth was formally examined by the Council. Questioned as to her contact with Sir James Croft and her proposed move to Donnington, Elizabeth stalled, saying "she did not well remember any such house," but then declared, "Indeed, I do now remember that I have such a place, but I never lay in it in all my life. And as for any that hath moved me thereunto, I do not remember." When Croft was brought before her, Elizabeth recovered her memory: "And as concerning my going unto Donnington Castle, I do remember that Mr Hoby and mine officers and you Sir James Croft, had such talk," but, she added defiantly, "what is that to the purpose my lords, but that I may go to mine houses at all times?"[18]

On April 3, Renard relayed to the emperor the queen's assurances that "fresh proof is coming up against her [Elizabeth] every day, and there are several witnesses to assert that she had gathered together stores and weapons in order to rise with the rest and fortify a house in the country [Donnington] whither she had been sending her supplies."[19] In her first Parliament, Mary had restored the ancient constitutional law by which overt or spoken acts of treason had to be proved before any English person could be convicted as a traitor. Mary could not convict Elizabeth on the evidence of intercepted letters because they were written in cipher and could be forgeries. She told Renard that she and her Council were laboring to discern the truth but insisted that the law must be maintained.

WYATT WENT TO the block on Tower Hill on April 11. Upon the scaffold, he addressed the crowd: "Whereas it is said and whistled abroad, that I should accuse my lady Elizabeth's grace and my lord Courteney; it is not so, good people . . . as I have declared no less to the Queens Council."[20] Having made his confession, he knelt down upon the straw and laid his head on the block. He then sat up again to tie the handkerchief around his eyes, raised his hands, and then returned to the block. At one stroke the hangman beheaded him. His corpse was taken to Newgate to be parboiled, after which it was cut into four pieces and each quarter displayed in a different part of the city.[21] His head, placed on top of the gibbet at St. James's, was stolen within a week.

The day after his execution, a group of councillors visited Elizabeth in the Tower.[22] Despite Wyatt's exoneration of her, pressure remained on the princess to admit her guilt. Mary still refused to proceed against her sister with insufficient evidence. Finally with Elizabeth maintaining her innocence, the decision was made to move her to Woodstock, a remote country house in Oxfordshire, "until such time as certain matters touching her case which be not yet cleared may be thoroughly tried and examined." Here she would be placed in the custody of Sir Henry Bedingfield, a Catholic gentleman of proven loyalty whose father had been steward to Katherine of Aragon during her last days at Kimbolton.[23] On May 19, Elizabeth left the Tower for Woodstock. As Mary stated in her instructions to Bedingfield, she was to be "safely looked unto for the safeguard of her person, having nevertheless regard to her. In such good and honourable sort as may be agreeable to our honour and her estate and degree."[24] It was an important caveat, one that Mary had not been afforded during her confinement in the infant Elizabeth's household at Hatfield.

Elizabeth would spend the next eleven months under house arrest. As Don Juan Hurtado de Mendoza, a Spanish noble, surmised to the bishop of Arras, "It was indispensable to throw the Lady Elizabeth into prison, and it is considered that she will have to be executed, as while she lives it will be very difficult to make the Prince's entry here safe, or accomplish anything of promise."[25]

CHAPTER 47

SOLE QUEEN

∴

On the word of a Queen I assure you, that if the marriage appear not before the court of Parliament, nobility and commons, for the singular benefit of the whole realm, then I will abstain—not only from this, but from any other.[1]

THIS WAS MARY'S PROMISE, MADE AT THE GUILDHALL AS WYATT threatened London. She would submit treaty to "the people" for ratification—a step her male predecessors had never taken. As Parliament prepared to meet in the days after the rebellion, such was the climate of fear and uncertainty that it was initially proposed that Parliament meet in Oxford. When it did meet, in London, Mary was not present.[2] In his opening address on April 5, Gardiner proceeded to make the case for the marriage treaty:

> whereas they [the conspirators] had said that his Highness wished to conquer the kingdom, in reality the kingdom was conquering Philip and his dominions . . . therefore trusted that they would not offer any opposition but rather render their humble thanks to the Queen for her affection and show their gratitude by deeds.[3]

In spite of their fears, both houses ratified the marriage treaty within ten days of Parliament's opening. Renard wrote a triumphant letter, mocking "the heretics and French who hoped there would be violent dissent."[4]

To secure English acceptance of the alliance, the emperor had conceded highly favorable terms. Although Philip was granted the right to enjoy the style and name of king of England, the treaty denied him regal power and limited his involvement to assisting the queen in the administration of her realm insofar as the "rights, laws, privileges and customs" of both kingdoms permitted.

Should Mary die before Philip, he would have no further claim to authority in England. The succession to the English crown was limited to Mary's right of inheritance, and only the children from their marriage might succeed them. Don Carlos, Philip's existing heir, did not have a claim. No foreign office holders could be introduced into English government, and England would not be involved in Habsburg wars, it being stated explicitly that England was not to be drawn into the wars between Emperor Charles V and Henry II, the king of France.

In the first draft of the marriage settlement, Philip had only to acknowledge that Mary was not bound to offer any more assistance in the Habsburg-Valois struggle than promised in two treaties signed by Henry VIII some ten years earlier. But at the last moment Gardiner inserted an additional clause stating that England "by occasion of this matrimony, shall not directly or indirectly be entangled with the war that now is betwixt Charles and the French King." Moreover, Philip shall "see the peace between the said realms of France and England observed, and shall give no cause of any breach."[5]

The treaty specifically sought to separate Mary as queen of England from Mary, Philip's spouse, so as to underline that her power and status would not be diminished by the marriage. Mary was to be "sole Queen." The act ratifying the treaty stipulated,

> that your Majesty as our only Queen, shall and may, solely use, have, and enjoy the Crown and Sovereignty of, and over your Realms, Dominions, and Subjects . . . in such sole and only estate, and in as large and ample manner and form . . . after the hitheration of the said marriage, and at all times during the same . . .

It was an attempt to address concerns about the status of a married queen regnant, given the traditional subjugation of women. As Renard reported on January 7, the pretext for summoning Parliament had been "furnished by two English lawyers who have been prompted to say that by English law, if his Highness marries the Queen, she loses her title to the crown and his Highness becomes King."[6] There were no precedents, and Wyatt's rebellion had been inspired by fears that Mary's marriage would lead to enslavement by the Spanish. But at the formal betrothal in March, Mary had once more pledged her commitment to the national interest:

> The Queen knelt down and called God to witness that she had not consented to marry out of carnal affection or desire, not for any motive except her kingdom's honour and prosperity and the repose and tranquillity of her subjects, and that her firm resolve was to keep the marriage and oath she had made to the crown.[7]

While the marriage treaty prescribed Mary's independent sovereignty, another act passed in the same Parliament, the Act Concerning Regal Power, stated that Mary held her regal power as fully and absolutely as her male predecessors had. According to an account written twenty-five years later by Sir William Fleetwood, recorder of London, this additional act was passed after a conspiracy that proposed that Mary "take upon the title of Conqueror" so that she might "at her pleasure reform the monasteries, advance her friends, suppress her enemies, establish religion, and do what she like."[8] Given the unprecedented nature of female rule, there was no existing statute, including Magna Carta, that limited the authority of a queen.

Fleetwood described how, having been presented with the proposal, Mary read it "over and over again, and the more she read and thought of it, the more she misliked it," believing it a breach of her coronation oath, by which she had promised "to keep to the people of England and others your realms and dominions the laws and liberties of this realm." She then "cast it into the fire," after which the chancellor "devised the said Act of Parliament."[9]

To prevent confusion among "malicious and ignorant persons," the bill for the act, drafted by Gardiner, declared that "the regal power of this realm is in the Queen's Majesty as fully and absolutely as ever it was in any of her most noble progenitors Kings of this realm." It was passed in the Commons and two days later in the Lords.

> Be it declared . . . that the Law of this Realm is and ever hath been and ought to be understood, that the Kingly or Regal office of the Realm . . . being invested either in male or female, are, and be, and ought to be, as fully, absolutely and entirely deemed, judged, accepted, invested and taken in the one as in the other.[10]

The act clarified the ambiguity of Mary's status as queen regnant. By throwing the proposal into the fire, Mary had declared her intent to be a parliamentary queen. Her sovereignty would be dependent on and prescribed by statute law. Thus Mary had chosen to follow the precedents of her male progenitors. The inauguration of female sovereignty could not have been placed in safer hands.

As Mary made her speech at Parliament's dissolution in May, she was interrupted five or six times by shouts of "God save the Queen!" as most of those present were "moved to tears by her eloquence and virtue."[11]

MARY NOW WROTE to Philip, informing him that Parliament had ratified the marriage articles and expressing her "entire confidence that his coming to England should be safe and agreeable" to him.[12]

Though Philip had pledged to be an obedient son and follow his father's will, the marriage held few personal attractions for him. Mary was eleven years his senior, and he referred to her as his *cara y muy amada tía* (dear and beloved aunt). Further, he disavowed the treaty, declaring that he was not bound by an agreement that had been reached without his knowledge. He would sign it so that the marriage could take place, "but by no means in order to bind himself or his heirs to observe the articles, especially any that might burden his conscience."[13]

As the prince prepared to leave La Coruña for England, Charles wrote to the duke of Alva, who was accompanying him, "For the love of God, see to it that my son behaves in the right manner; for otherwise I tell you I would rather never have taken the matter in hand at all."[14]

CHAPTER 48

GOOD NIGHT, MY LORDS ALL

With parliament dissolved and the marriage treaty ratified, preparations began in earnest for Philip's arrival and the royal wedding, which was to take place at Winchester Cathedral, the episcopal seat of Bishop Gardiner. The gallows scattered throughout the City of London, where the condemned rebels had hung, were taken down; the cross at Cheapside was repaired and a scaffold erected for the celebrations to welcome the prince.[1]

Mary had commissioned a suit to be made for Philip's entry into Winchester and for the wedding itself, together with hangings for the royal bed embroidered with the arms and devices of Spain and England. Some 350 Englishmen had been selected as Philip's household officers, among them individuals who had supported Mary in July 1553, such as John Huddleston. All had been assembled before the chamberlain of the royal household and asked to swear an oath of allegiance, and they, together with a hundred archers who were to join the guard Philip brought with him, now traveled to Southampton to await the prince's long-anticipated arrival.[2]

Finally, on June 16, Mary and her entire court set out from Richmond for Winchester and there took up residence in the Episcopal Palace of Bishop's Waltham, which had been specially prepared ahead of her arrival.

The decision to hold the wedding ceremony outside London had been driven by fears of disorder in the capital. Rumor and discontent were rife. Seditious prophecies were published in London to the effect that Philip's delay in embarking for England was caused by his reluctance to marry Mary and that the Spaniards would not let him come.[3]

As Renard reported on July 9, "the officers appointed for his Highness' service have been living at Southampton at great expense for a long time and are now beginning to leave that place, speaking strangely of his Highness."[4] Two aldermen in the City of London were ordered to keep watch every night and one or two constables until three or four in the morning for fear of "some disturbances among the citizens in detestation of the Spanish affair."[5] Pensions were distributed by the imperial ambassador to "render his Highness's coming secure," and the sum of 5,000 crowns was distributed among a number of gentlemen and officers who had served the queen in the last rebellion, "in order to keep them well disposed." In the hope that all would go smoothly, Simon Renard drew up guidelines for Philip, suggesting how he might ingratiate himself with the English people:

Notes for Prince Philip's Guidance in England

Item: when his Highness enters the kingdom, he will be well-advised to caress the nobility and be affable, show himself often to the people, prove that he wishes to take no share in the administration, but leave it all to the Council and urge them to be diligent in the exercise of justice, caress the nobles, talk with them on occasion, take them out to hunt with them. If he does so, there is no doubt whatever that they will not only love his Highness, but will adore him.

Item: it will be well to show a benign countenance to the people and lead them to look for kindness, justice and liberty.

Item: as his Highness knows no English it will be well to select an interpreter and have him among his attendants so that he may converse with the English. And let his Highness endeavour to learn a few words in order to be able to salute them. Then, as time goes on, he will be able to decide what he had better do in order to achieve his purposes.

> *Item:* no soldiers from the ships must be allowed to land here, in order not to confirm the suspicion inculcated by the French, that his Highness wishes to conquer the realm by force.[6]

At three in the afternoon of Thursday, July 19, Philip finally landed at Southampton. A great throng of nobles and gentry met his ship, and the earl of Arundel presented him with the Order of the Garter, which was buckled just below his knee, and a mantle of blue velvet fringed with gold and pearl. The prince was rowed ashore the following day in a magnificent state barge covered with white and black cloth, furnished with fine carpets and a chair of brocade, and manned by twenty men dressed in the queen's livery of green and white.[7] An English household of 350, headed by the earl of Arundel, had been made ready for the prince, but Philip had brought his own, immediately causing tension between the English and the Spaniards.

In London the populace marked the Spanish prince's safe arrival with officially organized bonfires and feasting, as well as "ringing and playing." Two days later, processions, Te Deums, and more ringing of bells were ordered in every parish of London.[8] Philip sent the count of Egmont to Winchester to "inform the Queen of his arrival, visit her, tell her of his health and assure her of his affection." The next day Gardiner arrived with a large diamond as a gift from Mary. Philip reciprocated with a diamond of his own, though unfortunately it was noted to have been "considerably smaller." Mary also sent "a very richly wrought poignard, studded with gems, and two robes, one of them as rich and beautiful as could be imagined."[9] Mary issued a proclamation summoning all those who were to attend the wedding:

> Forasmuch as (God be thanked) the Prince of Spain is now safely arrived and come unto this the Queen's highness' realm of England, her grace's pleasure therefore is that all noblemen and gentlemen, ladies and others appointed by her Majesty to attend upon her grace against the time of her marriage, do with all convenient speed make their repair to her grace's city of Winchester, there to give their attendance upon her highness.[10]

At the Church of the Holy Rood in Southampton, which had been lavishly adorned for his visit with brocade, gold fabrics, and embroidered canopies, Philip heard Mass and gave thanks for his safe voyage. Later, at the house that had been prepared for him, he addressed the English councillors who had gathered there. He had come to live among them, he said, not as a foreigner but as a native Englishman, not for want of men or money but because God had called him to marry their virtuous sovereign. He thanked them for their expressions of faith and loyalty and promised that they would find him a grateful and loving prince. Then, turning to the Spanish nobles in his entourage, he expressed his hope that, as they remained in England, they would follow his example and conform to the customs of the country. As he finished speaking, he raised to his lips a flagon of English ale and drank farewell to the men who were gathered before him.[11]

Having spent the weekend resting in Southampton, Philip set out on the twelve-mile ride to Winchester, through pouring rain, escorted by a guard of a hundred men wearing his livery. About six in the evening, Philip entered Winchester, mounted on a white horse and wearing a rich coat of cloth of gold, a feather in his hat and dressed in a suit embroidered with gold, "the English and Spanish nobles, one with another, riding before him."[12] At the cathedral, amid a fanfare of trumpets and bell ringing, the bishop of Winchester, the lord chancellor, and five other bishops greeted him. After praying in front of the sacrament Philip was taken by torchlight to his lodging in the dean's house to prepare for his first meeting with the queen.

At about ten in the evening, Philip walked through the gardens to the Bishop's Palace, where he and Mary were to meet. Surrounded by three or four councillors and her ladies-in-waiting, Mary came out to the door of her chamber and "very lovingly, yea, and most joyfully received him." She was dressed in a gown of black velvet over an underskirt of frosted silver adorned with magnificent jewels. Hand in hand they sat down and for about half an hour remained in pleasant conversation. Philip spoke in Spanish, Mary replied in French. Philip then rose and kissed the other ladies present, and his attendants kissed the queen's hand. As he departed, he said, "Good night, my lords all," in English, as Mary had just taught him to do.[13]

At three the following afternoon, the prince made his first public visit to the queen. Accompanied by a number of English nobles, he walked on his own behind them, "in a cloak of black cloth embroidered with silver, and a pair of silver hose." Entering the courtyard of the Bishop's Palace to the sound of music, he passed into the Great Hall, where Mary received him in the presence of the people. Taking him by the hand, she led him into the Presence Chamber, and there they talked for a quarter of an hour under the cloth of estate, "to the great comfort and rejoicing of the beholders." Philip took his leave and went to Evensong at the cathedral, returning afterward to his lodging alone.

According to the Scotsman John Elder, who was present at court, Philip struck observers in England as the image of a true king:

> Of visage he is well favoured . . . with a broad forehead, and grey eyes, straight-nosed and manly countenance. From the forehead to the point of his chin, his face groweth small. His pace is princely, and gate [gait] so straight and upright, as he loseth no inch of his height; with a yellow head and yellow beard. And thus to conclude, he is so well proportioned as nature cannot work a more perfect pattern; and, as I have learned, of the age of 28 years; whose majesty I judge to be of a stout stomach, pregnant-witted and of most gentle nature.[14]

It was a marriage that promised much, though it remained to be seen whether Mary's hopes for both a political partnership and a personal union could be realized.

PART FOUR

A King's Wife

CHAPTER 49

WITH THIS RING I THEE WED

∴

PHILIP AND MARY WERE MARRIED ON JULY 25, 1554, THE FEAST OF Saint James, the patron saint of Spain. It was a marriage intended to recast England in Europe and breed a new line of Catholic princes. And it was the first wedding of a reigning English queen.

The ceremony was one of unparalleled pomp and extravagance. Winchester Cathedral was decorated resplendently with banners, standards, streamers, and tapestries, all emblazoned with Spanish regalia. A raised wooden platform, covered with carpets, reached from the main door of the church to the choir, at its center a dais in the shape of an octagon, the setting of the solemnization of the marriage.[1] The arrangements for the wedding were based on those of Mary's mother's marriage to Prince Arthur. The ceremony was to be traditional and performed in Latin by Bishop Gardiner, assisted by five other bishops, all attired in copes and miters.

At about eleven in the morning, Philip arrived at the cathedral, accompanied by many Spanish knights and wearing a doublet and hose of white satin, embroidered with jewels, and a mantle of cloth of gold—which Mary had sent him—ornamented with jewels and precious stones, together with the ribbon of the Order of the Garter that had been presented to him at Southampton.[2] Half an hour later Mary arrived, dressed in a gown of white satin and a mantle to match Philip's, which "blazed with jewels to an extent that dazzled those who gazed upon her." On her breast she wore a piece of jewelry called "La Peregrina," set with two diamonds, one the gift from Philip in June, the other from Charles V, which had previously been set in the ring given to the Portuguese princess Isabella, whom he had married after breaking off his betrothal to Mary in 1525. Mary's sword was borne before her—a sign that she was monarch—by the earl of Derby and the marquess of Winchester. The lord chamberlain, Sir John Gage, carried her train.

Once the full party had assembled, Don Juan Figueroa, regent of Naples, handed to Gardiner two pronouncements by which Charles V bestowed on his son the Kingdom of Naples and the Duchy of Milan. Gardiner at once declared to the assembly, "it was thought the Queen's Majesty should marry but with a prince; now it was manifested that she should marry with a King."[3] Then the banns were bidden in Latin and in English, with Gardiner declaring that if "any man knoweth of any lawful impediment between the two parties, that they should not go together according to the contract concluded between the both realms, then they should come forth, and they should be heard."

According to the official account recorded by the English heralds, Mary was given to Philip "in the name of the whole realm" by the marquess of Winchester and the earls of Derby, Bedford, and Pembroke.[4] The pair exchanged vows in Latin and English: "This gold and silver I thee give: with my body I thee worship; and withal my worldly Goods I thee endow."[5] Mary then pledged "from henceforth to be compliant and obedient . . . as much in mind as in body"—in direct contradiction to Gardiner's insistence that in the marriage contract Philip must undertake to marry as a subject.[6] And whereas Mary endowed Philip with all her "worldly goods," Philip merely endowed Mary with all his "moveable goods."[7] Her wedding ring "was a round hoop of gold without any stone, which was her desire, for she said she would be married as maidens were in the old time, and so she was."[8]

Philip and Mary then proceeded hand in hand under a rich canopy borne by six knights. At the choir, a psalm was sung while the king and queen knelt before the altar, a taper in front of each of them. They then retired to their canopied seats on the raised dais to listen to the Gospels, reemerging to kneel before the altar for Mass. The king of arms solemnly proclaimed Philip and Mary king and queen, declaring their titles and style:

> Philip and Mary by the grace of God King and Queen of England, France, Naples, Jerusalem, and Ireland; Defenders of

the Faith; Princes of Spain and Sicily; Archdukes of Austria; Dukes of Milan, Burgundy and Brabant; Counts of Habsburg, Flanders and Tyrol.[9]

Their joint style had been difficult to agree on. The English Council had strongly resisted Philip being named before the Queen, but he had insisted "that no law, human or divine, nor his Highness's prestige and good name, would allow him to be named second, especially as the treaties and acts of Parliament gave him the title of King of England."[10] England was now part of a much larger European empire.

AT THREE IN THE afternoon, to the blare of trumpets and cheers of the crowd, the royal couple walked hand in hand—the sword of state borne before the king by the earl of Pembroke—under a canopy back to the queen's palace for the wedding banquet.[11]

Philip and Mary took their places at a raised table at the head of four long tables where the Spanish and English nobility were seated. Mary was served on gold plates, Philip on silver to indicate his subordinate status. Musicians played at the end of the hall throughout the banquet. When the feast was over and the queen had drunk a cup of wine to the health and honor of the guests, the party moved to an adjoining hall for dancing and entertainment. There was "such triumphing, banqueting, singing, masking and dancing, as was never seen in England heretofore, by the report of all men."[12] The king then retired to his chamber, the queen to hers, where they dined in private.

The evening ended with the blessing of the marriage bed. As one of Philip's gentlemen wrote soon after, "the Bishop of Winchester blessed the bed, and they remained alone. What happened that night only they know. If they give us a son, our joy will be complete."[13]

CHAPTER 50

MUTUAL SATISFACTION

∴

ON AUGUST 4, THE BISHOP OF ARRAS WROTE TO RENARD, EXPRESSING his "incredible content, that the marriage for which both had worked, for so long, was accomplished, to the mutual satisfaction of both parties" and that the king "was behaving in every way so well, that he had gained the approbation of all in England." He foresaw many difficulties ahead but hoped that with gentleness and benignity they might not prove too great.[1]

After ten days of honeymooning in Winchester, the royal couple began their journey back to London, stopping en route at Windsor on the third for Philip's installation as knight and cosovereign of the Order of the Garter.[2] The earl of Arundel once again deputized for Mary, investing Philip with the robe, while Mary placed the collar around his neck.

On the eleventh they moved to Richmond as final preparations were made for their formal entry into the capital.

AT TWO O'CLOCK on Saturday, August 18, Philip and Mary were met at Southwark by the lord mayor and aldermen and crossed into the city by London Bridge. Behind them followed the lords of the Council, foreign ambassadors, and the nobility of England and Spain, all on horseback, two by two in rank order. The lord mayor of London knelt down before them and gave the queen the mace, a symbol of power and authority in the city. The king and queen remounted their horses and, with two swords of state before them, rode into the city.

Some weeks before, Mary had issued a proclamation ordering all her subjects to extend "courtesy, friendly and gentle entertainment" to the Spaniards, "without either by outward deeds, taunting words, or unseemly countenance" giving any insult to the visitors. Londoners were in a benevolent mood, and there was little ill feeling displayed toward the new king. The city had been decorated with splendid pageants for the occasion. At London Bridge two vast figurines greeted the royal couple. The mythical giants Corineus Britannus and Gogamogog Albionus, warriors from Geoffrey of Monmouth's twelfth-century history of Britain, held between them a tablet on which were written verses lavishing praise on Philip and giving thanks for his safe arrival:

O noble Prince sole hope of Caesar's side
By God appointed all the world to guide
Right heartily welcome art thou to our land
The archer Britayne yeldeth thee her hand,

And noble England openeth her bosom
Of hearty affection for to bid thee welcome.
But chiefly London doth her love vouchsafe,
Rejoycing that her Philip is come safe.[3]

The king and queen rode on into Gracechurch Street, where Henry VIII was portrayed, a scepter in one hand and a book in the other, upon which was written *"Verbum Dei,"* "the Word of God." It was the image that had appeared on the title page of the Great Bible of 1539, the first authorized version in English, which had shown Henry distributing the English Bible to his subjects—anathema to Catholics, who believed that scripture in the vernacular undermined the sanctity of its meaning. Such a provocative image of Protestant triumphalism was hardly what might be expected in a pageant welcoming a Catholic king and queen. After Mary and Philip had passed, Gardiner threatened the painter, Richard Grafton, with imprisonment in the Fleet. Grafton responded that he thought he had done well, declaring, "If I had known the same had been against your lordship's pleasure, I would not have so have made him." Grafton was ordered to paint out the book and replace it with a pair of gloves.[4]

At the end of Gracechurch Street stood a triumphal arch adorned with statues and paintings, created by the merchants of the steelyard. On the left stood the figure of a woman, Hispania, supporting a castle; on the right stood Britannia with the arms of England. The pageant was decorated with pictures of battles on land and sea and the insignia of England and Spain. At the top of the arch was a mechanical image of King Philip on horseback and the inscription "In honour of worthy Philip the fortunate and most mighty Prince of Spain, most earnestly wished for."[5] At Cornhill, another pageant, surmounted with images of the royal couple, featured representations of four noble Philips from history: Philip, king of Macedonia, father of Alexander the Great; Philip, the Roman emperor; Philip the Bold; and Philip the Good of Burgundy. The third pageant, in Cheap, depicted Orpheus and the nine Muses. Near them men and children, dressed like wild beasts, lions, wolves, bears, and foxes, danced and leaped, this spectacle "pleasing their majesties very well."[6]

The royal couple moved on to the little conduit at the west end of Cheap for the fourth pageant. Described as "the most excellent pageant of all," it showed Philip and Mary's shared genealogy from Edward III of England. Under a great tree was an old man, signifying Edward III, lying on his side with a white long beard, a closed crown on his head, and scepter and ball in his hands. On top of the tree the queen was shown on the right and the king to the left, and underneath letters of gold read:

England, if thou delight in ancient men
Whose glorious acts thy fame abroad did blaze
Both Mary and Philip their offspring ought thou then
With all thy heart to love and to embrace
Which both descended of one ancient line
It hath pleased God by marriage to combine.[7]

Philip was presented not as the Spaniard of popular fears but as an Englishman. Mary's own Spanish lineage was also ignored, and she was depicted as being wholly English. Their marriage was cast as one of concord and reconciliation: being both descended from John of Gaunt, duke of Lancaster, their marriage had united the divided Lancastrian house. The pageant highlighted the fact that Katherine of

Aragon, Charles V, and Philip could be traced back to Edward III through John of Gaunt; while Roman Catholicism, which for twenty years had been reviled as foreign and traitorous, was represented as the true patriotic faith of England.

At St. Paul's a sumptuously dressed scholar presented the king and queen with a book, while at Fleet Street, Mary and Philip witnessed the final pageant. Set around a castle decorated with the "arms of all Christian realms," four characters—a king and a queen (Philip and Mary), Justice bearing a sword, and Equality holding a pair of balances—were each crowned by a figure that descended on a rope from the top of the pageant. An inscription below read:

When a man is gentle, just and true,
With virtuous gifts fulfilled plenteously
If Wisdom then him with her crown endure
He govern shall the whole world prosperously.
And sith we know thee Philip to be such,
While thou shalt reign we think us happy much.[8]

TWO WEEKS LATER, Philip wrote to his sister, the princess regent of Spain, telling her, "We have visited London, where I was received with universal signs of love and joy."[9] But despite the welcoming pageantry, anti-Spanish feeling was never far away.

On August 20, two days after the celebrations, the city authorities were ordered to take the pageants down for fear of vandalism.[10] At the time of the royal couple's entry into London, the Tower chronicler described how "there was so many Spaniards in London that a man should have met in the streets for one Englishman above four Spaniards, to the great discomfort of the English nation."[11] And Renard told the emperor, "They, the English, loudly proclaim that they are going to be enslaved, for the Queen is a Spanish woman at heart and thinks nothing of Englishmen, but only of Spaniards and bishops."[12] It was going to be difficult, he told Charles, to reconcile Spaniards with Englishmen. The language was an obstacle, the English hated foreigners, "and the slightest altercation might be enough to bring about a very dangerous situation."[13]

CHAPTER 51

THE HAPPIEST COUPLE IN THE WORLD

He [the king] treats the Queen very kindly, and well knows how to pass over the fact that she is no good from the point of view of fleshy sensuality. He makes her so happy that the other day when they were alone she almost talked love-talk to him, and he replied in the same vein.[1]

—Ruy Gómez de Silva, prince of Éboli, to Charles's secretary, Francisco de Eraso, August 12, 1554

In a private letter to a friend, Ruy Gómez de Silva, a member of Philip's entourage, revealed a somewhat different view: "To speak frankly with you, it would take God himself to drink this cup . . . and the best one can say is that the King realises fully that the marriage was made for no fleshly consideration, but in order to cure the disorders of this country and to preserve the Low Countries."[2]

Philip had intended to stay in England for only a short time, though Mary was probably unaware of this. On the eve of his arrival in England, the French had defeated imperial forces at Marienburg, the gateway to the Netherlands. Brussels had looked vulnerable to French attack, and Philip had brought 4,000 troops to go on to the Netherlands. Charles had instructed Philip to take only a few of his servants ashore with him in England and, immediately after the marriage and having spent just six or eight days with his bride, to sail straight to Flanders.[3] But then the military situation improved, and the emperor decided to delay his son's journey to Flanders: "You had better stay where you are and be with the Queen, my daughter, busying yourself with the Government of England, settling affairs there and making yourself familiar with the people, which it is most important you do for present and future considerations."[4] Mary was delighted that Philip was to remain in England, and in a letter to her father-in-law she declared:

> I see a proof of your Majesty's watchful care for the realm's and my own interests, for which, and above all for having so far spared the person of the King, my husband, I most humbly thank you . . . always praying God so to inspire my subjects that they may realise the affection you bear this kingdom, and the honour and advantages you have conferred upon it by this marriage and alliance, which renders me happier than I can say, as I daily discover in my husband and your son, so many virtues and perfections that I constantly pray God to grant me grace to please him and behave in all things as befits one who is so deeply embounden to him.[5]

IN A LETTER to a friend in Salamanca, a Spanish courtier wrote of Philip's first months in England:

> Their Majesties are the happiest couple in the world, and more in love than words can say. His Highness never leaves her, and when they are on the road he is ever by her side, helping her to mount and dismount. They sometimes dine together in public, and go to mass together on holidays.

But, he continued:

> the Queen, however, is not at all beautiful: small, and rather flabby than fat, she is of white complexion and fair, and has no eyebrows. She is a perfect saint and dresses badly. All the women here wear petticoats of coloured cloth without admixture of silk, and above come coloured robes of damask, satin or velvet, very badly cut.

The dominant style at the English court and that favored by Mary was French. Her clothes were not to Spanish tastes, and, as the Spaniard added, neither were the English revelries:

> There are no distractions here except eating and drinking, the only variety they understand . . . there is plenty of beer here, and they drink more than would fill the Valladolid river. In the summer the ladies and gentlemen put sugar in their wine, with the result that there are great goings on in the palace.[6]

Philip's efforts to secure the goodwill of the English were being undermined by tensions between the Spanish household Philip had brought with him and the English entourage that had been prepared for his arrival. "The English hate the Spaniards worse than they hate the devil," wrote one of his household. "They rob us in town and on the road; and one ventures to stray two miles but they rob him; and a company of Englishmen have recently robbed and beaten over fifty Spaniards. The best of it is that the councillors know all about it and say not a word."[7]

Philip looked to resolve the issue by retaining the English in formal ceremonial positions, such as cupbearers, gentlemen waiters, and carvers, while Spaniards remained in his personal suite. But complaints and tensions continued. Philip would write to Francisco de Eraso, his father's secretary, of the embarrassment caused by the two households, "not so much on account of the expense as of the troubles it gave me." Of the English servants, Philip expressed major reservations: "They are accustomed to serving here in a very different manner from that observed at his Majesty's Court, and as you know I am not satisfied that they are good enough Catholics to be constantly about my person."[8]

By the beginning of September, Renard was reporting, "very few Englishmen are to be seen in his Highness's apartments."[9] Given the acrimony, a number of Spanish noblemen and gentlemen obtained permission to depart. As the Spanish correspondent put it, "we are all desiring to be off, with such longing that we think of Flanders as a paradise."[10]

On Sunday, November 25, Spanish courtiers staged a cane play—a *juego de cannas,* a joust in which canes replaced lances—before the queen and English noblemen at Whitehall. The king rode in red, everyone else in yellow, green, white, or blue, "with targets and canes in their hand, hurling rods one at another, and the trumpets in the same colours and drums made of kettles, and banners in the same colours."[11] It was a spectacular display of color and sporting prowess, but it did little to win over English hearts, as the Count Gian Tommaso Langosco da Stroppiana noted: "It left the spectators cold, except for the fine clothes of the players, and the English made fun of it."[12]

Months later, it emerged that the cane play had been the occasion of a treasonous conspiracy. A man named Edward Lewkner alleged that he had arranged with Sir Francis Verney and Captain Edward Turner to kill Philip and his Spanish attendants during the contest.[13] He claimed that more than three hundred people had been involved in the plot, which was to have been carried out in the third round of the tournament. But when only two rounds were staged, the plan could not be executed.[14]

DESPITE THE TREASONOUS plottings against him, Philip quickly began to appropriate the images of royalty. Substantial sums were spent on embroidered cloths of estate, badges, and heraldic devices decorated with the king's and queen's initials.[15] In September 1554, new coins were issued on which both Mary and Philip appeared in profile, "the double face."[16] The king's was pictured on the dominant left-hand side, the position hitherto reserved for the reigning monarch, with a single crown floating above them both. One pamphleteer complained that Philip was being turned into a "King of England indeed," his name appearing on proclamations and on charters and "on the coined money going abroad current."[17]

Before Mary's wedding, Stephen Gardiner had stipulated that English subjects be explicitly assured that after the marriage Philip would be "rather as a subject than otherwise; and that the Queen should rule all things as she doth now."[18] Yet two days after the wedding the Privy Council stipulated that "a note of all such matters of

Estate as should pass from hence should be made in Latin and Spanish from henceforth."

Mary also issued an instruction, written in her own hand, to the lord Privy Seal, "First to tell the King the whole state of the Realm with all things appertaining to the same, as much as you know to be true. Second to obey his commandment in all things" and to declare his opinion on any matter the king wished "as becometh a faithful counsellor to do."[19] The Spaniards' view of the marriage was quite different from that of the English. They believed that Philip would provide the male element lacking in Mary's monarchy: he would "make up for other matters which are impertinent to women."[20]

The focus of Philip's energies quickly became reconciliation with Rome. He petitioned the pope to augment Cardinal Pole's powers so that he might negotiate for a general settlement with regard to Church property.[21] Finally the pope was persuaded. "It would be far better," he agreed, "for all reasons human and divine, to abandon all the Church property [in England], rather than risk the shipwreck of this understanding."[22] Philip sent Renard to Flanders to reason with Pole, who agreed not to exercise any jurisdiction without the king and queen's consent.[23] On November 3, 1554, the Council consented to admitting Pole into the realm. Lord Paget and Sir Edward Hastings were sent to conduct him from the imperial court, and Parliament was summoned to repeal Pole's attainder and condemnation for treason.

England's imminent return to Roman Catholicism was a tremendous coup for the Habsburgs. As Renard wrote to the emperor:

> I thought it my duty to write at once to Your Majesty, well knowing that this long looked for miraculous event, so big with consequences of the greatest importance to Christendom, will give you great pleasure. . . . Your Majesty too well understands how great was the joy felt by the King [Philip] and all his court for it to be necessary that I should describe it. Indeed, he had good reason to render thanks to God that such fruit, fertile in the increase of authority for him, should already come of the match, encouraging us to hope that God means to incline the enemy's [France's] heart to the desire of lasting peace.[24]

A week later, the king and queen returned to Westminster Abbey for the opening of Parliament. According to Count Langosco da Stroppiana, the waiting crowds called out, "Oh how handsome the King is! . . . Oh! What a good husband he is! How honourably and lovingly he treats the Queen!"[25] At the abbey the king and queen knelt and kissed the cross. The new bishop of Lincoln, John White, preached an English sermon, which was then summarized in Latin. The text was from Jeremiah. It said that those who had separated from the Roman Church did not harbor thoughts of peace any more than those guilty of sedition or disobedience to the king and queen. In conclusion the bishop urged the "firm establishment of our true Catholic religion."[26]

CHAPTER 52

TO RECONCILE, NOT TO CONDEMN

A year has passed since I began to knock at the door of this royal house, and none has opened to me. King, if you ask, as those are wont to do who hear a knock at the door: who is there? I will reply, it is I, who, rather than consent that this house should be closed to her who now possesses it with you, preferred banishment and twenty years of exile. And if I speak thus, is it not a sufficient claim to be permitted to return home and to approach you?[1]

—Cardinal Pole to Philip,
September 1554

Since his appointment as papal legate on August 5, 1553, Cardinal Pole had been petitioning Mary to allow him to return to England. He had traveled as far as Brussels but had been prevented from going any farther as the emperor wanted to secure Philip's marriage to Mary before England embarked on the path of Catholic restoration.

Pole, however, argued that nothing should stand in the way of the Church's immediate and unconditional return to Rome.[2] He believed the queen's marriage to Philip was "even more universally odious than the cause of the religion," and Mary feared his hostility to it.[3] As the months passed and there was no sign of his zealous advice being heeded, the cardinal's letters to Mary became more and more strident. "It is imprudent and sacrilegious to say that matters of religion must be cleverly handled, and left until the throne is safely established," he wrote; "what greater neglect can there be . . . than by setting aside the honour of God to attend to other things, leaving religion to the end?"[4]

In many ways Pole and Mary were kindred spirits. Both had suffered for their faith and lived through years of isolation in fear of death. Pole had been in exile for much of his life; both had lost their mothers to Henry VIII's cruelty. But England had changed in his twenty-year-long exile, since Henry's break with Rome and the execution of his elder brother, Henry, Lord Montague, and his mother, Margaret Pole. Years of antipapal propaganda had left many English people hostile to the idea of a return of papal authority. A generation had grown up knowing only the king as head of the Church. Meanwhile, Church lands had fallen into secular hands and their "possessioners" were not prepared to give them up. Finally, though, with the Spanish marriage concluded and a compromise reached, Parliament repealed Pole's attainder for treason and the cardinal could return to England.

On November 20, some fifteen months after his appointment as legate, Pole landed at Dover. Two days later, he journeyed to London, accompanied by an ever-increasing train of English noblemen and councillors. With Londoners lining the banks of the Thames, Pole took to the river at Gravesend, his large silver cross, an emblem of his legatine authority, prominent in the state barge. At noon he arrived at Whitehall, where he was met on a landing stage by Philip. With the sword of state borne before them, the king and cardinal proceeded to the Presence Chamber, where the queen awaited them. Pole had not seen Mary since she was a young princess. He knelt in front of the queen; she "received him with great signs of respect and affection; both shed tears."[5]

A week after his arrival in England, Pole appeared before both Houses of Parliament at Whitehall. Having expressed his gratitude for the admission into the realm of a man hitherto "exiled and banished," he outlined the cause of his coming. The pope had, he claimed, "a special respect for their realm above all other." While others nations had been converted gradually, "this island the first of all islands, received the light of Christ's religion."

It was a spurious appeal to English nationalism, a providential version of history, intended to make Roman Catholicism suitably English. England was, in Pole's view, the chosen Catholic nation. God "by providence hath given this realm prerogative of nobility above other," and Mary was deemed its savior. "When all light of true religion seemed utterly extinct, as the churches defaced and altars overthrown . . . in a few remained the confession of Christ's faith, namely in the breast of the Queen's excellency." When people conspired against her and "policies were devised to disinherit her, and armed power prepared to destroy her . . . she being a virgin, helpless, naked and unarmed, prevailed, and had the victory over tyrants." Mary was the Virgin Queen who had restored the national religion.

With carefully chosen words Pole assured Parliament that his commission was "not one of prejudice to any person":

> I come not to destroy but to build. I come to reconcile, not to condemn. I come not to compel, but to call again. I come not to call anything in question already done, but my commission is of grace and clemency to such as will receive it, for touching all matters that be past, that shall be as things cast into the sea of forgetfulness.[6]

Two days later, a delegation from Parliament presented themselves at Whitehall, where Gardiner made their supplication:

> We the lords spiritual and temporal, and the commons of this present Parliament assembled, representing the whole body of the realm of England and dominions of the same, do declare ourselves very sorry and repentant of the schism and disobedience committed in this realm and the dominions of the same, against the said See Apostolic . . . that we may, as children repentant, be received into the bosom and unity of Christ's church. So as this noble realm, with all the members thereof, may in unity and perfect obedience to the See Apostolic.[7]

At five in the afternoon of Saint Andrew's Day, November 30, Pole was conducted in full pontifical robes from Lambeth Palace to Westminster. There, with the Lords and Commons and the king and queen kneeling before him in their robes of estate, he formally absolved the country from its years of schism:

> We, by apostolic authority given unto us by the most holy lord Pope Julius III, his Vice-regent on earth, do absolve and deliver you, and every [one] of you, with the whole Realm and the Dominions thereof, from all Heresy and Schism, and from all and every judgement, Censures and pains, for that cause incurred; & also so we do restore you again unto the unity of our Mother the holy Church . . . in the name of the Father, of the son and of the Holy Ghost.[8]

According to John Elder, it "moved a great number of the audience with sorrowful sighs and weeping tears to change their cheer." England had returned to the Catholic fold. It was a moment of high ceremony and emotion.

That evening Mary gave a banquet for the king and his gentlemen, and after supper there were dancing and masques. The king had that day shown "liberality to the ladies of the court, who were dressed in the gowns he had given them."[9] The news of England's return to the fold quickly reached Rome, whereupon the pope ordered processions, "giving thanks to God with great joy for the conversion of England to his Church."[10]

THE SUNDAY AFTER the reconciliation with Rome—the first day of Advent—Mary, Philip, and Pole attended a High Mass sung by the bishop of London at St. Paul's Cathedral. The crowds "both in the church and in the streets, were enormous, and displayed great joy and piety, begging the cardinal for his blessing."[11]

After Mass, Gardiner preached at St. Paul's Cross, basing his sermon on the Book of Romans:

> Now also it is time that we awake out of our sleep, who have slept or rather dreamed these twenty years past. For as men intending to sleep do separate themselves from company and desire to be alone, even so we have separated ourselves from the

> See of Rome, and have been alone, no realm in Christendom like us.

He continued:

> During these twenty years we have been without a head. When King Henry was head perhaps there was something to be said for it, but what a head was Edward, to whom they had to give a protector! He was but a shadow. Nor could the Queen, being a woman, be head of the Church . . . now the hour is come . . . the realm is at peace . . . It is time for us also to awake.[12]

At the end "all those present, over fifteen thousand people, knelt down" to receive Pole's blessing, crying out "Amen, amen!" "A sight to be seen it was, and the silence was such that not a cough was heard."[13]

CHAPTER 53

THE QUEEN IS WITH CHILD

∴

UPON HIS ARRIVAL AT WHITEHALL ON NOVEMBER 24, CARDINAL Pole had addressed Mary with the opening words of the Ave Maria: "Hail, thou art highly favored, the Lord is with thee: blessed art thou among women," the words by which the Angel Gabriel had heralded the Virgin Mary's conception of Jesus. Pole's greeting was, it seems, equally prophetic. Shortly after he left, Mary sent a messenger after him. She had felt her child stir when Pole greeted her; she knew she was pregnant.[1]

It followed weeks of rumor and fevered speculation. Renard had written in his dispatch in mid-September, just two months after the wedding, that one of the queen's physicians had told him that the queen "is probably with child." The English ambassador in Brussels, Sir John Mason, reported weeks later, in response to the emperor's question "How goeth my daughter's belly forward?" that although he had heard nothing formally from the queen, others had told him "her garments wax very strait."[2]

With the pregnancy now seemingly confirmed, letters were sent from the Council to bishops ordering Te Deums to be sung and special prayers offered for this "good hope of certain succession" and to give thanks for her "quickening with child, and to pray."[3] The news was proclaimed across Europe. "The Queen is with child," announced Ruy Gómez; "may it please God to grant her the issue that is so solely needed to set affairs right here and make everything smooth . . . this pregnancy will put a stop to every difficulty."[4] Every aspect of Mary's appearance was scrutinized and reported on. Writing to the emperor in November, Renard told him, "There is no doubt that the Queen is with child, for her stomach clearly shows it and her dresses no longer fit her."[5] And later the same month: the "lady is well with child. God be thanked! For she has felt the babe and presents all the usual signs on her breasts and elsewhere."[6]

In the days before Christmas, Mary wrote to her father-in-law:

> As for that child which I carry in my belly, I declare it to be alive and with great humility thank God for His great goodness shown to me, praying Him so to guide the fruit of my womb that it may contribute to His glory and honour, and give happiness to the King, my Lord and your son, to your Majesty, who were my second father in the lifetime of my own father, and are therefore doubly my father, and lastly that it may prove a blessing to the realm.[7]

Charles responded with enthusiastic expectation: "Be it man, or be it woman, welcome shall it be; for by that we shall be at the least come to some certainty to whom God shall appoint by succession the government of our estates."

It was a sentiment shared by many. As long as Mary remained childless, there was grave anxiety in the kingdom, as John Mason explained during his audience with the emperor: "It maketh all good men tremble to think the Queen's highness must die, with whom, dying without fruit, the realm were as good also to die."[8] The future of the Catholic restoration would depend on the fruitfulness of the marriage.

MARY WAS EXPECTED to give birth on or before May 9. The chamber and nursery were made ready, the chief gentlewomen of the kingdom summoned to witness the birth, wet nurses and rockers put on standby, and the royal cradle "sumptuously and gorgeously trimmed" and a Latin verse and English translation inlaid upon it:

> *The child which thou to Mary, O Lord of might! hast send,*
> *To England's joy, in health preserve, keepe, and defend!*[9]

A series of letters announcing the baby's safe arrival was prepared and signed by Mary herself, ready to be sent to the pope, the emperor, the king of France, the doge of Venice, and the queen regent of Flanders. In most, the sex of the child and date of delivery were left blank to be filled in by clerks at the last minute, but the letter to the pope specifically informed "his Holiness" of the "happy delivery of a prince."[10]

Because of the dangers of childbirth, provision was made in the event of Mary's death for Philip to be made guardian of the realm during the minority of the expected child. He would still be confined within the limits of the marriage treaty and could not call Parliament, declare war, or arrange for a marriage of his heir without the consent of a council of eighteen peers.[11] The final bill of regency justified the need to avoid the "dolorous experience of the inconstant government during the time of the reign of the late King Edward the sixth." For this and other reasons, the king was to have charge of "the rule, order, education and government" of any children and the "rule, order and government (under such issue or issues)" of the realm during the minority of the heir.[12]

Finally, at the beginning of April, the king and queen moved to Hampton Court in advance of Mary's confinement. Mary preferred Windsor, but it was considered too far from London for her to be secure. At Hampton Court she would have the protection of her full guard and have closer access to the troops from the city and the arsenal at the Tower.

Two weeks later, Mary underwent the usual ceremonies in advance of "the lying-in" and withdrew to her chamber with her ladies and gentlewomen. On Saint George's Day, April 23, she showed herself at a window of the palace as she watched Philip lead the celebrations of the Garter, in which the king, Gardiner, the lord chancellor, knights and lords, and numerous clerks and priests, dressed in copes of cloth of gold, processed with three crosses, singing "Salve Festa Dies." As Mary looked out from her chamber she turned side-on to show off her great belly—"that a hundred did see her grace."[13]

While Mary prepared for the birth, Elizabeth was summoned to court from Woodstock.[14] She arrived in late April and repaired to the prince of Wales's lodging, which had been built for her brother,

Edward. It was more than two years since the sisters had seen each other, but after arriving at court Elizabeth was kept waiting three weeks before Mary agreed to see her. Then, at ten at night, Elizabeth received her summons. With guards bearing torches, she was escorted through the garden to the privy lodging and, accompanied by Susan Clarencius, Mary's favorite woman, was ushered into the queen's presence.

Elizabeth knelt while Mary spoke over her, chiding her for her refusal to acknowledge her offense in Wyatt's rebellion. "You will not confess your offence, but it stands stoutly in your truth. I pray God it may so fall out," she told her. "If it doth not," Elizabeth answered resolutely, "I request neither favour nor pardon at your Majesty's hands. . . . I humbly beseech your Majesty to have a good opinion of me, and to think me to be your true subject, not only from the beginning hitherto, but for ever, as long as life lasteth."[15]

As Mary and Elizabeth were finally reconciled, the country held its breath for the birth of its heir.

AT DAYBREAK ON Tuesday, April 30, bells rang out the news that Mary had safely delivered. Henry Machyn wrote in his diary, "the Queen's grace was delivered of a prince, and so there was great ringing through London and divers places, Te Deum laudamus sung."[16] Soon after midnight, "with little pain and no danger," she had given birth to a son.

The news was received with unadulterated joy. Shops were shut as people rushed to church. Bonfires were lit and tables of food and wine set up as spontaneous street parties erupted all over London.[17] "How fair, how beautiful and great a prince it was as the like had not been seen," as one preacher noted.[18] Reports quickly spread to courts across Europe. Thomas Gresham, the English ambassador to the Netherlands, reported how news had reached Antwerp that "the Queen was brought to bed of a young Prince on 30th April," and the city's great bell was rung in celebration. The English merchants fired their guns across the water, and the regent sent the English mariners 100 crowns with which to celebrate the news.[19] By the evening of May 2, the imperial court was "rejoicing out of measure" to hear of the prince's birth.

CHAPTER 54

HER MAJESTY'S BELLY

∴

THE BELLS WERE SOON SILENCED AND THE BONFIRES EXTINGUISHED. The rumors were false. The queen had not gone into labor, and fresh calculations had to be made. As the Venetian ambassador, Giovanni Michieli, reported in late May:

> Everything is in suspense, and dependant on the result of this delivery, which, according to the opinion of the physicians, unless it takes place at this new phase of the moon two days hence, may be protracted beyond the full [moon] and [its] occultation, on the 4th or 5th of next month; her Majesty's belly having greatly declined, which is said yet more to indicate the approaching term.[1]

Days passed, but the labor pains did not begin. Speculation continued to fill letters and ambassadorial dispatches. Ruy Gómez observed on May 22 that he had seen the queen walking in her garden with such a light step that "it seems to me that there is no hope at all for this month."[2] Renard wrote, "Everything in this kingdom depends on the Queen's safe deliverance." If she did not bear a child, he foresaw "trouble on so great a scale that the pen can hardly set it down . . . the delay in the Queen's deliverance encourages the heretics to slander and put about false rumours; some say that she is not with child at all."[3] Philip had already expressed his doubts. Writing in April to his brother-in law Maximilian of Austria, he declared, "The Queen's pregnancy turns out not to have been as certain as we thought. Your highness and my sister manage better than the Queen and I do."[4]

The summer turned increasingly bleak; the weather was so bad "that the like is not remembered in the memory of man for the last fifty years."[5] Mary grew more and more reclusive, sitting in one place for hours at a time, wrestling with depression and anxiety, neither leaving her chamber nor giving audience to anyone.[6] To those who saw her she looked pale and ill, weeping and praying that her labor pains begin. Her prayer book survives, the pages worn and stained around a page bearing a prayer for the safe delivery of a woman with child.[7]

As the weeks passed, the mood became one of despair. Some said the queen was dead; seditious talk was everywhere. Every few days new libels against her were thrown into the streets, stirring up fears and encouraging rebellion. By June, the earl of Pembroke and a number of troops had to be brought in to keep order in London. Protestant pamphleteers alleged that the king kept company with whores and commoners' daughters while Mary was confined to her rooms. Rumors circulated that Mary had never been pregnant at all "but that a supposititious child is going to be presented as hers"; or that the fetus had been a pet monkey or a lapdog; or that the Queen had delivered "a mole or lump of flesh and was in great peril of death."[8] Posters were nailed to the palace door and abusive papers thrown into the queen's own chamber. Others said the queen had been deceived by a tympany or some other disease to believe herself to be pregnant but was not. Some thought that she had miscarried, others that she was bewitched.[9]

The French ambassador, Noailles, scoffed at the solemn prayers and anxious anticipation, believing the queen's pregnancy to be an elaborate farce. He had been informed by two of Mary's intimate female attendants, Susan Clarencius and one of the midwives, "that the Queen's state was by no means of the hopeful kind generally supposed, but rather some woeful malady, for several times a day she spent long hours sitting on her floor with her knees drawn up to her chin," a position that no pregnant woman could have assumed without considerable pain. The midwife, "one of the best midwives in the town," believed the queen, "though pale and peaked," was not pregnant. "The said midwife, more to comfort her with words than anything, tells her from day to day that she has miscalculated her pregnancy by two months, the royal physicians either too ignorant or fearful to tell the Queen" the truth and so would refer only to a "miscalculation" in the time of her delivery.[10]

In a letter to Eraso, Ruy Gómez wrote, "All this makes me wonder whether she is with child at all, greatly as I desire the thing to be happily over."[11] Philip shared Gómez's sentiments and grew restless. "From what I hear," Michieli wrote in a dispatch, "one single hour's delay in this delivery seems to him a thousand years."[12] He had been expected in Flanders since May, and on June 6 the emperor was still postponing the interment of Queen Joanna, Philip's grandmother, in the hope that his grandson would arrive at any time. Philip had made preparations to leave as soon as the child was born and Mary was out of danger. According to Michieli, the hope of childbirth "has so diminished that but little reliance can now be any longer placed on it"; he concluded that "the pregnancy will end in wind rather than anything else."

By the end of June, the doctors had given up trying to predict when the queen would be delivered. On the twenty-sixth, Michieli wrote, "There is no one, either of the physicians or the women, or others, all having been deceived, who at present dare any longer form any opinion about it, all persons resigning themselves to such hour and time as shall best please our Lord God."[13]

The delay was interpreted in different ways. In mid-June two gentlemen "of no ordinary repute" were imprisoned in the Tower, charged with "having spoken about this delivery licentiously, in a tone unbecoming their grade."[14] People closest to Mary believed that a miracle would come to pass "in this as in all her Majesty's other circumstances, which the more they were despaired of according to human reason and discourse, the better and more auspicious did their result then show itself." The queen's child would prove to the world once and for all that her affairs "were regulated excessively by Divine Providence."[15]

AT THE END of July, daily processions and prayers for the royal baby's delivery were halted. On August 3, with no public announcement and on the pretext that Hampton Court needed to be cleaned, the court moved to the far smaller residence of Oatlands, allowing for the large retinue of gentlewomen, rockers, and nursery staff to be dismissed. As the Venetian ambassador wrote:

> Although no one dares to proclaim it . . . the fact is that the move has been made in order no longer to keep the people of England in suspense about this delivery, by the constant and public processions which were made, and by the Queen's remaining so many days in retirement . . . to the prejudice of her subjects; as not only did she transact no business, but would scarcely allow herself to be seen by any of her ladies who, in expectation of childbirth, especially the gentlewomen and the chief female nobility [who] had flocked to court from all parts of the kingdom in such very great number, all living at the cost of her Majesty.[16]

There had been no baby. Like her mother forty years before, Mary had been deluded into believing that she was pregnant. Wise after the event, Michieli described how "from her youth" she had suffered from the "retention of menstrual fluids" and the "strangulation of her womb." Her body swelled, and her breasts enlarged and sent out milk. "It was this which had led to the empty rumour of her pregnancy."[17]

THE OUTCOME OF the pregnancy had been of central importance to the peace negotiations between the French king and emperor, held under English auspices at La Marque in May. The latest round of hostilities, which had erupted in 1551, had reached a stalemate. The birth of an heir to the English throne would have given the emperor immense benefit, but if the queen and child died, the advantage would be with the French.

For the English, a great deal was at stake: the revival of England's prestige in continental politics, an improvement of relations with France, and, of greatest importance, the prevention of a new war in which Spain might try to involve England. But as the negotiations continued, it became clear that neither the Habsburgs nor the Valois were willing to give much ground. As the talks reached an impasse, news came at the beginning of June of Mary's failed pregnancy and of the election of Giovanni Pietro Carafa, a seventy-nine-year-old Neapolitan and great enemy of the Habsburgs, as pope. The conference came to an abrupt end: the French had lost their fear.

Now, with no immediate prospect of an heir, Philip prepared to depart England for the Low Countries. Nervous of informing Mary of his intentions, he rehearsed how he would tell her in a draft letter, sent probably to Ruy Gómez: "Let me know what line I am to take with the Queen about leaving her and about religion. I see I must say something, but God help me!"[18] Philip decided to leave most of his household in the hope of convincing the queen that he would return quickly. Yet, as the Venetian ambassador reported, "it is said more than ever, that he will go to Spain, and remove thence his household and all the others by degrees."[19]

Philip would be leaving England with the Catholic restoration achieved and the enforcement of Catholic obedience under way. Six months before, the medieval treason laws, repealed by Edward VI, had been restored. The secular authorities were empowered once more to deal ruthlessly with religious opponents: seditious words and activities would be punished. With the rising threat of disorder and rebellion, the restoration of Catholicism was to take on a ferocious edge: heretics would be burned alive.

CHAPTER 55

BLOOD AND FIRE

∴

ON MONDAY, FEBRUARY 4, 1555, JOHN ROGERS, CANON OF ST. PAUL'S, was led out to Smithfield, condemned as a heretic. Great crowds lined the streets to watch the procession, among them his wife and eleven children. As he stood at the stake, he was offered a pardon on condition that he recanted, but he refused. He exhorted the people to stand firm in the faith that he had taught them. When the fire took hold of his body, he "washed his hands in the flame as he was in burning."[1] As Renard related, "Some of the onlookers wept; others prayed God to give him strength, perseverance and patience to bear the pain and not to recant; others gathered the ashes and bones and wrapped them up to preserve them."[2]

Rogers's death was followed just days later by those of two country parsons—Laurence Saunders, the rector of All Hallows in Coventry, and Dr. Rowland Taylor, the rector of Hadleigh, Suffolk—and by the former bishop of Worcester and Gloucester, John Hooper. Each was burned in the district in which he had first officiated.

Hooper, like the other condemned martyrs, had denied papal supremacy over the Church and the Real Presence of Christ in the Eucharist. He was imprisoned in the Fleet on September 1, 1553, and remained there for more than seventeen months. At the end of January 1555, he was brought before Stephen Gardiner and a number of other bishops and urged to give up his "evil and corrupt doctrine" and to conform to the Catholic Church.[3] If he recanted, he would have the queen's mercy. He refused, and on February 9 he was burned. Standing on a high stool and looking over the crowd of several thousand that had gathered to watch him, he prayed.

An eyewitness described how "in every corner there was nothing to be seen but weeping and sorrowful people."[4] Faggots were laid around the stool and reeds placed in and between Hooper's hands. Then the fire was lit. The wind at first blew the flames from him and, having burned his legs, the fires were almost extinguished. More faggots and reeds were brought, and finally the two bladders of gunpowder tied between his legs ignited. In the end he could move nothing but his arms; then one fell off and the other, with "fat, water and blood dropping out at his fingers' ends," stuck to what was left of his chest. It had taken forty-five minutes of excruciating agony to kill him.[5] It was a horrific death and a sight that would be repeated nearly three hundred times during Mary's reign.

A WEEK AFTER Hooper's death, six other men—William Pygot, a butcher from Braintree; Stephen Knight, a barber at Malden; Thomas Haukes, a gentleman in Lord Oxford's household; William Hunter, a nineteen-year-old apprentice; Thomas Tomkins, a weaver from Shoreditch; and John Laurence, a priest—were denounced to Bishop Bonner as Protestant heretics. Having been defrocked, Laurence was brought to Colchester on March 29. He had been shackled in prison with such heavy irons and so deprived of food that he was too weak to walk to the stake and had to be carried there and burned sitting on a chair. His young children went before the fire and cried out, "Lord, strengthen thy servant and keep thy promise." Laurence and the other five men had been offered the chance to recant, but all remained defiant. As Thomas Haukes declared, "No, my Lord, that will I not; for if I had an hundred bodies I would suffer them all to be torn in pieces rather than recant."[6] He was condemned on February 9 and burned four months later.

At the request of his friends, who feared the extent of his pain in the fire, Haukes agreed that, if it were tolerable, he would lift his hand above his head before he died. Having been strapped to the stake and engulfed by the flames, he raised his hands and clapped them together to the cries and rejoicing of the crowd.[7]

IN EARLY 1555, the Privy Council sent a writ to Sir Nicholas Hare, master of the Rolls, and other justices of the peace in the county of

Middlesex for the execution of William Flower, signifying to them that "For as much as the said Flower's offence was so enormous and heinous, there further pleased for the most terrible example he should before he were executed have his right hand stricken off."[8]

William Flower had been condemned for striking a priest with a wood knife in St. Margaret's Church, Westminster. He was burned on April 24, 1555, as the Council's letter had instructed. Most of the burnings in the summer were in London and Essex, in the diocese of Edmund Bonner, bishop of London, who soon became synonymous with the persecution. Orders were sent to find anyone guilty of heresy and report them to the authorities. Towns and villages were searched to find those who held heretical opinions and refused to observe the Catholic faith. Many of the victims were agricultural laborers and artisans denounced by their neighbors or their families, the victims of private grievances or local disputes.

Margaret Polley, a woman living in Pembury near Tonbridge, was the first woman to be burned in Mary's reign. She had maintained that there was no reference to the Roman Catholic Church in the Bible and denied the Real Presence in the Mass. She was burned on July 18, 1555, along with two other martyrs in a gravel pit just outside Dartford in Kent. The local farmers brought cartloads of cherries to sell to the spectators.[9] Other women followed. Alice Benden of Staplehurst in Kent was reported to the authorities by her own husband and disowned by her father. She had refused to attend church as, she said, too much idolatry was practiced there. For nine weeks she was incarcerated in the bishop's prison, living only on bread and water and with no change of clothes. In John Foxe's description, she became "a most piteous and loathsome creature to behold." When offered the chance of freedom if she reformed, she declared, "I am thoroughly persuaded by the extremity that you have already showed me, that you are not of God, neither can your doings be Godly." She remained imprisoned and was burned with six others in Canterbury in June 1557.[10]

As the months went on, the persecution spread beyond Bonner's diocese to Wales, East Anglia, and the North. In the diocese of Chester, George Marsh, a young widowed farmer from Cumberland, had been ordained as a priest during the reign of Edward VI. After

Mary's accession he returned from London to Lancashire, denounced the Mass and papal supremacy, and was subsequently arrested. He was condemned as a heretic and sentenced to be burned at Spittle Broughton, just outside the north gate of Chester, on April 24, 1555. Offered a pardon if he recanted, he refused, saying he loved life and wanted to live but not at the cost of betraying Christ. Having walked to the site of his execution in shackles, a chain was fastened around his waist. On his head was placed a jar filled with tar and pitch so that when the flames reached it the contents would pour down. It was a gusty day and a gradual death, as very slowly the flames engulfed his body.[11]

On the island of Guernsey, a woman named Katherine Cowchen lived with her two daughters, Perotine Massey and Guillemine Gilbert. Perotine had informed the authorities that a local woman, Vincent Gosset, had stolen a gold goblet. In revenge Gosset denounced Cowchen and her two daughters as heretics. All three were convicted of heresy and sentenced to death by burning. Perotine had not told the authorities she was pregnant. When the faggots were lit, the fire caused her to give birth to her baby son, who fell onto the burning faggots. One of the spectators rushed forward to save the baby and pulled him out of the fire, but the local sheriff ordered that the baby be thrown back. He was burned with his mother, grandmother, and aunt.[12]

NEITHER MARY NOR Pole had expected to burn so many; they wanted the heretics to be reconciled rather than die and for the burnings to be carried out judiciously and without vindictiveness. Mary ordered that a councillor be present to supervise each burning in London and that during each execution "some good and pious sermons be preached." Writing in December 1554, she had declared:

> Touching the punishment of heretics, I believe it would be well to inflict punishment at this beginning, without much cruelty and passion, but without however omitting to do such justice on those who choose by their false doctrines to deceive simple persons, that the people may clearly comprehend that they have not

> been condemned without just cause, whereby others will be brought to know the truth, and will beware of letting themselves be induced to relapse into such new and false opinions.[13]

However, willful disobedience to the Catholic Church—heresy—was the worst of sins and needed to be extirpated, lest it "infect" more.

But rather than extinguishing Protestant sentiment, as Mary intended, the burnings served only to define more clearly the Protestants as a dissident group. Moreover, the courage of the martyrs stirred the admiration of many of those who saw them die. Such was the "murmuring about the cruel enforcement of the recent acts of Parliament on heresy which had now begun, as shown publicly when Rogers was burnt," reported Renard to Philip after the first London burnings, "I do not think it well that your Majesty should allow further executions to take place unless the reasons are overwhelmingly strong and the offences committed have been so scandalous as to render the course justifiable in the eyes of the people."[14] Four months later, Michieli made similar observations:

> Two days ago, to the displeasure as usual of the population here, two Londoners were burnt alive, one of them having been a public lecturer in Scripture, a person sixty years of age, who was held in great esteem. In a few days the like will be done to four or five more; and thus from time to time to many others who are in prison for this cause and will not recant, although such severity is odious to many people.[15]

Increasingly, Protestantism was associated with resistance to Spanish domination and the defense of English liberty, with Philip being held responsible by many for the burnings. However, just days after John Rogers's execution, Alfonso de Castro, Philip's confessor, preached a sermon at court with the king's sanction, attacking the burnings and "saying plainly that they learned it not in scripture, to burn any for conscience sake; but the contrary, that they should live and be converted."[16] Renard advised Philip that haste in religious matters should be avoided:

> Religion is not yet firmly established and . . . the heretics are on the watch for every possible opportunity to revive error and compromise the good beginning that has been made. They use as an argument the cruel punishments which they assert are being applied, with recourse to fire rather than doctrine and good examples, to lead the country back [to Catholicism].[17]

Although Philip did not play the direct role many attributed to him, he did nothing to forestall the persecution, and the burnings continued. But for Mary, to halt the process would have been to condone heresy, and this she could never do. It was an affront to her conscience that had been forged in the fires of persecution in the years before she had become queen. As the Venetian ambassador, Giovanni Soranzo, observed, during her brother's reign Mary had not conformed to the new religious service, "her belief in that into which she was born being so strong that had the opportunity offered, she would have displayed it at the stake."[18]

CHAPTER 56

EXTRAORDINARILY IN LOVE

∴

My lord and good father. I have learnt by what the King, my Lord and good husband, has told me and also by the letter which you were pleased to send me that for a long time past the state of your affairs has demanded that your Majesty and he should meet in order to be able to confer together and reach the appropriate decisions. However, you have been pleased to put off the moment of separating him from me until now, for which I humbly thank your Majesty. I assure you, Sire, that there is nothing in this world that I set so much store by as the King's presence. But as I have more concern for your Majesties' welfare than my own desires, I submit to what regard you as necessary. I firmly hope that the King's absence will be brief, for I assure your Majesty, that quite apart from my own feelings, his presence in this kingdom has done much good and is of great importance for the good governance of this country. For the rest, I am content with whatever may be your Majesty's pleasure.[1]

—MARY TO CHARLES V,
JULY—AUGUST 1555

ON AUGUST 27, MARY AND PHILIP RODE FROM HAMPTON COURT through London to Greenwich, accompanied by the lord mayor and aldermen, the English and Spanish nobility, and Cardinal Pole. Mary had planned to travel by barge and Philip to ride through the city, but at the last moment she chose to give Londoners the "satisfaction of seeing her likewise in his company."

The streets thronged with people, joyful not only to see the king and queen together but to be reassured, after months of rumors during her supposed pregnancy, that their queen was not dead. As Michieli wrote, "when they knew of her appearance, they all ran from one place to another, as to an unexpected sight." It was "as if they were crazy, to ascertain thoroughly that it was her, and on recognising and seeing her in better plight than ever, they by shouts and salutations, and every other demonstration, then gave greater signs of joy."[2] Two days later, Philip departed by river to commence his journey to Dover and then to Flanders. Mary watched at a window from the palace at Greenwich as the barge prepared to leave, and Philip waved his hat in her direction, "demonstrating great affection."[3] It was, for Mary, a sorrowful parting:

> The Queen . . . chose to come with him through all the chambers and galleries to the head of the stairs, constraining herself the whole way to avoid, in sight of such a crowd, any demonstration unbecoming her gravity, though she could not but be moved when the Spanish noblemen kissed her hand, and yet more, when she saw the ladies in tears take leave of the King, who, according to the custom of the country, kissed them one by one. On returning, however, to her apartments, placing herself at a window which looks on the river, not supposing herself any longer seen or observed by anyone, it was perceived that she gave free vent to her grief by a flood of tears, nor did she once quit the window until she had not only seen the King embark and depart, but remained looking after him as long as he was in sight.[4]

Philip and his retinue stayed at Canterbury for several days, awaiting good weather and the arrival of Flemish ships at Dover. Men were out on the road nearly every hour, carrying letters between the king and queen, and messengers waited about the courtyard of Greenwich Palace night and day, "booted and spurred ready for a start." As Michieli reported, "the Queen not content with having sent two of her chief chamberlains in the King's company for the purpose of being acquainted with all that takes place, writes to him daily in her own hand, and despatches courtiers, demonstrating in every way her great desire."[5] But Philip wrote less and less. When Michieli had an audience with the queen on September 13, she told him "very passionately with tears in her eyes, that for a week she had had no letters from him [Philip]."[6] Meanwhile, Michieli's informant described how Mary mourned as if grief-stricken, "as may be imagined with regard to a person extraordinarily in love."

> The Queen remains disconsolate, though she conceals it as much as she can, and from what I hear mourns the more when alone and supposing herself invisible to any of her attendants. During this absence Cardinal Pole will reside with her, lodgings having been assigned to him in the palace, that he may comfort and keep her company, Her Majesty delighting greatly in the sight and presence of him.[7]

In letters to Philip, Pole recounted how Mary spent her day, passing "the forenoon in prayer after the manner of Mary [Magdalene], and in the afternoon admirably personates Martha, by transacting business."[8]

Two weeks after the king's departure, Simon Renard left England. With Philip's arrival, his confidential relationship with the queen had ended. He had asked to be recalled, but Charles had refused, replying that he must stay in England to give Philip the benefit of his considerable knowledge of "the condition of affairs" derived from his long residence there.[9] By March 1555, Renard was given leave to depart. Mary said of him in a letter to Charles V, "He was here with me through very dangerous times and that he showed himself during the marriage negotiations to be a most indispensable minister, inspired by the greatest desire to serve us and the greatest zeal for my affairs."[10] She presented him with more than 1,200 ounces of plate as a token of gratitude.[11]

Having arrived at court for the queen's confinement in late spring, Elizabeth remained with Mary until the autumn. By September, Noailles observed, she was "more in favour than she used to be, going every day to mass with the Queen and often in her company."[12] In mid-October, she obtained leave to withdraw and left the court for Hatfield. At the same time many of Philip's household servants, soldiers, and pages also began to withdraw, "with a mind," Michieli noted, "not to revisit this country for a very long while."[13]

By December, all those who remained were instructed to join the king in the Low Countries. Federico Badoer, the Venetian ambassador to the emperor, reported:

> The King's confessor [Alfonso de Castro] has arrived here, and repeated a variety of foul language uttered by the English, indicating their ill-will towards his Majesty and the Spanish nation [and says] that on seeing him and the rest of the attendants depart, they made great rejoicing well-nigh universally; and he goes saying that the Queen's wish again to see the King is very great, nay boundless.[14]

Philip sought to stay in touch with English affairs through a body of advisers—a Council of State—that he established on his departure. The councillors were to reside at court, consider "all causes of state and financial causes and other causes of great moment," and write to Philip three times a week.[15] The reports, in Latin, were written by First Secretary Sir William Petre and then returned by Philip's secretary, annotated with comments in the margin or at the foot of the page. "It seems well done"; "the King is most grateful to be told"; "the King explains his wishes in letters to the councillors": such were typical of Philip's comments on matters ranging from prospective legislation and the nomination or recall of ambassadors to the condition of the shires and the defense of the realm.[16] Important statutes and proclamations continued to be sent to the king for his signature, but as he turned his attention to the Netherlands, his correspondence became less frequent.

In October 1555, Charles resigned the lordship of the Netherlands to Philip and in January 1556 the crowns of Aragon and Castile. He sent a message with one of his gentlemen to Mary "with congratulations on her being able for the future to style herself the Queen of many and great crowns, and on her being no less their mistress than of her own crown of England."[17] Philip now desired power in England in his own right, not simply as a regent for the heir. He began to put pressure on Mary that he be crowned and even suggested this might be a condition of his return to England.[18] On October 12, Badoer wrote that "the King of England had informed his wife that he was most anxious to gratify her wish for his return, but that he could not do so without being given an honourable share in the government of the realm."[19]

Yet Mary hesitated to propose his coronation. Parliament was full of opposition, and, as she relayed to Badoer, "she knew it to be impossible to form either of these important resolutions without greatly endangering her crown, but that she hoped in the course of a short time to comfort the King with what he seems to desire."[20] At the end of December, Mary wrote to Philip, "apologising for her non-adoption of any of the resolutions desired by him in the matter of the coronation, or with regard to waging war on the Most Christian King [of France]."[21] Rumors were circulating of Philip's lascivious antics abroad, and Mary began to lose hope of her husband's imminent return.[22] As Noailles recounted in a letter of December 30, Mary "told her ladies, that she had done all possible to induce her husband to return, and as she found he would not, she meant to withdraw utterly from men, and live quietly, as she had done the chief part of her life before she married."[23]

CHAPTER 57

COMMITTED TO THE FLAMES

ON THE MORNING OF MARCH 21, 1556, THOMAS CRANMER, THE sixty-six-year-old former archbishop of Canterbury, was burned alive in the town ditch in Oxford. Thrusting his hand into the flames, he spoke the words "For as much be as my hand offended, writing contrary to my heart, my hand shall first be punished therefor."[1]

Cranmer was the highest profile of the Marian martyrs and one Mary had always been determined to condemn as a heretic. It was he who had encouraged her father's break with Rome; he who had, as archbishop of Canterbury, declared Katherine of Aragon's marriage invalid; and he who had performed the wedding of Henry VIII and Anne Boleyn. Upon Mary's accession he had been condemned with Lady Jane Grey and three of Northumberland's sons for high treason for his support of Jane's accession, but his sentence had not been carried out.

Mary bore Cranmer a deep and personal grudge, and even though Church law said that as a repentant heretic he should be pardoned, she was determined that he burn. She wanted his death to be for heresy, not for secular offenses. Given his status as archbishop of Canterbury, she had had to wait for the restoration of papal jurisdiction. For two and a half years he had languished in prison, awaiting his inevitable fate.

IN MARCH 1554, Cranmer, together with Hugh Latimer, the former bishop of Worcester, and Nicholas Ridley, the former bishop of London, were moved from the Tower of London to Oxford and placed in the Bocardo, the town prison. Several weeks later, a disputation on the Eucharist was held at St. Mary's Church during which each of the Protestant leaders made their case to an audience of nearly a thousand Catholics. It was never intended to be a fair hearing; the prisoners were to be delivered to the commissioners "so that their erroneous opinions being by the word of God justly and truly convinced, the residue of our subjects, may be thereby the better established in the true Catholic faith."[2] After four days of debate, the Protestants were told they had been defeated. They were declared heretics, excommunicated, and returned to their prison cells. For the next seventeen months, Cranmer remained almost completely isolated in the Bocardo.

On September 12, 1555, Cranmer's trial for heresy began at St. Mary's Church. He faced fifteen charges: six dealing with his matrimonial affairs, six others with his repudiation of papal authority, and three with heretical doctrines. He refused to recant and to acknowledge papal supremacy and the Real Presence. The trial ended, the case had to be referred to Rome, and Cranmer was sent back to the Bocardo. Three weeks later, Ridley and Latimer faced their trial. Both refused to recant; both were condemned to death. On October 16, they were taken to a stake sunk into a ditch outside the northern wall of the city near Balliol College. Cranmer was brought out of his cell to watch. For three hours Dr. Richard Smith, an Oxford theologian, preached as Ridley and Latimer waited for their deaths. Finally they were fastened to the stake and the faggots were lit. "Be of good comfort mister Ridley, and play the man," Latimer called out, "we shall this day light such a candle by God's grace in England, as (I trust) shall never be put out."[3] Latimer was quickly engulfed by the flames.

Ridley's death was much slower. The faggots had been stacked so thickly that the fire could not burn through them. His legs burned, but the flames did not rise above his body to the gunpowder around his neck. "Let the fire come unto me, I cannot burn!" he cried.[4] Faggot after faggot was thrown around Ridley's head and further fuel added to the fire. Finally the gunpowder was ignited and he died.[5]

ON DECEMBER 4, Cranmer's fate was decided in Rome. He was deprived of his archbishopric "and of all ecclesiastical dignities," and permission was given for his execution. On January 27, the Venetian ambassador, Giovanni Michieli, reported that "the sentence against the late Archbishop of Canterbury will soon be executed, he remaining more obstinate than ever in his heresies."[6] A few days later, under pressure of interrogation, Cranmer admitted to every fact brought before him and signed his first submission. He stated that he would accept the supremacy of the pope because the king and queen had ordered him to do so and he would always obey his sovereigns.[7] Within days he signed a second recantation conceding more:

> I, Thomas Cranmer, doctor in divinity, do submit myself to the catholic church of Christ, and to the Pope, supreme head of the same church, and unto the King and Queen's majesties, and unto all their laws and ordinances.[8]

Mary must have been informed of his recantation but chose to ignore it; she was determined to be rid of the man who had caused her and her mother so much suffering.

On February 14, Cranmer was publicly degraded from holy orders in the church of Christ Church College. It was a ritual humiliation conducted by his old enemy Edmund Bonner, the bishop of London. After his crimes had been read out, Cranmer was forced to put on the vestments of an archbishop and then of a priest, after which each was stripped from him. His head was shaved to remove his tonsure, and his fingers were scraped to remove the holy oil that had ordained him. Then, dressed in a townsman's cloak and cap, Cranmer was handed over to the secular authorities, who returned him to the Bocardo. He made two more recantations, but to little effect. On the twenty-fourth a writ was issued to the mayor of Oxford ordering that "in a public and open place" Cranmer be "for the aforesaid cause committed to the flames in the presence of people; and have that Thomas Cranmer actually consumed by that same fire, for a manifest example to other Christians of the detestation in which such crimes are held."[9]

In his fifth and sixth recantations, Cranmer condemned himself in the most abject terms; he was "a blasphemer, persecutor and insulter . . . who surpassed Saul in wickedness and crime"; he was "unworthy of all kindness and goodness but rather deserving of . . . divine and eternal punishment." He continued that he had been "the cause and originator" of Henry's divorce, "which fault was in truth the seedbed of all the woes and disasters of this realm," and was therefore guilty "of the murder of so many upright men . . . the schism which split the whole kingdom . . . the slaughter of so many minds and bodies such that my reason can hardly grasp." He was, he maintained, "the most wicked all the earth has ever born."[10]

THE MORNING OF Saturday, March 21, 1556, was wet and dull. Given the weather, the sermon, normally delivered before the burning at the stake, was preached in St. Mary's Church.

Cranmer was expected to deliver his seventh recantation, retracting his rejection of the Real Presence in the Eucharist. Dr. Henry Cole, provost of Eton, first preached the sermon explaining the reasons for Cranmer's execution. Then, standing on a raised platform in a packed church, Cranmer began:

> And now I come to the great thing, that so much troubleth my conscience more than any thing that ever I did or said in my whole life, and that is the setting abroad of a writing contrary to the truth: which now here I renounce and refuse as things written with my hand, contrary to the truth which I thought in my heart, and written for fear of death, and to save my life if it might be. . . . And for as much be as my hand offended, writing contrary to my heart, my hand shall first be punished therefor: for may I come to the fire, it shall be first burnt. . . . As for the Pope, I refuse him as Christ's enemy and Antichrist, with all his false doctrine.[11]

The church descended into noise and protest. Cranmer was pulled from the stage and dragged through the streets to the place of execution, where Ridley and Latimer had suffered, and fastened to the stake with an iron chain. He held his hand in the flames, crying out, "Unworthy right hand!"[12] that which had signed the recantations. The sixty-six-year-old was soon dead. What had been intended to be a great coup—the public recantation of the architect of the English reformation—had been ruined.

The government immediately set about limiting the damage. The following day, Passion Sunday, Dr. Cole preached a denunciation of Cranmer in the church where he had spoken the day before. Within days John Cawood printed *All the Submissions and Recantations of Thomas Cranmer*, which ended with Cranmer's final expected recantation, rather than the one he had actually delivered. As the Venetian ambassador observed:

> On Saturday last, 21 March, Cranmer, late Archbishop of Canterbury was burnt, having fully verified the opinion formed of him by the Queen, that he had feigned recantations thinking to save his life, and not that he had received any good inspiration, so she considered him unworthy of pardon.[13]

CHAPTER 58

A GREAT AND RARE EXAMPLE OF GOODNESS

∴

AT THREE ON THE AFTERNOON OF MAUNDY THURSDAY, APRIL 3, 1556, Mary, accompanied by Cardinal Pole, her Council, and her chaplains, entered the Great Hall at Greenwich Palace. Gathered at the entrance were Mary's chief ladies and gentlewomen in long linen aprons and towels around their necks. Each carried a silver ewer full of water and bunches of flowers. Mary wore a gown of purple velvet, its sleeves touching the ground. On either side of the hall were forty-one poor women, one for every year of the queen's life, seated on benches, their feet on stools. The women's right feet had been washed in preparation for the ceremony, first by a servant, then by the under almoner, and then by the grand almoner, the bishop of Chichester.

Kneeling before the first of the poor women, Mary took the woman's right foot in her hand, washed it and dried it, and, having signed it with the cross, kissed the foot with "reverence and solemnity." To each of the women she did the same, moving one by one along each side of the hall, always on her knees, accompanied by one of the noblewomen attending her with basin and towel.

Rising to her feet, Mary went again to each of the poor women, this time with a large wooden platter filled with pieces of salted fish and two large loaves of bread. Having distributed the alms she returned with a wooden bowl filled with either wine or hippocras and then gave each of the women a piece of rich cloth and a leather purse containing forty-one pennies. Finally she presented to the women the apron and towel that each of the noblewomen had worn. She then left the hall to remove her purple gown. Half an hour later she returned, preceded by a servant carrying the gown. As the choristers sang, she went around the room, twice examining the women one by one; returning for the third time, she gave the gown to the woman she had deemed the poorest and oldest of them.

THE FOLLOWING DAY, Good Friday, the queen came down from her oratory for the Adoration of the Cross. Kneeling at a short distance from the cross, she moved toward it on her knees as she prayed and kissed it "with such devotion as greatly to edify all those who were present." Then, reciting prayers and psalms, Mary began the ceremony of the benediction of the cramp rings and the touching for the "king's evil," a healing ritual for sufferers of scrofula. An enclosure had been formed to the right of the high altar with four benches placed in a square. Mary stood in the center and knelt down before two large, covered basins, each filled with gold and silver rings. One basin contained Mary's own rings, the other those of private individuals, each labeled with its owner's name.

After the basins were uncovered, Mary began reciting prayers and psalms, and then, taking the rings in her hand, she passed them from one hand to the other. She then withdrew to an altar in a private gallery. There she knelt, made her confession to and received absolution from Cardinal Pole, and then proceeded to bless the four scrofulous women who had gathered before her. The first sufferer was brought before her, and, still on her knees, Mary pressed her hands in the form of a cross on one of the woman's sores "with such compassion and devotion as to be a marvel." When all four sufferers had received the royal touch, Mary made the sign of the cross with a gold coin and placed it on a ribbon around their necks. After washing her hands, Mary returned to her oratory. As Marc Antonio Faitta, the secretary to Pole, concluded,

> Having been present myself in person at all these ceremonies, her Majesty struck me as affording a great and rare example of goodness, performing all those acts with such humility and love for religion, offering up her prayers to God with so great devotion and affection, and enduring for so long a while and so

> patiently much fatigue; and seeing thus, that the more her Majesty advances in the rule of this kingdom, so does she daily afford fresh and greater opportunities for commending her extreme piety, I dare assert that there was never a Queen in Christendom of greater goodness than this one.[1]

By exercising her "healing power," Mary had demonstrated once again that a female monarch could conduct the ceremonies previously prescribed only to a "divinely appointed" king.

CHAPTER 59

STOUT AND DEVILISH HEARTS

For many consecutive days a comet has been visible, as it still is, and with this opportunity a gang of rogues, some twelve in number . . . went about the city saying we should soon see the day of judgment, when everything would be burnt and consumed. These knaves, with a number of others, availing themselves of this device, agreed to set fire to several parts of the city, to facilitate their project of murder and robbery.[1]

—GIOVANNI MICHIELI,
MARCH 17, 1556

ON MARCH 5, 1556, A BLAZING COMET APPEARED IN THE SKY OVER London. Night after night for a week it shone, and Londoners looked up at it with "great wonder and astonishment."[2] These were fearful and uncertain times; "the stout and devilish hearts of the people of England" were once again ready "to work treason and make insurrections."[3] Yet what was initially thought to be civil unrest in London would reveal itself to be much more: a plot to overthrow Mary.

Born of political disaffection and Protestant intrigue, the conspiracy sought to exploit the popular discontent that had been growing since the previous summer. "The greatest rain and floods that ever was seen in England . . . [in which] both men and cattle drowned" had led to poor harvests and famine across England.[4] Mary's pregnancy had been unsuccessful, the peace conference at La Marque had failed, and the religious persecution continued with the burnings of Bishops Ridley, Latimer, and Cranmer. Renard warned that "unless steps are taken to remedy this state of affairs, it is impossible that trouble will not ensue . . . all the executions have hardened many hearts, for it has been seen how constant, or rather stubborn, these heretics prove at the stake." He had, the ambassador concluded, "never seen the people in such an ugly mood as they are at present."[5] Rumors of sedition and incipient rebellion became commonplace amid growing fears that Philip was to be crowned. When Parliament met in October 1555, rumors circulated that the demand of a subsidy was for the king's coronation.[6]

A few days into the parliamentary session, the Privy Council, fearing insurrection, closed all houses of public dancing and gambling in London on the grounds that they provided opportunities for seditious assemblies.[7] At the same time, three Suffolk men were imprisoned in the Tower, one of them having declared on the day Parliament opened that "to free the kingdom from oppression it would be well to kill the Queen."[8] Seditious pamphlets, written by English exiles and filled with accounts of Habsburg tyranny in Naples and Milan, circulated on the streets of London.[9] By the end of October, the queen had abandoned all hope of persuading Parliament to consider Philip's coronation. She remained determined, however, to pass bills allowing crown lands and revenues to be returned to the Church and for the estates of Protestant exiles who had fled abroad to be confiscated.

The death on the night of November 12 of the lord chancellor, Stephen Gardiner, made Mary's task even more difficult. His health had been failing since the spring, and he had struggled to speak at the opening of Parliament. Without her primary supporter, Mary was left to face the Commons alone. Her determination to restore the crown lands was matched by the Commons' reluctance to let them go for fear that they would have to give up their own gains.[10] Though Mary succeeded in passing this bill, the other great measure, the exiles bill, was defeated after Sir Anthony Kingston, a member of the Commons, locked the doors of the chamber, forcing a division. Three days later, Parliament was dissolved and Kingston was imprisoned in the Tower.

By the new year, discontentment had deepened. In January, as the pace of religious persecution quickened, the Council decreed that the queen's pardon should no longer be offered to heretics at the stake because of the contempt with which the offer was habitually treated. Moreover, it ordered that those in the crowds at the burnings who were understood to be "comforting, aiding or praising the offenders, or otherwise use themselves to the ill example of others" would be imprisoned.[11] On January 27, seven people—five men and two women—were burned at Smithfield and a few days later five more at Canterbury. In February, the Treaty of Vaucelles, by which hostilities between France and Spain were to be suspended for five years, left England marginalized, as it had been excluded from the negotiations. Philip, in his first act as king of Spain, was blamed for the blow to national prestige. As the comet appeared in the sky in March, Philip's astrologers advised that a major rising was to be expected in England.[12] It was in these circumstances that the plot to depose Mary, hatched on both sides of the Channel, began to take shape.

LED BY SIR HENRY DUDLEY, a cousin of the late duke of Northumberland, and with the complicity of the French ambassador, Antoine de Noailles, the conspiracy sought to break the Spanish alliance and replace Mary with Elizabeth.[13] After setting fire to several areas of the city to disguise their purpose, the plotters—among whom were Sir Anthony Kingston, released from the Tower after two weeks' imprisonment, and Christopher Ashton, Dudley's father-in-law—planned to rob the Exchequer of £50,000 in silver bullion and flee to the Isle of Wight in two of the queen's ships, already commandeered. There they would raise forces and effect a national rebellion while Dudley sailed from France with a number of other exiles. But before the plan could be executed, Thomas White, an Exchequer official, leaked the plot to Cardinal Pole.[14] At first the Council waited, giving the conspirators time to begin executing the plot, while secretly moving bullion out of the Exchequer. Finally, on March 18, the government acted. The chief conspirators were arrested and sent to the Tower.[15] The Venetian ambassador reported on the twenty-fourth:

> The suspicion about the conspirators who purposed setting fire to several quarters of the city for the sake of plunder, had a different root and origin to what was reported, a plot having been lately discovered of such a nature that, had it been carried into effect as arranged, it would doubtless . . . considering the

> ill-will of the majority of the population here on account of the religion . . . have placed the Queen and the whole kingdom in great trouble, as it was of greater circuit and extent than had been at first supposed.[16]

Lengthy inquiries followed throughout March and April as the web of conspiracy became ever wider, revealing links to Exchequer officials, fugitives in France, and gentry and officials across the country, including Sir Anthony Kingston, Sir William Courtenay, Sir John Pollard, and Richard Uvedale, captain of the Isle of Wight. On April 4, Dudley and most of his fellow conspirators were declared traitors, although by remaining in France Dudley escaped arrest. Two weeks later, the rebel John Throgmorton and Uvedale were hanged and quartered at Tyburn. Kingston died on his way to London. Eventually ten men were executed.

The plot had thrown the popular discontent and the willingness of France to intervene against Mary into sharp relief. All the plotters were heretics; many of them were associates of Sir Thomas Wyatt, who had been released from the Tower six months before. Their common cause, as with Wyatt's rebellion two years before, was the unpopularity of the Spanish marriage, added to which was the new fear that Philip might be crowned king of England.

The conspiracy left Mary in a state of profound distress. The queen "rages against her subjects," wrote Noailles. "She is utterly confounded by the faithlessness of those whom she most trusted, seeing that the greater part of these miserable creatures [Dudley's conspirators] are kith and kin or favoured servants of the greatest men in the kingdom, even Lords of the Council."[17] Such was Mary's fright that she would not allow Cardinal Pole to leave her for the ceremony of his consecration to the archbishopric of Canterbury, due to take place in his cathedral on March 25. He was instead consecrated in the Friars' Church at Greenwich.[18] By the summer there was reported to be something of a "siege mentality" at court. Mary no longer appeared in public, living instead in a state of seclusion, the palace full of armed men and the queen so afraid that she dared not sleep more than three hours a night.[19] "All the nobility and gentry of the country have been desired to keep on the watch and ready to present themselves on the first summons."[20]

In the midst of such uncertainty, Mary grew ever more anxious for Philip's return, as Michieli related:

> For many months, the Queen has passed from one sorrow to another, your Serenity can imagine what a life she leads, comforting herself as usual with the presence of Cardinal Pole, to whose assiduous toil and diligence, having entrusted the whole government of the kingdom, she is intent on enduring her trouble as patiently as she can.[21]

Two months later, he wrote:

> The Queen's face has lost flesh greatly since I was last with her, the extreme need she has of the consort's presence harassing her . . . she having also within the last few days lost her sleep.[22]

In the middle of March, on the queen's instructions, the English ambassador, Sir John Mason, asked Philip "to say frankly in how many days he purposed returning" to the kingdom. Mason gently suggested that the king would "comfort the Queen, as also the peers of the realm, by his presence, saying that there was no reason yet to despair of his having heirs."[23] In April, Mary changed tack, sending Lord Paget as her envoy. As Badoer wrote, "I understand that the chief object of his discourse was to inspire the King with that hope, on his return to England, of being crowned, which has never yet been given him by the Queen his consort."[24] In a letter to the emperor on July 15, Mary made clear her despair and disillusionment:

> It would be pleasanter for me to thank your Majesty for sending me back the King, my lord and good husband, than to dispatch an emissary to Flanders . . . However, as your Majesty has been pleased to break your promise in this connection, a promise you made to me regarding the return of the King, my husband, I must perforce be satisfied, although to my unspeakable regret.[25]

Mary now spent her time in "tears, regrets and writing letters to bring back her husband," oscillating between a sense of anger and abandonment.[26] Increasingly she became frustrated with Philip and was reported to be "scratching portraits of her husband which she keeps in her room."[27] Finally, she wrote to the emperor once more, pleading that he hasten his son's return and arguing that it was for the safety of the realm:

> My Lord and good father, I wish to beg your Majesty's pardon for my boldness in writing to you at this time, and humbly to implore you, as you have always been pleased to act as a true father to me and my kingdom, to consider the miserable plight into which this country has now fallen. . . . Unless he [Philip] comes to remedy matters, not I only but also wiser persons than I, fear that great danger will ensue for lack of a firm hand, and indeed we see it before our eyes.[28]

CHAPTER 60

OBEDIENT SUBJECT AND HUMBLE SISTER

∴

On May 26, more than two months after the collapse of Dudley's conspiracy, two of Mary's most trusted servants, Sir Henry Jerningham and John Norris, were sent to Elizabeth at Hatfield with a posse of troops. An armed guard was put around her house, and her lady mistress, Katherine Ashley, her Italian teacher, Giovanni Battista Castiglione, and three other women of her household were arrested and taken to London. A search of Ashley's chambers at Somerset House found incriminating anti-Catholic and anti-Spanish literature. According to the Venetian ambassador, all confessed to knowing of Dudley's plot. Mary's courier Francesco Piamontese was sent to Philip in Brussels to seek his counsel with regard to Elizabeth.[1]

The advice Mary received was heavily influenced by Habsburg interests. Although there was evidence that Elizabeth had been involved in treasonous activity, any action against her would threaten her succession. In default of Elizabeth as heir, the English throne would go to Mary, queen of Scots, who was betrothed to the dauphin of France. If Philip were to triumph in the Habsburg-Valois struggle, this was something he had to prevent. Once again, English dynastic interests were to be subsumed to Habsburg strategic ones. Piamontese returned to London with an unequivocal message from the king: no further inquiries should be made into Elizabeth's guilt, nor any suggestion made that her servants had been implicated in the plot with her authority.

Hastings and Englefield were sent to Elizabeth to inform her of her servants' confessions but also to "console and comfort her on behalf of her Majesty" and to assure her that Mary trusted in her innocence.[2] The armed guard was stood down, and Elizabeth was presented with a diamond ring, a symbol of purity, as a gesture of the queen's goodwill.[3] But, unable to feign total trust in her sister's fidelity, Mary ordered that she be placed in the guardianship of Sir Thomas Pope, a loyal privy councillor and steadfast Catholic, who was put in charge of her household. As the Venetian ambassador related, Elizabeth was "in ward and custody," but in "decorous and honourable form," as Philip had decreed.[4]

IN JULY, ANOTHER conspiracy came to light, this time involving a young schoolmaster. Impersonating Edward Courtenay, the man issued a bogus proclamation at Yaxley in Suffolk, declaring that Mary was dead and that he, Courtenay, was king and "ye Lady Elizabeth" was queen.[5] In the event, the rebellion never got off the ground and the pretender was executed. Once again Elizabeth had been invoked at the heart of a conspiracy seeking to depose Mary, yet this time, in line with Philip's instructions, the assumption was made that Elizabeth was innocent. At the end of the month, the Council wrote to Sir Thomas Pope, informing him of the wicked behavior of the conspirators "and how for that intent they had abused her grace's name" by proclaiming Elizabeth the queen.[6]

Elizabeth responded with extravagant declarations of loyalty. Writing to Mary on August 2, she contrasted "the old love of pagans to their prince" to "the rebellious hearts and devilish intents of Christians in name, but Jews in deed, towards their anointed King." She invoked Saint Paul to confirm that rebels were indeed devilish, and continued:

> Among earthly things, I chiefly wish this one: that there were as good surgeons for making anatomies of hearts that might show my thoughts to your Majesty as there are expert physicians of the bodies, able to express the inward griefs of their maladies to their patient. For then I doubt not but know well that whatsoever other should suggest by malice, yet your Majesty should be sure by knowledge, so that the more such misty clouds obfuscate the clear light of my truth, the more my tried thoughts

should glister to the dimming of the hidden malice . . . And like as I have been your faithful subject from the beginning of your reign, so shall no wicked persons cause me to change to the end of my life. And thus I commit your majesty to God's tuition, whom I beseech long time to preserve . . . your majesty's obedient subject and humble sister, Elizabeth.[7]

During the autumn of 1556, relations between the two sisters seemed to continue to improve. Elizabeth was freed from Sir Thomas Pope's supervision and invited to spend Christmas at court. She left Hatfield escorted by two hundred liveried gentlemen on horseback and on November 28, amid cheering crowds, entered the City of London, proceeding to her residence at Somerset House. Three days later, she was received by the queen with honor and amicability. But then suddenly, without any warning, all changed: the invitation for Christmas was withdrawn, and on December 3, Elizabeth retraced her steps back through the city to Hatfield. She was no longer welcome at court.[8]

PHILIP'S SUPPORT OF Elizabeth had come at a price. With slight prospect of an heir to the English throne born of Mary, he had looked to secure a marriage for Elizabeth that would preserve his interest in England and the Catholic restoration. The intended bridegroom was Emmanuel Philibert, prince of Piedmont and titular duke of Savoy.

The twenty-eight-year-old duke was Philip's cousin, a loyalist imperialist and committed Catholic who was determined to rid his duchy of the French force that had occupied it since 1536. He had come to England in December 1554 as the recognized candidate for Elizabeth's hand. But Elizabeth had proved unamenable: she did not want to commit to Habsburg interests and the Catholic cause. By the winter of 1556, the idea had been revived and Philip pressured Mary to force Elizabeth to submit to his will. Mary threatened Elizabeth with a parliamentary declaration of her bastardy and an acknowledgment of Mary, queen of Scots, as her heir if she would not comply.[9] Elizabeth remained resistant, and Mary sent her sister from court.

A letter written in French in Mary's own hand at the beginning of 1557 reveals the tension between Mary and Philip over Elizabeth. He had sought to persuade Mary by arguing that she was bound by her faith and conscience to bring about Elizabeth's marriage to Philibert. But, as Mary explained in the first draft of her letter, her conscientious scruple against Elizabeth's marrying went back to her sister's birth in 1533. She then crossed out the passage and replaced it with the more benign statement that she did not understand his argument. In response to Mary's assertion that the marriage could not be carried out before parliamentary consent, Philip argued that if Parliament refused, he "would impute the blame to me." Mary begged him not to do that, saying that otherwise "I shall become jealous and uneasy about you, which will be worse to me than death," adding, "for I have already begun to taste [of such jealousy and uneasiness] too much to my great regret."

Mary was a submissive wife yet also a shrewd politician: it would not be possible, she declared, for the marriage to be carried out in his absence. He would need to come to England; then they could pray together to God, "who has the direction of the hearts of kings in his hand."[10]

CHAPTER 61

A WARMED OVER HONEYMOON

∴

AT FIVE IN THE AFTERNOON OF MARCH 20, 1557, PHILIP FINALLY returned to England. A thirty-two-gun salute greeted him at Greenwich Palace amid shouts of "God save the King and Queen."[1] The following day, the bells of London rang out in celebration. A series of entertainments—banquets, dances, and masques of welcome—culminated on the twenty-third in a grand civic festival as Philip, Mary, and the nobles and ladies of the realm rode through London. It was, as one diplomat described it, "a warmed over honeymoon."[2]

Yet despite the festivities, there was little disguising the true purpose of Philip's visit. The king had returned for money and an English declaration of war against France, a prospect very few Englishmen were happy with.

MONTHS EARLIER, the Habsburg-Valois conflict had reignited. In September 1556, the duke of Alva, Philip's viceroy in Naples, had launched an invasion of the papal states some thirty years after the armies of Charles V had destroyed Rome. Denouncing Charles V as a "heretic, schismatic and tyrant" whose aim had been to oppress the Holy See and Philip as the "son of iniquity," the eighty-year-old Italian Pope Paul IV persuaded the French to join him in an attempt to drive Habsburg forces out of Italy.

Philip's attention immediately turned to England. He sought to relieve the pressure in Italy by striking at the Franco-Flemish frontier. He was effectively bankrupt and desperately needed money and men and an English declaration to defend the Low Countries.[3] Philip's envoy, Figueroa, presented his demands at a series of meetings with the Privy Council held in the queen's chambers at St. James's in mid-November.[4] Though the Council approved sending money and naval support, it was not prepared to commit troops or renew the Anglo-Flemish treaties for fear of provoking war with France.

On the night of January 5–6, the French launched a surprise attack on the town of Douai on the Flemish frontier. The Treaty of Vaucelles was broken, and on the thirty-first war was formally declared between France and Spain.[5] Although there was no direct threat to England, Mary had already begun to prepare the country for war. In January, sheriffs of several eastern and midland counties were summoned to report on how many troops could be mustered; royal pensioners were equipped with new standards bearing the arms of Philip and Mary "with a great eagle above"; ships were ordered to be refitted, and further reinforcements were sent to Calais.[6] The English navy had been greatly expanded during the previous eighteen months, and two large new ships, the *Philip and Mary* and a new *Mary Rose*, were ready by the beginning of 1557.[7] The Council grudgingly approved the raising of 6,000 foot and 600 horse, which they were bound by treaty to send to Philip if the Netherlands were attacked.

On January 20, a muster of royal pensioners at Greenwich Park took place in front of the queen. With trumpets blowing and standards unfurled, the men at arms rode past her three abreast. Their standards, combining Philip and Mary's arms, symbolized the union of the two powers against the common enemy. On one side, the Castilian colors of red and yellow surrounded the white hart of England; on the other was the black eagle of the Habsburgs with gilded legs.[8] After the muster a tumbler performed many feats "that her grace did like." She "did thank them all for their pains" and went back into the palace much heartened.[9]

Henry II of France had sent clear instructions to Noailles: the principal thing he desired was to be kept on "friendly terms with the Queen of England . . . so that in that direction, if possible, nothing should happen to thwart me, and so that during these wars I may not have them [the English] for open and declared enemies."[10] Within days, Mary was informed of Philip's imminent departure for England and that the French, by breaking the truce, had left him no choice but to raise land and sea forces to prevent the pope and the French from waging war in the Kingdom of Naples.[11] Mary begged Philip "not to be afraid to come [back]," assuring him that his presence would "enable him to obtain what he wants."[12]

WHEN PHILIP RETURNED to England in late March 1557, both he and the queen petitioned the Council for a declaration of war. On April 1, Mary summoned the councillors to her and, in Philip's presence, made a speech outlining the reasons for war, with Mary now choosing to play up her wifely obligations:

> She expounded to them the obedience which she owed her husband and the power which he had over her as much by divine as by human law, citing to them many examples from the Old and New Testament, and begged them to consider the greatness and prosperity of the kingdom of France, which was already menacing the whole world. So that if they did not decide to aid her husband, who was beginning to be the weaker party (because of the recent misfortunes of the Emperor his father), they might be sure that the King of France, having driven the King her husband from Italy, as he was about to do through lack of help, would soon afterward turn to them and drive them out of their own house.[13]

The councillors asked for time to deliberate and returned two days later to deliver their verdict: it "ought not and could not declare war."[14] They would approve financial and naval support to Philip but would not promise troops or declare openly against France.[15] The realm, they maintained, was in no condition to wage war: food was scarce, the coffers were empty and the people discontented. It would be disastrous to cut off England's trade with France because neither Spain nor Flanders could supply all that was needed. Finally, they stated that the marriage treaty expressly forbade Philip to draw England into his struggle with France.[16]

Mary was furious. She ordered the councillors to meet again and draft a reply that would "satisfy her and her husband."[17] The Council remained defiant, and the stalemate continued. Yet Mary was determined to fulfill Philip's demands.[18] As Noailles reported, Mary would force "not only men, but also the elements themselves, to consent to her will."[19] On April 13, before the court removed to Greenwich for Easter, Mary summoned the councillors privately to her room and threatened each of them, "some with death, others with the loss of their goods and estates, if they did not consent to the will of her husband."[20] They now offered money and troops, but Philip refused to be satisfied with anything less than an open declaration of war.

CHAPTER 62

A PUBLIC ENEMY TO OURSELVES

∴

ON APRIL 23, 1557, SIR THOMAS STAFFORD, AN ENGLISH PROTestant exile, landed on the Yorkshire coast at Scarborough with two French ships and a force of up to a hundred English and French rebels and seized Scarborough Castle.[1] His aim was to depose Mary, an "unrightful and unworthy Queen" who had "forfeited the right by her marriage with a Spaniard."[2]

Styling himself "protector of the realm," he came, he said, to deliver his countrymen of the tyranny of strangers and warned of an influx of Spaniards who would enslave the people. He would "defeat the most devilish device of Mary," who "most justly deserved to be deprived from the Crown, because she being naturally born half Spanish and half English, beareth not herself indifferently towards both nations, but showing herself a whole Spaniard, and no English Woman, in loving Spaniards, and hating Englishmen." For the defense of the country, he promised that the crown would revert "to the true English blood of our own natural Country."[3]

The government reacted quickly. Within five days, the earl of Westmoreland had retaken the castle, and on April 30 a proclamation was issued in London announcing Stafford's capture. He was tried, condemned, and executed for treason at Tyburn a month later.

The rebellion provided the catalyst for the declaration of war with France. Writing to Emmanuel Philibert, duke of Savoy, from London on April 28, the Spanish commander, Don Bernardino de Mendoza, declared, "As for the breach of the truce, the French have spared us the trouble."[4] And in London, on June 7, 1557, the queen's heralds formally proclaimed war with France:

> Although we, the Queen, when we first came to the throne, understood that the Duke of Northumberland's abominable treason had been abetted by Henry, the French King, and that since then his ministers had secretly favoured Wyatt's rebellion . . . we attributed these doings to the French King's ministers rather than to his own will, hoping thus patiently to induce him to adopt a truly friendly attitude towards us . . . the other day he sent Stafford with ships and supplies to seize our castle of Scarborough . . . for the above reasons, and because he has sent an army to invade Flanders which we are under obligation to defend, we have seen fit to proclaim to our subjects that they are to consider the King of France as a public enemy to ourselves and our nation, rather than to suffer him to continue to deceive us under colour of friendship.[5]

When the English herald conveyed England's declaration of war to Henry II, he made clear who he believed was the real instigator of the conflict between England and France: "The Queen . . . did what she has done against me under compulsion, her husband having given her to understand that unless she declared herself he would depart that kingdom, and never return hither to see her . . . she was forced to do what she has done." He declared that as the herald had come in the name of a woman it was unnecessary for him to listen any further, "as he would done had he come in the name of a man." Laughing, he asked his ambassadors to "consider how I stand when a woman sends [a declaration] to defy me to war, but I doubt not that God will assist me."[6]

WITHIN WEEKS OF England's entry into the war, Philip left England. Mary accompanied him to Dover, from which he set sail, and at three in the morning of July 6, the king and queen parted company at the quayside. They would never see each other again.

Several days later, an English force of more than 1,000 led by the earl of Pembroke followed the king across the Channel. Many of the officers were former rebels and plotters, including Sir Peter Carew, Lord Robert Dudley, the son of the duke of Northumberland, Sir

James Croft, and Sir Nicholas Throckmorton. War provided opportunities for service and honor and allowed those involved with sedition and rebellion to make their peace with the government. Initially the English army had some success. On August 10, a French force advancing to raise the siege at Saint-Quentin was heavily routed. Although the English missed the battle, men under the earl of Pembroke took part in the capture of the city some weeks later. "Both sides fought most choicely," wrote one Spanish officer, "and the English best of all."[7] The news was greeted in England with widespread celebrations.[8] It looked to have been a successful end to the campaigning season, but the French were intent on quick revenge and believed that the winter would be the best time to attack the garrison at Calais, the last English territory in France, as the marshes would be frozen.

ON NEW YEAR'S DAY 1558, 27,000 French troops attacked Calais. On the third, Thomas, Lord Wentworth, now lord deputy of Calais, described the dire situation in a letter to Philip:

> Sire: I have received your Majesty's letter informing me that the French are moving against Calais. Indeed they have been camping before this town for three days. They have set their batteries in position, and have stormed the castle at the entrance to the port, and also the other castle on the road leading to France. Thus they have occupied all our territory, and nothing remains for them to do except to take this town. If it is lost, your Majesty knows what great facility it would give them to invade your territories of Flanders.[9]

By the seventh, the French had entered the castle and Wentworth surrendered. The diarist Henry Machyn recorded the loss:

> The x day of January, heavy news came to England, and to London, that the Fre[nch had won] Calais, the which was the heaviest tidings to London and to England that ever was heard of, for like a traitor it was sold and d[elivered unto] them the [blank] day of January.[10]

The garrison was ill prepared and undermanned. French forces led by Francis, duke of Guise, had been able to take it by surprise by launching their attack in midwinter.[11] The garrisons of Guisnes and Hammes held out until January 21, when forces under William, Lord Grey, short of ammunition and food, also surrendered. Just a few months after the victory at Saint-Quentin, the French had inflicted a catastrophic defeat on the English.

The recriminations began almost immediately. Lord Wentworth, it was claimed, was a heretic and had intrigued with others within and outside of Calais. Many Englishmen believed that Philip had done less than he could to assist the garrison, while the Spanish argued that the fortress had been lost through English incompetence. As the last remnant of the English claim to the continental monarchy, Calais had a highly symbolic value, arguably outweighing its economic and military importance. Calais had been captured by Edward III in 1347 and was the sole remnant of the Anglo-French empire that had endured from the Normans to the Wars of the Roses.

But neither the Council nor Parliament was prepared to sanction the granting of funds to send forces to recover Calais. "We feel compelled to urge you," Philip wrote to the Privy Council, "to be swayed by no private interests or passions, but only by your care for the welfare of the kingdom, lest its reputation for power and greatness, earned the world over in former times, be lost now through your own neglect and indifference."[12] Yet it was less English pride than Habsburg strategic interests that dictated Philip's concerns. As he wrote to Pole of the loss of Calais, "that sorrow was indeed unspeakable, for reasons which you may well imagine and because the event was an extremely grave one for these states."[13]

CHAPTER 63

THE GRIEF OF THE MOST SERENE QUEEN

∴

A war between your Highness [the Pope] and King Philip must produce the gravest danger and harm to the whole Christian Commonwealth . . . only Satan, could have sown the seeds of this dissension.[1]

—CARDINAL POLE TO POPE PAUL IV

BY DECLARING WAR ON FRANCE, IT WAS ALMOST INEVITABLE THAT England would be drawn into conflict with Henry II's ally, Pope Paul IV. For several months Cardinal Pole had sought to prevent military action and bring about a peaceful settlement, but to no avail. Writing to the pope, he explained:

> If to all good men this war between your Holiness and King Philip is most painful, by reason of the very many and grievous perils and damages with which it seems to threaten not one realm alone, but the entire Christian commonwealth, to me of necessity it is the more bitter, the more I find myself bound by all the ties of devotion and reverence to your Holiness, and by those of love to the King.[2]

Meanwhile, the pope was aggrieved that Mary had not shown any regret over the war against the papacy, nor had she exerted herself to prevent it. As Cardinal Giovanni Morone, the vice protector of England, reported, he had "been told on good authority" that she had aided Philip with money, which had "greatly exasperated" the pope, who was refusing to dispatch English business.[3]

On April 9, 1557, as the Privy Council was debating whether to declare war on France, Pope Paul IV had withdrawn his nuncios and legates from Philip's dominions. Pole was specifically mentioned and deprived of his legatine power, and the See of Canterbury was deprived of its legatine status.[4] Mary was horrified. "The grief of the most serene Queen," Pole wrote in his first anguished protest to Rome, "may be more easily estimated by the Pope, he having had experience of her extreme piety in bringing back this kingdom to obedience to the Church than he, Pole, can write it."[5] In letters to the pope, Mary and the Council stressed how much damage would be done to the realm by the withdrawal of the legate at such a critical stage in the process of Catholic restoration and likened the realm to a convalescing invalid who faced the withdrawal of his physician.[6] Given Mary's faith and fidelity to the Holy See, petitions to Rome would, it was believed, succeed in revoking the decree as far as it related to Pole.

On June 12, the Venetian ambassador in Rome, Bernardo Navagero, reported that the Roman Inquisition was investigating Pole as a suspected Lutheran.[7] The new pope held deep suspicions about Pole's religious opinions. In the 1530s, Pole had belonged to a group, the Spirituali, who had hoped for reconciliation with the Lutherans and sought an accommodation with them on the issue of salvation by faith alone. But by the 1550s, Pope Paul IV saw such doctrinal compromises as heresy. On June 14, 1557, Pole was formally recalled to Rome.[8] In acknowledgment of Mary's obedience to Rome and his concern for the restoration of the English Church, Paul IV announced that he would relax his general policy toward England and appoint a new papal legate, the eighty-year-old Franciscan friar William Peto, formerly the confessor of Katherine of Aragon.[9]

Mary learned the news as she was accompanying Philip to Dover on the eve of his departure.[10] She was outraged. When the papal nuncio bearing the official briefs reached Calais in July, he was refused admission into the realm. Mary would ensure that she never received the official notification of Pole's recall or Peto's appointment. Pole wanted to go to Rome to clear his name, but Sir Edward Carne, Mary's ambassador in Rome, warned him that he would be imprisoned by the

Inquisition.[11] Mary had no intention of letting him go and expressed her amazement that a man who had performed such distinguished services for the Church and whose presence was so essential to the task in hand should be withdrawn. She was confident that the pope would realize that she knew best about affairs in her kingdom and would grant her request, praying that he restore the legation of Cardinal Pole and beseeching him to "pardon her if she professed to know the men who are good for the government of her kingdom better than His Holiness."[12] If any disturbance should take place in England, she protested, it would be for that reason. At the same time, Peto declined the legateship on the grounds of age and infirmity.

By mid-August there was a deadlock. The pope had no intention of giving way and restoring Pole's legation, even though no charges had been leveled against him, while Mary refused to send Pole to Rome in exchange for Peto. Instead, she dispatched fresh instructions to Carne as to how to react if actual charges of heresy were made against Pole. If Pole were found guilty of heresy, Carne was to declare that Mary would be his "greatest enemy," but unless or until proof of such a crime could be found, she would take him for a good and Catholic man. Moreover, Mary argued, as an Englishman and archbishop of Canterbury, Pole must be tried in England, as Cranmer had been two years before. If the pope refused the request, Carne was instructed to leave Rome, but only after informing all the cardinals that "the Queen and Council and the whole kingdom of England, will never swerve from their devotion, reverence and obedience to the See Apostolic and to his Holiness' successors, although for a certain period they were compelled not to obey Pope Paul IV."[13] Charges were not made and diplomatic relations were not broken off, though rumors circulated around the curia that England was about to go into schism once more.

The conclusion of peace between Philip and the pope on September 12, 1557, was greeted with great jubilation in London.[14] By one of the articles of the Treaty of Cave between the pope and the Habsburgs, it was agreed that Pole's legation would be restored, though this never happened. Pole's position remained unchanged, and he continued, unsuccessfully, to petition the pope for vindication. He talked of the "sword of grief" with which the pope had pierced his soul.[15] The man who had absolved England from heresy three and a half years earlier was now a fugitive heretic. Pole could not accept that Paul IV, his former friend, had turned against him. He wrote to the pope, begging him to say he had only been testing Pole's loyalty "as Christ is wont to place his dearest children in purgatory to try them."[16]

Just four years before, Mary had described herself as the Holy See's "most obedient and affectionate" daughter; his Holiness had no more loving daughter than herself. Now, as the last months of her life drew near, her relations with the pope became significantly strained.[17] It was a great irony that upon Mary's death, the pope would initially express gratification upon the accession of Elizabeth as an improvement on her sister.[18]

CHAPTER 64

READINESS FOR CHANGE

∴

IN 1557, GIOVANNI MICHIELI, THE VENETIAN AMBASSADOR, LEFT England. In his final report, the *relazione,* he gave a detailed account of the character and concerns of the then-forty-one-year-old queen.

Above all, he praised Mary's devotion and piety. "Besides her noble descent," he wrote, she was "a very great and rare example of virtue and magnanimity, a real portrait of patience and humility, and of the true fear of God." Indeed, few women in the world were known to be more "assiduous at their prayers than she is," always keeping to the canonical hours and observing Communions and fast days. She had lived a life "little short of martyrdom, by reason of the persecution she endured."

In her youth, he reflected, Mary "was considered not merely tolerably handsome, but of beauty exceeding mediocrity." However, the queen's aspect was now "very grave," with "wrinkles, caused more by anxieties than by age, which make her appear some years older." Though "like other women," she could be "sudden and passionate, and close and miserly," she maintained a "wonderful grandeur and dignity."

Despite being "valiant" and "brave," Mary was prone to "deep melancholy"—a product, Michieli surmised, of "monstrous retention" and "suffocation of the matrix [womb]," a disease thought to be caused by the retention of menstrual fluids and a condition from which she had suffered for many years. But "the remedy of tears and weeping, to which from childhood she has been accustomed, and still often used by her" was no longer sufficient and now she required to be "blooded either from the foot or elsewhere, which keeps her always pale and emaciated."

Principal among Mary's distresses were those that arose from her love for Philip and her resentment of her sister, Elizabeth. Philip's constant traveling left Mary bereft, "not only of that company, for the sake of which (besides the hope of lineage) marriages are formed," but the separation "which to any person who loves another heartily, would be irksome and grievous" is felt particularly by a woman so "naturally tender." Her "fear and violent love" for Philip left her constantly in a state of anxiety. If to this were added jealousy, the ambassador continued, "she would be truly miserable," as to be parted from the king was one of the "anxieties that especially distresses her."

Added to this was her "evil disposition," as Michieli described it, "towards her sister Elizabeth"; although the queen pretended otherwise, "it cannot be denied the scorn and ill will she bears her." When faced with Elizabeth, "it was as if she were in the presence of the affronts and ignominious treatment to which she was subjected to on account of her mother," Anne Boleyn. Worse still, Mary saw "the eyes and hearts" of the nation already fixed on Elizabeth as her successor, given Mary's lack of an heir. Much to Mary's dismay, she perceived that no one believed "in the possibility of her having progeny," so that "day by day" she saw her authority and the respect induced by it diminish. Besides this, "the Queen's hatred is increased by knowing her to be averse to the present religion . . . for although externally she showed, and by living Catholically shows, that she has recanted, she is nevertheless supposed to dissemble and to hold to it more than ever internally."

Mary had, the Venetian reflected, become a queen of regrets. She had been "greatly grieved" by many insurrections, conspiracies, and plots that continually formed against her at home and abroad, and she mourned the decline of the "affection" universally evinced toward her at the beginning of her reign, which had been "so extraordinary that never was greater shown in that kingdom towards any sovereign." The country was, Michieli said, "showing a greater inclination and readiness for change" than ever before. The "fruitlessness" of Mary's marriage was a source of profound regret, and the lack of an heir threatened the restoration of Catholicism and the obedience of the English Church to Rome, which was now sustained by her "authority and presence." But, Michieli added, "nor is it to be told how much hurt that vain pregnancy did her."

If the queen predeceased Philip, he would be deprived of the kingdom; but more important was the fear that the king's "enemies" would seek to occupy England "or cause the realm to fall into their hands." Michieli ended his *relazione* with a list of possible claimants for the English throne: first, Elizabeth, whose right was based on the will of Henry VIII and the Act of Succession; then Mary, queen of Scots, who claimed an absolute hereditary right; and the two sisters of the late Lady Jane Grey, who claimed precedence over Elizabeth on account of the will of Edward VI. Yet, as Michieli concluded, even if Mary were to be "undeceived," which "as yet she is not," about the possibility of having children, she wished to avoid naming a successor and "will rather leave it to time to act, referring the matter after her death to those whom it concerns either by right or by force."[1]

CHAPTER 65

THINKING MYSELF TO BE WITH CHILD

∴

WITHIN SIX MONTHS OF MICHIELI'S RELAZIONE, MARY AGAIN believed she was pregnant. This time she waited until her sixth month and then in January 1558 sent word to Philip.[1] "The news of the Queen, my beloved wife," Philip wrote to Pole, "has given me greater joy than I can express to you, as it is the one thing in the world I have most desired and which is of the greatest importance for the cause of religion and the care and welfare of our realm." It has "gone far to lighten the sorrow I have felt for the loss of Calais."[2]

Weeks later, Don Gómez Suárez de Figueroa, count of Feria, was sent to England. He was to express Philip's delight at the news of his wife's impending labor but also to try to discover if it might be true. Many believed it was not, and this time no preparations were made for her confinement. Upon arriving in England, Feria quickly came to the conclusion that Mary was only "making herself believe that she is with child, although she does not own up to it."[3]

Yet Mary remained convinced, and on March 30, as she approached what she believed to be the ninth month of her pregnancy, she made her will:

> Thinking myself to be with child in lawful marriage between my said dearly beloved husband and lord, although I be at this present (thanks be unto Almighty God) otherwise in good health, yet foreseeing the great danger which by God's ordinance remain to all women in their travail of children, have thought good, both for the discharge of my conscience and con-

> tinuance of good order within my realms and dominions, to declare my last will and testament.

In the event of her death, the crown would be left to "the heirs, issue and fruit" of her body, while Philip, her "most dear and entirely beloved husband," would be appointed guardian and regent for the prince or princess.

BY MAY, MARY'S HEALTH had deteriorated: she suffered from intermittent fevers, insomnia, headaches, and loss of vision. It was clear that there was no pregnancy. Writing to Philip, Feria described how "she sleeps badly, is weak and suffers from melancholy; and her indisposition results in business being handled more slowly than need be."[4]

Over the summer Mary grew progressively weaker. In August, she caught influenza, then endemic in the country, and was moved from Hampton Court to St. James's Palace. Forced to acknowledge the seriousness of her condition, she added a codicil to her will: "feeling myself presently sick and weak in body," she admitted that it was unlikely she was with child. "Forasmuch as God hath hitherto sent me no fruit nor heir of my body, it is only in his most divine providence whether I shall have any or no." If God did not grant her an heir, she would be "succeeded by my next heir and successor by the Laws and Statutes of this realm."[5] She stopped short of acknowledging Elizabeth by name but exhorted Philip to protect and care for England "as a father in his care, as a brother in his love and favour . . . and a most assured and undoubted friend to her country and subjects."

On October 29, Antonio Surian, the Venetian ambassador, who was with Philip, wrote to the doge and Senate:

> A few days ago, his Majesty received news from England that the Queen was grievously ill, and her life in danger, which intelligence, most especially at the present moment being of very great importance, so disquieted his Majesty, and all these lords, that it was immediately determined to send the Count de Feria to visit the Queen, in the name of her consort but as when the count was about to depart, fresh advice arrived that her

> Majesty's health had improved his departure was delayed . . . the matter to be treated by him is the marriage of Milady Elizabeth, to keep that kingdom in any event in the hands of his Majesty's confidence.[6]

By the terms of the marriage treaty, Philip's prerogatives in England would cease with Mary's death. In April, the marriage between Mary, queen of Scots, and the French dauphin, the future Francis II, had finally taken place. If Mary Stuart's claim to the English throne could be secured, France's position would be strengthened immeasurably and tip the balance in the Habsburg-Valois struggle. Even if Elizabeth succeeded, Philip feared that her Protestant sympathies would lead to a diplomatic realignment that would leave Spain isolated.

Feria was instructed to visit Elizabeth on the king's behalf, present his compliments, express Philip's hope that the amity would continue between Spain and the Tudor dominions, and ingratiate himself with the men around her. Elizabeth responded favorably, declaring that she would always be grateful to Philip because "when she was in prison [the king] had shown her favour and helped to obtain her release," but dismissed the suggestion that she might marry the duke of Savoy.[7] Meanwhile, Feria was "to try and dispose the Queen to consent to Lady Elizabeth being married as her sister, and with the hope of succeeding to the crown."[8]

The first few days of November saw some alleviation in the queen's condition, and as Parliament met, the Council petitioned her to make "certain declarations in favour of the Lady Elizabeth concerning the succession." On November 6, Mary bowed to the inevitable: she "consented" and accepted Elizabeth as her heir. It was what she had fought to avoid most of her life, but now, realizing that death was near, she had no choice. Sir Thomas Cornwallis, the comptroller of the royal household, and John Boxall, secretary to the Privy Council, were sent to Hatfield to give Elizabeth the news. Mary asked that Elizabeth pay her debts and keep the Catholic religion as it had been established.[9] She knew it was a futile plea.

While Mary lay dying, the court began to move to Hatfield, as "many personages of the kingdom flocked to the house of 'milady' Elizabeth, the crowd constantly increasing with great frequency."[10]

CHAPTER 66

REASONABLE REGRET FOR HER DEATH

∴

JUST BEFORE MIDNIGHT ON WEDNESDAY, NOVEMBER 16, 1557, MARY received the last rites in her chamber at St. James's Palace. A few hours later, between five and six in the morning, she died. She was forty-two.

During her last few days, the celebration of Mass had been at the center of her conscious existence, and as dawn broke on Thursday morning, she had lifted her eyes at the Elevation of the Host for the final time. According to one later account, she had "comforted those of them that grieved about her, she told them what good dreams she had, seeing many little children, like Angels playing before her, singing pleasing notes."[1] Hours later, the lord chancellor, Nicholas Heath, announced to Parliament that Mary was dead. Any sorrow that might have been felt was quickly overshadowed by rejoicing for the accession of a new queen.

At Whitehall, Elizabeth was formally proclaimed as heralds rode out to the cross at Cheapside to make the announcement before the lord mayor and aldermen of the city.[2] By midafternoon, "all the churches in London did ring, and at night did make bonfires and set tables in the street, and did eat and drink and made merry for the new Queen Elizabeth, Queen Mary['s] sister."[3] Just six hours after Mary's death, Elizabeth was proclaimed queen.

Across the river at Lambeth Palace, Cardinal Pole also lay dying. The news of the queen's passing appeared to hurry his own demise. For nearly a quarter of an hour he remained silent, absorbing what he had just heard; "though his spirit was great, the blow nevertheless having entered his flesh, brought on the paroxysm earlier, and with more intense cold." Turning to Ludovico Priuli and Thomas Goldwell, bishop of St. Asaph, two of his closest attendants, he remarked on the symmetry, the "great conformity," as he described it, of their lives. She, like himself, "had been harassed during many years for one and the same cause, and afterwards, when it pleased God to raise her to the throne, he had greatly participated in all her other troubles entailed by that elevation."[4] Just twelve hours after Mary's passing, he too died, unreconciled with and condemned by the pope.

A messenger was sent to Philip with news of his wife's death. Just weeks before, both his father, the Emperor Charles V, and his aunt Margaret of Flanders, the regent of the Netherlands, had also died. "You may imagine what a state I am in," he wrote to his sister in Spain; "it seems to me that everything is being taken from me at once." Of Mary he added, "May God have received her in His glory! I felt a reasonable regret for her death. I shall miss her, even on this account."[5] Mary remained second to Habsburg strategic interests; Philip's comments were made in the middle of a paragraph detailing progress in the peace negotiations at Cercamp. He instructed Feria to secure the jewels that Mary had bequeathed him in her will and to represent him with suitable dignity at her obsequies.

WITHIN HOURS of Mary's death, the preparation of her body began. Her heart and bowels were removed, her belly opened and filled with preservative herbs and spices. She was placed in a lead coffin and then a wooden chest. For the next three weeks, her corpse lay in state in the Privy Chamber of St. James's Palace, which had been hung with black cloth and adorned with the royal arms. The coffin stood upon trestles, covered with a pall of rich cloth of gold. Every day her gentlewomen prayed about the coffin and heard Masses, and through the night her hearse was illuminated with burning candles.

In life Mary had received visitors in her Privy Chamber under the cloth of estate; now, in death, mourners looked upon her body and paid their respects. Though dead, Mary would remain in possession of sovereignty until her burial some weeks later. As was customary during the weeks of transition, a lifelike, life-size wooden effigy dressed in the coronation robes and bearing the orb and scepter acted in place of the dead monarch. A fifteenth-century guide, "What Shall Be Done on the Demise of a King Anointed," gave instructions to "make an image like him clothed in a surcoat, with a mantel of estate, the laces goodly lying on his belly, his sceptre in his hand, and a crown on his head, and so carry him in a chair open, with lights and banners, accompanied with lords and estates as the council can best devise."[6] Around it the routines of court life continued. As Feria noted, "the house is served exactly as it was before." Food was placed on the royal table; gentleman ushers officiated with their white wands; guards stood at doors of the chamber within which sat the five-foot-five wooden figure.[7]

The marquess of Winchester, the most senior of Mary's surviving councillors, was put in charge of the funeral arrangements. The ceremony, conducted according to "King Henry VIII's funeral book," was to be traditional, Catholic, and expensive.[8] Preparations continued for nearly a month as the dead queen remained in state at St. James's. Finally, on December 10, with the arrangements made and mourning clothes and funeral accoutrements prepared, a solemn procession of black-robed heralds, lords, ladies, and household officers entered the privy apartments. Mary's coffin was held aloft and carried to the Chapel Royal, where the high altar had been trimmed with purple velvet. At three in the afternoon lords and ladies assembled in the Presence Chamber and Great Chamber along with the officers of the household. The bishops went into the Presence Chamber, censed the coffin, and said prayers. The coffin, borne under a canopy of purple velvet, was then taken up by eight gentlemen and in ordered procession made its way to the chapel.

Three days later, the funeral cortege made its final journey to Westminster Abbey. Banners of the English royal arms led the king and queen's household officers, who, dressed in black, marched two by two in rank order. Behind them five heralds bore the masculine regalia of sovereignty—the banner of English royal arms embroidered with gold, the royal helmet, the royal shield, the royal sword, and the coat of armor, as if a king were being buried. A wheeled chariot bearing Mary's coffin followed, accompanied by the painted effigy "adorned with crimson velvet and her crown on her head, her sceptre in her hand and many goodly rings on her fingers."[9] At each corner of the funeral chariot a herald on horseback bore a banner of the four English royal saints. After the chariot followed the chief mourner, Margaret Douglas, countess of Lennox, and Mary's ladies-in-waiting, all in black robes, attending her in death as they had in life.[10]

The procession halted at the great door of the abbey, where it was met by four bishops and an abbot, who censed the coffin before it and the effigy were taken inside. There Mary's body laid overnight in the hearse that had been specially built to receive it, watched over by a hundred gentlemen in mourning clothes and the queen's guard, each holding burning torches.[11]

The next morning, the funeral Mass was sung and John White, bishop of Winchester, preached the funeral sermon.[12] He had been present at Mary's death and related how "if angels were mortal, I would rather liken this her departure to the death of an angel, than of a mortal creature." He then delivered an oration, praising Mary's virtues:

> She was a King's daughter, she was a King's sister, she was a King's wife. She was a Queen, and by the same title a King also. . . . What she suffered in each of these degrees before and since she came to the crown I will not chronicle; only this I say, howsoever it pleased God to will her patience to be exercised in the world, she had in all estates the fear of God in her heart . . . she had the Love, Commendation and Admiration of all the World. In this church she married herself to the realm, and in token of faith and fidelity, did put a ring with a diamond on her finger, which I understand she never took off after, during her life . . . she was never unmindful or uncareful of her promise to the realm.

He continued:

> She used singular mercy towards offenders. She used much pity and compassion towards the poor and oppressed. She used clemency amongst her nobles. . . . She restored more noble houses decayed than ever did prince of this realm, or I did pray God ever shall have the like occasion to do hereafter.

The bishop said little about Mary's religious policies but defended her sincere faith. "I verily believe, the poorest creature in all this city feared not God more than she did."[13]

It was a powerful speech based on two verses from Ecclesiastes: "I praised the dead which are already dead more than the living, which are yet alive" and "for a living dog is better than a dead lion." He sought to disguise his words with apparently harmless analogies, but his meaning was clear: a dead Mary was better than a living Elizabeth. After this encomium, the best that White could say of Elizabeth was that she was royal like Mary and held the realm "by the like title and right." He concluded by "wishing her a prosperous reign in peace and tranquillity"—"if it be God's will."[14] The next day the bishop was informed that "for such offences as he committed in his sermon at the funeral of the late Queen," he was to be confined to his house at Elizabeth's pleasure.[15]

At the offertory of the Mass that followed, the regalia was offered at the altar, one by one, and the queen's coat of armor, sword, shield, and banner of arms returned symbolically to God. The effigy and other tokens of royalty were removed from the coffin, which was carried to the chapel of Mary's grandfather Henry VII. A vault had been opened in the north aisle of Henry VII's chapel into which the coffin was lowered. After earth had been cast on top, Mary's household officers broke their white staffs of office and threw them into the grave. The heralds cried, "The queen is dead, long live the queen!" and people tore down the banners and cloth hangings for souvenirs. With trumpets blowing, the mourners and peers, officiating clergy, and Mary's officers all departed to dine at the abbot of Westminster's lodging, the last act of the regime.[16]

VERITAS TEMPORIS FILIA

... Witness [alas!] may Marie be, late Queen of rare renown
Whose body dead, her virtues live, and doth her fame resowne....

She never closed her ear to hear the righteous man distress
Nor never spared her hand to help, when wrong or power oppress

Make for your mirror [Princes all] Marie, our mistress late. . . .
Farewell, O Queen! O pearl most pure! that God or nature gave,
The earth, the heavens, the sprites, the saints cry honor to thy grave.

Marie now dead, Elizabeth lives, our just & lawful Queen,
In whom her sister's virtues rare, abundantly are seen.
Obey our Queen, as we are bound, pray God her to preserve,
And send her grace life long and fruit, and subjects true to serve.

—"Epitaph upon the Death of Quene Marie, Deceased" [ca. 1558][1]

The forging and recasting of Mary's reputation began immediately upon her death. One Richard Lante was imprisoned for printing this elegy without license, and the verses were swiftly reissued with a final stanza in praise of Elizabeth.[2] Mary had requested that her executors "cause to be made some honourable tombs or decent memory" of her and her mother, but this, her dying wish, was ignored. Instead the anniversary of Mary's death came to be remembered solely as "Elizabeth's Accession Day," an annual day of celebration and thanksgiving. Official prayers hailed the new queen, who had delivered the English people "from the danger of war and oppression, restoring peace and true religion, with liberty both of bodies and minds."[3]

Mary quickly became a figure of opprobrium, as Protestants returning from exile sought to ingratiate themselves with the new regime. In *The First Blast of the Trumpet against the Monstrous Regiment of Women*, written on the eve of Mary's death, John Knox condemned her as a "horrible monster Jezebel" and described how during her reign Englishmen had been "compelled to bow their necks under the yoke of Satan, and of his proud ministers, pestilent papists and proud Spaniards."[4] Knox argued that women were incapable of effective rule as they were by nature "weak, frail, impatient, feeble and foolish: and experience hath declared them to be inconstant, variable, cruel and lacking the spirit of counsel and regiment."[5] Female rule was "the subversion of good order, of all equity and justice." Yet Knox quickly had to refine his views to accommodate the accession of a Protestant queen.[6]

In his *Actes and Monuments of These Latter and Perillous Dayes*, John Foxe, the most infamous returning exile, celebrated the passing of Mary's reign. "We shall never find any reign of any Prince in this land or any other," he wrote, "which ever shows in it (for the proportion of time) so many great arguments of God's wrath and displeasure." His detailed account of the lives of the Protestant martyrs graphically portrayed "the horrible and bloody time of Queen Mary."[7]

Coinciding with the rise of the Accession Day festivities was the promulgation of an order that a copy of Foxe's *Actes and Monuments* be installed in every "cathedral church."[8] By 1600, Catholicism was firmly understood to be an "un-English" creed and Protestantism an entrenched part of England's national identity.

Foxe's account would shape the popular narrative of Mary's reign for the next four hundred and fifty years. Generations of schoolchildren would grow up knowing the first queen of England only as "Bloody Mary," a Catholic tyrant who sent nearly three hundred Protestants to their deaths, a point made satirically in W. C. Sellar and R. J. Yeatman's 1930s parody *1066 and All That*.[9] Mary's presence in a recent survey of the most evil men and women in history is testament to Foxe's enduring legacy.[10]

But there is, of course, a different Mary: a woman marked by suffering, devout in her faith and exceptional in her courage. From a childhood in which she was adored and feted and then violently rejected, a fighter was born. Her resolve almost cost her her life as her father, and then her brother, sought to subjugate her to their wills. Yet Mary maintained her faith and self-belief. Despite repeated attempts to deprive her of her life and right to the throne, the warrior princess turned victor and became the warrior queen.

The boldness and scale of her achievement are often overlooked. The campaign that Mary led in the summer of 1553 would prove to be the only successful revolt against central government in sixteenth-century England. She, like her grandfather Henry VII and grandmother Isabella of Castile, had to fight for her throne. In the moment of crisis she proved decisive, courageous, and "Herculean"—and won the support of the English people as the legitimate Tudor heir.

Mary was a conscientious, hardworking queen who was determined to be closely involved in government business and policy making. She would rise "at daybreak when, after saying her prayers and hearing mass in private," she would "transact business incessantly until after midnight."[11] As rebels threatened the capital in January 1554 and she was urged to flee, Mary stood firm and successfully rallied Londoners to her defense. She was also a woman who lived by her conscience and was prepared to die for her faith. And she expected the same of others.

Her religious defiance was matched by a personal infatuation with Philip, her Spanish husband. Her love for him and dependence on her "true father," the emperor Charles V, was unwavering. Her determination to honor her husband's will led England into an unpopular war with France and the loss of Calais. There was no fruit of the union, and so at her premature death there was no Catholic heir. Her own phantom pregnancies, together with epidemics and harvest failures across the country, left her undermined and unpopular. Her life, always one of tragic contrast, ended in personal tragedy as Philip abandoned her, never to return, even as his queen lay dying.

In many ways Mary failed as a woman but triumphed as a queen. She ruled with the full measure of royal majesty and achieved much of what she set out to do. She won her rightful throne, married her Spanish prince, and restored the country to Roman Catholicism. The

Spanish marriage was a match with the most powerful ruling house in Europe, and the highly favorable marriage treaty ultimately won the support of the English government. She had defeated rebels and preserved the Tudor monarchy. Her Catholicism was not simply conservative but influenced by her humanist education and showed many signs of broad acceptance before she died. She was an intelligent, politically adept, and resolute monarch who proved to be very much her own woman. Thanks to Mary, John Aylmer, in exile in Switzerland, could confidently assert that "it is not in England so dangerous a matter to have a woman ruler, as men take it to be."[12] By securing the throne following Edward's attempts to bar both his sisters, she ensured that the crown continued along the legal line of Tudor succession. Mary laid down other important precedents that would benefit her sister. Upon her accession as the first queen regnant of England, she redefined royal ritual and law, thereby establishing that a female ruler, married or unmarried, would enjoy identical power and authority to male monarchs. Mary was the Tudor trailblazer, a political pioneer whose reign redefined the English monarchy.

Upon her accession Mary adopted the motto *Veritas Temporis Filia*—Truth is the Daughter of Time—in celebration of her establishment as England's Catholic heir and the return of the "true faith." In 1558, her younger sister wrested the motto from the dead queen, for the Protestant truth. It was not the only thing Elizabeth took from her predecessor. After Mary's death, the coronation robes of England's first queen were hastily refurbished—with a new bodice and sleeves—to fit its second.[13]

In certain things she is singular and without an equal; for not only is she brave and valiant, unlike other timid and spiritless women, but so courageous and resolute, that neither in adversity nor peril did she ever display or commit any act of cowardice or pusillanimity, maintaining always, on the contrary, a wonderful grandeur and dignity . . . it cannot be denied that she shows herself to have been born of a truly royal lineage.

—The Venetian ambassador
Giovanni Michieli

ACKNOWLEDGMENTS

THIS WAS THE BOOK I ALWAYS WANTED TO WRITE. FROM THE earliest days of my doctoral research I was driven by a desire to tell Mary's remarkable story, to push her to center stage as England's first queen and bring her out from the shadow of her younger sister, Elizabeth. I hope I have gone some way to achieving this.

In writing this book I have incurred many debts to scholars, writers, librarians, and friends. The staff of Cambridge University Library has been endlessly efficient, helpful, and friendly, as have those of the British Library and the National Archives. I must also thank Henry Bedingfeld for allowing me to view his family records at Oxburgh Hall. Various colleagues have provided help, inspiration, and guidance during the course of my research, including my former tutor David Starkey, Judith Richards, Jeri Mcintosh, Diarmaid MacCulloch, David Loades, Nicola Stacey, Stephen Alford, Richard Rex, Mia Rodriguez-Salgado, and Ian Archer. I should also like to thank the master and fellows of Corpus Christi for providing a supportive research environment and my colleagues in the Department of History at Royal Holloway, University of London. Teaching often aids research, and various students have, over the past few years, asked important questions, resulting in interesting discussions.

My agent, Catherine Clarke, has provided great encouragement, guidance, and support throughout. Susanna Porter, my editor at Random House, has always remained enthusiastic about the book, as has Jillian Quint. For assistance in the editing of the text, I owe great thanks to Lynn Anderson, who has been immensely efficient and incisive, and to all at Random House.

This book has been long in the making and would simply not have started or finished without the support of friends and family. Its completion is very much a shared achievement. To some I must offer specific thanks: to Kate Downes for her enthusiasm and invaluable support for me and the book; to Miri Rubin and Gareth Stedman Jones for their generous encouragement and inspiring discussion; to Alice Hunt for endless "Mary" chats and great friendship; to Judy Forshaw and Richard Swift for wine, dinners, and continued interest in the book. Sandra and David Swarbrick and Paul and Jenny Baker have provided constant love and support, and they, together with Chez Hall, James McConnachie, Alexander Regier, Jonathan Hall, Naomi Yandell, Pedro Ramos-Pinto, and all at Herbert Street, have provided great friendship. Alistair Willoughby and Andrew Burns have been generous readers of the manuscript, as has Rebecca Stott, who has been a valuable library comrade and friend during the final stages of writing. I owe particular thanks to Victoria Gregory, Rosie Peppin Vaughan, Jo Maybin, and Rebecca Edwards Newman, upon whom I have depended enormously. Isobel Maddison and her husband, Peter, have shown immense loyalty and patience, have supported me through difficult times, and have been crucial to the book's completion.

My thanks go to Amy and Emily Whitelock, Martin Inglis, and Eric Nason for their support and encouragement. It is with much sadness and regret that my grandfather Kenneth Whitelock, who bought me so many history books as a child, is not alive to read mine. Finally I would like to thank my parents, Paul and Celia Whitelock, for their love and concern. Having taken me on endless trips to castles and stately homes as I was growing up, it is doubtless they who inspired my initial desire to ponder the past.

NOTES

Abbreviations

Aff.Etr.	Archives du Ministère des Affaires Étrangères, Paris, France (Correspondance politique, Angleterre)
APC	*Acts of the Privy Council*, ed. J. R. Dasent et al., 46 vols. (London, 1890–1914)
AR	*The Antiquarian Repertory*, ed. F. Grose, 4 vols. (London, 1807–09)
BL	British Library
Cal. Pole	*The Correspondence of Reginald Pole*, ed. T. F. Mayer, 4 vols. (Aldershot, 2002)
CPR	*Calendar of Patent Rolls*
CS	Camden Society
CSPD	*Calendar of State Papers Domestic*
CSPF	*Calendar of State Papers Foreign*
CSPS	*Calendar of State Papers Spanish*
CSPV	*Calendar of State Papers Venetian*
DNB	*Dictionary of National Biography*
EETS	Early English Text Society
EHR	*The English Historical Review*
Foedera	*Foedera, Conventions, Litterae . . .*, eds. T. Rymer and R. Sanderson, 20 vols. (London, 1704–35)
HJ	*The Historical Journal*
HMC	Historical Manuscripts Commission
LP	*Letters and Papers, Foreign and Domestic, of the Reign of Henry VIII*, 1509–47, eds. J. S. Brewer et al., 21 vols. and addenda (London, 1862–1932)
NA	National Archives
PPC	*Proceedings and Ordinances of the Privy Council of England, 1386–1542*, ed. N. H. Nicolas, 7 vols. (London, 1834–37)
PPE	*The Privy Purse Expenses of the Princess Mary*, ed. F. Madden (London, 1831)
Statutes	*Statutes of the Realm*, eds. A. Luders et al., 11 vols. (London, 1810–28)
St.P.	*State Papers of King Henry the Eighth*, 11 vols. (London, 1830–52)
TNA SP	The National Archives, State Papers

AUTHOR'S NOTE

1. Beatrice White, *Mary Tudor* (London, 1935), p. vii.
2. A. F. Pollard, *The History of England from the Accession of Edward VI to the Death of*

Elizabeth (1547–1603) (London, 1910; reprinted New York, 1969), p. 172; D. Loades, *Mary Tudor: A Life* (Oxford, 1989), p. 8.

3. G. R. Elton, *Reform and Reformation: England, 1509–1558* (London, 1977), p. 376.

INTRODUCTION: RESURRECTION

1. James also brought the coffin of his mother, Mary, queen of Scots, from Peterborough and placed it next to that of Margaret Beaufort, mother of Henry VII, to emphasize his lineage.
2. Marjorie Chibnall, *The Empress Matilda: Queen Consort, Queen Mother and Lady of the English* (Oxford, 1991), p. 102.

CHAPTER 1. PRINCESS OF ENGLAND

1. BL, Harley 3504, fols. 232r–233v.
2. *AR* I, pp. 305–306.
3. "The Sarum Rite," in E. C. Whitaker, *Documents of the Baptismal Liturgy*, ed. Maxwell E. Johnson, 3rd ed. (London, 2003), pp. 284–307.
4. BL, Harley 3504, fol. 232.
5. NA, PRO, OBS 1419; *CSPS* II, 23, p. 24.
6. *CSPS*, supplement to vols. I and II, p. 34.
7. *LP* I, i, 394, p. 184.
8. *CSPS*, supp. to vols. I and II, pp. 34–35, 42–44.
9. Ibid., p. 42.
10. Ibid., p. 43.
11. *CSPS* II, p. 38.
12. Ibid., p. 38.
13. *AR* I, pp. 304–305, 333, 336; BL, Harley 3504, fols. 272r–273r.
14. *AR* I, p. 305.
15. Sebastian Giustiniani, *Four Years at the Court of Henry VIII*, ed. and trans. R. Brown, 2 vols. (London, 1854), I, p. 181.
16. Ibid., p. 182; "token of hope" is David Loades's phrase; see *Mary Tudor: A Life* (Oxford, 1989), p. 9.

CHAPTER 2. A TRUE FRIENDSHIP AND ALLIANCE

1. Giustiniani, *Four Years*, I, p. 181.
2. E. Hall, *The Union of the Two Noble and Illustre Famelies of York and Lancaster* [hereafter Hall, *Chronicle*], ed. H. Ellis (London, 1809), p. 584.
3. A. F. Pollard, *The Reign of Henry VII from Contemporary Sources* (London, 1913), III, pp. 2–5.
4. James Gairdner, ed., "Journals of Roger Machado," in *Historia Regis Henrici Septimi* (London, 1858; 1966 reprint), pp. 170–75.
5. G. Kipling, ed., *The Receyt of the Ladie Kateryne* (Oxford, 1990), p. 4.
6. *CSPS* I, 305, p. 262.
7. Kipling, *The Receyt of the Ladie Kateryne*, pp. 39–51.
8. BL, Egerton 616, fol. 17; trans. in M. A. E. Wood, ed., *Letters of Royal and Illustrious Ladies of Great Britain*, 3 vols. (London, 1846), I, pp. 138–40.
9. S. and H. M. Allen, eds., *Opus Epistolarum Des. Erasmi Roterodami* (Oxford, 1906), I, no. 214.
10. *CSPS* II, 17, p. 19.
11. *LP* I, i, 1475, p. 675.
12. *LP* I, ii, 2299, p. 1027.

13. *LP* I, ii, 2268, p. 4451; BL, Cotton Vespasian F III, fol. 15, printed in H. Ellis, ed., *Original Letters, Illustrative of English History . . . from Autographs in the British Museum and . . . Other Collections*, 11 vols. (1824–46), 1st series, I, p. 88.

CHAPTER 3. ARE YOU THE DAUPHIN OF FRANCE?

1. *AR* I, p. 306; *PPE*, p. xxi.
2. *CSPV* II, 1287, p. 558.
3. *Foedera*, XIII, p. 624.
4. Ibid., p. 632; *LP* II, ii, 4480, p. 1376.
5. Giustiniani, *Four Years*, II, p. 226.
6. *CSPV* II, 1085, p. 463.
7. Giustiniani, *Four Years*, II, p. 226.
8. *LP* II, ii, 4480, p. 1376.
9. *CSPV* II, 1088, p. 465.
10. *LP* II, ii, 4468, p. 1372.
11. Giustiniani, *Four Years*, II, p. 240; *CSPV* II, 1103, p. 474.
12. Ibid.

CHAPTER 4. A VERY FINE YOUNG COUSIN INDEED

1. *LP* III, i, 689, p. 230.
2. *LP* III, i, 869, pp. 303–306; 870, pp. 307–14; *CSPV* III, 67, pp. 47–50; 68, pp. 50–55; 69.
3. *LP* VIII, 263, p. 101.
4. BL, Cotton Caligula D VII, fol. 238v.
5. BL, Cotton Vespasian F XIII, fol. 129; *LP* III, i, 873.
6. *CSPV* II, 1298, p. 596.
7. *LP* III, i, 118, p. 37.
8. *LP* VIII, 263, p. 101.
9. *LP* III, i, 896, p. 323.
10. *LP* III, ii, 2333, pp. 987–91.
11. *LP* III, ii, 1443, p. 587.
12. *LP* III, i, 1150, p. 424.
13. *CSPS* II, 355, pp. 365–71.
14. *CSPS*, further supplement, p. 74.
15. Ibid., p. 71; D. Starkey, *Henry VIII: A European Court in England* (London, 1991), p. 91.
16. *CSPS*, further supplement, p. 74.
17. Hall, *Chronicle*, p. 635; *CSPS* II, 423, p. 430.
18. *CSPS* II, 441, p. 448.
19. R. Withington, *English Pageantry: An Historical Outline*, 2 vols. (Cambridge, 1918), I, p. 97; Hall, *Chronicle*, pp. 635–41; *LP* III, ii, 2233, pp. 987–89; *CSPS* II, 43, pp. 443–45.
20. *LP* III, ii, 2322, p. 983; 2333, p. 987; *CSPS* II, 427, pp. 434–37; 430, pp. 438–40.
21. *PPE*, p. xxxii.

CHAPTER 5. THE INSTITUTION OF A CHRISTIAN WOMAN

1. BL, Cotton Vespasian C III, fol. 177; *LP* IV, i, 184, p. 662.
2. J. L. Vives, *De Institutione Feminae Christianae*, eds. C. Fantazzi and C. Matheeussen, 2 vols. (Leiden, 1996), I, pp. 3, 11.
3. Ibid., p. 51.
4. J. L. Vives, "De Ratione Studii Puerilis, Epistola I," in *Opera Omnia*, ed. G. Majamsius, 8 vols. (Valencia, 1782), IV, p. 256. For a translation, see J. L.Vives, "Plan

of Studies for Girls," in *Vives and the Renascence Education of Women*, ed. F. Watson (London, 1912), pp. 137–50.

5. Watson, ed., *Vives and the Renascence Education of Women*, p. 147.
6. Printed and translated in J. W. O'Malley and L. A. Perraud, eds., *Collected Works of Erasmus: Spiritualia and Pastoralia* (London, 1998), p. 214.
7. BL, Royal 17 C XVI, fol. 2. In his "lady's book of hours" there is a copy of "The Prayer of St Thomas of Aquine," translated by Mary in 1527, when she was twelve.
8. *PPE*, p. xxiii.
9. See, e.g., *PPE*, p. 30.

CHAPTER 6. GREAT SIGNS AND TOKENS OF LOVE

1. *CSPS*, further supplement, p. 325.
2. *LP* IV, 600, pp. 266–68.
3. *St.P.* IV, p. 200; *LP* IV, i, 767, p. 337.
4. *LP* IV, i, 882, p. 388; *CSPS* III, i, 103, pp. 174–79.
5. *CSPS* III, i, 33, p. 82.
6. *CSPS* III, i, 60, p. 108.
7. G. Mattingly, *Catherine of Aragon* (London, 1942), p. 168.
8. BL, Cotton Vespasian C III, fol. 50.
9. Ibid., fol. 162.
10. *CSPS* III, i, 103, p. 175.
11. *St.P.* I, p. 160; *LP* IV, i, 1378, pp. 612–13.
12. *LP* IV, i, 1379, p. 616; 1380, p. 617.
13. *CSPS* III, i, pp. 1018–19.

CHAPTER 7. PRINCESS OF WALES

1. *LP* IV, i, 1484, p. 667.
2. *CSPV* II, 479, p. 188.
3. *CSPV* III, 1053, p. 455.
4. Hall, *Chronicle*, p. 703.
5. See P. Williams, *The Council in the Marches of Wales under Elizabeth I* (Cardiff, 1958), pp. 3–43, and F. Heyburn, "Arthur, Prince of Wales and His Training for Kingship," *Historian* 55 (1997), pp. 4–9.
6. BL, Cotton Vespasian F XIII, fol. 72, printed in Ellis, *Original Letters*, 1st series, II, pp. 19–20.
7. *LP* IV, i, 1691, pp. 752–53; 1577, pp. 707–11.
8. BL, Harley 6807, fols. 3r–6r (noted as John Fetherstone).
9. BL, Cotton Vitellius C I, fol. 8v.
10. BL, Cotton Vespasian F XIII, fol. 72, printed in Ellis, *Original Letters*, 1st series, II, pp. 19–20.
11. BL, Cotton Vitellius C I, fol. 9r.
12. BL, Cotton Vespasian F XIII, fol. 240r.
13. G. Duwes, *An Introductory for to Learn to Read, to Pronounce, and to Speak French* (1532?), ed. R. C. Alston, facsimile (Menston, 1972), sig. B62.

CHAPTER 8. PEARL OF THE WORLD

1. *LP* IV, i, 2079, p. 934.
2. *CSPV* III, 902, p. 395.
3. BL, Cotton Caligula D IX, fol. 272.

4. *CSPV* III, 1406, p. 607.
5. BL, Cotton Caligula D IX, fol. 272.
6. *LP* IV, ii, 2840, pp. 1, 271.
7. *LP* IV, ii, 3105, p. 1412.
8. *CSPV* IV, i, 105, p. 58.
9. *LP* IV, ii, 2981, p. 1337; *PPE,* p. xlviii.
10. The commission for this treaty is in *Foedera,* XIV, p. 195, dated April 23, 1527.
11. *CSPV* IV, i, 107, p. 61.
12. J. Lingard, *The History of England . . .*, 10 vols. (London, 1854), IV, p. 237, n3.

CHAPTER 9. THIS SHEER CALAMITY

1. G. Cavendish, *The Life and Death of Cardinal Wolsey by George Cavendish,* ed. R. S. Sylvester (London, 1959), p. 83; *LP* IV, 4942, p. 2145.
2. G. Ascoli, *La Grande-Bretagne devant l'Opinion Française depuis le Guerre de Cents Ans jusqu'à la Fin du XVIe Siècle* (Paris, 1927), p. 234.
3. H. Savage, ed., *The Love Letters of Henry VIII* (London, 1949), pp. 32–34.
4. *CSPS* III, ii, pp. 193–94.
5. *LP* IV, ii, 3140, p. 1429.
6. Ibid.
7. *LP* IV, ii, 3147.
8. *CSPS* III, ii, 113, p. 276.
9. *St.P.* I, pp. 194–95.
10. Ibid.
11. *CSPS* III, ii, 131, p. 301.
12. Ibid.
13. Wood, ed., *Letters of Royal and Illustrious Ladies,* II, pp. 201–203.
14. *CSPS* III, ii, p. 443.
15. *LP* IV, 4736, p. 2055.
16. *LP* IV, ii, 4875, p. 2109.
17. Ibid.
18. Wood, ed., *Letters of Royal and Illustrious Ladies,* II, pp. 32–33; T. Hearne, *Sylloge Epistolarum* (London, 1716), pp. 122–23.
19. *LP* IV, ii, 5016, p. 2177.
20. *CSPS* III, ii, 600, p. 861.
21. Cavendish, *Wolsey,* pp. 78–91.
22. *LP* IV, iii, 5694, p. 2520; *CSPV* IV, 482, pp. 219–20.
23. *LP* IV, iii, 5702, p. 2526; *CSPV* IV, 482, pp. 219–20.
24. *LP* IV, iii, 5702, p. 2526.
25. Ibid.; *CSPV* IV, i, 482, p. 259.
26. *LP* IV, iii, 5791, p. 2589.

CHAPTER 10. THE KING'S GREAT MATTER

1. *CSPS* IV, i, 83, p. 133.
2. G. Burnet, *The History of the Reformation,* ed. N. Pocock, 7 vols. (Oxford, 1865), IV, p. 35.
3. *CSPS* IV, i, 132, pp. 189–90.
4. *LP* IV, iii, 6667, p. 3004.
5. Hall, *Chronicle,* p. 780.
6. P. Friedmann, *Anne Boleyn: A Chapter of English History, 1527–1536,* 2 vols. (London, 1884), I, p. 130.

7. *CSPS* IV, ii, 584, p. 3.
8. *CSPS* IV, ii, 681, p. 112.
9. *CSPS* IV, i, 373, p. 633.
10. *CSPS* IV, ii, 1003, p. 527.
11. *LP* V, 308, p. 145; *CSPS*, IV, ii, 753, p. 199.
12. *LP* V, 216, p. 101.
13. *LP* V, 308, p. 145.
14. *LP* V, 238, pp. 110–111.
15. *LP* V, 238, p. 110.
16. *CSPS* IV, ii, 739, pp. 171–76.
17. *CSPS* IV, ii, 765, p. 212.
18. *CSPS* IV, ii, 775, p. 222.
19. Ibid., pp. 223–24.
20. *LP* V, 375; *CSPS* IV, ii, 778, p. 228.
21. *CSPS* IV, ii, 778, p. 228.
22. *LP* V, 187, p. 89.
23. *LP* V, 216, p. 100.
24. *CSPV* IV, i, 82, pp. 287–88.

CHAPTER 11. THE SCANDAL OF CHRISTENDOM

1. *LP* V, 696, pp. 335–36.
2. *LP* V, 1377, p. 591.
3. *LP* V, 1117, p. 501.
4. Hall, *Chronicle*, XXX, pp. 790–94.
5. *LP* V, 1484, pp. 623–24; 1485, pp. 624–26.
6. *LP* VI, 230, pp. 103–04; 614, pp. 282–83.
7. *CSPS* IV, ii, pp. 510–11.
8. *CSPS* IV, ii, pp. 597–559.
9. Ellis, ed., *Original Letters*, 3rd series, II, p. 276.
10. 24 Hen. VIII c.12; *Statutes*, III, pp. 427–29.
11. *LP* VI, 584, pp. 264–66; *CSPV* IV, 912, pp. 418–19.
12. *CSPS* IV, ii, 1073, p. 678.
13. *LP* VI, 759, p. 339; 760, p. 340.
14. *CSPS* IV, ii, 1062, pp. 646–67.
15. Ibid.
16. *LP* VI, 351, p. 168.
17. *LP* V, 513, p. 239.
18. *LP* V, 478, pp. 226–27.
19. *LP* VI, 720, p. 150.
20. *CSPS* IV, ii, 1058, p. 630.
21. *CSPS* IV, ii, p. 649.
22. *LP* VI, 568, pp. 252–54.

CHAPTER 12. THE LADY MARY

1. *LP* VI, 1112, p. 465.
2. *LP* VI, 1111, p. 464; Hall, *Chronicle*, pp. 805–806.
3. *CSPS* IV, ii, 1127, p. 795; *LP* VI, 1139.
4. BL, Harley 416, fol. 22; *LP* VI, 1207, p. 500.
5. TNA SP 1/79, pp. 121–22; *LP* VI, 1186, pp. 491–92.

6. *LP* VI, 1249, p. 510.
7. *LP* VI, 1528, p. 617.
8. Ibid.
9. Ibid., pp. 617–18.
10. *CSPS* IV, ii, 1161, p. 882.
11. TNA SP E 101/421/14; *LP* VII, 372.
12. *LP* VI, 1392.
13. *CSPS* IV, ii, 1144, p. 839; J. Foxe, *Actes and Monuments of These Latter and Perillous Dayes . . .* (London, 1583), book 9, p. 1396.
14. *LP* VI, 1558, p. 629.
15. Ibid.
16. *LP* VII, 14, p. 8.
17. *LP* VII, 171, p. 69; 530, p. 214.
18. *LP* VII, 214, p. 84.
19. *LP* X, 1134, p. 476.

CHAPTER 13. SPANISH BLOOD

1. BL, Arundel 151, fol. 195; *LP* VI, 1126.
2. *LP* VII, 83, p. 33.
3. BL, Cotton Otho C X, fol. 176 (much burned), printed in A. Crawford, ed., *Letters of the Queens of England 1100–1547* (Stroud, 1994), pp. 178–79.
4. *LP* VII, 162, p. 66.
5. *LP* VII, 232, p. 94.
6. *LP* VII, 83, p. 32.
7. *LP* VII, 171, p. 68.
8. *LP* VII, 83, p. 32.
9. *LP* VII, 296, p. 127; H. Clifford, *The Life of Jane Dormer, Duchess of Feria*, ed. J. Stevenson (London, 1887), pp. 81–82.
10. *LP* VII, 871, p. 323.

CHAPTER 14. HIGH TRAITORS

1. H. A. Kelly, *The Matrimonial Trials of Henry VIII* (Stanford, Calif., 1976), p. 169.
2. 25 Hen. VIII c. 21, 22; *Statutes*, III, pp. 471–74.
3. LS Her. VIII c. 12; *Statutes*, III, p. 450; J. A. Froude, *History of England from the Fall of Wolsey to the Defeat of the Spanish Armada*, 12 vols. (London, 1856) 11, p. 171.
4. A. Neame, *The Holy Maid of Kent: The Life of Elizabeth Barton, 1506–1534* (London, 1971), p. 338.
5. M. St. C. Byrne, ed., *The Lisle Letters*, 6 vols. (Chicago and London, 1981), II, p. 130.
6. Neame, *Holy Maid of Kent*, p. 338.
7. BL, Cotton Titus B I, fol. 415.
8. BL, Cotton Otho C X, fol. 169v.
9. BL, Cotton Otho C X, fol. 202.
10. *LP* VII, 662, p. 254.
11. Ibid.
12. BL, Cotton Nero B VI, fol. 89r.
13. BL, Cotton Otho C X, fol. 254 (damaged by fire); *LP* VII, 1036, pp. 403–405.
14. *LP* VII, 1036, pp. 403–405.
15. *LP* VII, 214, p. 84.
16. *LP* VII, 530, p. 214.

CHAPTER 15. WORSE THAN A LION

1. *LP* VIII, 189, p. 71.
2. *LP* VII, 1193, p. 463.
3. *LP* VIII, 200; *CSPS* V, i, p. 134.
4. *LP* VIII, 263, p. 101.
5. *LP* VIII, 429, p. 167.
6. BL, Cotton Otho C X, fol. 176 (much burned), printed in Hearne, *Sylloge Epistolarum*, pp. 107–108.
7. *LP* VIII, 429, p. 167.
8. Ibid., p. 165.
9. *LP* VIII, 948, p. 370.
10. *LP* VIII, 1, p. 2.
11. 27 Hen. VIII c. 13, *Statutes*, III, p. 508.
12. Quote from eyewitness William Rastell in N. Harpsfield, *The Life and Death of Sir Thomas More . . .*, ed. R. W. Chambers and E. V. Hitchcock (London, 1932), App. I, p. 245.
13. C. Wriothesley, *A Chronicle . . . by Charles Wriothesley, Windsor Herald*, ed. W. D. Hamilton, 2 vols. (London, 1875–77) [hereafter *Wriothesley's Chronicle*], I, p. 29.
14. *LP* VIII, 726, p. 272.
15. *LP* VIII, 1105, p. 432.
16. *CSPS* V, i, 148, p. 435; 210, p. 548.
17. *CSPS* V, i, 218, pp. 559–60.
18. *LP* VIII, 666, p. 253.
19. *LP* VIII, 556, p. 210.
20. *LP* IX, 776.
21. *LP* IX, 873, p. 293.
22. *LP* IX, 862, p. 290.

CHAPTER 16. SUSPICION OF POISON

1. Crawford, *Letters of the Queens of England*, pp. 179–80.
2. Hearne, *Sylloge Epistolarum*, pp. 107–108.
3. *LP* X, 59, pp. 20–21.
4. Ibid., p. 21.
5. Ibid.
6. *LP* X, 141, pp. 49–50.
7. *St.P.* I, p. 452; *LP* X, 37, p. 14; 41, p. 16; 141, p. 51.
8. *LP* XI, p. 51.
9. *LP* X, 59, p. 22.
10. *LP* X, 141, pp. 51–52.
11. Ibid., p. 51.
12. *LP* X, 54, p. 19.
13. *LP* X, 141, pp. 47–48.
14. *LP* X, 373, p. 148.
15. *LP* X, 141, p. 52.
16. *CSPV* II, 16, p. 33.
17. *LP* X, 59, p. 22.
18. *LP* X, 199, p. 69.
19. *LP* XI, 141, p. 48; 199, p. 69.
20. *LP* X, 307, pp. 117–18.

21. *LP* X, 307, p. 117.
22. *LP* X, 307, p. 116.
23. *CSPS* V, ii, pp. 12–13; *LP* X, 199, p. 69.
24. *LP* X, 307, pp. 116–17.

CHAPTER 17. THE RUIN OF THE CONCUBINE

1. *LP* X, 284, pp. 104–106.
2. *LP* X, 39, pp. 14–15.
3. *LP* X, 282, pp. 102–103.
4. *LP* X, 199, p. 70.
5. *LP* X, 282, p. 103.
6. *LP* X, 199, p. 70; *LP* X, 351, p. 134.
7. *LP* X, 282, p. 103.
8. *LP* VII, 1257, p. 485.
9. *LP* X, 752, p. 315.
10. *LP* X, 601, p. 245; *CSPS* V, ii, p. 84.
11. *LP* X, 601, p. 245.
12. Ibid.
13. Ibid., p. 243.
14. T. Amyot, "Transcript of an Original Manuscript, Containing a Memorial from George Constantyne to Thomas Lord Cromwell," *Archaeologia* 23 (1831), p. 64.
15. *LP* X, 908, p. 377.
16. Ibid.
17. Ibid., p. 378.
18. Ibid.; *Wriothesley's Chronicle,* I, p. 38.
19. *LP* X, 911, p. 382.
20. L. Wiesener, *La Jeunesse d'Elisabeth d'Angleterre* (Paris, 1878), p. 7.
21. *CSPS* V, ii, p. 574.
22. *LP* X, 908, p. 377.
23. *Wriothesley's Chronicle*, I, p. 43.
24. *LP* X, 901, p. 373.
25. *Wriothesley's Chronicle*, I, pp. 43–44.
26. *LP* X, 908, p. 377.
27. *St.P.* VII, p. 684; *LP* X, 726, p. 306.
28. *LP* X, 699, pp. 287–95.
29. *LP* X, 726, pp. 306–308.

CHAPTER 18. MOST HUMBLE AND OBEDIENT DAUGHTER

1. Hearne, *Sylloge Epistolarum,* p. 140. Only a fragment of this letter survives after the Cotton Library fire of 1731. BL, Cotton Otho C X, fol. 283r; *LP* X, p. 968.
2. BL, Cotton Otho C X, fol. 267v; Hearne, *Sylloge Epistolarum,* p. 147.
3. Hearne, *Sylloge Epistolarum,* p. 146; BL, Cotton Otho C X, fol. 268r (badly burned).
4. BL, Cotton Otho C X, fol. 287r for June 8; Hearne, *Sylloge Epistolarum,* p. 149.
5. BL, Cotton Otho C X, fol. 269v; Hearne, *Sylloge Epistolarum,* pp. 125–26.
6. Hearne, *Sylloge Epistolarum,* pp. 124–25; BL, Cotton Otho C X, fol. 269v (badly burned).
7. BL, Cotton Otho C X, fol. 263b, printed in Wood, *Letters of Royal and Illustrious Ladies,* II, pp. 250–52.
8. Hearne, *Sylloge Epistolarum,* p. 127.
9. *LP* XI, 7, pp. 7–8.

10. *CSPS* V, ii, 70, p. 184.
11. Hearne, *Sylloge Epistolarum*, pp. 137–38.
12. *CSPS* V, ii, 70, pp. 183–84.
13. Ibid.
14. *LP* X, 1134, pp. 475–76.
15. *CSPS* VI, i, 43, pp. 81–85; 47, p. 106.
16. R. Morice, "Anecdotes and Character of Archbishop Cranmer," in J. G. Nichols ed., *Narratives of the Days of the Reformation, Chiefly from the Manuscripts of John Foxe the Martyrologist*, 67, CS 77 (London, 1859), p. 259.
17. *LP* X, 1137; Hearne, *Sylloge Epistolarum*, pp. 142–43.
18. *CSPS* V, ii, p. 183; Hearne, *Sylloge Epistolarum*, p. 142; *LP* X, 1137, p. 478.

CHAPTER 19. INCREDIBLE REJOICING

1. Hearne, *Sylloge Epistolarum*, pp. 128–29; Wood, *Letters of Royal and Illustrious Ladies*, II, pp. 258–59.
2. *LP* XI, 7, pp. 7–8.
3. Ibid.
4. *CSPV* V, ii, 71, p. 195; *LP* XI, 40, p. 24.
5. *CSPS* V, ii, 71, p. 195.
6. *CSPS* V, ii, p. 199.
7. *LP* XI, 576, p. 229; 597, pp. 241–42.
8. *CSPS* V, ii, 85, p. 220.
9. *LP* XI, 148, p. 65.
10. *LP* XI, 7, p. 8; *CSPS* V, ii, 94, pp. 237–38.
11. *LP* XI, 7, p. 8.
12. *LP* X, 219, p. 96.
13. 28 Hen. VIII, c. 7, *Statutes*, III, pp. 655–62; *LP* XI, 40, p. 24.
14. *LP* XI, 221, p. 97.
15. *CSPS* V, ii, 94, p. 238.
16. *LP* XI, 1246, p. 507.
17. *LP* XII, i, 901, p. 406.
18. *LP* X, 1353; *LP* XII, i, pp. 367, 368, 779.
19. *Reginaldi Poli ad Henricum Octavum Britanniae regem, pro ecclesiasticae unitas defensione* (Strasbourg, 1555), fol. lxxxxiv, cited in T. Mayer, *Reginald Pole, Prince and Prophet* (Cambridge, 2000), p. 21.
20. *LP* XII, i, 1032, p. 471.
21. *Wriothesley's Chronicle*, I, pp. 59–60.
22. Byrne, *Lisle Letters*, III, pp. 576–77.
23. BL, Cotton Titus B, fol. 481; see also *LP* XII, 815, p. 361.

CHAPTER 20. DELIVERANCE OF A GOODLY PRINCE

1. BL, Cotton Nero C X, fol. 1; J. G. Nichols, *The Literary Remains of King Edward VI*, 2 vols. (London, 1857), p. xxiii; Crawford, *Letters of the Queens of England*, p. 199.
2. *Wriothesley's Chronicle*, I, p. 66; BL, Add 6113, fol. 81.
3. *LP* XII, ii, 890, p. 310.
4. *Wriothesley's Chronicle*, I, p. 64.
5. Simon Thurley, "Henry VIII and the Building of Hampton Court: A Reconstruction of the Tudor Palace," *Architectural History*, 1988, pp. 29–37.
6. *Wriothesley's Chronicle*, I, p. 66.
7. *LP* XII, ii, 911, p. 318.

8. *LP* XII, ii, 923, p. 325.
9. *Wriothesley's Chronicle*, I, p. 68; *LP* XII, ii, 911, pp. 318–20.
10. *LP* XII, ii, 970, p. 339.
11. Hall, *Chronicle*, p. 825.
12. *LP* XII, ii, 972, p. 339.
13. *LP* XII, ii, 1060, pp. 372–74.
14. Foxe, *Actes and Monuments*, book 8, p. 1087.
15. BL, Cotton Titus B I, fol. 121; *LP* XII, ii, p. 1075.
16. *LP* XIII, i, 1011, p. 373.
17. *PPE*, pp. 61, 67, 69.
18. Clifford, *Life of Jane Dormer*, pp. 61–62.
19. Byrne, *Lisle Letters*, V, p. 305.

CHAPTER 21. THE MOST UNHAPPY LADY IN CHRISTENDOM

1. *LP* XII, ii, 1004, pp. 348–49.
2. *LP* XIII, ii, 77, pp. 28–29.
3. Hearne, *Sylloge Epistolarum*, p. 141.
4. Ibid., p. 139; *LP* XIII, i, 1082, pp. 395–96.
5. *CSPS* VI, i, pp. 25–26.
6. Ibid., p. 26.
7. *LP* XII, i, 1141, p. 526.
8. *LP* XIV, i, 980, pp. 451–52.
9. TNA SP C 65/147, m. 22.
10. *Wriothesley's Chronicle*, I, p. 92.
11. *LP* XIV, i, 372, p. 143.
12. *LP* XIII, ii, 1148, p. 477; *LP* XIV, 377, p. 143; *LP* XV, 134, pp. 42–43.
13. *LP* XIII, 1148, p. 477.
14. *CSPS* V, ii, 61, p. 151.
15. *LP* XIV, i, 103, p. 41.
16. Ibid.
17. Hearne, *Sylloge Epistolarum*, pp. 149–51.
18. *LP* XIV, ii, 744, p. 275.
19. *LP* XIV, ii, 733, pp. 269–71.
20. *LP* XIV, ii, 52, p. 15.
21. *LP* XIV, i, 603, pp. 235–38.
22. *LP* XVI, 117, p. 59; 160, pp. 73–74; 175, pp. 80–81; 270, p. 115.
23. *LP* XVI, 270, p. 115.
24. *LP* XVII, 182, p. 83.
25. *LP* XVII, 371, p. 221.

CHAPTER 22. FOR FEAR OF MAKING A RUFFLE IN THE WORLD

1. *LP* XIV, ii, 754, p. 283.
2. *Wriothesley's Chronicle*, I, pp. 109–110.
3. Burnet, *History of the Reformation*, IV, pp. 425–26; *LP* XV, 823, p. 389.
4. *LP* XV, 823, p. 391; Burnet, *History of the Reformation*, IV, pp. 425–26; J. Strype, *Ecclesiastical Memorials; Relating Chiefly to Religion, and the Reformation of It, and the Emergencies of the Church of England, under King Henry VIII, King Edward VI, and Queen Mary the First . . .*, 3 vols. (London, 1721), I, p. 360.
5. Burnet, *History of the Reformation*, IV, p. 426; *LP* XV, 823, p. 389.
6. *LP* XV, 823, p. 391; Burnet, *History of the Reformation*, IV, pp. 425–26.

7. Burnet, *History of the Reformation*, IV, p. 427.
8. Ibid., p. 430.
9. Strype, *Ecclesiastical Memorials*, I, p. 360.
10. *LP* XVI, XII, pp. 4–5; J. Kaulek, ed., *Correspondance Politique de MM. de Castillon et de Marillac* (Paris, 1885), p. 218.
11. *LP* XV, 766, p. 363; Kaulek, ed., *Correspondance Politique*, pp. 189–90.
12. *LP* XV, 804, p. 377.
13. *LP* XV, 823, pp. 389–91.
14. BL, Cotton Otho C X, fol. 242; *LP* XV, 824, pp. 391–94.
15. Hall, *Chronicle*, p. 839.
16. *LP* XV, 908, pp. 450–51; 930, pp. 454–60.
17. *LP* XV, 908, pp. 450–51; 925, pp. 456–58; 930; pp. 456–60.
18. See Foxe, *Actes and Monuments*, book 8, p. 1199.
19. Ibid., p. 1201.

CHAPTER 23. MORE A FRIEND THAN A STEPMOTHER

1. *LP* XVI, 578, pp. 269–73; *Wriothesley's Chronicle*, I, pp. 121–22.
2. *LP* XVI, 223, p. 100.
3. *LP* XVI, 449, p. 222; *CSPS* VI, i, 149, pp. 305–306.
4. *LP* XVI, 314, p. 149.
5. *CSPS* VI, i, 161, p. 324; *LP* XVI, 835, p. 401.
6. *CSPS* VI, i, 166, pp. 331–32; *LP* XVI, 897, p. 436.
7. BL, Cotton Otho C X, fol. 250, printed in N. H. Nicolas, ed., *PPC*, p. 352.
8. HMC, *Bath Papers*, 5 vols. (London, 1904–1980), II, pp. 8–9.
9. *LP* XVII, 124, p. 50.
10. *CSPS* VI, i, 232, p. 472; *LP* XVII, 124, p. 50.
11. *CSPS* VI, i, 211, pp. 410–11; *LP* XVI, 1403, p. 653.
12. *LP* XVII, App. B, no. 13, p. 723.
13. *CSPS* VI, ii, pp. 223–24.
14. *LP* XVII, 251, pp. 124, 140.
15. *LP* XVII, 260, p. 140.
16. *LP* XVII, 1212, p. 669.
17. *CSPS* VI, ii, 87, p. 190; 94, p. 223.
18. *LP* XVIII, i, 894, p. 490.
19. *LP* XVIII, i, 873, p. 483.
20. *LP* XIX, i, 118, p. 64; 296, p. 189.
21. Wood, *Letters of Royal and Illustrious Ladies*, III, pp. 181–82.
22. Nicholas Udall, ed., *The First Tome or Volume of the Paraphrases of Erasmus upon the Newe Testamente* (London, 1548), vol. III, fol. ii.
23. F. Madden, ed., "Narrative of the Visit of the Duke of Najera to England in the Year 1543–4; Written by his Secretary, Pedro de Gente," *Archaeologia* 23 (1831), p. 353; *LP* XIX, i, pp. 7, 9.
24. J. O. Halliwell-Phillipps, ed., *Letters of the Kings of England, Now First Collected from the Originals*, 2 vols. (London, 1846), II, pp. 8–9.
25. BL, Harley 5087, no. 6, trans. Halliwell-Phillipps, *Letters of the Kings of England*, II, pp. 7–8.

CHAPTER 24. THE FAMILY OF HENRY VIII

1. 35 Hen. VIII c. 1; *Statutes*, III, p. 955.
2. 28 Hen. VIII c. 7; *Statutes*, III, pp. 655–62.

3. 35 Hen.VIII c. 1; *Statutes,* III, pp. 955–58.
4. *LP* XIX, i, 780, p. 477.
5. *LP* XVII, 124, p. 50.
6. *LP* XVIII, i, 804, pp. 454–55.
7. *LP* XIX, ii, 424, pp. 238–42.
8. TNA SP 1/190, fol. 156, printed in Crawford, ed., *Letters of the Queens of England,* pp. 216–17.
9. *LP* XIX, ii, 35, p. 16.
10. *LP* XX, i, 1263, p. 627.
11. *LP* XX, ii, 89, p. 43.
12. *LP* XX, ii, 788, pp. 376–77.
13. *LP* XX, ii, 639, p. 295.
14. *CSPS* XIII, 51, p. 109.
15. *LP* XXI, i, 1215, pp. 603, 1309.

CHAPTER 25. DEPARTED THIS LIFE

1. *CSPS* VIII, 204, p. 318.
2. Foxe, *Actes and Monuments,* book 8, p. 1242.
3. Ibid.
4. Ibid., p. 1243.
5. Ibid.
6. Ibid.
7. *LP* XXI, i, 605, p. 307.
8. *LP* XXI, ii, 769, p. 403.
9. *LP* XXI, ii, 555, pp. 283–89.
10. Lord Herbert of Cherbury, *The Life and Raigne of King Henry the Eighth* (London, 1649), p. 567.
11. TNA SP E 23/4/1, fol. iv.
12. *LP* XXI, ii, p. 360.
13. See Foxe, *Actes and Monuments,* book 8, p. 1290.
14. Strype, *Ecclesiastical Memorials,* II, pp. 10–11; part ii, pp. 3–4.
15. *CSPS* IX, p. 6.
16. *CSPS* IX, p. 101.
17. BL, Add 71009, fol. 45r.
18. W. K. Jordan, ed., *The Chronicle and Political Papers of King Edward VI* (London, 1966), p. 4.

CHAPTER 26. THE KING IS DEAD, LONG LIVE THE KING

1. P. L. Hughes and J. F. Larkin, eds., *Tudor Royal Proclamations,* 3 vols. (New Haven and London, 1964–1969), I, p. 381.
2. Society of Antiquaries, MS 123, fol. 1r.
3. *APC* II, pp. 7–8; College of Arms, MS I 7, fol. 29; Nichols, ed., *Literary Remains,* I, p. lxxxvii.
4. *APC* II, pp. 7–8; College of Arms, MS I 7, fol. 29, printed in Nichols, ed., *Literary Remains*, I, p. lxxxvii.
5. BL, Harley 5087, no. 35, printed in Nichols, ed., *Literary Remains,* I, pp. 39–40.
6. Strype, *Ecclesiastical Memorials,* II, ii, p. 9.
7. Martin A. Hume, ed., *Chronicle of King Henry VIII of England . . . Written in Spanish by an Unknown Hand* (London, 1889), p. 154.
8. A. Strickland, *Lives of the Queens of England,* 6 vols. (London, 1854), II, p. 443.

9. Strype transcribes a manuscript account of Henry VIII's funeral ceremonies in his *Ecclesiastical Memorials*, II, ii, pp. 3–18. Also see J. Loach, "The Function of Ceremonial in the Reign of Henry VIII," *Past and Present* 142 (1994), pp. 56–66.
10. Jordan, ed., *Chronicle of Edward VI*, p. 5.
11. College of Arms, MS I 7, in Nichols, ed., *Literary Remains*, I, p. cclxxx.
12. *CSPS* IX, p. 47.
13. R. Holinshed, *The Firste (–Laste) Volume of the Chronicles of England, Scotland and Irelande* (London, 1577), p. 614.
14. College of Arms, MS I 7, fol. 32, in Nichols, ed., *Literary Remains*, I, p. ccxci.
15. Nichols, ed., *Literary Remains*, I, p. ccxc.
16. *CSPS* IX, p. 47.
17. College of Arms, MS I 7, fol. 32, in Nichols, ed., *Literary Remains*, I, p. ccxci.
18. For the text of the *Liber Regalis*, see L. G. Wickham Legg, *English Coronation Records* (London, 1901), pp. 81–130.
19. Wickham Legg, *English Coronation Records*, p. 230.
20. J. E. Cox, ed., *Miscellaneous Writings and Letters of Thomas Cranmer* (London, 1846), pp. 126–27.
21. Hughes and Larkin, eds., *Tudor Royal Proclamations*, I, no. 275, p. 381.
22. Cox, *Writings of Thomas Cranmer*, II, p. 1267.
23. College of Arms, account in Nichols, ed., *Literary Remains*, I, p. ccxcv.
24. Jordan, ed., *Chronicle of Edward VI*, p. 5.

CHAPTER 27. FANTASY AND NEW FANGLENESS

1. C*SPS* IX, p. 38.
2. Ibid., p. 15.
3. Ibid., p. 495.
4. *CPR Edward VI*, II, pp. 20–23.
5. Bodleian Library, Tanner MS 90, fols. 157–168.
6. BL, Lansdowne 1236, fol. 26, in Ellis, *Original Letters*, 1st series, II, pp. 149–50.
7. Chapuys, dispatch to Antoine Perrenot, the emperor's minister, May 18, 1536. Referring to Jane Seymour, he wrote, "She is the sister of a certain Edward Seymour, who had been in the service of his Majesty [Charles V]." *LP* X, 901, p. 374. Edward Seymour had entered the emperor's service in early 1521 on the recommendation of Henry and Wolsey; see *LP* III, i, 1201, p. 452.
8. P. E. Tytler, ed., *England under the Reigns of Edward VI and Mary*, I, pp. 51–52, 60–61.
9. BL, Cotton Otho C X, printed in Strype, *Ecclesiastical Memorials*, II, pp. 58–59.
10. See E. Cardwell, *Documentary Annals of the Reformed Church of England, etc.*, 2 vols. (Oxford, 1844), I, pp. 4–31.
11. *CSPS* IX, p. 101.
12. Ibid., p. 298.
13. Strype, *Ecclesiastical Memorials*, II, pp. 59–60.
14. Ibid.
15. E. Rhys, ed., *The First and Second Prayer Books of Edward VI* (1910), p. 225.
16. *CSPS* IX, p. 351.
17. Ibid., pp. 360–61.
18. Ibid., p. 330.
19. Ibid., pp. 374–75.
20. Ibid., pp. 385–86.
21. Ibid., pp. 381–82.
22. Ibid.

CHAPTER 28. ADVICE TO BE CONFORMABLE

1. *APC* II, pp. 291–92.
2. Foxe, *Actes and Monuments,* book 9, p. 1332.
3. Ibid., p. 1333.
4. This remembrance was undoubtedly drawn up as a very definite response to Mary's letter of defiance dated June 22. Foxe, *Actes and Monuments,* book 9, pp. 1332–33.
5. Foxe, *Actes and Monuments,* book 9, pp. 1332–33.
6. *CSPS* IX, pp. 406–407.
7. Ibid., pp. 360–61.
8. Ibid., p. 394.
9. Ibid.
10. Ibid., p. 419.
11. John Hooker, *The Description of the Citie of Excester* (Devon and Cornwall Record Society, 1919), p. 61.
12. The articles are printed in A. J. Fletcher and D. MacCulloch, eds., *Tudor Rebellions* (Harlow, 2004), pp. 139–41.
13. TNA SP 10/8/30 (*CSPD Edw VI,* 327, p. 126).
14. *"De Mario vel Marianis me valde ang it, immo prope exanimat,"* in Tytler, *England under the Reigns of Edward VI and Mary,* I, p. 188.
15. Burnet, *History of the Reformation,* VI, pp. 283–84.
16. *CSPS* IX, p. 407.
17. Ibid., pp. 406–408.
18. TNA SP 10/8 no. 51 (*CSPD Edw VI,* 348, pp. 132–33), printed in Wood, *Letters of Royal and Illustrious Ladies,* III, pp. 213–14.

CHAPTER 29. THE MOST UNSTABLE MAN IN ENGLAND

1. *CSPS* IX, p. 453.
2. Hughes and Larkin, eds., *Tudor Royal Proclamations,* I, 351, p. 483.
3. R. Grafton, *A Chronicle at Large and Meere History of the Affayres of Englande . . .*, II, p. 522.
4. *CSPS* IX, p. 449.
5. *CSPS* X, pp. 5–6.
6. *CSPS* IX, p. 446.
7. Hughes and Larkin, eds., *Tudor Royal Proclamations,* I, p. 352.
8. *CSPS* X, p. 6.
9. Ibid., pp. 5–6.
10. TNA SP 10/9 no. 57 (*CSPD Edw VI,* 428, p. 158).
11. *CSPS* X, p. 5.
12. Ibid.
13. Ibid., pp. 56–57.
14. *CSPS* IX, p. 489.

CHAPTER 30. WHAT SAY YOU, MR AMBASSADOR?

1. *CSPS* X, p. 82.
2. Ibid., pp. 127–28.
3. *CSPS* IX, p. 450.
4. Ibid., pp. 449–51.

5. *CSPS* X, p. 117.
6. Ibid., pp. 94–96.
7. Ibid., pp. 124–35.

CHAPTER 31. AN UNNATURAL EXAMPLE

1. See *CSPS* X, p. 140.
2. Tytler, *England under the reigns of Edward VI and Mary,* I, p. 347.
3. Foxe, *Actes and Monuments,* book 9, pp. 1335–37.
4. *CSPS* X, pp. 172–73.
5. Foxe, *Actes and Monuments,* book 9, p. 1583.
6. *CSPS* X, pp. 205–209.
7. *CSPS* X, pp. 209–12; Foxe, *Actes and Monuments,* book 9, pp. 1333–34.
8. *CSPS* X, pp. 212–13; Foxe, *Actes and Monuments,* book 9, p. 1334.
9. *CSPS* X, p. 219.
10. *APC* III, p. 215.

CHAPTER 32. NAUGHTY OPINION

1. J. G. Nichols, ed., "The Diary of Henry Machyn, Citizen and Merchant Taylor of London . . . ," (London, 1848), p. 5.
2. *CSPS* X, p. 264.
3. Jordan, ed., *Chronicle of Edward VI,* p. 55.
4. *CSPS* X, pp. 258–60.
5. *APC* III, p. 239.
6. J. G. Nichols, ed., "Chronicle of the Grey Friars of London," CS, old series, 53 (London, 1852), p. 69; *APC* III, p. 239.
7. *APC* III, p. 239.
8. Ibid., p. 267.
9. Foxe, *Actes and Monuments,* book 9, p. 1337.
10. Ibid.; see also Jordan, ed., *Chronicle of Edward VI,* p. 67.
11. Jordan, ed., *Chronicle of Edward VI,* p. 56.
12. *CSPF Edward VI,* p. 75.
13. Jordan, ed., *Chronicle of Edward VI,* p. 56; BL, Harley 353, fols. 130–136v, printed in Nichols, ed., *Literary Remains,* I, pp. ccxxiv–ccxxxiv.
14. *CSPF Edward VI,* 393, pp. 137–38; *CSPS* X, pp. 310–17.

CHAPTER 33. MATTERS TOUCHING MY SOUL

1. Jordan, ed., *Chronicle of Edward VI,* p. 76.
2. Ibid., p. 333.
3. Ibid., pp. 338–39.
4. Ibid., pp. 333–34, 336–41.
5. Ibid., p. 343.
6. Ibid., p. 349.
7. Ibid., p. 348.
8. Jordan, ed., *Chronicle of Edward VI,* p. 78.
9. T. D. MacCulloch, ed., "The *Vita Mariae Angliae Reginae* of Robert Wingfield of Brantham," *Camden Miscellany* 28; CS, 4th series, 29 (London, 1984), p. 247.
10. *CSPV* X, p. 391.
11. Nichols, ed., "The Diary of Henry Machyn," p. 20.

CHAPTER 34. MY DEVICE FOR THE SUCCESSION

1. 5 Edw. VI c.1; *Statutes*, IV, I, pp. 130–31.
2. *CSPS* XI, pp. 8–9.
3. Inner Temple Library, Petyt MS 538, vol. 46, fol. 9, printed in Nichols, ed., *Literary Remains*, I, p. cxc.
4. Cited in S. T. Bindoff, "A Kingdom at Stake, 1553," *History Today* 3 (1953), p. 647.
5. *CSPS* XI, p. 46.
6. Nichols, ed., *Literary Remains*, pp. 571–72.
7. Inner Temple Library, Petyt MS 538, vol. 47, fol. 317.
8. *CSPS* XI, p. 57.
9. MacCulloch, ed., "The *Vita Mariae*," pp. 247–48.
10. BL, Royal 18 C XXIV, fol. 373v.
11. *CSPS* XI, p. 70.
12. A. Vertot, *Ambassades de Messieurs de Noailles en Angleterre*, 5 vols. (Leyden, 1763), II, pp. 35–38.
13. *CSPS* XI, p. 65.
14. Vertot, *Ambassades*, II, pp. 50–53.
15. E. Lodge, ed., *Illustrations of British History, Biography, and Manners, in the Reigns of Henry VIII, Edward VI, Mary, Elizabeth and James I, Exhibited in a Series of Original Papers . . .*," 3 vols. (London, 1838 ed.), I, pp. 226–27.
16. J. Burtt, ed., "Letters Illustrating the Reign of Queen Jane," *The Archeological Journal*, XXX (1873), p. 276.

CHAPTER 35. FRIENDS IN THE BRIARS

1. J. G. Nichols, ed., "The Chronicle of Queen Jane and Two Years of Queen Mary," (hereafter *CQJQM*), (London, 1850), p. 3.
2. *CSPS* XI, p. 80.
3. See A. Plowden, *Lady Jane Grey: Nine Days Queen* (Stroud, 2003), p. 84.
4. "Epistle of Poor Pratte to Gilbert Potter," in *CQJQM*, pp. 115–21.
5. *CSPS* XI, pp. 76, 79.
6. Ibid., p. 73.
7. *CSPS* XI, p. 74.
8. *CSPS* XI, pp. 73–74.
9. Suffolk Record Office, Eye Borough Records, Ipswich MS EE 2/E/3, fol. 26v; Foxe, *Actes and Monuments*, book 10, p. 1406.
10. Suffolk Record Office, Eye Borough Records, Ipswich MS EE 2/E/3, fol. 27r; Foxe, *Actes and Monuments*, book 10, pp. 1406–07.
11. BL, Lansdowne 3, fols. 48v–49.
12. *CQJQM*, p. 5.
13. Ibid., pp. 6–7.
14. *CSPS* XI, p. 88.
15. *CQJQM*, p. 8.
16. F. Madden, ed., "The Petition of Richard Troughton," *Archaeologia* 23 (1831), p. 25.

CHAPTER 36. TRUE OWNER OF THE CROWN

1. MacCulloch, ed., "The *Vitae Mariae*," p. 252.
2. *CSPS* XI, pp. 106–107.
3. Ibid., p. 79.

4. Hughes and Larkin, eds., *Tudor Royal Proclamations,* II, p. 3.
5. Oxburgh Hall, Bedingfeld Papers.
6. C. V. Malfatti, ed. and trans., *The Accession, Coronation and Marriage of Mary Tudor as Related in Four Manuscripts of the Escorial* (Barcelona, 1956), pp. 14–15.
7. *APC* IV, p. 296.
8. Malfatti, ed., *Mary Tudor*, pp. 16–17.
9. Ibid.
10. Hughes and Larkin, eds., *Tudor Royal Proclamations,* II, p. 3.
11. *Wriothesley's Chronicle,* II, pp. 88–89.
12. Nichols, ed., "The Diary of Henry Machyn," p. 37; Malfatti, ed., *Mary Tudor*, p. 20.
13. *CSPS* XI, p. 115.
14. Ibid., p. 108.
15. J. Stow, *The Annales of England* (London, 1592), p. 1035; *Wriothesley's Chronicle*, II, pp. 88–90; *CQJQM*, pp. 9–12; Nichols, ed., "The Diary of Henry Machyn," p. 37.

CHAPTER 37. MARYE THE QUENE

1. *CSPS* XI, pp. 259–60.
2. *CSPV* V, 934, p. 532.
3. Ibid., 934, p. 533.
4. MacCulloch, ed., "The *Vitae Mariae,*" p. 252.
5. BL, Add 5841, fol. 272.
6. J. Loach, *Parliament and the Crown in the Reign of Mary I* (Oxford, 1986), p. 1.
7. *CSPS* XI, pp. 109–110.
8. Vertot, *Ambassades*, II, pp. 82–100.
9. Aff. Etr. IX, fols. 50, 53, quoted in E. H. Harbison, *Rival Ambassadors at the Court of Mary I* (Princeton, 1940), p. 54.
10. Aff. Etr. IX, fol. 53, quoted in Harbison, *Rival Ambassadors,* p. 54.
11. MacCulloch, ed., "The *Vitae Mariae,*" p. 269.
12. Ibid.
13. *Wriothesley's Chronicle*, II, pp. 91–92.
14. Ibid., p. 92.
15. Ibid., p. 93.
16. MacCulloch, ed., "The *Vitae Mariae,*" p. 271.

CHAPTER 38. THE JOY OF THE PEOPLE

1. *Wriothesley's Chronicle*, II, p. 93.
2. *CSPS* XI, p. 151.
3. *Wriothesley's Chronicle,* II, pp. 92–95; MacCulloch, ed., "The *Vitae Mariae,*" pp. 275–76.
4. *Wriothesley's Chronicle*, II, p. 94.
5. *CSPS* XI, p. 151; *Wriothesley's Chronicle,* II, p. 94.
6. *CSPS* XI, pp. 134, 209.
7. *Wriothesley's Chronicle*, II, p. 95.
8. *CSPS* XI, p. 151.
9. *Wriothesley's Chronicle*, II, p. 95.
10. *CSPS* XI, p. 215.
11. Ibid., p. 172.
12. Ibid., p. 180.
13. Ibid., p. 252.
14. Ibid., p. 130.

15. Ibid., pp. 130–31.
16. Ibid., p. 293.
17. Ibid., p. 132.
18. Ibid., p. 153.

CHAPTER 39. CLEMENCY AND MODERATION

1. Nichols, ed., "The Diary of Henry Machyn," p. 38.
2. R. Garnett, ed. and trans., *The Accession of Queen Mary: Being the Contemporary Narrative of Antonio de Guaras a Spanish Merchant Resident in London* (London, 1892), p. 99.
3. *Wriothesley's Chronicle,* II, pp. 90–91; Garnett, ed., *The Accession of Queen Mary . . . de Guaras,* p. 99.
4. *CQJQM,* pp. 18–19; Tytler, *England under the Reigns of Edward VI and Mary,* II, pp. 230–33; BL, Harley 284, fol. 127.
5. *CSPS* X, i, 184, p. 210.
6. *CSPS* XI, p. 168.
7. Ibid., p. 113.
8. Ibid., p. 168.
9. Ibid., p. 215.
10. Ibid., p. 131.
11. Ibid., p. 134.
12. Ibid., pp. 156–57, 210; Nichols, ed., "The Diary of Henry Machyn," pp. 39–40.
13. *Wriothesley's Chronicle,* II, p. 102.
14. *CSPS* XI, pp. 169–70; Nichols, ed., "Chronicle of the Grey Friars," p. 83.
15. *CSPS* XI, pp. 173–74.
16. Hughes and Larkin, eds., *Tudor Royal Proclamations,* II, p. 5.
17. *CSPV* V, 813, pp. 429–30.
18. *CSPV* V, 836, p. 447.
19. *CSPS* XI, pp. 169–70.
20. Ibid., p. 169.
21. Ibid., pp. 195–96.
22. Ibid., pp. 220–21.
23. Ibid., p. 221.
24. Ibid., p. 240.
25. Ibid., pp. 252–53.
26. Ibid., pp. 393–95.
27. Ibid., p. 395.
28. See ibid., p. 440.

CHAPTER 40. OLD CUSTOMS

1. *CSPS* XI, p. 214.
2. Hughes and Larkin, eds., *Tudor Royal Proclamations,* II, 393, p. 11.
3. Strype, *Ecclesiastical Memorials,* III, p. 34; Nichols, ed., "The Diary of Henry Machyn," p. 43.
4. *CQJQM,* p. 31.
5. Strype, *Ecclesiastical Memorials,* III, p. 34.
6. *CSPS* XI, p. 238.
7. Ibid.
8. Ibid., pp. 238–39.
9. *CSPV* V (15), p. 430. Mary stopped using the title "Supreme Head" at the end of 1553,

but the break with Rome was not officially reversed and England absolved until the third Parliament in November 1554.

10. *CSPS* XI, p. 220.
11. J. R. Planché, *Regal Records; or, A Chronicle of the Coronations of the Queens Regnant of England* (London, 1838), p. 3.
12. College of Arms, MS I 18, fol. 117.
13. *CSPS* XI, p. 262; TNA SP 11/1/16.
14. Planché, *Regal Records,* pp. 4–12; Garnett, ed., *The Accession of Queen Mary . . . de Guaras,* pp. 117–19.
15. Planché, *Regal Records,* p. 6.
16. *CQJQM,* p. 28.
17. Garnett, ed., *The Accession of Queen Mary . . . de Guaras,* pp. 118–19.
18. J. Mychel, *A Breviat Chronicle* (London, 1554) (STC ggjo.j), sig. Oii.
19. *CSPS* XI, p. 259.
20. *CQJQM,* p. 29.
21. Stow, *Annales,* p. 1044.
22. *CQJQM,* p. 30.
23. Ibid.

CHAPTER 41. GOD SAVE QUEEN MARY

1. Planché, *Regal Records,* pp. 12–13; Society of Antiquaries, MS 123, fol. 4v; Malfatti, ed., *Mary Tudor,* p. 32.
2. *CSPS* XI, pp. 239–40.
3. Malfatti, ed., *Mary Tudor,* p. 33.
4. Planché, *Regal Records,* pp. 16–23; Society of Antiquaries, MS 123, fols. 6r–8v.
5. Garnett, ed., *The Accession of Queen Mary . . . de Guaras,* p. 121.
6. Malfatti, ed., *Mary Tudor,* p. 34.
7. *CQJQM,* p. 31.
8. *CSPS* XI, p. 262.
9. Garnett, ed., *The Accession of Queen Mary . . . de Guaras,* pp. 122–23.

CHAPTER 42. INIQUITOUS LAWS

1. *CSPV* V, 813, p. 431.
2. BL, Cotton Titus B II, fol. 148.
3. *CSPS* XI, p. 305.
4. Ibid.
5. *Cal. Pole,* II, 760, pp. 231–32.
6. *Cal. Pole,* II, 765, pp. 235–37.
7. *CSPV* V, 807, p. 425.
8. *CSPS* XI, p. 418.
9. Ibid.
10. Hughes and Larkin, eds., *Tudor Royal Proclamations,* II, pp. 35–38.
11. Bonner's articles, printed in W. H. Frere and W. M. Kennedy, eds., *Visitation Articles and Injunctions of the Period of Reformation,* 3 vols. (London, 1910), II, pp. 344–45.
12. Frere and Kennedy, eds., *Visitation Articles and Injunctions,* II, pp. 347–55.
13. Strype, *Ecclesiastical Memorials,* III, ii, pp. 37–42.
14. Charles Lethbridge Kingsford, ed., *Two London Chronicles from the Collections of John Stow* (London, 1910), p. 31; Nichols, ed., "Chronicle of the Grey Friars," p. 85.
15. Nichols, ed., "The Diary of Henry Machyn," p. 49.

16. A. G. Dickens, ed., "Robert Parkyn Narrative of the Reformation," *English Historical Review* 62 (1947), p. 82.

CHAPTER 43. A MARRYING HUMOR

1. *CSPS* XI, p. 266.
2. Ibid., p. 282.
3. Foxe, *Actes and Monuments*, book 10, p. 1418.
4. *CSPS* XI, pp. 386–87.
5. Vertot, *Ambassades,* II, pp. 144, 174–82.
6. *CSPS* XI, p. 131.
7. BL, Arundel 151, fol. 195; *LP* VI, 1126, p. 472.
8. *CSPS* XI, p. 165.
9. Ibid., pp. 126–27.
10. Ibid., pp. 177–78.
11. Ibid., p. 213.
12. Ibid., pp. 289–90.
13. Ibid., p. 288.
14. Ibid., p. 310.
15. Tytler, *England under the Reigns of Edward VI and Mary,* II, pp. 260, 263.
16. *CSPS* XI, p. 328.
17. Ibid., p. 331.

CHAPTER 44. A SUITABLE PARTNER IN LOVE

1. *CQJQM,* p. 32.
2. *CSPS* XI, pp. 363–65.
3. MacCulloch, ed., "The *Vitae Mariae,*" p. 278; *CSPS* XI, pp. 312–13.
4. *CSPS* XI, p. 364.
5. Ibid., p. 372.
6. Ibid.
7. Grafton, *A Chronicle at Large,* (London, 1569), p. 1327.
8. *CSPS* XI, p. 467.
9. Ibid., pp. 409–10.
10. *CQJQM,* p. 34.
11. Aff. Etr. IX, fol. 99, cited in Harbison, *Rival Ambassadors,* pp. 115–16.
12. *CSPS* XI, p. 407.
13. *CQJQM,* p. 34.
14. Ibid., p. 35.
15. Ibid.

CHAPTER 45. A TRAITOROUS CONSPIRACY

1. *CSPS* XI, p. 426.
2. Aff. Etr. IX, fol. 99, cited in Harbison, *Rival Ambassadors,* pp. 115–16.
3. Harbison, *Rival Ambassadors,* p. 108.
4. *APC* IV, p. 382.
5. *CSPS* XII, pp. 30–35.
6. Ibid., p. 31.
7. TNA SP 11/2/8, fols. 12–13v (*CSPD,* Mary, 30).
8. *CSPS* XII, pp. 40–41.

9. J. Procter, "The Historie of Wyate's Rebellion," in *Tudor Tracts,* ed. A. F. Pollard (London, 1903), pp. 212–13.
10. Procter, "Wyate's Rebellion," p. 213.
11. *CQJQM*, p. 37.
12. Procter, "Wyate's Rebellion," p. 230; John Elder, *The Copie of a Letter Sent into Scotlande* (London, 1333), reprinted in *CQJQM*, appendix X, pp. 38–39.
13. *CQJQM*, p. 39.
14. TNA SP 11/2/9, fols. 14–15v.
15. Proctor, "Wyate's Rebellion," p. 237.
16. Malfatti, ed., *Mary Tudor,* p. 43.
17. *CQJQM*, p. 40.
18. Cited in S. Brigden, *London and the Reformation* (Oxford, 1989), pp. 539–40.
19. MacCulloch, ed., "The *Vitae Mariae,*" p. 281.
20. *CSPV* VI, i, p. 1054.
21. Foxe, *Actes and Monuments,* book 10, pp. 1418–19.
22. Procter, "Wyate's Rebellion," p. 240.
23. Kingsford, ed., *Two London Chronicles,* p. 32.
24. *CQJQM*, p. 43.
25. *CSPS* XII, p. 86.
26. *CQJQM*, p. 48.
27. Ibid., p. 51.
28. *CSPS* XII, pp. 86–88; Nichols, ed., "The Diary of Henry Machyn," p. 55.
29. *CQJQM*, p. 54.

CHAPTER 46. GIBBETS AND HANGED MEN

1. *CSPS* XII, p. 120.
2. *CQJQM*, p. 59.
3. *CSPS* XII, p. 106.
4. Nichols, ed., "The Diary of Henry Machyn," p. 56.
5. *CSPS* XI, p. 168.
6. *CQJQM*, p. 55.
7. Ibid., pp. 56–59.
8. Strype, *Ecclesiastical Memorials,* III, pp. 82–83.
9. Tytler, *England under the Reigns of Edward VI and Mary,* II, pp. 426–27.
10. Strype, *Ecclesiastical Memorials,* III, p. 95; Tytler, *England under the Reigns of Edward VI and Mary,* II, pp. 310–11; Nichols, ed., "The Diary of Henry Machyn," p. 57.
11. *CSPS* XII, p. 125.
12. Ibid.
13. Foxe, *Actes and Monuments,* book 12, p. 2092.
14. L. S. Marcus et al., eds., *Elizabeth I: Collected Works* (Chicago and London, 2000), pp. 41–42.
15. *CSPS* XII, p. 167.
16. *CQJQM*, pp. 70–71.
17. Foxe, *Actes and Monuments,* book 12, p. 2092.
18. Ibid., p. 2093.
19. *CSPS* XII, p. 201.
20. *CQJQM*, pp. 73–74.
21. Nichols, ed., "The Diary of Henry Machyn," pp. 59–60; *CQJQM*, p. 74.
22. *CQJQM*, p. 5.
23. BL, Add 34563, fol. 6r; Revd. C. R. Manning, ed., "State Papers Relating to the

Custody of the Princess Elizabeth at Woodstock in 1554," *Norfolk Archaeology*, 4 (1855), pp. 133–226.

24. Manning, ed., "State Papers," p. 158.
25. *CSPS* XII, p. 162.

CHAPTER 47. SOLE QUEEN

1. Foxe, *Actes and Monuments,* book 10, p. 1419.
2. Hughes and Larkin, eds., *Tudor Royal Proclamations,* II, no. 40.
3. *CSPS* XII, p. 201.
4. Ibid., pp. 216–17.
5. TNA SP 11/1/2, fols. 50–53v.
6. *CSPS* XII, pp. 15–16.
7. Ibid., p. 142.
8. J. D. Alsop, "The Act for the Queen's Regal Power," *Parliamentary History* 13, no. 3 (1994), p. 275. Original is at BL, Harley 6234, fols. 10–25v, which is transcribed in Alsop's appendix.
9. Alsop, "The Act for the Queen's Regal Power," pp. 275–76.
10. *Statutes,* IV, I, p. 222; 1 Mariae, St. 3. c. 1.2.
11. *CSPS* XII, p. 242.
12. BL, Cotton Vespasian F III, Art. 24, no. 19, in French, printed and transcript in Wood, *Letters of Royal and Illustrious Ladies,* III, pp. 290–91.
13. *CSPS* XII, p. 5.
14. Ibid., p. 185.

CHAPTER 48. GOOD NIGHT, MY LORDS ALL

1. Strype, *Ecclesiastical Memorials,* III, p. 127.
2. *CSPS* XII, p. 279; *APC* V, p. 131.
3. *CSPS* XII, p. 309.
4. Ibid.
5. Strype, *Ecclesiastical Memorials,* III, p. 127.
6. *CSPS* XII, p. 295.
7. Malfatti, ed., *Mary Tudor,* p. 49.
8. Nichols, ed., "The Diary of Henry Machyn," p. 66.
9. *CSPS* XIII, p. 1.
10. Hughes and Larkin, eds., *Tudor Royal Proclamations,* II, 413, p. 45.
11. Vertot, *Ambassades,* III, p. 287.
12. John Elder's letter in *CQJQM,* p. 139.
13. Ibid., p. 136.
14. Ibid., pp. 165–66.

CHAPTER 49. WITH THIS RING I THEE WED

1. College of Arms, MS WB, fols. 157r–158r; Malfatti, ed., *Mary Tudor,* p. 51.
2. BL, Add 4712, fol. 79–80.
3. John Elder's letter *CQJQM,* p. 141.
4. Marriage of Queen Mary and King Philip: English heralds' account printed *CQJQM,* pp. 167–72.
5. Bodleian, Wood MS F 30, fol. 49, cited and transcript in A. Samson, "Changing

Places: The Marriage and Royal Entry of Philip, Prince of Austria and Mary Tudor, July–August 1554," *The Sixteenth Century Journal* 36, no. 3 (2005), p. 763.

6. Bodleian, Wood MS F 30, fol. 49r, transcript and cited in Samson, "Changing Places," p. 763.
7. Ibid.
8. John Elder's letter in *CQJQM*, p. 6; *Wriothesley's Chronicle*, II, p. 120.
9. *Wriothesley's Chronicle*, II, p. 121; Hughes and Larkin, eds., *Tudor Royal Proclamations*, II, pp. 45–46.
10. *CSPS* XII, p. 269.
11. Ibid., 11, p. 10.
12. John Elder's letter in *CQJQM*, p. 143.
13. *CSPS* XIII, 11, p. 11.

CHAPTER 50. MUTUAL SATISFACTION

1. C. Weiss, *Papiers d'état du Cardinal Granvelle*, 9 vols. (Paris, 1844–52), IV, p. 285.
2. John Elder's letter in *CQJQM, CSPS* XIII, p. 443.
3. John Elder's letter in *CQJQM*, p. 146.
4. *CQJQM*, p. 79.
5. John Elder's letter in *CQJQM*, p. 147.
6. Ibid.
7. John Elder, in *CQJQM's letter* p. 150.
8. Ibid., p. 151.
9. *CSPS* XIII, 53, p. 43.
10. Withington, *English Pageantry*, p. 190.
11. *CQJQM*, p. 81.
12. *CSPS* XIII, 60, p. 49.
13. *CSPS* XIII, 5, pp. 3–4.

CHAPTER 51. THE HAPPIEST COUPLE IN THE WORLD

1. *CSPS* XIII, 30, p. 26.
2. *CSPS* XIII, 7, pp. 3–6.
3. *CSPV* V, 925, p. 527; *CSPS* XII, pp. 291–93.
4. *CSPS* XIII, 12, p. 13.
5. *CSPS* XIII, 33, p. 28.
6. *CSPS* XIII, 37, pp. 30–34.
7. Ibid.
8. *CSPS* XIII, 102, p. 95.
9. *CSPS* XIII, 56, p. 45.
10. C. H. Williams, ed., *English Historical Documents 1485–1550* (London, 1967), V, p. 210; *CSPS* XIII, 37, p. 31.
11. Nichols, ed., "The Diary of Henry Machyn," p. 76.
12. *CSPS* XIII, 111, p. 105.
13. Nichols, ed., "The Diary of Henry Machyn," p. 108; *CSPF*, Mary, 514, p. 231.
14. Harbison, *Rival Ambassadors*, p. 198.
15. TNA SP E 351/3030.
16. *CQJQM*, p. 82.
17. A supplication to the Queen's majeste (1555) (STC 17567), fols. 23v–24.
18. *CQJQM*, p. 35.
19. BL, Cotton Vespasian F III, no. 23.

20. Archivo General de Simancas, Estado 1498, fols. 6–7; quoted by G. Redworth in "Matters Impertinent to Women: Male and Female Monarchy under Philip and Mary," *English Historical Review* 112, no. 447 (June 1999), p. 598.
21. *CSPS* XIII, 75, pp. 63–64.
22. *CSPS* XIII, 94, pp. 79–80.
23. *CSPV* V, 955, pp. 582–83; 957, pp. 584–86.
24. *CSPS* XIII, 115, p. 108.
25. *CSPS* XIII, 97, p. 81.
26. *CSPS* XIII, 97, p. 82.

CHAPTER 52. TO RECONCILE, NOT TO CONDEMN

1. *CSPS* XIII, 63, p. 53.
2. *CSPV* V, 776, p. 398.
3. *CSPV* V, 856, p. 464; *CSPS* XI, p. 263.
4. *CSPS* XI, pp. 420–21.
5. *CSPS* XIII, 111, p. 105.
6. *CQJQM*, p. 159.
7. John Elder's letter in *CQJQM*, p. 160; Foxe, *Actes and Monuments*, book 10, pp. 1476–77.
8. Foxe, *Actes and Monuments*, book 10, p. 1478.
9. *CSPS* XIII, 115, p. 109.
10. Grafton, *A Chronicle at Large*, pp. 550–51.
11. *CSPS* XIII, 118, p. 112.
12. Foxe, *Actes and Monuments*, book 10, p. 1479. See John Elder's letter in *CQJQM*, pp. 162–63.
13. *CSPS* XIII, 127, p. 122.

CHAPTER 53. THE QUEEN IS WITH CHILD

1. *Cal. Pole*, II, 998, p. 380.
2. Tytler, *England under the Reigns of Edward VI and Mary*, II, p. 455.
3. Strype, *Ecclesiastical Memorials*, III, pp. 204–205; Nichols, ed., "The Diary of Henry Machyn," pp. 76–77.
4. *CSPS* XIII, 71, p. 60.
5. *CSPS* XIII, 92, p. 78.
6. *CSPS* XIII, 116, p. 110.
7. *CSPS* XIII, 130, p. 124.
8. Tytler, *England under the Reigns of Edward VI and Mary*, II, p. 455.
9. Foxe, *Actes and Monuments*, book 11, p. 1597.
10. *CSPF*, Mary, 367, p. 172; Tytler, *England under the Reigns of Edward VI and Mary*, II, p. 469.
11. *Statutes*, IV, I, pp. 255–57; 1 and 2 Phil. & Mar. c.10.
12. *Statutes*, IV, I, p. 256; 1 and 2 Phil. & Mar. c.10.
13. Nichols, ed., "The Diary of Henry Machyn," p. 85.
14. *CSPV* VI, i, 67, pp. 57–58.
15. Foxe, *Actes and Monuments* (1563), 5, iii, p. 1731.
16. Nichols, ed., "The Diary of Henry Machyn," p. 86.
17. *CSPV* VI, i, 72, p. 61; *CSPS* XIII, 184, p. 169.
18. Foxe, *Actes and Monuments*, book 11, p. 1596.
19. *CSPF*, Mary, 354, pp. 165–66.

CHAPTER 54. HER MAJESTY'S BELLY

1. *CSPV* VI, i, 89, p. 77.
2. *CSPS* XIII, 193, pp. 175–76.
3. *CSPS* XIII, 216, p. 224.
4. Cited in H. Kamen, *Philip of Spain* (New Haven, 1997), p. 62.
5. *CSPV* VI, i, 174, p. 148.
6. *CSPV* VI, i, 174, p. 417.
7. BL, Sloane I, 583, fol. 15.
8. *CPR,* Mary, III, pp. 184–85.
9. Foxe, *Actes and Monuments,* book 11, p. 1597.
10. Vertot, *Ambassades,* IV, pp. 341–44.
11. *CSPS* XIII, 212, p. 222.
12. *CSPV* VI, i, 116, p. 93.
13. *CSPV* VI, ii, 174, pp. 147–48.
14. *CSPV* VI, i, 142, p. 120.
15. Ibid.
16. *CSPV* VI, i, 174, p. 147; 184, p. 162.
17. *CSPV* VI, ii, p. 1080.
18. *CSPS* XIII, 229, p. 240.
19. *CSPV* VI, i, 190, p. 167.

CHAPTER 55. BLOOD AND FIRE

1. Foxe, *Actes and Monuments,* book 11, p. 1493.
2. *CSPS* XIII, 148, pp. 138–39.
3. Foxe, *Actes and Monuments*, book 11, pp. 1520–21.
4. Ibid., p. 1510.
5. Ibid., p. 1511.
6. Ibid., p. 1592.
7. Ibid., pp. 1592–93.
8. Ibid., p. 1567.
9. *APC* V, p. 118.
10. Foxe, *Actes and Monuments,* book 11, p. 1981.
11. Ibid.
12. Ibid., p. 1945.
13. *CSPV* VI, iii, appendix, 136, p. 1647.
14. *CSPS* XIII, 148, pp. 138–39.
15. *CSPV* VI, 116, p. 94.
16. Cited in Kamen, *Philip of Spain,* p. 62.
17. *CSPS* XIII, p. 151.
18. *CSPV* 934, p. 533.

CHAPTER 56. EXTRAORDINARILY IN LOVE

1. *CSPS* XIII, 228, pp. 238–39.
2. *CSPV* VI, i, 200, p. 173.
3. *CSPV* VI, i, 204, p. 178.
4. Ibid.
5. *CSPV* VI, i, 209, p. 183.
6. *CSPV* VI, i, 213, p. 186.

7. *CSPV* VI, i, 200, p. 174.
8. *CSPV* VI, i, 217, p. 190.
9. *CSPS* XIII, 52, p. 42.
10. *CSPS* XIII, 239, p. 247.
11. BL, Cotton Titus B II, fol. 62.
12. Vertot, *Ambassades,* V, pp. 126–27.
13. *CSPV* VI, i, 246, p. 213.
14. *CSPV* VI, 318, p. 285.
15. BL, Cotton Titus B II, fol. 60.
16. TNA SP 11/6/17, fol. 27v; SP 11/8/71 (i), fols. 121–122v.
17. *CSPV* VI, i, 353, p. 319.
18. *CSPV* VI, i, 245, p. 212; 257, p. 227; 315, p. 281.
19. *CSPV* VI, i, 245, p. 212.
20. *CSPV* VI, i, 332, p. 300.
21. *CSPV* VI, i, 332, pp. 299–300.
22. *CSPV* VI, 309, p. 278.
23. Vertot, *Ambassades,* V, pp. 169–73.

CHAPTER 57. COMMITTED TO THE FLAMES

1. Lord Houghton, ed., *Bishop Cranmer's Recantacyons*, with introduction by J. Gairdner, *Miscellanies of the Philobiblon Society*, 15 (1877–84), pp. 108–10.
2. Letter of Warrant from Mary to mayor and bailiffs of Oxford quoted in G. Townshend and S.R. Cattley, eds., *Actes and Monuments of John Foxe* (8 vols., 1837–41), 6, pp. 531–32.
3. Foxe, *Actes and Monuments*, book 11, p. 1770.
4. Ibid.
5. Ibid.
6. *CSPV* VI, 365, p. 329.
7. Cox, ed., *Miscellaneous Writings and Letters of Thomas Cranmer,* II, p. 563.
8. Ibid.
9. P. N. Brooks, *Cranmer in Context* (Cambridge, 1989), p. 112.
10. Cox, ed., *Miscellaneous Writings and Letters of Thomas Cranmer,* II, pp. 564–65.
11. Foxe, *Actes and Monuments,* book 11, p. 1887.
12. Ibid., p. 1888.
13. *CSPV* VI, 434, p. 386.

CHAPTER 58. A GREAT AND RARE EXAMPLE OF GOODNESS

1. *CSPV* VI, i, 473, pp. 434–47.

CHAPTER 59. STOUT AND DEVILISH HEARTS

1. *CSPV* VI, i, 429, p. 378.
2. Strype, *Ecclesiastical Memorials,* III, p. 286; Nichols, ed., "The Diary of Henry Machyn," p. 101.
3. John Bradford's letter in Strype, *Ecclesiastical Memorials,* III, ii, p. 129.
4. Nichols, ed., "The Diary of Henry Machyn," pp. 94–95.
5. *CSPS* XIII, 161, pp. 147–48.
6. *CSPV* VI, i, 215, p. 188.
7. *CSPV* VI, i, 274, p. 243.
8. *CSPV* VI, i, 258, p. 231.

9. *CSPV* VI, I, 297, pp. 269–270.
10. *CSPV* VI, i, 289, p. 259.
11. *APC* V, p. 224.
12. *CSPV* VI, i, 427, p. 376.
13. *CSPV* VI, i, 434, p. 384.
14. Ibid.
15. *CSPV* VI, i, 434, pp. 384–85.
16. *CSPV* VI, i, 434, pp. 383–84; *CSPF,* Mary, 496, pp. 222–23.
17. Vertot, *Ambassades,* V, pp. 361–63.
18. *Wriothesley's Chronicle,* II, p. 134.
19. *CSPV* VI, i, 440, p. 392.
20. *CSPV* VI, i, 458, p. 411.
21. *CSPV* VI, i, 525, p. 495.
22. *CSPV* VI, i, 570, p. 558.
23. *CSPV* VI, i, 427, p. 376.
24. *CSPV* VI, i, 460, p. 415.
25. *CSPS* XIII, 273, p. 271.
26. Vertot, *Ambassades,* V, pp. 361–63.
27. Aff.Etr. XIII, fol. 24, as cited in Harbison, *Rival Ambassadors,* p. 301.
28. *CSPS* XIII, 279, p. 276.

CHAPTER 60. OBEDIENT SUBJECT AND HUMBLE SISTER

1. *CSPV* VI, i, 505, p. 475.
2. *CSPV* VI, i, 510, p. 479.
3. L. Wiesener, *La Jeunesse d'Elisabeth d'Angleterre* (Paris, 1878), p. 343.
4. *CSPV,* VI, i, 514, p. 484.
5. Strype, *Ecclesiastical Memorials,* III, p. 336.
6. Ibid.
7. BL, Lansdowne 1236, fol. 37, printed in Marcus et al., eds., *Elizabeth,* pp. 43–44.
8. Nichols, ed., "The Diary of Henry Machyn," p. 120.
9. Wiesener, *La Jeunesse d'Elisabeth,* p. 304.
10. BL, Cotton Titus B II, fol. 109.

CHAPTER 61. A WARMED OVER HONEYMOON

1. Nichols, ed., "The Diary of Henry Machyn," p. 129.
2. C. Erikson, *Bloody Mary* (London, 1978), p. 463.
3. *CSPV* VI, ii, 743, p. 835.
4. *CSPV* VI, ii, 723, pp. 808–809.
5. *CSPV* VI, ii, 787, p. 902; 790, p. 907; 795, pp. 916–17.
6. "Instructions," Jan. 22, 1557, Aff.Etr. XIII, fols. 137, 139, cited in Harbison, *Rival Ambassadors,* p. 315.
7. BL, Cotton Otho IX, E321–342, fol. 88; T. Glasgow Jr., "The Navy in Philip and Mary's War, 1557–1558," *Mariner's Mirror* 53, no. 4 (1967), pp. 321–42.
8. Nichols, ed., "The Diary of Henry Machyn," p. 124.
9. Ibid.
10. Aff.Etr. XIII, fol. 157, quoted in Harbison, *Rival Ambassadors,* p. 317.
11. *CSPS* XIII, 289, pp. 285–87.
12. Aff.Etr. XIII, fols. 160, 180, quoted in Harbison, *Rival Ambassadors,* p. 321; *CSPV* VI, ii, p. 956.
13. Aff.Etr. XIII, fol. 182, quoted in Harbison, *Rival Ambassasdors,* pp. 323–24.

14. Aff.Etr. XIII, fols. 182–183, cited in Harbison, *Rival Ambassadors,* p. 324.
15. *CSPV* VI, ii, 864, p. 1019.
16. Aff.Etr. XIII, fols. 182v–183, cited in Harbison, *Rival Ambassadors,* p. 324.
17. François de Noailles to Montmorency, April 5, 1557, cited in Harbison, *Rival Ambassadors,* p. 324.
18. *CSPV,* VI, ii, 743, p. 835.
19. Aff.Etr. XIII, fols. 166–168, cited in Harbison, *Rival Ambassadors,* p. 319.
20. Aff.Etr. XIII, fol. 191, cited in Harbison, *Rival Ambassadors,* p. 326.

CHAPTER 62. A PUBLIC ENEMY TO OURSELVES

1. *CSPV* VI, 870, p. 1026.
2. Strype, *Ecclesiastical Memorials,* III, ii, p. 261.
3. Ibid., pp. 261–63.
4. *CSPS* XIII, 299, pp. 290–91; *CSPV* VI, ii, 873, pp. 1028–29.
5. *CSPS* XIII, 306, p. 294.
6. *CSPV* VI, ii, p. 927.
7. *CSPS* XIII, 339, p. 317.
8. Nichols, ed., "The Diary of Henry Machyn," p. 147; Strype, *Ecclesiastical Memorials,* III (1721), p. 382.
9. *CSPS* XIII, 349, p. 321.
10. Nichols, ed., "The Diary of Henry Machyn," p. 162.
11. George Ferrers, "The Winning of Calais by the French" (1569), reprinted in Pollard, ed., *Tudor Tracts 1532–1588,* pp. 290–98.
12. *CSPS* XIII, 395, p. 348.
13. *CSPS* XIII, 382, pp. 340–41.

CHAPTER 63. THE GRIEF OF THE MOST SERENE QUEEN

1. Reginald Pole, *Epistolae Reginaldi Poli*, ed. A. M. Quirini, 5 vols. (Brescia, 1744–1757), V, p. 24.
2. *CSPV* VI, ii, 849, p. 994.
3. *CSPV* VI, ii, 772, p. 880.
4. Pole, *Epistolae Reginaldi Poli,* V, p. 144.
5. *CSPV* VI, 899, p. 1112.
6. Strype, *Ecclesiastical Memorials,* III, ii, pp. 231–37.
7. *CSPV* VI, 898, pp. 1109–11; 913, pp. 1131–33.
8. *CSPV* VI, 937, pp. 1166–70.
9. *CSPV* VI, ii, 937, pp. 1166–67.
10. *Cal. Pole*, 111, p. 464.
11. *CSPF,* Mary, 641, p. 320.
12. *CSPV* VI, ii, 981, p. 1240.
13. *CSPV* VI, 991, p. 1248.
14. Nichols, ed., "The Diary of Henry Machyn," pp. 150–51.
15. Pole, *Epistolae Reginaldi Poli*, V, p. 34.
16. *CSPV* VI, iii, 1209, p. 1482.
17. *CSPV* V, 813, p. 429.
18. C. G. Bayne, *Anglo-Roman Relations, 1558–1565* (Oxford, 1913), p. 24.

CHAPTER 64. READINESS FOR CHANGE

1. *CSPV* VI, ii, 884, pp. 1043–85.

CHAPTER 65. THINKING MYSELF TO BE WITH CHILD

1. *CSPV* VI, iii, 1142, p. 1427.
2. *CSPS* XIII, 382, pp. 340–41.
3. *CSPS* XIII, 413, p. 367.
4. *CSPS* XIII, 425, pp. 378–79.
5. BL, Harley 6949, is the transcript of the will and is printed in D. M. Loades, *Mary Tudor: A Life* (Oxford, 1989), pp. 370–83.
6. *CSPV* VI, iii, 1274, p. 1538.
7. M. J. Rodriguez-Salgado and S. Adams, eds., "The Count of Feria's Despatch to Philip II of 14 November 1558," *Camden Miscellany* 28 (1984), pp. 330, 334.
8. *CSPV* VI, III, 1274, p. 1538.
9. *CSPS* XIII, 498, p. 438.
10. *CSPV* VI, iii, 1285, p. 1549.

CHAPTER 66. REASONABLE REGRET FOR HER DEATH

1. Clifford, *Life of Jane Dormer,* p. 71.
2. Holinshed, *Chronicles of England,* II, p. 1784.
3. Nichols, ed., "The Diary of Henry Machyn," p. 178.
4. *CSPV* VI, iii, 1286, p. 1550.
5. *CSPS* XIII, 502, p. 440.
6. "Ceremonial of the Burial of King Edward IV, from a Ms of the Late Mr Artis, Now in the Possession of Thomas Astle, Esq," *Archaeologia* II (1779), pp. 350–51.
7. *CSPS* I, 1, p. 3.
8. TNA SP 12/1, fols. 32–33.
9. Nichols, ed., "The Diary of Henry Machyn," p. 182.
10. Strype, *Ecclesiastical Memorials,* III, i, pp. 466–67; Nichols, ed., "The Diary of Henry Machyn," p. 182; A. P. Harvey and R. Mortimer, eds., *The Funeral Effigies of Westminster Abbey* (Woodbridge, 1994), pp. 55–57.
11. Nichols, ed., "The Diary of Henry Machyn," pp. 182–83; TNA SP 12/1, fols. 69–80.
12. Strype, *Ecclesiastical Memorials,* III, ii, pp. 277–87.
13. Ibid.
14. "A Sermon Made at the Burial of Queen Mary," BL, Cotton Vespasian D XVIII X, fol. 104; for published version, cited in Strype, *Ecclesiastical Memorials,* III, ii, pp. 277–87.
15. *APC* VII, p. 45.
16. Nichols, ed., "The Diary of Henry Machyn," pp. 183–84.

EPILOGUE. VERITAS TEMPORIS FILIA

1. BL, Harley, 1813, pp. 259–60. *The Epitaphe vpon the Death of the Most Excellent and oure late vertuous Quene, Marie, deceased, augmented by the first Author* (London, 1558?), in *Old English Ballads 1553–1625, Chiefly from Manuscripts,* ed. Hyder E. Rollins (Cambridge, 1920), pp. 23–26, at p. 26. See Marcia Lee Metzger, "Controversy and 'Correctness': English Chronicles and Chroniclers, 1553–68," *The Sixteenth-Century Journal* 27 (1996), pp. 437–51, at p. 450.
2. E. Arber, ed., *A Transcript of the Register of the Company of Stationers of London, 1554–1640,* 5 vols. (London, 1875–77), I, fol. 35.
3. "A fourme of prayer with thankes giuing, to be used every yeere, the 17. of November, beyng the day of the Queenes Maiesties entrie to her raigne, London

1576," reprinted in W. Keatinge, *Liturgical Services, Elizabeth* (London, 1847), pp. 548–58.

4. J. Knox, *The First Blast of the Trumpet against the Monstrous Regiment of Women* (Geneva, 1558), p. 32.
5. Ibid., p. 10.
6. Ibid., p. 9.
7. Foxe, *Actes and Monuments* (London, 1583), p. 2098.
8. R. Garcia, "'Most Wicked Superstition and Idolatry': John Foxe, His Predecessors and the Development of an Anti-Catholic Polemic in the Sixteenth-Century Accounts of the Reign of Mary I," in *John Foxe at Home and Abroad*, ed. D. Loades, pp. 79–87.
9. W. C. Sellar and R. J. Yeatman, *1066 and All That: A Memorable History of England Comprising all the Parts You Can Remember . . .* (London, 1930), pp. 64–65.
10. M. Twiss, *The Most Evil Men and Women in History* (London, 2002), pp. 85–97.
11. *CSPV* V, pp. 532–33.
12. J. Aylmer, *An Harborowe for Faithfull and Trewe Subiectes* ("Strasborowe" [i.e., London], 1559) (STC 1005) sig. H3v.
13. Janet Arnold, *Queen Elizabeth's Wardrobe Unlock'd* (Leeds, 1988), pp. 52, 55.

SELECT BIBLIOGRAPHY

UNPUBLISHED SOURCES

Manuscripts

Bodleian Library

Rawlinson MS B 146; Tanner MS 90; Wood MS F 30

British Library

Add 4712; Add 5841; Add 5935; Add 6113; Add 21481; Add 24124; Add 27402; Add 33230; Add 34563; Add 48126; Add 71009; Arundel 97; Arundel 151; Cotton Caligula D VII; Cotton Caligula D IX; Cotton Caligula E V; Cotton Cleop E VI; Cotton Faustina C II; Cotton Nero B VI; Cotton Otho C X; Cotton Titus B I; Cotton Titus B II; Cotton Titus C VII; Cotton Vitellius C I; Cotton Vitellius V I; Cotton Vespasian C III; Cotton Vespasian C XIV; Cotton Vespasian F III; Cotton Vespasian F XIII; Egerton 616; Harley 284; Harley 416; Harley 589; Harley 3504; Harley 5087; Harley 6068; Harley 6234; Harley 6807; Lansdowne 3; Lansdowne 103; Lansdowne 1236; Royal 14 B XIX; Royal 17 B XXVIII; Royal 17 C XVI; Royal 18 C XXIV; Royal App. 89; Sloane I; Sloane 1786; Stowe 142; Stowe 571

The National Archives

E36; E101; E179; E351; LC 2; LC 5; LS 13; PROB 11; SP 1; SP 10; SP 11; SP 12; SP 46

College of Arms

MS I 7
MS I 18
MS WB

Oxburgh Hall

Bedingfield Papers: Papers relating to Henry Bedingfield

Suffolk Record Office

EE2/E/3: Eye Borough Records
HA 411: Cornwallis family papers

Society of Antiquaries

MS 123

Inner Temple Library

Petyt MS 538

PhD Theses

Braddock, R. C. "The Royal Household, 1540–1560: A Study in Office-holding in Tudor England" (PhD thesis, Northwestern University, Illinois, 1971).

Bryson, A. "The Special Men in Every Sphere; The Edwardian Regime, 1547–1553" (PhD thesis, St. Andrews, 2001).

Carter, Alison J. "Mary Tudor's Wardrobe of Robes" (MA thesis, Courtauld Institute, 1982).

Drey, Elizabeth Ann. "The Portraits of Mary I, Queen of England" (MA thesis, Courtauld Institute, 1990).

Hamilton, D. L. "The Household of Queen Katherine Parr" (DPhil thesis, University of Oxford, 1992).

Lemasters, G. A. "The Privy Council in the Reign of Mary I" (PhD thesis, University of Cambridge, 1971).

Merton, C. "The Women Who Served Queen Mary and Queen Elizabeth: Ladies, Gentlewomen and Maids of the Privy Chamber, 1553–1603" (PhD thesis, University of Cambridge, 1992).

Starkey, D. "The King's Privy Chamber, 1485–1547" (PhD thesis, University of Cambridge, 1973).

Whitelock, A. "In Opposition and in Government: The Households and Affinities of Mary Tudor, 1516–1558" (PhD thesis, University of Cambridge, 2004).

PUBLISHED SOURCES

Primary

Aylmer, John. *An Harborowe for Faithfull and Trewe Subiectes, against the Late Blowne Blaste, Concerning the Government of Women* (London, 1559).

Bonner, Edmund. *Homilies Sett Forth by the Righte Reverence Father in God* (London, 1555).

———. *A Profitable and Necessarye Doctryne* (London, 1555).

Brewer, J. S., et al., eds. *Letters and Papers, Foreign and Domestic, of the Reign of Henry VIII, 1509–47*, 21 vols. and addenda (London, 1862–1932).

Brown, R., et al., eds. *Calendar of State Papers and Manuscripts, Relating to English Affairs, Existing in the Archives and Collections of Venice, and in Other Libraries of Northern Italy*, 9 vols. (London, 1864–98).

Burnet, Gilbert. *History of the Reformation in England*, ed. N. Pocock, 7 vols. (Oxford, 1865).

Byrne, M. St. C., ed. *The Lisle Letters*, 6 vols. (Chicago, 1980).

Calendar of the Patent Rolls Preserved in the Public Record Office: Philip and Mary (London, 1937).

Cavendish, G. *The Life and Death of Cardinal Wolsey by George Cavendish*, ed. R. S. Sylvester (London, 1959).

Clifford, Henry. *The Life of Jane Dormer, Duchess of Feria*, ed. J. Stevenson (London, 1887).

Collins, A., ed. *Letters and Memorials of State in the Reigns of Queen Mary, Queen Elizabeth,*

King James, King Charles the First, Part of the Reign of King Charles the Second and Oliver's Usurption, written and collected by Sir Henry Sydney, 2 vols. (London, 1746).

Cox, J. E. *Works of Archbishop Cranmer*, 2 vols. (Parker Society, 1846).

Crawford, A., ed. *Letters of the Queens of England 1100–1547* (Stroud, 1994).

Dasent, J. R., et al., eds. *Acts of the Privy Council*, 46 vols. (London, 1890–1914).

Du Bellay, Jean. *Ambassades en Angleterre de Jean Du Bellay . . . Correspondance Diplomatique* (Paris, 1905).

Duwes, G. *An Introductory for to Learn to Read, to Pronounce, and to Speak French [1532?]*, ed. R. C. Alston, facsimile (Menston, 1972).

Elder, John. *The Copie of a Letter Sent into Scotland* (London, 1555).

Ellis, H., ed. *Original Letters, Illustrative of English History . . . from Autographs in the British Museum and . . . Other Collections*, 1st ser., 3 vols. (London, 1824).

An Epitaphe upon the Death of the Most Excellent and Late Vertuous Queen Marie (London, 1558).

Foxe, J. *Actes and Monuments of These Latter and Perillous Dayes . . .* (London, 1583).

Frere, W. H., and W. M. Kennedy, eds. *Visitation Articles and Injunctions of the Period of Reformation*, 3 vols. (London, 1910).

Gairdner, J., ed. "Journals of Roger Machado, Embassy to Spain and Portugal, AD 1488," in *Historia Regis Henrici Septimi* (London, 1858; 1966 reprint).

Giustiniani, Sebastian. *Four Years at the Court of Henry VIII: Selection of Despatches Addressed to the Signory of Venice*, ed. and trans. R. Brown, 2 vols. (London, 1854).

Grafton, R. *A Chronicle at Large and Meere History of the Affayres of Englande and Kinges of the Same* (London, 1569).

Grose, Francis, ed. *The Antiquarian Repertory*, 2nd ed., rev. E. Jeffery, 4 vols. (London, 1807–09; first published 1775).

Guaras, Antonio de. *The Accession of Queen Mary: Being the Contemporary Narrative of a Spanish Merchant Resident in London*, ed. and trans. R. Garnett (London, 1892).

Hall, E. *Hall's Chronicle Containing the History of England, during the Reign of Henry the Fourth, and the Succeeding Monarchs, to the End of the Reign of Henry the Eighth, in Which Are Particularly Described the Manners and Customs of Those Periods*, ed. Henry Ellis, 2 vols. (London, 1809).

Halliwell-Phillipps, J. O., ed. *Letters of the Kings of England, Now First Collected from the Originals*, 2 vols. (London, 1846).

Harpsfield, Nicholas. *Archdeacon Harpsfield's Visitation of 1557*, ed. L. E. Whatmore (London, 1950–51).

Haynes, S. *A Collection of State Papers Relating to the Affairs in the Reigns of King Henry VIII, King Edward VI, Queen Mary and Queen Elizabeth from the Year 1542 to 1570 . . .* (London, 1740).

Hearne, Thomas. *Sylloge Epistolarum* (London, 1716).

Herbert of Cherbury, Lord. *The Life and Raigne of King Henry the Eighth* (London, 1649).

Holinshed, R. *Chronicles, &c.*, ed. H. Ellis, 6 vols. (London, 1807–08).

Hughes, P. L., and J. F. Larkin, eds. *Tudor Royal Proclamations*, 3 vols. (New Haven and London, 1964–69).

Jordan, W. K., ed. *The Chronicle and Political Papers of King Edward VI* (London, 1966).

Kaulek, J., ed. *Correspondance Politique de MM. de Castillon et de Marillac* (Paris, 1885).

Kipling, G., ed. *The Receyt of the Ladie Kateryne* (Oxford, 1990).

Knighton, C. S., ed., *Calendar of State Papers, Domestic Series, of the Reign of Edward VI, 1547–1554*, rev. ed. (London, 1992).

———. *Calendar of State Papers, Domestic Series, of the Reign of Mary I, 1553–1558, Preserved in the Public Record Office*, rev. ed. (London, 1998).

Knox, John. *The First Blast of the Trumpet against the Monstrous Regiment of Women* (Geneva, 1558).

Lodge, Edmund, ed. *Illustrations of British History, Biography, and Manners, in the Reigns of Henry VIII, Edward VI, Mary, Elizabeth and James I, Exhibited in a Series of Original Papers . . .*, 3 vols. (London, 1838 ed.).

Luders, A., T. E. Tomlins, J. France, W. E. Taunton, and J. Raithby, eds. *Statutes of the Realm*, 11 vols. (London, 1810–28).

MacCulloch D., ed. "The *Vita Mariae Angliae Reginae* of Robert Wingfield of Brantham," *Camden Miscellany*, 28 Camden Society, 4th series, 29 (London, 1984), pp. 181–301.

Madden, F. "Narrative of the Visit of the Duke of Najera to England in the Year 1543–44; Written by his Secretary, Pedro de Gente," *Archaeologia* 23 (1831), pp. 344–57.

Madden, F., ed. "The Petition of Richard Troughton . . . to the Privy Council," *Archaeologia* 23 (1831), pp. 18–49.

———, ed. *The Privy Purse Expenses of the Princess Mary* (London, 1831).

Malfatti, C. V., ed. and trans. *The Accession, Coronation and Marriage of Mary Tudor as Related in Four Manuscripts of the Escorial* (Barcelona, 1956).

Marcus, L. S., J. Mueller, and M. B. Rose, eds. *Elizabeth I: Collected Works* (Chicago and London, 2000).

Marillac, Charles de. *Correspondance politique de MM. de Castillion et de Marillac*, ed. J. Kaulek (Paris, 1885).

Mayer, T. F., ed. *The Correspondence of Reginald Pole*, 4 vols. (Aldershot, 2002).

Morice, R. "Anecdotes and Character of Archbishop Cranmer," in *Narratives of the Days of the Reformation, Chiefly from the Manuscripts of John Foxe the Martyrologist*, ed. J. G. Nichols, Camden Society 77 (London, 1859), pp. 234–72.

Mueller, J. A., ed. *The Letters of Stephen Gardiner* (Cambridge, 1933).

Mychel, J. *A Breuiat Cronicle . . .* (London, 1554).

Nichols, J. G. *The Legend of Nicholas Throgmorton* (London, 1874).

———. *The Literary Remains of King Edward VI*, Roxburghe Club, 2 vols. (London, 1857).

Nichols, J. G., ed., "Chronicle of the Grey Friars of London," *Camden Miscellany*, Camden Society, 1st ser., 53 (London, 1851).

———. "The Chronicle of Queen Jane and Two Years of Queen Mary, and Especially of the Rebellion of Sir Thomas Wyat," *Camden Miscellany*, Camden Society, 1st ser., 48 (London, 1850).

———. "The Diary of Henry Machyn, Citizen and Merchant Taylor of London, from 1550–1563," *Camden Miscellany*, Camden Society, 1st ser., 42 (London, 1849).

———. *Narratives of the Reformation*, Camden Society, 1st ser., 77 (London, 1859).

Parkyn, Robert. "Robert Parkyn's Narrative of the Reformation," ed. A. G. Dickens, *English Historical Review* 62 (1947), pp. 58–83.

Planché, J. R. *Regal Records: or, A Chronicle of the Coronations of the Queens Regnant of England* (London, 1838).

Pocock, N., ed. *A Treatise of the Pretended Divorce between Henry VIII and Catherine of Aragon by Nicholas Harpsfield*, Camden Society, new ser. 21 (London, 1878).

Pole, Reginald. *Epistolae Reginaldi Poli*, ed. A. M. Quirini (Brescia, 1744–57).

Proctor, John. "The Historie of Wyate's Rebellion," in *Tudor Tracts, 1532–1588*, ed. A. F. Pollard (London, 1903), pp. 201–57.

Robinson, H., ed. *Original Letters Relative to the English Reformation . . . Chiefly from the Archives of Zurich*, Parker Society, 2 vols. (Cambridge, 1846–47).

Rodriguez-Salgado, M. J., and S. Adams, eds. "The Count of Feria's Despatch to Philip II of 14 November 1558," *Camden Miscellany*, 28 (1984).

Rymer, T., and R. Sanderson, eds. *Foedera, Conventions, Litterae . . .*, 20 vols. (London, 1704–35).

State Papers Published under the Authority of His Majesty's Commission, King Henry the Eighth, 11 vols. (London, 1830–52).

Stow, J. *The Annales of England* (London, 1605).

Strype, J. *Eccesiastical Memorials, Relating Chiefly to Religion, and the Reformation of It, and the Emergenices of the Church of England under King Henry VIII, King Edward VI and Queen Mary I,* 3 vols. (London, 1721).

Turnbull, W. B., ed. *Calendar of State Papers, Foreign Series, of the Reign of Mary I, 1553–1558* (London, 1861).

Tyler, R., et al., eds. *Calendar of Letters, Despatches and State Papers Relating to the Negotiations between England and Spain; Preserved in the Archives at Vienna, Simancas, and Elsewhere* (London, 1862–1954).

Tytler, P. E., ed. *England under the Reigns of Edward VI and Mary . . .*, 2 vols. (London, 1839).

Underhill, Edward. "The Narrative of Edward Underhill," in *Tudor Tracts*, ed. A. F. Pollard (London, 1903).

Vertot, R. A. de, ed. *Ambassades de Messieurs de Noailles en Angleterre* (London, 1681–1714).

Vives, J. L. *De Institutione Feminae Christianae*, ed. and trans. C. Fantazzi and C. Matheeussen (New York, 1998).

Weiss, C. *Papiers d'État du Cardinal Granvelle* (Paris, 1844–52).

Wood, M. A. E., ed. *Letters of Royal and Illustrious Ladies of Great Britain*, 3 vols. (London, 1846).

Wriothesley, C. *A Chronicle during the Reigns of the Tudors from* 1485 *to* 1559, *by Charles Wriothesley, Windsor Herald*, ed. W. D. Hamilton, 2 vols., Camden Society, new ser., 11 (London, 1875–77).

Secondary

Alexander, G. "Bonner and the Marian Persecutions," *History* 60 (1975), pp. 374–92.

Alford, Stephen. *Kingship and Politics in the Reign of Edward VI* (Cambridge, 2002).

Alsop, J. D. "The Act for the Queen's Regal Power," *Parliamentary History* 13, no. 3 (1994), pp. 261–78.

———. "A Regime at Sea: The Navy and the 1553 Succession Crisis," *Albion* 24, no. 4 (1992), pp. 577–90.

Anglo, Sydney. *Spectacle, Pageantry and Early Tudor Policy* (Oxford, 1965).

Bayne, C. G. *Anglo–Roman Relations, 1558–1565* (Oxford, 1913).

Beer, B. L. *Northumberland: The Political Career of John Dudley, Earl of Warwick and Duke of Northumberland* (Kent, Ohio, 1973).

Bindoff, S. T. *Kett's Rebellion* (London, 1949).

———. "A Kingdom at Stake, 1553," *History Today* 3 (1953), pp. 642–48.

———. *Tudor England* (London, 1950).

Bourgeois, G. "Mary Tudor's Accession and Cambridgeshire: Political Allegiance and Religion," *Lamar Journal of Humanities* 21 (1995), pp. 37–49.

Brigden, Susan. *New Worlds, Lost Worlds: The Rule of the Tudors* (London, 2000).

Bush, M. L. *The Government Policy of Protector Somerset* (London, 1976).

Carter, Alison J. "Mary Tudor's Wardrobe," *Costume, The Journal of the Costume Society* 18 (1984), pp. 9–28.

Chibnall, Marjorie. *The Empress Matilda: Queen Consort, Queen Mother and Lady of the English* (Oxford, 1991).

Davies, C. S. L. "England and the French War, 1557–9," in *The Mid-Tudor Polity, c. 1540–1560*, ed. J. Loach and R. Tittler (Basingstoke, 1983), pp. 159–96.

Dodds, M. H., and R. Dodds. *The Pilgrimage of Grace: 1536–1537 and the Exeter Conspiracy*, 1538 (Cambridge, 1915).

Doran, S. *England and Europe 1485–1603* (London, 1996).

Doran, S., and T. S. Freeman, eds. *The Myth of Elizabeth* (Basingstoke, 2003).

Dowling, M. *Humanism in the Age of Henry VIII* (Beckenham, 1986).

———. "Humanist Support for Katherine of Aragon," *Historical Research* 57, no. 135 (May 1984), pp. 46–55.

Duffy, E. "Mary," in *The Impact of the English Reformations, 1500–1640*, ed. P. Marshall (London, 1997), pp. 192–229.

———. *The Stripping of the Altars: Traditional Religion in England c. 1400–1580* (London, 1992).

Duffy, E., and D. M. Loades, eds. *The Church of Mary Tudor* (Ashgate, 2006).

Edwards, J. *The Spain of the Catholic Monarchs, 1474–1516* (Oxford, 2000).

———. "Spanish Religious Influence in Marian England," in *The Church of Mary Tudor*, ed. E. Duffy and D. M. Loades (Ashgate, 2006), pp. 201–27.

Edwards, J., and R. Truman, eds. *Reforming Catholicism in the England of Mary Tudor: The Achievement of Friar Bartolomé Carranza* (Aldershot, 2005).

Ellis, T. P. *The First Extent of Bromfield and Yale, Lordships A.D. 1315* (London, 1924).

Elston, T. G. "Transformation or Continuity? Sixteenth-Century Education and the Legacy of Catherine of Aragon, Mary I, and Juan Luis Vives," in *"High and Mighty Queens" of Early Modern England: Realities and Representations*, ed. C. Levin et al. (New York, 2003), pp. 11–26.

Emmison, F. G. *Tudor Secretary* (London, 1961).

Erickson, C. *Bloody Mary* (London, 1978).

Fenlon, D. B. *Heresy and Obedience in Tridentine Italy* (Cambridge, 1972).

Fletcher, A. J., and D. MacCulloch, eds. *Tudor Rebellions* (Harlow, 2004).

Freeman, T. S. "'As True a Subject Being Prysoner': John Foxe's Notes on the Imprisonment of Princess Elizabeth, 1554–5," *English Historical Review* 117, no. 470 (2002), pp. 104–16.

Freeman, Thomas S. "Providence and Prescription: The Account of Elizabeth in Foxe's 'Book of Martyrs,' " in *The Myth of Elizabeth*, ed. S. Doran and T. S. Freeman (Basingstoke, 2003), pp. 27–55.

Friedmann, P. *Anne Boleyn: A Chapter of English History, 1527–1536*, 2 vols. (London, 1884).

Froude, J. A. *The Reign of Mary Tudor*, ed. W. Llewelyn Williams (London, 1910).

Gammon, S. R. *Statesman and Schemer: William, First Lord Paget, Tudor Minister* (Newton Abbot, 1973).

Glasgow, Tom, Jr. "The Navy in Philip and Mary's War, 1557–1558," *Mariner's Mirror* 53, no. 4 (1967), pp. 321–42.

Harbison, E. H. "French Intrigue at the Court of Queen Mary," *American Historical Review* 45, no. 3 (April 1940), pp. 533–51.

———. *Rival Ambassadors at the Court of Queen Mary* (Princeton, 1940).

Harvey, A. P., and R. Mortimer, eds. *The Funeral Effigies of Westminster Abbey* (Woodbridge, 1994).

Hoak, D. E. "The Coronations of Edward VI, Mary I, and Elizabeth I, and the Transformation of the Tudor Monarchy," in *Westminster Abbey Reformed 1540–1640*, ed. C. S. Knighton and R. Mortimer (Aldershot, 2003), pp. 114–51.

———. "Rehabilitating the Duke of Northumberland: Politics and Political Control, 1549–1553," in *The Mid-Tudor Polity*, ed. J. Loach and R. Tittler (Basingstoke, 1983), pp. 29–51.

———. "Two Revolutions in Tudor Government: The Formation and Organisation of Mary I's Privy Council," in *Revolution Reassessed: Revisions in the History of Tudor Government and Administration*, ed. D. Starkey and C. Coleman (Oxford, 1986), pp. 87–115.

Houlbrooke, R. "Henry VIII's Wills: A Comment," *The Historical Journal* 37, no. 4 (1994), pp. 891–99.

that reads *San Francisco Botanical Gardens*. Two layers of fencing and turnstiles, fortress-like, as if the plants inside required prison-level security to preserve them from the outside world.

Today, at 12.11 p.m., I walked through those gates, produced my local ID so as to avoid the tourists' entrance fee, and wandered through the greenery to my bench. To that spot where that which is expected is also that which is cherished. I took my familiar steps and thanked God it's not just the dreary parts of life that are repetitive.

I have no coffee today, here on my perch. Enough of it has already worked its way into my system. It often does on mornings like this, which, though unremarkable, follow restless nights. I have too many of those, though there's no discernible reason why I should. My job isn't exactly the high-stress sort, and outside of work all is generally as peaceful as I could hope for. But still sleep is often slow in coming, and there doesn't seem to be anything I can do about it. I've tried the tablets, descended at times to drink, even given a shot to the soothing tones of a new-age SureSleep app downloaded to my phone for ninety-nine cents. But nothing really helps (and Apple won't refund the ninety-nine cents). Insomnia is like an unwanted family member on a holiday visit. The more you wish he would leave, the more obstinately he remains.

So no coffee, but I have my notebook and my pencil – the productive equipment, and the food and the drink, of the poet. Which is what I consider myself and what I am, despite the fact of my rather more worldly employment. And the absence of a single published poem. A badge of honour, I'm convinced. True poets never publish. To publish a poem is to sell one's soul, to befoul and dirty one's words with consumerism and industrial approval-seeking. This is a realization almost all real poets come to, generally after their thirtieth or fortieth rejection letter. And however it may sound, it's not hypocrisy, this: it's the fruit borne of a slow evolution of genuine understanding. The kind of understanding I am proud to call my own, after many years of careful refinement.

Since I've been sitting here I've jotted down two lines of my latest poetic effort.

The tree-bough leans, its leaves an applause
Cheering in the wind

It's what I've managed so far. And I'm not one to be too precious: it's a bit shit. The muses have yet to find me at the pond today. No flashes of inspiration illumine me, no sudden bursts of creativity. That can be a frustrating thing; it's driven some poets to madness. But today there are ducks in the water – a mother with three children paddling after her from one small bay to the next, seeking what only ducks know is there to be sought. That's enough. I've learned that poems come when they will, they're not things that can be forced. Being a poet is mostly about the waiting. Waiting for the right thought to take the right shape, then capturing it in words like pixels capture sights for a camera. And there are rice yeast tablets and kale extract drinks to sell in between, so I'm not going to find myself homeless.

Then, clockwork: he's there again. The little boy. One of those once-surprises that's become a predictable repetition of the good and welcome sort. I like that I see him every day, visiting this place just like me. I like his kiddish overalls. The white shirt that's become a dusty brown is on display again, the armpits stained. His hair is dirtier than before. The stick again is in his hand, the tip piercing the water.

He seems to gaze vacantly out over the tiny expanse of our miniature sea. He doesn't notice the ducks.

He never notices the ducks.

I squint my eyes. It looks like there's a spot of blood on his arm, poor thing. Happens to kids.

It glistens in the midday light. Blood on the arm of the little boy. And like the ducks, like the wind, he doesn't seem to notice.

3

The Boy in the Park, Stanza 2

The evening is coming,
The morning is gone;
Little boy with his playful heart
And castle and crozier and soldier.
Leaps, not knowing
where they shall land –
How little boys do play until
The day of youth is done.

4

Wednesday Afternoon

I've gone back to the shop and taken up my dutiful post. A steady stream of customers, none of them terribly interesting. None of them offensive. I ate a sprout and beancurd wrap for a bite, taken from our refrigerator in the back. Why pack a lunch when you work at a health food shop? I wouldn't take the tablets if they were free (and Lord knows they aren't), but the food's a nice perk; at least, once you convince yourself that terms like 'curdled' and 'fermented' are actually positives and not the repellent horrors the words more obviously suggest.

I've developed the habit of eating when I return to work, after my outings, in the last five minutes of my lunch break (though my boss, Michael, doesn't really mind if I nibble at the counter once my shift resumes). Eating at the pond always seems a touch vulgar. A cup of coffee, that's different. Sip and watch and enjoy. But gnawing into a sandwich or wrap, face smothered in the cellophane wrapping with bits of lettuce and mayonnaise clinging to your chin . . . it seems like the trees, if they had voices, would snicker down and say, 'All well and good that you visit like this, but honestly, couldn't you do that sort of thing at home?'

So it's here in the store that I'm chewing on my sprouts and former beans, and here that I'm pondering what came before. I am, I realize, a touch confused by what I saw in the park. It didn't hit me then, but it's stuck with me since. This boy and I have been sharing the pond for a year and a half, and I've never seen him injured before today. Not a bump, never even an obvious scratch. Then today, that bloodied arm . . . it's troubled me more than it really should.

I think I'm most disturbed that he didn't notice it. Or at least, he gave no visible signs of having noticed. There was blood that descended from a patch of raw skin above his left elbow, emerging just beneath the tattered hem of a short sleeve, which isn't something a person simply stands oblivious too. Especially a child. I'm left wondering what caused it. A bad scrape from a fall? Rough play? In any case, what I'd seen was too much blood for a little child – the amount of blood you expect to draw tears. But there were no tears.

There was no expression on his shadow-hidden face. None that I could make out. The blood dripped a little, but his attention remained at the tip of his stick, tracing figure eights in the algae at the surface of the water. He appeared unfazed and unemotional.

I'm plucked back into the present by a woman who wants to know about dietary supplements. 'The kind for losing weight.' I walk her over to a whole shelf we have cunningly dedicated to this particular myth. HEALTHY RAPID WEIGHT LOSS is the sign we've affixed to the top of the section: words so oxymoronic that I'm surprised we've never been sued for deception.

The woman gasps, mystified at the array of bottles. It's the gasp that comes with a look of excited enthusiasm I've seen many times before.

'Which would you recommend?' she asks. *There are so many! Clearly, these are going to change my life!*

She's in her mid thirties, pudgy but not fat. Not as fat as the men who usually come to browse this section, who absolutely never want to talk to anybody about their options (if caught gazing at the weight-loss shelf, they usually swerve just to the right, where we've cleverly placed the Protein Muscle Bulk powders so as to save them the embarrassment of admitting what they were really looking for). The whipped cream of the woman's mocha Frappuccino is piled high beneath a domed plastic lid, a crowning chocolate-covered coffee bean beginning to sink into its sugary pillow. She seems entirely oblivious to the irony.

'A lot of people are going for the cinnamon extract,' I say non-judgementally, pointing to a green bottle. 'But others swear by the basic fibre capsules. They fill up the stomach with harmless bulk.' A brown bottle. 'Keeps you from wanting so much when you eat. So the theory goes.'

And they'll each do you about as much good as closing your eyes, clicking your heels three times and hoping the fat will make a pilgrimage to Oz.

I artfully keep that last bit to myself. My job is to get her to pick a bottle, any bottle, and politely charge her the 450 per cent mark-up we make on what is mostly encapsulated sawdust with a token sprinkling of your favourite herb. I smile warmly, something I've practised. She goes for the brown bottle and I nod in knowing approval. *A wise choice, ma'am. That's the one I would have suggested all along.* A few minutes later I have gratefully relieved her of $39.50. If she loses a pound from a fistful of fibre capsules three times a day, I'll personally double back her money. But at least she won't be suffering from irregularity.

My mind is back in the park. He remained a few minutes, there, the boy. Standing motionless on the far side of the pond like he always did, though not for quite as long, I think, as usual. When I saw his wound I felt the urge to say something. *Are you all right? Did you fall? Do you need that looking at?* But I sat quietly, instead, and I wished I'd had a coffee. Maybe that was selfish. I'm not used to looking after other people's children. And after all, it's just a scrape.

A few moments later, the boy plucked up his stick, turned and walked back into the greenery, into the depth of the park.

Tough breaks, kid. Everybody falls. Given the calmness of his demeanour, it was a lesson he seemed to have learned with grace and dignity.

Once he'd gone I closed my notebook. The muses had still not come and there was no more time to wait for them. My two lines remained an unaccompanied duo. I rose from my bench, said farewell to Margaret's ghost, and walked away.

That was hours ago. I must really be bored to have spent the afternoon dwelling on it as I have. The clock on the wall says 5.49 p.m. and I can't imagine anyone is coming supplement shopping between now and six, so I flip the sign to 'Closed' and lock up. It's enough for today. There's a bus ride ahead. Home, and diamonds, and memories.

5

Taped Recording
Cassette #014A
Interviewer: P. Lavrentis

The recording hisses slightly as it begins, but she is content. The sound quality overall is good.

A rustle of papers before the dialogue ensues. When the voices emerge, their interactions pick up mid-stream; a continued recording from a continuing conversation. Not the first Pauline Lavrentis had had with him, and far from what would be the last.

'I want us to return to yesterday.' Her voice creeps out of the small speakers. In recordings she hears what always sounds an odd echo of herself. Her voice emerges as that of a woman of indeterminate age, though certainly without the lilt of youth she'd once had. It's free of the humour she likes to feel she possesses, and the emotion by which her husband has always characterized her. That dispassion is intentional now, of course – speaking in just this way, in just this tone, has become a crafted skill – but it still sounds odd to her in the recordings, and she assumes it probably always will.

A pause.

'What about yesterday?' The voice that responds is a male's, its own ambiguous qualities creeping through. Definitely not a child's tones, but not an old man's either. Somewhere in the vast expanse in between.

'You said you killed your wife.'

A far longer pause. Plastic squeaks: the back of a chair bending under readjusting weight. Pauline leans towards the small recorder in its playback, straining to catch every sound.

'I had to admit it eventually,' the male voice finally responds. 'Can't keep everything bottled up. That's what you're always telling me, isn't it?' More fidgeting.

'It's good to talk,' she answers with words she'd spoken a hundred times before, 'to open up about ourselves.' But not everything about this interview is usual. Some of her words are rarer, less customary on her lips. 'I've been troubled by what you said.'

'No shit.' The male voice is flippant, now. The change happens quickly, seamlessly. 'Can't say I'm not troubled by it myself, lady. Terrible. Just a terrible, terrible thing. A man shouldn't kill his wife.'

'It's not the killing that's troubling me, Joseph.'

A hesitation.

'You're . . . not bothered I killed my wife?' Genuine confusion sounds in the man's voice. The cassette captures a different, halting rhythm to his speech. 'That's just sick.'

'Killing is very—'

'No, seriously,' his words slice across hers. 'You ought to be fucking revolted. I told you I killed my goddamned wife! Held a pillow over her head till she stopped breathing.'

'I remember what you told m—'

'What sort of callous bitch are you?' His voice is angry now. Pauline recalls how swiftly it had changed, the features of his face altering along with it. 'You're always doing this! Playing with me. Finally getting me to open up, then you toy around.' A pause. His breathing is heavy and angry. 'Bitch.'

On the cassette, Pauline allows a silence to linger. The man's breath continues to resonate. Several seconds pass. When Pauline begins to speak again, her voice has a different tone to it. A deliberate strategy, and on hearing it now on tape, Pauline is certain it was the right one.

'Perhaps that isn't where we should begin, today. Perhaps it's too much.' She'd let her focus remain vague, unclear whether she was speaking to the man or to herself. But then, more definitively, 'Did you love her? Your wife?'

The question provokes a hesitation, captured on the miniaturized magnetic tape. 'That's . . . that's a ridiculous thing to ask. Of course I loved my wife.'

'And you remember that – that love?'

The pauses grow longer and more frequent. 'You ask foolish questions. How could I not remember being in love? Obviously I remember it. We were head over heels. Full of romance. All that.'

'It sounds very lovely,' Pauline answers. Now, as then, his initial response provoked images of perfection. The kind of perfection she'd felt when she'd first met her husband, on those first dates when romance was everything and the world slipped away from her attention. For a time. And that was the key: for a time. Reality always steps back in. Pure romance is meant to give way to the sturdier, though sometimes less flattering, realities of genuine love.

'Always been a traditional man,' the male's voice continues, 'loving the lovely. She was the traditional woman, too, the kind any guy would want.'

A silence lingers between them. Finally, the sound of Pauline leaning in towards the recorder.

'I told you before that something was troubling me about your recollection of the murder.'

'I haven't forgotten. Your reaction was just . . . sick. Most people, *normal* people, would be horrified. But you, you're "troubled".'

'It's not that I don't find killing repulsive, Joseph,' she continues. 'I do.'

'Then are you going to get to just what it is that's "troubling" you?' Sarcasm clings to his syllables.

There are more sounds of bodily readjustment. When Pauline's voice returns, it comes from a place closer to the microphone. She'd positioned her body carefully, the memory still fresh in her mind. She'd brought her face closer to his, lined it up directly with his eyes.

'I'm troubled, Joseph, because there's a fact of this case that simply doesn't mesh with what you've confessed.'

'There's lots of details. Not everything "meshes" in real life, and murder isn't an everyday occurrence that follows ordinary rules.'

'No, but usually the pieces fit together, once we look at them. The details of the crime, and of the criminal.'

'You can't expect me to remember every little detail perfectly.'

'It's not a little detail, Joseph.' Her instinct, Pauline recalled, had been to offer a compassionate smile, something almost maternal. She'd forced herself to hold it back.

The man's voice grunts in impatient displeasure.

'Just get to the point, would you?'

'Joseph,' she answers, slowly, 'the simple fact of the matter is, you didn't kill your wife.'

Thirty-seven seconds of sustained silence. Not even the sound of breathing. As if the microphone has dropped out.

Then, the last word recorded on cassette #014A.

'Bitch.'

6

Thursday Lunchtime

I've chosen a frou-frou coffee for my lunch break today: double latte with caramel syrup and whipped cream. There's no particular reason I've switched from my usual black filter selection; perhaps it's the slightly overcast sky, the nip of a chill in the air. Some days are bright on their own. Some need to be brightened up and sweetened, however artificial the sweetener.

I walk towards the park along my usual route. I have a full hour for lunch today – an extra fifteen minutes occasioned by the manager training in a new employee. 'I'll stay in and watch the counter with her for a bit,' he said. 'She can use the practice on the till. Have a good walk.' That's Michael. Not a bad man. Looks like death warmed over: pale, gaunt, waxy eyes and a head of hair so sparse that at a polite distance you can make out individual strands emerging like sprouts from a desert dry scalp. And he still manages to run a successful shop that sells health supplements and vegetable-based 'miracle' hair products.

Today is a 'Free Day' in the SF Botanical Gardens, meaning that as I approach I see larger than usual crowds strolling over the Great Meadow. They have these, every so often: days in which there is no entrance fee, even for non-residents – so the throngs of tourists ambling through Golden Gate Park have a chance to see one of the finer places in the city. A noble, civil attitude. I support it wholeheartedly. As long as it doesn't become everyday and we locals get entirely run out.

Cindy is in the entrance booth, the one marked *Tickets*. 'Good morning, Dylan,' she says with a broad smile as I walk by. Cindy volunteers Tuesdays and Thursdays, and normally checks my driver's licence each and every time I arrive, even though she's known me for two years now. She's a law student up the hill – a career that makes for that kind of attitude, I suppose. But she's delightful in every other way. I smile back as I pass by, noting her kind eyes behind the massive orange plastic rims of her eyeglasses and the nod as she beckons me onwards. No IDs required today. Not on a Free Day.

It takes two left turns, a brief jaunt down a main pathway (today covered in people), and then a right onto a short, planked path into the trees before I arrive at the dirt walkway that leads to my pond. All in all, no more than five minutes from the entrance. Five minutes, and I'm in another world.

I set the caramel latte on the bench beside me, bid hello and a pleasant afternoon to the memory of Margaret, and pull out my notebook. Its home in my back pocket has left an indelible imprint on my khakis, every pair of them; and the shape of my ass has left the notebooks slightly bent. Every one of them. There are stacks, piled up at home. A lifetime of poetry, thus far read only by me.

I am not alone this afternoon. Free access and not-too-miserable weather have brought others into what is normally a rather secluded area. A group of children plays with stones off to my left, down at the water's edge, their parents chatting idly behind them, visibly relieved that for the moment their offspring don't require active observation. Further in the distance, a clutch of tourists with enormous cameras stops and starts along the beds by the water. I've never understood the fascination with taking pictures of plants, but these kinds of visitors are the standard, not the exception. The kind that take photos of flowers rather than actually *see* them – smell them, feel the way they reflect the light into your eyes, standing before their simple, unadorned magnificence. Surely this is a far greater thing than converting them to pixels. But I suppose there's a whole generation, now, who simply do not know how to encounter anything directly. Human experience is mediated by a small screen held up between face and reality. Only what it captures is truly real. The memories of life have become confined to a span of 2.5 x 5 in (3.5 x 6 if you've got the latest model). On the periphery, nothing truly exists.

There has to be something tragic in this, there just has to be. I know we're more connected than we've ever been, that it's become the norm for the anonymous 'us' of the world to tweet and post and link to a degree that wouldn't have been imaginable a generation ago. And I'm not against occasionally stepping into the public library and accessing the Internet with a swipe of my ID, to visit an online story or revel in the latest news of the day. But I cannot be the only one who feels more detached there than anywhere else. When I'm sitting beneath my trees and the water ripples beneath me, I feel more connected to the world than in any other spot. Even when there's not another dot of humanity around me. But when I 'connect', when wires and satellites link my data stream to that of everyone else in creation, it's then that I feel the most lost. The most alone.

And they make you pay for the experience.

Still, today is not about being alone. The tourists with their eyes pressed to their cameras may not notice the wide beauty of the periphery they're avoiding, but for me the periphery is what's interesting. Because there, at the edge of my vision, the branches wiggle again at the water's edge.

In the usual spot.

I sit forward, unsurprised but eager. I've been looking forward to seeing him, to seeing the scrape that had upset me yesterday bandaged and a boy back to being a boy. Sure, the injury may have been unpleasant, but there are times when unpleasantness brings rewards. Now the boy will have war wounds to prove his courage and offer bragging rights before his peers. Every boy needs to have those: stories connected to little scabs, scars, offering fleshy proof that 'I was brave, guys, and all grown up.' Men seem to need them, too, though their scars tend to be deeper, their falls more brutal, and the evidence of maturity even more fleeting.

He dutifully emerges, as if on cue, and promptly takes his customary three steps down to the edge of the pond. Then, as always, he stands like a statue, his stick in hand, its tip just piercing the water. The familiar scene. My own comforting reassurance of normalcy. My heart loosens with gentle satisfaction.

But my breath chokes in my throat. The blood, I immediately realize, is still on his arm, just as fresh as yesterday. It glistens in the grey light seeping down from the overcast sky: moist, liquid, fresh. Even at the distance, I can see a stream of it flow along the path of his dirty skin towards his hand, trailing brown edges where the red blood meets dust and grime.

There is no bandage. His wound hasn't been cleaned. Hasn't been tended to at all.

But it's not just the blood that stops my breath and keeps it halted. The blood's not even the worst of it. There's more, today. I'm glued at first on the injury I remember – *poor child, still all scraped up* – but finally my glance wanders a few inches to my left. Initially, I think it's the shadows, a trick of the light; but then a sunbeam pierces the clouds and I see directly. The boy's other arm is overwhelmed by something oval, black. I think at first it's a patch of some kind, maybe a dark bandage over a different scrape. But it's not fabric. Almost mirroring the wound on his left arm, I can see now that the large mark on his right is a bruise, deep and discoloured. The kind so dense it looks like it digs down to the bone. It extends over the whole of his forearm, from his elbow to the hand that clutches his favourite stick. Blues and purples and almost-greens that should never be the colours defining the skin of a boy.

I can't fully focus. This isn't right. A child so small should not be walking around with such wounds. I try to look into his face, into his eyes, to see if they're watering, filled with pain. They ought to be filled with pain. But I can't make out his features through the shadows and distance. Only the basic outline of his face, a few details – the bumps of his ears beneath his hair, the shadow that barely defines his nose. If only I could see him a little better; but the sunbeam is interrupted by tree branches high above, restricting its light to his shoulders and below.

I really have to approach him. Someone must take him to get cleaned up somewhere, at the very least. Get that scraped arm washed off.

But the boy senses my thoughts – his motions are almost that synchronized – and turns. Three steps and he is gone, the bristly green leaves of the *Cryptomeria japonica* brushing closed behind him.

EVENING

I cannot sleep. Not tonight. It's not my usual insomnia, either. My normal night-time torture is more gentle: a sustained, unwavering, yet calm refusal to let sleep come, with no specific cause and no specific cure. I've grown accustomed to the ruthless consistency of its long-game attack. I know what it's like to have no thoughts fill my head but still find sleep a foreigner, and to start counting sheep at number one, knowing I'll easily make it to a thousand without my eyelids growing the slightest bit heavier. One sheep after another, waiting their turn without drama or protest, each mocking the sleep I crave.

But tonight's insomnia is different, a punctuated sort of thing. Pokes and prods that bolt me to alertness every time I start to fade. And my body is actually fading, that's the strangest part. I'm genuinely tired tonight. Exhausted. But each time my body starts to give way, to give in, my mind pounces and shoves sleep off.

I am thinking of the boy. He's all I'm thinking about. Those arms, bloodied and bruised. The fact that I did nothing. I don't understand his silence and I can't fathom his threshold for what must be tremendous pain, but mostly I feel guilty that I saw a child with wounds he shouldn't have had, whom no one had tended to since the day before, and now I'm here comfortably in bed – awake or otherwise – and I didn't so much as say a word to console him. I feel ashamed, and embarrassed with myself.

This all must change, I resolve, and the change must begin with my behaviour. It's not socially responsible just to sit on one's own in such circumstances. I must take my courage in my hands and get my posterior off my bench.

Tomorrow, I'm going to say something.

7

Friday

The new day hasn't begun well, and that's not entirely a surprise. The organic Vitamin-C-and-Zinc tablets in the yellow jars are selling themselves, but my mind is otherwise occupied. The sun is brighter today – none of the half fog / half overcast sky that sullied yesterday – so I ought to be in brighter spirits. My mood so often follows the weather outside the window: bright when it's bright, grey when it's grey. But I've spent the morning grey when it's orange, troubled, as I knew I would be, from the moment I awoke, by the memory of the boy.

Memory allows the space for analysis, and in the scope of such analysis I recognize that there are a few features about this child that should, just possibly, not have me in quite such a state over his present circumstances. He's never looked entirely in top form, not on all the many occasions I've seen him. That's the first reality that sinks in. He's never been one of those made-up children that urban parents produce as if from a factory or mail-order supply. The kind sculpted out of name-brand 'playwear' that's stain-, wrinkle- and pleasure-resistant, trained to hold their autographed football rather than throw it, 'because the grass is so dirty, Junior, and leaves marks.' The boy is rougher than that. A little out of place for the middle of San Francisco, as if the Midwestern prairies had lost one of their member in this peninsular metropolis; and this child, who would have looked at home on an Oklahoma farmstead, had found himself wandering through the cultured greenery a stone's throw from Silicon Valley. Out of his environment, caught askance out of time, with a body and a posture not quite sure what to make of this different jungle. The kind of boy who inserts himself into a tyre swing and kicks until his feet are above his head and the arcs so high the rope goes slack when it crests. Who sits in the muddiest patch of the field, just to sense what it's like to feel the liquid sludge seep over his ankles. Who's never owned a ball, because balls cost money; but has also never wanted one, because he's always had access to sticks, and sticks are so easily horses, and rocket ships, and swords and sceptres.

But children don't wander alone from Little House on the Prairie to the Inner Sunset, I know this full well. The fact that he's not an Abercrombie Child doesn't mean he's not from around here. Not everyone in the City on the Bay is rolling in start-up fortunes and Union Square attire, and it's possible to be poor and haggard in the city. Perhaps more normal than I generally appreciate. It's the glitter that catches the eye, they say. Beneath it there's usually a lot more glue and bare cardboard than we care to notice.

I'm stuck in these memories, such as they are. Second day running he's done that to me. And in the mix of them, I find myself calling back to the most unlikely of things; the one feature that really nags at my attention. To my puzzlement it's not the blood, not even the bruise. Instead, what troubles me is the fact that he's never looked me squarely in the face. I've often thought this peculiar, even penned it into one of the poems in my notebook. Kids normally look at everything. From the moment their eyes first open children are absorbing the universe, striving to interpret it. Relishing every sight – which to young eyes are usually new sights, never before seen – and adding them to the canvas of their experience of life. What sort of child doesn't fit this bill?

But this child, this one unique, odd child, has never so much as lifted his eyes up to mine, though I've always sat in what is quite clearly his field of vision. Day after day, and not so much as a passing glance or a corner of his eye caught out of a corner of mine. But he's never had a bloodied arm before, either, or black marks.

My thoughts drift, and I wonder who takes care of him when he leaves the water's edge, when he makes his way home. Who touches his face and speaks soothing words to him? And why haven't they bandaged the broken skin?

Every boy deserves soothing words when he's done himself harm. Soothing words, a bandage, and the love that makes blood a little less terrifying.

LUNCHTIME

With thoughts like these occupying my internal attention, work before lunch sits in my mind like a kind of haze. I'm fairly certain I sold a good stock of pills to several people, at least enough to keep my manager smiling. But I did it all while staring out the glass storefront at the bright sunshine of this new day, only physically present in the little shop. The higher part of me was somewhere else. I was anxious. Anxious to get back to the park and settle my internal bets about the boy's welfare. I wanted to see if he would be there again. If he was, I wanted to survey his condition; and assuming that it still contained any troubling elements, I was resolved to speak. I had even prepped my remarks in advance so as to be fully prepared for the encounter.

Hi kid. My name is Dylan. I usually sit over there around lunchtime. I would point back towards my bench. *I saw you hurt your arms. Are your parents around? Can we get them to take a look at it?*

During the night I'd determined this was probably a good approach. Casual, not too confrontational. Caring, I hoped, without being creepy.

But they're only plans. Burns once wrote a poem about plans – something to do with mice and men. One every poet has to learn. I forget it now, but the gist sticks with me. Plan and plan and plan, and eventually something will come along to best your intentions. So lunchtime has come, and I'm resolved to put my own into immediate action before Burns's mice have the chance.

I walk towards the park with unusual haste, each foot planted before the next with a few extra inches in my stride. I don't have the full hour today that I had yesterday – apparently Michael's new hire has become proficient enough on the till that more extended training isn't required, so it's to be my usual forty-five minutes and I want to make the most of it. Today, unlike most days, I actually have things to do.

My ID is already in my hand as I approach the ticket window and hold it up for Anna. She's the one who works Fridays, whose hair is dyed a hazard-cone orange with roots that are almost black, gelled into little spikes that give her head the overall appearance of a badly spray-painted cactus. There are three slashes boldly shaved at angles through her left eyebrow, which I'm vaguely certain is a signal of something, but I have no idea what (perhaps she's in a gang? though this seems unlikely. I'm not sure how many gang members have day jobs taking tickets in botanical gardens). Her grey T-shirt says BACK OFF in enormous lettering, and she's affixed her *Welcome to the Botanical Gardens, My Name is Anna and I'm Happy To Help You* badge just above the final F of OFF.

Anna glances at my ID with relative detachment. She's not so much interested in the name, Dylan Aaronsen, or the photograph that is obviously me. Her real interest is in the zip code provided at the end of my address – proof I'm a resident, which she then notes down on a sheet of paper that for some reason charts the number of daily visitors from each zip code in the region. I've often tried to imagine why this could be of interest to anyone; but I've also taken an oddly irrational pleasure in seeing more tick-marks by my own suburban zip code (94131) than by many others. On other days, I've entertained the idea that this says something rare and telling about what kind of people we are in Diamond Heights. The kind of people who like plants more than the Union Square elitists of 94108 and the Mission hippies of 94110. I've never seen a single mark next to the zip codes that lie along the beaches. That's telling, too. Let them have their sand. We 94131'ers like our nature, and enough to travel a good hike to get it.

But today my mind is on other things. I at last step into the gardens, my ID returned to my wallet, and start to walk with purpose. These grounds normally cause me such delight, but today they are simply an avenue towards a destination.

Five minutes later. I'm at my bench. I don't sit down in a usual way: today isn't about a gentle relaxing into place and breathing a little more deeply for the peace of it. I sit today with purpose, as if my butt plopping onto the wood will trigger the events I want to happen next.

The sun is bright and the water is dead still. There are no throngs of visitors this afternoon. Not every day draws the crowds, and it's an unpredictable game, guessing what factors pull them in and what fend them off. It's not always an exact correlation of sunshine-to-crowds or fog-to-emptiness. I'd have thought it would have been, that's the sort of formula that makes sense; but today is a case in point against.

It takes a few seconds, given my swirl of thoughts, but I eventually calm myself down and shake off the various annoyances of the walk: the noise of the traffic along the road, the seemingly unnecessary ritual at the gate. I'm able to take in a few, deep, wonderful breaths of the fresh park air, scented with a touch of the must that comes off the still water. I'm refreshed. And in that relaxed state I realize that my stillness here is a little unusual.

I am, in fact, not only absent a crowd today. I'm entirely alone. Entirely. And the reality of that strikes out at me all at once.

The boy isn't here. It's past time for him to be here, and he isn't here.

This isn't right. This isn't how these days go, I tell myself, agitated. My mind is immediately analytical. *I come, I sit, and he appears. That's the pattern.* I'm used to the pattern.

My pulse is quickening. I can sense my heart thumping in my chest – and for an instant I feel absurd. *Why this fuss?* It's just a kid with a scraped arm and a bit of a bruise. God's sakes. *You're obsessing.*

Yet I'm infinitely relieved when a second later I hear

a rustle in the trees. I glance across the pond to the boy's usual spot, expecting my consolation – but there is nothing there. A strange tingling starts to build up in my spine. Then, two college-aged students emerge from a different spot, giggling at each other with heavy book bags over their shoulders. They are the sources of my noise.

I have to calm myself down. I've become entirely too worked up over this whole thing. I don't know this boy from Adam. His life is none of my business. I focus on the college students instead. They're amused by whatever stories they're telling themselves. They're that age, so it's probably something to do with alcohol, workloads, or sexual escapades – the only three categories of mental focus for the 18- to 22-year-old college crowd. For an instant, I desperately wish I was in college.

Then, to my relief, the longed-for moment comes. Branches rustle again, and from his spot the boy finally emerges onto the landscape of the pond.

I can feel the breath ease within me, like a great release from an over-inflated tyre. *He's here.* And I can sense my curiosity pique as I squint in the sunlight to examine him from afar.

And then the colour starts to drain from my face – I can feel it disappearing – as I gaze upon what, despite everything, I was not prepared to see.

The blood still drips down his left arm. The bruise still covers his right. And today there is a great, blue patch of swollen skin beneath one of his eyes. Strange, that in the shadows from the trees I can't make out the eyes themselves – I couldn't tell you their colour, the length of the lashes around them – but the bruising on his face broadcasts just fine across the distance.

No, enough of this, I say to myself. *A boy shouldn't look like that.*

More giggles come from the college students. They've now planted themselves on a patch of grass off to the left, facing each other, and are oblivious to the world. If they weren't they would see him, and they would be as concerned as I am.

I rise from my bench. My words are scripted, and I know the little dirt pathway that leads around the pond to the spot where he's standing. But I don't want the child frightened by my bursting out of the woods without a little hint of warning.

'Hey, kid,' I call out from just in front of my bench. My voice echoes slightly over the water. The boy doesn't seem to hear. His expression remains fixed, gazing out over the lilies.

'My name's Dylan.' I start to move in his direction. My plan has begun. Burns may have ploughed over the nest of his mice and sent their intentions awry, but mine are being put into motion. I'll be able to offer the boy some help, if he'll let me. At least he isn't running in fear at the sound of my voice.

But suddenly I freeze. I've barely made it a few steps, but I can't move; my feet seem anchored to the soil. Something happens that has never happened before. An arm emerges from the greenery behind the boy. I can't see the body it's connected to, but it's a large arm. An adult arm. And it reaches out with a practised violence – the kind of motion that can only be called that: violent – and grabs the boy by the back of the overalls. The arm pulls and the boy is yanked in reverse, his stick falling from his grasp.

'Stop!' I shout, but in an instant the boy is gone, his body gathered into the dense branches, out of sight, the heels of his shoes dragging in front of him.

8

Taped Recording
Cassette #014B
Interviewer: P. Lavrentis

As the recording resumes on its B-side, the tension between the male's voice and Pauline's is high.

'Didn't kill my wife?' Joseph yells, spitefully. 'I don't know what in the godforsaken pits of your deranged mind you're talking about, but this is going way, way past anything that "therapy" is supposed to be good for. You can't just baldly call me a liar. Why would I lie about something like this?'

'I'm not necessarily saying you're lying, Joseph,' Pauline answers, 'but—'

'Not lying? You're flat out telling me that the one thing I'm flat out telling you isn't true. What else would you call that?'

A slight pause. Hearing the recorded hesitation, Pauline recalls how she'd searched for the right word. 'A mistake.'

'A mistake!' A hand slams down on a table. 'A mistake! This isn't like you're asking me to do math problems in my head, woman! I killed my wife. Took a pillow, slammed her head down onto the floor. Held it over her face and watched her body writhe until it didn't move any more. Dead. Telling you this isn't a *mistake* of my memory!'

His words are enraged. There is genuine disbelief in them, utterly uncomprehending of the blanket rejection of his claims.

Pauline's voice returns, with the same practised calm she had trained herself to manifest in situations like this. 'There are reasons I'm calling it a mistake, Joseph, but it will do little good for me to explain them outright. It's better if you can come to it yourself. Maybe you—' Her voice hesitates, then she seems to start again afresh. 'Why don't you start by telling me more about her. Your wife.'

The man's breathing steadies. 'What do you want to know?' Then, with a snort, 'What can I tell you that you're not just going to call more lies, or "mistakes"?'

Pauline doesn't fall prey to the provocation but answers calmly. 'What do you remember about her? About the two of you together?'

'I remember plenty. All the normal stuff.' Joseph's words are gruff.

'So tell me about that,' she prompts. This is good territory; the opportunity to speak about 'normalcy' has a tendency to calm people overcome with the unusual. She remembers the moment, sat there across from him. 'Tell me about the normal stuff.'

'Falling in love. Romance. The way we'd look at each other.' His voice slows, as if his words are retreating into memory, but he grows more stolid and sturdy as he continues.

'We were so happy. When it was just us, with no one else around. It was like there were only two of us on the planet. The sun and the stars and the moon disappeared, and there was only her and me. It would be like that wherever we were, whatever the circumstances. She'd look into my eyes, and I'd look into hers, and the universe would just melt away.'

He hesitates. His voice bears the traces of embarrassment, as if speaking this way, in his current position, is a sign of weakness and immaturity.

'That sounds very comforting,' Pauline says encouragingly. Hearing her own words played back to her now, they seem mildly inadequate. His emotions were coming through. She could have prompted him more. Encouraged him.

'She was nothing but love and warmth,' he continues, and Pauline is drawn back to the moment. He hadn't needed further prompting; he'd swept himself away. On the cassette his embarrassment is instantly gone. 'Blonde hair, she had, and big blue eyes. Soft cheeks and a killer laugh. She'd take my hand in hers, wrapping her fingers through mine, and take me on walks. I'd never gone on walks before her, never been interested. But walks with her were like dreams. We'd go out together, sit on a big blanket and have picnics. Can you imagine that? In this strange world, having picnics out in the countryside?'

Pauline's voice offers a soft, noncommittal chuckle. The kind that broadcasts pleasant encouragement without meaning anything on its own.

'She would make the most amazing treats for me. Out of nothing. I don't know how she did it. It's not like we had cash flowing out our pockets night and day, but somehow she'd fabricate the most perfect foods for those outings. Sweets. Savouries. And there would always be a little card tucked into the picnic basket. Something handmade, brilliantly drawn, with some inside joke written out inside. We would laugh until we were in giggles.' His voice trails off again. Then, in barely more than a whisper. 'She was one of a kind. Nobody else like her. I wanted it to be just us. Us and no one else.'

Pauline lets the remembered narrative halt, allows some silence to buffer her next question.

'Do you ever wonder, Joseph, whether you were too lucky?'

It was the question to which Pauline had known this whole line of discussion would have to lead. His response, however, had been hostile and resistant.

'There you go again!' his voice taunts from the recording. 'I tell you something simple, something straightforward, and you go off toying about with words. Playing your games.' He's vocally irritated. 'What's that even supposed to mean, "too lucky"?'

'I mean,' Pauline's voice comes back calmly, 'do you ever sometimes feel that this perfect marriage, this perfect woman, that they're almost too perfect to be . . .' She allows her voice to trail off.

Joseph doesn't pick it up. Pauline hadn't wanted to push. Instead, she'd made the decision to shift tack once again.

'Something must have happened, if everything was once that idyllic.'

The man's breath picks up pace, and his words are harder when they return.

'Everyone has another side to them. Everyone, even her.'

Silence. She lets Joseph recollect, uninterrupted, before he speaks again.

'I got to the point where I knew there must be someone else. I don't know the exact moment it hit me, but after I'd figured it out it all made perfect sense. She was in love with another man.'

'You'd had suspicions?'

Joseph's voice hardens. 'I had reasons to be suspicious.' He doesn't elaborate.

'And?' Pauline finally asks.

'I don't know when it started. Probably'd been going on for years. But that was it. That's when I knew.'

'Knew what, Joseph?'

'Knew I had to kill her. Knew she couldn't be allowed to live.'

The statement comes as a definitive finish, and a long silence follows. Pauline's voice, however, returns with a new, slightly firmer tone.

'Joseph, I've looked at your file. I even did a little research last night, from home, to examine things further.'

She recalls that she'd looked down at her stack of notes as she'd delivered the comment, a strategy to suggest definitiveness. Certainty, even of things unknown. It was a true comment, as far as it went – Pauline had indeed spent at least an hour the night before, just before sleep, with Joseph's file open on her knees, the comforter of her bed a makeshift reading desk as she tried to ponder a way forward for the next day's interview.

'They won't let me see my file,' the man's voice answers.

'That's standard procedure.'

'So . . . what's in it?'

'There are records from the trial. From your previous escape attempts. But mostly it's notes from conversations like these. From talks you've had with other people. Some from talks with me.'

'Fat lot of good they do, any of them.' Joseph's voice is disgusted.

'There's also biographical data about your life.'

Four seconds of silence. Joseph's voice is vaguely confused, vaguely annoyed when it returns. Pauline now leans towards the recorder again, eager to relive every sound from the tensest moment of that interview.

'It can't be complete,' he says. 'My file, my details. I haven't told them everything. I thought that's why we were here. You want to drag the rest out of me.'

'It is. But some things aren't buried away inside.' There is a soothing compassion to her voice, now. The balance between firmness and tenderness at this moment was critical. 'Some things can be checked on externally.'

The cassette almost manages to capture her slow draw of breath before her next words.

'Joseph, I know you don't want to hear this. Especially after all you've just recounted, I know it's going to be hard to hear it again.'

His breathing audibly deepens on the recording, as if he's steeling himself for something.

'You didn't kill your wife,' Pauline repeats.

'Screw you! This again! How would you know?' Pure rage is captured in the magnetic reverberations. 'I've never told anyone what I did! I've always passed it off as someone else's crime. But you told me you wanted me to be honest!'

'And I do.'

'Then – *dammit*. I just opened up to you! It's you who's the liar. A liar and a hypocrite.'

The sound of another chair bending under a repositioning of body weight. It comes from the right speaker, the one on the side of Pauline's voice.

'I want you to be honest with me, Joseph. Honest enough to admit that you did not kill your wife.'

'Damn you! I told you yesterday that I di—'

'I want you to be honest enough', her voice breaks through his, 'to admit that you've never been married, Joseph. That you never had a wife at all.'

9

Friday

I am racing towards the boy's spot by the pond as fast as I can run. The pathway is narrow, but I've walked it plenty of times – enough to know where the large roots jut out from the ground, where there are protruding stones and dips in the soil. My footing is sure.

It can't be more than thirty yards, but it's thirty yards blind, where I can't see his position through the thick of green overgrowth and artfully planted forestry. To my left the whole time, as I circle anticlockwise around its circumference, is the pond. It glistens and sparkles through the branches at the edge of my vision.

I'm out of breath when I arrive at the spot. It's more to do with adrenalin than with the run itself, surely, but I'm panting heavily.

There is no one here. I step over to the water's edge. The stick is lying on the muddy shore, half in the water, half out. *His stick*. I pick it up, as if it presents some tangible connection to the boy – and I'm not surprised that it does. I've always been a deeply tactile person. My grandmother's crocheted shawl brings back more memories of her than any photographs, because when I fold my fingers through its loops and draws, I can feel her. I can feel the warmth of her wrapping me up in it, rocking me on her knees. 'Little Dyl, little Dyl,' falling out from between false teeth whenever I needed a little boost. Rocking and humming a tune I never quite remember, though I can almost hear its music, surrounding me in that wonderful, loving, protective cocoon.

I curl my fingers around the stick. It doesn't have bark so much as it has skin, leathery and dry, knobbed and creased. The pads of my fingers trace its stalk a few inches, taking in its unique texture. There is a patch, a little over halfway up its length, where the roughness becomes smooth. The echoes of a tight, repeated grip. The boy and I are momentarily connected: this is something he touched, and I can feel the imprint of his little hands.

It's while I'm crouched down, senses taken up in this tactile encounter, that I notice the two parallel tracks in the mud. They're there, just beside where the stick had lain. Lines scraped into the earth; and suddenly I realize what they must be. Trails left by small sneakers, heels dragged at an angle as the feet that wore them were pulled in reverse. These are the concrete evidence of whatever it was I had witnessed from across the pond.

The lines, I notice, are perfectly parallel. No wiggling. No remnants of protesting squirms. The boy hadn't resisted when he was pulled.

I lurch upwards. The tracks lead straight back into the branches, and I thrust myself in after them. The boy must be here, he and whoever grabbed him. It's an emotional thought, but I entertain it. I want to entertain it. *They can't have gone far. I can still find them.*

Yet there is no one in the trees. The shoe trails stop as the ground turns from pond-side mud to vegetation-covered earth, and I feel myself growing frantic as my only clues to his whereabouts fade away into the mix of ground cover and rotting leaves. I scan around me for any signs of his presence.

'Kid!' I cry out again, and I'm aware of the strange sound of panic in my voice. 'Kid!'

No one answers, and I'm not surprised. Somewhere inside, I think I know the boy is gone, but I can't simply stop looking for him. I take a few steps further into the trees, knowing that after five yards a major, paved pathway bisects this part of the park. Within a few seconds the soles of my shoes touch the black tarmac.

There is movement now – bodies strolling this way and that, taking in the sights. My glance flits from one to the next. *Be him, be the boy and whoever took him.* But there are no small children. Only happy couples, a few loners. A druggie. More college students on lunch breaks, necking.

I'm frantic now. I start to jog along the path, glancing

at each group of people I pass. They look at me with puzzled expressions, and I can't blame them. I feel foolish, flustered like this over someone else's child, running around like a madman with a stick in his hand.

But that arm shouldn't have appeared from the trees. The boy shouldn't have been pulled away.

'Have you seen a small boy, about this high?' I ask an elderly couple dressed in matching cardigans, who until that point had been entirely captivated by the knuckled, crevassed bark of an enormous Monterey Cypress. I hold my hand slightly above waist-height. The boy is small.

They shake their heads. The woman has wrinkled skin and a compassionate, grand-maternal smile. 'Your boy run off, son? Don't worry. They do that. Probably just playing hide and seek. This is a great place for it.'

I think about smiling back, but my feet are already moving me away.

Why do I need to find this child? I quiz myself, my breathing growing shallower, faster. *Let him be. There's probably a perfectly good explanation.* A concerned parent pulling a child back from perceived danger at the water's edge. A family spat that looked worse than it was without context. (What parent doesn't occasionally grab his child by the clothes and pull him back into line? And what child wouldn't go limp in resignation as he's hauled to a punishment for a rock fight with his sister, or a toy stolen from his brother?)

I start to calm myself down – to force the matter with

a slower pace and deep, controlling breaths. But I keep walking, keep scanning the surroundings.

Little boy, little boy
Little boy in the park . . .

The words of one of my poems come back to me in my search. I don't know where they come from, why they hit just now; but this is a routine experience for a poet. Poetry emerges from memories into moments, generally uninvited and unannounced. And these stanzas are familiar, though suddenly tainted with new meaning.

Little boy standing, lost . . .

I strain to see him, the verses repeating in my mind. My pace gradually slows to a stop. I stand beneath an overhanging elm. The vastness of the park stretches out before me.

I've reached the last couplet of my poem. I don't want to say the words.

Little boy weeping . . .
Little boy weeping . . .

10

Saturday
Office of Lieutenant Brian Delvay

It is discouraging to walk into the office of a law enforcement officer and immediately sense a spirit of mistrust and disbelief, but this is precisely what I feel as I enter into Lieutenant Brian Delvay's office at mid-morning. I'd asked to speak with someone involved in missing persons, and after being kept waiting for almost an hour while others in the office conferred and passed the request from one set of ears to another, I'd finally been led through the back to a small room in which Delvay was waiting for me. I don't know if he's a man who doesn't enjoy his job, or if for some other reason he's just become a rather jaded character, but there was little eagerness in his eyes as I approached his workspace, and there's little there now that I'm sitting before him.

He produces the requisite form from a drawer in a clanking, metal desk. He lays it flat on the surface, cracks his knuckles, and takes up a pen in his right hand. This all appears to be a routine of which he's long since grown tired. He fills out a few lines in silence before finally raising his head to look directly at me. His hair is greasy, lumped strands flopping down from what were probably neatly combed rows when he left home this morning. I can smell that he's a heavy smoker. He looks like he spends too much time at the gym. His arms are disproportionately massive in comparison to the rest of his torso.

Behind us, the door to his office still open, there are noises of the general melee of others going about their business.

'I'm told you want to speak with me about a missing person.' He places the tip of his pen inside one of the fields on what looks like a bespoke form. 'Can you tell me your relationship to whomever it is you believe has gone missing.'

I immediately dislike the flippancy in his tone.

'I'm not related,' I answer. 'I'm reporting the abduction of a little boy.'

Officer Delvay squints his brows and scribbles down a few words.

'A boy, then. How long has the boy been missing?'

'Since yesterday afternoon at twelve forty-nine p.m.'

He looks up. 'That's awfully specific.'

'That's the last time I saw him. I know the time because it was just at the end of my lunch break. I'm there every day. In the Botanical Gardens. I saw him, and then he was gone.'

I'm not surprised that there's a look of suspicion in his eyes. The words sound strange even to me, and were I not sure of what I'd witnessed I would be inclined to disbelieve myself.

'What's this boy's name?' Delvay asks.

'I don't know.'

He peers at me for a few seconds, then returns to writing on the form. I'm pleased that he's taking down the details. I wasn't able to do anything directly for the boy yesterday, but this feels like a concrete step in his favour. Something I can actually contribute to his well-being, being penned on an official document by an officer of the law.

'It's strange to me that you're filing a report without knowing the boy's name,' the officer finally says.

'I've never met him before,' I answer honestly. 'I've only seen him in the park.'

Officer Delvay's eyebrows wander up his face. He can't seem to help it. Surprise is evident on all his features. He scribbles on the form in earnest, which I take as an act aimed more at calling himself out of his surprised stare than of actual note-taking. It's clear I'm not convincing him.

'If you don't know the child, don't even know his name and you've only ever seen him in a park, then how can you know he's missing?'

I squirm a little in my seat. I'm entirely aware how strange this whole scenario is.

'Because I haven't seen him in the park lately. I always see him there. It's been a daily thing. For as long as I can remember.'

'You – *watch* this boy in the park?' The officer is now squinting out a sentiment other than simple curiosity.

'It's nothing like that,' I answer. God forbid he should believe I would do, or even think, anything untoward to a child. The notion is repugnant. 'I go there every day to sit and write. And he's always there. Always.'

Officer Delvay sets down his pen and leans back in his chair. He looks exasperated, annoyed.

'I don't know what to tell you. We can't file a missing persons report on a child we can neither name nor identify, and whom you don't even know is actually missing.'

'But I saw him taken.'

Delvay stiffens. He grabs his pen again. 'You personally observed a child being abducted?'

'I saw a hand grab him and pull him back from the edge of the pond.'

The officer contemplates this for a few seconds. His words are choppy when they come. 'Pull him back?' he asks. 'From a pond?' Suddenly his tone is tainted with sarcasm. 'Maybe it was one of his parents.'

'I don't know his parents. I've never set eyes on them.'

The pen is flat again. Delvay's expression is broadcasting unsalvageable disbelief. 'Why doesn't that surprise me?'

'Why aren't you taking this more seriously?' I ask. I'm deeply annoyed.

'I'm sorry, but I'm taking it as seriously as I can. You're suggesting you witnessed someone pull back a young child from a spot too close to the water of a pond, who could easily have been his parent. You don't know. That's not an abduction. That might just be good parenting.'

'But he was hurt.'

'All the more reason to keep him from playing off on his own. And by the water!'

I can feel my body sagging in frustration. Officer Delvay is trying to look sympathetic, but it is evident he isn't feeling it.

He hesitates, then looks directly into my eyes. 'While you're here, maybe you can tell me, for the report . . . are you on any medications?'

I'm startled by the question. 'Medications?'

'Anything new? Anything that might be, I don't know, impairing your judgement?'

I'm confused for a few seconds, but suddenly his meaning registers. He thinks I'm drugged up. Thinks I'm inventing all this. Here I am, trying to help an innocent child, and this worthless police officer is asking questions about my mental clarity and what pills I might be popping to cloud it.

'No,' I snap, rising to my feet, 'I'm not taking any *medications*.' I stress the final word. We both know it's code for what he's really suggesting, and I might as well have said 'crack' or 'meth'. Me, a man who works in a health food shop!

'And I don't appreciate the insinuation,' I add, straightening my shirt in the only act of demonstrative protest I can think of. 'I've come here to be of help, and to ask for yours. Not to deal with your jaded attitude. There's a boy in trouble.'

I make to sit back down, but Delvay is now standing. There is an air of finality to his demeanour. He's showing me the door, figuratively and literally.

'I'm sorry, there's really nothing we can do. If you've ever got something substantive, you can always come back, Mr . . . Aaronsen, is it?'

I nod. I'd given my details to the desk clerk when I first arrived. 'You'll make a proper note of all this, at least?' I ask as I leave.

'You can be sure of that. I'll put everything in the file.'

That, at least, makes me feel a little better. Because I'm quite certain that the boy is missing, and that at some point others are going to become aware he's missing, and these notes are going to be important.

11

Sunday

I am not sorry that I went to the police yesterday. Not sorry, though I do feel a bit the fool. What I must have looked like, an almost middle-ager in a stressed state, trying to attract police interest to a case in which an unknown child, of unknown parents, with no name, vanishes from nothing more than a pattern of being present beside a pond to which I'd grown accustomed. I'm not a nutcase, but hell, after that display I'd be hard pressed to prove it.

I am, however, more than a little annoyed at the officer's implication that the only explanation for the oddity of my report is that I must be an addict high on some mind-polluting cocktail. I know the circumstances are strange, but surely a more serious consideration is warranted. I can't recall the last time I felt as if I'd been so summarily dismissed out of hand.

I should have ironed my clothes. Maybe worn a suit. On the television the men who walk into police stations in suits always get paid more attention. I'll have to remember that if I'm ever back.

Still, I don't apologize for the action. A knot in my gut was telling me that something wasn't right, and it still is. I may not know that boy, but I know that these last two days are the only days I can remember that he hasn't been in the park. Supportable by credible evidence or not, I know that something is wrong. There are certain things in life that you know with a type of knowledge that doesn't rely on factual data. A kind of knowing that comes from a place other than the brain, and is all the more forceful because of it.

Yet as certain as I am that some sort of action has to be taken, one cannot wholly abandon the necessary course and flow of life. I'm back at the health foods counter this Sunday afternoon, as bereft of his presence as the past two. I have to calm myself down. We sell a powdered concoction that advertises itself as a 'non-medical, natural Prozac alternative'. Something made from two parts garden weeds and one part homegrown (but organically certified) fungus. I'm agitated, but not an idiot. I'll try that, perhaps, if two days become twenty.

It's funny, really, how quickly emotion can shift intensity. Two days ago I was running through the park, convinced of the absolute, immediate need for desperate action – to save *someone* from *something*. Yesterday I was still flustered, and today I remain deeply concerned; but my pulse is back where it should be. I've counted up our stock of OrganoVit and protein shake powder (if I'm the only one who thinks the name 'Brown Rice Proto-Power Blast' is odd, maybe I really am off my gourd). I've balanced the ledger from my last two shifts. I've moved a respectable amount of stock. The day has, despite it all, become normal.

I must simply tuck down and ignore the one glaring, horrible abnormality. I was at my bench again for lunch. I had a coffee (back to black; it's the new orange). I had my notebook with me, though I didn't crack the cover. No verses since before . . .

But the boy didn't appear. Of course. Why would he? The boy is gone. And I'm the only one who seems to know.

12

Taped Recording
Cassette #021C
Interviewer: P. Lavrentis

The recording begins with a fluster of clicks and the scrape of the plastic recorder being slid across a table top. Five seconds in, a rustling of papers, then a sustained silence.

'I'm glad you've finally agreed to talk to me again.' The voice that breaks the silence is Pauline's. Her tone is, as in the previous recordings, the practised, soft monotone of unreadable openness.

'Only because they told me I had to.'

'You don't have to talk to me, Joseph. Not if you don't want to.'

'That's not what the others say.'

'You have to meet with me, that's different. That's

part of the sentence. But Officer Ramirez told me you said you had something you wanted to tell me. That you wanted actually to speak.'

A pause, seven seconds.

'I don't want to tell you anything.'

Pauline doesn't answer.

'But,' Joseph's voice carries on a moment later, 'I don't think you're going to leave me alone if I don't.'

'You can speak openly with me, you know that.' An innocuous statement; a practised non-response to a provocation.

'I don't like what you said to me last time we met,' Joseph says in return. 'I don't like being lied to. Not when things are this serious.'

'Why do you think I lied to you?'

'Don't mess with me about this, bitch!' The words are a flash of shouted rage. There is a clanking and thunder on the small cassette – a fist smashing into a metal table sending it rattling. Pauline recalls vividly the ferocity that had overtaken him, the way it shook his whole body. She'd forced herself not to react, to take bracing breaths of her own, culling the adrenalin down. She'd repositioned the recorder equidistant between them on the table. A few seconds later silence returns to the cassette, then her own voice. In repetition.

'What makes you think I lied to you, Joseph?'

'You know what. You know full well. It's insulting for you to treat me like an idiot. To tell me I wasn't married.'

'More insulting than the thought of killing your wife?'

'Don't twist my words. I'm admitting I killed her. I know it was a bad thing. Wrong. But you're twisting reality.'

'Joseph, I've studied your file. Other people have studied your file. Your whole life was examined at the trial. You've never been married.'

A long silence. Sixteen seconds.

'Things get left out of files.'

'Not things like this. Not things like marriage, which can be verified so easily. And certainly not in a murder trial.'

'Everything about that trial was stacked,' the man protests. 'It was a farce. You know it, I know it. Nothing there had any bearing on reality.'

'You've said that to me before,' Pauline answers, committing herself to nothing. 'But . . .' she hesitates. Through the tape, she can almost hear herself shifting tack.

'Let's go this route,' she prompts. 'Tell me why, precisely, you think you killed your wife.'

'I don't *think*, I—'

'I know. You're sure. But I want you to tell me why you're so sure. What specific memories do you have?'

Joseph's voice is vaguely distant when it comes back, as if he is searching his memory while he forms his words.

'Her cheating had got to be too much. I couldn't take it any more. I felt betrayed. All a guy ever wants is a woman to stand by his side, and if she can't do that . . .'

'How did you know she was cheating?'

'It's hard to pinpoint how a man knows these things. You just do. The good times were good, but a wife is supposed to be there for you. Not just for the picnics and the nights out on the town, but all the time. Even when you're down, when life's hard.'

'And she wasn't always there for you?'

'It was like she'd be gone when I needed her most. Consistently. When I really needed her. The treats and kisses and tendernesses didn't make up for that. I'd hit tough times and she'd be nowhere to be seen. Evaporated.'

'Almost like she wasn't—'

Pauline had so hoped he would finish the sentence, the way it needed to be finished. Instead, he'd simply cut her off, continuing his rant.

'On the rare occasions she would actually stick around for the tough moments, she'd go all silent.' His tone grows more resentful. 'Cutesy quiet and noncommittal. She wouldn't stand by me when I needed her.'

'That . . . that can't have been easy, Joseph.'

'I guess I was fine for the romantic trysts and jaunts, but I wasn't enough to satisfy her all the time. When things were difficult, she didn't want a damned thing to do with me.' He hesitates. 'That's how I knew there was someone else. Someone she was more attached to. And, well, after a while you reach a point where you've had enough.'

The recording captures the long lull that Pauline had permitted in their conversation. Finally, in more subdued tones, she speaks. 'Let's talk in more concrete terms, just for the moment. The actual killing, Joseph. Tell me what you remember about it.'

'More than's in all your precious court transcripts?' he mocks. It's clear he has no respect for whatever is in the court documentation.

'Yes, more than what they contain. Tell me in your own words. Killing a person is traumatic, Joseph. I'm sure it's vividly in your memory. Tell me precisely what you see when you look back on that event.'

A pause. 'You're sure this isn't just a little bit sick, you wanting me to relive all that? You get some twisted pleasure in the gory details?'

She doesn't reply. The question isn't really a question.

'I remember her eyes,' Joseph finally says. 'They were alive, just like always. Mad at me, upset maybe. Not sure what was going on, but they definitely weren't peaceful and loving like they sometimes were. I don't know. The way eyes look on the face of someone who knows they're going to die.'

'She knew she was going to die?' Pauline asks.

Joseph doesn't directly answer the question. 'Then I remember them when I was done. Her eyes. They weren't alive any more. They just stared at me. They didn't blink. They were finished.'

She allows some time for them both to reflect on this statement.

'You said, "when you were done", just now,' she eventually says. 'What did you mean by that?'

'Sometimes I think you just aren't listening to me at all,' the man's voice answers, sighing with frustration. 'Done killing the bitch. I thought that was obvious.'

'Joseph, I need you to try to be more specific. What, precisely, do you remember doing to her?'

Pauline recalls, now, the mounting frustration she'd felt at this point in the conversation. He was so close, so very close.

'I told you last time. I smothered her with a pillow. Held it over her face until she couldn't breathe. Until she stopped moving.'

'No, Joseph,' Pauline's voice counters. 'There was no pillow.'

'Ah! You admit it!' Another fist on the table. Joseph's voice is energetically animated. Vindicated. 'Your word games have caught you out! You admit I killed her. You admit I had a wife! See, you can't lie to me. Not about this kind of stuff.'

'No, Joseph. You've never been married.'

'You just acknowledged the murder! You can't say I got the details of the killing wrong – "there wasn't a pillow, Joseph",' he squeaks out the words in mocking, mimicking tones, 'and then tell me there wasn't a killing!'

Another silence. Twelve and a half seconds.

'Joseph, there was no pillow. There was no wife. But you're right, there was a murder.'

The longest silence on cassette #021C. Forty-one seconds. Each one of them had been agonizing. Pauline's skin had been pinpricks of expectation. She'd watched Joseph's face contort from surprise, to anger, to confusion, and finally to a muddled, confounded blankness.

'I don't understand,' he finally answers.

'Joseph, please listen carefully to my next question. Can you do that? Can you promise me you'll listen to what I'm going to ask you, and think before you respond?'

He shuffles. 'Whatever. I'll listen.'

'Thank you, Joseph. I appreciate that. Now, I'm going to need to ask you what you remember about the boy.'

13

Monday

Damn, if I'm not sick and tired of poetry. I can't think of how many years I've been writing it; there are at least forty notebooks full on my shelves at home – but for what? How many times can 'dancing sunlight crest the hills' or 'artful emotion hug the embrace of day'? I've done all the metaphors. I've called love everything it can be called, and only on days like today do I start to realize that I haven't come close to saying anything at all about it. Saying what it really is. Not that I would know; but I know enough to be certain that no stanza ever written has done it the tiniest fleck of justice.

I fling my black Moleskine down in disgust. Margaret's bench receives it silently. It's taken this angry assault before. Every so often I go through a poet's tizzy, convinced momentarily of the senseless uselessness of it all and avowing never again to waste the earth's depleted paper supply with more vulgar verse. The fit is generally accompanied, like today, with the flinging away of the notebook in disgust. Twice my pencil has even been tossed into the foliage as an extra act of rebellious defeatism.

But I always go back for the notebook, if not for the pencil. It's far easier to rebel for a moment than for a lifetime. I long ago figured out that the reason the hippie movement died out was because it just takes so much bloody energy constantly to protest everything, no matter how much pot and free love might be involved. When it comes to my own literary rebellions, the weaker but more practical half of my brain always figures that I'd better not actually leave my scraps behind, lest, at the most basic of levels, I find myself in my next fit of disillusionment without anything to fling away in disgust.

For the moment, though, *screw it*. I've been sitting here for the past twenty minutes, trying to wrest a few good lines out of the bowing branches and larger than usual flock of waterfowl on the pond this lunchtime, but it isn't working. Today the Black Princess water lilies just look like aquatic weeds and the ducks like pond rodents with their butts up in the air as they poke their bills beneath the surface for some revolting, muck-smeared bug.

For an instant I realize that this is nonsense, that the difference between poetry and pessimism rests entirely in the state of wonder with which a person looks at the world around them. But I'm not feeling any wonder today. Today, I'm just seeing the duck butts.

I'd feel wonder, I'm sure, if I knew what had happened

two days ago. Then I'm sure my life would feel normal and I'd be able to operate in my usual style, all my emotions appropriately intact. Instead, I have the sinking feeling in the pit of my belly that I might not feel anything at all until I know what's come of my boy.

My boy.

I'm too much a poet not to notice the shift into the personal possessive.

I gaze out over the pond. One of my pencils is down there, below my perch, somewhere in the greenery, rotting away.

Beyond, on the far shore, I see the spot where the boy ought to be standing. He isn't, of course. He wouldn't be. But his stick is lying in the mud, its point touching the water.

And for just an instant, I think that this is wrong. That I'm sure I took that stick with me when I ran after him. That it shouldn't be there at all.

Memories are strange beasts, impossible to control. I am not sure what keys one into place now, at this precise moment. Maybe it's the abnormality of the situation, evoking a normalcy from the depths of my mind to try to counterbalance it, to set things into their customary equilibrium – but for just an instant both stick and circumstance disappear. It's no longer today. The spot is the same, vaguely, but the day is different. I am back in the midst of wonderful moments. At one supremely wonderful day. The day I first saw him.

It's eighteen months ago, perhaps. Maybe twenty. I've been visiting my bench by the pond for at least six weeks, and I've started calling it that. 'My bench'. I've staked my claim. Planted my flag. Clichéd my rhetoric, perhaps, but I've found my spot.

I took my time settling on just which one would be called my own, back in those days. There are hundreds of benches in the park, I don't think that's an exaggeration, and they come in every conceivable type of setting. Open air, in the midst of large quadrangles. Tucked amongst tended flowerbeds. In stone form within the Succulent Garden, surrounded by the potent scents of rosemary and a hundred other herbs. Hidden in darkness beneath the redwoods. Alongside accessible footpaths.

There are even more just like this one, alongside ponds, of which there are four or five in the gardens and dozens in the park as a whole. So that factor alone can't account for my taking to this bench in the way I did. It is, like so much in life, in the mixture of things. Just the right amount of shade, without being dark. Near the water, but far enough from its edge to avoid the bugs. Blooming, colourful plants amidst the greenery below, but not so many as to feel you're sitting in the middle of your grandmother's flowerbed. That, and it's a bit off the beaten path – a cliché that's perfectly literal in this case. The path to this spot isn't beaten down by the same amount of foot traffic as so many others. It's still a bit raw, a touch wild.

For a moment I think again of the stick, of the present, but memory has too powerful a hold.

Since the day I first arrived here, since I found this perch and christened it my own (with all due respect to Margaret, whose claim is more memorialized than present) there was very little to surprise me. I cherish that as well. What sort of people are they that spend their lives chasing after surprises? Some may crave the burst-through-the-woodwork spontaneity of the unknown, but I've always preferred the peace that comes from comfortable regularity. Some have called me predictable. I've always thought them incomprehensibly daft. Is it 'predictable' to cherish the familiar face of a friend? Or a scene one has grown to love?

But one surprise did, in fact, come into my otherwise unsurprising retreat. Two days ago, in the past-that's-present, the way memories go. A Monday, so vividly clear now. I was just starting what I hoped would be one of my longer poems, an exercise in iambic pentameter (I don't usually write in meter), and I was distracted mid-iamb by a rustling of the otherwise silent greenery.

I didn't know where to look, at first. There's so much of it. Part of the appeal of this place is that the pond is completely encircled by trees and dense shrubbery, embraced by it. A flutter in the branches could have come from anywhere.

But sight is far more precise than sound. Green everywhere, rustling leaves everywhere – but a small figure that stood only in one spot. A little landing at the edge of the water, almost immediately across the pond from my perch on the bench. The foliage reaches out nearly to touch the shore, thick and dense; but just at its edge is a foot and a half of hard-packed mud that leads into the water itself.

And on the muddy shore stood a little boy.

I'd never seen him before, which is part of what made his impression on me so interesting. Not being a man with children, or with any cause to be around children regularly, it could realistically be said that most boys are boys I've never seen before. For that matter, apart from customers in the shop, most people of any age are people I've never seen before. I am not the socialite that culturally advanced mothers hope their sons one day will become, climbing up civic ladders on the shoulders of fleets of 'friends' who bear that title after a single lunch together or chat over a Starbucks counter. I have two friends: Greg, whom I haven't actually seen in six years, but who sends an email on most major holidays and with great faithfulness a week or two after my birthday; and Allen, a co-worker with whom I've grown close enough that I suppose by most standards we've crossed the amorphous line that distinguishes acquaintances from friends. He owes me three drinks down at the Mucky Duck bar on 9th. That's a good measure, I should think. Only friends owe each other drinks.

But this boy, who in the present moment is the cause of my angst, was then a complete stranger to me. I'm not even sure just how or when he appeared on the shore of my pond. When I looked up, he was there. He can't be more than four or five, though I'm hardly the best judge of ages (I still consider Allen's daughter, Candy, to be three, the age she was when I first met her five years ago).

I find myself at a loss for words to describe him – a strange position to be in, for a poet. He's a touch over half my height, scrawny, brownish hair in a fluff over his ears. His arms look a bit like wires, but dirty wires, well used. He wore a white T-shirt under his overalls on Monday, and again yesterday. I can't say it was clean, or that it might smell too nice were one close enough to catch a whiff. But boys play, don't they? He's a long way off from puberty and the special reek boys develop when the hormones hit, but sweat is sweat and will stain the clothes of a boy as well as a man.

His overalls are the lighter, rather than the more common darker, denim blue, just a little too short for him. Probably in a growth spurt.

You've probably seen this kid. At least, I felt I'd seen him before, or at least the image of him. Mark Twain had him in mind when he dreamed up Tom Sawyer — this exact boy. Add a straw hat and a Mississippi steamer and you've got the principal casting for Huck Finn sorted. Throw in a lovable golden dog and you've got Travis Coates getting ready to run after Old Yeller. Put him in the Catskills and you've got Sam Gribley on his side of the mountain. He's that boy, all those boys. A bit out of place for modern times, perhaps, but the traditional image in all its details.

Yet there's something more about him. Something as

unknown as known. Something I couldn't quite grasp, back then. Or now. I haven't been able to get a good look at his face – not yet, not even after all these months. The shadows in this part of the park sometimes play havoc. Maybe that's part of it. But a faceless child is a little . . . well, eerie.

I was sure, though, at that first sighting, that I'd see it soon enough. Each day the boy came back. Same spot, same still posture. Playing with a stick, though barely that. He just stood there, really, but he seemed content enough.

And I returned too, again and again. It became my habit. Nothing to do with him. Yet I would still sit on my bench, my notebook open on my knee and pencil knuckled tightly in my hand – and I would gaze out over the water. Waiting for him to appear.

14

Monday Afternoon

No, the stick definitely should not be there. My comforting recollections have puffed out of existence as fast as they came and I'm bound back to the present. Here, now, I'm absolutely certain that I picked the stick up when I went looking for the boy after The Disappearance. I'm sure I walked with it into the trees. I don't know where I left it, but I know I never returned to the boy's spot.

But there it is. Today. Impossible. *Wrong.*

I'm already walking down that path again as the thoughts come – the familiar ring around the pond. Walking this time, though, not running. I arrive after a few moments, half expecting the vision to be gone. An illusion. The stick, though, is lying where I'd seen it, its wispier tip still in the water.

I reach down to pick it up, and I'm momentarily taken over, again, by that stark feel of wood on skin. Rough, natural, completely earthy. But there's more to the feel: today there is memory. The kind of memory that resides in fingertips and nerve endings more clearly than brain synapses. This is not a lookalike, not a similar piece of forested remains. I have felt this stick before. I have held it.

Two days ago.

I'm not sure it's possible for a heart to 'suddenly' beat twice as fast as it had been a moment before. I've read this in books, but I've always shied away from using the expression in my poems. It doesn't seem like organs should really work that way. But my pulse is certainly racing forward right now at a speed it wasn't before this moment. Maybe there is meaning in certain catchphrases, just like there is good in certain evils, truth in certain lies.

It's important that I don't panic. What happened on Monday was close to panic, and the outcome was less than fruitful. I have to keep my wits about me. *Be calm*, I command myself. And then, with a familiar retort, *Don't repeat Nashville.*

It's my own stock phrase (we all have to have them) for moments of too-intense emotion. *Don't repeat Nashville.* Had I never gone there, never ventured out to see the music scene and taste a culture I'd never known, I'd be a happier man. But I went. Curiosity is a hard cat to kill. I went, and I heard the music, and I saw the scene. And I discovered Jaegermeister, as well as the tolerance I thought I had for Jaegermeister. My closest friend at the time, Greg, should have known better than to let me drink the way I did; but Greg had also simultaneously discovered Jaegermeister, so we were sort of together in the proverbial boat.

The boat tipped when Greg's stomach turned inside out. That's how I remember it: not just vomiting, not just retching. It was as if his stomach simply inverted itself. In a single instant, what had been inside was out – and it was everywhere. Disgusting, and everywhere.

I was sure that Greg was dying. Stomachs aren't supposed to do that. The quantity and the suddenness were unbelievable. Everything was tinged a surreal brown from the drink, and that didn't help; but in the amalgamation of it all I simply lost my wits. I panicked. I started to perform CPR on him after he fell to the floor, and had to be ripped off his chest once everyone else in the bar convinced the bouncer this wasn't a good idea, as Greg hadn't lost consciousness or stopped breathing. I, however, was in a panicked frenzy. I punched at the bouncer, on impulse I suppose, but this was an even poorer choice of action than the CPR. The fist that swung back at my head was like an iron cannon. I can still see the lights that flashed through my vision as I planted my face into the wet, wooden floor. None of the shake-it-off-and-swing-back magic of action films. One punch and I was levelled. Levelled until consciousness returned. When it did, attention had shifted entirely away from me and was focused on Greg, who seemed to be tottering on his feet in the midst of a huddled crowd. I can't explain why (I've tried so many times, for years), but I was convinced the whole bar had surrounded him, to finish the upheaval of his flesh that his drinking had started. They weren't there to help him: they were going to hurt him. They were menacing beasts, that's how I saw it. My Jaegermeister vision. So I crawled up onto my knees, then my feet, and snuck to the back room to a payphone and called the police. My friend was being assaulted. Violently. They were trying to kill him. Get here quick. I read the address off the typeset note behind the plastic sheath of the payphone.

The police arrived a few minutes later with guns drawn. Two shots were actually fired, thank God not at any people but as warnings into the floor when the bouncer and an associate, charged up on emotion and surprised at the sight of firearms, initially lunged at the intruders. But the badges that the officers held high stopped them before real damage was done.

Greg was fine. Sick as a rat, and had to have his stomach pumped; but I was jailed for the first time in my life. *A fucking monumental overreaction, dipshit. If you can't hold your liquor, stay the fuck out of a bar.* That's how the booking officer put it. Not wrongly. I still cringe when I think of it.

I cringe right now. I've already charged into the police station over this boy. I've already run around the park accosting elderly couples. Overreaction. *Stop it. Don't pull another Nashville.* But there's a force inside me, the same, perhaps, that possessed me on the floor of that

Southern bar. *Don't stop. Something is wrong. Something is very, very wrong.*

I peer down at the ground beneath my feet. The parallel lines of heel scuffs I'd noticed two days ago are still there, though slightly less distinct now. Mud doesn't hold shape for long. The only witness to the *something* that I know I saw is fading. Soon there will be nothing left at all. No testimony. No—

I can't finish the thought, and it's not for overemotive speculation. There's something else, there in the mud, something I've only just spotted. Less distinct than the fading trails, but there. Footprints. Little ones, the size a child's shoes would make. Right there, following the same path as the trails.

And more importantly, the footprints are pressed on top of the trails. First they point forwards, out to the water; then back, towards the trees.

I squeeze my hand so tightly around the stick that its rough edges begin to cut into my palm. I'm shaking. I don't know why, but I'm instantaneously certain. The boy has been back. He's come back here, and he's left me his stick.

In the next seconds I try to figure out what this could mean. Why return at all? It certainly hasn't been at his usual times; I've been here every day. And he's never before left anything behind. Not until—

They say realization 'hits' you, and I know exactly

what they mean. It comes at me like a two-by-four straight across the eyes.

He's come back to leave a message. He's reaching out to me.

There is no reason I should think like this. Part of me knows immediately that it's illogical. Spectacularly unlikely. When I'd called out to him before he hadn't responded, hadn't shown any sign at all he'd heard. Yet maybe he had. Maybe my voice had reached him and in the midst of his – I struggle to find an emotion to apply to his consistently emotionless visage – in the midst of his *whatever*, he knew that someone was concerned about him. And he's come back to leave me a message.

But I'll be damned if I know what message a stick is supposed to leave. *Be a little more concise, you little bastard.* I can't be too sweets and butterflies with this kid. After all, I don't know him from Adam. But then, the jarring thought is a little harsh. It's not anger I am really feeling, it's concern.

There's more. Something else draws my attention, not far from the footprints. There is a fleck of white down past my knees. It's one colour that doesn't belong on a mud-patch at the edge of a pond. Greens, browns, oranges, some reds and blues: these are all the colours of nature. But this kind of white is unequivocally unnatural. Manmade. It attracts my eye, and I allow my head to follow.

It's beneath a leaf; just an edge, a corner. I reach down to grab at it with muddied fingernails. The leaf falls away.

A slip of paper. Printed. A receipt.

A receipt.

I look over its contents. The words sink into my understanding, the shock coming all at once.

And now I know the boy is talking to me.

15

Taped Recording
Cassette #021D
Interviewer: P. Lavrentis

'What the hell are you talking about, "the boy"?' Joseph's voice emerges from the speakers the instant the play button is pressed and the back side of the cassette rotates into motion.

'You promised me you would think before you answered,' Pauline replies. 'Try to control your anger. Please, think about the question.'

The sounds of agitated fidgeting: plastic chairs bending, feet scraping and tapping over a concrete floor. Gruff breath.

'I don't need to think. I don't have any idea what you're talking about.'

'I want you to reflect again, Joseph, on what I told you before. About the person you killed.'

'My wife,' Joseph quickly recollects.

'That's what you've said. But I want you to go back in your mind. Take full account of what I've told you.'

It is hard, listening again to the circuitous route Pauline had had to take with him. But she'd known then, and remains certain now, that it was the right one. Too direct a path, and the usual roadblocks would stop everything.

On the recording, Joseph senses the circular path, too.

'Your nonsense about my marriage,' he says, harking back to Pauline's earlier words. 'The lies you want me to accept, right when I'm finally ready to tell you the truth.'

'The fact that you've never been married, Joseph. That you've never had a wife. I want you to think about that, then look back again at the killing.'

Silence.

'Thinking doesn't change what happened.'

Pauline's voice is a shade more tender. 'No, but it can change how we remember what happened. What actions we've taken.'

'It's like you said before, killing is traumatic. You don't forget those things. My memories are fresh. It happened exactly like I told you it happened, and you've got to accept that and help us all figure out what's supposed to happen next.'

'We can't really do that, Joseph,' she answers, 'until

you're able to come to grips with some things that so far you're refusing to accept.' Firmness. Necessary, but delivered without too sharp an edge.

'I'm not *refusing* anything,' he answers defiantly.

'Perhaps not refusing, no. Maybe that was the wrong word. But you have, as yet, been unable to enter into the reality of your circumstances.'

'You're playing mind games again.'

The briefest hesitation. Pauline had faced a dozen choices, at that moment, as to how to react to his loaded choice of words. 'It's funny you should phrase it like that, Joseph. What do you mean?'

'I mean you're messing with my head. That's all this is. Messing with my head and playing games.'

'Tell me about the boy.' The command is abrupt. Pauline's ability to shift instantly between softness and firmness is a tool she's honed just as finely as the investigators whose work generally led people here.

'I don't know a boy!' Joseph shouts. 'Why the hell do you keep talking about a boy?'

'The boy who was so wounded, so brutalized.' Pauline's words are strong, evocative.

Joseph snorts: the sound of a staggered, shocked intake of breath.

'Wait, you're suggesting . . . you're asking . . .' His breathing comes in sudden, jerking heaves. 'Fuck you! I would never kill a child! I'd never *want* to kill a child! You're a hell of a lot sicker than I'd imagined. And you're supposed to be the one here to help!'

'You did kill him, Joseph. That's really the point, isn't it?'

'Listen here, I don't have to take this—'

'Everything else, all the other anger, the other actions, all your rage. They ultimately lay behind your killing that child, didn't they, Joseph?'

'You're a fu—'

'They soaked him in blood, Joseph. They soaked that little boy in blood, and he died. Isn't that what really happened? Isn't that what you really want to tell me?'

There is a sound of metal slamming violently into concrete: a table upturned and thrown into a wall. A brief rattle of plastic – of the recorder crashing to the floor.

The cassette ends.

16

Monday Afternoon

The receipt is for something that can only relate to my current predicament. Neatly printed, though smudged under a bit of forest-floor grime, are the words: 'Child's Juice Box – $3.95.'

Child's juice box. I know – I rationally, intellectually know – that other children drink from juice boxes, that this isn't the exclusive prerogative of the boy I've watched by the water (and whom I've never seen drink anything, from a box or otherwise). And yet something in me screams out, *Dylan, it's his. The boy's. He left it for you!*

I can't explain the feelings that come into one's head when absolute certainty collides there, somewhere in the frontal cortex, with absolute doubt. They don't always make rational sense. They don't have to. They connect As to Bs in ways that otherwise might not occur to you. And they come with a powerful, assaulting force.

I find myself leaning on the boy's stick now, rather than simply holding it, as these feelings course through me. The stick bends beneath my weight – it's a boy's stick, it isn't meant for supporting grown men. But I need a support, something to prop me up and reassert firm reality in this surreal moment when the whole world feels monumentally stranger than it did a few seconds before. Than it ever had since I first saw him, all those months ago, and every day since. Week after week. Like clockwork.

I remember that early on I'd found his presence increasingly distracting. To be frank, he was a little creepy. I mean, what sort of boy hikes to an inner-city pond just to stand by the water and stare at it? Maybe he's . . . I don't know what the acceptable word is these days. Slow? Simple? I'm not sure forty-six is yet old enough for me to have a 'my day', but I still feel that 'in my day' children didn't behave like that. I imagine my childhood to have been filled with more rambunctiousness and tomfoolery (two very good, poetic words) than slow, deliberative pondering by ponds.

The kid certainly has never been quick, in the most literal of terms. I can't think I've ever seen him move, not more than to step out of the foliage; then, some time later, back into it. No playful motions in between. Not up until the events of these past days.

Creepy.

But I can't be too weirded out by the boy. This is San Francisco. If it isn't creepy and strange, it doesn't belong here. We send that sort of thing over to Berkeley where they can pretend it's rebellious. Here, we live in the great modern-day paradox in which the odder a thing is, the more we all join together in pretending it's absolutely, unremarkably normal. You want to surgically introduce plastic inserts into your tattooed head so you develop ridges over your scalp like a lizard? We have a shop for that (actually, many; and we've conveniently assembled them all together over in the sad remains of Haight-Ashbury, where poetry once had a Mecca). You want to run your earphone cable through your six nose rings in a criss-cross, shoelace pattern? Why not? It's hardly that radical nowadays, and you've got to store that cable somewhere. We would have a nudist beach if that wasn't terribly passé and Victorian. We do, however, have men who stand naked at stoplights in the Castro, performing aerobics as police officers drive casually by and ignore this particular form of free-thinking personal self-expression. And we have a whole series of salons that offer 'Asian Face Slapping' as a rejuvenating health option – a fact I haven't even had to make up, though every time I walk by one of the signs ('Face Slapping: $45') I think I've lost my marbles.

So in the bigger picture of things, a boy who spends a few minutes each day staring blankly at the water isn't that strange. Maybe he comes here for the same reason I do. To not see all that – even for just a few moments. To find a scene of peace, where normal is what water does when left alone. Lapping quietly, without slapping anything.

But why have I never been able to see his face? Why does he always stand just there, where shadow obscures, where the sun doesn't reach?

And when I ask these questions, why can't I breathe?

I stare at the receipt again. It's printed on the usual, flimsy paper. The ink is an off-blue, almost purple, with a faint stripe of pink along one edge indicating that it had come somewhere near the end of the roll. The leaf under which it was resting has left a few speckles of sap that make the paper stick to my hand, and the dirt from my skin smudges it further with every motion of my fingers.

But I can read the text with its words that are so strangely cataclysmic. *Child's Juice Box – $3.95.*

And then I notice the date. Yesterday. I check my phone just to be sure, but yes, the date printed on the date is yesterday's. The time, 10.44 a.m.

I move my thumb. The name of the shop is all in caps: MO'S MARKET. And there, just beneath it – yes. I smudge away the dirt. It's what I think it is. A token.

An address.

The name of a town.

17

The Boy in the Park, Stanza 3

Little boy weeping, blood on your arm
Trees bow and hollow;
The games we sing, the songs
we play—
The crying wind, the fighting day.
The waters burn, the quiet flees
    The blood on your arm . . .
    The blood on your arm . . .

18

Monday Evening

The name of the town printed on the receipt is Redding, California, and it's not a place with which I have any direct familiarity. I'm gazing over its statistics on the Internet, now, trying to change that. The receipt compels me. I feel that prompt learning is necessary.

The town sits 220 miles north of San Francisco, about a four-hour drive if one pushes on the pedal a little more than one should. Nothing spectacular, nothing eminent or noteworthy, at least that I can make out online. A strip of cheap hotels alongside the interstate (Super 8s, Red Lions, Ramadas, that sort of thing), the requisite town historical museum. Some connection to old railways and older mining. It looks like any one of a hundred towns in the countryside, out where urban sprawl and the gated communities of plastic suburbia give way to the rustic farm towns of which California was once made up, and in most places still is. The sort of place anyone might call home. Anyone, that is, who falls into that modern-day 'Western' mix of driving a pickup truck and wearing leather boots, but still sipping a Starbucks latte while talking into a smartphone. God, I love country folk. Too old-world for the nonsense of big city livin' – a fact routinely shared on what they call 'social media' while walking between a saddle store and an organic soap supplier.

I've already scanned the online edition of the local Redding paper, the *Redding Record Searchlight*, for any mention of a missing child. Nothing. The police station's website has two notices of recent thefts – one of a car, the other of something called a 'Self-Propelled Broadcast Seeder', which I take to be some kind of farm equipment. I guess people will steal anything. But nothing about a child. No abductions. No losses. No notices from worried parents.

And it's a bit discouraging that Google Maps has no named listing for Mo's Market in Redding. I wasn't expecting that. But I type in the address from the receipt and a pin drops onto a corner about a mile from the town centre, so at least the address is valid. I switch the view from map to satellite mode. The resolution is grainy; Redding apparently isn't the kind of place that warrants the higher resolution optics of a Los Angeles or a London. But the pixellated, rough outlines are clear enough. The intersecting streets look fairly wide. A residential neighbourhood. Yes, the building at the corner does look like it might be a shop.

It happens. I feel a strange charge within me. An impulse, someone might say, though it's more focused than that. A drive. Yes, a compelling drive, almost like a silent, felt command.

I look down at my fingers. They've moved the trackpad cursor. They're typing. Up on the monitor I see a small box emerge above the pin for Mo's Market's address, and in the 'Directions To Here, From:' field characters are appearing.

6414 Gales Road, Diamond Heights, CA.

I'm typing my address.

But I suddenly have to stop. I don't get to my zip code. A pain overtakes me – dramatic, immediate, unexpected. My left hand seizes up, my fingers agonizing with every motion. I can't explain it. I would think heart attack, but it's the wrong kind of pain. I've been told the signal of The Coming Doom is a deep, core pain radiating out to a limb. This isn't that. It's as if my arm is raw. Like it's been tenderized, beaten, scraped.

I reach my other hand over to rub at the sore flesh, but the instant my fingers make contact with the fabric of my shirtsleeve I let out an agonized yelp. The pain is magnified a thousandfold.

The last thing I concretely remember is peering down and seeing the bloody fingerprints. Three of them, where three fingers of my right hand had tried to touch my arm. The blood is not from my fingertips; it does not lie atop the cloth. It is seeping up from underneath. As my vision begins to blur I move my focus to the cuff of my sleeve. There is blood there, too, dripping out from the cross-stitched hem, falling in crimson drops onto my keyboard.

It glistens strangely in my living-room light, wet and raw. The blood on my arm.

The blood on my arm . . .

REDDING

19

Wednesday

Redding is as unimpressive in the first person as it is on the Internet. Not to speak ill of a fine, small town. I've been here the better part of a day and not been treated poorly. The waitresses in the little dive I found for lunch were friendly, and service at the front desk of the Ramada has been unremarkable, which is not a bad thing to say for the modern-day service industry. I mean it as the compliment it is.

It's taken me nearly the full day to acclimatize. I'm a city boy, used to the urban hills and general melee of San Francisco. As much as I crave the quiet and solitude of my park, I confess it's comforting to hear the hum of traffic beyond it, just out of sight. To know that the great mass of civilization is there, just at arm's length, even if I'd rather not interact directly with any of it.

It's something different to find oneself in a farming

town. Here it's the chatter of a road or a shop that's the oasis, the something different in the midst of a vast landscape of disquieting quietude. The earthy silence of life outside the city is all-enveloping, combatted by open-windowed driving in trucks with radios booming at twice the volume any ears could actually manage pleasurably. I'm convinced the loudness isn't for pleasure; it's for warding off the silence of the fields, the hills, the pastures that spread out indefinitely into the distance. The silence that sounds rather romantic in literature, but which haunts city folk, and maybe even country folk, more than they'd like to admit.

But apart from settling in, my first day has been mostly wasted. I arrived late-afternoon after a lengthy drive through the flats that emerge an hour north of the Bay and continue almost to the Oregon border, where suddenly the mountains reemerge in a display of spectacular natural showmanship. Redding sits right at the conjunction of these two. Stare south and it's flat as far as your eye can gaze. Turn north and the earth rises up in great heaves towards heaven, as if a tall enough peak could pierce the sky and cause paradise to sag a little closer to earth.

I found my hotel quickly enough – I'd booked the room in advance, on the road, from my phone. There's an app for that, and a map that led me right to it. I'd picked one on the edge of town, which in retrospect was a mistake. When I entered my room for a quick nap after the long drive it was like entering solitary confinement. Sensory deprivation. I couldn't hear anything; no traffic, no arguing vendors' voices. Nothing. It was overwhelming and immediately oppressing. I clicked on the television to compensate – just a little background noise would do me – but the help it provided was minimal. Funny that I so often belittle the fakery of city talk and chatter, but when those things themselves are faked, they fail to satisfy.

I barely slept, though I needed the rest. When finally I shot up off the plaid bedspread (just who is it who picks the patterns for cheap hotel linens?), tired of 'resting', it was too late to do much of what I'd come here to do.

As to that: I can't fully explain why I'm here. The moment I saw the receipt, the name of this town, something inside took over. I had to take the next step. And then, from the second the blue line connecting Diamond Heights and Redding appeared on my screen, I knew it would be the route I was following. I knew I wanted to see what lay at the end.

I knew it would relate to the boy.

I feel foolish thinking like this, here and now. There is nothing here, and there's no real reason I should be here, rather than home. Hundreds of people pass through my park every day; any one of them could have dropped that receipt. It's not a real clue. And for his part, the boy is surely a San Franciscan. I've seen him there, in the city, every day for a year and a half. That he should have any connection to this place is to take one piece of evidence in defiance of all others. I'm becoming a fool.

But logic has no answers to sell a belly, and it's in my belly that I feel this . . . *conviction.* This is the spot to be. So I'm here, and I have three nights on my hotel booking. Michael was understanding at the shop ('You've never asked for vacation days before, ever, Dylan. Of course you can go'), and it's not as if I have any other pressing engagements. Maybe the trek out of the city will do me some good.

This drink in my hand isn't going to help with that, of course. Jack Daniel's. God, it's foul stuff, but the closest place to my hotel to get an evening meal is a bar, and this seems like the kind of thing you should order in a bar in a town like this. It's certainly not the place to order a velvety Pinot with a touch of vanilla on the nose, though I can't imagine I'd order that even if I could. I'm not sure what I'd rather be drinking, really, but God knows it isn't this. The things we do in the name of conformity.

In the evening hours after my nap and before this drink, I drove around the town. Orientated myself. Kind of quaint, really, Redding. And just at the spot where the pin had fallen on the map, I'd found Mo's Market. Not listed online, but still a reality. Closed, of course. It was 7.26 p.m. when I pulled up to its corner, and it isn't a large-scale supermarket sort of place, or posh Whole Foods organo-fest. It looks like a little mom-and-pop, wire mesh over the windows to protect the Half Buck Chuck inside, presumably from small-town teenagers for whom it's just as desirable a contraband as any other booze. I'll go by again tomorrow morning when it opens. Maybe someone inside will know something. Maybe I'll meet Mo, whom I imagine to be a rather gruff, maybe even a bit burly fellow. Strikes me this is how the owners of shops like that probably look. A little overweight, friendly enough, good-spirited, with a short-barrelled shotgun behind the counter 'just in case'.

My Jack is gone. It's the second one, and I'm surprised I've managed them both. I'd have thought the taste of cask-distilled paint thinner would have stopped me hours ago.

The glass seems so tiny in my hand, shimmering in the heavy light over the bar counter. My hands themselves look tired. Older than they should. My head is starting to hurt. My arm is throbbing. I am wondering why I'm really here.

It's not that I've forgotten about the blood. I couldn't, even if I wanted to – and I do desperately want to. The blood I found on my arm. Lord, I want to forget about that, to insist it never happened.

There is the real possibility that it didn't. That it was just a dream or hallucination. Those can be as vivid as what I remember, I'm sure that's true. But I've never had one before, so it's hard to convince myself that's what it was.

I must have blacked out just after the . . . I'm resigned to calling it the 'vision'. The last thing I remember was the blood that appeared beneath my finger marks on my sleeve, dripping down from my cuff. Things got hazy, fast. Then there wasn't anything. My next memory is of waking up, face down on my keyboard, my fingers still perched near the keys.

There was no blood on the keyboard, of course, though I remembered seeing it drip out of my cuff onto it. Nothing on my sleeve, either. I all but tore off my shirt to see beneath, but my arm was fine. No wound, no cut. Nothing. Just the fuzz that's been there for decades – not quite smooth, not quite hairy.

It took a cup of coffee to bring me back to normalcy, to shake away the terrible feelings of what I forced myself, immediately, to write off as a dream. Too much concern over the boy, starting to infect my thoughts once I'd gone drowsy. Or maybe I'd simply pulled a Dickens, taking in late-night food and suffering the after-effects of a spot of bad mustard or a bit of sausage. Have to watch out for that.

But there was something crusted, crimson, beneath my fingernails. That was very real, even after I woke up. I noticed it in the kitchen as I boiled the kettle and screwed open the lid to my tired jar of Nescafé. Rusty, crumbling, beneath the nails of both hands.

A shower and three rounds of soap did away with it, but I don't want to pretend it didn't freak me out a little. A vision of blood, then no blood, then blood caked beneath my fingernails. That's not . . . usual. Of course, what was under my nails may well not have been blood. I'd been in the park, I'd been digging in the dirt and manhandling sticks. It was the remnants of mud, almost certainly. Mud I'd seen beneath my nails in an evening of too much emotion and strain. Mud that my mind translated into blood, which reminded me of the boy, which . . .

That's the explanation I've come to, anyway. By the time I returned to my computer to finish typing in my address so that Google could spit out a travel route to Redding, it had become a firm resolution. It's the only sensible explanation. And I'm sticking to it.

20

Thursday

It's morning. I woke early today, made myself two cups of Hotel Room Coffee and had a shower, then drove towards the middle of town to find a Starbucks and a real coffee. Not the Beanery in Inner Sunset, mind, but it did the trick. Genuine caffeine, priced highly enough to make it feel gourmet.

My only agenda item this morning is to return to Mo's. The sign behind the wire mesh in the window said the shop opens at 7.00 a.m., and I intend to be there as 'Closed' is flipped over to 'Open'.

I remember the route back to the intersection of Victor and Hartnell clearly enough that I don't need to reenter the address in my phone and chart the route via GPS. There aren't that many streets around, and my memory isn't yet that bad.

I know I'm going to discover something with Mo.

Assuming he's there, of course. But even if he isn't, I'm absolutely certain that this isn't a dead end. It's nice to begin a day with that level of conviction, with the surety that mysteries are going to be solved and fog is going to drift away into clarity.

Mo was not what I imagined. I think my vision of mom-and-pop shop owners has been too strongly influenced by East Coast television crime dramas. I had in mind that Mo's surname would be 'Marconi' or 'Gianelli', or something similarly ethnic that would accompany a pot belly and gruff-but-friendly bulk. It turns out that the Mo of Mo's Market is in fact Mo Bates, whose family is from no more exotic a locale than Fresno, and that definitely doesn't count.

I was at the door of the shop at 7.00 a.m., as planned, and the only segment of my encounter that went according to the stereotype in my mind was the hand that appeared behind the wire mesh to flip over the 'Closed' sign and proceed to unlock the three bolts on the heavy, glass door.

The hand was a woman's, and that startled me more than it should. I was expecting to see Mo – but maybe I shouldn't have been. Why would the owner be the one unlocking the shop? That's work for the grunt labourers. I unlock the shop back in San Francisco almost every day.

'Good morning,' the woman said as she pulled open the door. 'Bright and early today, are we?'

She spoke with the kind of automatic pleasantness

that suggested we were long and fast friends. In appearance she resembled Betty Crocker, only with more grey in her hair and no apron. I seriously doubted she had a knack for making cakes. She was wearing blue jeans – an almost universal custom in this town – and a felt shirt with a patch over the breast pocket that read 'Mo'.

'You're Mo?' I asked. The atmosphere was already friendly, I didn't feel the need to casually banter up to my question. And I was surprised, and wanted an explanation. Maybe Mo was short for Maureen, or Molly.

'No, hon,' she answered with a laugh. 'That'd be my husband. But as I've got older, I've filled out to his size. Can't say I'm going to win any beauty pageants, but it saves on the clothing budget.' She laughed heartily at her own joke. 'My name's Susan.'

'Hello Susan,' I answered. 'I'm Dylan. Just visiting the area.'

'Here on business?'

'No,' I hesitated as I answered, wondering for a moment what sort of business drew people to Redding. 'A personal reason, really. I'm trying to find someone.'

'Well we're not a one-stoplight sort of town, but we're not a big city either. Can't say I know everybody, but Mo and I have been here more 'n forty years, so maybe I can help.' She strutted back to the counter and took up what I presumed to be a familiar perch on a torn, upholstered stool behind the till. 'Who is it you're lookin' for?'

It was there that the conversation had become difficult.

I needed to let her know I was looking for a boy, but the fact that I wouldn't be able to provide a name, any personal details or a relationship – essentially my only pieces of information were an 'about this height' and a guessed age – would strike anyone as odd. It had certainly done so with the police officer back in San Francisco. And I thought mentioning that I'd tracked this place down via a receipt would make matters sound even more suspicious. I needed to walk a careful line.

'I'm actually looking for a family I got to know a little a while back,' I answered, trying to keep my voice relaxed, informal. 'I met them on a trip up here with some friends, maybe a year ago, to go hunting.' Now *that* sounded like something people came to Redding to do. 'We ran into them in a restaurant – one of those accidental encounters. I know they told me their names, but I didn't really take note at the time. Wasn't sure I'd ever be back. But they were such nice people, and now that I'm up here again, well, I was hoping I might be able to track them down and say hello.'

Susan reflected on my words for a few moments and I wondered whether she was going to buy my story. It sounded plausible enough to me, but isn't that how liars generally get caught out? Lies always sound convincing to the people telling them.

'Well, that ain't a lot to go on,' Susan finally answered. I could feel my muscles relax. She was at least contemplating my request. 'What sort of family?'

'Just a small one,' I answered. 'Mother and father, I'd

guess just on the older side of middle aged.' That was all a lie. I knew nothing about any parents. 'And they had a little boy. About this high.' I made the appropriate gesture. 'I'd guess maybe he was four or five. Cute kid. Looked like Dennis the Menace in his overalls.'

I'd gotten in the pertinent details. Lord help me if the kid was from a single-parent family.

Susan mused on the description. Then, in a great, heaving yell: 'Maury, get yourself down here! Customer's got a question!'

My nerves were already going, so the sudden shout caused me to leap back a little, and Susan answered the jump with a smile. 'He's a lazy bastard, but he's got a better memory than me. You just hold on a minute, son. He'll be right down.'

Not long later, Mo had appeared. 'Mo Bates,' he said, extending an open hand and shaking firmly when I met it with mine. A callused grip. He was in his late fifties or early sixties, I would say. Not bulky, with a slight stoop. He looked as if he'd just woken up, but there was also something about his face, his attire, his body language – something that suggested he always looked like this, even when he'd been awake for hours.

Mo, it turned out, was as friendly as Susan, and I repeated my story to him without any additional embellishments. Too many lies only muddle the stew: a lesson learned by anyone who's ever watched an episode of *Law and Order*. I was determined to keep my story simple.

'Can't really say I can be of much help,' Mo finally

answered. 'We came up here from Fresno after we was married, Susan and me, and that was a lifetime ago. Lots of families since then. I can't think of one with us now with a kid like you mentioned. Doesn't mean they aren't out there, just they're not ringing any bells.'

'Maybe they come by sometimes, to shop?' I asked. I was feeling too much disappointment, as if my only lead was slipping away from me. I needed Mo and Susan to have some sort of information I could use. 'Maybe the father comes by to, I don't know, get the kid a juice box?'

'We sell those all the time,' Susan answered. She seemed pleased to be responding for her husband. 'Usually to the kids themselves. Most parents don't like that they're almost solid sugar.'

'And no boy like the one I've mentioned might have bought one?' I realized, even as I asked, that this was a very specific question; more specific than a general memory of an encounter from a year ago should warrant. But I had to ask it.

'Like I say, nothin' rings no bells,' Mo answered. 'Sorry. There's lots of families here.'

I struggled for anything else I could ask, but there really wasn't anything. Short of producing the receipt from my pocket and saying, 'I want the kid who purchased this, who wears overalls and whom I have seen every day in a park in San Francisco for a year and a half, whom I don't otherwise know.' And that would have certainly called forth the shotgun from behind the counter – the one part of the stereotype of the shop that I'm still convinced is probably true.

I lingered a few minutes, pretending to peruse the store while I tried to dream up another approach, but when none came I bought a packet of sunflower seeds and a Diet Pepsi, thanked Mo and Susan, and left.

21

Taped Recording
Cassette #033A
Interviewer: P. Lavrentis

Joseph's voice does not emerge at any point from either side of cassette #033. It is the only one in the archival drawer marked with his case number on which he doesn't speak.

Unlike most of the cassettes, the B-side of #033A is in fact entirely blank. Only the front has been used, and that only for Pauline Lavrentis's personal notes.

A five-second pause precedes her first comments.

'I've been unable to convince Joseph to speak with me again since our last encounter more than two weeks ago. He had to be sedated at the end of that session. The guards were good about that. Two of them were in the interview room before he could do more than toss the table against the wall. His cuffed hands kept him from doing any real damage, but the pattern of increasing aggression is something we've all had to take note of.

'I'm not sure if it's the sedatives or the content of our discussion that has had him in silence for the past weeks. I'm told he's not giving the silent treatment just to me. The cell block guard hasn't heard so much as a word from him, and Valdez has allowed me to speak to the inmates on either side of his cell as well as those across the corridor. None of them can recollect him talking – even to himself – since our last session.

'This may be a positive development. The confrontation of our last conversation was necessary. It's time Joseph is brought to a place where he can directly face what he's done, without any of the gloss he normally superimposes on it. His silence may simply be a retreat into real recognition and an inability to process the truth. Given my discussions with him thus far, this is likely to be a stubborn, combative process. But I think we can make progress. He hasn't wholly walled off his emotions. He obviously feels guilt, just not yet for the right things.'

A six-second pause. Within those seconds, Pauline relives all the emotions, all the analytical thoughts, that had whirled through her head as she'd made this recording. It had been a period of crux in her interactions with Joseph: the escalating introspection, leading to that confrontation with the one fact he didn't want to admit. And now the crux had been reached, every word, every gesture to follow would impact what direction things went next.

They could go everywhere. They could go nowhere. She would do everything in her power to see that it was the former, but ultimately as much was in Joseph's hands as in hers. It was a strange partnership, a delicate dance – in which the steps had to be taken together, by two dancers who had never met before being thrust together on the floor of this strange ballroom.

'The warden has assured me that next week we'll have a session together.' Her voice suddenly re-emerges from the cassette. 'That Joseph will be compelled to come, if he doesn't volunteer.'

Another pause, three seconds.

'Perhaps that will be enough time to help him remember.'

22

Thursday

My complete lack of success at the Market has left me stranded in Redding with nothing else to go on. It's starting to become clear that coming here was a fool's errand – but then, of course, I think I've known that from the beginning.

I still have two more nights on my hotel booking, though (they make the rates cheaper online if you book multiple nights at a go; a sneaky trap I should have been the wiser to), and I have no pressing need to return to the city. So I've been driving somewhat aimlessly through the middle of town, criss-crossing streets on both sides of the interstate. Seeing if anything of interest may crop up. So far, the most intriguing thing has been a billboard that reads, in ten-foot-high font, 'You missed the olive store! Five exits back on I-5.' They must be damned good olives if they expect anyone to turn around and drive five exits back on the freeway to buy them.

But I haven't wholly abandoned the *raison d'être* of my visit, and my downtown trek is revealing in its own right. The longer I'm in the middle of the town, the less likely it seems I'm going to find anything useful here. I begin to analyse this in rational terms. What do I know about the boy? Admittedly, not much; but what I do know possesses certain characteristics. Overalls, dirty clothes, tousled hair. Plays with sticks. Fine, these are not one-of-a-kind attributes, any of them, but they do coalesce around a certain type of locale. An outside-of-town locale. Even in a small place like Redding, those are the traits of a boy who doesn't live in the middle of the shopping or restaurant plots, or even on the blocks of neighbourhood houses that surround them. Those are on-the-outskirts-of-town attributes. Or even out-of-town, out-in-the-country, though I hope it's not one of those. Out in the country opens up an impossibly vast landscape. But the outskirts of town is different. Redding is of a size that easily allows the possibility of driving around its outskirts, and with two days to do it I can take my time. Be thorough.

So I call up the map on my phone, find my way to the roads that ring the town and start this newly conceived phase of my investigation. I have a renewed sense of optimism about me. There are houses out here – farmhouses, remote houses, some trailers – set at a distance from the heart of this small outpost of civilization. The kinds of places where kids play in nature, where not washing your clothes for days doesn't set you at odds with neighbours. Where there aren't neighbours, at least not the kind it doesn't take deliberate travel to visit.

These are the kinds of places such a boy would live. If I'm going to find him, it's going to be out here.

23

The Boy in the Park, Stanza 4

A lingering stain
When the play is gone;
A home unkept, unwanted.
Where fire burns at timber's edge,
Stretch townsfolk's grasp
        past neighbour's reach –
Where games are ended
And rage alone can find you.

24

Thursday Afternoon

I've been driving in loops and circles for hours. It's a stop-start kind of game. I can't just pull up to houses, remote on the outskirts of town, and go knocking on doors. 'Hey, have you got a kid? About this tall? Wears overalls?'

Why the fuck do you want to know? would probably be the nicest of the answers I'd receive. There would probably be fists. Or guns.

So I'm forced to take a different approach. Some of the houses I see, off on their own little plots outside Redding, aren't candidates. They just look wrong. The sorts of places that wouldn't have children at all, or where I can immediately see a different lifestyle in evidence than the sort this boy evokes in me (and I've learned that not all small-town country homes are dumps: some of these are remote palaces. But this boy doesn't come from a palace).

When I spot a house that has the right balance of run-downness, with signs of childhood presence like a swing set or some overturned toys in the yard, I park at a good distance and wait. Better to watch and wait than confront, though this takes time. Suddenly I'm happy I have my multi-day booking at the Ramada. Two days might not even be enough.

Sometimes the wait is brief. I parked at a distance from a double-wide trailer home as my first stop: a plastic jungle gym crumpling beside it and a massive trampoline behind. I was there only twenty minutes before a man emerged, kissed his wife tenderly on the add-on wooden porch before driving away, presumably to work. Two minutes later, three small girls emerged. They wore flowered summer dresses and made for the trampoline en masse. The mother followed a few seconds later, a glass of something in her hand, and took up a perch on a folding chair to watch them play. Pretty little family. But no boys.

Sometimes the wait is much longer. My third stop this afternoon had real potential. A farm-style house, the kind with a wrap-around covered porch and a hanging bench swing. A large maple tree overhangs the front yard, and there's even a tyre hanging from one of its sturdier branches. I could almost feel my anticipation rising.

I sat in my car a good 500 yards down the road for over two hours, waiting for any signs of life. I was just about to give up and leave when a yellow school bus emerged from a bend behind me on the road and overtook my parked location. I glanced at my watch and saw the time was 4.11 p.m. – the right sort of time for a school bus to be returning children home.

This one stopped in front of the perfect house, a red STOP sign swinging out into the centre lane from a hinge so squeaky I could hear it from my car, and out the kerbside door emerged two girls and a boy. I lurched forward in my seat, straining to see. He was the right height, the right general build. My pulse sped up. But just as fast as it came, hope vanished. This boy's hair was a dark black, sprouting out from beneath a baseball cap.

The boy does not have black hair.

I waited until they had gone inside, then started my engine and drove off. The adrenalin spike was making my skin itchy, but the close encounter was enough to have me riveted. I needed to find another house.

I'm parked now beside a large, unploughed field. It's mostly dirt, a few weeds staking their claim along the gentle ridges that are the lingering remains of its last planted season. I think I remember that farmers allow fields to lie fallow every so often, to gather back minerals depleted from previous plantings and make themselves ready for their next working run. This must be one of those fallow fields. I can't help but make a poet's mental note, that 'fallow fields' sounds romantic and beautiful, but in reality they're ugly things: dust patches with weeds that look uncared-for and unloved.

I've positioned my car next to one, however, because just down the road, sitting adjacent to this field in a grassy patch between it and the fully planted field beyond, is another candidate house. Not as picture perfect as the last one (there is no porch here, but there are still play things in the yard), though definitely a possibility.

I've been here for forty-five minutes. The light is starting to turn that slanted orange colour that precedes sunset, making all the greens seem a little more intense, the browns rusty and in general the whole earth more vivid. I imagine that I have only another twenty minutes before the sun goes down, and after that less than fifteen before things go truly dark. Thirty-five minutes in total before I have to write off this activity until tomorrow.

I'm doing these mental computations when I notice that bending my fingers (embarrassingly, I still use them to count when doing up sums) is causing me pain. That it's causing me *too much* pain is what kicks the adrenalin into gear once again. Another blast of it. I'm almost getting used to the sour taste in my mouth.

The pain is fierce, intense, shooting through my arm.

I'm panic-stricken even before I swivel my head to look at the arm. It's the right, not the left one that bothered me before. I can't see anything, but my eyes are starting to water from the agony. With my other hand I undo the button at the cuff and roll up the sleeve – and then I see why.

My right arm is covered in a massive, black bruise. It's as if my flesh has been replaced by a swirl of mottled, vanquished skin that's turned the colours of bleakest night-time. I try to move my wrist, to reposition my arm, but the agony is so fierce I let out a cry and freeze before I move another inch.

The blood comes to my attention a second later. My left arm, the same as two days ago. Two days ago in what I'd convinced myself was a bad dream. It's seeping out of the cuff of my sleeve again, sponging its way through the cloth all the way up to my elbow. Dark, crimson. I can smell it, metallic and pungent. It drips down onto my lap. My eyes are watering from the grief, both arms immobile. I am terrorized.

And I look up, and it's him. My vision is blurry, but it's him. Not at the house I've been scoping out, but on the hilltop to the right, outside my passenger-side window, beyond the fallow field. It's the boy, standing in his overalls and his white shirt. His hair is dancing in the breeze, shimmering gold in the evening light.

25

Thursday

Despite my agony, my skin freezes the instant I see him. I can't believe it; as much as I've been hoping to chase down his trail, actual sight of the boy, here, so far from the park, seems momentarily impossible. It simply cannot be. But his features are unmistakeable: the same clothes. The same dishevelled hair.

I cannot restrain the explosion that takes place in my mind as I catch sight of him. The eruption of emotions is automatic, outside my control. Apart from the day I saw him abducted, there has been only one other occasion on which the sight of the boy truly troubled me – horrified me. In this instant, as it horrifies me again, my mind launches back to that place, sixteen months ago. The one time I'd been afraid of the boy.

I had that day completed a poem, so there was a special joy I'd carried with me into the park. I wrote out the final stanzas in the early morning; it was as if the last verses, the verses I'd been striving so hard to locate over the previous weeks, had woken me up and called me to attention. It was that intense. Creativity is sometimes like that: a force that emerges from within a person, like an erupting volcano or exploding geyser, rather than some well-honed skill that we polish and sharpen. The last lines of my poem burst out of me, out of nowhere, and I managed to do all that a poet really ever needs to do: be there to catch them and translate them onto the page.

I don't often finish poems. I've always found them easier to begin than to conclude, and I've imagined that this is because poems are generally so emotional, and emotion never really ends, does it? It's far easier to speak of a glimmering moment of love, a chance encounter with beauty, than it is to wrap these things up nicely with a little bow, a final full stop and an implied 'The End'. Maybe authors of stories and books have an easier time coming up with endings, but the vast majority of my poetry is the unfinished sort. Were I ever to sell out and publish any of what I've written, it would be under the title *Unfinished Works*. I decided on this some time ago. It's a title that's poetic in its own right, with the added benefit of being accurate.

But this tendency makes actually completing a poem, arriving at its ultimate and final stanza, something that brings me a real and unusual joy. I knew it wasn't true, but I was able to convince myself that the sun was shining brighter that day because of it. The ducks in the park were swimming more merrily. The breeze was of exactly the right strength, direction and temperature. The bird-song was more symphonic. That is what finishing a poem will do to you.

I hadn't even brought my notebook with me to my bench. What would have been the point? I wasn't going to start in on a new poem so soon after reaching such a milestone, and I certainly didn't need my pages to remember the one I'd just finished. All poems are inscribed first and forever on the poet's heart. The version on the page is merely for other people.

There were plenty of them – people – around my pond that day. There usually are on a good, sunny day; though I was perfectly willing to imagine they were also there to rejoice with me, with my accomplishment. But there was, of course, only one person with whom I really wanted to celebrate. The little boy, who for two months had been my companion at this spot. My lunchtime partner in the beauty of that secret place. Maybe he's home-schooled; that's the only reason I could think that he would have such predictable lunchtime freedom, the ability to come to the park each day to relax. Good parents, the kind that provide for their children like that.

I wanted to think he would be pleased for me, with me, at the day's poetic marker. Of course we'd never spoken, so this was a silly wish. But we were connected by the pond, and the pond stirs up so many of my poems. I like to think there's a bond.

As he emerged from the brush at his usual spot, I felt a smile edging its way onto my face. Of course he'd come, like always, and of course I was pleased to see him.

He moved to the water's edge. He planted the tip of his stick in the water.

I've done it, I mentally willed him to hear. *I've finished my poem. It's a good day.*

And this was where things went wrong. This is where the unexpected happened – and on my good day.

The boy did what he never does: he turned to face me squarely. He was in the shadows, as always (the sun never seems to shine in that little cove of the pond), and I could not directly make out his expression, but I could sense his anger. He was overwhelmingly, infuriatingly, angry. Rage broiled within him. I don't know how I knew this, it was more a feeling than an observation. But his shoulders shook, his body seemed almost to vibrate. And then he lifted his stick out of the pond, held it perpendicularly in front of him with both hands and raised a knee. Before I could shout out to stop him, he slammed the stick down over his knee. It broke in half with a crack that echoed over the water. He held up both halves, high above his head. I could feel his fury, his defiance.

He threw the remains of his stick into the pond. Its glassy top became a storm. The ducks fluttered and kicked away from the disturbance. And the boy turned and stormed off into the woods.

I was left alone, my sense of accomplishment as broken as the stick and my peace as vanished as the boy himself.

And I was afraid.

26

Thursday

I am afraid of the boy now, too – the way he's suddenly appeared, there on the hilltop. I'm frightened and I'm angry, still in my own agony. But then, in an instant, I forget my own pain, my own inexplicable injuries in the car. I forget them because there, on his hilltop, I can see that the boy still bears his own marks. The marks that first led me after him. There is still the blood on his one arm, the bruise on the other; and though his face is a blur, his eyes concealed, I can still see the swelling on his cheek. The boy who had once turned from me in anger is beckoning me now, calling out to me in his silence.

I can barely breathe. *This isn't possible. I don't understand what I'm—*

But I can't finish. My eyes have fallen back to my arms, suspended in pain over my lap, but the signs of torment are gone. There is no bruise above my right hand, in place of the rolled-up sleeve. There is no blood on my left – not at the cuff, not seeping through the fabric, not dripping onto my trousers. I curl back my fingers to check my nails, just to be sure, but they're clean. I can smell the cheap soap from the hotel shower, still fragrant, overperfumed on my skin.

I have no pain as I wiggle my fingers. I don't understand what is happening. For an instant, I feel completely lost. Without grounding.

But I look back up. The boy is still on the hilltop. That is something I can understand. Resolve overtakes me and I grab at my car door. I'm shaking with nerves, so I have to try for it twice before I get a good grip, pull the lever and thrust it open. I forget my seat belt is still fastened, and nearly choke as I try to lunge out from beneath its restraint. *Shit!* I mutter the profanity to myself and fumble for the plastic release. A second later I'm standing outside, the door wide open, praying deeply within: *Don't be gone! Don't be gone!*

He isn't gone. I look up to the top of the hill on the far side of the unploughed field, and the boy is still there. He's waiting.

I lurch forward, and for an instant I'm startled by my own action. I'm being driven, that's how it feels – like someone else is at the helm of my craft. But I know it's just instinct: *Go! Follow!* My elusive prey (God forbid, calling a child 'prey') is there, in the distance. *Don't lose him!*

I start to walk towards the hill on which he's standing. It's not a high hill, but high enough that I can't see beyond it. A significant bump in the flatness.

He turns as I walk, and my heart squeezes fear into the depths of me. *What if he walks away and out of sight before I have a chance to reach him? What if I can't find him when I get there? What if it's like it was by the pond?* I begin to walk faster, compensating for my new concern; but the footing of the field is uneven. I can't run. I want to, but I know not to try. I have to keep glancing down at my shoes with every other step, to make sure they find solid footing and don't send me flat onto my face; and every time I do, I'm terrified that the boy won't be there when I look back up.

But the boy doesn't budge from his spot on the hilltop. He simply turns. He's not facing in my direction now. He doesn't quite have his back to me, but almost. He's gazing outward, down towards whatever lies on the other side. And he's motionless in his new position, just as he was in his old.

God, my legs hurt. My thighs start to burn. *I have to ignore this.* I need to get there. Get there before he disappears.

The boy is gone, of course, when I arrive. Somehow, I expected this. It seemed inevitable. I hate that I knew it was coming. I hate that I know so well this child I've never met. That I know his movements.

I peak the hill perhaps five or six minutes after starting

to make my way towards it. It's grassy, uncultivated. Purple flowers dance around my knees; there is a fresh scent to the air, the kind fabric softeners try to bottle in pastel liquid form.

And there is a breeze that blows gently through my hair.

27

Taped Recording Cassette #041D Interviewer: P. Lavrentis

The cassette whirs to life with static and motion before the sound settles to a quiet that precedes the beginning of the dialogue.

'Joseph, I'm glad we're seeing each other again.' Pauline's voice. 'It's been several weeks.'

'I'm here because they're making me, bitch.' Joseph's words are like poison. 'They've got me chained up like a dog, thanks to our last episode together.'

'You've been erratic lately. You became aggressive at the end of our last meeting, if you remember. They felt it was necessary to take some precautions, for your own sake as much as for theirs.'

'I wouldn't hurt anyone,' he snaps back. 'Not any

more. Everyone knows that – or they should, anyway. I wasn't going to hurt you. I just get angry and I have to let off the steam.' He hesitates. 'I'm sorry I threw the table. I know I shouldn't have done that.'

A pause of fifteen seconds. Pauline doesn't respond, and the lack of an answer is deliberate.

'Have you used our time apart to think about our last discussion?' she finally asks. 'To reflect on some of what was said, prior to that outburst?'

Joseph doesn't immediately respond. There is a rattling sound, fingers tapping on a table top.

'I've thought about it, sure,' he finally answers. 'Not much else to do in here. Just think and eat, and take a little exercise when they let you.'

'When you've thought about it, how have you felt?' she presses. 'Have any memories started to come back to you?'

Again, silence. Fourteen seconds. Then:

'I don't remember a boy. No matter what you say, no matter how many times you say it, there wasn't a boy. There just wasn't.'

A sigh is caught in the recording, gentle, coming from Pauline's lips. Audibly it could be taken as sign of either disappointment or frustration, or possibly both. She remembers, though, that it was an altogether different emotion that sagged out of her lungs. Distress, as concealed as she could keep it.

But Joseph isn't finished. 'Though I've been thinking about my wife, and maybe . . . well, maybe you're right.'

'Right?' A new tinge of hope.

He hesitates. 'Right that, well,' he sounds embarrassed by his admission, 'maybe I wasn't married. I'm not saying I'm sure about that, but I've been trying to think about our life. You know, the wedding, the honeymoon, that kind of stuff.'

'And you don't have memories of these things?' Pauline asks.

'It's not like that. I have memories of them, just like I have memories of our picnics and our nights out.'

'It's a lot to piece together.' The sounds of Pauline shuffling the papers on the table into order – a little gesture aimed to encourage the man opposite her that things are coming together. 'Let's start with just one of those events. What can you tell me about your wedding?'

'I remember the church, a little white one. I remember her dress. I remember a trip to Florida for a honeymoon. Jet boating on the swamps. That's what I'd always wanted.'

'Joseph, that sounds beautiful. Perfect.' She pauses. 'Almost too perfect.' Another pause. 'Does that thought ever occur to you? Like what you're remembering is something out of a storybook. Just like when you told me about falling in love with her.'

Joseph protests, but his voice isn't as vehement as on other occasions. 'You've said that before. When you thought I was lying.'

'Not lying,' Pauline corrects. 'It's just that memories that sound like they're from storybooks, well . . . sometimes they *are* from storybooks, Joseph.'

'Again, your damned mind games,' he protests. But once again, the words lack teeth. There is curiosity in his voice. 'What's that even supposed to mean?'

'Sometimes, Joseph, what works its way into our memory are pictures we get from other places. Not things we've actually seen, but things we've imagined. Or heard about. Stories we've been told, or sometimes told ourselves.'

'That sounds unlikely.' Joseph's words are soft.

'These kinds of memories,' Pauline continues, 'they can be very powerful. But usually there's something not quite right about them. Something that isn't like our other memories. They look a little different, or they—'

'They look a little fuzzy?' Joseph asks over the top of her. An intake of breath can be heard from her lips.

'Why do you ask that, Joseph?' Pauline's voice is clearly interested, though she is attempting to remain dispassionate.

'It's just that all these memories, well, they're, I don't know. Blurry.'

'Blurry?'

'They don't start out that way. They start crisp, like photographs. But then when I try to look close at the photographs, they go out of focus. I don't know.' He hesitates. 'Maybe it's just the drugs they've got me on.'

'I don't think it's the drugs, Joseph. I think you're actually making some real progress.'

'Whatever,' he answers. His voice has become dismissive. 'Anyway, I'm just saying that maybe you're right. Maybe I wasn't married. I can't trust these things.

I'm pretty sure I was, but I won't call you a liar any more for saying I wasn't.'

'So what do you think happened, then? If you're not here for killing your wife, what do you think brought you to this place?'

'I know I killed her. That much isn't fuzzy at all. I *remember* the killing. Okay, maybe she wasn't my wife. Maybe a girlfriend. Maybe a whore. Who knows. But I killed her. We both know I did.'

'We know that—'

'And there was no fucking boy!' he interrupts, returning to the subject that clearly bothers him the most. 'There was my wife – the woman. And maybe an old man. But no boy.'

'You remember an old man?' Pauline questions. The intensity is back in her voice. As the cassette whirls, her pencil is scraping across her yellow notepad. This is precisely the moment in the interview that the hearing will focus on. The panel will be interested in every word, so she transcribes as she listens again to her own conversation.

'I said maybe. Damn, I wish you'd actually listen when I talk to you. *Maybe*.'

'Who is this man, Joseph?'

Another silence. Twelve seconds.

'Joseph?'

'Maybe there wasn't a man. I can't remember. I told you, some things are blurry. I've been in here too long. Maybe I'm just thinking of one of the guards.'

'No, Joseph, I don't think you are.'

'You don't know anything!' His voice is all at once enraged again. 'And I'm done talking.'

'Joseph, please, we're making progress—'

'GUARD!' The word is shouted. A fist slams down. Two seconds later, the sound of a door opening and footsteps drawing near. Chains rattle as a decisive click brings the recording to a close.

28

Thursday

There is simply nowhere that the boy could have gone. From this vantage point, the solitude of the hilltop is patent. No trees – not for a good 200 yards off to the left. Behind, just the dirt field I've traversed to get here. And in front of me the hill slopes downward again, and . . .

I spot it in the dimming light. It's not that it's that far away, it's just small, and my eyes aren't used to these surroundings.

It's another farmhouse, like a few others I've seen today. A sloping roof over a single storey, a porch on the front that's had a covering added after the fact. There's a swing-set off to the side. Even at this distance I can see it's rusted. Two equally rusted cars are sprouting grass from long-gone windows, side by side in a little automotive graveyard a short distance from the house itself. The paint on the home looks like it was once green, or perhaps yellow. It's hard to tell now: it's chipped and faded into an almost unidentifiable shade. The roof sags in the middle. The porch buckles at its edges.

It's the kind of rundown country house that fits the stereotypes that make it feel familiar, even if you've never seen it before. I have that sentiment now, though it's not the house that I'm interested in. I'm interested in the boy; in finding out where he could have gone. Obviously, he was headed to this house: it's where his gaze was directed once he'd turned, here, at the top of the hill. But I can't see him anywhere. Can't see any sign of him or of anyone else.

But I can hear. Down there at the bottom of the hill, in the unspectacular abode, there are voices. They emerge from within the walls, indistinguishable but obviously animated. Inhabitants.

I'm suddenly conscious that I'm perfectly visible from where I'm standing, and if there are people in that house (and from the jumbled voices, I can tell there are a few of them) then it would only take one of them glancing out from behind those dirty windows to see me here, spying on them.

I do the only thing that seems sensible in the moment. I drop to my belly in the grass of the hilltop. Just like I've seen in a hundred films: I drop to take my cover. But the grass is too tall and from this vantage point I can't see anything else. I rise up slowly, onto my knees, then into a crouch. This isn't working, either. I'm either exposed or blind, and neither is what I need. I need to find a better spot. I want to get closer to the house. I want to hear the voices.

Off to my left, not too far away, the hillside meets the treeline of a wood. I'm guessing that's going to be the place that gives me the best access. A bit more cover, and the treeline descends the slope towards the house which means I'll be able to get closer. I start to sidestep my way in its direction, keeping low, beneath the level of the wild grass and flowers. The voices still rise up from below, still indeterminate. I can smell the thistles.

It takes me a good five or six minutes to reach the trees – it's not easy to move in that hunched-over position. But I eventually arrive. Thinking that the transition from grass to tree is probably the most exposed part of my journey, I glance down at the house to make sure no one is standing in the window, gazing out, and when I'm convinced I have a moment unobserved, I jump up and into the wood.

The pine scent of the trees is intense. It's all shadows and darkness now – the sun has gone down and the dusky light of the hillside doesn't make its way through the treetops. That's okay. At this moment I feel better in the shadows. But it's harder to hear the voices here, and I know I need to work my way down the hillside and find just the right perch at the edge of the wood. I desperately need to find out just who's inside, and what they're saying.

I walk all the more slowly now, given the darkness and the unclear ground. The last thing I need is to twist an ankle or – God forbid – break something out here. Explaining that would be a hard one, especially if I had to hobble to the door of this house and ask for help. I can't let my eagerness get the best of me. So I move slowly, breathing deeply to calm my nerves, and work my way down the hillside. The house is now probably only a hundred yards away, out of the woods and below.

I don't think I'm going to get a better spot than this. Any further down and the treeline starts to bend away from the property, defining a nice, lawned area that surrounds it. I'm at the closest point where the pines will cover me, and it's close enough that the voices are now louder. I make my way to the very edge of the wood, back down on my knees. There's a bed of leaves and needles beneath me, musty and earthen. Beyond, I have a direct line of sight. All the better. I can see the dirty windows with dull light behind them.

And I can make out the voices clearly.

29

Thursday

The voices aren't the kind I want to hear, or that anybody would want to hear. I've flattened myself onto my belly, lying on the rug of pine needles and brush, and I've propped myself up on my elbows. The forest is quiet, the hillside quieter. The voices from the house echo up to my position as if amplified by the curvature of this plot of earth.

'You little bastard, you think I wouldn't find out?' An angry voice. Male. Adult. The words are slurred, like there's drink behind them.

'Don't yell at him like that!' a woman shouts back. Her voice is wet. She's crying. 'He didn't mean anything by it!'

'He never fucking does!' A crash. Something slams into a wall. In the darkness I can make out the wooden panelling behind the porch shake from the impact.

'He never *means* anything!' the man shouts again. 'None of you do!'

'Stop throwing things!' the woman sobs back. 'You broke it. That's our only table. What do you expect to eat off of tonight?'

'Don't you go making me out the bastard in this!' The man's ranting borders on incoherent. I've never heard speech like this. 'We've got more serious problems to worry about than a *goddamned table*!'

Something in my stomach is churning as these words drift up to me at my perch in the forest. I don't know what I was expecting to hear, what I was expecting to find here, but the dialogue has a degree of hate behind it that physically repulses me. I've never known words to attack like a bodily presence – like a fist or an illness. I feel as if I might vomit.

The man's voice returns. 'Tell me what I'm supposed to do with this little fucker.' A moment's pause, and I can imagine him turning towards the boy, who must be in there with them. My little boy from the park, the boy with the stick, in this strange hell. 'Eh, little fucker? What am I supposed to do with you?'

'Don't talk to him like that! He's just a child!' the woman weeps. I can tell from her voice that she's exhausted, but her fear keeps her going.

'Just a child who goes around telling lies about his pops to his friends,' the man answers. 'Lies his teachers hear.'

'He doesn't mean to, he just—'

'Do you realize I got a phone call at work today? From his school principal? Asking if everything was okay at home?' The man's voice is back at a full, hateful yell. He is on a tirade. 'At my fucking work! Said she had "concerns" and wanted to know if everything was okay at home!'

'They're just checking up on—'

'Said he'd told another boy he'd been beaten!' Fire is in the man's words now. 'I was being accused over the phone, at work, by some school bitch!'

The woman is whimpering. 'What did you tell her?' My stomach is turning over. I can taste vomit at the back of my throat.

'I told her I didn't know what in God's name she was talking about,' the man answers, 'but that she could stay the hell out of our family's business. I'm a free man in a free country. How I raise my son is my own affair.'

There is a pause in his slurred speech and my body tenses. Strange, but I have a powerful feeling that this silence is even worse than the angry words. I can sense something bad is coming.

So can the woman, and it is her voice I hear next.

'No, no – don't do that. Don't touch him!'

I hear another slam, see another shaking of the walls. The woman whimpers. I can almost see her, thrust aside on the interior, pushed out of the way.

'I'll show you what it's like to get beat, you little shit!' the man roars.

'No!' The objection is the woman's, but it's cut off by

the sounds of fists meeting flesh. Of a smaller body being tossed onto the floor. 'Stop it!' she shouts again. Her voice is panicked. Then it, too, is cut short by a fist that audibly knocks the wind from her cries.

I can take no more of this. There is bile and acid in my throat, my skin is covered in a cold, slimy sweat; but my sense of rage is stronger than my repulsion. The little boy in the park, with his overalls and his stick that I held in my own hands: this is his life. This is what he has brought me here to see. To hear. To bear witness.

And now I've seen and I've heard, and I won't stand for it. I won't let him suffer like this. I must act. Must take matters into my own hands. I wouldn't have thought myself capable of such spontaneous action, but these are not normal circumstances.

I push myself off my elbows and rise onto my knees. The adrenalin coursing through me now is so potent it might as well have replaced my blood. My thoughts are a stretched elastic band, pulled to the point of snapping, ready to launch all of me into a flurry of action. I tighten my thighs, prepare to thrust myself to my feet and storm the hill. Storm the hill to save the boy.

But a hand comes down on my shoulder, firm and solid. I almost cry out, completely shocked at the surprise of human contact here in this secret spot in the forest, but a second hand swiftly covers my mouth and with a grip like steel cuts off my breath and prevents any sound.

30

Thursday

I feel like my heart might explode in my chest, and I writhe to see who's assaulting me in this way. In my terror I don't know who I'm expecting. I'm not expecting anyone. *I have no idea what is happening*. Then the terrifying thought explodes into my mind: I've been caught. *Oh God, I've been caught and . . .*

The hands that have grabbed me in the darkness slowly, steadily, turn my head. In under a second I'm facing my captor. It's a man holding me: he's younger than I am. Just barely a man. Amidst my fear I place him as a teenager. Maybe eighteen or nineteen. Buzz-cut. He hasn't shaved today and has a shadow of a country goatee. And he has a fearsome, solid look in his eyes, which are a deep jade-green. His look is older than his face.

He gazes straight at me. His own chest is rising and falling quickly: the moment has him tense as well. Then, keeping one hand over my mouth he takes the other from my shoulder and raises a finger to his own lips. *Shh*, he mimes. Then he whispers. 'Be quiet. Don't let them hear you inside.'

I can barely move. I've never felt such fear. Every muscle in me is clenched to the point of snapping the bones beneath it. Yet I also have the strangest sense this young man isn't here to do me harm. There is no real logic to this, no reason my terror should give way. I am, after all, being held down with a hand over my mouth.

The young man keeps his eyes locked on mine for a few seconds, allowing me to regain my lost breath and composure. This calms me further. He gives me a look that says, *I'm going to remove my hand. I'm not going to hurt you. Don't yell.* And then he does. And I don't.

We're face to face on our knees in the forest. The noises of violence are still wafting up to us from below. The scent of must is still in the air. I have no idea how long he's been there, behind me, watching.

'I know what you want to do,' he finally whispers. His glance turns towards the house. He looks angry. 'I can see it in your face. I know because I want to do it too.'

'I want to stop them,' I spurt out. Whether it's fear or the situation below, I respond to his prompt rather than protest my assault. This man isn't a threat, it's just something I sense within me. And I can't forget the boy.

'Whatever's going on in there. I want to put an end to it.'

He turns back to me. 'You're going to have to get in line.'

31

Thursday

It takes me a moment to absorb the young man's meaning. I'm still on an adrenalin high of proportions that tower over anything I've experienced before. And I continue to be nauseated by the noises from the house as well as shocked at the presence of this other person in the woods with me.

I can't find words to speak, so he takes the initiative. He talks in a whisper, but there is a force behind his words and the kind of overconfidence common to adolescence caught at the border of adulthood.

'I've been scoping out this place for a while now. This is the best spot.' He motions to our surroundings. I'd apparently chosen wisely.

'This,' he continues, motioning towards the house and the noises coming from it, 'this isn't an uncommon thing. They fight like that all the time. Believe me. *All the time.*'

I can't respond. What I'm hearing isn't fighting. It's assault. No, it's an . . . an abomination. It's indescribable. And if this young man's been monitoring this house for a while, then it has to be a long-standing thing. Something he's grown to loathe as much as I have in only a few minutes. I can't imagine how he's shown the restraint not to act before.

'We have to stop it,' I finally force the words out of my throat.

'Yeah, I'm with you on that,' he answers. There is resolve in his face – it's vivid, like a signpost. This isn't the first time he's thought of this. I'm running on instinctual reaction, but I can tell in this instant that he's operating on plans he's worked out before.

'Do you know them?' I ask.

He hesitates, but nods. 'Yeah. I've known them long enough. Everyone in these parts has. We've all known them longer than any of us would like. And it's always like this.' He nods again towards the house and the vile noises. 'Always has been.'

'Why hasn't anyone stopped them?'

'People are people. Easier not to see anything. Definitely easier not to hear anything.'

Not to hear. I'm imagining the boy inside, taking the brutal beating the man is dishing out. It's impossible not to hear this. I can't fathom the inhumanity of anyone whose ears would not stir them to rage on hearing such sounds.

We can't just sit here and talk about this. We have to do something, and we have to do it now.

The young man can sense my urgency. 'Yeah, I know. It's time.'

'What are we going to do?' I'm all at once conscious that I'm no example of remarkable fitness, no powerhouse street fighter. I'm not quite six feet and barely break 200 pounds. It took one punch to level me in Nashville, albeit from a rock of a man. And I realize in this instant that I have no idea just what it is I expect us to do. We could storm down to the house – we'll have to do that, one way or another – but then, what precisely? The man inside is clearly drunk, and violent. Am I going to stop him? Me, an angry post-pubescent at my side, and what army?

'Don't worry, buddy,' the young man answers. 'I haven't come unprepared. I've been planning this a while.'

He shakes his back and a pack falls loose behind him. He picks it up and drags it between us. It's made of a heavy, coarse fabric. Old and well used.

He unties the yellow cords that close it as he speaks. 'I was planning to do this alone, but a second body'll make it go even better. That is, if you've got the balls to do what needs to be done, old man.'

I'm almost ready to answer – to assure him I do, to make a snide remark about his age comment; the kind of contextually inappropriate humour that helps calm nerves, like soldiers joking with each other that the cook overboiled their eggs, while driving a tank into battle – when he reaches into his bag and pulls out a handgun.

Humour abandons me, even the dark kind. My whole body stiffens.

I know nothing about guns, so I don't know what type this is, but it looks fairly old. Not an antique, by any means, but not what you'd see on a SWAT member's hip either. It's the kind with a rotating cylinder and six bullets. A moment later he reaches in and extracts another. A rifle, with a vinyl strap.

'You in?' he asks, holding out the handgun to me. His eyes bore into mine, determined. 'I mean, you don't have to be. I can do this myself. That's always been my plan. I'm not letting him go on like this another day. But if you want in, man, you're in.'

I hesitate. I've never actually held a gun in my life. Never contemplated holding one.

But in my mind I see the boy, standing beside our pond. I see him holding his stick. I see the blood on his arm, the bruise over his hand, the puffy skin on his cheek, and suddenly I know where they all come from. I hear the thundering voice of a shouting father in the house below us. *'I'll show you what it means to get beat, you little shit . . .'*

I look into the man's eyes. 'I'm in.'

'Fucking excellent,' he answers. I take the handgun from his grip.

'You have to show me how to use this.'

'Nothing to show. Point, pull the trigger and shoot if you need to. I'm guessing you can figure out which way is forward.' There is a black grin on his face. It's a darker humour now, then stark seriousness. 'It's loaded. There's no safety, so don't go dropping it.'

I take a deep breath. I feel strangely ready to defend the boy down in that house.

The young man starts to get up, but before he does I reach out a hand. 'Hold on just one second.' My breathing is getting shorter, faster, and the tangy adrenalin is returning; but there's a question I want to ask.

'What do I call you, if we get caught up in the thick of it down there?' He doesn't seem to catch my meaning. 'Your name,' I say. 'Shouldn't we know each other's names, if we're going to do this together?' Still no response. I decide to take the initiative. I switch the gun to my left hand and hold out my right in the darkness. 'My name's Dylan.'

Finally he reaches out his own. 'Good to know you, Dylan. I'm Joseph.'

32

The Boy in the Park, Stanza 5

Little boy longing, eyes in the dark,
No tears – no silent beckon.
In night a deeper darkness
falls
Till vengeance comes with mounted wings
And creeping heart and passion
For the little boy longing . . .
The little boy longing . . .

33

Thursday – Nightfall

Joseph and I have no more time at our disposal to exchange pleasantries, to get to know one another any further, or even to prepare. The sounds of violence from the house have not abated. If anything they've grown worse. Yells, grunts, cries. Body parts smacking other body parts; bodies themselves ricocheting off furniture and walls.

'I'm ready if you are,' I say, firming up my grip on the gun. In my peaceful, mundane and ordinary life, this isn't a grip I'd believed my hands would ever take.

Joseph is already up. He's shaking the dirt off his knees. It's almost a ritual. He looks me straight in the eyes.

'I've been ready for a long, long time. I know these kind of people. It's time to make that bastard pay.'

He seems to want to offer me that much of an

explanation, though I really don't feel any is necessary. I was ready to barrel down the hill alone, simply shouting and screaming. Joseph has given us the means to do something more about the situation.

'We'll find the old man, and we'll get him cornered,' he says as I raise myself off the ground and up to full height. He tosses his pack, now empty, into the darkness. 'Make him learn that this kind of shit doesn't fly. That there's a price to pay.'

I nod, strangely content with this plan. Joseph had instructed me on use of the handgun with guidance on how to 'shoot, if you need to', which I take to mean that he believes it might not be necessary, and there's a certain, comforting reassurance in this. It should be enough without. If I were that father and a teen and a grown man stormed into my home with firearms drawn, it would scare the life out of me without the need for a single bullet to be fired. Sometimes the threat of retribution is worse than retribution itself. I feel a sense of anticipation at instilling that kind of fear in someone who is clearly evil enough to deserve it.

'What about the others?' I ask Joseph as we both take our first steps out of the trees and onto the hillside. He passes me a strange look, then shakes his head.

'The woman's not to be brought into this. She isn't like him.'

I nod. That's enough. We're focused. We know what we're doing.

We start to run. The shouts emanating from the house

at the bottom of the hill are like magnets, pulling us in. Joseph has the rifle held in both hands, sturdy across his chest. I have the revolver in my right hand. I'm trying to hold it in front of me, but my arm is flailing a little as I run, striving to maintain my balance. All sunlight is gone, now. The moon has emerged from somewhere, casting a silverish hue on the scene around us.

We run faster. My legs are on fire, my heart is thrashing. My mind is chanting a mantra in its rhythm: *I will protect that boy, I will protect that boy, I will protect that boy.*

Gravity increases the speed of our descent. We're plunging, racing towards the house. *I will protect that boy.*

And then I see him. The boy, right in front of me. I'm moving and he is still – yet somehow he remains just in front of me, even as I run. Directly in my line of sight. Before my face. It's not something I can explain.

I will protect this boy.

He stares straight at me. He's never been this close. In that blur of motion I can see freckles on his upper arms, above the bruises and the blood. I never knew he had freckles. I can see the torn label of his overalls and the scuff marks on its metal clasps. I can make out individual strands of his hair.

But he has no face. He is standing right in front of me, only feet away, the earth around us is a blur of motion, but he has no face. Only a grey space, formless, there where his boyish features ought to be – a space into which I cannot bear to look. I want to, but the void repels me.

The rest of him I cannot avoid. He is covered in blood, now. It's no longer just on his arms. It's everywhere. A bullet wound eviscerates his chest. I look closer, see there is more than one. They're not mere wounds. The boy has been destroyed. It's as if he is coming apart.

And for the first time, I hear his voice. I cannot see a mouth, but it is clear the voice comes from him. A voice like no other I've ever heard, a sound so guttural and deep and feral it seems to come groaning out of the earth itself.

'Things aren't what you think,' he says to me. The world around us remains a blur. I'm still in motion, still following Joseph's lead; but the boy is perfectly still in my vision.

'You don't have to do this.'

It's this that the boy in the park says to me on the hillside. He spreads his palms, his shattered body growing more tortured, more vile, with each second. He is falling to pieces in front of me.

'It doesn't have to be like this.' The words repeat in thunder, and my eyes are suddenly filled with tears. I feel the boy urging me to stop. Begging me to plant my feet on the grass beneath them and put a stop to everything. To be at peace. Not to take the few steps that remain.

But it's too late. I'm in motion. *I will protect this boy.* My feet can't be halted. I'm barrelling forward in unrestrained fury, Joseph a few steps ahead of me. His rifle is forward and my own gun is drawn, and I feel the crunch of wood as we charge up the steps of the porch.

As Joseph slams his body into the door and I hear it shatter at his attack, I glance back to take a final look at the boy. The boy in the park. The boy I've come here to save. The boy I suddenly feel I am somehow betraying.

Behind me, the hillside grass shimmers in the moonlight. I can't see the boy, and my last thought as I follow Joseph through the door is to wonder whether he's ever really been there at all.

PART TWO

THE FARMHOUSE, 1974

34

The Porch

The Christmas tree is thin and sparsely decorated, but beautiful. There is no tinsel, no store-bought ornamentation – only a few hand-crafted stars and angels, and one Play-Doh wreath ornament in gaudy red and green that was a kindergarten project a few years ago and takes pride of place. There's nothing else festive or seasonal about the interior of the house. But there's always a tree, and it's always gathered from the nearby woods and brought into the living room during the second week of December. Some things are tradition, tried and true.

The tree is visible through the window, from the position outside on the porch where the mid-sized man is standing. There are no gifts beneath it. Not yet. Those will come at the last minute, if they come at all. Last year there hadn't been any, but there were promises made that this year would be different. Of course, promises had been made last year as well.

Promises. Always with the promises. Andrew Warrick, the man on the porch, fixes his gaze through the window. He's paused before entering the house, a moment of reflection that he supposes is meant to calm his nerves. But he looks at the tree in disgust and his emotions are anything but calm. The symbol has become one he resents. It was supposed to represent joy and hope, that's what everyone said, but in reality the tree was just another monument to obligations the world felt entitled to place on his shoulders, adding to a list that only ever seemed to grow longer and more oppressive. The list that seemed ever more to rule his life.

That's what this season was really about, he'd decided. Chores. Not love and joy and merriment – he wasn't sure where that myth had got started, or what sort of fools bought into it. Chores, plain and simple. The annual Christmas laundry list. *Get a tree. Get decorations. Buy gifts. Entertain friends.* Take all the work a man is normally expected to do, all the weight that normal day-to-day life places on his shoulders, and add more. Colour it in red and green, sing silly songs about it, but demand that the chores get done. *Merry Christmas.*

It was all too much, and Andrew Warrick is well past tired of dealing with it.

His shoulders slouch as the thoughts collide in his head. It's not just Christmas in its own right that eats at him. If it were only that, a man could bear it. But

Christmas is a reminder, one that comes every year at this same time and wags an accusing finger in his direction. A reminder of his lot in life. A beacon of failure in a world that just never lived up to a man's expectations.

It hadn't been Andy's dream to live on the outskirts of nowhere in a rundown house with a rundown wife and one scrawny kid. No man dreams of that. A man dreams of a good house, with a two-car garage and a gas grill on the porch, with a picket fence and a big lawn you've got enough money to pay someone else's kid to mow. He dreams of a job that doesn't break his back and summer holidays to places more exotic than 'into the city', which normally meant into a Denny's or an Olive Garden, on a good year, in the shopping district of the nearest bigger town. A man dreams of a cruise ship at least once in his life, with his hot wife in a two-piece bikini on his arm, his other hand filled with one of those drinks that has an umbrella coming out the top, which isn't gay in those circumstances because he's drinking it on a cruise ship in the Caribbean.

Those are the kinds of dreams a man dreams for his life, and Andy had once been set to attain them. He was no dumb kid, back in his day – he'd had brawn and muscle and enough smarts to get by. And looks, and a good solid appetite for the kinds of girls who would one day become those hot, bikini-clad, arm-hugging wives. Christ, he'd dated the prom queen in high school. Jennifer Erwin. She'd been like a local goddess, the kind of girl every teen male drooled over in private and sometimes in public. And she'd actually come to *him*, asked *him* out (or, in keeping with his manliness, *strongly suggested* that he ask her out, which he'd promptly done). That's how drawn to him she'd been. A badge of honour. Andy had been marked for success. No man who's dated the prom queen is supposed to end up burdened with a nonsense life once the crowns have come off.

But hell, how things had changed. The Christmas tree taunts him through the window. The wood of the feeble porch moans beneath his feet. A nonsense life was exactly what he'd obtained. He didn't know how it had happened, but it had become a reality he wasn't able to escape.

Andy couldn't even afford his own truck, that's how bad things had become. Worked like a bastard, sweat and grease and muscle, and couldn't man up to buy his own truck. He had to drive a hand-me-down he'd inherited when his old man had died, and it had been worn out back then. The old man hadn't even given it, either: hadn't so much as left a will or even a note saying 'my stuff goes to my boy'. He'd died like he'd lived, a selfish bastard. Andy had simply taken the truck. No one was going to ask any questions about it. He'd thought about taking more, but there hadn't been anything else to grab. The few books lining a shelf in his father's bedroom weren't of interest and, apart from those and a few dishes, he'd lived in a barren house.

Good riddance.

Still, to not even have your own truck . . .

The old man was certainly to blame, at least in part.

For things to go wrong so fast in his life it must have been the working of more than just his own foul luck. There was no love lost between Andy and his father. He neither misses nor mourns him. But he does blame him. Had he been a little less self-righteous and detached, maybe things would have gone differently. Maybe. Who knows.

It is cold, and Andy shivers on the porch. For an instant, he feels the need to console himself. It's not all that bad. *Things could be a lot worse*, he reminds himself, as he does from time to time. He stares through the window at the scrawny tree inside. *Ain't got the job I want or the life I'd dreamed of, but things could definitely be worse.*

But the comfort of the thought immediately turns to bitter resentment. When did the fact that things 'could be worse' start making people feel better about the shit they have to face in the present? Andy isn't a stupid man, though he'd never gone further with his education than high-school graduation an eternity ago. These sorts of questions bother him. Yes, he could be homeless. He could have some crippling disease. But none of that changed the fact that his life was crap, right here, right now.

Crap enough that he'd come to love a bottle better than Kate, the woman he'd had the misfortune to marry back when she'd told him she was pregnant. She hadn't even been a good lay. A quickie up in the hills after half a case of beer. Definitely *not* the prom queen. The next day he'd thought her name was Karen, and had sent her packing as soon as he caught his first look at her in bright daylight. *A cow of a woman. Absolutely no redeeming qualities*. He couldn't for the life of him figure out why he'd gone after her, but skirt's skirt. Sometimes, with enough booze, that's all the explanation a guy needs.

Andy stops himself. He's being unfair. He'd had a drink in the old truck on his way home from work, not his first of the afternoon – that's why he's thinking like this. His thoughts are too harsh. Kate isn't a cow, and there are some redeeming qualities in there. He knows he should be more understanding. When she cleans up she's got a pretty face, in a homely sort of way. And she's never tried to cheat on him. Not every man can say that, not with women the way they are these days. He's got more friends at work who've been cheated on than who haven't, and there's a certain pride to be had in not falling into their ranks.

Andy is tired from a long day's work, worn out in body and soul. He's prone to being harsh when the day gets towards its close.

Still, she'd got herself pregnant, back on that first night. Five years ago, it was now, almost six. That was a hard sin to overlook. Women were supposed to take precautions against that sort of thing, but he'd been forced to recognize that he couldn't expect that kind of common sense from a woman as thick-headed as Karen. Kate.

No, we were both drunk. Andy stiffens at the troubling collision of thoughts. Something inside compels him to accept some responsibility for their actions, for the pregnancy and the birth of their child; but he'd been raised firmly, and if there was one thing his old man had been clear on, it was that it's the woman's job to be watchful about that sort of thing. The responsibility Andy feels gets pushed aside. It wasn't his fault. *None of this is my fault.* She should have been paying more attention.

She'd offered to get rid of it, the baby, once the doctor confirmed the home test. That still enraged Andy. *You want to kill my kid?!* he asked her. That had been the first time he'd struck her, and not one inch of him had felt bad about it. Not then, not now. You don't threaten to butcher a man's kid in the womb and not expect to have the idiot nonsense beat out of you.

Not that he ever enjoyed the beatings. No one did. Not in the receiving, not in the giving. But certain things are necessary. That had been a lesson learned early, too, and learned well.

He'd married Kate without a ring, and the kid had come.

And now there is a Christmas tree in the corner. It stares at Andy through the window, accusing him for his thoughts. *Cry me up a river*, it taunts. *You've got the kid now. You'd better get a damned gift to put under here.*

That's the way Christmas works. That's what it is. Obligations. Obligations on a life that couldn't fulfil them if it wanted to.

Andy feels like bursting through the door, picking up the tree by its scrawny trunk and flinging the whole sorry sight out into the snow – cancelling the season, banishing the sense of guilt that haunts him. As if getting rid of the decoration would abolish the reminder it bore of all that had gone wrong in his life. As if what were left would be better.

But it's been a long day, and Andy's not a fool. The disappointment doesn't go away when Christmas ends each year and the next fake holiday begins. That's not the way a broken life works.

He looks down from the window. There's grease on his hands from the shop, and what he really wants, more than revenge or release or the absence of the season, is another beer. And if there's one thing in this house that's never in short supply, it's beer.

35

The Kitchen

The soup on the back burner is leftovers: two days' worth, blended in with a few spices and a fistful of herbs from the garden. But the steaks in the frying pan are new – a special surprise. She'd found them on sale three days ago and hidden them in the freezer when she got home. Back behind the frozen peas where no one would ever look. Hidden so they could come out today and make for a Friday treat.

They're sizzling now, and Kate Warrick's nostrils draw in a long, full lung of the scent. She can't remember the last time she cooked steak. They hadn't been able to afford it in . . . well, she honestly couldn't remember. That's what had made the sale such a surprise. Genuine steak, at almost the cost of chuck beef. She'd even asked the Safeway butcher if the pricing label was a misprint, sure that her luck couldn't be this good. He'd smiled politely and assured her, 'Just a little special offer for the season.' And she'd felt real Christmas joy in that moment. The spirit of giving, of goodwill: all of it. Bound up in butcher's paper and a price tag a third of what it should be.

Her husband would be so happy with this. Kate wasn't often able to surprise Andy, but he would be genuinely pleased tonight. She knew he'd had a long week at the garage, that he always got depressed at this time of year. His spirits weren't where she wanted them. But then this little gift came along, an unexpected blessing in the Fresh Meats refrigerator, and she had been soaring with the thought that she could do something to change that. She could be the Good Wife, bringing joy to her husband. And she meant to do it well.

Kate was cooking the steak just the way she remembered he liked it, from back when they'd had such things a little more often. Sautéed in a little of the bacon fat she always kept in a coffee can in the refrigerator, a tradition she'd learned from her mother, sprinkled with pepper and Lays Seasoning Salt. She'd never cared for the red combo-seasoning herself – a little too tangy for her liking – but she knew he favoured it above just about any other spices that money could buy. The fact that it was half the price of anything else didn't hurt, either. So she added it liberally, watching it soak into the fat and oils and turn a crusty brown from the heat.

Just before she served the meal she'd drop a pat of cold butter on top of each steak. That was the real trick.

Your magic touch, babe, Andy had once called it. Kate smiles at the memory. Some memories – the good ones – feel a thousand years old, as if they're part of the very fabric of her existence. This sentiment of 'the good old days' is a fable, she knows. She and Andy haven't been together that long. It's been just almost six years. Since before Tom was born, a little after he was conceived. But the memory of how he likes his favourite food makes Kate feel centuries old, looking back on days of real happiness.

Suddenly, a thought pries open eyes that had been closed with the pleasant memories. Will this be Tom's first time having steak? It's not quite a nonsense question, and for some reason it makes Kate doubly excited. It might well have been a few years since they'd last eaten this rare treat, and their son would have been too young then. Still on mashed vegetables and puréed chicken out of jars. Not that a boy's first steak is generally considered a milestone in a growing life, but still. A first is a first.

Kate's smile deepens. This is an unexpected source of happiness. To please her husband, to treat her son. The day is getting better with each thought.

Beyond the kitchen door the Christmas tree is in the front room, and knowledge of its proud place in the corner reassures her further. Andy took Tom out and got it last week, just as he'd said he would. There hadn't been any dramatics. They'd gone out in the snow, bundled in as many warm clothes as they had, Andy with an axe in his hand and Tom filled with excitement and a well-defined vision in his head of what the perfect tree would look like. He'd narrated its dimensions to her the night before: the way its branches would angle to their point, the colour its needles would have, the amount of space that would linger between branches, allowing room for decorations. He had it all worked out. And they'd found just the right one. Tom had pronounced it 'perfect in every way' as he'd followed Andy back into the house later that evening, snowflakes falling from its needles onto the threadbare floor. Her son had been positively beaming. Even Andy had looked content.

Kate had decorated the tree the next day as best as she could. It took some creativity to make something out of nothing. They weren't the sort of family that had an enormous cardboard box of Christmas ornaments down in the basement. But she had paper, scissors, string and imagination, and she'd decorated this tree the way she'd decorated each they'd shared over the past six years. And it was all perfect.

There are some moments in even the worst life when happiness forces its way through the grief, where paper angels are perfect ornaments and the scents of sizzling steak tantalize even a raw nose.

36

The Living Room

The day had been blissful and playful. As a boy, Tom Warrick supposes this is the way all days are supposed to be – the natural state of a twenty-four-hour period. He knows they're not, and he's had plenty which weren't, but this one was. Every dimension of it had been just the way he wanted.

Before him the Christmas tree is idyllic. Mother had produced the most exquisite of all angels and snowflakes and stars from ordinary sheets of white paper, and with her sewing needle and a bit of thread had fashioned loops to hang them from its branches. Each one looked like it belonged precisely where she'd placed it, like the tree had been incomplete until just that snowflake was hung from just that branch, over and again until the ideal tree had found its ideal form. Tom sits in his favourite corner of the little living room and gazes at it with awed wonder.

My tree is the way all trees should be. It is the tree by which all others should be judged.

My tree. The words comfort him. He'd gone up the hill with Father and helped pick it out, just a few days ago. Of all the trees in the forest, they'd found this one. It wasn't big, but it was just the right size for them. It met the very specific requirements that Tom had formulated. It was the shape of the kind of longish triangle that he associated with a slice of pizza – not too fat, but not too skinny and tall. And it was the green of the finger paint that they used at school, if you mixed just a little yellow in. A bright and sunny green, even out in the snow. He liked the darker green of some of the other trees, too – the kind of green with some blue or even black in it – but they didn't shine the way his tree did. There hadn't been any question. This was the one.

Father had approved, even said, 'Yeah, that ain't bad, kid, not bad at all,' and then Tom had been certain it was the tree for them. (Father had also said 'Just call me Dad, or Pops', as he'd done many times before; but Tom had heard the titles 'Mother' and 'Father' in a story at school, and had been told these were 'cultured' words, and loved the sound of them – so that's who they had become. They would just have to live with it.)

The snow had been fresh that afternoon as they'd hiked. The whole morning it had fallen in small, blue-white flakes; the kind that are almost like powder, that come when the weather is really cold. The kind that crunch under your shoes. It had made the afternoon magical. The sun had finally come out by the time Father came home, and when he and Tom had hiked into the woods it was like entering into a fairy tale.

Tom is truly happy, now, all these memories swirling like a happy fog in his mind. *This is* my *tree*. A boy feels real pride in a tree he's brought into the house with his own two hands. There is a sense of genuine possession, and not the selfish kind (not being selfish is something being stressed very much in school these days). This tree had once been lonely and cold in the snow. Tom and Father had rescued it and brought it into a home, dressed it in lovely adornments (thanks to Mother's help, of course), and made it part of the family. Being proud of that isn't selfish. Being proud of that is kind.

In Tom's hands now is a small book, and his attention falls back to its stiff pages. He'd swiped this one from the Blessing Box at school two days ago. The Blessing Box is a big yellow bin brought in each year by a local charity, and people are supposed to put things into it, not take them out. Toys, food, clothes. Whatever. Then the charity – a group that looked after the poor – would give the things to people who didn't have anything.

Tom feels a little bad that he's stolen the book from the Blessing Box, but he'll put it back before Christmas. There aren't really any books around his house, and the school library doesn't start lending until students are in the fourth grade. And besides, people sometimes call him poor, so maybe the box is really for him anyway.

His love for books has always been strong. He loved

the picture ones when he was smaller – the kind with unbendable cardboard pages and glossy cartoons that didn't get ruined if you spilled milk or juice on them – and he still likes them. But he's been learning to read, almost two years ahead of schedule, the teachers say, and he's soaking up everything he can get his hands on. He read a book last week (also taken from the box, and since returned) about a cat with boots. Tom had enjoyed the sounds of the words, and there were some funny illustrations (though the pages were thinner, made from paper and not cardboard, and while the illustrations were still colourful he noted that they looked like they *would* be ruined if he spilled anything on them; this seems to be a trend with more grown-up books, and so he's especially careful with them). The story itself, however, had struck him as a bit absurd. The cat's adventures weren't the issue. They were fascinating and interesting. But the author, which is what people who write books are called, had got one important detail very wrong. Every boy knows that a cat wears socks or mittens, not boots.

This book, the one in his hands now, is about trains. Tom can't make out all the words, but he can at least get the sounds of them if he goes back and forth over the letters a few times. And a lot of the words he knows, and they make sense when he strings them together and thinks about them, and when he uses the pictures to help.

This story isn't as funny as the one with the booted cat. It's more serious, but he likes what he's able to make out. He knows there's a big hill in this story, and the main train engine is scared. There's a big hill in front of him, big like the sky, and he doesn't think he can make it over that hill. It's impossible. It's too steep for such a little train. But then he changes his mind. He thinks he can. He thinks he can . . .

37

The Kitchen

The scents of the pending meal are swirling together now in almost magical combination. The outside of the steaks are just starting to turn the darker red that signals the approach to medium-well, which is how Andy likes them. The fat around the edges is changing to the caramel-gold that even looks smooth and buttery and wonderful. The soup is simmering away, its herbs fragrant in the air. Kate has tossed a few handfuls of the frozen peas into a saucepan with a bit of oil and some salt and they've started to wrinkle with the heat and warm to the right temperature. The three pats of cold butter to go atop the finished steaks have already been cut, and she's set them on a plate in the refrigerator to keep them solid until the moment is right.

She's timed everything perfectly. Andy gets off work at 6.00 p.m. and always stays behind at the garage for a beer with his friends. Maybe two. But he's always home by 7.00, since 'Supper's always at seven, ever since I was a kid.' Andy doesn't have many childhood traditions he's keen to maintain, but a seven o'clock supper is an inviolable one.

It's 6.58 now, and by her estimation the steaks need another three minutes to be at their perfect point of readiness. As Andy will be home any second, she's delighted that everything is in order for his surprise. She's laid the table already. Put out the good tablecloth to cover up the scratched surface of the wooden table, then set three places with a fork and a steak knife over a folded paper towel that serves quite nicely as a napkin. She's pre-filled their glasses with cold water and two ice cubes each, and she's even picked a handful of flowers from the hill out back and used another glass as a vase to decorate the centre of the table. It really will be a wonderful meal.

She looks down at herself. She's wearing a simple frock, like most days, and the old apron over the top of it is covered in grease and handprints. Some of the grease has splashed up onto her rose-coloured sleeves and some has fallen below the hem of the apron onto the lower inches of the dress. She wonders for a moment whether she ought to go change into something else. She could even get out her Sunday clothes – but those were packed away in plastic at the back of their closet. It had been so long since they'd gone out together, or since Sunday had actually meant going into church and being seen by others. No, it would take too much time. And it didn't matter, really. It was the meal that was meant to be the surprise, not her clothes.

Kate runs her fingers through her hair, straightening her appearance. She hears a creaking from outside, from the porch. The time has come. Andy is home. In a moment she'll welcome him and Tom into . . .

She stops herself. Tom. She'd almost forgotten. Where was he now? She probably should have called him a few minutes ago, told him to go wash his hands and tidy himself up from whatever outdoor adventures he'd been up to during the afternoon. She'd want him looking nice when his father saw him.

And then a moment of brief panic overtakes her. Tom hasn't been outside. She remembers, just now, that he'd asked her earlier if he could stay inside instead of going out to play.

'Why inside, hon?' she'd asked him. 'What are you going to do kept up in here?'

'I've got a book, Mother,' he'd answered. He'd produced a thin book from his backpack and shown it to her. She didn't ask where he'd got it from. She suspected he swiped books from the school now and then, but she also knew he was honest enough to return them, and since she and Andy couldn't afford to buy him books of his own, she chose to turn a blind eye to the minor transgression. It was good that he had the interest, which his teacher said was a sign of a creative intellect. This was the only real way it could be fostered.

'You *sure* you want to sit inside and read instead of going out and running around?' she'd asked. Tom had nodded in aggressive surety. He was absolutely positive. And she couldn't resist the enormous smile on his face as he crossed his legs, cracked open the cover and stuffed his nose into its pages.

That had been then. In the present moment, the memory brings Kate a deepening sense of fear. Since she hasn't called Tom to get ready for supper, it means he'll still be there – in the corner with his book, oblivious to the world. Right where she'd left him. His tufts of hair will be sprouting out from the top of its pages, his face somewhere in his story, and he won't hear his father approaching. He won't have heard the groaning of the wood on the steps just now.

Which means Andy is going to walk into the house and find him there. In the corner.

Reading.

And in an instant, Kate knows this means that the evening she had planned, the evening she'd thought lay ahead of them, was over.

38

The Living Room

It's seeing Tom in the corner with a book that sends Andy over the edge. Outside, on the porch, he'd only been taunted by the tree and the memories of the better life he'd once thought he'd have, but to enter into the house and be confronted with his own flesh and blood, rubbing in the insult – it's too much.

Books are all this kid's good for these days. Of all the stupid, childish, useless things. Tom may only be five, but Andy had been five once and he sure as hell hadn't wasted his father's time with books. By five Andy knew tools. By five he'd help his old man on the car, or fix the truck, or do his bit with good, proper chores around the house. By five a boy is supposed to be learning the skills to become a man.

But not this one. His son is too otherworldly bookish to have two wits of common sense about him, not to mention any semblance of a work ethic. A useless child. A useless child who flaunts his uselessness like a badge of honour.

And Andy's simply had enough.

'Fucksakes,' he mutters as he walks into the house and slams the front door behind him. His anger builds as he moves, every step fuelling his disappointment and disgust. As the door thunders closed, Tom's face pops up from behind his book. The cheerful blue train engine on its cover looks absurdly out of place in this house.

For an instant Tom's eyes look happy, like a boy's eyes are supposed to look when they see their father. He's been startled out of his reverie, but his thoughts are still in storyland and filled with dreams. But then Tom sees Andy, and immediately his face changes.

'That's right,' Andy says, louder, 'you can wipe that little smile off your face. You ought to feel ashamed of yourself.' He stands in the centre of the room. He has an arm extended, a grease-covered finger pointing towards his son in the corner.

'Let me guess, you've been buried in that book all day and haven't done shit around the place.'

Tom doesn't answer. His face is a full shade whiter now, his eyes wider. Andy doesn't really expect a response. Kid may be learning how to read faster than others, that's what they tell him, but he doesn't talk much. Especially not when he knows he's in trouble. Then the boy's as good as a mute.

Taking a hammer and a few nails to the loose boards on the back steps doesn't require talking, though. Andy had shown his son how to use the hammer. Twice. He'd shown him where the nails are kept, in a glass jar in the garage. And he'd shown him the wobbling steps and given clear instructions.

He decides to give Tom a chance to prove he's not a total waste of space. He knows the boy will fail the test – he always does – but he'll give him the chance anyway.

'The steps?' he asks his son. 'You do what I asked you with them? You pick up the hammer like a man?'

Andy doesn't feel it's necessary to elaborate. Tom damn well knows what he's been told to do. And Andy knows, even as he hints at the one, singular thing that he'd asked Tom to take care of, that his son hasn't done it.

The boy timidly shakes his head. The movement starts slowly, as if he's afraid to move at all, and especially to have to make this gesture. But soon his head is swinging back and forth in a dejected negative. For what it's worth, he looks genuinely upset. He knows he's failed.

For a moment, Andy isn't sure what's coming next. His whole body is tense, poised at the precipice of something. He knows this knife-edge well, what it's like to teeter between control and the complete loss of it. He teeters as long as he can.

But his mind is already spinning. The words *Damned little bastard* float through his consciousness on repeat. All day he's been at work. All day, providing for this *damned little bastard* and his mother, and the *damned little bastard* can't so much as lift a finger unless it's to please himself with a book or a stick or a toy.

It doesn't take long. It never does. Just a few seconds. Andy's frustration mutates into rage. He lurches the two steps over to Tom's corner and grabs the book out of his son's hand. Tom pushes himself further back, shaking.

'You relax once you've done some *goddamn work*!' Andy shouts. He can hear his old man's voice in his, the same voice that used to shout the same things at him, when he was cowering in his own corner doing whatever it was he did that had set his old man off. It's a disgusting thought, realizing he's become his father, but Andy is caught up in the moment.

He takes the thin book in both hands, open to the place where Tom had been reading, and rips it apart at the spine. The flexing of his muscles, the physical vibration of the paper and glue tearing away from their bond – they're like a charge in his skin. The rage increases. He flings the remains of the book at the far side of the room. They fly into the branches of the Christmas tree before falling to the floor.

The tree shakes. Two paper angels fall from their branches and flutter down to join the remains of the book.

Andy turns back to Tom, crouched in his corner. His heart is thumping, his blood flowing in torrents that thunder in his ears. And *that little bastard* has been asking for a good dose of correction for some time.

Andy reaches down to his belt buckle. It's the usual

way, and he can already feel this is going to be one of the usual encounters. A father's duty. The way people learn. The way he learned . . .

But he stops himself before his belt is undone. The normal course of events is interrupted, and the strangest distraction halts him. There's the scent of something coming from the kitchen. Something rich and hearty that at first he can't identify. Something unexpected. But then his nostrils and taste buds collaborate to piece together the evidence. Bacon fat. Spices. The blood-rich scent of red meat, and not just any meat. *Steak*.

Andy's blood courses again, on fire in his veins. He simply can't believe what his senses are telling him. He's infuriated, and his nose is bearing a new insult. An incomprehensible reality, a fuel for his rage.

I work my damned hands off to get us enough money to get by, and that bitch goes and spends it on steak!

He can see Kate's face in his mind. That cow, that sad excuse for a woman. That sorry, deceptive, lying, home-wrecking wretch of a wife. He can imagine her sneaking around their room while he's asleep, stealing cash from his wallet. That's probably how she's done it. He's had his suspicions for a while. Stolen his money then gone out lady-shopping and spending it on indulgences, thinking he'd never be the wiser. No wonder they still lived in a shit-hole like this! No wonder they could never up themselves to a better lot in life. A good man is satisfied with a burger. *And the bitch wastes my money on . . .*

He isn't able to finish the thought. His anger has taken over. His thoughts have become a pure mess of rage and fury, no longer coherent phrases or emotions but simply a mass of uncontrollable fire. And he doesn't want to control it. He wants to let it out, to let it run its course. It's the only thing that helps. The only thing that can make a situation like this better. And it's the only thing that can teach a lesson no words could ever convey.

His buckle has come undone and he's unthreading the belt as he moves. Tom is pressed into his corner, shaking at the beating he's certain will come, but Andy is no longer aimed at him. He's wrapping the belt around his wrist and elbowing his way through the kitchen door. Into that room where his wife has betrayed him yet again.

I'll show her what happens to bitches who steal.

39

The Living Room

Only whimpers manage to make their way through Tom's throat. There's no point in screaming out. He's learned that there's never anyone around to hear. There's no point in crying, either. Tears are supposed to attract the people who love you. They're supposed to call them to your side, to wipe away the wetness on your cheeks and say things that make the pain better. But nothing ever makes Tom's pain better, and the only person that loves him is in the other room. She's in the other room and can't get to him. And he can't get to her.

Tom can hear her, though, and every time he does he repeats the same little, compassionate whimper. It's all he can offer her.

He knows the different sounds that come from the different corrections. Before, he didn't know which sounds went with which, only that they were all bad.

But since Father had started correcting him, too, Tom had learned how to identify them. They were like a little catalogue in his mind, linked together through experience.

There was one sound made when the belt was swung and the leather strap snapped against your clothes. It made a different sound if it hit skin – more of a pop. There was another sound altogether when Father swung the buckle end and that hit you. That was more of a thud, like when you drop a rock onto a carpeted floor. Then there was a sound for when he wrapped it round his wrist and punched. That's the sound Tom hears now. That's how Mother is being corrected. It's kind of a muffled sound, usually with a grunt behind it, and there's usually a lot of heavy breathing since it takes more work for Father to correct them like this.

Tom hears the grunts and the breathing. He hears his mother's cries, which eventually fade to sobs. He's expected that. She usually stops crying out after the first few seconds, just like now. Just like Tom, when it's his turn. Because crying out is like shedding tears: it's supposed to attract the people who love you. It's supposed to call them to your side to make the pain better.

But Tom can't help her. He cowers in his corner. He whimpers. The edges of his vision start to go hazy and white. He so wishes he could help her, but he's just too small. He tried once, and that's what started his father correcting him, too. He'd walked into the bedroom when Mother was being corrected – the popping kind of sound, with the belt hitting her skin – and shouted out, 'Stop it! Don't do that to Mommy!' (This was before the story at school and the advent of Mother and Father.) He'd yelled the words as loudly as he could, certain that instructions yelled that loudly would be listened to and his father would stop whatever he was doing. Tom didn't know quite what it was, but the tears covering his mother's face were enough for him to know she didn't like it, and that meant it was bad. But she was also shaking her head at him, like she didn't want him to be there. He'd never encountered that before. Tom had never known his mother ever to want him to be anywhere but at her side; but as he'd burst into that room, she looked like she wanted him to go away.

His father's look had been different. He'd never seen a grown-up look like his father looked, just then. He looked like a monster, even though Tom know that his father wasn't a monster and that monsters weren't real. But he was as scary as a monster. There was sweat on his cheeks, and his eyes looked sharp. When Tom was done shouting, he looked right at him. He had his belt in his hand, and it was raised high over his head. Slowly he'd let it down and turned to his son.

'The fuck do you want, you little brat?' he'd asked. His words were so mean. Like they were from someone else's voice.

'Stop doing that to Mommy,' Tom had repeated. He'd stomped his foot. That was another sign of how serious he was. He didn't know what was going on, but he'd shouted and stomped, and so now it would have to stop.

But his father hadn't stopped. Instead, he'd turned towards Tom and lunged at him. He'd crossed the room so fast that Tom almost thought he was flying. But people can't fly.

But then, he'd never thought people could do the things to each other that he then learned his father could do. He'd ripped off Tom's T-shirt – actually ripped it, a great tear all the way down the left side – and thrown him onto the bed.

And then Tom had heard the snapping sound again. Only this time, when it came, his whole world exploded. His skin went on fire. It started in his back, but went like a lightning bolt through his whole body. He wanted to scream, but he didn't have any breath.

He heard more snaps. Felt more explosions. And he heard his mother sobbing softly, 'I'm so sorry. So sorry.'

And Tom is sorry now, too. Sorry he can't do anything for his mother in the kitchen. Because they are grown-ups, and he is a boy. Just a little boy.

But one day I'll be big, Tom says internally, and despite himself there are tears flowing down his cheeks now. His vision has gone blurry, the way it does when he gets so upset, but his mind is clear. *One day I'll be big, and I'll help her.*

40

Christmas Day – Two Weeks Later

The day is finally here, and Tom is as excited as he can remember being. The promise of gifts hadn't been a lie. This morning, as he bounds into the living room with a heart full of boyish hope, he spots them. Right where tradition says they should be.

Three presents, wrapped beneath the tree.

He literally shrieks with joy. For a moment Tom worries that the noise will get him in trouble. His father doesn't like a lot of noise, and he definitely doesn't like yelling. But then Tom isn't worried. It's Christmas. However bad things can get on other days, nobody gets mad or hits on Christmas.

The shriek attracts Mother, who appears a moment later from the kitchen, beaming. There are good scents coming from behind the door: sweet cakes. Cinnamon. Something with cooked pumpkin. There is flour on

Mother's hands and she shakes it off on the dress she always wears for special occasions.

But Tom can barely keep his focus on her. The presents are crying out to him, almost like they know his name.

'Is Dad coming?' he asks. He's decided to stop calling him 'Father' for the day – a special Christmas gift between the two of them. He didn't have enough money to get his dad anything else, and his father's never been one for homemade gifts. Mother said Tom could claim joint credit for the present under the tree she'd actually bought and wrapped, with his father's name written on a small card attached to it, and this made Tom happy. But he knew that 'Dad' instead of 'Father' would be a kind of extra present itself, and that made him even happier.

His mother pats his fluffy hair, washed and towelled dry the evening before. Her face is a smile, and most of the blue marks are gone. What's left are the lines that are starting to show, which she once described to Tom as laugh lines. 'But you don't laugh that much, Mother!' he'd answered, and she'd laughed at that. When she did some of the lines got deeper, so maybe there was truth in what she'd called them. But Tom had the suspicion some of the lines came from other things, too.

'Your father will be here in a second. Why don't you get the gifts out from under the tree. You can pass them out once we're all together.'

Tom complies eagerly. The presents are very different by feel, though all wrapped in the same light paper. His mother's handiwork. Each has the name of its recipient penned in beautiful handwriting – the kind called cursive – on a small card that's been decorated with a sketched image of a tree, a ribbon, or a star.

Tom's father's gift is heavy, hard and oddly shaped. Mother's is hard, too, but not quite as heavy. It has strangely pointed ends. Tom's is the lightest of the three, and not hard at all. It's soft and with no distinctive shape. Squeezable inside the coloured paper.

The temptation to tear into it is almost overwhelming. When he presses his fingers in, the paper yields beneath them and Tom knows if he presses just a little further, just the tiniest bit, it will tear and he'll be able to catch a glimpse of whatever is inside. He's rarely ever been so tempted to do something he knows he shouldn't. But he's resolved to be on his best behaviour today, so instead he sets out the gifts in the centre of the floor. They're only a few feet away from their previous location beneath the tree, but now they're assembled in opening order, right there where they can't be missed. Tom sits immediately beside them, as if moving too far away might result in them disappearing altogether.

Andy arrives after a few minutes. He's still in his pyjamas, unshaven and dishevelled, his hair oddly matted on his head. For an instant he looks like he wants to be left alone, but at the sight of his boy and wife seated around the bundle of gifts, a smile crosses his face.

'You waited for your old man, didn't you?'

'Of course we did!' Tom cries out. He grabs the heaviest gift, shoots up onto his feet and rushes it over to his father. Andy smiles again and takes it from him.

'Open it, Dad!'

Andy might not like the season, but the moment is a hard one to protest. Another smile finds its way onto his unshaven face and he complies, sitting on the old sofa and tearing away at the paper. He even makes a little show of it, flinging the torn-away scraps into the air so that they flutter down like big, lop-sided snowflakes. Tom giggles.

The hard object beneath the wrapping is finally exposed. It's what Andy wanted. A bottle, the biggest size, of his favourite. Maker's Mark. The kind of bourbon too expensive to buy. The kind you had to get as a gift – even if it's a gift you have to tell your wife you expect to be given. She'd complied, like a good wife should.

'Hey, that's great,' he says, and is already screwing off the cap. 'Not bad at all. Good job, hon.' He nods at his wife as he takes a swig directly from the large bottle.

'It's from Tom, too,' she says, smiling at their boy. 'From the two of us together.'

'Well, then,' Andy answers, 'then the not bad goes to both of you.' Tom beams. He likes hearing his father say nice things about him.

'Go on then,' Andy continues after another swallow, nudging at Tom with his bare foot. 'Give your mother hers.'

Tom is eager to play the deliveryman and rushes his mother's gift to her lap. She kisses him on the forehead, smiles into his eyes for a moment, then rips into the paper with childlike zest. She flings the scraps of paper into the air just like Andy had done – a new family tradition emerging. Tom giggles again, and bats at some of the scraps as they fall.

The object beneath Kate's paper is a rolling pin, wood. New, rather than a hand-me-down. It's shrink-wrapped in plastic and still has the bright red label on it. Tom looks up at her anxiously, waiting for her reaction.

She beams with happiness. Not because she particularly wanted or needed the gift – the old rolling pin she has in the kitchen works just fine; they're not the sort of thing that wears out – but because it's clearly made Tom happy to watch her open it. That's more than enough.

'Maybe that'll increase the chances of getting a good meal out of you more than once or twice a year,' Andy mutters. He grins. It's a joke. He's the only one who laughs, but it's a joke all the same. Kate wrinkles up her face in a smile.

'I can certainly try.' She pauses. 'Thank you, love.' Then, to Tom. 'And you to, my little love. Thank you both for my wonderful present.'

Tom probably hears her thanks, but doesn't seem to notice. He is waiting, excited, fidgeting like an anxious puppy.

Can I? Can I now? Can I please?

'Well, go on then, boy!' Andy finally says. He laughs again, and this time Kate joins him. It's rare that their son is so obviously excited and filled with visible happiness.

Tom dives at his gift. He digs his fingertips through the paper, and he feels the soft object beneath before he can see it. Within a few seconds the paper is shredded – he doesn't have to make a show of tossing it about like his parents had, this happens all of its own accord through the intensity with which he dismantles the wrapping. Then, when the paper is gone, he beams at the gift that he holds up in front of his face.

It's exactly what he'd wanted.

A brand new pair of overalls. The light-blue kind. They're what he asked for. *And I got them!* Tom couldn't remember the last time he'd got what he asked for, but this, today, it made up for everything.

Tom clutches the overalls to his chest, elated, shooting broad-toothed smiles at both his parents. He looks like he might burst with happiness. Then, without missing a beat, he drops his gift to the floor and strips down to his underpants, right there in the middle of the living room. He picks up the overalls and shakes them open, then crawls into them. The metal clasps come together in front of his chest. He adjusts their position until they're just right, then looks up to his parents.

He is beaming. They're a size too large, but he's a growing boy and overalls don't have to be just perfect. In any case, Tom wouldn't notice if he was tripping over the cuffs or if they only came down to his knees. He knows only that he feels genuinely happy, that he got the one gift he truly longed for, and that Christmas is the best day of the whole year.

He is, for this bright, Christmas moment, a beaming, beautiful little boy.

THE SCHOOLYARD, 1975

41

At School – Two Months Later

Of all the spots in the world that involve other people, school is one place where Tom feels truly happy. Lee Kragan Elementary is for big boys, and he's been promoted into the First Grade a full year early, which means he's bigger than he sometimes thinks. Not size-big, but brains-big. And Mrs Curtis always makes him feel like he's earned his place in her classroom with the twenty-three other children, all of whom are a solid year older than Tom. 'You wouldn't be here if this wasn't the spot for you, bright and clever as you are,' she said on his first day in her class, and she'd repeated it more than once since. Mrs Curtis is the kind of teacher who likes to say nice things, and does it effortlessly.

Tom wears his overalls almost every day. It would be absolutely every day without exception if he could, but they had to be washed every so often. Mother was pretty insistent on that. So once a week, or sometimes twice, depending on the intensity of play, he'd appear in jeans and a T-shirt. He felt like a different boy when he had to dress in those old things. But it was only ever a temporary measure. He'd always be back in the overalls the next day.

This insistence on his favourite outfit isn't, however, helping fend off the accusations of some of the older boys who like to tease him for being poor. Before, they'd taunt him for not having a better family car, or for the holes in his jeans. Now it's for his new outfit. Tom considers overalls to be the epitome of class, style and function. They're the perfect attire: they're not like trousers that fall down when you're too active or require a belt. They can be worn with or without a shirt. They're quick on and quick off. And you can even go through growth spurts – he gets those now and then – and they still fit, since they're supposed to be a little baggy and loose. Perfect.

But some of the boys call them 'country crap' – employing a word Tom thinks they really shouldn't use – and like to tease him, especially since he wears them so often. 'Only set of clothes you got, eh, poor boy?' they would say. 'Can't afford anything else, poor boy?' And then on the days the overalls were in the wash and he'd wear jeans, 'What's wrong, poor boy? Your country crap outfit go missing? Wouldn't think it'd be hard to find one set of clothes in a house that ain't got nothin' else in it.'

The boys might be mean, but they were also inconsistent. They teased him when he wore his overalls, and they teased him when he didn't. Tom felt like they should pick one or the other.

On one occasion, a few days after Christmas when this was all first starting, the taunts bothered him and Tom went home crying. Mother hadn't been there, and he still had tears on his cheeks when Father got home from work. 'What's this all about?' he'd asked, generally disapproving of tears. Tom explained the situation: the taunts, the insults, the mean words. He'd expected to get a lecture from his father, but he didn't.

'You need to grow a pair. Those kids are just a bunch of stuck-up shits,' his father had answered, then left the room.

Tom didn't know what the first part was supposed to mean, but he was *sure* that 'shits' was a word he wasn't supposed to say. However, he liked that it was what his father thought of those boys, and so he thought it too. 'They're just a bunch of shits,' he would say – to himself – whenever the taunts began, and it made them not hurt quite so much.

The other great benefit of overalls is that they cover so much of your body, which is a useful feature for a child. Tom isn't quite sure how other boys cover up all the signs of their own corrections, since he's been told by his father that they are never to be shown in public, and he can't think of a time he's seen them on anyone else in school. But Tom always has marks here and there – a bruise, a cut – that come from 'being shown the difference between right and wrong'. And overalls do a fine job of covering them up. Legs: fully covered. Back and chest: check.

Only the neck and arms are exposed, and that is just a matter of a T-shirt. Tom has a few of those. The yellow and grey ones are long-sleeved, so work well if he has any marks on his lower arms. The white ones (he has two of those) are short sleeved, so there are some days he can't wear them. But they're his favourites. He loves the feel of the wind over his skin; and when he plays, he loves how the grass and dirt and leaves rustle against his wrists and elbows.

So he tries to be as good as he can, to keep the corrections to a minimum. And when they come, he's learned how to position his body so that most of the blows go to his back or his legs. It's really just a question of how to hold yourself, and you learn some tricks after a while. Lean a little to one side and a blow that would have gone to the arm goes to the shoulder instead – and the shoulder's okay. T-shirts cover that easy. Even the stomach or chest are okay, though those hurt more and for a longer time. But they're still better than marks on the arms, which mean long-sleeve shirts and less freedom.

Because if there is one thing that Tom loves, it's being free. There are plenty of things in his life that don't feel very free: schoolwork, chores, arguments, punishments. But none of those cancel out the freedom that only a boy can know, when he's given a few minutes to himself. He'll grab a stick, a pocketful of stones, and the whole world will fade away. The little shits at school can call him 'poor kid' till they're blue in the face. In those moments Tom is a prince and a king. He's a knight with a thousand-strong army on horseback behind him. He's a jouster with an undefeated record. He's an astronaut with a ray gun and a spaceship and a whole universe at his fingertips.

And in those moments, Tom knows there is nothing poor about that.

42

The Schoolyard

It's one of the days with the taunting. The morning had already been hard. Father had been in a foul mood. He'd been drinking even before Tom woke up and had yelled during breakfast. Tom hadn't said anything. He'd eaten his Cream of Wheat and drunk his glass of milk quickly, then grabbed his paper-bag lunch and gone outside to wait for the bus. He felt mildly bad for leaving Mother to deal with the yelling, but she'd told him before that was the best thing to do on these kinds of mornings, and he tried to do what she said. Mother was a grown-up, and grown-ups know better. Most of them, at any rate.

But the day hadn't got any better. At recess a group of five older boys from the second grade – a group Tom knew well from experience – had cornered him near the large, metal slide on the far side of the playground. It was a favoured spot for such encounters, as the teachers patrolling the schoolyard generally concentrated their attention on the paved-in section on the near end, with the swings and jungle gym, where most of the students congregated. This was as far as one could get without going out of bounds and having the whistle blown at you.

'There he is,' the leader of the little pack had chided. 'Mister Overalls.'

Tom wasn't sure why they called him that. The nickname was an innovation. They seemed to think it was an insult, but he couldn't understand how.

'Mommy can't afford any new clothes for you, Mister Overalls?' The name might be new, but the taunts were familiar.

Tom knew better than to answer. They used this taunt a lot, and early on he'd actually responded. 'These *are* new!' he'd protested. 'They were a Christmas present!' That had only earned him more jeers and a few elbows at his ribcage. Something about getting leftovers for Christmas when other boys got remote-controlled cars and skis.

So Tom just let them jeer. They did the normal things: threw a few small rocks at his ankles, tried to chase him around the slide. But the best reaction is no reaction. He'd heard that once from Mrs Curtis, and it was good advice. If he didn't say anything, didn't react, the boys got bored quick enough and left him alone. And so they did.

He sits on the bottom of the slide, now. They've gone, at last. It hadn't been a long go of it today. But still, after his morning, and forgetting to do his homework – with a lecture and disapproving look from the teacher in response . . . it was a crummy day.

'You don't look so great,' comes a voice from behind his shoulder. Tom doesn't have to turn to identify it. He's only got one real friend, and the sound of his voice always makes him feel content.

'It's nothing,' he answers as the other boy walks into view. 'You know, just those boys.' Anyone who knows Tom knows how he's treated by the older boys, so there's no need to explain. If it wasn't a taunting it was a teasing, and if it wasn't a teasing it was a bout of name-calling. All very predictable.

'They're a bunch of fuckers,' his friend says definitively.

Tom cringes, then can't help himself and bursts into an enormous grin. He knows with absolute certainty that they're not supposed to use words like these, that they're the kinds of words that can get you detention. But there are no teachers around, and that one always sounds so *horrible*. It makes him convulse with laughter, and when he realizes he's laughing and hears the word again in his head, he laughs even harder.

His friend laughs too, and for a few seconds they just sit there, giggling at the foot of the slide.

'Yeah, I guess that's what they are,' Tom finally says when the laughter has died down. The teasing of a few minutes ago doesn't seem so bad now.

His friend is pleased to see him smiling and pats him on the shoulder.

'That's better.' They pause for a few seconds. Tom looks happier. His friend always has this effect on him. Things get bad, people are mean, but friends make you feel calm inside.

'We've only got a few minutes of recess left,' his friend suddenly says. 'You want to go play?' He points towards a grassy spot on the north side of the playground where they often go to act out the next instalment of their long-standing Knights and Warriors game.

Tom grins again. Even the worst days can get better.

'That sounds great, Joseph,' he answers. 'But today, I get to be the warrior.'

43

The Boy in the Park, Stanza 6

Then comes the play,
The light returns:
Day is not forever hid.
There comes the voice, touch is felt
In tender caresses to
        Too-torn flesh
And a heart that cries, that
Mourns its burial within.

PART THREE

REDDING

44

Thursday – Nightfall

Joseph and I have been running deeper into the woods for the past ten minutes. Once we at last left that god-forsaken house we simply aimed at the forest and ran. Ran as fast as either of our legs would carry us. Mine are larger than his, so my strides are longer; but Joseph is younger and far more fit. I'm straining to keep up. My body is tortured with pain, though I can't determine whether it's from the run or the horror of what we just experienced. That much shock, delivered to the system all at once, will do things to the body that cannot be explained.

These ten minutes of motion feel like hours. I'm certain every step is going to be the last I manage before I collapse, and finally I can go no further. My heart is mere seconds from exploding in my chest. And the most repugnant thing is that, having seen what I've just seen, that thought is more realistic and vivid than I'd ever have imagined it could be.

'Joseph!' I cry out. 'Stop! I can't go on. I need to catch my breath.'

My feet are already slowing, gasps of air interjecting themselves between my words. A horrible reality comes with the act. Though I'm physically no longer able to keep running, slowing down is causing the images of what we're fleeing to become more vivid. Our flight had kept them at bay, the sheer movement of it; but as my feet lose their pace the farmhouse seems closer than when they were in motion. When I stop it feels like it's almost on top of me, that all this running has only brought us full circle and if I angle my head slightly I'll be confronted with the horror all over again. I know this can't be so – that we've been running in a straight line and putting more and more distance between us and that place. But I can't analyse the feeling now. I'm too short of breath and my mind is filled with too much horror.

'Joseph!' I cry out again. He hasn't seemed to hear and I'm afraid I might lose him out here in the middle of nowhere, but there's no longer any option except that I draw to a halt. The body has its limitations, and even adrenalin can only extend them so far. Once my feet are finally still I slump down to support my palms on my knees and draw in the most air possible with each wheeze. I've never undergone such exertion before. I don't know if Joseph is even aware I'm not behind him, but in this spot it's quite possible my frail life is ending.

A few seconds later, though, between my wheezing, I hear his footsteps on the crunching groundcover, back-tracking to my position.

'You all right, old man?' he asks. He's out of breath as well, I can hear him panting above me. But there's a thrill to his voice, too. An excitement coming across through the exertion. His emotions are still on fire.

I'm not sure what to say to him, and for an instant I'm grateful that my heaving breath makes it hard to speak. I'm not sure what my first words should be. I want to shout at him. I want to scream. I want to demand an explanation, because more than anything else I simply don't understand what happened between our crouch on the hillside and our arrival here. I'm alternately horrified and outraged. But I'm also confused, because in the mix of my indignation I have to admit that there is something else. Something of the same excitement I hear in Joseph's voice. A giddiness that is entirely inappropriate to our circumstances.

One should not feel giddy when he's just stained his hands with death.

'You just going to crouch around here all night?' Joseph asks, his voice in motion as he darts around my position. My eyes are still on the ground, my breath finally slowing to a controllable level. I notice the decomposing twigs and leaves of the forest floor. A beetle scurries out from beneath the tip of one of my bloodstained shoes and darts for cover beneath a brown oak leaf.

'I just need . . . just need another second,' I answer. *And an explanation*, my mind demands. *And some answers.* I close my eyes, trying to quiet the thoughts, but that only brings images. Faces of pure terror. Weapons in motion. Bodies falling to pieces.

I can't handle it. I fling open my eyes. The leaves at my feet are unmoved, but my breath is tensing again.

'I need to know something,' I force out between gasps, trying in vain to calm myself. Joseph grunts a 'huh' from a position that sounds like it's in front of me and I push my hands off my knees and start to rise to face him.

'I need you to tell me wha—'

But I can't finish the sentence. I halt, half-crouched and half-standing. It's not my lack of breath that stops me, but the sight that befalls my eyes. For the first time since we'd fled the farmhouse I catch direct sight of Joseph, I look into his face, and the sight stops everything. My words, even my racing breath. For a second I am completely frozen.

Joseph's eyes are wild. I feel I'm looking into the face of a beast – and I don't mean that as a poetic aphorism for a particularly mean or wily person. I mean I feel like I'm looking into the face of a wild animal, a creature: something untamed and feral. His hair has been scattered in every direction from the run, the blood that covers his face splotching and smeared from the sweat of the exertion. There is red in the hair, too, stained rust and brown now as it dries. His chest is heaving in violent jerks. His cheeks flex in and out with his breath and the tensing of the muscles in his jaw. It's a scene out of a bad vision, a grotesquerie from a disturbed mind.

But it's in his eyes where the beast is the most evident. The moonlight is reflecting off them in a dull glow, and in all my life I've never seen anything like it.

I know, somewhere inside, that eyes don't really change. The poet in all of us talks about eyes 'looking tender', 'growing mournful' or 'taking on a happy expression', but eyes are actually fairly featureless. They never change shape or texture, they never flex or grow slack. The face around them, sure; but eyes themselves are constant and fixed. Perhaps that's what makes them so perpetually captivating. They're the one part of our being that really can't change with our moods and emotions, and so we notice them all the more when those emotions are in flux. Even when tears flow over them or lids conceal them, eyes never really alter.

But in this moment, Joseph's eyes *are* different. I can't explain it, I can't identify it, but they're not like they were before. They're the same jade-green I noticed when I first saw him, before our attack, of course; but staring into them now is like staring into a different soul. Or the absence of a soul, if such a thing were even possible. There's a hollowness to them. The place where I'd seen humanity and determination is now taken up by something else. Something ferocious, uncontrolled.

And it's in more than his eyes. His gaze is darting about our surroundings with flash-like speed, his body is following his glance with each turn. Joseph is hopping, spinning. It's a strange, incomprehensible dance.

He dances in the forest light and I'm suddenly more afraid than I was before. I'm afraid because I'd stormed off that hill and into that farmhouse with a righteous man keen to help me do a righteous deed, who'd grounded me in the need to act. And I'd escaped that horror with a righteous man who could be my support in coming to grips with what the deed had cost.

But righteous men don't look like wild beasts. Their eyes aren't hollow, and they don't let fear make them dance in forests.

45

Thursday – Night-Time

My fear finally gives me strength. Given Joseph's strange visage I realize I can either let it stunt me or I can try to act, and I find the resolve to do the latter. It comes, in part, from looking beyond Joseph's face – by far the most frightening part of him. When I glance over his whole body I'm reminded that as bold and fearless as he is, he's a teenager. He can't yet be twenty. Being fearless when you're a teenager rarely means you aren't actually afraid.

I right myself, recognizing that something has to happen to change this situation. I need Joseph to be sensible. Stable. Despite his youth, thus far he's been the one with the concrete plans and I need to ask him what the hell it is we're supposed to do now. That means bringing him out of whatever trance he's worked himself into. So I reach out a hand to calm him, bringing my open palm towards his shoulder in what I hope will be taken as a sign of friendship and empathy.

The instant I make contact with his shoulder, Joseph swings. I don't think he means to: it's an automatic, instinctual reaction. The touch is like a trigger, and his whole body rotates left in one violent surge: a coiled spring released on contact. His right arm is in a hook that's spinning round his torso, ending in a fist flying towards my face. It happens so quickly that there's no time for me to respond. I'm defenceless as his fist comes for me.

He freezes with only inches to spare. His eyes – still wild and ferocious – meet mine, and a confused recognition grabs his features just in time for him to stop his swing. His breath is racing in pace with mine, and for a few seconds we linger like that: wild eyes connected, his clenched fist hovering inches from the left side of my face, a few silver moonbeams casting their dim light into the blackness of the forest depths around us.

I want to yell at him for this unprovoked behaviour. I want to fling a torrent of angry words back the way he flung his fist at me. I want to spit at him, to cry out in judgement of the fact that I joined him in the house and he is now acting like such a stranger. Like an ass. But the words that work their way up out of my chest and into my lips aren't those. They come in a whisper, in an entirely different tone.

'Joseph,' I finally ask him without breaking our stare, my tone trembling, 'what have we done?'

The question pours out of me with a mournful sob. I don't mean it to, but my words take this force all of their own. It's a genuine question – I don't comprehend, not fully, what just happened – but it's also a cry of agony. An agony I've never before felt.

My sobs don't seem to affect Joseph's solid dispassion. 'We did what we needed to do, Dylan,' he answers, finally lowering his arm and unclenching his fist. His eyes are back to dotting around the darkness. 'What needed to be done. Nothing more.'

'Nothing more!? Joseph, that was, that was . . .' I can't find the right word, not for a few seconds. But then it comes. '*Slaughter.*'

He turns back to face me, his features hard. 'You can call it what you want. I call it standing up for what's right. Doing the hard work that sometimes needs to happen.' He draws closer, looks straight into my eyes. 'Where there's great evil, *that kind of evil*, steps need to be taken.'

I'm looking past Joseph as he talks. Past our surroundings, back to the sights of the farmhouse that are so vivid they might as well be my current surroundings. I'm repulsed, revolted by what I've seen. By what he's – no, *we've* – done. It's abhorrent. The earth, out of pure revulsion, should open up and swallow us alive.

Yet what's even more incomprehensible to me is that even in this moment I can't completely disagree with Joseph. I, too, feel that in the mix of it all we've accomplished something acceptable, or at the very least something necessary. I remember hearing once that there is a distinction between 'just war' and 'good war'. I'm not suggesting what we had just been involved in was a battle or a war, but the distinction suddenly makes sense to me. What we did certainly wasn't good; no one could possibly call it that. But it might have been just. It must have been. Because if there wasn't justice behind it . . .

But can justice really involve so much blood? So much pain?

And then there is the one question. The one that causes my stomach to turn over and knot up. The question mark hovering over one action that cannot possibly be righteous or just.

'Joseph, what about . . . her?'

His body cringes. To hear that final word physically repels him, and in an instant his eyes are wild again in that way I can't explain. The rational man of a moment ago – the man of virtue-minded deliberation on the necessary response to evil – is gone. What stands in his place is a hollow, empty beast.

'What about her?' he spits out. Even his words feel vacant. Then he shakes his head. Denial. Rejection. 'What "her" are you talking about?'

I can't believe he's asking me the question. My anger starts to flare.

'Her!' I shout. 'The woman! For Chrissakes, the woman in the house, Joseph!'

He cringes again each time I mention her. His head is shaking. It's an irrational motion: like a child refusing to accept that there are vegetables on his plate that he doesn't want to eat. If he says they're not there, then they're not there. That's the way it works in a child's mind, and it makes a kind of sense at that age. Denial is a powerful force. It's a power strong in Joseph's mind now, visible in his motions.

But she was there. Joseph's denials can't change that fact. I'd seen her with my own eyes.

'The man had to die!' Joseph shouts, and I notice that he completely avoids answering my question. 'I don't mind that it had to be bloody. I can live with that.'

My anger deepens and I take a step towards him in the darkness.

'I'm not talking about him! I'm talking about—'

My sentence is cut off. Before I can say 'her' another time, Joseph is swinging at me again, but it's not his fist that rounds towards me. He's swung the rifle over his shoulder and is aiming it straight at my face. There is still blood crusted on the barrel and stock. It's purple, almost black, in the shady moonlight.

46

Taped Recording Cassette #057A Interviewer: P. Lavrentis

The cassette whirs to life in the usual way. The small speakers crackle before the conversation picks up from the last point in the dialogue.

It is Pauline whose voice first emerges from the speakers.

'Tell me, Joseph, about the actual night of the murders.' Despite the content of her question, her voice is calm and non-judgemental.

'Murders?' the male voice answers. Joseph sounds taken aback. 'Why do you say murders? It's not like I'm a serial killer. I told you I only killed the woman.'

Pauline Lavrentis's voice is ever so slightly hesitant in response. 'Okay. Maybe that was the wrong way for me to begin.' A lull indicates her reflection on what words ought to come next. She remembers that hesitation. He'd thrown up a wall; she'd had to get around it. 'Let's set that aside for now. Tell me what you remember, in as much detail as you can, about that night.'

A long pause seems longer on the cassette, which rotates slowly in the absence of sound before Joseph finally answers.

'That's hard to talk about.'

'I know, but it's important. It's important that we look back at what happened out there at the farmhouse.'

'I was angry, I guess,' he answers. 'Angry that nothing was being done, and that so much evil was being allowed to take place.'

'Is that what drove you? Your anger?'

'The anger was just part of it. An aftereffect. What got me going was what happened inside those walls.'

'And you wanted to do something about that, since what was happening there made you mad?'

'I wanted to kill him!' Joseph snaps. His voice is suddenly harsh. 'That's all there was to it. Not rocket science. I wanted to kill him. To make him pay.'

'Now that's very interesting,' Pauline says. She permits a note of encouragement into her voice.

'You always say the stupidest things when I tell you something that really matters,' Joseph bites back. 'Like you're "troubled" when I confess I'm a murderer, or it's "interesting" when I say I wanted to kill.'

'Joseph, listen to me,' she presses, 'what's interesting

isn't that you said you wanted to kill. We both already knew that.' She pauses, waiting – hoping – for him to recognize where she's leading, but when he doesn't she carries forward.

'Do you realize that you've just said "him"?'

Joseph hesitates. Then his anger snaps again.

'Of course I did! Why the fuck are you hanging on that? I wanted to kill him. Kill him because of the things going on in that house.'

'I know what was motivating you, Joseph. It's just that in the past, even until just a few moments ago, you've always insisted that you killed a woman. A her. But you've just said you wanted to kill "him." To make "him" pay.'

Seconds pass in silence.

'Maybe I . . . maybe I meant her.' Joseph's voice bears the hallmarks of confusion. His words slur slightly together. 'It could have been a her, actually. Now that you mention it. I've always said it was a woman.'

Pauline interjects. 'No, Joseph, don't let these thoughts get away from you, and don't fall back on old patterns. I'm trying to tell you that you're making progress.'

Joseph snorts, but doesn't say anything. The lull between them feels uncomfortable.

'Tell me the sequence of what happened,' Pauline finally prompts.

Joseph shuffles in his chair. 'I'd found the bastard, that's what happened. Found him in his little hidey hole, even though he thought he'd never be rooted out. He was a damned fool, that one. I knew what sort of things he was responsible for.' Joseph halts at his own words, as if they suddenly resonate with him in a new way. Then, 'Yes, I guess it was a him. Yeah. You're right. It was a man.'

She sighs, and it is definitely a sound of pleasure. Of relief. The goose bumps that had risen along her back at the thought of him closing up entirely, she recalls, had tingled as they receded.

'So the face you're seeing now, the one you wanted to kill, back then . . . it's a man's face?'

'God, I hated that bastard,' Joseph answers. 'With everything in me. More than I've ever hated anything or anyone else in my life.'

'So you knew him in advance of the attack?' Pauline is keeping her voice at a neutral register, but she can't fully conceal her enthusiasm. They are, at last, making what she considers progress. 'There must have been some past between you, for you to harbour such strong feelings.'

'Do you have to actually know a man to hate him?' Joseph asks back. 'Can't it be enough that he is who he is? When he's that . . . *vile*.' The word is slippery as he utters it. Venomous.

'Some men are simply deserving of hate, whether you know them or not. And in the end, who really does?'

47

Thursday

I've never before had a gun pointed at me. I've sometimes wondered what it would feel like, if it ever happened. In films people usually cower in a kind of whimpering, emasculated terror, begging for mercy and making promises of whatever they can think of to deter the individual holding it. Money, servitude, favours. Or they're belligerent bastards who don't care whether they live or die, who manage to say something threateningly witty despite the circumstance.

In the moment, my reaction is neither of these. I don't whimper or beg or plea, but nor do I respond aggressively. In fact I can't get out any words at all. All I see is the barrel. I'm puzzled by the fact that it seems to be so still: perfectly aimed at a spot between my eyes, even though Joseph, holding it, is a heaving wreck of movement. And I'm amazed at the thought that this very gun, the one he's holding, had been able to do so much damage. Such a tiny hole at the end of that barrel, barely a pinprick. And yet I'd seen it wreak such terrible things.

I find it extremely odd, but I really don't feel afraid. And I can't say that I have any profound thoughts, either – no flashing-of-the-life-before-one's-eyes sort of event. It's the strangest thing, but in this moment what shoots into my mind is a memory, calm and wonderful and peaceful. A memory evoked by the trees around us more than the gun barrel in my eyes. My body is a mix of panic, adrenalin, fear and fury, my skin caked in sweat and dust and blood, and in the forest I experience a moment of perfect calm.

It's a little over two years ago. I'm not in the forest, but in the heady melee of my arrival in San Francisco, with all the bustle and change involved in a move. Yes, in the present reality of circumstance I'm on my knees in the woods, but in this instant I am also content and joyful in the city. That's the way memory works. Here in this scenario of impossible violence and a gun in my eyes, I'm back at that instant where I at last found a spot to call my own. I'm kneeling in hell, but the thoughts that fill my mind are of that joyful day when I finally found heaven.

I wasn't sure, when I first entered the city, whether I ever would. Everything in that foreign place is concrete and noise: roads, corridors, traffic, people. And I don't mind all that, I really don't. But everyone needs a place of their own. A place apart that's a refuge from the noise of the world.

And I'd at last discovered mine. I'd found it within a great wilderness that sits right in the middle of the bustle. Golden Gate Park: the Central Park of the City by the Bay. It's a vast expanse of the most exquisitely cared-for greenery, fifty-three city blocks from east to west and between five and six from north to south. It's stunning that the city cares so much for green space that it's allowed its heart to be vastly gutted for this purpose – but what bliss has come about as a result.

I blink, and for a moment I see the black night and dark, towering trees of the forest. I see the gun barrel and I can hear the fluttering gasps of Joseph's breath. But a light flashes in my mind and the greens around me are once again tended, bright and glorious.

My first visit to the park was actually a drive-through. I experience the moment again now – the taste of the outside air sneaking into my car, the sound of the birds unseen in their trees. Though it's mostly a haven for pedestrians, there are a few roads that criss-cross the park, and 19th Avenue, the main drive from the peninsula up towards the Golden Gate, bisects it almost perfectly through the middle. I hadn't realized what was there the first time I drove my car from the bridge towards the southern neighbourhoods of the city – the Sunset, Merced Manor, Ingleside, Daly City. From the street you can only see a border of greenery, a sign that there is something next to the road other than houses, but there's no indication of just how magnificent the space is that lies on either side of the road.

My eyes began to be opened when I got onto my feet and found one of the first great wonders of the park. Hidden just out of sight in a bend in that very road, past which thousands of cars drive every day on their commutes, is the largest standing stone cross in North America. The Prayer Book Cross, erected in honour of the first English-language Christian services on the West Coast, back on St John the Baptist's Day in 1579. Now, I'm not one for the Prayer Book (no Episcopalian roots in me), but I can't imagine a person who wouldn't stand in awe of this cross. It's the size of a small office building, absolutely massive, atop a hill that wants to tower over the landscape around it, and maybe once it did, before the park was planted. But the trees that surround it now have become thick and monumental in their own right, so this extraordinary sight – literally a hundred yards from the swerving traffic of 19th Avenue – is almost completely unknown even to locals.

I relished in the sight the first time I saw it. I thought I was dreaming when I found the enormous waterfall (fake, of course) that flows from its base down to the main ground level at the bottom of the hill.

This is a place that cares about beauty, in the middle of busy life.

I'd been back just about every day since, checking out

all the varied wonders that Golden Gate Park contains. Two Dutch-style windmills. A polo field. A paddleboat-laden lake with Chinese pagodas and a peaking island at its centre known as Strawberry Hill. A rose garden. A statuary park. A lawn bowling club. Countless fountains. A Japanese tea garden.

Isn't it strange, that a man with a gun in his face should remember a Japanese tea garden? That with the blood still wet on my skin, I recollect in such vivid clarity the sloping red roofs of the pagodas?

Finally, after all that wandering, I'd found my spot. The Botanical Gardens occupy a plot of land running along the park's southern edge from 9th to 18th Avenues, a triangle set aside for the most beautiful sights in a venue full of beautiful sights. From the first moment I stepped into it I knew I had found my refuge.

It was another three months of wandering before I settled on the pearl of it all. Three months, just to explore the Gardens! Even with all that, I'm sure there are paths I've not covered. Little alcoves and expertly curated scenelets that I've yet to see. But once I found the pond I lost the drive to explore. I know there's more beauty out there, but it took just one look to know this was something different. This was *my* beauty. And once you've found the beauty that touches your heart, you don't keep looking. You let it take hold of you, and you give yourself to it without qualification.

I'm looking into Joseph's gun again, now. The blood caked on its shaft isn't beautiful. Joseph isn't beautiful.

I'm fairly certain I'll be dead within a few seconds – that's usually the outcome once situations have gone so far that a rifle is aimed at your eyes. But I know there's beauty out there. I've seen it and tasted it and revelled in it. And it's strange, but that memory actually brings me an overwhelming peace.

48

Thursday

Joseph doesn't kill me, in the end. He keeps the rifle levelled on me for what might have been a few minutes or only a few seconds. Memories have the power to shift vast expanses of time into mere instants. But by the time my memory is fading and the vision of the park receding, Joseph is lowering the rifle.

His head is shaking. He's scolding himself, and I don't think he can bear to look at me.

'I'm . . . I'm sorry,' he mutters, his face turned away from mine. 'I didn't mean that. I shouldn't have pointed the gun at you.'

I contemplate answering, but there's little to say.

'It's just, well, you know. Nerves,' he continues. His face darts about the dark trees again. He's all nervousness. 'You know, people could be looking for us. You were shouting.'

Now I do want to say something, to assure him of a fact that to my surprise is actually true: I'm not angry. I'm not upset with him for holding me at riflepoint. I should be, by any and all accounts. But it stirred up the most beautiful memory, and I can't quite force myself to be mad at him, despite the threat his actions so obviously implied.

'We're under a lot of stress,' is all I manage. I don't know how to say those other things. I've never been good at sharing emotion in anything other than a poem.

'You know I wouldn't hurt you, Dylan,' he answers. I'm not too emotional to acknowledge the irony of the comment, coming from a man who'd had both a fist at my face and a gun between my eyes within the past fifteen minutes. But he'd stopped himself both times. I think he's being honest.

But he still hasn't answered my question, the one that initiated this moment. I want to know one thing above all else, and it's the one thing that it's now abundantly clear we won't be discussing, at least not here.

There was no woman. There is no 'her'.

Finally Joseph looks squarely at me.

'Are you hungry?' The question is absurd. Of all the situationally inappropriate comments he could make, he goes and . . . but then I realize that yes, actually. I'm not just hungry.

'Starving,' I answer. Perhaps violence requires more than a usual intake of nutrients. It's not something I've ever thought of before, but the fact is I'm completely famished.

'I don't suppose you have any food in that pack of yours?' I ask.

Joseph shakes his head. 'Left it back on the hill before we went in. Didn't want to be toting extra weight.'

That ruled it out. Neither of us was willing to even suggest returning to the landscape around the farmhouse.

'Well we can't just sit here,' I say. 'But we're in no condition to walk into town.' He looks at me, puzzled, and I motion towards my clothes and then to his. We're both caked in blood.

Joseph grins, broad and ironic. 'No, guess we can't.'

His amusement troubles me, but he doesn't give me time to ponder it. He's already reaching out a hand to lift me onto my feet.

'Come on. I know a place we can go.'

49

Taped Recording Cassette #057A Interviewer: P. Lavrentis

The conversation on the cassette is moving faster now than usual, but not too fast for the words to be clear and distinguishable in the recording.

There is an expectation in Dr Pauline Lavrentis's voice. It is evident that she regards the last few moments of their conversation to have been critical and doesn't want to lose the momentum.

'You say you hated this man,' she says. 'The one you went there to attack. And I believe you truly did hate him. Is that why you did what you did that night?'

There are sounds of Joseph squirming in his seat. 'I did what I did because it needed to be done, that's all. I've told you that before.'

'Those are vague words, Joseph. Be more precise. What was it that needed to be done?' A bit chiding. He'd needed to be goaded on.

'You have the trial transcripts, for fuck's sake! Everybody knows what happened.'

'That's right, I have the papers,' Pauline answers, 'and I've read them several times through. But you've never accepted those records, Joseph. Not since you've been here. You've always insisted they aren't the real story.'

'Lies, that's what they are.' Joseph's voice has become angry again. 'Never known half the story, and they're always cocksure of everything. That's the way everyone is. So sure of themselves when they don't understand a fraction of what's really going on.'

'Tell me, then, in your own way, what it was you felt "had to be done" that evening at the farmhouse.' Pauline's voice is soothing, but urging. 'I'm giving you that chance. No buffers, no other people involved. No one claiming to know the story. For right now, I'll know only what you tell me, nothing else.'

Joseph lingers in reflection for a long while before answering. Thirty-seven seconds.

'I'd heard more than I could bear. That's all.' A hesitation. When he speaks again, there is a pleading agony in his voice. 'Nobody could bear what I'd listened to. I mean, have you ever heard a man talk to his wife like that?'

'Like what, Joseph?'

'Like a damned animal. No, worse than an animal.

Worse than a beast. Have you sat outside a house like I sat outside that one, listening to him beat her? Watched her emerge the next morning, blue and red and broken? Have you?' Joseph is shouting his questions. Spittle can be heard flying off his lips.

'No, Joseph,' Pauline answers soothingly. There is authentic sorrow in her voice. 'I wasn't there. I haven't had those experiences.' She can't help feeling, as she listens to the recording now, the same gulp of oxygenless emotion that had choked her throat as he spoke.

'Then you can't fucking know what I was feeling, not even the littlest bit. None of you can.' He draws in a deep breath. 'I'd been listening, watching for a while. When he didn't think anyone was there, or that anyone knew what he was up to – I knew. I'd made sure I could be a witness to all of it.'

'You'd found a way to keep an eye on him?'

'I'd found a place where he never knew I was watching. I could see and I could hear. I was never far away. And I kept waiting for it to stop. Waiting for things to change. But when they didn't, then I knew that I had to stop him.' He hesitates. 'Yes, definitely a him. You were right before.' Then, matter-of-factly, as if the statement fixed a great many things, 'I didn't kill my wife. I'm sorry I said I did.'

'It's okay. What you're acknowledging right now, it makes a lot of things clearer.'

Joseph takes in another deep breath. His next words flow like data being read off a prompter. 'I did what had to be done. *What had to be done.* No one else was going to, that much had become clear. I'd let enough time pass that if anyone else was going to step up to the plate and act appropriately, they would have. But there's a limit to everything. So I got some guns and took the responsibility that others wouldn't.'

'Where did you get the guns?' Pauline asks.

'It's not hard to get weapons, not out there. Everyone's got 'em. I snatched a few from neighbouring houses, I think.'

'So you definitely had a plan for this. You'd worked it out in advance?'

'Yes, I guess I must have. If I went round looking for the guns and things. Probably had it worked out in my mind what I was going to do.'

The sound of Pauline's pencil taking down a note scratches across the recording. She has the note before her now, as she listens. *Worked it out in my mind. A plan.*

'And then?' she finally asks. 'What came of your plan?'

'Well,' Joseph answers, 'it must have come off just fine.'

'Meaning?'

There is no pause at all.

'He's dead, isn't he?'

50

Thursday

It takes us nearly forty minutes to arrive at the place Joseph has in mind. He seems familiar with the forest, but we'd run away from the farmhouse in a frantic beeline, and it takes him a little while to reorientate himself and figure out just where we are and which direction we need to go. But once we're in motion, Joseph guides us expertly through the dark terrain.

It's hard to describe the blackness of a forest at night to someone who's never experienced it. It isn't just dark, the way towns get dark, or the way a hillside is dark in the starlight. Forests at night are like the world beneath a blanket. Only on rare occasion does a moonbeam make it through the trees as far as the ground, which otherwise is too black even for shadows.

Yet Joseph moves swiftly, as if he knows every log, every rise and fall of the forest floor. I struggle to keep up. I chide myself for not having thought to bring a flashlight, and then the scolding makes me laugh. When this day began, I had never thought I'd be in a forest. I'd never thought I'd have had a gun in my hand and . . .

We arrive at the spot at what I assume must be shortly before midnight. At first I can't make out just what it is we've come to. It seems at first to be only a black blob in the darker blackness around it. Then it looks like a mound. Maybe a hill. But as my eyes adjust and I draw closer, I can see it's not a hill but a pile – a pile of odds and ends that have clearly been assembled here intentionally. It looks like there's a bed frame in the mix. Definitely some corrugated metal roofing sheets, laid at angles. Some old, broken chairs. A tyre or two. The rubbish of the forest, always a favoured spot to get rid of household extras without paying removal fees to the state, had been gathered and assembled into this place. For what purpose I had no idea.

'Come on in,' Joseph says as we draw closer. The words confuse for just an instant, and then his meaning becomes clear. He lifts back a sheet of plywood – once painted but now mouldy and warped – and reveals a hollow space inside the pile.

This is a shanty. A kind of dwelling. What a child would call a fort, but what it suddenly seems, in this instant, might actually be Joseph's home.

He's holding up the plywood sheet, looking impatient. 'You coming in or not?'

There's no reason for me not to comply, so I walk up

to what passes as the entrance, duck low and shimmy into the interior space. Joseph follows, releasing the plywood with a thud.

It takes him a few seconds to get it going, but in short order Joseph has lit a propane lamp that hangs from a jagged nail, its sharp end pointing ominously outward, protruding from what I think is the remains of a wooden pallet. The kind forklifts use to shift heavy loads. As the lamp comes up to its hissing brightness, I'm able to take in the surroundings. We're seated (there isn't really room to stand comfortably, so I'd sat automatically once I'd made my way in) on two layers of blankets that are heavily stained and mouldy, but which provide a decent amount of insulation from the earth below. The shape of the space that surrounds us is close to a dome, perhaps four feet in height by a circumference of six, and the 'walls' are a mixture of rubbish-heap oddities. A wire bed frame is the largest single element, and Joseph – I'm assuming it's Joseph who's crafted this place – has woven a tattered blue tarpaulin through the wires to give it a semblance of solidity. Another segment of wall is made up of a stack of furniture pieces, which include chair backs and drawers from a bureau. I don't recognize every feature around me, but the 'roof' overhead is clearly a star-shaped criss-crossing of two-by-fours and one-by-fours over which Joseph has flung a large sheet of heavy clear plastic, tying it down with some of the same yellow cords I remember seeing on his pack. It looks like it might almost be waterproof, though I'd hate to be the one to put it to the test.

'It isn't much,' Joseph says, noticing my wandering eyes, 'but it isn't bad. Pillow there in the corner if you need to lay down and catch some sleep.'

The pillow looks as old and worn out as everything else in the shanty.

'Joseph,' I finally ask, 'do you . . . live here?'

It had never occurred to me that this muscular teenager, who spoke with a degree of country simplicity but was clearly capable, and even occasionally bordered at the precipice of profound thoughts, might be homeless.

'Haven't for long,' he answers, 'but for the moment it's as good as home.' He smiles, and there's a kind of pride on his face. He doesn't view this creation as anything to be ashamed of. 'Got a cooler over there and there's some food in it. A couple of beers too. Pass us some, would you?'

I look around until I find the cooler. Inside there are a handful of plastic-wrapped sandwiches, the kind sold at service stations and generally considered the last resort of the food-starved traveller. I find myself wondering whether these have been stolen, swiped by Joseph on trips into town in order to stock the larder of his strange little dwelling.

But if he's a shoplifter, he's clearly a good one. There are also six or seven cans of Coors Light in the cooler, along with a brick of cheese and a two-pound package of raw hamburger meat. Perhaps in addition to a propane lamp Joseph also has some means to cook, out here in the middle of the forest.

I grab a sandwich for myself and one for Joseph, together with two beers, and close the cooler. A moment later and we're both wolfing through our makeshift meal in this makeshift hut.

'We'll be safe now,' Joseph says after he's polished off the last of his sandwich. 'Nobody knows about this place.'

He doesn't seem inclined to offer me much more than that. No explanation for these surroundings, no expansion on what 'being safe' really means. But it's clear there is more to Joseph than I know, which really shouldn't surprise me. I've known him only a few hours, and not a single minute has been anything other than exceptional.

Suddenly I am overwhelmingly tired. I must look it, too, because Joseph's next words are, 'Yeah, it's time for rest. You take the pillow. There's a blanket just there.'

'What about you?' I just manage to ask as my eyelids go down with remarkable speed and weight.

'I'll lie down over here. I'll be fine.'

And he seems to smile, and look almost compassionate, as I retreat beneath my eyelids and escape to an almost instantaneous sleep.

51

Friday

In the morning I awake in an inconsolable panic. Before there is a thought in my head there is sweat covering my body and my breath is already coming in short flutters. It takes a few seconds for me to register my surroundings, to piece together the events of the previous evening and try to sort out why I've awoken in such a state, but when I do the panic just increases.

I'm in the woods. Somewhere behind me is the farmhouse. And in the house are bodies.

I can barely breathe.

I roll over, the surreal surroundings of the forest shanty only adding to the abnormality of my emotions. Joseph is still lying on the other side of the hut. The sun is starting to rise – a few beams of light are working their way through the plastic sheeting above us – but he's still sleeping. His chest rises and falls slowly.

I let my head fall back down onto the damp-stained pillow. I'm not a man prone to self-pity, but for an instant I despair over my lot. Two days ago I was at home in Diamond Heights. I was in my shop. I was in the park. Yes, things had become a little odd, but at least the surroundings were familiar. But now I'm here, lying in the forest, and for the first time in my life I have blood on my body that isn't my own.

But then my self-pity begins to change. I feel like weeping, like bemoaning my lot; yet I'm here for a reason, and that reason fends off the tears.

I'd come to Redding for the boy. I'd run into that house for the boy. I'd done the things I'd done with Joseph – all for the boy. And he'd come to me, he'd shown me the way. He'd brought me to that hilltop, with the blood on his arm and the bruise that ate at his flesh. And he'd spoken to me.

And I hadn't seen him since.

He'd spoken to me as we charged down the hill towards his home and his torture, or at least I think he had. The boy's always been concrete, ordinary if compelling, in all my encounters. But that one was surreal. I remember him motionless and stalwart even as the world was sliding by and my feet in a flurry of movement. I remember a deep voice. I remember words that seemed out of character.

It's possible, and the longer I ponder on it, quite probable, that this was my imagination. I was as charged up as I've ever been, about to do something beyond my immediate comprehension, and I think I simply wished his face into existence. Because he wasn't as real then. Not like he'd been by the pond. Not like he'd been on the hilltop.

And not like he must be now, wherever he is.

He wouldn't have told me to stop, not when I was about to save him. He wouldn't have asked me to retreat.

But now he isn't talking to me at all, and I feel the most immense loneliness without him. I wonder where he's gone, and what it is going to take to find him.

52

The Boy in the Park, Stanza 7

But how long stay the buried down
In darkness cold and unknowing?
Until the prey becomes
the beast
And tigers roar with claws unfurled;
Killing hope yet ending the tears,
Of the little boy weeping . . .
The little boy weeping . . .

53

Saturday

We've been in the woods almost two full days. Joseph has been proved right: no one has found us here, and the surroundings have been almost tranquil. We've been working our way through the food in his cooler, and Joseph is convinced that it will be easy to get more. He's got the rifle so we can hunt, and there's always the option of going back into town and swiping more supplies from various shops in an act that Joseph describes as if it's a familiar pattern.

I, though, am becoming more and more anxious as the hours pass. Two days here is about as much as I can handle.

'Joseph, we can't just sit here like this.'

He peers at me from a log. We're sitting outside his shanty. It's a bright day and the air is crisp, and Joseph's face bears the marks of genuine surprise.

'Why not?' He seems to think it reasonable that we can stay here as long as we want. Maybe forever.

'Joseph, eventually people are going to discover what we've done. They're going to find the bodies, and then they're going to start looking for who did it.'

'They don't know it was us.'

'But they're sure as hell going to look everywhere.'

'We're far away,' he protests. I shake my head.

'You know we're not that far. This place may feel remote, but if they start a manhunt – which they will – they're definitely going to include the woods. It won't take them long to find this place.'

Joseph looks uneasy, but doesn't say anything. Not at first.

'We could go to the city,' I suggest. 'San Francisco's only a half-day's journey. I have a car, parked back the way we came.'

He ponders the idea, but it's clear he doesn't like it.

'No, if you're right then the city's too close. For that matter, anywhere in the state's too close. Like you said, people are going to be looking for us.'

I'm pleased he's understood my point and the need for us to remove ourselves from the surroundings, but I'm disappointed at his rejecting the idea of San Francisco. It's the place I know best, and the thought of returning there is comforting.

'We're going to have to go a lot further,' he continues. 'If we're going to get away, we should do it well.'

'Where do you suggest?' I'm now asking him for thoughts on my own plan.

'I'm thinking. Give me a minute to sort things out.'

It's a little strange, that the teenager is the one telling the adult to give him time to sort out the details. But I don't have any immediate suggestions, myself. I can't think of the last time I've been outside of the state of California. For an instant, all geography fails me. In the map in my mind there is simply nothing beyond the state lines. California, then blackness.

'Well, I guess that'll do,' Joseph finally says, responding to a thought that's occurred only in his mind.

'You've got an idea?'

When he turns to me something of the humanity and determination I remembered from our first encounter are back in his eyes. Just a touch of them. Glimmering in the jade-green.

'I've always liked country music,' he answers. 'You ever been to Nashville?'

54

Sunday

We are going to be on the road for a while. Several days, at least. Maybe a week, depending on the route we take. A week in the cramped confines of my little car, two men and the uncontainable cloud of an event too massive to be held in any small space.

I can tell, after only our first few hours on the road, that the darkness hovering over us is going to become as oppressive as any acts we've committed – and now that we've fled the woods and the little pretend home where we'd pretended nothing had happened, we're confronted anew with reality. It's back, with all its fearful force and oppressive bulk. We can't go on simply sitting in its shadow. A person can only take it so long. From one perspective the darkness is mysterious and haunting and inviting; when you're peering in, it's where dragons and monsters and adventures lie. But once you're there, you realize that darkness is cold and empty. That there are no dragons, only dust and empty rooms.

I still have my Moleskine in my pocket. The realization comes to me as a sudden comfort – an embrace. I have my notebook and my pencil and unending time on the road with nowhere to escape to but the world of my thoughts. I can let the memories of the past hours haunt me, or I can make them fruitful. That's what true poets do. Joseph can drive and I can regain my identity; and with it, I hope, a trace of my calm.

These aren't going to be hours of the contemplation of flowers and birdsong, of course. But not all poems are like that. It's nice, under normal circumstances, to see the beauty of the world in ways that others don't – to behold leaves as dancing wings fluttering at the ends of branches, to see the greens of nature as the varied brushstrokes of the canvas of the world. There's a reason a lot of poetry is gaudily over-beautiful. It's because poets know what it means to see beauty. They can be forgiven if sometimes they forget that writing about it can too easily come off like sucking on saccharin, everything turning sickly sweet.

But a poet can't suffer in his heart and write only of beauty with his pen. The internal and the external are supposed to collide in the ink of a poem. In my mind I have the whole canvas of nature; the beauty of my bench in the park is always with me, always in my thoughts, even here in the cramped car with blood-soaked clothes and Joseph silently at the wheel. I'm watching the wings of the wilderness dance in the breeze, but I'm letting them flap their way into the darkness of my new reality. I'm seeing the sun shine in the memories of flowerbeds, yet I'm aware of the darkness that now follows me around, and which I fear may do so forever, even into the brightest sunshine.

In the lamplight of the passenger seat my pencil is recording it all, the pages taking in their stories. And though for the moment it's only in my memory, only in the perfect image in my mind, I've noted – maybe for the first time – that the remarkable reflection of the world in my pond is, for all its beauty, upside down. Inverted. Shimmering, but wrong. The treetops there don't point up to heaven. They are mesmerizing and beautiful, but they point down, down into the belly of the earth where there is only darkness and fire.

And suddenly I'm more afraid than I've ever been in my life. More afraid than I was when I first saw the little boy's wounds. More afraid than I was in the forest, or in the house. More afraid than I was when Joseph held the gun to my face in his rage. I'm afraid because for a moment, just the briefest moment, I wonder whether all my poems amount to anything at all. Whether poetry itself is only a deception. Whether stories are only lies that belittle the darkness. I'm confronted with a reality too terrible for my heart to imagine. Sometimes, a story is just the thing we tell ourselves to escape the ordinariness of a life that has no tale to tell at all.

VACAVILLE, CALIFORNIA

55

Conference Room 4C
California Medical Facility – State Prison

There are three chairs on one side of a beige table in the small room. Behind each is a civil official in civilian attire: a grey-haired man in the middle, who is a full three inches taller than both the others and whose demeanour suggests he's at the head of the small panel; an auburn-haired woman in a violet business suit to his right, who is tapping her plastic pen on her papers in frustration already, before they've even begun; and a black man of almost equal age to the first, in a darker suit, to his left. His is the sternest look of the three: hard, holding back what appears to be a desire to launch into an angry yell at any moment. Instead, he busies himself by scrolling through messages on his phone, laid flat on the table in front of him.

Despite the fact that there are three microphones on the table, one aimed at each of them, a stenographer sits at a small desk to the side. The stenographer is making no effort at avoiding the clichés of her profession: a tight dress that would still be considered skimpy if it were six inches longer, hair done up in a multi-layer nest. She has her keyboard comfortably in front of her and the control monitors for the microphones close beside it.

The door to the room is locked. This is to be a closed inquiry, uninterrupted. A few jugs of water and a tray of fruit lie on the panellists' table, in case refreshment is required during the day.

The only other person in the room is a woman, at a separate table some six feet away from that of the panel. Her table is smaller, though it also contains a microphone, and she is positioned to face the others directly. There is a single glass of water before her.

'If we're all here and accounted for,' the grey-haired man in the middle of the larger table says, ensuring he aims his mouth at the microphone, 'then I say we call these proceedings to order.' The microphone does not magnify his voice. Its purpose, like that of all the others, is only to record.

'Let's roll through all the official stuff first,' he mutters, nodding towards the stenographer. His look is one of mild annoyance, as if this is an unwanted step before their real work begins; but he also appears to be well tried in such proceedings and aware it's an inflexible requirement. He loosens a burgundy tie that clashes badly with his soft blue suit.

'My name is Benjamin Tolbert,' he announces, 'appointed chairman of the inmate conduct review panel.' He nods to the woman at his right, offering a business-like smile that deepens the creases at the corners of his eyes.

'Christina Vermille,' the woman says, a slight southern twang to her vowels. 'Deputy consultant for the committee.' She speaks rapidly, as if efficiency is of the utmost importance. Her spectacles have fashionable rims, and in general she presents herself as an extremely well-kept woman.

Finally, the black man adds his own credentials to the recording. 'Tyrone Davis. Warden.' His manner is clipped and direct. He doesn't look up while he speaks, and the thinning hair at the top of his head is showing some grey. He is a man of bulk, almost all of it muscle, and every facet of his demeanour is one of frustration.

'And that brings us to you,' the chairman says, nodding towards the woman at the table opposite them. 'Would you please state your name and position for the record?'

'Dr Pauline Lavrentis, forensic psychologist here at Vacaville.'

Tolbert takes a moment to scratch a few notes onto a yellow legal pad before looking up at Pauline. She sits cross-legged at her small table, every inch of her the professional. Her jacket is navy blue and trousers beige, her hair a sandy grey that says wisdom rather than age.

She wears a gold chain around her glasses, but on Pauline it doesn't seem either grannyish or passé. She is a woman who exudes confidence and comfort – a surety in her work, her person, and, in this room, her credentials.

'Thanks for that,' Tolbert replies. 'Now I don't want any of us to feel too formal about all this. We're all on the same side here. Just trying to figure out what happened, and why, and where we go from here.'

'I understand,' Pauline answers. 'I'm happy to give whatever assistance I can, beyond my printed notes and the recordings, which I believe the committee already has in its possession.'

'We have,' the chairman confirms. 'We've all had the chance to listen to them, as I trust you've also done, to refresh yourself of the details of the case before we move forward.'

Pauline merely nods her confirmation. It had not been easy to listen to the recordings, to re-live all the conversations that had led up to this moment, but she'd known it would be a necessity, especially if she wished to make the strongest possible argument, and even more especially given what she hopes to accomplish at this hearing. The nuances will be important. Essential.

The chairman glances through a few sheets at the top of the stack of papers before him. He turns to the warden. 'Let's start with the core details and go from there, shall we?'

The other man, the warden, finally looks up from his phone. His eyes are heavy, and faced fully on they reveal a frustration that isn't with the people in this room. He is frustrated with a situation that seems to be escalating beyond his ability to control it.

'The facts are straightforward,' he says, following the chairman's prompting. 'Your patient's aggressive behaviour,' he nods towards Dr Lavrentis, 'has escalated exponentially, leading to his third escape attempt since his incarceration began. This last was at just after two fifteen in the morning a week and a half ago, during the third night watch.' The frustrated look intensifies. 'What sets this one apart is the degree of violence that it involved.' These words obviously eat at him.

Pauline nods. She's aware of the details, and shares the warden's disappointment. If, perhaps, for reasons that differ from his. Her relationship to the inmate is not the same.

'This attempt was made in conjunction with two other men,' the warden continues. 'None made it past the fences, though they got a hell of a lot farther than they should have done' – he appears as if he's making a mental note, jotting down details on precisely who's to be lambasted for precisely what failures in security – 'and the attempt involved physical attacks against our guards.'

A moment's silence overtakes the meeting. Any time an inmate's actions involve attacking a guard they automatically invoke harsh responses.

'What we need to know', the grey-haired chairman continues, taking over from the warden, 'is just what's going on in the mind of your patient, Dr Lavrentis. We all recognize that his situation here is going to have to change. His actions mandate that. But some additional information may help us chart a course for his future incarceration.'

'May I ask a question about the other inmates who made the attempt with my patient?' Pauline interposes. She reaches forward and draws the microphone closer to herself. She is familiar with being recorded. She grabs a pencil and readies herself to jot down notes from the replies.

'One is a twice-convicted felon,' the suited woman on the committee answers. 'Three times down for fraud on smaller counts before the two felony charges stuck. Felony assault and felony burglary. The other for repeated counts of aggressive social disorder.'

'But they ended up here?'

'Both were unstable enough that their lawyers pled them to cells with us rather than in San Quentin.'

Pauline jots down the details. 'Violent?'

'Aren't they all?' the warden snaps back, rhetorically.

'All very fascinating,' the chairman continues, 'but our purpose here this afternoon is learn more about progress with inmate #10481-91, since he is the most troubling of the three. He's the one who had the shank, the one who attacked the guard. He's been in your diagnostic care for some time, is that correct, Dr Lavrentis?'

Pauline rises slightly in her seat, adopting a yet more formal, professional posture. She speaks with confidence and an authority borne of long experience in her field.

'That's correct. I've been working with him, on and off, for the past eight months. I took over after Dr Grainger left for Colorado.'

'And how was that . . . work . . . going?' The voice of Christina Vermille is tainted with what sounds like suspicion of the whole process. Pauline accepts the question, and the tone, without being fazed by either. Vermille's role on the committee is to question everything, including the efficacy of the confinement and treatment. Suspicion is entirely appropriate.

'I consider that we were making progress,' Pauline answers honestly. 'He'd been beginning to confront the reality of his crimes.'

'Beginning? In all this time he hadn't done so before?'

'I'm afraid it's no surprise that he hadn't. That's the nature of his personality and his actions. He's a man of intense repression.'

'Repression or not,' the warden kicks in, 'he's an individual who's unstable and whose crimes more than justify his confinement here. Who's been involved in two prior escape attempts, and now, with this.' His hands are in the air in a sign of self-evident emphasis.

Pauline says nothing. The warden extinguishes his interjection with a sigh and lets his arms collapse back onto the table.

'The warden is right. Your patient's record indicates a pattern of increasing instability. Yet you still consider that you were having success?' Vermille presses.

'I do. Progress in these matters is often very slow,

especially given the psychological effects of incarceration itself. But we were seeing signs of real steps forward.'

'Though I take it that none of those signs included a proper confession? An admission of his acts?'

Again Pauline doesn't answer. She's too experienced to fall prey to leading questions. The panel is well aware of the content of her reports, and the fact that they don't include bringing her patient to such an admission. Not to the degree that any of them would like.

'Sounds like this is a man who doesn't want to take responsibility for those actions,' Vermille continues. A nod of agreement from the warden, and even the wizened and grandfatherly visage of the chairman is bobbing in affirmation.

'Actually, it's quite the opposite,' Pauline counters. Her fingers are interlaced on the table before her. Her eyes bear directly into those of the other woman, then sweep slowly and deliberately to each of the men.

'Accepting responsibility is precisely what he was trying to do. Especially over our last few conversations. I got further with him in those sessions than over the past several months.'

'But we have reports his aggressive tendencies increased during that precise period, and I remember the experiences personally,' the warden interrupts. 'My guards had to sedate him multiple times when his temper flared beyond limits they felt were safe. And you won't have forgotten that he attacked you as well, Doctor. Threw a table at you, if I remember the incident report correctly.'

'It wasn't *at* me,' Pauline counters. The encounter refreshes itself in her mind – the tension of the inmate's body; the acrid smell of the sudden spike of adrenalin in his sweat in the small room. 'He was simply acting out. Even the guards that entered the room noted that he threw the table to the side, not in my direction.' She gazes across the three faces opposite her, recognizing this was a hard sell. 'He wasn't intending to harm me, of that I'm certain. It was an outburst, and in someone with his condition, a controlled outburst is actually a good thing. It comes with the territory.'

'He brutally assaulted a cell-block guard during this latest escape attempt,' the warden adds. His words are now accusations. 'Is that also something that "comes with the territory", Dr Lavrentis?'

She sits in silence. Finally she leans towards the microphone again.

'Controlled aggression, the kind we were able to deal with in sessions, is an important part of trying to get to the root of his issues. One of the main factors in his condition is an inability to come to grips with his own emotions.'

'So,' the female panel member interjects, 'the lack of control we read about in the trial records still exists?'

Pauline ponders the question thoughtfully. 'Yes, in a sense. His profile remains largely unchanged. He is generally calm, but then things snap into focus. Something brings him to the breaking point, and he folds. And that's when the outbursts come.'

'So he maintains as much control as he can for as long as he can,' the warden interrupts, 'but then eventually snaps and goes violent. This is the profile of a killer. It's the profile he had when he first arrived here.'

'The way out of this condition,' Lavrentis answers, pushing back, 'starts with coming to grips with one's own actions. One's behaviours, and the evidence of them from one's past. For all the time I've known him, the patient has denied every element of his crimes.'

'Even that he's a criminal,' the chairman adds, noting a detail from one of his printed pages. 'It says here he's generally denied ever having been involved in the crimes for which he was convicted.'

'That's right, and a denial of guilt, one that's not made just to the authorities as an excuse but to one's own self – a genuine, absolute belief that you've not done anything wrong – that's the thickest layer of skin to get through. Until recently, I couldn't even scratch the outer layer of it. He'd deny his crimes outright, insist everything spoken against him was a lie. But then the first of those concrete signs of progress you were asking for, Mr Chairman.' Pauline glances at Tolbert. 'He began to concoct other crimes to replace them.'

'In other words, lying,' Vermille interjects. 'I don't see how that counts as progress.'

The chairman holds up a hand to stop her. 'Hold on just a moment, Christina. Dr Lavrentis, what sort of other crimes are you talking about?'

'Most recently, he confessed to murdering his wife.'

There is a confused silence from the panel's table. It seems that no one was expecting this.

'His wife?' the warden asks. He's already flipping through his papers, his face confused. 'We have no records of him being married.'

'He never was.' Pauline is content with the wide eyes before her. Surprise, and for a moment at least, a genuine willingness to listen. 'He constructed the wife as a first step towards admitting guilt.'

Vermille can't restrain herself. 'Sounds like a fishy first step, Doctor.'

'That's your judgement.' Lavrentis smiles, attempting to ensure the other woman doesn't take her words as an insult. 'But it's a huge leap from convincing yourself you're an innocent, wrongly accused victim, to admitting you've committed one of the most heinous acts possible. That he constructed a fake person to have done it to was a mental buffer. A way to edge a little closer to the truth, without yet being able to grasp the full horror of what he'd actually done.'

The female investigator leans back in her chair.

Benjamin Tolbert rests his gaze pensively on a fixed point at the far side of the room, pondering Lavrentis's answer. Finally, he turns to face her.

'Would he ever have done that? Understood the full scope of his actions? Was he close?'

Pauline sags slightly. It is her first visible indication of frustration.

'We had just got there.'

56

Conference Room 4C
California Medical Facility

'Dr Lavrentis, I am ready to admit that I'm finding your answers to this committee to be elusive and evasive.' The accusation comes from Christina Vermille, whose whole demeanour radiates her annoyance with the psychology-speak she's hearing from the other woman. 'We've asked for a straightforward answer to a straightforward question. Did the patient ever take full responsibility for his actions? And if so, was it in a spirit of regret or of defiance?' Lavrentis leans forward to answer but Vermille holds up a hand and continues her own remarks before she has a chance.

'The pressing need for a direct answer to these questions should be obvious to a woman of your professional stature, Pauline. If a man who's repressed his violent past has suddenly had it return to him, if he knows what he did and has become comfortable with it, at the same time as his pattern of aggression begins to increase, then we have a man who is a very real threat to the general population of this institution, guards and fellow prisoners alike. Thus far we've treated inmate #10481-91 as a delusional individual who thinks the worst thing he did in life was steal his neighbour's skateboard as a boy. But if he's realized he's something else, and is already acting on that . . .' She allows the conclusion to be drawn without saying anything further.

Pauline Lavrentis waits patiently until she is done.

'I do not disagree with you on any of your points of fact, Ms Vermille,' she finally answers. 'But I must respectfully disagree with the implication that recognizing his crimes leads a man to becoming once again the violent individual he once was. It's actually quite the opposite. The most dangerous condition of all is that of denial. All the anger, all the violence, they're still there. They haven't just vanished. They're lurking under the surface, and at some point they're going to boil up and explode.'

'This is a somewhat regular occurrence?' the chairman asks.

'It is an absolute pattern, sir. Predictable and assured. That is why we spend so much time trying to get these kinds of patients to acknowledge their crimes. It's not to revert them back to their criminal state, but to lead them through an honest awareness of it to a place where they can address its underlying causes.'

Vermille slumps back in her chair, unhappy but unwilling to press the point.

The warden looks directly at Pauline.

'Dr Lavrentis, I have a guard with a shank wound in his abdomen. That's a simple fact, and it's an unacceptable one.' He leans forward. 'The only real question facing this panel is how severe the response should be. You can talk of progress all you want, but this man is a danger. We're trying to figure out whether an indefinite stay in solitary confinement is even enough, or whether we need to have your patient in restraints to prevent more "outbursts" with such violent ends.' The warden's voice is anxious and frustrated.

'I don't think that would be helpful,' Lavrentis answers. There is strain in her voice now, almost worry. 'You're talking about a response that could destroy a man in his state. His mental condition . . . he's fragile. We may be a penal hospital, but we're a medical facility all the same.'

'It's not only him that we have to consider. There are other patients. Staff. Their welfare must be taken into account in all of this. His increasing instability makes him an increasing threat.'

Pauline nods with a certain resignation. The arguments are reasonable. Yet there is a pressing look on her face, as if there is more that the panel needs to understand.

'Isolation could break him. I know he's caused problems, but the damage this could effect, it could be permanent.'

The chairman leans towards her. 'Tell me, Pauline,

what sets this man off, when he has outbursts like this?'

She considers Tolbert's question.

'There can be a number of factors, Mr Chairman. But in this case, he was discovering something about himself that he simply couldn't handle.'

'You mean the details of the murders,' Tolbert replies. 'I can see why. I can't even look at the crime-scene photos, and I've been doing this a lot of years.'

Pauline is shaking her head. 'It's not just the killings, though that's a critical part of it.'

'What else is there?' Vermille asks.

'He was having to come to grips with something worse than what he'd done. He was being forced to discover who he really is.'

57

Taped Recording
Cassette #058A
Interviewer: P. Lavrentis

The final cassette in the case-file drawer is marked #058 and begins with an unusual jumble of mechanical noise. On analysis, it is the sound of fingers fumbling in a rush with the mechanism of the recorder itself. The cassette-change between the preceding recording and this was evidently managed in extreme haste, resulting in a few foibles of grip. Joseph is already speaking, mid-stream through an ongoing sentence, as the noise subsides and his words become audible.

'. . . and when I broke through the door, my plan was only to kill the old man.'

'Can you say that again? You had a plan to kill the man in the house.'

'Fuck's sake, woman, am I talking to myself here? I thought it was your job to listen.'

Pauline doesn't respond. She's given Joseph time to take a few deep breaths, which had calmed him down only a little. The anger on his face, she remembers, had been fixed as if in plastic.

A pained edge remains in his voice when it returns.

'I only intended to go after the man, no one else. I need you to know that. Anything else that may have happened, that was an accident. I had one target only, and it was him.'

'I'll make sure I take a note of it.'

'Good. Get it in the documents. Make sure that whoever looks at these things knows what really went down.' There is a new intensity to Joseph's words, but then a halting pause, and then an abrupt change of tone. 'Actually,' he says, 'I wasn't intending to kill him at all.'

Pauline hesitates. 'You weren't? You just told me your plan was to kill the old man. Those were your exact words, Joseph.'

'I know what I said!' he barks. 'I just wanted to scare the shit out of him, really. That's all I was planning. Maybe out a kneecap or an ankle or something small like that. Make the bastard bleed a little. But mostly I wanted him to feel real fear, and you don't have to die to feel real fear.' The last statement emerges from the recorder with a kind of knowing, learned force behind it. They are the words of first-hand experience.

'What changed?' Pauline asks. 'What happened that caused such a different outcome than the one you'd anticipated?'

'It was when I saw him. *That* was the change. The sight of his face. Oh God, I ran through that door and saw him – perched in his seat like some despotic king on his throne. He had such a smug look. He didn't give a damn about any of it. After all I'd just heard him doing, minutes before! He had the content look of a man who was *proud* of everything he'd ever done in life.'

'That must have been terrib—'

'It was like I went blind, just then,' Joseph continues, not seeming to take any notice of her consoling interjection. Pauline recalls the moment vividly. Joseph had suddenly been, for all intents and purposes, utterly oblivious to her presence.

On the cassette, his words are pouring out of him. 'It was like something took me over, and it started invading my eyes. Everything went white around the edges of my vision. The whole world was on fire, burned away from me. I don't know a better way to say it. I could still see, but I couldn't, all at the same time. The only thing that wasn't a blur was him, and I felt . . . I felt . . . I don't know how to describe what I was feeling.'

'Can I take a guess?' Pauline asks. Even now, she fidgets in her seat on hearing her own question through the speakers. It isn't her normal pattern to suggest answers to her patients' questions or speculate about their emotional states, but the circumstances had pressed her into an unusual position. She had wanted to help him. God help her, she still did.

'A guess?' Joseph's voice questions back. 'No one's stopping you.'

'I think what you were feeling is rage,' she says. 'It's an anger that goes deeper than normal anger. An uncontrollable violence deep inside, that bursts out of you like an explosion.'

The increase to Joseph's breath is audible in the recording. 'Yes! It was exactly that. And damn, it was *rage* like I've never known. It took me over, like something besides me was controlling my body.'

'And what did you do when this rage took you over?'

'I shot and I shot and I shot,' Joseph answers, his words racing. 'I shot until the trigger no longer produced the effects I wanted, then I spun the gun around and swung with its butt like a bat.' He takes a deep, coursing breath. 'I crashed it into him. I could hear the crunch of bones. I could *hear* it, but I couldn't really see. My vision was even blurrier then, all white light and nothing. But I kept going, and each shot, each swing and impact, it was like . . . *righteousness*!' Joseph's voice roars out the word like a lion. It's so loud the speakers rattle as the magnetic recording overloads their threshold. 'Real righteousness, at last! And justice. Finally, justice!'

A long pause. Twenty-three seconds. Heavy breathing. The words have physically depleted him.

'Do you remember what happened after that?' Pauline's voice is exceptionally soft and gentle. As she listens now, her eyes are moist. This was the moment. All her work had been pointing to this, and yet somehow she hated to have had to bring him here.

'I remember . . . I don't know how much later it was, but it was like waking up. That's what I'd call it. Like coming to. My eyes had never been closed, but suddenly I started to be able to see again. That bright white haze went away and normal sight returned, and . . .'

'And?'

'There was blood everywhere. God, it was more than I'd ever seen. I'd been to horror films before, but I'd never imagined anything like this. It was even on the ceiling. And I . . . I remember I couldn't breathe.'

'Why couldn't you breathe, Joseph?'

A six-second pause. When Joseph's voice returns, the anger is gone. It quavers, two notes struggling for dominance, as if it's on the verge of a sob.

'I couldn't breathe because when I looked down, I didn't see his eyes staring up at me.'

'The old man's?'

Joseph's voice is catching now. He can't seem to get proper lungfuls of air. His words are short. The moisture in Pauline's eyes has crested her lids, two saline drops sliding down her makeup-less cheeks as she relives the moment anew.

'It . . . it, it wasn't him.' As Joseph tries to breathe in, the sound of his lower lip fluttering against his teeth just makes it onto the recording.

'Whose eyes did you see?' Pauline asks, her voice now

even softer. In this instant, it sounds almost as sorrowful as his.

The sob comes. Joseph can't hold it back any longer. It can be clearly heard, mournful and agonizing, choking in his throat.

'I saw hers,' he forces out around it.

'The woman's,' Pauline offers.

'I'd been so overcome, oh God,' Joseph sobs. 'I didn't know I was doing it. But I'd killed them both. All that blood, it wasn't just his. I wanted it to be his, in that moment, but I'd done, done *that*, to both of them. She didn't deserve it! God, she didn't deserve anything!' Joseph's voice is little more than a howl now, mournful and broken. The cassette struggles to relay the agonizing mixture of sounds. 'But it was her eyes that were staring up at me,' he finally adds, 'not his. The eyes of the only woman I'd ever loved.'

'Whose eyes were they?' Pauline asks. Her voice has drawn in close. It is tense. *Talk to me.*

'We used to be so happy. When it was just the two of us, with no one else around. Like we were the only two people on the planet. The sun and the stars and the moon would disappear, and there was just her and me.'

Joseph's voice is changing, now. It's slipping as his mind drifts into a memory, and the words come as if he's reading them from a page.

'She'd take me on walks. She'd hold my hand in hers. And we'd sit together on a big blanket and have picnics.'

'Whose eyes were they?' Pauline asks again, urgent.

She can't let him lose this momentum. *Come on, Joseph. Take the step!*

'And she would make me the most amazing treats.' Joseph doesn't seem to notice her. 'We never had cash flowing out of our pockets, but she'd make the most perfect sweets. And little presents, and all the pain would go away.'

'Tell me who she was.'

'And she'd look into my eyes, and I'd look into hers, and the universe would just melt away.'

'Whose eyes, Joseph?'

'Hers, bitch! I told you!' The rage is back. A fist slams on the table. The man is pure fury, howling like a lion again. 'The woman's!'

'Which woman, Joseph? *Whose eyes?*'

'My mother's eyes!' he yells out. His roar is bestial. Fists slam on the metal table over and over again. A chair slides away and ankle restraints can be heard clanking against their bolt in the floor. 'My mother's fucking eyes!'

And then the recording is only sobs and tortured, moaning gasps for breath, and Pauline's voice, further away from the microphone now, saying to unnamed others, 'It's okay, don't come in. The situation is under control. Leave us be.'

Eventually the howling subsides and the breathing slows. There is only a whisper, repeated over and over again until the cassette clicks to its end.

'I saw my mother's eyes.'

58

Conference Room 4C
California Medical Facility

The committee chairman peers across the room at Pauline. Her explanation has been as compelling as thorough. They've read all the documentation and listened to all the cassettes.

'So the inmate did finally acknowledge that he had killed his own family, that night twenty-eight years ago?' he asks.

Pauline nods. 'He was beginning to understand. The details weren't full in his memory yet, but yes. He'd started to accept it. The transition from denial to invention to honesty was in motion. The woman he'd admitted killing before, when he'd convinced himself he'd murdered his wife – he had become aware that this was actually his mother.'

'And his father?'

'He'd totally written his father out of his memory, and I haven't yet been able to bring him to recognize him, not fully, in the recollections of what he did. All he remembers, in flashes of recognition, is the hatred that he had for the man. But we know from the trial transcripts, from the testimony of neighbours, schoolteachers and others in the town that the father was extremely abusive, both mentally and physically. It's no surprise he's simply erased him from his memory.'

'Why all the focus on his mother?'

'That's where his guilt comes from,' Lavrentis answers. 'He'd intended to act out towards the man, since his father had been the source of the abuse, but his rage got the better of him. It was a wild outburst. I'm not sure he even knew at the time what he was doing, and all these years later he has only flashes. Images. His rage became unfocused and he simply shot at everything. Hit everything. Attacked everything. You might say that his mother got caught in something akin to crossfire. But when he realized he'd killed her, the woman he was trying to protect, it broke him.' She pauses, uncrosses and then re-crosses her legs, trying to find the right words to sum up. 'For the longest time, his only defence against his guilt was to write the whole experience out of his memory. He was an innocent man. He'd never done anything wrong, certainly nothing like this. But his conscience was starting to bring him back to reality.'

There is a heavy silence while the details are processed.

The stenographer types the final syllables of Pauline's comments into her keyboard.

Finally, the warden leans forward, his elbows on the table.

'This is compelling and helpful, but one question still remains unanswered. One that goes directly to his stability and mental fitness.' The warden's eyes bore directly into Pauline's. 'At any point since his arrival, Doctor, since your interactions with him began, has inmate #10481-91 ever acknowledged who he really is?'

'In what sense do you mean, sir?'

'I mean, in all your recordings, in all your notes, he consistently refers to himself as Joseph.'

'That's right,' Pauline answers. There is a firmness, an unnamed emotion that moves in her breast. 'It's the only name he's ever used with me.'

'Were you ever able to bring him to acknowledge that his real name is Tom Warrick?'

Pauline Lavrentis leans back in her chair. For the first time, frustration glazes over her features.

'No, sir. We never got that far.'

PART FOUR

ON THE ROAD

59

Wednesday

It's impossible to describe what it's like to travel, day in and day out, hour after hour, down endless stretches of road with another person, and not be able to speak with them about the one thing that is the most pressing on both of your minds. It's the strangest sensation, sustained and unwanted, to be having what must be the same thoughts about the same things, and yet not share a single word about them. But this is precisely how Joseph and I have been travelling for the past two-and-a-half days. It's the most forced and awkward situation I've ever known, and the longer the trip continues the more impossible it becomes.

The problem is that the journey to Nashville provides occasion for far more silence than is healthy for either of us. Nearly 2,400 miles of roadway at speeds that, in my little car, rarely top sixty. And since for reasons he hasn't explained but which aren't entirely mysterious to me, Joseph wants to avoid the major interstate freeways, it's an even more circuitous route than it might otherwise be. A journey through the American heartland, which by car is mostly unending stripes of tarmac laid out over desert and plateau and not much else. All that time to not talk about the only thing that really needs discussing.

We've occasionally clicked on the radio to try to break up the silence lingering between us, but so much of the stretch between California and Tennessee is made up of great patches of land that don't offer any radio reception to speak of – at least, not the kind either of us are interested in listening to. Political talk shows and zealous religious sermons aren't high on either of our priority lists. So we sit, mile after mile. Apart from engine noise the car is almost always silent and the environment inside is constantly awkward.

From time to time we try to break up the monotony by starting conversations that, even as we begin them, neither of us believe are going to be particularly successful. As we passed the Grand Canyon Joseph turned to me and asked if I'd ever been there before, ever seen that great slash that cuts its way through the earth with such unparalleled grandeur. When I confessed that I hadn't, that I'd only read about it in books but always been fascinated by it, this provided the occasion for fifteen or twenty minutes of Joseph narrating his experiences of having once been there as a child. The place sounded fabulous. In his description the Grand Canyon was far deeper than I'd imagined it could be, and far wider than seemed realistically possible, and a man could walk right up to the edge and dangle his toes over an abyss that might as well reach down into the belly of hell. Or he could hire a mule and trek down narrow pathways to the bottom of the gorge, a journey that drained every ounce of human energy on the descent and absolutely required the animal to make it back to the top. Or you could pay for a spot in a raft and brave the rapids that had cut the canyon out of solid rock, and were still cutting it deeper even today.

Joseph's words painted a beautiful picture – a portrait better than any photograph I'd ever seen, even though I vaguely recollected these features from the books I'd read. Joseph, I was learning, doesn't talk at length that often, but when he does he has a remarkable way with words. His description of the canyon was almost surreal, too real for reality. But he did it with his eyes on the road, as if it were an ordinary feature of his life to think about such things, and in such terms.

I found myself filled with longing. This teenager has been to the Grand Canyon and it has clearly affected him, yet here I am teetering on middle age, and I have so few experiences in my portfolio that relate or could compare. I wonder what it must be like to breathe the air of such a place, what it must be like to see those colours directly, foreign and strange and other-worldly.

But this conversation, like all of those that we share, had a limit that was quickly reached. Before too long Joseph had said all that he had to say about his visit to the canyon. I had the feeling that he could go on, perhaps, if he were in the mood to wax reminiscent. But he was content simply to describe the crags and valleys and the shapes of the stone; and once that was done and all had been set forth he dropped back into a silence that I have come to understand is familiar and comfortable to him.

We contemplated stopping at the Grand Canyon Visitors' Centre and providing me with the opportunity to see it at last, but it was night-time as we neared and neither of us felt that staring into the darkness at a canyon's edge was going to be particularly more awe-inspiring than staring into it from a car window. We kept driving.

In due course, in turn, I asked him about San Francisco, the city that had become my home and to which I've taken such a liking. I asked whether Joseph had ever been there before. It seemed likely that he would have been, given that it's such a short distance from Redding, whereas the Grand Canyon is so much further. But to my surprise, Joseph has never been down the road to the city, never seen the bridges, the islands. He hasn't driven through the vineyards and farmlands that stand between the northern border of the state and the great bay in which San Francisco is perched on its little jetty of a peninsula. He hasn't passed through the country towns, he hasn't arrived in that many-hilled wonderland to ride on a trolley car or walk along the wharf and eat a crab out of its own shell, prepared in front of him on a sidewalk by a vendor from a little cart on wheels.

In this, as in so many other things, Joseph's life is a

mystery to me. I hadn't understood why it was that he had a shanty in the forest. That had been the first real surprise. Presumably he had been homeless, and so maybe he still was. He had offered no explanation for the situation, not then and not in the car since. But clearly if he was a homeless young man, he had come from a family that wasn't entirely destitute. A family that had been able to give him trips to great canyons and distant states – the kind I'd only ever been able to dream about through books – even if it had deprived him of some of the more wonderful sights that sat essentially next door.

Our conversation about San Francisco provided a chance for me to talk with him about some of the things that I loved, and it was cathartic for me to have the opportunity. I shared with him my impression of the colourful streets with their brightly painted houses all done up in rows, the most famous ones Victorian and elegant but the vast majority stucco and plaster, still quite beautiful but without the old-world charm. He asked what I did for work and I described my mundane life in the supplement shop. Joseph at first didn't know what supplements were, and after I had spent ten or fifteen minutes describing the concept – powders made from plants and other natural substances that people think in some sense supplement a normal healthy life – he still didn't seem fully to understand the concept.

'Why supplement health, instead of just being healthy?' he asked. It was a question I'd asked myself many times before.

I replied with the normal answer. The same one I would often give customers. 'We all try to live healthy lives. We all try to eat well and take in the nutrients that we need. But life is busy and frenetic and hectic. We try, but we don't always succeed. This is a way of supplementing those efforts with a little extra push, to give the body and the mind what they need.'

I sighed satisfactorily when I had finished this spiel. It was well rehearsed and usually convincing, and very similar to the one I'd first encountered in the slew of books I'd read, which had built up my knowledge of the subject. But Joseph's brow simply rose and his head shook slightly from left to right.

'It seems a bit like make-believe. A fantasy,' he answered me. 'Pretend play time for adults.'

I laughed, because this was about as good an analysis as I had ever heard, and fundamentally I supposed that I agreed with Joseph. All those books on supplemental health, all the conversations with others, and it still seemed as much a fantasy as anything close to a reality.

And so we drove into the hours, into the rising of the sun and its setting, always through the night – never staying in hotels but keeping the wheels in motion – having these sorts of conversations that weren't really conversations. More than small talk, but nothing which revealed the depths of our souls, one to another. And certainly nothing that ever touched on that great, terrible common experience that bound us together here in the car. That was a subject tacitly off limits, and we both seemed to know it.

We couldn't, however, escape it altogether. Words might be implicitly banned, but there were more physical dimensions that had to be dealt with. We'd left California covered in blood, and that certainly wasn't a situation that could be maintained. In that first night it had to be taken care of, and the perfect opportunity presented itself in the form of a river that ran alongside the highway. We'd agreed to stop once we saw that there were various turn-outs that would allow easy access (in order 'to get out and clean up a bit,' we said to each other, carefully avoiding the word 'blood' in our description of just what needed cleaning, despite the obvious fact that it was caked over both of us), and as it was the dark of night and there was little traffic we pulled to the side of the road and went down into the water with all our clothes on. Cold as stepping into ice water, but that proved useful in its own way. In addition to washing the blood out of our clothes and off our faces and arms, it also well and truly woke us up – something needed after the adrenalin had retreated and exhaustion threatened the safety of our drive. I remember the moon had been back, that night. There's a wonderful silver sparkle to a river in the moonlight. It almost dances. In that strange darkness the clear water beneath the sparkles is black, so the blood streaming away from our bodies was invisible. The river didn't judge us by changing colour, stained by our actions. It just received us dirty and handed us back pure.

But that necessary act was about as far as our shared experience had been allowed to intrude into our journey.

The rest of the time we pretended the memory wasn't with us.

Finally, though, I felt an urge to know *something* more about the young man next to me in the car. It was one of the periods in which I was behind the wheel and Joseph was sat knees-up in the passenger seat, his feet against the dash and shoes on the floor beneath him. The posture seemed to give Joseph a measure of calm. He appeared almost to be content in the moment, with some of the worry that hung over us leaving his features. Perhaps it was the scenery outside the window, which I recall at that moment had been especially beautiful, poignant. Perhaps it was the sunshine, now full and bright, but Joseph was almost cheerful. And in this spirit I thought I would take advantage of the moment and ask him something about himself that *meant something* – more than places he'd visited and things that he'd seen. Something that might tell me just who was this young man with whom I'd bloodied my hands.

'You haven't told me about your family,' I said. I tried to keep my voice cheerful, since Joseph had appeared to be homeless when we'd been together in the forest, and that meant the question might be touchy. But it was also an ordinary enough sort of question between friends that I felt, with the right tone of voice, just might be accepted.

Joseph shrugged. He didn't answer, not immediately, but I couldn't help noticing as I glanced at him across the car that a little of that bright spirit fled as soon as the question had been asked.

'I dunno,' he finally responded. 'Not sure there's really much to talk about. What can you really say about a family?' He took a few seconds in silence, pondering his own question. 'Family's family. They just are what they are.'

I thought about this for a moment. At first it seemed a sensible enough thing to say; though I've always hated this saying, 'It is what it is' being a too-frequently-employed nonsense phrase I've always considered a bit defeatist. And general criticisms aside, in this case it was a nothing thing to say. An answer that revealed nothing, that didn't expose a single thing about his family life. Though maybe that fact was in itself revealing.

'Any brothers or sisters?' I probed.

He shook his head, 'Just me. That was always enough for the parents.'

I nodded. I also was an only child, part of an elite club that included a huge swath of the world's population, but which always made those of us within it feel a little special. That's how we were supposed to feel: unique. It's what we'd been told in school, and certainly what we were told by our parents. *'You don't need a little sister or brother, Dylan. You're enough for us just as you are, all by yourself.'*

'I'm with you on that one,' I decided to add, allowing a little levity into my voice. It was a kind of puerile comment, far more new-generation in style than I normally spoke, but I felt like this might resonate well with the not-yet-twenty lad beside me. 'What about your parents?' I finally asked.

This time I could feel, more than see, the shift in Joseph's form, as if his whole body tightened at the question. But again he didn't say anything, not immediately.

'Are they still alive?' I followed up. A reasonable enough question. Many people's parents are, many people's aren't.

'No,' he answered. 'Not the last time I saw them.'

A puzzling answer, if ever I'd heard one, to what was otherwise a fairly ordinary question.

My parents are still alive, though I haven't seen them in a very long time – can't actually think of the last time I went to visit them. 'I'm sorry to hear that,' I answered to Joseph. 'That must be difficult for you.'

'Everybody dies,' he replied, matter-of-factly, with a simple shrug of his shoulders.

I couldn't argue with his logic, though it was clear there was pain behind his otherwise unemotional words.

My own parents brought good memories into my mind, not bad. Loving people, both of them, who care for each other deeply. That's the way they always look in my memory. They are alive but very old and very far away, and we're not really in frequent touch. No fallings-out, just the way the modern world works. Every time I think of them, every time they come into the forefront of my memory, it's like a portrait out of a picture frame in a shopping centre. An ideal husband and wife gazing longingly into each other's eyes. Even there, sitting in the car fleeing the scene of a murder, that image brought me tremendous comfort. There was real love, real joy, real support.

I glanced in Joseph's direction. He was gazing vacantly out the side window. 'Do you want to talk about them?' I asked, wondering if his silence was an invitation for friendly dialogue.

'There isn't anything to say,' he answered, and his voice seemed a full pitch lower than when he'd spoken a moment ago. 'Nothing to say that changes anything.'

'What would you change?' I asked, innocent and curious. He swivelled his head towards me, and he probed me with a gaze unlike any other he'd had since I'd met him. Those fierce eyes were not fierce in this instant, but questioning. Intently. Almost uncomprehending. *You should know*, they seemed to telegraph across that little space. *You should know full well.* But I didn't know. I didn't understand.

Once the gaze had been broken he turned back to looking out the window. 'My memories aren't pleasant,' he said. 'Family isn't a subject I've ever liked to talk about.'

My insides clenched a little. I felt compassion. I felt sorry for this young man.

'But at least it's done with,' he continued.

I let some silence pass between us. His parents were no longer alive, but that seemed to be a good thing for Joseph. Whatever his relationship with them had been, it clearly hadn't been comfortable; and while death is never an easy thing – and I'm sure that, however they died, the result is that he misses them – nevertheless it seems that in death they had left him with more peace than when they'd been alive. And maybe that was good enough. Maybe that's the way that consolation comes through grief.

So I turned my attention back to the dashed yellow lines marking the centre of the highway as I continued to drive, and for a while no more words were necessary, and no more words were spoken.

60

Thursday

We've pulled in at a roadside service station to fill up the car and grab a few supplies for the next leg of our journey. According to the atlas Joseph extracted from my glove compartment, we've probably got another fifteen to twenty hours ahead, and neither of us is able to make that without a little food. Thus far it's been McDonald's and Burger Kings all the way, and without actually conferring on the matter we both agreed silently that the limit of fast food had been reached. We needed to stop for something different.

So, having cleaned ourselves up as much as we could – there's very little blood left on our bodies now – we've exited the car, filled up the tank, and have both gone into the service station to buy some snacks and proper food. Not that filler-station food is known for being that much more nutritious or delicious than what one gets from a fast-food window, but it's different, and at this stage in our monotony different is as welcome as good.

Joseph goes immediately for the pre-wrapped sandwiches and an enormous case of canned beer – the same provisions, I immediately recognize, with which he'd stuffed his cooler back in the forest in California. I suppose once we know what we like, we know what we like.

A more practical streak catches alight in me, however, and though I'm also anxious to find something to fill my stomach, I make my way first towards the toiletries section of the shop where I grab a cheap toothbrush and a travel-size tube of toothpaste. I feel dirty inside and out, and the thought of clean teeth and fresh breath is almost as inviting as a full stomach.

Then it's to the coffee counter, again before the food, priorities being priorities. I remember I haven't had a good cup of coffee since before I met Joseph, since before the tragedy at the farmhouse. But as I arrive at the counter, marked by a bold display saying 'Coffee!!!' with three exclamation points – as if this were a point of particular elation for any who would walk into the store – I realize in a heartbeat that I'm not to have any good coffee here either. That which is served comes in one of two forms: from a push-button machine on the counter, which dispenses something that it persists in calling 'Cappuccino' but which is simply a foamed concoction of powdered milk heated to just above lukewarm while powdered coffee is sprinkled on top with a little hot water. Or, as a second option, coffee that comes out of a round glass carafe, the kind found in old restaurants and diners, which looks like it was brewed in the early hours of the night and has sat, half-empty on the burner, for all the hours that have passed since. It's a hard decision between two obviously putrid choices, and I weigh it carefully. Ultimately I chose the tar-like substance in the glass carafe. It's undoubtedly five times the strength coffee should be and will bring winces and unpleasant thoughts when I drink it, but at least it's real coffee and not a powdered chemical substitute. I fill one of the large paper cups, snap on a plastic lid, and head for the food aisle.

Joseph is still filling up a basket with snacks. 'You ever feel like eating something besides a bologna and American cheese sandwich?' I ask him, my voice half in jest, as I see what he's gathered together. Even in the world of service-station sandwiches there's more variety on offer than just that. But his basket has five of them, arrayed in a nice little row.

'Hey, I likes what I likes,' he says, a fake Boston accent suddenly emerging from his nineteen-year-old lips, emulating some film he must once have seen.

'Well, as long as you *likes* to let me pay for that case of beer you've got under your arm,' I joke back, trying – and failing – to mimic his accent, 'then they might actually let us out of here in one piece.'

He grins at me. Being underage hadn't been a problem when his aim was to steal whatever he took from little shops, but since we are here fully intending to pay, it is going to have to be me who brings the alcohol up to the counter. I only hope that the uninterested man at the till hasn't already seen it under Joseph's arm.

I glance over the food on offer. The choice is remarkably slim. I take two sandwiches of my own, one a chicken tikka masala and one a BLT, together with a banana and two apples that for some reason are wrapped in cling film and look to be almost as old in fruit terms as the coffee is in coffee terms. But still edible, and probably mostly clean.

When finally our baskets have been filled, when we've both held them for each other while we daringly brave the men's toilets and come out mostly unscathed from the filthy experience, we bring them up to the front of the shop and lay them next to the till.

'I'll put all these on my card,' I say to the man who's already examining the pricing labels on each item and typing them manually into the register. No laser scanners in this dive.

But there is a television, mounted up on the shelf behind the counter, presumably to occupy this man's attention for the long expanses of time between the arrival of visitors such as ourselves. It looks older than the man, but it functions and it's powered on. And on that little television, in black-and-white forms scattered beneath the static haze of a foil-enhanced aerial, is a news report.

I've never been afraid of the news. I rarely watch it. But in this instant the report sends my heart into terrorized palpitations.

We're in Texas now, hundreds of miles away from the scene, but right before my eyes, even subtitled to remove any doubt, is a place I recognize. *Redding: California.* In the north of the state. Only a stone's throw from the Oregon border.

The volume isn't loud, but neither is there much noise in the shop apart from the teller's fingers pressing into his buttons, a soft beep emerging with each one. I can just make out the newsreader's voice as the report is broadcast live across the air.

'One of the most grisly crimes seen in this part of the state in decades,' she says, somewhere in the middle of her prepared text. 'A double homicide in a small town inexperienced in dealing with the discovery that two of its citizens have been brutally murdered.'

Brutally murdered. The words drive through me like spikes. I can feel my skin go cold – all of it, over every inch of my body – and then I can't seem to feel it at all.

'Local authorities in this largely peaceful neighbourhood have never before faced a crime scene bearing witness to such violence,' the report continues. 'Full details on the nature of the crime have not yet been shared with us, but a source from the inspecting unit, who wishes to remain anonymous at this stage, indicated to us that the bodies of the two victims had been, to quote, "brutalized". While the word torture wasn't used in his remarks to us, this reporter proposed it in a question back to him, and it wasn't denied.'

Now it isn't just my numb skin that's reacting. My

ears start to ring with a tinny, tingling noise that invades my perception. It surrounds the newsreader's words, fading out the other sounds around me. I can no longer hear the beeps from the till, though the man behind it is still pounding away at his keys. I can hear only this ringing, my own raspy breath, and the voice coming from the television.

The display on the screen suddenly shifts to a situational shot, taken from the top of a hill, and I recognize the spot immediately. It's the same spot where I'd stood, where the boy had led me, when I first glanced down its far side and saw the farmhouse. And there it is, just as I remember it, now in black and white and grainy, but unquestionably the same house. I can almost see, between the spot where the camera is positioned and the front porch of that house, two trails in the high grass leading out from the forest, carved by Joseph and myself as we charged up to the door which even now is visibly shattered, its remnants hanging in place from a single hinge.

'There are no suspects as yet in what is a crime with no known motivation,' the newsreader continues, 'though an investigation is underway involving both local and state forces, and which may be expanded as more materials come to light.'

These words both comfort and panic me. The comfort comes from the fact that no suspects are yet charted. They don't know my name. They don't know Joseph's. They haven't pieced together our presence there. And maybe they never will.

And yet panic. Terror. The investigation is only beginning and it's already spread beyond the confines of little Redding to the whole of California. *State forces.* This means it involves officials in my own city, in San Francisco, and I wonder for the briefest of instants whether this means I'll never be able to return there. That thought is almost impossibly frightening.

The investigation is going to expand. *Expand.* With that, my stomach forms into a rock. How far will they go to look for the as-yet unknown assailants? The assailants standing here in this Texas shop buying sandwiches and beer and a travel-size tube of toothpaste, joking in fake accents and running away from a crime that has shocked an entire nation.

61

Thursday

'Joseph, did you see the news report?' I ask the question the moment we're back on the highway. For some reason I didn't feel inclined to ask it when we first sat back into the car, fired up the engine and made our way off from the station. I wanted there to be some distance, however minimal and ultimately meaningless, between the service station and us before I raised it. But when I do, the question drops out of me with a powerful fervency.

'On the little television in there,' I continued, 'just where we were paying. Did you see? Did you hear?'

Joseph is driving now and he keeps his eyes on the road, both hands firmly on the wheel.

'Pass me one of them beers,' he says, avoiding my question, sounding very countryish. I'm infuriated.

'Listen to me!' I say to him, reaching out and rapping

my knuckles on the dash in front of the wheel, trying to gain his proper attention. 'Listen to what I've just said! There was a news report, there on the television in the shop. Did you see it or did you not?'

I demand that he answer me. I will not have it that he simply ignores such a question about such a thing.

'Yeah, I saw it,' he finally says, annoyed, 'now give me a damned beer. I'm not going to ask again.' He removes his right hand from the wheel and holds it out towards to me, waiting. And I, not knowing quite what else to do, tear through the cardboard top of the case and hand him one of the semi-cold cans.

'They know about everything,' I say as I pass him the beer. He cracks open the top with a flick of his finger and downs a full swallow of his drink, still saying nothing. 'They know about what we've done.' I stress each word as I emphasize the point. Joseph is failing to appreciate the gravity of what this means.

'They don't know shit,' he eventually says back. He takes another swig of his beer. 'Nothing that matters.' Finally he glances over and looks straight into my eyes for an intense second. 'Nothing that connects to you or to me.' Then his eyes are back on the road, as if this answers every question and solves every problem. But I know that it doesn't. My heart is racing. I'm consumed with tension and fear.

'Joseph, it said that they're initiating a manhunt.'

'Of course they are!' he lets out. There's an almost jesting tone to his voice. 'But we knew that! You said they would, back when we were in the forest. That's why we left my house.'

I'm briefly startled by hearing him refer to the pile of old rubbish in the woods as his 'house', but it's not the issue of the moment.

'I knew they would start looking, Joseph, but didn't you hear: they're coordinating. It's not only the local police. They're not just looking in the forest. They've got the state patrol on board, and it said they're bringing in others!'

Joseph shrugs. He reaches a hand into one of the paper sacks into which our goods were packaged by the man at the till and extracts a sandwich. Examining it to make sure it's one of his bologna monstrosities, he works a finger through the cellophane, his beer now tucked between his knees, and pries it open. A moment later his mouth is filled with soggy white bread, bologna, and something that in only the vaguest of ways resembles cheese.

'I'm not sure you fully understand what this means, Joseph.' I feel I might need to explain the details of an actual manhunt to this younger man. 'The *others* they're going to bring in are police from other states, maybe even interstate organizations. Joseph, they're going to be looking for us *everywhere*!'

He chews on his sandwich. The scent of bologna, something I don't find pleasant under normal circumstances, is particularly revolting in this instant.

'Let them look,' he says, 'just what do you expect

them to find, Dylan?' There's exasperation in his voice. He's as annoyed with my spiked energy as I am with his lack of it. 'We didn't touch anything in the house when we were there. We brought the weapons in and we took them out. The people are dead and the job is done. They'll look and they'll look, but what are they going to find? There's millions of people in this country – fifty states full of them. The fact they're looking doesn't mean they're going to find shit!'

He allows his eyes to turn towards me again. This time they're filled with surety. This is all obvious to him. A complete picture. We're safe. Events are certain. There's nothing to worry about. As if to emphasize the point he reaches his left hand down and grabs his beer, takes another long swig, then turns his attention back to the road with a grunt of finality. 'Have a drink, old man, and relax.'

I have no appetite now, nor do I want anything to drink. Certainly not a Coors Light. And I'm not convinced, no matter what Joseph says. If he was living in the woods, so close to that house, they *will*, as I knew from the beginning that they would, find his little shanty. And that means they'll likely be able to narrow down who it was that lived there. At least enough to get a general picture, a description of a man: so tall, so high, so young. The kind of man that shopkeepers have seen swiping sandwiches and beer when he thought they weren't looking. Maybe they won't know his name, his identity, but that kind of description attached to a nationwide manhunt . . . there may be hundreds of millions of people out there, but there aren't that many who look like that.

I recognize the danger this means. Joseph doesn't. He's chewing on his damned bologna sandwich and I just want to drive a fist into his face. But I know from our previous discussions that pushing Joseph too far, too fast, only forces him to a breaking point; and the last thing that I need is a yelling match, or some sort of silent treatment for the next 400 miles in the car. So I force my breathing into a steadier rhythm. I watch the dashed yellow lines disappear beneath us as we drive. I let thirty seconds pass. A minute. I even grab a beer – not because I want it, but because I think the casual, ordinary action might open up Joseph to some sort of reasonable discussion, friend to friend, peer to peer. Coors Light drinker to Coors Light drinker.

I snap open the top, take a swill. It's every bit as repugnant as I anticipate. I let another thirty seconds pass. I turn my body so that it's angled towards him. It's clear I want to speak. I draw in my breath, but before the words can come out Joseph lifts up both hands from the wheel and taps them down again with a kind of change of pace about him.

'You know what?' he says to me, his voice suddenly interested and engaging in a way that I hadn't heard it since I first met him in the forest. 'You've never told me what you like to do.'

This comment throws me totally off guard. 'What I

like to do?' I'm not even sure how to formulate a question in response, though everything in me in this instant is a question.

'Yeah. You've told me about where you live. About where you work. You've told me about streetcars and buildings – but you've never told me what you like to do.'

Again I'm baffled at this young man's ability to avoid the points that need to be discussed in favour of things that have no bearing on our dire circumstances.

'Joseph, it doesn't matter what I like to do. Right now we need to talk about—'

'On an ordinary day,' his words pierce through mine, 'what do you do with yourself? I mean when you're not at work, when you're not selling your drugs or your "supplements" or whatever it is you call them. Are you a fisherman? Do you play video games? Do you hang out in bars?'

I sink back into my seat and force myself to take another, rather longer, drink of the beer. Joseph is not going to talk about the news report. He's making that as obvious as he can in his own way. But he is talking, and that in and of itself is something unusual. I'm loath to give it up simply because it's not about the topic that I feel is most pressing.

'No, Joseph,' I sigh, 'I don't hang out in bars. I've never been able to find them all that interesting.' In fact the first bar I can remember being in in years was the one I'd sat in in Redding, having a Jack Daniel's the night before I'd started my search around the outskirts of town.

'So what, is it video games or book clubs – what do city men do?' He turns to me. He's making light, trying to be friendly. I resign myself to whatever this conversation is to become. Reaching into the paper bag I extract one of the sandwiches, also examining it closely, though in my case to ensure that it is *not* one of made of bologna.

'I like to take walks,' I finally answer.

'Walks? In the city?' Joseph looks perplexed. 'What's there to walk to in the city? You see one street, you've seen every street.'

This causes a slight smile. There is a naiveté to Joseph, though there is a truth to his words as well. One city street is much like every other street, though of all the cities I've ever known San Francisco is the one with the most varied beauty between one street and the next. Victorian homes here, skyscrapers there, pyramid buildings, Chinatowns, old military garrisons. Yet Joseph has a point, and he's not wrong. Not in my case.

'Not on the city streets,' I say. I decide against the sandwich before I start unwrapping it. The conversation has become more interesting. 'I like to walk in the park.'

'Ah, you've got a park in San Francisco! That's nice.' Joseph seems to think the idea quaint, and I can understand that, coming from someone who's grown up in the actual outdoors.

'It is a big one, your park?' he asks.

I smile despite myself. Even the mention of the park,

and even in these circumstances, brings me joy. 'Huge,' I answer. 'I've been walking around it for a couple years now and there are still more paths I haven't put my feet on than those I have.'

'Doesn't sound bad,' Joseph answers, his mouth full again.

'It's actually quite wonderful. And there's its best spot, which I especially like to visit.'

I would have brought this up with Joseph before, in one of our many non-conversations of the drive, but I was certain he never would have listened, never would have cared. That it would have been ten seconds of me describing my haven to a wall of complete disinterest and silence. But in this moment Joseph seems not only interested but captivated, and though I'm nearly certain that this interest stems from his desire not to talk about the news report – which must frighten him just as much as it frightens me – nevertheless he's listening. And I'm keen to talk.

'The one spot I really love,' I continue, 'it's a little pond beneath these beautiful Asian trees. And there's a little bench by the pond and I go and sit there just about every day at lunch.'

'Why at lunch?'

'My only free time in the day,' I answer. 'Forty-five minutes off at lunchtime. I can make it there and back with enough time to have a solid half-hour at the pond. I just sit there and enjoy the scenery. Refresh myself before I head back out into the world.'

Joseph ponders these words as if they're comprehensible to him, but still slightly strange. 'With all that park out there, don't you get bored sitting all the time at that same pond?'

I chuckle to myself. I'm not sure how to answer the younger man. I remember youth. Youth is filled with the need to constantly see new things, mark new ground, conquer new territory. And to youth it's impossible to describe the stability that one starts to crave with age. Yes, there is still a thrill that comes from climbing up a new mountaintop every once in a while, but what solace and joy there is in finding a place that is always yours, always beautiful. That, no matter what may be happening around you, provides you with comfort. The heavens may break open, the world may bomb itself into oblivion, terrorists may rip apart the fabric of society itself; but in that park, by that pond, on that bench, all is always well.

'No,' I finally say to him, 'I don't get bored, but there's no reason for us to chat so much about this, Joseph.' I find it odd that I am the one wrapping up this conversation. 'We don't have to dwell on these things.'

'Hey, that's up to you, man,' he answers. He's already made it through his first beer and tosses the empty tin nonchalantly over his shoulder into the back, then reaches over to grab another.

As he does so, I'm reminded of the main reason I go to my park. I'm reminded of the one thing that I always crave to see there. I'm reminded of the connection which that pond and that bench in that park have to this moment, in this car on this road. I'm reminded of the boy. I'm reminded of the wounds. I'm reminded of my desire to help – my trip, my journey. And I'm reminded of the terror to which my little pond ultimately drew me.

62

Thursday Night

There comes a point when truth can no longer be avoided. Joseph and I have been making the most of our journey, which the map indicates should, before too long, be coming to its end. We're driving through the night now, and likely by lunchtime tomorrow we'll have made our target: the Nashville that Joseph suggested from the forest in California. And all this way we've avoided talking about what we did there, though the newsreader on the television prompted it, and though my constant desire has been to raise it. We've relegated it to the shadows, to the clouds that sit over the top of us, to the silent spaces between our conversations.

But shadows eventually creep in on the light, and clouds that big can't linger for too long in such a little space. As we settle into a long night and all conversation comes to a natural ebb, the quiet of the road lulls me into the kind of half-sleep where memories so often come. And this night, they come with a vengeance.

We stormed the house, Joseph and I, just like we'd planned. It was meant to be a righteous act and that's where the righteousness lay, because even as we ran up to the porch we could hear the abuse inside getting louder. There were sounds of fists meeting flesh, of profanities and depredations. If there had been any doubt in my mind before, as we concocted our reckless plan of action in the woods, it was gone by the time we got to the door. I no longer had any reservations: it was good that we were there, that we were running with weapons into a scene where those who needed defending had no means of doing so on their own. It was good that Joseph had his shoulder forward and was slamming his body into the door, and that it splintered away beneath him with such ease.

It was good. And it felt good – genuinely, nobly good – to be doing it.

The house into which we'd thrust ourselves was a dump. A shack, really. It looked like it had been neglected for years, with only a few traces of family warmth left in its timbers. There were echoes of a child in some of the decorations – a few school photos, a framed crayon drawing, that sort of thing – but there was an evident, overwhelming aura of absence at the same time. It hit me the moment we burst in. The child wasn't there any more. The parents were living in an empty nest, and they'd started to let it go to the birds.

That fact troubled me instantly. And it troubles me

now. Because I'd gone there for the boy, and the boy wasn't a memory. He wasn't a thing of the past. He was suffering, and I'd seen him wounded and broken. But this house didn't feel like the place that a boy lived.

The man we were after had been in a chair: a tattered, worn out Lay-Z-Boy that had seen its best days a decade ago. Or, if I am to be more precise, he was falling into the chair as we entered. Whatever fit he'd been in as we'd listened outside, it had resulted in the woman fleeing the room (I could only presume; she wasn't in sight when we made our entrance), and he was slumping into his recliner, a bottle in hand.

Self-satisfied bastard.

The bottle fell out of his grasp as we stormed his little fort. The man was unshaven, grey, and looked older than I'd expected. A man with such a young boy should be – younger. At least I thought so. But I'm no master of ages, and I know that men in particular can father children well into their older years. In any case, I didn't have long to consider it. Joseph and I were still in motion, and he was putting the whole of our plan into action.

He yelled at the man with a fierce anger. It was clear that the observation Joseph had made of this family from the hillside, of which he'd spoken with me so briefly before our charge, had affected him deeply. He had a powerful hatred towards this man, and at first it came out in a torrent of fierce words. I was surprised at the string of profanities this young man knew, and how they came out in an uninterrupted stream.

Then the man, utterly shocked to see us, rose from his chair. I'm not sure if he made a move towards Joseph or if it just appeared like he did, but Joseph reacted. The rifle swivelled on his shoulder strap and he slammed its butt into the man's chest, flinging him against the wall.

As his body flew back into the timbers, the abuser's eyes were wide discs: horrified. He wheezed from the blow, his body sliding down towards the floor, but he still managed a few desperate words.

'What the hell are you doing?'

Maybe that's how violent, abusive men respond to attackers invading their space. Not with pleas of fear and cowardice, but with words that are almost an accusation. I was expecting terrorized shock.

But Joseph wasn't interested in tones or temperaments or in answering questions. He advanced on the man, his words bubbling out between spittle from his lips.

'I know what you've done, you bastard!' In the small, wooden room his words were thunder. 'I know what you've done your whole stinking, self-righteous life! The whole world knows, though you've convinced yourself you've done it all in secret!'

I'm still not sure how to assess the expression on the man's face as he bore this accusation. He was surprised, of course. But, once again, it wasn't the kind of surprise I'd anticipated. It's a hard thing to qualify in words. I was expecting absolute shock and incomprehension. *Who are you? What are you doing here? Why are you doing this to me?* That sort of thing. But it wasn't that kind of surprise. In amidst his shock there was recognition, clear and concrete, and that fact caught me off balance.

'Did you think you'd get away with this forever?' Joseph shouted, taking another menacing step towards the man, whose back had slid fully down the wall and who was now perched against it, his legs splayed in front of him. 'Did you think there wouldn't be a price to pay?'

My world started to break apart with the man's answer.

'I never thought I'd see you back here,' he said. 'I thought you were gone for good.'

I still can't precisely identify the mixed emotion of those words. Surprise was there. Anger, too. Fear. Disgust. But the contents of the words themselves, they're what threw me. I simply couldn't comprehend what the man was saying. Joseph had told me he'd watched the house, that he'd observed it from the woods. He'd obviously left something out. This man, the one he'd hurled to the floor, the one he and I both knew was violent and wretched and a wraith more than a man, was someone who had met Joseph before. Someone who knew him. And the two of them had a past.

'Of course you didn't think you'd see me again, you bastard,' Joseph spat back at him. 'You thought you'd got rid of me when I ran off. Probably never happier than when you saw my room empty and I didn't show up at the supper table at seven o'clock on the spot.'

'You got that one right, you little shit!'

His words shocked me again. There's a strange shattering that can take place inside the human mind, when reality seems to break apart like a fracturing mirror, suddenly reflecting not the single image you expect but two or three or four angular variations on a theme. That's what this unexpected dialogue did to my understanding of our circumstances. I'd thought I'd known what was going on, but there were new pictures being reflected back to me. I'd thought we were aiding the innocent by attacking a stranger, but the man wasn't a stranger, not to Joseph. I'd thought we were here for justice, but the words were starting to make it sound like my newfound companion was here for something else.

The man's answer turned Joseph's cheeks red. He shouted back at him, 'Did you think I was just going to forget what you did to us?'

The man didn't respond with words. Instead he leaned forward, never breaking eye contact with Joseph, looming above him, and spat onto the floor between them. Defiance and disgust. They were the only realities to him.

'No more than you deserved,' he finally added.

The response was revolting, but Joseph didn't seem to hear it.

'What you did to *her*!' he shouted back, his words overlapping the old man's. 'What you're *still* doing to her! Did you think I was just going to let you go on like that!?'

The man's eyes went red, and he stared up at Joseph with fierce defiance.

'I don't give a fuck what you think about the way I raised you, or how I treat her. I'm a free man in a free country, and how I choose to raise my family is my own—'

He stopped his well-rehearsed rant as Joseph swung the rifle barrel-forward and aimed it at his face. There was an instant of terror: the muscles at his shoulders tensed, his features went taut. But a second later his venom returned.

The mirror of my understanding broke apart again. *'The way I raised you . . .'* The words didn't make sense. *'How I choose to raise my family . . .'* New splinters in the glass, and the image became more fragmented.

The man stared up defiantly at the rifle Joseph had aimed at his head.

'Nice try, kid. You and I both know you've never had the balls.'

That's all it took. They were, as older stories might go, the magic words. Joseph broke. He brought the gun's barrel down a few inches and without a second's hesitation fired. The round blasted into the old man's right knee with a sickening crunch, and he howled in pain.

A second shot took his other knee. Joseph's face was wild.

'What the fuck are you doi—'

The man's panicked cry didn't make it through the third shot, which took out his left shoulder, slamming him into the wall again. His face was now utter disbelief.

I don't know what it was that provoked me to fire. Joseph had clearly disabled the man, but there was still a flame in the abuser's eyes, even in the midst of his disbelief and pain. Maybe that's what it was. A flame that I knew he had used to abuse the boy, his wife – and God knows who else. A flame that needed to be put out, even if I didn't fully understand the circumstances I was in.

I fired at his other shoulder. My aim was not as true as Joseph's and I shot wide, blasting a hole through his forearm.

'That's right! That's the way!' Joseph shouted. I glanced at his face. He had a manic look on his features, a smile that didn't belong there.

His next shot was meant to kill, and Joseph executed it perfectly. He aimed the gun squarely at the old man's chest and pulled the trigger twice. Straight into his heart. I've said before that I'm no expert on guns, so I have no idea what calibre it was that he fired, but the heart seemed to explode. His chest was eviscerated.

I couldn't breathe. Kneecaps and shoulders and fore-arms were one thing, but this was something different. This was a life, deliberately taken. I felt new acid in my throat. My skin went slick and cold.

But Joseph didn't stop. The shots had obviously done the job, but it wasn't enough. He spun his rifle around again, butt forward, and began to beat the man as he lay on the floor. It was as brutal a scene as my mind could ever have imagined. No, I could never have imagined a scene like that. He went after the man's head, his face, his torso. Every swing brought new blood, new horror, and long after it was clear that the man was gone, Joseph kept beating him. The whole time his voice was a brutal, angry roar.

For an instant I caught sight of his face. I'd never known anything so wild. But it was also as if something in him had disappeared. What was moving and acting now was a shell, more than it was a man. The teenager who'd found me in the woods wasn't in possession of himself. Joseph had gone hollow.

And that's the only way I can explain what happened next. We'd been there what seemed like ages, though probably it had only been a few minutes. The woman, the dead man's wife, heard the noise and suddenly came into the room. She did the only thing any rational person could have done at that moment, at the sight of such carnage. She released a scream of absolute, sheer terror.

Joseph spun his gun automatically and fired. I don't think he thought about it – the shell of him just acted on impulse. The single bullet that flew out of the rifle pierced the woman's chest while she was still screaming. But Joseph didn't seem to notice this either, didn't seem even to see. His eyes were open, but his vision was somewhere else. He ran over to her body as it fell to the floor and began the same brutal beating he'd just enacted on the old man. His voice was uncontrolled rage. 'Why? Why didn't you stop him! Why didn't you protect me? You were supposed to be there when I needed you!'

There were tears streaming from his eyes. For a second his was the face of a small child, innocent and confused, pleading for help. Despairing that it had never come.

But there was no more innocence behind the tears. Joseph was an enraged beast, and he attacked until all life was gone. And then he kept going.

I watched in horror. The scene was a nightmare in parts I couldn't connect. I watched the man die, for which I felt disgust but little remorse. I watched the woman die, which filled me with absolute revulsion. But I also witnessed another death. I stood there, stunned, as all the life ebbed from the room, but it was only when Joseph stood up from delivering his last blow and turned to me that I fully realized what that meant. As his face met mine, for the most fleeting of instants, I had the strangest feeling that he was as dead as the others. He was standing, he was heaving from the exertion, but I had the overwhelming sensation of looking at a man whose life had just been voided and cancelled out.

And I'm not sure if it was then that I first noticed it, but I became aware that he was wearing overalls. The shirt beneath them had been white before it had been soaked in this bath of blood. And the way he held the rifle at his side – it was almost like a stick, its barrel on the floor in a pool of his mother's blood, as if piercing the water of a clear and tranquil pond.

In that instant, I saw the boy. But I didn't see him saved. I saw him die, there in that room. The innocent boy I had known and loved from my bench. The boy in the park. The boy whose life had now forever been taken away.

63

Friday Morning

When the sun starts to come up and I look across at the driver's seat, Joseph's hands still clutched firmly at the wheel and his eyes attentively on the road, I see him differently than I've ever seen him before. Poets often write that dawn brings new revelations along with each new day, and this morning those words make an immediate, indisputable sense. Something new has been revealed.

I'm not certain how much of my memory of what we did in California is accurate, how much of it is influenced by the adrenalin that was coursing through me like a drug, or the shock that lingered afterwards. I know that all those things can modify vision and recollection, and I don't feel I'm in any position to trust myself resolutely. But when I look at Joseph now, he seems a different person. He is present to me in a way he hadn't been before. And I no longer wonder where that little boy I was seeking has gone.

I don't know precisely how he's connected to the man in the car with me. Obviously they're not the same person. That can't possibly be true. The boy is young and Joseph is older. The boy is innocent. Joseph has just done such terrible things. And yet the connection seems tangible to me, even if inexplicable. Maybe there are more things that are possible in this life than I am given to understand. For the moment, I'm willing to let that be.

The end result of this awareness is that I view Joseph a little more tenderly. I'd been so frustrated with him in the hours before, so annoyed that he wouldn't talk, that he wouldn't accept and respond to what we'd done. But I feel satisfied now just to be quiet with him. To be connected to him. And I don't know why.

The human mind is a strange thing. We link together stories that aren't really connected. We piece together little bits of data from here and there, stringing them together like popcorn on the thread of a Christmas garland, so that they make a nice stream – whether or not the pieces actually have anything to do with one another. So whether or not it's true, whether or not it's accurate, Joseph is bound together with this boy for me, now and forever. He's bound together with the pain I saw in that boy's body, with the agony I felt when I saw him on the hill. He's bound together with the justice we had to deliver, even as he's bound together with the tragedy that actually unfolded.

And I'm sorrowful. I'm sorrowful that Joseph is now connected up in my mind with all these things. But I'm comfortable with the sorrow. That's the other odd thing about the human mind. Once we think we can explain something, it loses the fierceness with which we looked at it before, and the grief that it formerly threw at us. That's how I feel with Joseph now. I'm saddened, but I accept the man before me. I don't feel any need to press for more information, for details about his family or his reflections on how the manhunt will go. I'm content to be with him, the two of us together, as we drive off into whatever lies ahead.

Soon enough we'll be in Nashville, the place he wanted to go. And whatever comes will come. That's the way of life – at least of our lives – and for one moment, at least, I'm content to let it be.

NASHVILLE

64

Friday Evening

We've arrived in Nashville at long last. The drive has been interminable, almost impossibly lengthy, but we've finally got here. And I have to admit, even with all we've been through, I'm thrilled at the sight.

My love for all things country and western is something I'm generally ashamed to admit in polite company. It seems like the sort of thing that people of a certain breeding aren't meant to enjoy; that the qualifications for finding it inspiring or even enjoyable are a degree of poverty, at least a few months spent living in a trailer park or a shack, and a general disillusionment with anything other than 'the old-fashioned American way'. I can't say that I fit under any of those headings. But I can say, and I do, that I've always loved the music. Finally we've arrived in a place where I can admit it freely; where not to do so would put me in the minority of the unusual and the out of place.

This is something I've learned, during the drive, that Joseph and I share. A fact that came out in one of our pleasantries-but-nothing-serious conversations. It turns out he's been wanting to come to Nashville for years. Our circumstances have provided him with the opportunity to fulfil a dream, of sorts, and they haven't dampened his spirits towards making the most of it.

For me visiting Nashville has never been so much a deliberate desire as an 'Oh, I suppose that would be fun if it ever happened' sort of thought in the back of my head now and then. The same way I think it might also be fun to one day walk the Great Wall of China. But Tennessee is closer than China, and now that we're here and I see the city lights and the home of this whole culture that sits at the fringe of normalcy, I'm delighted we've come. I'm delighted he's wanted to visit here, too. That this may be the scene of new beginnings.

Our arrival early this morning spurred a few facts to the forefront of our attention. We'd got by just about as long as two human males could without showers and in clothes that had only been river-washed. My shirt felt stiff enough to serve as body armour, and the grunge of the rest of my attire didn't bear mentioning. There was more to it than just the filth, too. What had been washed away in the river was horrific, but what lingered in the threads and creases of our clothes was of the same substance. It continued to connect us to that same, horrible reality. When your clothes have been soaked in another person's blood, it's not the sort of thing you just wash out and make like it never happened. Those are the clothes you throw away.

Once we were in the city, then, it was definitely time for some new attire and we prioritized a shopping trip to K-Mart and some discount clothing without any horror attached. It was also a chance to pick up something suitable to a city environment, since the place in which we'd found ourselves was hardly a country backwater, despite the images that the very name 'Nashville' conjures up. Perhaps that was my first real surprise with this city. I'd suspected the Capital of Country to be all blue jeans and cowboy boots, maybe even with a few dusty roads. In reality, it's a city of fashion and glamour like any other, with hybrid cars and boutique espresso houses, indistinguishable in most ways from any major metropolis. Except that there is a recurring Western theme to the neon and polished main street signage, and one can wear a ten-gallon hat over a business suit without it being taken as satirical.

That shopping trip took precedence during the morning. Next came finding a place to stay, which we did without any significant problems. We're holed up for the time being at the Rock Fork Inn, a little motel off the Murfreesboro Pike. They rent rooms by the week and we've opted for two weeks, paid up front. I don't know how long Joseph plans for us to stay in Nashville, overall, but the hotel's rate is ridiculously cheap. It's not the kind of place that advertises on the internet, and I'm half convinced that the 'Cash Highly Preferred' sign at the reception desk indicates a degree of under-the-table operation I'm quite content not to know anything more about. But it's suitable enough, and with our plans up in the air two weeks seems a good starting point. Maybe we'll be here longer. I don't think the clerk at reception is going to be upset with another fistful of cash passed his way if that becomes the case – and there's plenty of money in my checking account to withdraw as needed. If we choose to leave sooner, it's not as if we'll be out of a fortune.

'I get the shower first,' Joseph said when we got into our room. Two sagging double beds and a vomit-coloured floor, a faux-wood dresser opposite them on which is perched an old television. Nothing flat-screened or plasma here. This is the kind of television that takes a good thirty seconds to 'warm up' after you switch it on, which has a remote with large, plastic manual buttons, a knob on the front of the set that offers adjustment for 'vertical hold' and a plaque that reads '*Colour* television' as if this were an altogether surprising and unusual feature. Like something out of my youth. There are probably collectors out there who would consider this vintage and pay a small fortune for it.

I nodded and Joseph went off to the shower. I waited my turn patiently, not attempting to navigate the ancient television but instead simply staring from the corner of my bed to the rug-like curtains that hung from bent aluminium poles over the window. I don't think I had any particular thoughts with me, then. Not at first. I was eager to get beneath warm water with soap and a good washcloth. I had more to wash off me than just the remnants of dirt. I was hoping the memories that were buried inside might be water-soluble as well.

Then, as if in a great lunge of emotion, I felt the overwhelming, immediate desire to be out of my old clothes. The new were still in the K-Mart bag at the bedside and I wasn't prepared to put them on before I'd cleaned myself properly, but I felt I couldn't stay bound up in my old things a minute more. Not a single second. They pulled at me like they weighed a thousand pounds, and I had to be rid of them. I rose from the bed, tore off my shirt with more energy than I can ever remember employing in undressing, and wriggled my way out of my trousers. A few seconds later and I'd kicked off my socks, my shoes already on their sides on the floor, only leaving covered the portion of my body that shyness wasn't willing to expose, even in my desire to be rid of everything associated with *that place*. I kicked the other garments away, banishing them, and as much as I could of the past, into the far corner of the room. And I was done with them.

I sat back down, the curtains once again before my gaze from the corner of the bed. I looked down at my hands. Quietly, without any particular focus, I curled my fingernails back towards myself. I'd cleaned them fairly well in the river the other day – well enough not to be a source of questioning looks at petrol stations or McDonald's windows. But here in the light of the hotel room I saw them more closely. And beneath the nails blood was crusted, rust-coloured and crackling.

I picked at it, one fingernail burrowing under another to scrape away their contents. But the dried blood split apart rather than fell away, breaking into smaller and smaller particles that seemed only to burrow themselves more deeply into the crevasses of my nails. When I'd finished, they looked little different than they had when I'd begun.

My fingernails, still caked in blood.

For an instant, I had the strangest feeling I'd seen my hands like this before. But then – the oddest thing – I couldn't remember when. Or in what context. Or if it had ever happened at all. Or even why I was here.

65

Sunday

Breakfast this morning was two eggs and bacon, with sides of sausage and a plate of waffles for Joseph. We've both ordered the same thing for the two mornings we've been here. Habits form quickly. Our cholesterol may never be the same, but our stomachs are happy. It's amazing what a good breakfast will do to a day, no matter what else may be conspiring against it as the sun starts to rise.

It's nearing lunchtime now, and we've been wandering the downtown side streets off Lower Broadway for a few hours. Yesterday we roamed the waterfront, which is particularly beautiful and feels more like a glamorous corner of Manhattan than a city in Tennessee. Today it's Broadway and some of the more touristy sections of what is nevertheless billed as 'Real Nashville'. Real. Another one of those routinely misleading words. I've always believed that anything that feels the need to identify itself as 'real' usually isn't, just as most things marked 'authentic' are fakes and 'original' are copies. And the glass facades and boutique shops of Nashville's Lower Broadway feel just about as 'real' as I would expect.

But Joseph and I aren't unhappy strolling through the glass and plastic and fakery. We walk mostly in silence. We chit-chat here and there ('Hey, do you like those kinds of boots?' as we pass a shop window, or 'I've never fancied hats that big' as we walk by another), but nothing of substance. We'd exhausted whatever substance we have between us in the car. What's left are moments of casual banter and a generally friendly sentiment that lingers on.

And perhaps what's strangest: I don't feel the pressing desire to talk I once had. I know something was weighing on me before. Something terrible and haunting and overwhelming. But it's slipping into the past, and I'm happy to let it go. Sometimes I'm not even sure I remember what it was.

Finally, though, Joseph stops me as we approach a corner onto 5th Street. He reaches a hand out to my upper arm and gently turns me to face him. There is a serious expression in his eyes.

'What is it?' I find myself asking automatically. It's unlike Joseph to make physical contact – the one time I tried the hand-on-the-shoulder move with him he nearly took out my face with his fist. That memory hasn't faded. But he's got a firm clutch now and a pensive look.

'I've been thinking. We probably need to do something about our identities.'

A peculiar statement, and I'm not sure what he means. 'What about them?'

'Maybe we should think about concealing them. Not let people know who we really are.'

Nerves start to electrify the skin on my back. Just the slightest hint of fear. Memories that an instant ago were gone, part of the vague cloud of forgetting that lines the human mind, return. I can hear the newsreader's words, back from the television at the service station in Texas: '*an expanding manhunt*'. Joseph had told me he wasn't worried, but now he's suggesting we hide who we are, here, half a country away.

'Do you think anyone from . . . from, *back there*, is going to get to us down here?'

'We've come a long way,' he answers, 'but people are going to be looking.' He says this as if it doesn't conflict with his previous dismissal of anything that the police might do. 'Might as well not make it easy for them to find us.'

I let my gaze fall to the pavement beneath our feet. Of course Joseph is right. He's only suggesting what I probably would have proposed earlier, if he hadn't so compellingly told me to forget about any potential search. I'd convinced myself he was right, that there was no way the police in California would connect either of us to the crime; and if we weren't connected, what would it matter if anyone knew we were here?

I should have been more forceful in the car. I should have gone with my gut.

I notice there is still mud on my shoes.

'Don't look so glum about it,' Joseph says, his tone suddenly light. His clutch on my shoulder turns to a friendly tap before he draws his hand away. 'Haven't you ever pretended to be someone else? That's all we're really talking about.'

There's a smile on his face when I look back up to him. Devious. Pleased at the craft of creating a new identity. That's just like Joseph, finding something amusing at a moment when I want to let out a scream and run away to a different planet.

'Not really,' I answer, 'I haven't pretended like that since I was a kid.'

'Well, it's not rocket science. You won't have forgotten how. We just pick new names and use them from now on when we're in public.' He thinks for a second, then adds, 'And maybe best that we use them when it's just us, too. To get in the habit, so we don't slip up when there are people around.'

This sounds reasonable enough. We don't need to be broadcasting our location to all and sundry. And what can it hurt to try on a few new names while we're in a town of new adventures? It might make the starting-over nature of our time here all the more concrete and real. Something that can really get under the skin.

I don't have any idea what sort of name to choose. But in this, as in so much else, Joseph has a knowing look about him, as if he's already got it covered. So I ask him the obvious question.

'What should I call you, then?'

He has a wide grin.

'It's gotta be something simple, right? Forgettable. Some ordinary name you'd call your best friend.'

I peer at him, waiting for his choice.

'I don't know,' he finally says. 'I've always liked the name Greg.'

And I shrug my shoulders. That's that. Joseph is a thing of the past. I am standing with my best friend, one of my only friends, really. I'm standing with Greg.

66

Monday

Greg and I have passed another day in relative calm. Actually, all our time here has been profoundly uneventful, with no external excitement of any kind. It's only what's within me that makes it seem otherwise. What can you say of a street that's beautifully cared for, cleaned and clad with music-themed shops yet still makes you feel that the world is ending and your soul is being consumed, if not that it's a sign of something eating at you, rather than the street itself? And I've had those feelings, on and off, every day. Every hour we've been here. They pursue me. Though increasingly, with every hour, I'm less certain why.

I try, every so often, to rationalize them away. Vivid memories of a horrible story crash into my mind. Joseph (I have to keep reminding myself to call him Greg) was at a house somewhere far away. I was with him, too, but he was so . . . brutal. Not me. The brutality was all him. Yes, I shot too – but only once. And mine wasn't a death blow in that macabre scene. Had it just been me there the old man would have had a wounded arm and a badly bruised conscience, and that seems like an entirely reasonable price to exact for the awful things he'd done. It wasn't me who went further. It was Joseph, Greg, who killed him. Who beat him senseless. Who killed the woman. It was he who had become a savage. If I didn't feel that our fates had become inextricably interconnected in that moment, I'd flee from his presence right now. Why stay in town with someone who holds that kind of rage within him? When will it emerge again? And when it does, what is to keep it from being aimed at me? He's already pointed a gun at my face once.

But then these memories flee. They're like a poem in my mind: a flash of powerful intensity, overwhelming emotion and crisp visions which then fade, get dismissed, and retreat before the reality that remains after the poem is done. But this poem is truly horrible – one of the worst I've ever internally recited. And nothing voids the sense of guilt that looms over my shoulders every time its images come. I was there too. I played my part. And when I fail to catch my mind before it wanders too far, I find myself wondering if there will ever be another moment in my life when I don't see blood on my hands.

I allow myself a moment to appreciate this irony. I'm in Nashville, spiritual home of a genre of music built around the unshakeable principle that life just sucks, no matter what you do about it, and the sorrow of life is always following just behind you, like the flatbed of your pickup truck. That's always seemed absurdly defeatist to me – until now. Now it seems surprisingly realistic. Maybe Nashville has a force to it that breeds this kind of sentiment into the minds of any who pass through.

But it's fair to say that it isn't just me who's feeling the pressure. Greg is too. The more we try not to do anything, to be anyone, the more oppressive it all feels. I don't know how others manage going into hiding, but I've not found it the simple 'just put on the airs of someone else and lay low' craft I'd presumed it would be. It's difficult to abandon yourself, almost physically painful to give up the someone you've always known yourself to be and become no one – even for reasons of necessity. When you're a child and you amuse yourself by playing pretend, part of the joy is knowing that it's all just that: pretend, and that when you're done being a knight or soldier you get to go back to being your real self. But when you're putting on a new personality and aren't sure when, or even if, you'll be able to go back to your real identity, suddenly fun is no longer a part of the game.

It's Greg, though, not me, who finally reaches the tipping point.

'You know, Allen,' – that's what he decided he would call me – 'I think we need to get out.'

'Out?' I dread the thought of another lengthy car ride. 'I thought Nashville was far enough away. Where do you suggest we go?' Travel any further east and we start getting to bigger and bigger cities, and that seems a foolish move.

'No, not out of the city,' he answers, 'out, as in "let's go out". Out for a drink. A bit of fun.'

The word 'fun' seems absurd to me.

'You know,' he continues, 'blow off some steam and relax a little. We're both under stress.'

It's another one of those comments that makes me want to slap Greg across the face. There are so many moments like these, where his levity is just inappropriate to the situation and clashes with my internal fears. And yet there's always something marginally sensible about his suggestions. We are stressed, that's absolutely true. And if there's a way to relax, to unclench the muscles that feel like they've been held in a state of constant tension for over a week, we would probably benefit from it.

In the process of my analysis I must be shrugging my shoulders positively, since Greg smiles in approval at my apparent agreement. He slaps my shoulder again: a solid, friendly slap between friends.

'I saw a bar a few streets back that looks like just the right sort of place,' he says. 'You up for something like that?'

'A bar?' He knows I'm not a fan of bars.

'Don't think of it as just a bar,' he answers, 'think of it as an experience. You like country western, and you can't have country western without a saloon and a few bar-stools, right?'

It's my turn to smile. It's to be an experience, then. And it doesn't sound bad. 'All right. Let's give it a try.'

'Fantastic.' Greg turns on his heels so he's facing back the way we came. 'Let's go back to the motel, catch a nap till the sun goes down, then come back and have a proper night of it.'

He's grinning. He looks genuinely happy with the plan. And who am I to disagree?

67

Monday Evening

The time has come for us to make our entry back into the world of social exposure and living encounters with other people. Greg and Allen, our new cloak-and-dagger identities, intent on not remaining in hiding forever. And as darkness has spread out over the city and streetlights and neon signs have burst to life, I have to admit that I'm glad Greg has thought up this plan. I'm not sure I could have handled another night holed up in that motel room with only the sound of evening television and lust-inflamed grunts through the wall of the room next door. Time seems to stand still there, the present coming to bear an increasingly mystical, disjointed relationship to the past.

The bar Greg has found is as perfect as he said it would be, and he's absolutely right: it's a postcard picture of the 'genuine' experience. The sign saying Jake's

Hitching Post is in tangerine neon with blue accents, and the moment we walk in I feel we've found the ideal spot. The best bar in Nashville. Every stereotype I could have hoped for is here: raw wood floors, vinyl-topped bar-stools and an old-fashioned jukebox that still uses records rather than CDs or digital files. And there is country paraphernalia on the walls in abundance: a mounted deer's head (a twelve-pointer, by my count), a rope lasso in a glass case, even a pair of rodeo chaps that have been signed – illegibly – by some hero of the arena.

I love the place from the second we arrive. I'd been leery of our outing until just this moment, but now I'm finding myself truly excited about the evening ahead. The past immediately feels a little further away. Another continent and another world.

The music, too, is just the sort that I expect, and it does my heart good to hear it. The kind of proper country western you would have heard in the Eighties – Vince Gill and Holly Dunn and Dwight Yoakam – not the half-pop nonsense that passes for country today. I glance at Greg's face as we walk towards the bar and I see he's smiling at the music, too. So we share our taste in music, at least nominally. It's nice to see him, for a moment, looking happy.

At the bar we take stools side by side and prop our elbows on the highly polished surface. My wallet is thick in my back pocket. We'd stopped at an ATM along the way to charge up on cash for the evening ahead. I've always felt it's better to tip bartenders in cash than on a card. You get better service in return, and it's nice to throw down the bills every so often and feel the tinge of showmanship that comes with the act.

It's funny, but for all that Greg and I have shared on our journey to this place, for all that we've gone through together, I realize in this moment, as we sit side by side, that we still really don't know each other. The conversations I was so keen to have, about events and families and fears, they're important things. We've even covered some ground with them. But you can't rush getting to know a person. I might know that Greg is an only child who had trouble with his parents, but until this instant I didn't know what sort of music he liked, or which spot at the bar, or whether he props his feet on the metal ring of the stool or on the bar itself. The unimportant things. The things that make a person a personality. Circumstance has attached us at the hip, but we're still essentially strangers.

I'm not sure what causes me to notice the little television perched above the bar. It's in black and white, its picture a little hazy, and for an instant I'm reminded of a television I've seen somewhere else, perched high, just like this. It feels like it wasn't long ago. The memory brings bad feelings into my stomach, but in this instant I can't place their origins. My stomach rumbles.

It's hard to make out the audio over the music and tumult in the bar, but I lean in and can just catch the words. The image is of a uniformed police officer – a navy-blue shirt covered in a badge, medals and various stripes – before a podium, surrounded by other official-looking figures. A subtitle on the screen identifies him as Lieutenant Donald Rogers of the Shasta County Police Force in California. 'PRESS CONFERENCE' is marked out in bold letters just above his name.

I feel strangely as if I should be reacting to this. Like something in my stomach wants viscerally to feel something. Fear. Trepidation. But in this setting I can't really connect to those emotions. These things are taking place in a different world, and I'm in a new environment. I even have a new name.

A multiple homicide in northern California on 14th June, seven days ago, is believed to have been committed by a person or persons who have since fled the jurisdiction of the County, and likely have crossed state lines.

The officer on the screen reads from a written report. His voice is matter-of-fact, and he looks uncomfortable standing before cameras and reporters. Homicide is an ugly word. He doesn't seem to like saying it.

We are coordinating with the FBI to track down the whereabouts of the prime suspect in the case, an 18-year-old male named Thomas Warrick. The victims are the suspect's parents, and local investigators believe the homicides may have been revenge killings for what neighbours describe as decades of home abuse.

I feel an immediate sense of relief. This name means nothing to me. Though my palms are sweating and I can feel my heart thumping, it's clear this report is nothing to do with me. With us. I do know that I feel guilty, deeply guilty about my recent actions; but the details are all a blur. I'm sure it's being here that's causing the haze – Nashville. The bar. With a new name. With a new friend. My memory's gone a little cloudy. Though I don't really know my new friend that well. A bit of the pace to my pulse returns.

Thomas Warrick is considered extremely dangerous, and as the two weapons that forensics have determined were used in the attack, a .22 calibre rifle and a .38 handgun, have yet to be recovered, is presumed still to be armed.

I feel my pulse start to return to normal. It's the repetition of the name that does it. Thomas Warrick is a name I've never heard before. And I know names change, and we've been changing ours. But Greg was Joseph before he was Greg, just like I was Dylan before I was Allen. He wasn't Tom, or Thomas. This story isn't about him. It's nothing to do with us. Nothing to do with us. Our lives are, I think, connected to that house and that horror, but the police are not after us.

If located or if any information in your area is forthcoming, approach the subject only with caution. Accomplice or accomplices a possibility. The brutality of the crimes makes him, or them, the highest possible threat. We advise contacting our office or your local FBI station office prior to any direct action.

The press conference may or may not go on. I don't

know. I've lost interest, and my attention is back at the bar.

I look to my essentially-stranger friend. For an instant there is a real fondness in my heart. The world out there is so terrible, home to so much turmoil – the police report on the television is a case in point – that it's nice to have found someone keen to join you in a bar and escape from it all together. And it's pleasing to see that we share so much in common (not just the music; I notice in this instant that we both have our feet locked onto the metal rings of our bar-stools. I make a mental tally of this meaningless point of personality that draws us closer together). And our shared tastes become even more surprising when we find ourselves ordering the same drink.

'A double Jaegermeister, straight up,' we say, in an almost comical unison, as if we'd been practising the act.

I immediately laugh and turn to face him. 'You're joking. You like it too?'

Greg grins back. 'I can't say I really like it. It's just . . . well, to be honest, I've never had it before.'

'You're kidding me!'

He looks slightly embarrassed. 'Just never had the opportunity, I guess.'

'No, I mean you've got to be joking. Neither have I! What are the chances?' I'm shaking my head in amused disbelief. 'I mean, you're young, so it isn't really a surprise you haven't tried it.' I realize as I'm saying this that it's puzzling the bartender hasn't carded him. Greg doesn't look twenty-one by any stretch, but the bartender apparently isn't asking any questions. Maybe that's just how things roll in Nashville.

'But for me,' I continue, 'it's a bit more unusual. I've been drinking for a lot of years.'

'But still never tried the stuff?'

I shake my head. 'I guess it's a night for firsts.'

It feels satisfying to say this. The brown, herbally scented stuff arrives and Greg raises his small glass towards mine.

'Here's to firsts.'

We slam back the drinks in another act of spectacularly accidental synchronicity. The Jaegermeister burns and has a bitterness I wasn't expecting, but it's wild and wonderful at the same time, filled with berries and flowers and barks and spice. I'm strangely thrilled by it.

A few moments later we order two more. And then, later, another two. The longer the night goes on the more at ease we both feel. Maybe drink really does bring strangers together. Every so often I can almost feel Joseph's – Greg's – thoughts. Our minds, I think, must echo each other's after what we've been through. An aftereffect of seeing the same horrific sights. Of having our hands together in them. But now, with that behind us . . . why shouldn't we relax and find relief together?

But then there are moments when I find myself feeling suddenly fearful; and I look to my left and see Greg with the same look of fear in his eyes. In the worse, as in the better, we are of one mind. We slam back another drink. New, true friends.

And it's that sense of friendship, of brotherhood, that bursts my whole being into a panic when I see him start to convulse and fall to the ground.

68

Monday Evening

Greg is on the floor in under a second, and it looks like he is hyperventilating. He's overtaken, by what I don't know, and his chest begins to flutter. His skin appears clammy, even in the dark bar light. He hadn't appeared even remotely ill a moment ago, and I have no idea what may have overtaken him. But once again, in this shocked instant, I realize that I don't know Greg all that well. There's so much that I can't explain. Maybe it's the alcohol – I'm not feeling entirely well myself – or maybe it's a condition or a disease he's borne his whole life. Maybe it's just panic. I am helplessly uninformed.

As his chest dances with its spasms and convulsions, though, my own heart starts to squeeze with dread. Whatever its cause, something is wrong. Terribly, terribly wrong. I see Greg crumbling and I am overcome with sudden fear. Fear inside. Fear everywhere. *We're going to be found out. We're guilty. We're never going to get away.* I know in an instant that I'm panicked for him, but I'm overwhelmed for us.

His body hitting the floor causes me a strange pain. I can almost feel the impact in my own flesh; there where his shoulder hits the wood, I sense a blow. *I can't let him die* . . . I'm suddenly convinced that Greg is going to die. The world is ending and Greg is going to die. But I feel a personal attachment to him now. It happened quickly, but it's real. We're not strangers any longer.

Since I know with this absolute certainty that Greg is close to death, I act on my conviction. I have to save him. I can't lose him. *Not again.* The words blaze through my mind, though even as they come I don't know what they mean.

I fling myself off my bar-stool and lunge down into the floor after him. His body is writhing. I don't know what to do, but I know that every movie I've ever seen with a scene like this involves someone giving CPR to the person on the ground, and that seems like the sensible action to take. I've never been trained in the skill, but it can't be that complicated. I understand the basics. I place my hands over each other and begin to press them into his chest. I space out the compressions by counting the way I used to do as a child: *One-Mississippi, two-Mississippi, three-Mississippi* . . .

There is yelling around me now, yelling as if people in the bar are upset with me. Disgusted. I don't understand, but I won't be deterred. I think I'm doing what's right. I feel my chest constricting, my heart racing.

I don't get to my fourth compression before I'm wrested away from Greg's body. I'm not sure how it happens. Isn't that the very strangest thing? One second I'm there, about to rescue my friend, providing him with life-saving aid, and a second later I'm off to the side, watching. I don't think a hand has pulled me here. I really don't understand what's happening—

I'm suddenly overcome with a new emotion. The crowd has surrounded Greg on the floor, and all at once they look ominous. I don't know why for an instant I feel far from him, but I'm abruptly certain their motives aren't good. None of them are doing CPR. No one is trying to save him, or even help. They're just looming, sinister. One of them is in a uniform, and he looks the most sinister of all.

Now there is motion again, and my alert is heightened. An enormous bouncer is moving in from the doorway, bulky and lumbering. His face is red and angry and his eyes narrowed with intensity. I can't explain why, but I'm convinced his intentions are foul and I feel an uncontrollable urge to stop him before he gets to Greg. To fend him off before he can harm my friend.

I do the only thing that makes sense. I'm scrawny, yes, but a man has to do what a man has to do. I swing at the bouncer with all my strength. My knuckles are in a tight fist when they collide with the side of his face, and I try to push all my body weight into the punch. It's the only time I can ever remember hitting a man. I hope I'm doing it right.

The blow has absolutely no physical effect on him. I'm a fly batting at the thick hide of a horse. But it does alter the focus of his attention and he turns from Greg to me. I think that for an instant I realize what he's going to do, but I have no time to contemplate it. His bulky arm moves, and the fist that swings into my face is like an iron cannon. I'm on the floor in an instant: none of that shake-it-off-and-swing-back magic of action films. One punch and I am levelled. Levelled until consciousness returns, and I have no idea how long that takes.

As I come to the bouncer is no longer in front of me. I think I've been left alone. The floor stinks of stale beer. My head is exploding.

I loll my head to the side and try to get a look at Joseph. The whole right side of my face feels like it's been tenderized. It's hard to move, but I want to see him. I want to know he's okay. And then, through legs and feet, I catch sight of him. Joseph is still surrounded by the throng of people. He's writhing, but for an instant he turns his head towards me.

His face is marked with a massive bruise. The last image in my mind as I black out is that wound on his face. It's in the very spot where my own face aches, where the blow I just took had landed.

69

Monday Evening

I'm awake. Conscious. *How long have I been out? Am I still here?*

I try to look around me, to take in my surroundings. Above me the scene is surreal. There are neon signs. Big hats. A leather riding crop on the wall. Cigarette smoke in the air. The images don't make sense. This isn't San Francisco. I've never seen such big hats in San Francisco.

I try to move, but something is constraining my motion. I think I'm on the ground. On my back. That explains the strange perspective. There is pressure on my chest, like there is a foot or a brick on my ribcage.

I feel detached from myself. Did I lose consciousness? Did I black out?

But the feeling is deeper than that. Something within me has . . . I can't find the right words. Something isn't right. I feel broken. I can't figure out who or what I am.

It's the strangest feeling, not to know who or what you are.

I blink, and my vision changes. No, I'm not on the floor. I'm standing at the side of the room. Of course I am. I wouldn't be on the floor, that's a foolish place to be. I look down, though, and see myself on the ground, surrounded by a small mob. I don't recognize myself at first – I can't remember ever seeing myself in this way, looking on like an outside observer. It's as if I'm peering through a camera mounted on the wall, beholding a recording of myself.

No, I'm mistaken again. It isn't me. I know who it is. It's the one called Joseph. Or Greg. Yes, it's him on the floor, not me. We came here together, I think. Yes, that's right. We were in a car, then a hotel, then here. It's him, not me. It wouldn't be me. *I'm not the kind of person who can do what Joseph did.*

I can't remember what Joseph did. For a moment I feel like I should, like his actions should mean something to me and I should have them emblazoned in my consciousness. I think it was something terrible. Maybe that's why I'm lying there on the floor like that. That is, if it's me on the floor and not Joseph. Or Greg.

I don't know how long I've been here or how long I've been thinking these thoughts, but it seems like the police arrive extraordinarily quickly. They're bursting through the front door. Yes, that's the right poetic phrase. One launches through a window but bursts through a door. That's what these men do. But maybe they're not police, after all. They are forceful men with stern faces and large letters on their jackets, bold yellow on black: FBI. Ah, that explains it. The FBI are definitely the sort of people who would burst through doors.

There are guns drawn, and I can feel my insides churn. I've sometimes wondered what it would feel like to have a gun pointed at me – what my reaction would be. In films people usually cower in a kind of whimpering, emasculated terror, begging for mercy and making promises . . . but then, as I wonder, I think I've had a gun in my face before. That I probably didn't react like that. But why would I have had a gun in my face? It's not as if I live a life of—

The FBI men's march is towards me, and suddenly I suffer intense fear. Do you know what it's like to feel threatened? To suddenly be convinced of your own imminent demise? One doesn't think rationally or ponder one's moves. Instinct drives me and I make to lunge for these men, these intruders – but no, no, it's Joseph again, not me. He's the one doing the lunging. It's hazy, my head hurts, and I'm confused. Joseph is lunging, but I am moving, that much I do know.

Two shots are fired. Warnings, I think, at my, or his, or our, feet. God, it's confusing. The small throng of people from the bar back away and the jacketed FBI men move in. And then there are cuffs. They're cuffing Joseph, I'm watching them do it. But when they slap closed the cuffs on his hands, I feel steel clasp around my own wrists. At least, I'm very nearly certain they're my wrists.

I only catch murmurs of conversations in the room around us. 'That's the one. I'm off duty but I saw the

APB in the office today.' The man with the uniform at the bar is talking. His voice has an accent I find vaguely ridiculous. 'This guy was acting really suspicious. Talking to himself at the bar. Something about running away, about hiding in the woods. Seemed worth calling in.'

I don't know what this means. I go to the park, not the woods. There are no woods in San Francisco. The world has stopped making sense.

'Good you did.' Another voice now, this one coming from one of the FBI men. 'We'd got a ping on his debit card from an ATM two blocks away just a couple of hours ago. Your call narrowed down the search.'

I remember I used a debit card earlier. Very convenient. I always like to have cash on hand when ordering at a bar, and Joseph and I were going to get some drinks. But I think we were calling each other by different names.

One of the bigger men looms over me. He tightens the cuffs until they hurt my hands. 'A fucking monumental overreaction, dipshit.' I think he's talking to me. 'You want to act out at Mommy and Daddy, learn to hurl a few good insults or steal some cash.' He seems revolted at the sight of me, but I can't figure out why. Maybe I drank too much and made a fool of myself. That can sometimes happen. I can play the pretty fool when I have too much to drink, and I've been known to have some spectacular blackouts.

'And if you can't hold your liquor,' he adds, almost confirming my suspicion, 'then stay the fuck out of a bar when you're plotting your escape.'

He's lost me again. Escapes are for villains and showmen, but I'm a poet and poets don't make escapes. We dwell in moments. We linger and persist and contemplate. But I don't have the strength to try to interpret this man's strange speech. I can't be responsible for everybody.

Suddenly my heart aches. I feel sorrowful, then the sorrow becomes fear. Worse things are happening than the cuffs on my wrists and the officer's strange speech. Joseph is fading. As I peer at him across the floor he's fading, though I'm not even sure I know what that means. He's thinner, ethereal. He's a phantom, becoming a mist. And now I can't see him any more.

Maybe there are just too many people in here.

My head is going light, and suddenly all the attention is on me. I can feel my consciousness ebb. And for reasons I cannot fathom, the last words I hear before I black out again are those of one of the officers.

'Tom Warrick, you are under arrest on a Federal warrant for murder in the state of California.'

And it strikes me I know that name. Or perhaps Joseph knew that name. And I remember a boy, and a pond, and a park . . .

PART FIVE

VACAVILLE, CALIFORNIA

70

California Medical Facility – State Prison The Present Day

'Can you bring him outside, let him get a little light?'

The voice of Pauline Lavrentis bounces off the brick walls. They've all been whitewashed in the last month, a new coat of paint over a dozen coats before. The knobby surface of cinder bricks beneath has long since been rendered completely smooth by the paint, giving all the walls a sheened, reflective pallor.

'Of course, Doctor.' An orderly pushes the wheelchair through a mesh door into an enclosed courtyard marked 4-BG. Corridor number four, and one of the spots known colloquially as 'breathing grounds'. Places for inmates to escape the antiseptic interior of their cells and common halls and catch as much fresh air as their sentences will permit.

Passage through two gates is required to gain entrance, and ID badges must be shown each time, with records taken and access statistics recorded. Corridor four is for prisoners with aggressive tendencies and euphemistically titled 'behavioural issues'. It's for the crazies, and the violent crazies most often of all.

'Wheel him over there, if you would,' Dr Lavrentis continues to instruct the orderly. She has done this many times before. It's an old routine, even if it's been a while since the last time out. She knows the spots he likes. Those that tend to keep him calm.

The wheelchair is moved to the spot that inmate #10481-91 always prefers: the north-eastern corner of the cement courtyard, where at midday the sun casts a shadow just beside the plastic fountain donated by the Sisters of Mercy five years ago. The little unit once had a motor that kept water constantly cycling through a minuscule 'spring' that emerged from a plastic rock at its centre, on which a pair of plastic sparrows sits in permanent pose, but the motor had died after its first few months of use. The water in the fountain is now a heavy brown, bits of algae floating on its surface and more sticking to the bowl itself. But the inmate never seems to mind.

'That'll do.' Lavrentis taps the orderly on the shoulder. A maternal sign of thanks.

She looks down at her patient, his right ankle cuffed

to his wheelchair. This was one of the conditions of his right to visit this spot, granted as a special exception to his otherwise complete restriction to solitary confinement. Pauline hadn't been able to sway the board away from that decision, not after his last violent outburst, but after so many months of exceptional behaviour in solitary he'd been granted this one privilege – at her special pleading – without being given the right to return to the general population. But he is required to remain cuffed to the wheelchair, though Pauline knows he always prefers to sit on the sagging green plastic chair with a broken back that's near the little fountain. She thinks she can just manage to manipulate him in such a way that he can swivel onto that seat with his right leg still attached to the chair, and decides it's worth the effort. It takes a bit of doing, but after a few seconds he's seated on the squeaking seat, the wheelchair at his side.

Pauline had worked hard to obtain the requisite permissions for this exceptional visit. For months her requests on her patient's behalf had been refused out of hand. Men in solitary don't get time off for restful breaks in courtyards. But finally she'd managed this afternoon's privilege: only forty-five minutes, and only under lock and-key and constant guarding. It's a test run, and in a few days there will be a hearing to determine if visits like this can become more regular. But for the moment it is enough, and Pauline intends to make the most of it.

The transition into solitary confinement had been

disastrous for the inmate's mental state. She'd predicted it would be, and she'd been proved right. Pauline knows her former patient is gone, that this man only bears the marks of him. But she hadn't been able to halt the essentially automatic process that took over once his increasing violence led to an assault on a guard. At least they hadn't decided to keep him permanently bound.

Some people can bear solitary, others can't. There was never any question in Pauline's mind into which category this man fell. The moment his sentence had been altered, she had known he was already lost.

In some real, practical and diagnostic sense, there is nothing for her to do. No treatments left. No more therapies to pursue. But she has been working with him a long time. And as she sees him now, back outside – even if bound – she feels there is the slightest flicker of hope. If she can manage to make this more regular, there is the chance at least that he will find some peace. And she wants that for him. Just that. After everything.

She grabs a second plastic chair and walks it over to a position at a right angle to his. There's no place to set a recorder between them, and the sight of it seems to bother him these days anyway, so she clicks it on and places it out of sight in her breast pocket.

'I'm happy to see you here,' she says, kindly, sitting down and drawing her right leg over her left. Her eyes are genuine, the tone friendly.

The inmate looks up. He is startled, but his eyes are gentle.

'Oh, I'm sorry, ma'am. I didn't see you arrive. Must have been lost in my thoughts.' He smiles, a perfectly ordinary smile.

'What brings you to my pond today?'

71

Conference Room 6A
California Medical Facility

When the time comes for Pauline to go before the governance board with her request, the trial run of her patient's first visit to the courtyard having gone smoothly and without incident, she finds herself uncharacteristically hesitant. She's made similar requests many times before for other patients; she's always been a strong advocate for those in her care. Her nerves aren't caused by the content of her request.

She is anxious only because she expects to receive little sympathy. She knows, in the depth of her being, that her cause is important and the request reasonable. But she also knows this is going to be an almost impossible thing to prove. Inmates who attack guards with shanks that draw blood and pierce organs go into solitary and stay there a good, long time. Her patient has only been in such confinement for twenty months, and that isn't even close to long enough. But she knows that that continuing time in solitary is nothing more than torture for a man who is already gone.

There is another worry. If the panel is made up of the same members who had been on the review committee after the incident that had sent her patient into isolation, she doesn't expect a generous audience to hear her plea. Still, she is determined to try at what needs to be done, even if a try is all it will amount to. At least they'd finally agreed to hear her request, rather than refusing it outright as they'd done some nine times previously.

Pauline pushes open the door to meeting room 6A and finds the configuration almost identical to that of the previous interview session. These surroundings rarely change. A panel, a stenographer, and the interviewee.

It is only the panel that Pauline is interested in, and immediately her heart starts to feel its hope slip away. There at the centre of the table is the familiar visage of Benjamin Tolbert, again in the chair, his silver hair still several inches above the heads of the others. He wears what appears to be the same burgundy tie he'd sported at the previous hearing, though the suit today is brown rather than powder blue. It still clashes terribly.

To his left is Tyrone Davis. Pauline had expected that. The warden always has a place on panels like this. It's a fixed part of his remit, and he is responsible for input on all decisions relating to inmate arrangements, something today's session is certainly slated to deal with. He looks just as stern, forceful and cross as Pauline expected.

But the woman on the other side of the chairman is a surprise. This is not the fearsome visage of Christina Vermille, who had been there two years ago, and whom Pauline had seen on so many occasions since. In many ways, the delicately brown-skinned female who now sits at the head table is Vermille's opposite. A soft expression instead of hard, short hair neatly done up instead of long and let down, and a smile that seems moulded in her cheeks rather than the scowl that was a plastic fixture on the other woman's face. The placard on the table before her reads 'Alice Anonando', a name with an ethnic origin Pauline can't identify, but she begins to feel the slightest touch of her hope return.

'Let's just get right to it, shall we?' Tolbert says into the microphone. 'All our names have already been entered into the record from the proceedings sheet I provided, yes?' The stenographer nods in the affirmative. 'Very good.' He turns to Pauline. 'Dr Lavrentis, it is difficult for this panel to understand that you would even contemplate making this request.'

Pauline cannot miss the exasperation in the chairman's voice. He is genuinely flabbergasted.

'To seek permission for this inmate to be transferred out of isolation and granted routine recreational access to courtyard areas, less than two years after a pattern of increasing aggression led to a third escape attempt – one that included inflicting severe bodily injury upon a guard. I'm shocked you think it would even be seriously considered.'

The warden grunts. The expression on his face makes it clear he is in perfect agreement with the chairman.

Pauline leans in towards her microphone. 'I realize this is unusual.' Another sarcastic snort from the warden, and she tries not to pay it attention. 'I know I am making this request far sooner than might be usual, but I can honestly say that in my professional estimation inmate #10481-91 poses no further risk of violence, and that granting him a return to the general population and access to common recreational areas on a limited basis will pose no security or safety issues to the institution or its staff.'

Professional-speak, with all the right keywords included.

Warden Davis is incredulous. 'In your professional estimation? I'm sorry, Dr Lavrentis, but long experience or not, you cannot deny this man's character, or what he's done.'

'I am not denying it, Warden. I am, however, suggesting – with the full weight of over three decades of experience behind me –' she emphasizes this point as a means of pushing his indignation back a notch – 'that this most recent venture and its consequences have changed him. Permanently.'

'What does that mean?' Benjamin Tolbert asks.

'It means the events of that last outburst, and its consequences . . . they've broken him.'

'He wasn't broken before?'

'In a different way, yes,' Pauline answers, 'and we were making some real progress in overcoming some of his most fundamental issues. He was beginning to understand the nature of the rifts inside himself, and showing signs that he might be able to work towards repairing them. But that, that's . . .' She hesitates. 'That's gone now.'

The new woman, Alice, readjusts her position and leans in to her microphone. She forgets to switch it on and takes a moment fumbling with the button before the stenographer gives her the go-ahead from her desk at the side.

'Dr Lavrentis, can you explain to me what that means? Rifts?'

These are the new woman's first words, and Pauline is encouraged by what sounds, at least, like an empathetic question.

'You have to understand that in patients like this one, there is a degree of psychological fracture. A break within his consciousness. In this individual's case, that fracture has been multifaceted and severe for many years, and yet all the various pieces have still been connected. Interacting with one another. But this last trauma – the renewed thought of escape, the surge towards freedom, the violence he enacted against the guard – it was the breaking point. Internally he had perhaps made plans for crafting a new start to his life, but that new start began with a surge of violence, a shank pushed through the flesh of another human being, and more blood on his hands. As quickly as the hope had come, it was dashed. By the time that evening was over, what had been fractured in him for so long had become permanently broken. When he went into isolation, even the pieces were crushed.'

Alice shakes her head. 'I'm sorry, Dr Lavrentis. I'm not a psychologist, and I'm only becoming familiar with this inmate's case file. I might need some of that in more lay vocabulary. This wasn't the first escape attempt by your patient, though it was the most violent. What set this event apart?'

'I believe he had convinced himself that he was truly at the verge of walking back into his past,' Pauline answers. 'Rather, into an imagined version of it. Into a different life. That if he could just make it beyond these walls he could shake off everything and return to another existence. A peaceful life, with a different spirit, different circumstances. I note that on this occasion he attempted his escape with two other men. I can only assume he'd brought himself to believe they were his friends, rejoining him for a purer existence. In reality his friendships themselves are delusions he'd crafted in the first days after his crime, stirred back up and providing once again the same sense of hope.'

'The new faces of imagined friends?'

'Faces change for him all the time,' Pauline says. 'That, too, is a part of his condition. I think he'd hoped the return of familiar faces was going to help bring him into a freedom he remembered, or imagined, that he once knew. But it all fell apart, and to be placed in solitary confinement afterwards, with the prospect of remaining there indefinitely . . . it represented a point of collapse. Reality has simply disintegrated for him.'

'All that matters,' the warden interrupts, 'is that he's a man with an extraordinarily violent past.' The skin at his temples is flexing in annoyance. 'He's unstable, and in the estimation of *my* long experience,' he looks directly at Pauline as he says this, 'he most certainly poses an ongoing danger.'

Pauline forces herself to remain calm. She knows the warden has strong opinions, and doesn't fault him for his reading of the situation. Perhaps, were she in his position, she might read it the same way. But she isn't, and she cannot.

'It is true that Thomas Warrick was once extremely violent,' she says. It seems an appropriate moment to humanize him, especially for the new panel member, and to refer to him by name rather than number. 'And there are reasons for that violence that are spelled out in full, and rather gruesome, detail in his file. As a young child he suffered ongoing and extreme physical abuse at the hands of his father, as did his mother. This wasn't unknown to neighbours and others in their town, but this was the late Seventies. People didn't exactly report things with the same urgency in those days.'

'He acted out back then?' Alice asks. 'As a child?'

'We've never found evidence that he was violent as a boy, but this isn't uncommon in cases like his. As a small child the individual – despite being, as in Thomas's case, intelligent, curious, and bright for his age – is nevertheless powerless. His father was a big man who worked in a mechanic's shop: plenty of muscle and physical mass. Tom would have learned early, probably through experience, that any attempt to respond to his father's abuse with a physical reaction would only make matters worse.'

'The father would abuse him further,' Alice adds, grasping the point.

'Or would take it out on the mother. Tom, like most children in this kind of situation, was equally traumatized by witnessing the violence his father enacted on his mother, and so he would have learned, too, that any acting out on his part would have resulted in more beatings for her.'

'Damn,' Alice sighs. Pauline is extremely pleased. She has found a sympathetic hearer. Someone who, perhaps, is new enough to dealing with these kinds of cases that the pure ugliness of what is involved still affects her. Pauline is well aware that it doesn't have the same effect on the chairman or the warden. They've seen cases like this many times over.

'His violence began when he was a teenager,' Pauline continues. 'According to the trial that followed his capture after the murders, Tom Warrick had run away from home shortly after his seventeenth birthday. His schoolteachers were called upon to help pin down a date, tied into his sudden departure from class. His parents, the court presumes, had assumed he was gone for good, and there is testimony from neighbours to the effect that

Andrew Warrick, the father, had understood his son to be "a lost cause".'

'But I take it that wasn't the case?' Alice asks.

'Tom had indeed run away from home, but he hadn't gone far. Investigators eventually discovered a small makeshift hut he'd constructed for himself in the forest behind his family's property in the north of the state. He'd remained in the area, living close by, secretly. Just how he looked after himself – food, and the like – for almost eleven months is something that was never fully explained in the trial. But it became clear that he'd been living close enough by that he could watch his home.'

'Watch?'

'That's right,' Pauline affirms. 'Tom's intention had apparently been to monitor his home. He knew he'd escaped the direct abuse of his father by simply running away, but he stayed behind to see if it meant his father might also go easier on his mother. Maybe he thought he was the fuel that sparked his father's venom, and if he were out of the picture his mother would fare better.'

'But . . .' Chairman Tolbert interjects.

Pauline nods. He already knows the facts. 'But that wasn't how it happened. Tom observed, from afar, that the opposite took place. His father became more aggressive, and his mother suffered fierce and more frequent assaults.'

'Christ, that poor woman. That kid.' Alice is shaking her head.

'He had all his own traumas in his conscience, plus a

new feeling of guilt over the increased suffering of his mother. At some level, he felt responsible for what was happening to her. One day, he simply couldn't take any more. He attacked.'

'Not to deny the horrors that boy went through,' the warden interjects, 'but to say he "attacked" is putting it damned mildly, Dr Lavrentis. Tom Warrick was eighteen at the time, an adult, and he slaughtered them.'

Alice is leaning forward. She's read the file on the actual murders and the extraordinary violence they involved.

'He acted alone?' she asks.

'No accomplices were ever found,' Tolbert answers from the central seat at the table. He's known the details of this case for years. 'Nor were any ever expected, though for a time there was a search that included the possibility. But when the two weapons used in the murders were eventually recovered, there was only one set of fingerprints on them.'

'In his outburst,' Pauline continues, 'Tom Warrick simply lost control. All his suffering and pain burst something inside him, and the result was an extraordinary show of unrestrained, uncontrolled violence.'

Alice looks back down at the table, flips through the papers in front of her. 'And this was the result of what you've called his personality issues?'

'No,' Pauline objects, 'it's the other way around. Thomas had been a normal, healthy boy before the abuse. Even bright, by his school reports. Creative, advanced for his age, imaginative. That's something that's stayed with him throughout his life, through everything. He comes from a low-heeled background, but he learned early on to absorb other worlds through books, through stories, through whatever means were at his disposal. But despite that creative mind, the result of all that torment, and then the trauma of his outburst and violent acts – he found himself engaged in actions he had never thought or believed himself capable of committing. And his mind simply could not accept what he'd done. It was too much for it to hold, too much for his personality to take. So he created another personality to compensate. Someone else to blame for the crime.'

'And that other personality,' Alice asks, 'that's this . . . Joseph?'

'Tom often calls himself Joseph. I'm convinced that's the first personality that emerged. Or perhaps it's better to say the first split that took place within him. I haven't been able to get fully to the bottom of its origins but, often in cases like this, the initial personality that's created is modelled off the memory of someone the patient had trusted in his past. A childhood friend, a school mate. Someone in his life that he associated with comfort and safety. We've never found anyone named Joseph in Thomas's school records, so we don't know who that model may have been for him; but whoever it was, it was the image that became his first new personality. The first buffer between him and the reality of his situation. But as he fled the crime scene, moving east across the country in the weeks before his capture, the personalities began to multiply. With each, he was able to distance himself, mentally, a little further from his actions. Each new personality became a new intermediary, which put him a little further from the blood he had on his hands. So, before long, Joseph became Greg. Greg became Allen.'

Alice nods a developing understanding.

'And when did Dylan emerge?'

'Dylan first surfaced after the trial, after his conviction. He was extradited back to California from Nashville in July nineteen eighty-seven, and by the time the trial was complete and the sentence passed the next year, Dylan had taken over. He seems to be a composite of experiences that Tom had had in his youth, together with more he's absorbed from things he's read and heard – his voraciousness as a reader has never left him, and he's been one of the most frequent visitors to the prison library since he arrived. He loves poetry. There's a chance that Dylan comes from Dylan Thomas, whose works his records show he's checked out on numerous occasions, but I am unable to speak with certainty on this. He reads anything, everything, absorbing details of culture and social refinement he's never experienced elsewhere in his life.

'He's been particularly interested in San Francisco as long as I've been working with him,' Pauline continues, 'as well as in gardens, parks and lakes. He discovered a book in the prison library on the history of Golden Gate

Park and the San Francisco Botanical Gardens, and this seems to have strongly shaped the Dylan personality.'

'The man doesn't have a goddamned clue who or where he is,' the warden snorts. Pauline tries to ward off his dismissiveness with an affirmation.

'It's true that he has lost his hold on reality. But what he's dreamed up has become real for him, and so his everyday experiences here in the institution are grafted into his imaginary world. Prior to his transfer into solitary two years ago, after the escape attempt, he'd been on morning work duty in the Ward Four pharmacy. In his mind he's translated this into employment in San Francisco, working at a health food supplements shop. Mitch Whittaker, the inmate with oversight of the pharmacy, became Michael, Dylan's friendly boss.'

'He's nuts,' the warden states.

'The walk he used to take down the mainline corridor towards his cell block, following his work shift, became a stroll through the park towards a favourite place. And,' Pauline straightens herself as she comes to the real substance of her request, 'the forty-five minutes in courtyard 4-BG became his sanctuary. BG became "Botanical Gardens", and what he saw when he would sit there, by that small plastic fountain, was a tranquil pond in a forested retreat. The broken chair became a bench. His bench. It's where he found his calm.'

There is a moment of contemplation on the panel. Finally, it is Alice who speaks.

'And it's to this courtyard that you wish to request he be permitted access again, now?'

'That is correct,' Pauline answers. 'I honestly believe –' she gazes straight into the warden's eyes as she says this, willing him to understand – 'that he poses no further risk. He did before, it's true. I don't deny that. But Tom Warrick is gone, Warden. The fragments of him that remained, of that boy with all his tortured memories and violent past: they've died. There is no other way to put it. The man who injured your guard no longer exists. You saw how passive he was during his trial outing to the courtyard last week. He's not who he was before. All that's left is Dylan Aaronsen, a shop worker from San Francisco who thinks he's a poet.'

'And you don't think there's hope of helping him back?' Alice asks. There is real empathy in her voice.

Pauline shakes her head. Her shoulders slouch. She suddenly feels older than she did a moment ago. Depleted.

'No. That boy from so long ago is gone. I can't bring him back. All we can do is let the different person he's become live in his delusion. He wants to sit in his park and write poetry. That's all.'

And that is it. Pauline has said all she has to say.

Seconds pass in what seems a heavy silence. Finally, Benjamin Tolbert leans towards his microphone.

'The panel thanks you for your request and your testimony here this afternoon, Dr Lavrentis. What you've asked us to consider is unusual, to say the least. And weighty.'

Pauline doesn't know what these words forebode.

'We will need time to consider. You'll have a determination letter from the administrative office within two weeks.'

He signals to the stenographer, and at her flip of a switch the red lights on all their microphones go dark.

72

Friday – Two Weeks Later

I'm on my bench again this lunchtime. No surprises. The morning was the usual routine, but I've found my way back to my spot. To my perfect, ideal, sacred spot.

My bench is old, tainted from moisture. From it, I'm afforded the best view in the park. And in front of me, the pond. Not the blue-basined, sanitized sort of water feature too common in public spaces. The pond, though entirely manmade, is of a style *au naturel*. Just the right amount of vegetation colours its surface. A few stones peek up from the brown water, often serving as perches for birds. Surrounded by tall trees, the pond is generally hidden from the breeze, and so almost always the texture of glass – and just as reflective.

I sit on my bench, the poet in the midst of poetry. There is a poem here. I can feel it. Waiting to be found and spoken. One that will sing of something brighter than the dark world that gives it birth.

I've been coming here every day since I moved to San Francisco. Every day when I'm done with my morning shift selling herbal supplements that nobody wants and that I would certainly never take. So much nonsense, really.

But here a poet can come to sing his song to the greens and browns of nature, and witness it singing back.

There is a woman here, at my pond, today. There's something vaguely familiar about her; something maternal, kind. I feel like I might have known her once, but I realize that's silly, in a park with so many people in it and as socially reclusive as I generally am. So many women have that look. I'm sure she's here for the same reasons I am, whoever she is. To see the beauty that a secret spot can hold. To be comforted by the extraordinary wonder of life.

I'm not writing any poetry today. I haven't brought my notebook. I'm tired of that for now. I've learned that poems come when they will. Being a poet is mostly about the waiting.

But I am hoping for the one sight that fills me, that feeds me, here at this pond. Hoping it will come today, like it comes every day.

Of course it will come. He always does.

The birds are sitting on their stone in the middle of the shimmering water. Side by side. In love, I presume. That's the way with birds. I can almost hear the heavens singing above them.

And then, there he is, at his spot in the distance. I see

him. My heart speeds up, I'm so happy. The boy, at his spot on the muddy patch of shoreline just opposite. He wears faded denim overalls over a white shirt. He holds a stick in his right hand, with which he draws lazy figure eights in the surface of the water.

I breathe more easily at the sight of him. My boy, at his spot. Everything I've ever loved, everything I've ever hoped for or dreamed about or wanted, it's all bound up in this boy. This boy who loves books and trains and castles and knights. This boy who is so singularly innocent and pure.

Then, to his left, the other visitor I knew I would see today. He is not as familiar to me as the boy, not so frequent a visitor here. I don't really know when he started to appear. For the longest time, I don't think he did. But he comes now, and he's comfortable and welcome in his own way. He's become a part of my experience of the park, and he steps out of the greenery where I sometimes spot college students sitting down to read or make out.

He's a teenager, maybe eighteen or nineteen. Buzz cut. He hasn't shaved today and has a shadow of a country goatee. His eyes are solid and a deep jade-green.

They're both here. My two companions. For a moment, I'm lost in the presence of each of them.

The woman nearby is talking. I can't hear what she's saying, her voice is indistinct. Something about a Tom. And a Joseph. And a Dylan. It's nonsense-speak, really. Some people are just confused. But everyone, however odd, has a right to sit in the park.

I don't pay any attention to her. The young man is walking towards me. He's a tough teenager, been through a lot by the looks of it. He walks right up to my bench. Stares me straight in the face, his jade-green eyes on fire. It's the strangest thing. I look at him and I see myself. The perfect image. The mirror of me, down to the tiniest freckle.

'It's good to see you,' is all he says, and the words emerge from his mouth with my voice. I think about answering, but there is really nothing to say. Nothing that matters. Nothing that warrants interrupting what has to happen next.

So the young man turns and sits on my bench, next to me. He gazes out over the pond with me, our eyes taking in the same sights. The Asian trees sway in arcs high above us, and in symphony we answer our own greeting with one voice: 'Glad to be with you. Glad to know you.'

And now the boy is in front of me. He is so close I can see the sweat marks on his shirt, the scuff marks on the clasps of his overalls. I'm sure I used to have overalls like this as a kid – God, how I loved them back then.

He peers at me, intently. For a moment my mind is consumed with images, with memories of dreams that seemed so real I felt, once, that I could see blood on my arms. Yet the images fade. We're together, friends, in the park; and the park is not a place for such memories.

I feel like I want to speak, like I want to pour out my heart to these two. But the poet for once is not the master of words. 'I'm so sorry,' is all that emerges, and I am not entirely sure why. The words come out of my throat in a teenage voice. More almost follow, but the boy holds up a small hand. Behind it, his face is the exact image of my own. For the first time I can remember, I see his features clearly. He has my eyes, my nose. His cheeks are the perfect, puffy images of what mine once had been. He is joyful and happy and innocent. The playful and pure boy I once had been. The boy in the park.

And he doesn't want me to say anything else. My own eyes gaze thoughtfully at me, and in a single breath I exhale a world of grief and agony from somewhere deep in my belly. And the little boy looks hopeful, even looks content. As a little boy should.

He turns to face the pond with me, and sits on my bench. And we remain there, the three of us side by side, forever lost and yet strangely at peace, as leaves dance on the trees and the world speaks to us of beauty.

I have a stick in my hand. My overalls are done up tight. I can feel my hair flop on my forehead. The tip of my stick pierces the water, and I watch the ripples dance in the sunlight. And for an instant, for a blessed instant, there is no pain. No grief. No fear.

There is only this beautiful scene. Almost perfect. Almost free.

Note

There really is a bench, and a pond, and a secret escape in the Temperate Asia section of the San Francisco Botanical Gardens – perfectly majestic and surreal – on which I sat every day during a much-appreciated retreat, and wrote this novel.

And there really are children who are so tortured in their youth that they become what they wouldn't and shouldn't become, whose lives are torn away from them. I am not one of those, but to all who are the sympathy of this book is dedicated.

The Boy in the Park

1.

Little boy in the park,
Little boy standing, lost.
The waters quiet, the tree-wings
dance
For the little boy still, unmoving.
The little boy with stick in hand;
Little boy weeping . . .
Little boy weeping . . .

2.

The evening is coming,
The morning is gone;
Little boy with his playful heart
And castle and crozier and soldier.
Leaps, not knowing

where they shall land –
How little boys do play until
The day of youth is done.

3.

Little boy weeping, blood on your arm
Trees bow and hollow;
The games we sing, the songs
we play –
The crying wind, the fighting day.
The waters burn, the quiet flees
The blood on your arm . . .
The blood on your arm . . .

4.

A lingering stain
When the play is gone;
A home unkept, unwanted.
Where fire burns at timber's edge,
Stretch townsfolk's grasp
past neighbour's reach –
Where games are ended
And rage alone can find you.

5.

Little boy longing, eyes in the dark,
No tears – no silent beckon.
In night a deeper darkness
falls

Till vengeance comes with mounted wings
And creeping heart and passion
For the little boy longing . . .
The little boy longing . . .

6.

Then comes the play,
The light returns:
Day is not forever hid.
There comes the voice, touch is felt
In tender caresses to
Too-torn flesh
And a heart that cries, that
Mourns its burial within.

7.

But how long stay the buried down
In darkness cold and unknowing?
Until the prey becomes
the beast
And tigers roar with claws unfurled;
Killing hope yet ending the tears,
Of the little boy weeping . . .
The little boy weeping . . .

Acknowledgements

There are many people to thank for the fact that a book I wrote in solitude has found its way into your hands, and the hands of so many others. The book's two fiercest champions have unquestionably been Luigi Bonomi, my extraordinary literary agent, who was the first to lay eyes on the manuscript and then championed it with incredible zeal; and Kate Bradley of HarperCollins, whose fierce enthusiasm for the story, the book and my entrance into the HarperCollins world has been unmatchable. Both are wonderful people, whose love for books and mastery of the literary ethos makes it a superlative joy to work with them. They are each parts of extraordinary teams as well, and I owe profound gratitude to Kate Elton, Kimberley Young and Charlotte Ledger at HarperCollins, all of whom have helped shape this book into what you have in your hands; together with Alison Bonomi, Dani Zigner and the team at LBA Books. I am represented by the finest agent in the business and publishing this book with the finest of publishers: an author could not be happier.

The fact that *The Boy in the Park* has launched in multiple languages, and is appearing in more all the time, is due to the tireless work of my international rights agents at ILA: Nicki Kennedy, Sam Edenborough, Simone Smith, Alice Natali and all their colleagues. The fact that the cover is so beautifully haunting is the result of the work of its designer, the talented Stuart Bache.

Finally, my thanks to the Trustees of the San Francisco Botanical Gardens for the luxury of spending so much time in that wonderful place, writing these pages; and to the owner, staff and 'the regulars' at the Beanery coffee shop in San Francisco's Inner Sunset, just near the entrance to the park. The casual mention of the place in the novel belies the fact that, during the writing of the book, it was almost a second home.

And to the many, many people I have talked to, over the years, about what haunts, what disturbs, what frightens, and what brings peace. It is an honour to know all of you.

About the Author

A J Grayson drinks extraordinary amounts of coffee and likes to write on an old Corona Standard typewriter, though is enough of a technical enthusiast to buy whatever Apple dangles from its latest stick. Time not spent writing books is spent reading them, walking (perhaps unsurprisingly, in parks), working with youth and adults in various counselling settings, and teaching.

Please be in touch with AJ Grayson on Twitter, Facebook and Instagram @GraysonForReal.